CHAPTER I

'Gerry! Where are you?'

Dr Dorothy Laver pushed open the door of the sitting-room of Pond Cottage, Middle Lane, Hampstead. It was a pleasant blue and white room with long windows opening on to a balcony over which trailed a pale clematis in full flower on this June morning. Two daily papers were lying crumpled on the carpet by the side of an arm-chair and the ashtray was full of cigarette ends but there was no sign of her husband. Half an hour ago she had telephoned from the hospital to say that she would be home to lunch. Gerry had seemed all right then and had promised to have a drink ready for her. Either he had been putting on an act or one of his attacks had come on very suddenly.

Dr Laver emerged from the sitting-room and looked into the little study at the back of the house where Gerry gave English lessons to private pupils from a tutorial college when he was well enough.

This room, too, was empty, but Dorothy's quick and anxious glance instantly picked out the sheet of writing-paper on the desk. It was lying on the blotter at a slight angle and the thin ballpoint pen lay beside it as if the writer had been suddenly called away but intended to return. Only a few lines had been written in Gerry's small neat hand.

My darling Dolly, I can no longer endure to be such a

burden to you. I must once again take steps to end it and this time I promise I will not fail. By the time you return it will all be over and you will be free of me for ever and can marry any one of them you choose or enjoy the house with your lover in peace . . .

Dr Laver took in the contents of the letter with no change of expression on her face, but as she left the room there was the slight tensing of the hand muscles with which she always prepared herself to meet an emergency, whether it was a domestic crisis or a particularly difficult patient at hospital.

Her hands were clenched into fists when she looked into the kitchen and the downstairs lavatory and her own consulting-room and saw no Gerry. This meant that he would be upstairs. An ominous sign and she feared the worst. The messiest and the most thoroughly upsetting kind. Fortunately it was also the rarest. He had only once before done it this way. Her own telephone call had probably sparked it off. Knowing for sure that she would very soon be home he had felt safe in doing this. Or perhaps he had waited until he saw her car actually turn into Middle Lane. The bathroom was at the front of the house and there was a good view of the road from the window.

Dorothy Laver picked up her emergency bag before she ran upstairs. She would almost certainly need it. When she reached the turn of the stairs she heard sounds of groaning. Timed just right, she said to herself. It was extraordinary how she could be logical and aloof, deeply compassionate, guilty, and just plain scared all at the same time. You'd think you'd get used to it, she thought

One of Us Must Die

Dr Dorothy Laver and her husband lived together in great unhappiness in their beautiful Hampstead home. Their lives were bedevilled by the loss of their baby daughter fifteen years earlier. One of them was guilty of giving the child an accidental overdose, but both had been attending to her and it was impossible to say which one of them was to blame. The tension between them, heightened by Gerry's carefully staged suicide attempts and Dorothy's guilt feelings, had risen to breaking point. One of them must push the other over the edge of sanity. One of them must die.

Into this tense and claustrophobic situation new elements intrude: a girl about the age their daughter would have been who takes up residence in the house; Dorothy's wise, serene clergyman father, who may or may not be guilty of ending a human life; and the young electrician who falls in love with Dorothy and to whom she turns more and more for support.

When death does indeed occur, it is as innocent-seeming as the baby's death years before. But a new and horrible question-mark hangs over the survivors as the past tangle of guilt and suspicion is unravelled. One of them is guilty of murder. Once again, one of them must die.

ANNA CLARKE

One of Us Must Die

COLLINS, ST JAMES'S PLACE, LONDON

William Collins Sons & Co Ltd
London · Glasgow · Sydney · Auckland
Toronto · Johannesburg

First published 1978
© Anna Clarke, 1978

ISBN 0 00 231609 9

Set in Baskerville
Made and Printed in Great Britain by
William Collins Sons & Co Ltd Glasgow

as she reached the bathroom door. After all, it must be the tenth – or was it the eleventh? – time.

Deliberately she set herself the task of counting the previous suicide attempts. The little mental exercise reinforced the coldly rational part of herself and helped to steady her while she staunched the flow of blood, cleaned the slashed wrists, and put in the stitches. He had used a new razor blade and the cuts were straight and not very deep. The repair job was a simple enough one in itself. Dorothy Laver practised now as a psychiatrist but she had not lost her basic skills. What was so agonizing to her was not the gushing blood but the sickening stream of self-reproach that flowed from Gerry's lips while she was dressing the wounds.

'Why do you bother, why don't you just let me die . . . I'm not worth it . . . I'm a misery to you . . . I always will be . . . I've ruined your life . . . and you're so wonderful, Dolly, so strong, so good.'

And so on and so on. Drowning in self-pity, pouring out the old clichés over and over again, luxuriating in it. These were now the high spots, the greatest times in his life. It would not be quite so bad if he were no more than a weak hysterical creature who was completely dependent on her and whom she could treat as she treated her patients. Compassion and professional pride would carry her through. And it would be easier to bear if he truly loved her in spite of everything, if they were tied together with bonds of past affection instead of with hatred and guilt. For it was his hatred that was so hard to bear, his bitter resentment of her that was never openly expressed but always indirectly in these carefully timed and arranged suicide attempts. He had got it down to a fine art, she reflected as she scrubbed round the bathroom floor tiles to remove the remaining traces of blood. He knew her moods and weaknesses, her likes and dislikes. Being a doctor, she was all the more vulnerable. He tortured her conscience with these fake suicide bids as an experienced kidnapper or hijacker played on the conscience of a civilized society.

And her conscience was terribly sore, sore with a wound that would never heal, sore in a way that nobody else knew about except Gerry.

'How are you feeling now?' she asked him a few minutes later.

Gerry Laver was lying on his bed in his olive green dressing-gown, propped up against an edifice of pillows. On the bedside table stood a transistor radio tuned softly to Radio One and a small tray containing a whisky bottle and a jug of water. In the less damaged of his hands he held a cigarette and with the other he was rather awkwardly turning the pages of the morning's *Guardian* which was propped against his knees. He looked as elegant and placid and comfortable as the hero of a Noel Coward play.

'Fine,' he replied, looking up and smiling at her. 'Thanks to my clever darling Dolly.'

It was indeed as if he were acting to an unseen audience. But he was not forcing her into any particular role. She had played her part and given him his satisfaction by being unable to conceal her own horror and revulsion and he was no longer interested in her. At any rate not for the time being. Later on – it might be a week, it might be a fortnight, it might even, with great luck, be two or three months – the whole disgusting business would start again and there was nothing whatever that she could do to prevent it.

'Do you want any lunch?' Dorothy was so exhausted by the struggle within her that she had barely strength to ask the question. For a moment it looked as if she would have to repeat it because Gerry, seemingly completely absorbed in something he was reading, took no notice. Just when she could stand it no longer he shifted slightly and murmured without looking up: 'Later. Not just yet. I'll have a little something later on.' And then he laughed, quite naturally and happily as he read from the paper: 'Listen to this, darling. Man pours bucket of ice cubes over wife's lover. He's up in court for causing grievous bodily harm. How could you cause harm with ice cubes? It might cool his ardour and he'd probably get very wet, but otherwise . . .'

Dorothy heard no more. Her own impulse to attack Gerry could no longer be held in check and the violence of it horrified her. It had never been as bad as this before. She rushed out of the bedroom, just remembering to leave the door open in case he should call her, but not knowing how she would be able to respond if he did.

In the pretty blue and white sitting-room with the balcony she walked up and down until she was a little calmer and then swallowed a little white tablet and sat down on the settee, breathing deeply and commanding herself not to think about Gerry until the tranquillizer had begun to take effect.

But it took a second tablet and a glass of sherry and the best part of an hour before relief came at last. Dorothy kicked off her shoes and lay back on the settee with her eyes closed. It was fortunate that she did not have to go

back to hospital this afternoon and was not seeing any
patient at home until four o'clock. Two hours to recover.
She would sleep for an hour and then make tea and
sandwiches for herself and Gerry and gradually get back
into the normal routine.

But sleep did not come. The drug held her body in its
grip like a strait-jacket but her thoughts had no such
restraint. You can have your freedom from him, they kept
telling her. It is terribly easy. All you have to do is to let
it happen next time. Not to come to the rescue. To
arrive home too late.

CHAPTER II

The front doorbell broke into Dorothy's waking nightmare. Upstairs Gerry, drifting off into a comfortable
doze, scarcely heard it. Dorothy smoothed down her hair
and her skirt as she went to answer the ring and made an
effort to appear her usual self. That it was not a very
successful effort was immediately apparent from the
reaction of the young man who stood on the doorstep.

'Good afternoon,' he said. And then, apologetically:
'I'm sorry to disturb you.'

Dorothy tried a bit harder and achieved a little twitch
of the lips that might pass for a smile.

'Not at all. What can I do for you?'

He doesn't look as if he's selling anything, she thought;
he's not nearly brash enough. But perhaps it was a new
technique. And she didn't recognize him as a patient,
although it was not impossible that he was somebody

whom she had seen briefly at the hospital and who, resentful of receiving so little time and despairing of ever coming to the top of the waiting list for treatment, had sought her out at her private address. Except that he didn't look like a patient either, and certainly not the type who would go to such lengths. He was of medium build and medium colouring, and he spoke with a slight West Country accent. Could he possibly be canvassing in the by-election, wondered Dorothy. Surely not. He didn't look right for that either.

'Is Mr Laver in?' asked the caller, and Dorothy's dazed mental fumblings came to an end as she realized that it was Gerry who was wanted and not herself. She even experienced a momentary flicker of sympathy for Gerry, whom a few minutes ago she had been wishing dead. It was tough on him to be nearly always regarded as nothing more than an awkward appendage of his wife, as Dr Laver's husband. If they separated he might just have a chance to recover and lead a normal life. Perhaps she ought to try, even now, really to talk to him. Perhaps if she were to admit her own deep feelings of guilt, for everything, not just that first disaster . . . perhaps if she could bring herself to take the plunge and open up the forbidden subject after all these years . . .

'I'm afraid Mr Laver isn't very well at the moment,' she said in a much firmer voice. 'Was he expecting you?'

'At half past two,' was the reply. 'I have a tutorial arranged for then.'

'Oh dear.' Dorothy glanced at her watch. 'What a pity that you've had a wasted journey. Are you one of his regular pupils? I'm Mrs Laver, by the way.'

'I'm Peter Tarrant.' The young man suddenly held out

his hand and Dorothy took it for a moment. 'No, I'm not a regular student,' he went on. 'I've never seen Mr Laver before. The agency fixed it up for me. I'd better go then, if he's not well, and perhaps I can see him another time.'

'I'm awfully sorry,' said Dorothy. 'I hope you've not had very far to come.'

That was obviously all that needed to be said in the circumstances and Peter Tarrant ought to have taken his leave and Dorothy Laver ought to have shut the door and returned to her own affairs. But neither of them did so. They remained staring at each other.

'Is he very ill?' asked Peter at last. 'Is there anything I can do to help you?'

Dorothy made no reply. It was so rare for anybody to think that she could be in need of help that she was momentarily taken aback.

'I thought you looked very worried when you opened the door,' said Peter. 'I hope you don't think I'm being interfering, but I couldn't help noticing.'

Suddenly Dorothy smiled, quite naturally, and the young man blinked. She was in her late thirties, he supposed, tall, thin, and rather frail-looking, with short straight black hair and a pale skin. But her mouth, which was too large, and her eyes, which were violet-coloured and rather too close together for beauty, seemed to come alive when she smiled and fill her whole face with light and movement. If he had known the expression he would have called her a *belle laide*. As it was, he simply thought how extraordinarily fascinating a plain woman could sometimes look.

'It's nothing very serious,' she said, 'but he was taken ill rather suddenly and that's why he couldn't let you know in time. I was a bit dopey when you rang because I'd been resting and had just woken up and had not fully connected.'

This brought another apology from Peter. Dorothy cut it short. She was feeling quite wide awake now and extraordinarily light-hearted all of a sudden. To be treated by this pleasant and sympathetic stranger not as Dr Laver who was to be deferred to and depended on at every turn, but simply as an ordinary woman worried about her husband, had touched some deep spring of release in her. She felt irresponsible and free, as if she had been magically transported beyond the bounds of her own life and could show herself as whatever sort of person she pleased.

'I tell you what we will do, Peter Tarrant,' she said. 'I was just going to make some tea. You come in and wait while I do so, and I'll take some up to my husband and see whether he's fit to see you now for a little while. If he isn't, then perhaps I could help you a bit myself. I'm an idiot in some subjects but might be able to remember some useful tips in others. What do you need coaching in?'

Peter explained while they were in the kitchen, where he insisted on following her. He was trying to make up for an interrupted education by doing an Open University degree in Technology. The practical side did not worry him much, since he had worked at a variety of engineering jobs and was at the moment earning his living as an electrician, helping a friend who had a thriving one-man business. It was writing essays that was his problem.

'I've never been much good at getting things down on paper,' he said as he was quickly and efficiently cutting bread and butter for the sandwiches. 'It's all quite clear in my mind and I can explain it to somebody else if necessary, but I panic at the sight of a blank sheet of paper.'

'That's not an uncommon experience,' said Dorothy, laughing. 'You're in good company. But surely the Open University ought to be helping you?'

'Oh, they are. They're super. My counsellor has spent hours with me, but I still feel I need more practice. I can't afford to fail.'

'All the same, I don't think you ought to be spending money on private coaching,' said Dorothy, suspecting that the agency that sent Gerry his pupils was making a very comfortable profit out of them.

'It would be even worse to have to take the course over again,' returned Peter. 'There. Will these do?'

'Much better than I'd have made myself. Thank you very much.'

Dorothy put the sandwiches on a tray. 'If you like to wait in here,' she went on, indicating the sitting-room, 'I'll go up and investigate. Shan't be long.'

A little later she returned, still carrying the tray. 'He's fast asleep,' she said. 'I won't wake him. Let's see if I can help you myself. I'm free till a quarter to four. Excuse me chewing and drinking the while.'

It turned out that Peter had actually brought along an exercise for comment and advice. It was a report to an imaginary board of directors, comparing the merits of rival pieces of office machinery. The technical details were admirably clear and the conclusions, though rather naïvely presented, gave ample information on which to form a judgement. Dorothy studied it carefully while

Peter Tarrant poured tea and demolished the sandwiches as if he too had had nothing to eat all day.

'It's a lucky firm who gets you for technical adviser,'
she said at last, looking up from her reading and smiling
at him. The pleasant, undistinguished face opposite her
went very red.

'There's no need to be kind about it,' he muttered,
turning aside to put his cup down on the table. 'I know I
can't write.'

'I'm not being kind about it,' Dorothy exclaimed. 'I'm
telling you what I think. For what my opinion is worth,
that is.'

Peter looked up at her again and they glared at each
other for a moment. Then they both said 'Sorry' simultaneously and burst out laughing.

'As a matter of fact I've got rather a high opinion of my
own opinion,' said Dorothy. 'Shall we cut out the false
modesty all round and start again?'

'Yes, please.' Peter took another sandwich. 'I've got
quite a good opinion of myself too. In some respects.'

'What respects? Hi.' Dorothy grabbed the plate.
'Leave me something to eat, can't you?'

'I feel as if I've known you for years,' said Peter.
'Funny, isn't it? What respects? Well, I'm pretty good at
diagnosing faults in electrical equipment. I can grasp a
point quickly. I think I usually get my priorities right.
And I know when I'm beaten.'

'That last one is not necessarily a virtue.'

'You think it's better to go on banging against a brick
wall?'

'No, no. Of course not. One has to go on looking for
the way over or round it, however hopeless it seems.'

'Oh, I do that all right.'

Peter took another sandwich and Dorothy picked up the little batch of handwritten sheets again. She had indeed, in this strange and unexpected moment of release, allowed herself to become a different person. Or rather, two different people. One part of her was feeling happier and more carefree than she had for years; the other part was terrified by the rate at which this unsought-for acquaintanceship seemed to be progressing. She had always been completely faithful to Gerry. The lovers he endowed her with existed in his imagination alone. There was no time for any such involvements in Dorothy's life. After the death of her daughter Irene she had deliberately taken on more and more commitments, and so had Gerry. Friendships had been allowed to drop, social life had dwindled to nothing. They drugged themselves with work, avoiding all close personal contacts, sharing the same roof and the same table and the same bedroom but still managing to avoid each other. The terrible gulf of secret guilt and suspicion lay between them and there was no crossing it. The struggles and sufferings of her patients' lives were an open file to Dorothy; but her own case history was locked away, deep in the memory, where it festered and never healed.

She could not unlock it. She could not cure herself, neither could she find the will to ask for help. Gerry alone held the key, but he would never release her. On the contrary, he turned it ever tighter, rejecting the few tentative efforts she had made to bridge the gulf and always forcing her back into herself.

The strain of their life had been very severe, but Dorothy was the stronger and Gerry had been the first to crack. Five years ago he had broken down completely and made the first suicide attempt. On that occasion Dorothy had been frightened enough to ask a colleague for help. Drugs and a spell in hospital had brought Gerry back to the outward appearance of what he had been before. Since then Dorothy had kept up with everybody the fiction that he was going to get better; even with her father, who was nearer to her than anybody else in the world.

It took every bit of her energies to do her job, cope with Gerry, look after the house, and keep an eye on her father, who was elderly and in poor health and lived alone. For a man to awaken in Dorothy any personal interest he would have to have exceptional charm: like Gerry as he had been when she first knew him.

This man sitting by her now had no such charm. But he had something that mattered a great deal more. He had calmness and balance; in his presence one felt security and peace.

'What I think you'll have to work at,' she said, still keeping her eyes on the papers, 'is dressing up your reports a little so that the statements don't look quite so bald. It's a funny thing nowadays,' she added thoughtfully. 'People are obsessed with taking off all their clothes or baring their souls for everybody to see, but when it comes to language they seem unable to endure the simple statement, naked and unadorned.'

'And yet we are supposed to be so very permissive about language,' said Peter.

'Yes, but it runs alongside this frightful squeamishness about making a simple statement. Read the sociologists or economists. Listen to any current affairs radio discussions. No one ever says "yes" or "no" or "I don't know" or "it might be". They say "in point of actual fact we have to take into consideration the undoubted possibility that in the eventuality of . . ." '

'I can't write like that,' said Peter.

'Heaven forbid that you should.'

'But you said I ought to dress it up for the examiner.'

'I shouldn't have used that phrase. I should have said you could make some of the sentences sound less abrupt. Here for instance.'

Dorothy leaned forward to show him but he got up and came to sit on the settee beside her and they looked at the exercise together.

'And here.' Dorothy made a few more suggestions and then reached for a cigarette. The impulse to fling her arms around him was overwhelming. Just an ordinary uncomplicated person, she was thinking. I hardly ever meet any. It's wonderful. Like fresh bread and butter. 'You have a go at the next paragraph,' she said.

Peter did so, nervously at first but gaining confidence. Then he took out a pen and made a note of their redraft and compared it with his original.

'Well?' asked Dorothy.

'Yes. It's an improvement.'

'Not dressing-up. Just a spot of polishing. For heaven's sake don't lose your capacity to go straight to the point. It's an invaluable asset. Incidentally this recording-machine that you are recommending sounds a great improvement. I wonder if I could persuade them to buy one at the hospital for – ' She broke off abruptly. The last thing she wanted was to give any hint of her own position.

'You work in a hospital?' said Peter with quick interest.
'Yes.'

'Medical? Admin?'

'Yes,' said Dorothy again.

'Yes which?'

'Ssh.' She held up a hand. 'I thought I could hear my husband calling. Excuse me.'

This was not entirely an excuse for not replying to his question. She really had heard a faint sound coming from upstairs. She found Gerry awake and peering over the side of the bed.

'Dropped the stick,' he said sleepily. 'Wanted to bang on the floor for you.'

'I heard it. Are you feeling better? D'you want anything to eat yet?' She was arranging the pillows again, quickly and efficiently. There was no more emotion in her voice than if Gerry had been a casualty patient. If he had not been so dopey he might have noticed this and resented it. As it was, he simply murmured that he would like a cup of tea.

'I'll get it,' said Dorothy.

But when she was at the door he called her back: 'Doll.'

'Yes?'

'Thought I heard voices. Who is it?'

'The man's come to mend the washing-machine.'

It was extraordinary that it could slip out so glibly while her heart was pounding so and that Gerry could accept it without question, sleepy as he was.

CHAPTER III

When Dorothy came downstairs she found that Peter had taken the tray out to the kitchen and washed up.

'Thanks,' she said, suddenly feeling very embarrassed in his presence. 'He wants some tea. I'll make some fresh. This is rather stewed.'

Peter ran water into the electric kettle and plugged it in.

'Thanks,' said Dorothy vaguely, longing now for the whole little incident to be at an end and yet dreading his departure. Open University student, she was saying to herself; electrician; came through the Hampstead Tutorial Service – there's enough information there to track him down again. But what excuse can I make for doing so? You're crazy, woman, she told herself in the same thought; your life is bad enough as it is. Don't make an even worse mess of it. Nip this nonsense in the bud at once.

'Having trouble?' Peter was looking at the washing-machine. There was a screwdriver and a hammer lying on top of it, left from Dorothy's hasty and unsuccessful attempt to get the lid to shut properly.

Dorothy nodded. 'I meant to phone them about it but haven't had the time yet today.'

'I'll fix it if I can. Don't worry,' he added, instantly reading her mind. 'I won't stay too long. You said you were free till quarter to four.'

'Yes. I've got a – '

Again she pulled herself up. She had very nearly said 'a

patient coming'. She began to laugh and Peter looked up at her enquiringly.

'My husband wanted to know who was downstairs,' she said, 'and I didn't want him worrying because he'd forgotten about a student coming, so I told a lie and said it was the man come to mend the washing-machine. It's rather disconcerting to find you've been speaking the truth when you intended a falsehood.'

He made no reply and she was afraid that she had offended him by seeming to be putting him in his place as a tradesman. She went upstairs again wondering anxiously how she could put it right with him before he left. It would be unbearable not to part on the same terms of cheerful and equal fellowship that they had so miraculously achieved in this brief meeting.

Gerry was lying listening to the radio with his eyes closed when she came into the bedroom.

'Can you hold the cup?' she asked. 'Or shall I hold it for you?'

He did not immediately respond and she knew with sickening certainty that he had detected something odd about her. His sensitivity to her slightest change of mood or feeling was uncanny. It's going to be hell, she thought; even worse than ever.

'Does your hand feel strong enough?' she asked patiently.

'To hold a teacup? Yes.' He looked up at her for a moment and then shut his eyes again.

'I'm leaving it here then. Just by the radio. Don't knock it over. Are you sure you don't want anything to eat?'

'Later,' he murmured. 'Later. You're busy now. Men

mending washing-machines and patients and things. Busy busy Dorothy.'

'All right then.' The familiar helpless fury surged up in her again as she left the room, this time shutting the door behind her.

Her hands were still tightly clenched when she returned to the kitchen. Peter glanced at her curiously for a moment before returning to his work. A few minutes later he said: 'That ought to do if you give it a good bang. Don't let them try to sell you another. There's plenty of life in this yet. It's not a bad model.'

'Thanks,' said Dorothy. 'I'm very grateful.'

She wanted to offer to pay for the work but knew that she must not, and she was relieved when he spoke.

'Exchange of services. A repair job for a tutorial. OK?'

'Very much so. I've had the better bargain.'

'It's too early to tell. This may go wrong again to-morrow, but I've really learnt something from you. I wish you could take me on as a pupil. Would it be very unorthodox? Would your husband be very offended if you did?'

'It would be a bit difficult,' said Dorothy, thinking hard after her first reaction of wild delight. 'You see, I'm out at work much of the time. This happened to be a free afternoon. And I'm not qualified to teach English, which my husband is. Very much so. He was head of the English department in a big school until he had a bad breakdown some time ago. That's why he's doing this tutorial work. It's keeping his hand in until he's fit to take on a heavy job again.'

'I see,' said Peter, and again there was that curious glance, instantly withdrawn. 'It would be awkward if you were to steal his pupils. I don't think I'll trouble to ask them for another tutorial, though, if he really has forgotten about me, and I'll tell the agency I've changed my mind. You're quite right. I ought to make the best use of the Open University facilities instead of getting in a panic and chasing after private tutors. But you've helped me a lot this afternoon and I'm very grateful. Goodbye.'

And he held out his hand in the same abrupt manner as when he had first introduced himself. Dorothy took it and neither of them could let go. They made no further movement towards each other, but it was as if they were both clinging to a lifeline.

'I should like us to meet again, though,' said Dorothy with the sensation that the line had given way and she was plunging down the edge of the ravine, 'because I've not been quite honest with you.'

'No, you haven't, have you? I have got a wife, by the way. You'll have been wondering about that. At the moment we are having a trial separation. She doesn't like me studying and I don't like her choice of companions. If she's as satisfied with the trial as I am, it will be made permanent. She's got our house at present and I'm living in a couple of rooms in Camden Town. You're welcome to pay me a visit if you like but I must warn you that it's rather sordid. I'm sure you wouldn't mind that, but perhaps you'd like to make another suggestion, since I take it that it would be awkward for me to come here.'

Dorothy managed to withdraw her hand at last. 'Do you ever go for walks on the Heath?' she asked.

'I used to. There's not much time now between work and study, but I'll make it if you can.'

'My father lives in a block of old people's flats near Parliament Hill. I always go and see him Tuesday evenings and I shall be there tomorrow. If I leave him a little earlier than usual it will still be light enough for a stroll.'

They fixed the exact time and place. If Peter suspected that Dorothy's father was to be used as an alibi for a longer than usual absence from home he did not say so. After he had gone, however, Dorothy became intensely conscious that this was her intention. I'll tell Dad I'm going early to meet a friend, she said to herself; he knows how impossible Gerry makes it for me to bring anyone home. He can think I'm going to have a drink with Pauline.

But the thought of deceiving her father in this way worried her even more than the thought of keeping Peter's existence a secret from Gerry, and she stood still at the foot of the stairs for several minutes, holding her face in her hands and frowning.

CHAPTER IV

'You've not been listening to me, Doctor,' said the plaintive elderly voice.

Dorothy controlled a start. This was only too true. Mrs Bertram, the four o'clock patient, had been burbling away as usual and her own thoughts had been miles away. Desperately she tried to remember what had been the main theme of this session so far. The fear of cancer, which Mrs Bertram did not suffer from. The arthritis, from which she did, but not very badly. Or the detested son-in-law with whom Dorothy had a sneaking sympathy, as she had with so many of the close friends and relatives of her patients. These were the three main struts that supported Mrs Bertram's bored and idle life and they occupied roughly equal parts in her thoughts. If she had been a poor widow instead of a rich one, her neighbours, or even her cat, would have been performing the service that Dorothy was now providing, and her chances of becoming less depressed and anxious would have been very much the same as they were with her present expensive treatment.

Such patients were unrewarding but they were often the only ones who could afford to pay, and Dorothy needed the money. For there was of course very little chance that Gerry would ever be able to resume his career. In fact he had recently been talking of abandoning even that little effort of which he was capable, and Dorothy had an uneasy feeling that today was a turning point and that from now on he would never work again. He had a certain amount of insurance money and disability benefit and the house was his own, inherited from an uncle. But it was Dorothy's earnings that kept it going, clothed and fed them, paid for the cars and enabled them to live as if two large salary cheques were coming along regularly every month.

Dorothy loved the house. Since the death of Irene it had been the chief consolation of her life and remained constantly in her mind and heart as something to work and plan for. If she bought a vase or a picture for the sitting-room it was as if she were choosing a gift for a lover or a child. She was ashamed of this passion of hers and afraid of it too because it made her so vulnerable.

Nobody else knew how she felt. Only Gerry, who watched her and studied her and read her through and through. She would never be able to leave him because if she did she would lose the house. And she would never be able to leave him because she could not endure her feeling of guilt if she did.

Neither of these statements was ever uttered, but the truth of them both lay heavy between them in all their dealings with each other. Neither of these facts was ever forgotten.

It would be nice, thought Dorothy, to transfer Mrs Bertram to a junior colleague of hers who also needed the money, and take on a patient who was more capable of making progress, but there was no question of it.

'I am listening, Mrs Bertram,' she said in the voice of quiet authority that patients found so soothing. 'Please go on.'

The next few words gave her the necessary cue, and after a little while she repeated her usual reassurances and mild exhortations. They came easily enough, through long practice, and as usual the old lady went away considerably comforted.

If only someone would do the same for me, thought Dorothy as she took out the correspondence referring to the next appointment. But it's only till tomorrow evening, she told herself, and then I am going to tell Peter all about it. Or at any rate, all about some of it. She stopped reading and looked, unseeing, out of the window. It was she who was mad, not Gerry. If she couldn't bear the pressures of her life any longer then she ought to talk to someone at the hospital about them. Or to her father. Or even to Mrs Oliver, the cleaner, who probably saw and suspected more than most people because she came to the house every morning.

The trouble was that Dorothy had kept quiet about it all for so long, had patched up Gerry again and again, pretended to everyone that he was getting better. A convalescent mental patient was best helped by being treated like a normal person, not by emphasizing the differences. That had been her guiding principle with Gerry: to restore his self-esteem, his status in his own eyes and in other people's. But she had carried it too far and persisted with it long after she should have sought outside help. Not only was there this terrible secret between them, but she had also built up a barrier around them both that neither of them could break through. They were imprisoned behind it, destroying each other.

And now she was going to talk to a stranger because there had been that extraordinary flash of recognition and understanding between them. She knew nothing about Peter but what he had told her of himself, and that was not much. She had noticed him looking with interest at her pictures and china, and, for all she knew, he might be a would-be burglar who had made up the story about wanting English tuition to cover up an unsuccessful attempt to get into a house full of valuable knick-knacks. Except that he had written that exercise for discussion and he knew the name of Gerry and of the tutorial agency, and it would be easy enough to check with them or with the Open University people. It might be sensible to do this. But she didn't feel like being sensible. At the moment she didn't care if Peter Tarrant were a crook. She believed he could help her and that was all that mattered.

She skimmed through the letter on the desk in front of

her, replaced it in the folder and put it back in the drawer. It concerned another commonly-met-with type of patient. A sixteen-year-old girl referred as an emergency from a young people's rescue service. A child who had run away from home and was drifting about miserably from one group of communal-livers to another, hanging on to the edge of them, tolerated but not cared for, unable to settle anywhere or to make any permanent relationship of any kind. She had been picked up by the police after an eviction struggle and taken to the temporary refuge, where she had found a bottle containing a few sleeping tablets that someone had left lying about and had swallowed the lot.

As if I hadn't got enough of that already at home, thought Dorothy. But when the girl arrived she was more in control of herself than she had been with Mrs Bertram and for the next forty-five minutes gave every bit of her mind to the frightened and hysterical child. Irene would have been about this age if she had lived, thought Dorothy. She always said this to herself when she met a girl of the appropriate age group. These were the only times when she allowed herself any conscious recollection of the child who had died so long ago.

The case of Nina Farrell was probably a hopeless one. She was the offspring of a casual student affair, and her mother, disliking her from the first, had hung on to her in the hope of getting Nina's father to marry her. A sad old story. Nina's childhood had consisted mostly of waiting alone in the flat, hungry and frightened, for her mother to come home, and of being violently quarrelled over by her mother and her grandparents, who had refused to take her on themselves but would not stop interfering. Material conditions had improved when her mother eventually married a man much older than herself, but Nina was more unwanted than ever. She ran away from home a number of times, and on one occasion managed to track down her own father, only to be rejected yet again with unnecessary violence. She had no other relatives and no friends. There seemed to be nothing good and positive in Nina's experience of life on which to build. She really needed to start her life all over again and receive at least a modicum of love and attention in some caring surroundings. And there were so many like her. Dorothy was about to utter a few kindly reassurances and tell her to come to the outpatients department at the hospital on Friday when she caught the girl's eye and saw in it such an agony of pleading that her heart contracted.

'If you will come along and see me here at the same time next week,' she said instead, 'we'll be able to have another talk about it and perhaps by then I'll have some better suggestions about helping you.'

'Are you sure you mean it?' The girl looked at her suspiciously.

'Of course I do. Why should you think I don't?'

'Because most people don't.'

'Well, I do. I want to see you again at five o'clock next Monday afternoon, and I don't want any nonsense in the meantime, Nina. No more drugs and you are to stay in the hostel. And give them a bit of a hand with looking after the house. They could do with it.'

'I'll make them a cake,' said Nina unexpectedly.

'That's a good idea,' said Dorothy, mildly amused and hoping that the badly harassed warden would be co-operative about this.

'I'll bring you one too, shall I?'

'Yes, please,' said Dorothy.

Nina smiled suddenly, looking quite pretty in a pale and waifish way. When she had come into the consulting-room she had looked as if she would never smile again. I'm breaking all the rules today, thought Dorothy after the girl had gone. Letting sympathy run away with me and becoming personally involved with a patient who will have to be treated without payment. I wonder where it is all going to end?

CHAPTER V

'I've sometimes wondered,' said Peter, 'what doctors and priests and others who carry other people's burdens do when they find they can no longer stand it.'

'Well, now you know. They drag unfortunate technology students away from their studies and pour out the lot.'

They were sitting on a bench at the edge of a clump of trees. In the distance was the vast pulsing, sprawling mass of London. A little way down the hill a few boys were kicking a ball about in a desultory manner. They had not, after all, walked very far. Dorothy's appearance had belied her statement that she was not too tired. Peter had said nothing, but as soon as they came to the bench he had said: 'Let's stop and look at London a bit. This must be Dick Whittington's view.'

'Just about,' agreed Dorothy. 'Are you ambitious, Peter?'

'Yes. I certainly don't want to be an electrician all my

life any more than I wanted to be an unsuccessful farmer like my poor father. But we're not here to talk about me. Another time. You were going to tell me something about yourself.'

She had told him then, without any effort and without any reserve, about Gerry's breakdown and the suicide attempts. That was half an hour ago and they were still sitting on the same seat.

'I'll have to be going soon,' she said, 'or Gerry will be getting suspicious and phoning my father.'

Peter stood up. 'We'll walk slowly back to the car,' he said, 'and talk on the way. Why did you marry him? No, that's a silly question. Why does anyone marry? I mean, did you not realize that he was terribly jealous and possessive when you married him? Or did you know it but think you could cope?'

'Both, I think,' replied Dorothy thoughtfully. 'And also . . .' She hesitated a moment and then laughed. 'He's very good-looking. I was flattered that a man like that should take any notice of me. I didn't have many boy-friends when I was young. I was ugly and clever and emotional and intense. A ghastly combination, don't you think?'

Peter made no reply.

'What I like so much about you,' said Dorothy, 'is that you don't feel obliged to make some sort of feeble comment on what I've just said. If you've nothing to say, then you say nothing. It's wonderful.'

'I should think you must get very tired of hearing people's voices in your job. It must be worse in a way than to be always looking at diseased bodies.'

'I love my work,' said Dorothy defensively. 'I chose it.'

'Look out.' Peter caught her arm. They had come to a pathway and a boy on a bicycle was heading straight for Dorothy without looking where he was going. When he had passed they walked on together holding hands.

'I haven't felt like this for years,' she said. 'I feel about sixteen.'

'And I feel rather ancient. It's a great responsibility, being confidant to an eminent psychiatrist. I'm not sure that I'm quite up to it, simple-minded mechanic that I am.'

Dorothy glanced at him with a flash of anxiety, saw that he was laughing at her, flung his arm backwards and forwards, and then let it go and ran ahead towards her car.

He caught her up and put a hand against the driver's door to prevent her from opening it.

'When are we meeting again? Or is this just a one-off job?'

'Ah, so you are human after all, Mr Tarrant.'

'I – ' He drew a deep breath. 'Now listen. You wanted to tell me and you feel better for doing so. Right? If that's all it's to be, just say so at once and I'll know where I am.'

'What do you want it to be, Peter?'

'For the time being I'd just like to help you if I can. But not being a psychiatrist, I can't be detached about it. And your husband is obviously a very sick man and I don't somehow relish the thought of a regular discussion of all his symptoms, poor devil. But if that's the only way to help you, I suppose I shall have to stick it.'

'Let's get into the car,' said Dorothy. They did so, and

then she said: 'I wouldn't dream of inflicting it on you. As regards poor Gerry, this is definitely a one-off occasion. Just speaking it aloud has taken off the pressure. Now that I know somebody else knows, I'll be all right. Can't we meet again like this and talk about something else? Yourself if you want to. Or electrical engineering. Or music. Or dogs. Or cooking. Or absolutely anything you like. Oh, if you knew what heaven it is for me to talk to a really *sane* person!'

'So that's the attraction. I was rather wondering. I thought it couldn't be for my brains or my beauty. But, Dorothy, surely you do have some people in your life who are reasonably sane. Friends? Relations? People at work?'

'My hospital colleagues are mostly half-way bonkers themselves. It's an occupational disease among us. And friendship isn't easy to keep up in the circumstances. It was my oldest friend Pauline who actually introduced me to Gerry in the first place. I think she'd got her eye on him for herself and was shattered when he started taking an interest in me.'

'So you feel guilty about that too.'

'Not exactly, because he wouldn't have married her even if it hadn't been for me. But it's a constraint between us. So we don't talk about him much if we meet.'

'And relations?'

'There's no one close but my father. He's a retired clergyman. He's spent his life in tough parishes trying to sort out people's troubles. He's got emphysema and his heart's shaky and he's very tired and he's just had enough. He knows how ill Gerry has been, of course, so we can talk a little but I can't tell him the lot. I *can't.*'

'Well, it's not my business,' said Peter, 'and of course I haven't met your father, but all the same it's hard to believe that he hasn't guessed. And if it's from him that you've inherited your character, then he'll be the sort of person who would want to know, however tired and ill he is.'

'You may be right. I've told him about you, by the way. I hope you don't mind.'

'Of course not,' said Peter, but Dorothy, looking at him suddenly, thought he looked slightly taken aback.

'I didn't want to feel he was being used to cover up a secret assignation,' she added rather self-consciously. 'I said we'd met by chance and liked each other and wanted to continue the acquaintance. I said we were going for a walk on the Heath.'

'What did he say?' asked Peter with unconcealed curiosity.

'He said he hoped we'd enjoy ourselves.'

'That was all?'

'That was all.'

'Most remarkable.'

'Dad knows when to keep quiet,' said Dorothy. 'Like you. In fact you are rather alike. I wish you could meet him.'

'Why not?' said Peter.

'It's taking up too much of your time. Unless,' added Dorothy thoughtfully, 'he could tutor you instead of Gerry. That's an idea.'

Peter seemed to think well of it too.

'Do you know, I believe he'd enjoy having a little job like that,' went on Dorothy. 'And he'd be able to help you quite a bit. You'd have to watch him, though, and make sure he didn't get too breathless. Shall we meet an hour earlier next Tuesday and I'll take you to see him?'

The arrangement was made. Dorothy drove a little way and then said: 'I suppose I'd better drop you here.'

'Unless you want me to come and meet your husband too. I'm quite prepared to if it will make you feel any easier.'

'I don't think it would,' said Dorothy, thinking over the suggestion quite seriously. 'He's fiendishly jealous of anybody I talk to. Including Dad. And our daily help. And my patients. Not to mention all those lovers that he's invented for me. I think it would be easier if he goes on imagining them and doesn't have an actual face to stick his stories to.'

'You're sure he won't suspect my existence except as the man who came to mend the washing-machine?'

'Quite sure,' said Dorothy firmly.

This was a lie. Dorothy knew perfectly well that Gerry had guessed that some sort of new influence had come into her life, subtly changing her own attitude towards him. Not only this, but Gerry probably knew the exact time when this had taken place. But if Peter thought he was putting her in some danger, or even making things more difficult for her with Gerry, then he would probably feel he ought quietly to slip out of her life. Such a prospect was unendurable.

Peter gave her a very keen look, as if he saw through her pretence, but to Dorothy's great relief he said no more. I don't really like deceiving him, she told herself; when we know each other better and I feel more sure of him I'll explain why I had to tell that lie. And perhaps one day I will be able to tell him about Irene too. But not yet. I can't bear to speak about it yet. Not even to Peter, who understands so well.

CHAPTER VI

'How was your father?' asked Gerry glancing up from the crossword puzzle.

The radio was playing loudly and he did not trouble to turn it down as he spoke. He had been playing either the radio or the record-player more or less continuously ever since Dorothy had found him in the bathroom the previous day, and always the sort of music she disliked. In his saner and happier days he had disliked it himself. She didn't know now whether he used it as a sort of drug or whether he only did it to annoy her.

'Not too bad,' she shouted through a particularly noisy patch. And then, in a blessed interval of comparative silence, she added: 'I'm tired. I'm going to bed to read a bit.'

She retreated towards the door of the sitting-room. The radio clicked off.

'Just a moment,' said Gerry.

Dorothy turned at the door. His voice had sounded quite as usual and he was looking at her in what appeared to be a friendly enough manner. And yet it was at that very moment that she became conscious of the first icy shiver of a fear that was to become more and more intense.

'What is it, Gerry?' she asked, assuming a greater

weariness than she actually felt. 'Is anything the matter?'

'I've finished the crossword but for two clues,' he replied in the most mundane of tones. 'Perhaps you will have an inspiration.'

And he read out the clues. Dorothy instantly supplied one of the solutions. The word was 'murder'. As soon as she had said it she felt that little shiver of fear again. She was quite sure from his reaction that he had already solved it for himself and was only asking her in order to make her repeat the word aloud. Every little thing that Gerry did or said had a hidden purpose behind it. Even when well he had had a tortuous mind that delighted in subtleties and undercurrents of meaning. And now his words and actions were more calculated than ever.

He had wanted her to say the word 'murder'. Was this some new sort of blackmail? A hint that he proposed to accuse her openly of murder or attempted murder? Or was it a warning that she might herself be in danger from him? The sickness of his mind had not, up till now, taken the form of violence towards her or to anybody except himself, but nothing was impossible with somebody in Gerry's condition. The one thing that was quite clear was that both she and Gerry had reached some kind of turning-point in their relationship with each other and it certainly was not a turn for the better.

'What was the other clue again?' she asked, pretending to stifle a yawn.

Gerry read it out. ' "Direction in hospital room gave notice." Six letters, something A something N and if murder is right, it ends in a D.'

'No idea,' said Dorothy after a moment's pause.

'Pity, I thought you'd get it,' said Gerry staring at the

newspaper. 'Hospitals, you know.'

'Sorry, can't help,' said Dorothy abruptly and left the room before he could speak to her again. The solution was 'warned' of course, as he had obviously seen for himself, being a quick crossword-puzzle solver, but he was trying to get her to say this word too. 'Murder' and 'warned'. What was she supposed to make of that? Was it intended as a serious threat towards her or towards somebody else? Or was it nothing more alarming than a new variation of his cat and mouse game with her?

Dorothy pretended to be asleep when Gerry came up to bed. She knew that he was no more taken in by this pretence than she had been over the crossword clues, but it was a relief all the same, because she felt less able than usual to cope with Gerry this evening. Confessing part of her troubles to Peter had greatly eased her mind, but oddly enough it had at the same time lowered her resistance to them. She had been stronger alone, with nerves stretched to the uttermost. The tautness was gone and there was no longer a risk that she might snap; but she felt weak and frightened in a way that was quite new to her. Suppose Gerry were to track Peter down and attack him? Or, even worse, suppose he were to get at Dorothy through her father? Peter was tough and could defend himself. Mr Thorn was old and sick and vulnerable. Gerry's twisted mind would enjoy making Dorothy suffer through him.

And it would all be through her own fault.

Long after Gerry had fallen into a drugged sleep, Dorothy Laver lay awake with her mind chipping relentlessly away at the forms his madness might take.

Her last waking thought was that nobody, not even herself in her professional capacity, had the power to force him to go into hospital care until after the damage had been done.

In fact Dorothy was totally unprepared for the first manifestation of the change in Gerry. Two days after her talk with Peter on Hampstead Heath she returned late from the afternoon clinic to find Gerry very carefully and self-consciously dusting the blue and white plates that stood on the pine dresser in the sitting-room. He had never done this before, nor taken any part in the work of the household. Dorothy's first thought was that he was going to break some of the plates because she liked them. Accidentally, of course, because the self-inflicted wounds on his wrists were still bandaged and his movements were awkward.

But such little pinpricks were so much less bad than the evils that she had been imagining that her first reaction was one of relief.

'Hullo, darling,' she said cheerfully. 'Didn't Mrs Oliver come today?'

Dorothy looked around her. The room with its mixture of Regency and cottage-kitchen effects, and the climbing plants showing through the open window, was her greatest joy in the house. Mrs Oliver shared her pleasure in it. She was a middle-aged woman with an invalid husband and few pleasures in her life. She had worked for Dorothy for six years, and there was quite a strong bond between them, even though with Dorothy's hours of work they did not see very much of each other. Mrs Oliver always arranged the cushions in the high-backed rocking-chair in a certain way and Dorothy saw instantly that this had not been done.

'Hasn't Mrs Oliver been?' she asked again, and went on before Gerry could answer: 'I do hope that doesn't mean her husband is worse.'

'As far as I know,' said Gerry, replacing a plate and standing back as if to check that it was in the right place, 'there has been no change in the condition of that mysterious invalid husband of hers. We didn't even refer to him in our brief conversation this morning.'

'Then what – ' began Dorothy, but broke off abruptly.

Gerry had turned aside from the dresser and was standing behind the settee, resting both hands on the back and looking at her. He was smiling, but it was a travesty of the charming humorous smile that was one of the things that had first attracted her to him. It did not reach the eyes, and the look in the eyes was vicious.

This is another stage set for me, thought Dorothy, and the little lightning flashes of fear quickly came and went. I am intended to ask what has happened to Mrs Oliver, she thought, and he will let it out slowly, drip by drip, dragging it out as long as possible.

I won't play his game, I won't ask, she said to herself. But instantly the thought came: if I frustrate him in this way, what will he do in revenge?

She decided to try to compromise, steeling herself against whatever unpleasantness she was going to hear.

'Oh well,' she said in her brightest bedside manner, 'I'm sure there's some very good reason for it all. Tell me about it over supper. I suppose there'll be nothing prepared, but we can have an omelette or get something from the freezer.'

Dorothy was walking towards the kitchen as she spoke. She could better bear whatever revelations were to come if she was moving about busily rather than sitting or standing still.

'Such a busy little woman,' said Gerry following her, and she knew from the spiteful tone of voice that he was very annoyed because things were not going according to plan. 'Ever so sorry I can't be of more help to you,' he continued, moving about the kitchen immediately behind her. 'Oh – you want to use the bigger plates? I'm ever so sorry. Yes, it has cracked.' He picked up a plate that he had dropped. 'Irretrievably, I fear. What a clumsy person I am! I shall have to try hard to be more use to you in future, shan't I? Poor, poor Dorothy. Such a lot of work in this house. Much too much work for you. Much too big for us. I really think the time has come for us to look for a smaller house, don't you? Such a pity, after all the work you have put into it, and it is a credit to you, I must say, very unusual, very charming. Not exactly beautiful, but very striking. Striking and original, like Dorothy herself. Not to everyone's taste. But some people like it. I liked it myself. But it's too much work. Especially now. Yes, I really think we are going to have to relieve you of the work of this house.'

Dorothy, vigorously beating eggs, did not pay too much attention to him. Threats about selling the house were nothing new. They had distressed her when they first started but she had grown fairly hardened to them. She could, as a last resort, call in the law to her aid, but on the whole she did not believe he would ever take any action about it, partly because he would then lose the satisfaction of threatening her and partly because she believed he was not capable of the sort of sustained effort required for carrying through a matter such as the sale of a house.

Gerry must have sensed that his words were not having the desired effect, because he changed tack.

'Such a clever little woman,' he said as they sat down to eat at the kitchen table. 'She can even cook quite a nice little meal. Wonderful woman, your wife, they say to me. Or they think it even if they don't say it. Wonderful how she copes with everything. Big house and garden, that useless husband of hers, and that job. Oh that terrible job! Just one long series of crazy people! However does she do it? And patients coming to the house too. And men who come to mend the washing-machine.'

He stopped suddenly and allowed time for this last remark to sink in before he began to talk again, this time with an affectation of sympathy.

'Yes, that really was the last straw, wasn't it? Poor old Doll. Ruined your free afternoon. First of all you have to cope with me and then just as you are getting a bit of peace and quiet at last, damn it if the man doesn't come along to mend the washing-machine. By the way, that was pretty quick work on the part of the electricity people. Usually one waits weeks for a repair. But you'd only just phoned them. When did you actually phone them, Dolly?'

His voice was friendly, quiet, faintly puzzled. Only somebody who knew him very well indeed could have guessed at the deadly purpose behind it.

'Can't remember,' replied Dorothy, inwardly shivering but outwardly as placid as he was. 'Was it last Friday?

Or Saturday morning? Or . . . no, wait a moment . . . didn't I get one of the girls in the office at the hospital to phone for me?'

'It can't have been Friday or Saturday,' said Gerry, watching her slice through an apple before taking a bite out of it, 'because it didn't go wrong until Sunday morning.'

'Then I must have asked one of the girls.' Dorothy took another bite. 'These are quite nice,' she said with her mouth full. 'New Zealand, I think.'

'Poor Dorothy.' Gerry reached out to touch her hand as it lay on the table gripping the remains of the apple. Instantly she raised it to her lips and chewed at the apple core. 'Poor old Doll. So much on your mind you can't possibly be expected to remember about a trivial little thing like a repair to a household gadget.'

Dorothy picked up a knife and cut off a section of cheese. She didn't really want any but it steadied her nerves to keep doing something. If I can only go on eating until I know the worst, she was saying to herself, I may get through it. She was still quite in the dark about what Gerry was really driving at. It had seemed to be something connected with Mrs Oliver, and Dorothy wished now that she had let it remain there, because whatever unpleasantness was brewing up for her in that connection, it could not be as bad as having him go on and on about the washing-machine. Had he actually telephoned to check up on her call and been told there was no record of it? She could get out of that, she supposed, by throwing the blame on the vast impersonal organization of the Electricity Board, but he would be constantly nagging about the bill and asking when they were going to make a charge for the work done.

Gerry always had made a great deal of fuss about checking the household bills, even before his breakdown. He loved to find mistakes and would not rest until they were put right. Useless to protest that she was paying the bills in any case, that she didn't care about a few pence one way or the other, and that if they were never sent a bill for the repair, why not just keep quiet and be grateful? Dorothy swallowed bread and cheese and knew with horrible certainty that the subject of the washing-machine repair was going to be brought up again and again at every meal time and at other times too; it would be worried at until her nerves were raw and she could not endure another second of it, and then dropped until the next time.

'You must be wondering,' said Gerry, 'why I am taking such an interest in the matter. The fact is that if we are to be without a cleaner then it seems only right and proper that whichever of us has more time should bear the brunt of the household duties.'

'Without a cleaner,' repeated Dorothy, shocked but at the same time relieved that it had come out at last. 'Doesn't Mrs Oliver want to come to us any more?'

'I dare say she does.'

'Is her husband worse?'

'Not that I know of.'

'But she's given notice?'

'Oh no, my dear. You've got it wrong.' Gerry's voice was very sweet and patient. 'She isn't leaving us. It is we who are sacking her.'

CHAPTER VII

Dorothy pushed back her chair, got to her feet, and shouted and swore at him, ignoring Gerry's little smile of triumph and not caring what she looked like or how upset she sounded.

'What did you tell her?' she asked when she had exhausted the first upsurge of fury, but instantly went on: 'No, don't trouble to answer that. It will only be a lie. Oh, poor Mrs Oliver! Why should she have to suffer for our miseries! You are a poisonous bastard, Gerry. There was no need to drag her in.'

'My motives for dismissing Mrs Oliver were three in number.' Gerry stood up and ticked off the points on his fingers, as if he were addressing a room full of students. 'One, to save money. Two, to give me something to do. Three, to have the house completely to ourselves. I will amplify these in turn. The two first are closely linked. Saving money will become even more necessary if, as I fear, it becomes impossible for me to continue with the tutorial work. But it will then be even more necessary for me to have some sort of occupation. What more suitable than that I should take over the household duties in place of Mrs Oliver? Killing two birds with one stone. I shall not, of course, perform them with her efficiency at first, but no doubt I shall improve with practice. The third motive is rather more complicated and requires a detailed exposition . . . where are you going?'

Dorothy had gone out into the hall and was rapidly

turning over the pages of a little book that lay on the telephone table. 'Mrs Oliver's address,' she muttered. 'I'm sure I put it in the book. It's somewhere in Camden Town.'

'Why this haste?' asked Gerry. 'A little note thanking her for past services would, I agree, be appropriate during the course of the next few days, but – '

'Here it is.' Dorothy tore a sheet off the telephone message pad and copied the address on to it. 'I'm going round to see her at once. Poor Mrs Oliver. She must be dreadfully upset.'

Gerry followed her as she fetched her handbag from the sitting-room and took out the car keys, and then he accompanied her to the front door, talking all the time.

' "Dreadfully upset" is a more apt description of your-self at this moment than of the worthy Mrs Oliver. I do assure you, my dear Dorothy, that there is no need for this excessive concern on her behalf. She has been told very politely that we have no further need of her services and has been paid up to date with a little extra. She has, I imagine, some regrets but with her talents and the shortage of cleaning women she will have no difficulty in finding another job, and I find it hard to believe that she has not weathered far more serious catastrophes during the course of her life. It's perfectly absurd to rush off like this as if you have been summoned to a particularly agonizing deathbed. You really are making a fool of yourself, Dorothy.'

They were at the front door. She pulled it open, slammed it behind her, and got into the car, which fortunately she had not yet put away in the garage. She was trembling so much that she could scarcely hold the steering-wheel, and in backing out into the road she scraped against a lamp-post and broke the glass on a rear light.

The little accident steadied her. We shall never hear the end of that repair job either, she thought, although it's my car and I'm paying for it and it's nothing whatever to do with him. Half-way along Middle Lane she had to stop for a moment to allow a car to straddle the roadway while making a sharp turn into a drive. She knew the driver slightly and they smiled and waved at each other. It was reassuring to Dorothy, this little glimpse of a normal everyday world outside the horror that her own home had become, and she drove on more confidently.

Princes Street was undergoing a transformation. One side had been demolished and blocks of council flats were going up. The other side consisted of a Victorian terrace with the houses at one end either boarded up or vandalized and those at the other showing signs of human habitation. In this last section Dorothy found the number she was seeking, walked up the worn stone steps to what had once been quite an elegant doorway, and lifted what had once been a beautiful and unusual brass knocker. There appeared to be no bell in working order.

While she waited, her present misery and fear became mixed with a remoter, less intense kind of distress. She had spent her childhood in gloomy, decaying areas of large cities. Only in his last few years before retirement had her father consented to move to a pleasanter suburban parish. Dorothy's mother had been a social worker, equally dedicated to the unfortunates of this world. Neither of them had ever put any pressure on the child to follow in their footsteps, but on the other hand,

neither of them had ever fully appreciated the extent of
the conflict in their daughter's mind between her deep
compassion and longing to help on the one hand, and her
squeamishness and sheer physical revulsion from the
smell and sight of poverty on the other.

Princes Street brought back many memories. Dorothy
shut her eyes for a moment and had a vision of her own
lovely Hampstead home.

Except that it was not her own and never would be
while Gerry lived. Dorothy shook her head violently and
gave a little cry as the overwhelming longing for Gerry's
death assaulted her again and made her dizzy with its
force.

'Dr Laver! Who'd have thought . . . whatever is the
matter? Come in and sit down. Come on in now.'

Dorothy felt herself being guided through the doorway
and towards a chair. She sank back and shut her eyes.

'I'm terribly sorry, Mrs Oliver,' she said a moment
later. 'I felt quite faint for a moment. I'll be all right now.
What a thing to do – to turn up unexpectedly on your
doorstep and go and collapse on you!'

She tried to smile, but the big, haggardly handsome
woman standing in front of her did not respond in kind.

'You're ill, Doctor,' she said, 'and I'm not at all
surprised. Working yourself to death. Now what can I
get for you? I haven't any spirits in the house, only some
sherry, but I can go out and get something if you like.'

'Just some water, please,' said Dorothy.

Mrs Oliver fetched it and Dorothy took a small white
tablet from her handbag and swallowed it.

'It's only a very mild tranquillizer,' she said, smiling
with more confidence this time. 'If I'd had any sense I'd

have taken it before. Then I wouldn't have given you such a fright. Have I come at a very bad moment, Mrs Oliver? You weren't busy with your husband, were you?'

Mrs Oliver reassured her. Fred had had one of his better days and had gone out for a stroll and a drink. She hadn't been doing anything in particular, was thinking of letting down the hem of an old summer dress, that was all.

'Why don't you go on with it,' said Dorothy, 'if you don't mind me sitting here a little to recover.'

'I might as well, I suppose.'

Mrs Oliver found some scissors and began to cut away at the stitches round the hem. Dorothy watched her in silence for a moment or two. She had the impression that now the first shock of her own appearance was over, Mrs Oliver was feeling rather awkward and glad of something to occupy her hands. The room was a curious mixture of a few old pieces of solid mahogany and of cheap new furniture already beginning to look shabby. The armchairs in which they sat had been savagely scratched by sharp claws.

'Where's Bella?' asked Dorothy. She and Mrs Oliver had on several occasions chatted about the cat.

'Out in the yard,' was the reply. 'She'll be in presently.'

Mrs Oliver turned the dress round and proceeded to clip round the other side of the hem.

She's waiting for me to begin, thought Dorothy, and suddenly she wished with all her heart that she had never come. What Gerry had said was perfectly true. The job in Hampstead was a pleasant one for Mrs Oliver, but there were plenty of others to be had. Dr Laver was no doubt regarded with respect and possibly even a little affectionate concern, but Mrs Oliver had her own life and her own problems, and Dorothy was only on the fringe of them. It was Dorothy's crisis, not Mrs Oliver's, that had led to this untimely and increasingly embarrassing visit. There seemed to Dorothy to be only two courses of action open to her. She could pour out her troubles to Mrs Oliver as she had done to Peter, and in that case she would no doubt receive a great deal of affectionate sympathy which would be very comforting. Or she could explain away her collapse as convincingly as she was able, and back up whatever story Gerry had told.

The trouble with the first alternative was that Mrs Oliver could hardly be expected not to tell her husband about it, and he in turn would tell some of his cronies, and the thought of complete strangers discussing the miseries of Gerry and herself was intolerable to Dorothy, for Gerry's sake as well as for her own. Besides, as she had discovered after talking to Peter, this unloading of her burden seemed to weaken rather than to strengthen her; she seemed to be one of those rare people who disprove the rule that a trouble shared is a trouble halved.

On the other hand it was useless to pretend to Mrs Oliver that there was perfect harmony between Gerry and herself. Mrs Oliver had seen and heard too much.

Dorothy decided to plunge straight in without thinking any more.

'I'm afraid we've got in a muddle,' she said. 'I don't want you to stop working for us at all and I was very upset when my husband told me he'd told you not to come again. I think he must have been worried by something I said about having to cut down expenses, but in fact I'd been thinking about something quite different...'

Her voice tailed away. The trouble was that she had no idea what Gerry had really said to Mrs Oliver. The other woman, understanding Dorothy's confusion, came to the rescue.

'You're not to worry about it at all, Doctor,' she said warmly. 'I quite understand. Truly I do. Mr Laver was very kind and explained it all. He said he wouldn't be able to earn much for the next few months but he did feel up to doing the housework, so that it seemed only sensible for him to do it and save my wages.'

So Gerry was telling the truth about that, thought Dorothy in a bemused manner. How clever of him, to do something nasty that still enabled him to tell the truth.

'It does seem strange for a man to be looking after the house,' went on Mrs Oliver. 'I can't quite get used to it myself, but after all, why not, as Fred always says. He's quite happy to clean up when he's fit for it and get me a meal ready for when I come in from work, so why shouldn't Mr Laver feel the same? That's what I said to myself, Doctor, and although I've always liked coming to you, I quite understand. So you're not to worry about it any more. You've quite enough to worry about already. More than enough in my opinion. No, you're not to rush away again – not without a cup of tea. Not after having a turn like that. You sit and rest yourself, and now you know you haven't to worry about me you'll be feeling a little better. I'll soon have it made.'

And she left the room. Dorothy lay back and closed her eyes. One part of herself was deeply grateful to this nice, sensible, understanding woman for taking control of the situation and making it so easy for her. But the rest of her was panicking worse than ever. She felt as if a trap was closing round her, a trap set by Gerry. To have Mrs Oliver coming regularly into her home had been a considerable source of comfort and support. And now it was to be removed. Gerry's unpredictable behaviour and her own reserve had driven away all the acquaintances who once used to call. Between them they had made it a very unhappy house to visit. No wonder people stayed away. And now the house was to lose its last little focus of steadiness and sanity. There would be nobody left to cross the threshold except a few patients – sick and self-centred people – and Gerry himself. Except for business callers such as the gasman coming to read the meter.

Or the man coming to mend the washing-machine.

Dorothy shifted in her chair and gave a little moan. She was going to have to do something about it. She could not live in that house alone with Gerry any longer. She was too afraid. But what to do? Even if she could bring herself to the point of just walking out on him she would never dare to do it. Gerry could take too terrible a revenge.

Mrs Oliver came back with the tea-tray. Dorothy sipped and made conversation about Fred and the cat and the present miserable condition of Princes Street.

'It'll be better when they've finished building the flats and got people in them,' said Mrs Oliver, 'though I wish they didn't have to pull down all the old houses. I wish they'd just done them up a bit and put in bathrooms like they've been doing in Victoria Avenue.'

'Victoria Avenue?' Dorothy's heart began to thump. This was Peter's address. 'Is that far from here?'

'Just round the back,' said Mrs Oliver. 'Same sort of houses but some of them don't look at all bad now they're painted up. You get nice big rooms in these older houses – gives you a bit of space to turn round in. Mind you, I wouldn't mind a nice modern kitchen.'

Dorothy chatted a little longer, insisted on Mrs Oliver accepting a ten-pound note as a goodbye present, and begged her to keep in touch.

'Let me know what sort of job you find and whether you are happy,' she said.

'And you take care of yourself, Doctor. A good holiday, that's what you need. And Mr Laver too.'

'Perhaps I'll be able to persuade him to a week or two in the country,' said Dorothy. 'But he doesn't much like being away from home, you know.'

They were standing in the shabby handsome entrance at the top of the broken steps, opposite the steel framework of the building site. A thunderstorm was brewing. The evening sky was lurid and oppressive. Dorothy felt an overwhelming sense of desolation, as if the last doorway that might lead to hope was being closed on her. She came down the steps and stood leaning against the dusty privet hedge that encircled the stone front yard. The car was only a few yards away but for the moment her legs felt powerless to carry her so far. A sad little old man walked by, carrying a big load of washing for the laundrette. Then came two teenaged boys, one black and one white, moodily kicking a tin can along the gutter. A car and a post office van drove past, and after that there was no life in the street save for a black and white cat.

Dorothy bent down to stroke it, but it snarled at her and ran through the railings.

I wish I were dead, she said to herself, straightening up again and at last walking the few yards to the car. She got in and drove a little way, taking the first turning to the left and then the first left again, and drawing in to the kerb at the first vacant space. There was no road sign within view, but according to Mrs Oliver's remarks, this must be Victoria Avenue. Dorothy was not conscious of any intention of seeking out Peter, or even of hoping that she might run into him by chance. In fact she was conscious of nothing except extreme lethargy. The effort of shifting the car a hundred yards had totally exhausted her. I can't go any further, I'll just have to stay here, she said to herself.

She leant against the side of the car and shut her eyes. Her muscles felt paralysed but at the same time she was intensely conscious of every sound about her. This seemed to be a livelier road than the neighbouring Princes Street and quite a lot of traffic went by. There were also doors opening and footsteps passing and children crying and dogs barking. And after a little while came the first faint rumblings of thunder. When the crashes became very loud and the rain came down in sheets Dorothy opened her eyes. She had always enjoyed thunderstorms and even in her present condition felt a flicker of the familiar sense of release that came from the lightning and the lashing of the rain.

When the worst of it was over she still felt deadly tired but no longer paralysed. She put the car into gear, eased it carefully out into the centre of the road, and drove slowly along, glancing at the houses with Mrs Oliver's

remarks in mind. One side of the road was very dilapi-
dated, the other looked quite smart. Peter lived at sixty-
eight. An even number. The shabby side. But she was not
going to call on him, she told herself, and she drove on
without glancing at the numbers on the doors any more.

She had turned out of Victoria Avenue and was going
past a row of shops, some of which were still open, when
she saw him. He had his head bent against the still
driving rain and was carrying a big blue plastic bag. A
car moved off from the kerb and she was able to pull in.
She leant across to wind down the window of the passenger
seat and he looked up and saw her.

'Get in,' she said. 'I'll run you home.'

'I'm absolutely soaking,' he protested.

'It doesn't matter. The seat's wet anyway. I forgot to
shut the window. Laundrette?' She watched him heave
the bulging bag over to the back seat.

'Yes,' said Peter. 'It's not worth getting out the van to
drive round. And I might as well have saved the money
for the dryer. I ought to have waited till it stopped
raining but I hadn't taken enough to read and was getting
very bored. We'd better go round the block. You'll never
do a U-turn here.'

They drove round the block in silence.

'More trouble?' said Peter when they had stopped as
near as it was possible to get to No. 68. 'Were you coming
to see me?'

'Oddly enough, I wasn't.' Hastily Dorothy explained
the situation about Mrs Oliver and her own reactions to
it. 'It sounds idiotic,' she said at last, 'because it's not as
if she is a close friend or anything, but it meant a lot to
me, having a sensible person coming regularly to the

house, and after I'd left her just now I really felt as if I only wanted to die. It was terrible. Everything seemed to be blocked in every direction. I've always believed I could understand how people felt in a suicidal state of depression. But I couldn't. It's much worse than I'd thought. And that was only a few minutes of it. I suppose Gerry feels like that most of the time.'

'I don't think it will help you to try to imagine how Gerry feels,' said Peter sharply. 'I think you'd better stop that.'

'I'm sorry,' said Dorothy. 'Was I getting hysterical? I'm very sorry.' She swallowed convulsively. She was indeed very near to tears, and if they once started there would be no end to them.

'Were you proposing to go home now?' asked Peter.

'Yes. What else?'

'You could stay the night here if you like. I'll clear out and leave you, or stay and cosset you. Whichever you prefer.'

'It would only be putting it off,' said Dorothy doubtfully.

'True, but you might feel a little bit more able to cope with it in the morning.'

'I might go home and find him really dead in the morning,' she muttered.

'I was afraid you'd say that. So you want to go home now.' It was more a statement than a question.

'Yes,' whispered Dorothy, 'but I don't know if I'll be able to manage if he's cut his wrists again. Or done anything else.'

'In that case we shall just have to send for another doctor, shan't we?'

'We?'

'I'm coming with you. Just let me dump this wet washing. Like to see my pad?'

'Yes,' said Dorothy, wondering whether this was just his tactful way of ensuring that she did not run away while he was inside.

'Gosh, you really are organized!' she cried a moment later.

Peter had the two back rooms on the second floor. They were newly decorated and adequately furnished, but the most surprising thing about them was the big chart pinned on the wall of the bigger room. It was a timetable of his studies for the year, containing dates of radio and television programmes, tutorials and counselling sessions, together with numerous neat notes about books to consult, questions that needed revision or special attention, and various similar memoranda. On a large table was a tape-recorder, a radio, a pocket calculator, various types of graph paper and geometrical instruments, and a pile of books. Some sheets of paper covered with calculations and writing showed that he was at the moment struggling with some sort of exercise.

'How many hours a day do you work?' asked Dorothy after exclaiming again at this scene of industry.

'Eight at my job, four at my studies, which sometimes includes things like a couple of hours in the afternoon having a private English tutorial. Three hours spent travelling – mostly in traffic blocks. Two hours for eating and shopping and laundretting and suchlike. Seven to sleep. That's my twenty-four. A very chaste and sober life.' He made a face. 'I only hope I can keep it up for long enough to get my degree.'

'I can quite see that there's no room in it for a wife or even a mistress,' said Dorothy. 'And no room in it for wasting time with the likes of me. I'm going back home alone, Peter. I feel I can face it now. It's helped me no end, just having this glimpse of your tremendously orderly existence. Honestly it has. You don't know how much good it does me, just knowing you're there beavering away.'

'Come on,' said Peter. 'I don't think we ought to delay any longer.'

'But, Peter . . .'

'Hurry up.'

She protested all the way downstairs and out into the street. The rain had stopped and the evening felt fresh and clean.

'Are you feeling fit to drive?' he asked.

'Yes, but honestly – '

'Then you start off and I'll follow you in the van. When we get to Middle Lane I'll park on the other side of the road a little way back from your gate. Leave the gate open after you've driven through. If you find everything is all right, come out and shut it and that will be the signal for me to go away. But of course we won't speak to each other or make any contact. If you want me to come in, just stand at the gate and I'll come at once. If you don't appear within twenty minutes I shall come and investigate. Got that?'

'Yes. Thank you, Peter.'

'I shall be anxious to hear how you are, though, even if you do come out and shut the gate. Can I phone you at the hospital tomorrow?'

'Yes. I'll probably have a patient with me, so I'm afraid I shall sound rather formal.'

'That doesn't matter. As long as I know you're all right. Let's go.'

CHAPTER VIII

It was just on ten o'clock when the blue Vauxhall turned into Middle Lane, followed at some distance by the little Ford van. The road was not very well lit, but the sky was by no means dark, and the white gateposts of Pond Cottage showed up clearly. Peter kept his eyes on them until he began to feel hypnotized. The minutes passed and Dorothy did not appear. At a quarter past ten Peter got out of the van and walked up and down the road, trying to appear to anyone who might see him as if he were taking a casual stroll, but in reality feeling more and more anxious every minute.

At nineteen minutes past ten he walked through the open gateway of Pond Cottage and up the drive. Light shone from every window of the house, as if a party were taking place there. It made the total silence seem all the more uncanny. If murder or attempted murder had been committed here, surely there would be some sign or sound or feel of it. Surely it would not be like this, just a blaze of light from all the uncurtained windows of a silent house.

Peter came up to the front door and stood close to it, listening intently. There was no sound to be heard from within. He turned the handle and gave a little push. The door was unlocked. He opened it very cautiously, keeping well behind it and being prepared to spring backwards any moment. Dorothy had been very much afraid, and fear was catching. For all he knew he might be walking into a trap. Suppose this husband of hers really was a maniac, homicidal as well as suicidal, and had knocked her unconscious and was now lying in wait for her supposed lover. It was perfectly idiotic, of course, but all the same he could not help his imagination running a little away with him.

Maybe Dorothy herself had set a trap for him. After all, he knew nothing about her except what he could see for himself: that she was fascinating and very attractive in an odd sort of way; that she was under great stress and very much afraid. If what she had said of her husband was true, then he certainly ought to be in some sort of care other than that of his wife. But Peter had never even seen the man and all he knew of him was what Dorothy herself had told him. Could it all be a complete fabrication? Would it not be possible for an overworked psychiatrist herself to have some sort of mental breakdown that led her to imagine herself threatened and to invent fantastic stories? Or if it was true that her husband was making her life a hell but that she could see no way to free herself, then wouldn't she be longing for somebody else to free her?

Peter was almost sure that Dorothy was absolutely straight and really was going to the utmost lengths not to drag other people into her own troubles, but he could not quite suppress a little nagging doubt.

What he saw next increased it.

Since the front door seemed to be free of booby traps, and nobody appeared to be lurking behind it, he stepped into the hall. At the same moment Dorothy appeared from the kitchen at the back of the house. She did not immediately see him and he caught the expression on her face before she had brought it under control. It was a blood-chilling mixture of hatred and horror. Her mouth was slightly open, her teeth clenched; her skin was dead white and her violet eyes looked as black as her hair.

She saw him and the muscles relaxed and she once more looked intensely weary and anxious but quite sane.

'Is it time already?' she asked. 'I thought there was another minute to go.'

'It seemed a long time,' he replied. 'I was getting very impatient.'

'I'm sorry. He's not here, but I didn't want to call you until I'd made quite sure that he wasn't in the house.'

'You're sure now?'

'More or less. I've looked everywhere. Cupboards and all.'

That explains the lights on in every room, thought Peter. She left them on as she went round. She really is in a very bad way.

'Would you like me to come round with you to look again?' he asked.

'I don't think it's necessary. Thanks all the same. He left a note, you see. But I didn't trust it. That's why I was checking.'

Her voice was dull and lifeless. She shut her eyes and seemed to sway a little. Peter caught her arm.

'Come and sit down and tell me.'

In the sitting-room he turned out all the lights except

one reading lamp. Dorothy leant back on the settee.

'I found it in his study,' she said. 'I went there first. If he doesn't answer when I come in, it usually means I'm going to find a message there. This was a longer one than usual and rather different.' Her voice shook and she took several deep breaths before going on. 'I told you what it usually is,' she continued. 'Self-reproaches. Wants to end it all in order to stop being a burden to me. I always destroy them immediately. There weren't any self-reproaches this time. It was all directed against me. He's going to kill himself in order to – in order to – '

Again she had to pause and take a deep breath. 'In revenge for an injury that I once did him. He threatens to kill himself in such a way that it will look as if I have murdered him. That's what he says. He doesn't say how or when or whether it's going to happen in this house or somewhere else. That's why I felt I had to go all round the house before I called you. He might have been lurking somewhere and I'd have been dragging you into a trap.'

'I see,' said Peter. 'May I see the letter?'

'I'd rather you didn't. It seems . . . it seems treacherous to him somehow.'

'Treacherous! And you've been subjected to a threat like that! I'm all for loyalty and for standing up for people and covering up their weaknesses, but to carry it to these lengths . . . it's insane.'

'Yes, I think perhaps I am a little mad myself,' she said wearily. 'It's probably just because I hate him so much that I feel I've got to protect him and that I can't stand anyone, even you, to see his outpourings. Least of all you.'

Peter did not ask why. 'Listen,' he said patiently, 'I'm not asking to see this letter because I want to feel superior to your husband or because I have any pleasure in reading such things. I'm only asking so that I can try to form an opinion for myself of how serious the threat is and what we ought to do about it. You'll say I can't judge because I know nothing about mentally ill people. I say you can't judge because you're too emotionally involved. But between us we might manage to make some sort of objective assessment. Is that sense or isn't it?'

Without a word Dorothy fished in the pocket of the short raincoat that she was still wearing and drew out a few folded sheets of paper. Peter read in silence. He tried to prevent an expression of distaste from forming itself upon his face but was not sure that he had succeeded. The contents of the letter were exactly as Dorothy had said, much embroidered with abuse and interwoven with descriptions of her relationship with her 'lover'. Whether it was more revolting than it was horrifying Peter could not tell. Certainly it aroused both sensations, but also, in spite of it all, one could not help but feel pity for the man who had written it.

Dorothy's circumstances and Dorothy's feelings became very plain to Peter as he read her husband's letter. And yet the little niggling doubt about her remained and was reinforced when he asked the inevitable question.

'This last sentence – I don't get what he's referring to.'

Gerry had written: 'You really would like to die, wouldn't you, Dolly, so that you can stop feeling guilty about Irene.'

'Who is Irene?' asked Peter.

'That's the – the reference to the injury he thinks I

did him,' said Dorothy.

Peter made no comment on this evasive answer, but simply handed back the folded sheets of paper and said: 'I think we ought to call the police.'

'Oh no!' It was a cry of horror, much as he had expected.

'It contains a threat that has to be taken seriously,' went on Peter stolidly. 'A double threat. Against himself and against you.'

'I can't, I can't.' Dorothy became very agitated. 'That would mean everything coming out. It'll all be churned over again and again and we'll end up in exactly the same position as before. There's nothing on earth that anyone can do so long as it's all threats and no action.'

'But there has been action. He's made lots of suicide attempts. You said so.'

'Only token attempts. It used to be a crime, but it isn't now.'

'Then what happens if somebody finds an attempted suicide and reports it? Surely they are taken to hospital? Surely they are?' persisted Peter as Dorothy did not immediately reply.

'Yes, if they need treatment,' she said at last.

'And what then?'

'They pump out the stomach if it's poisoning or do whatever else is needed. Then they discharge them.'

'Oh come now, Dorothy! I know we're short of mental nurses and doctors and hospital beds but surely they don't just shove people back into whatever situation drove them to try to kill themselves without making any attempt to find out what's the matter and give them some help?'

'A quarter of an hour in outpatients once a month.

Once a week if you're lucky.' Dorothy's laugh held a ring of hysteria. 'Not exactly adequate for delving into the depths of a human soul and trying to put it in order. That's a twenty-four-hour-a-day job, you know.'

'I see,' said Peter soberly. 'I hadn't realized the situation was as desperate as that.'

'It is very desperate. Mental illness is the epidemic of our era. People like me can do no more than put a finger in the dyke to hold back the flood.'

'But surely in your position . . . you would have some pull when it comes to your own husband . . .'

'Get him into a hospital psychiatric department ahead of the queue, you mean? Certainly I could do that. There're only two objections. First of all, there's practically nothing they can do for him except give him the sort of pills he's having already. Secondly, he wouldn't stay. He's not certifiable, you know. You have to do quite a lot to be that. And with anyone other than me he sounds quite rational and plausible. He happens to have an excellent intellect. He'd make rings round any doctor who tried to prove him *non compos mentis*.'

'I'm sorry,' said Peter. 'I'm afraid I hadn't fully realized the position. All right then. We don't ring the police. We just wait on events. Is that what you suggest?'

'For tonight, at any rate,' said Dorothy. Her little burst of spirit had spent itself and she sounded dull with weariness again. 'And since he may come back at any moment I think you'd better go, Peter. It won't help if he finds you here.'

'I'm not leaving you alone.'

They wrangled about this for a minute or two.

'Then I'll call somebody else to stay with you,' he said

eventually. 'Somebody above suspicion. What about that friend of yours. Pauline, was it?'

'Oh no!' Dorothy shrank from the idea. 'I can't possibly tell Pauline. She married somebody else and is a widow now, but I believe she's never really stopped being in love with Gerry. We only keep friendly by not talking about things.'

'Then I'll phone your father. Now shut up. So he's old and tired and has a tough life behind him. What sort of a life are you having at the moment? How do you think he would feel if anything frightful were to happen to you and he hadn't even been given the chance to prevent it? Come on. What's his name? What's his number?'

Dorothy supplied them. Peter dialled the number.

'Mr Thorn? I'm sorry to be ringing so late . . . I hope you hadn't gone to bed . . . Good . . . My name is Peter Tarrant and I know your daughter – I believe she's mentioned me to you . . . Yes, I'm here with her at her home and she's in a spot of trouble . . . no, she's not ill, she's perfectly all right. It's about her husband. He's disappeared. Gone off and she doesn't know where. I don't think she ought to be alone here in case there's some bad news . . . oh good, I hoped you'd say that. I'll come and fetch you . . . fifteen minutes or so – traffic's not so bad this time of night . . . thanks very much. We'll be there.' He put down the receiver. 'Come on. I'm not leaving you alone here, even for half an hour.'

Another wrangle began. Before it had got very far the telephone rang. Dorothy lifted the receiver.

'Is that you, dear?' said her father's voice. 'Is Mr Tarrant still there?'

'Yes,' said Dorothy.

'Then keep him there. I'm getting a taxi. Shan't be long.'

And he rang off before she had a chance to reply.

Peter laughed when Dorothy told him. 'I'm going to like your father,' he said. 'He obviously knows just how to deal with you.'

CHAPTER IX

The Reverend William Thorn turned out to be almost disconcertingly like Dorothy in appearance, except that the thick hair was shining white instead of black and the eyes were faded violet. He was tall and upright and had the same way of holding his head. Faintly aloof, unconsciously arrogant, Peter told himself. A man who did not bend or break easily, probably a man who did not find it too easy to establish superficial relationships with people, but who seemed to have an outsize conscience, like his daughter.

'I quite agree that we don't want to do anything that might make it harder for Gerry to get over this,' he said when the situation had been explained to him.

Peter noticed that Mr Thorn did not appear either shocked or surprised when told about the numerous suicide attempts. It was evident that he had guessed that something of the sort had been going on, and Dorothy's protectiveness, as Peter had himself suspected, had been to a large extent unnecessary.

'I'd like to see this last letter of Gerry's, please,' said Mr Thorn.

'It's rather beastly, Dad,' said Dorothy.

'Is it? I dare say I've seen worse at one time or another.'

Reluctantly Dorothy handed the letter over and Mr Thorn read it without comment. Then he folded it up neatly and put it in his pocket. 'I'd better keep it safe,' he said. 'If anything has happened to Gerry it will be needed as evidence.'

How well he knows her, thought Peter again; she would destroy it if she got half a chance, even though it might be vital for her own protection if indeed Gerry had carried out his threat to kill himself in such a way that she would be suspected of murdering him. But how could he have done so? If he had got a gun and gone and shot himself on the middle of Hampstead Heath Dorothy would no doubt blame herself for it, but there would have to be some very solid evidence for Dorothy to be suspected of murder.

Peter spoke this thought aloud. Mr Thorn was inclined to agree that Gerry was still alive. But where? 'I suppose you made sure he wasn't in the garage,' he said.

Peter shook his head, annoyed with himself for not thinking of this obvious precaution.

'The car,' cried Dorothy. 'That must be it. We've got two Vauxhalls. Same model. Keys fit them both. Oh, what a fool I am!' She clenched her hands and banged at the sides of her head. 'It's obvious. He's gassed himself from the exhaust and rigged it up to look as if I've done it.'

'How?' asked Peter bluntly.

'How do I know how?' Her voice rose. 'He's so bloody clever he'd fix it somehow.'

'But why,' asked Peter in the same down to earth way, 'should he go to all that trouble to throw suspicion on you and then ruin it all by writing his confession in that letter?'

'Because he's mad. That's why.'

'Wouldn't we have heard the engine running if that's what he's done?' persisted Peter.

'Not necessarily. The garage is round the side. The doors will be shut. We were very preoccupied.'

She spoke in a jerky, breathless manner. Her hands were twisting together and there was a hint of that look in her eyes that Peter had seen when he came upon her unawares. His doubts returned, not in a little niggling way, but with a sharp stab. She could have been pretending all along, he thought; twenty minutes is quite a long time. And I wasn't watching the house and garden, only the gateway. I saw nothing but the gateposts.

Suppose after she found the letter – that's genuine surely – she searched everywhere and found him in the garage. Unconscious or semi-conscious. As on earlier occasions. Found him in time to bring him round. Again as on earlier occasions. And decided not to. Perhaps even hurried it on. Perhaps he'd left himself enough air to survive and she closed the opening to make sure. Then she'd have come to the gate and told me everything was all right. But she was too late. I came a minute too early. She couldn't get rid of me. She had to change her plans. I don't blame her. I only wish she'd been honest with me.

He stared at Dorothy and she stared back.

'Don't you think we ought to go and see?' said Mr Thorn, beginning to get up from his chair.

Dorothy jumped up and pushed him back. 'Not you, Dad. You oughtn't to be involved in this at all, in your condition. I'll go myself.'

'No,' said Peter reaching the door of the sitting-room before her. 'I think it would be best if I go.'

Again they stared at each other: their eyes were very nearly on a level.

'Very well,' said Dorothy. 'You'll need the spare key to the garage. He may have locked himself in. It's an ordinary wooden door like a shed. The old coachhouse.'

She went into her consulting-room and came back with a key.

'Do you always keep it in there?' he asked.

'Yes.' She was very abrupt.

But she was coming from the kitchen when I came in and saw her, thought Peter. Does that mean she really doesn't know what's happened? Or had she already replaced the spare key in the consulting-room?

'Thanks,' he said. 'I won't be long.'

At the front door she called after him: 'Don't try to move him if he's there. Call me at once.'

'Yes, Doctor,' he said and ran off round the drive to the side of the house.

Dorothy returned to the sitting-room and began to fuss over her father. 'I do wish you hadn't been dragged into this. Are you feeling all right, Dad? I hope you hadn't gone to bed when we phoned.'

'No, my love, I had not gone to bed,' replied Mr Thorn patiently. 'I don't need much sleep and I never go to bed till after midnight. And I am feeling perfectly all right. I will tell you at once if I'm not. I wish you had been equally honest with me, Dorothy. It is very grievous to learn that Gerry has been behaving in this way and that you've kept it all to yourself. I suppose he has been tormenting you by making you feel guilty about the child, which is all nonsense. You know that, don't you, Dorothy?'

'Please, Dad. Please don't talk about her.'

The pain in his daughter's voice was more than Mr Thorn could bear to hear. 'Well, there's no sense in wasting our breath on recriminations,' he said. 'We'll just have to carry on from here. I like your Mr Tarrant. Economical sort of person. Very self-controlled. Doesn't waste words or effort. But not without feeling. I hope he's not going to be any the worse for this little adventure.'

'I know I oughtn't to have dragged him in,' cried Dorothy, 'but he insisted on coming.'

'Just as I did. Well, we shall know the worst in a minute or two. Poor Gerry. What misery he causes. A most unhappy soul.'

Mr Thorn shut his eyes and took slow, controlled breaths, conserving his limited energies for whatever shock was to come. Dorothy paced about the room, clenching and unclenching her hands.

'What was that?' she cried suddenly, standing still just inside the window and peering out into the garden.

Mr Thorn stirred and opened his eyes but did not speak.

'I thought I heard voices.' Dorothy left the window and came to sit on the arm of her father's chair. 'I don't know how to bear it if he isn't dead,' she said quietly. And then she clutched his arm. 'Is that dreadfully wicked of me? Am I so very bad?'

'No, my love. Not bad.' He soothed her. 'Just terribly overstrained. But it's coming to an end now. It will soon be over. Do you understand that, Dorothy? We shall know in a minute what has happened. But whether

Gerry is dead or alive doesn't matter. As far as you are concerned it is finished. Just hold on to that. In one way or another this is going to end. I promise you, Dorothy.'

'Thank you,' she murmured. 'I'm sorry, Dad. I ought to have told you about it ages ago.'

'Yes. Never mind. It's nearly over now. Ssh. Listen. Can that be Gerry?'

Mr Thorn raised his head. The distant voices that Dorothy had heard sounded much nearer. There was a loud shout and then something that sounded more like an animal growl than a human voice.

'He'll kill him!' screamed Dorothy and ran out of the room and out of the house.

Mr Thorn gave a helpless little shrug and leaned back resignedly. If he tried to intervene it might bring on an attack and he would be more nuisance than help; Dorothy would have two patients to look after instead of one. There was nothing he could do, but the minutes of waiting seemed very long.

The shouting died away. Mr Thorn, listening intently, heard two voices coming nearer. One of them was Dorothy's; the man's voice was not so clear and it was not until they were actually in the house that Mr Thorn could make out who it belonged to. He got carefully to his feet and walked towards the sitting-room door. The waiting had become intolerable.

'Mind his head,' he heard Dorothy say, and then the man's voice said: 'All right. I can take most of the weight now.'

The voice was that of Peter Tarrant, not his son-in-law. Mr Thorn was conscious of a great sense of relief which he did not care to analyse too closely.

'In here,' said Dorothy.

Mr Thorn stepped back into the room and rearranged the cushions on the setee.

'Thanks,' said Dorothy as she and Peter eased Gerry's limp body into a comfortable position.

Mr Thorn bent over it. 'He's not dead,' he murmured.

'No,' said Dorothy, 'nor even fatally injured. You were wrong in thinking it's all coming to an end.'

And she gave a hysterical little laugh.

'I said in one way or another,' said her father. His glance moved from her to Peter Tarrant. 'Good God, man!' he cried in quite a different sort of voice. 'Are you badly hurt?'

There was blood running down one side of Peter's face. Some of it had dripped on to the collar of his jacket.

'I don't think it's much,' he said, putting a hand up to his forehead. 'I'll see to it in a moment. Is there anything more I can do, Dorothy?'

Dorothy was standing completely still, looking down on her husband's unconscious body. 'No, thanks,' she said. 'It's too late. It's a pity you didn't finish the job off properly while you were about it.'

Peter's eye caught Mr Thorn's and signalled an appeal.

'Dorothy,' said the old man sharply, 'you have two men here who need your skilled help. Are you going to give it them or shall I telephone for an ambulance?'

'I'm sorry.' Dorothy gave herself a little shake. 'Come up to the bathroom and I'll clean up that cut,' she said to Peter. 'There's no hurry about Gerry. He won't come round just yet.'

CHAPTER X

'He came at me when I was shutting the door of the garage,' said Peter about a quarter of an hour later. 'I can't remember exactly what he said. "Stop thief" was the gist of it. I said something like "Are you Mr Laver? Your wife's looking for you." And he said something more and then I noticed he'd got something in his hand. It looked like a breadknife. I got hold of his arm and managed to turn it round and to duck at the same time and he caught me with the blunt edge of the knife. Surprisingly hard.'

Dorothy gave a little shudder.

'Yes. Lucky,' said Peter. 'It's a beautifully sharp knife. I didn't fancy any more of that and I hit him on the jaw. He went backwards and unluckily caught his head on that stone you've got for propping open the garage door. That's the point when Dorothy appeared on the scene.' Peter turned to Mr Thorn. 'And the rest you know.'

'But where had he come from? How long had he been there?' Dorothy looked at Peter. 'Why didn't you notice him when you were watching the house? You could see the front drive.' She sounded reproachful rather than mystified.

'I couldn't see round to the garage,' he retorted. 'Why didn't you look in the garden yourself when you were hunting for him?'

'I did look. All round the back. I couldn't find him.'

'Then you must have been playing hide and seek with

each other. In and out the bushes. Very charming.'

'If you think I knew he was there all along and was setting a trap for you hoping he'd go for you and you'd kill him – ' began Dorothy furiously.

'Dorothy, my dear,' interposed her father.

'No, no. Let her go on,' said Peter. 'It's about time we got this straight. You accused me just now of not finishing the job properly.'

'I was hysterical.' Dorothy's fury subsided as quickly as it had flared up.

'Were you hysterical when I came into the house after waiting as we had arranged? You were coming out of the kitchen. You didn't see me for a moment. I was quite frightened by the way you looked.'

'I'd had a shock,' muttered Dorothy. 'That letter.'

'Yes. You'd found that letter at least fifteen minutes earlier. I think it was something else. Something you'd only that minute discovered.'

'Don't you think, Mr Tarrant . . .' began Mr Thorn in quiet protest.

'I've got to know,' insisted Peter. 'I'm in this business up to the hilt, whether I want to be or not. I could have lost my life over it. I don't mind taking risks and I'm not complaining. I want to help Dorothy if I can. But I don't want to be tricked into anything. I'd rather she didn't keep things so much to herself.'

'Yes, yes. You've got a point,' murmured Dorothy's father in some distress.

'While we were talking about Gerry poisoning himself with the exhaust fumes,' said Peter addressing himself to Mr Thorn, 'I couldn't help wondering whether Dorothy hadn't already found him in the garage while

she was alone here and had decided to let him finish
the job, leaving it for me to discover the corpse because
it would look better. We were to be kept talking here for
long enough to let him die. I've no idea how long it
takes for a man to kill himself that way, but I expect
Dorothy knows.'

He stopped and looked keenly at Dorothy. She was
curled up on the settee. They had carried Gerry on to
the couch in the consulting-room, put him to bed there,
and left the doors open just in case there should be any
sound of returning consciousness. There was nothing
much to be done for him yet, Dorothy said. The concussion was probably quite severe but there was no open
wound. When he came round it would be a matter of
painkillers and sedatives.

'If Gerry jumped out on you from the bushes, then I
couldn't have left him dying in the garage, could I?'
said Dorothy.

'No indeed. It couldn't have been that that was
worrying you when I came in.'

Dorothy did not immediately respond. Her fingers
pulled at a button on the back of the settee that was
slightly loose, worried at it until it came away.

'Damn,' she said. 'It's awfully hard to find someone
to mend these button backs.' And then she continued,
almost in the same breath: 'You're right, Peter, I was
practically hysterical when you came into the house and
it wasn't just because of the letter. It's odd that you haven't
guessed why. I should have thought it was obvious. I'd
just found that the breadknife was missing.'

Peter and Mr Thorn looked at each other.

'We might indeed have guessed,' said Dorothy's

father. 'And we might also wonder why Peter was not warned that Gerry was in possession of so lethal a weapon when he went off to look for him just now.'

'D'you think I'm not blaming myself?' cried Dorothy passionately, getting up from the settee and starting her pacing again. 'I don't know why I didn't warn Peter. I suppose I just took it for granted that Gerry was going to injure himself and nobody else. I just didn't think of mentioning it, that's all.'

'That sounds so feeble that I think it must be true,' said Peter.

'It is true! It sounds crazy but it's true. It's not the first time Gerry's used a knife. It just never occurred to me that he might use it on anyone but himself. And I really thought he might have rigged up something with the car. It's not the first time he's tried two things together either. He once had an electric heater in a bath full of water and had just swallowed half a dozen tablets when I found him.'

'Is the inquisition over now?' enquired Mr Thorn, trying to lighten the atmosphere. 'If so, then I think it's time we all tried to get some rest.'

'I'll take you home, Dad,' said Dorothy, very contrite. 'Or would you rather sleep here tonight?'

'I would most certainly rather sleep here. I wouldn't dream of leaving you. But how about yourself?'

'Oh, I'll doze down here and keep an eye on Gerry,' said Dorothy.

'That's not good enough,' said Mr Thorn, and Peter said almost simultaneously: 'Can't you get a nurse in from an agency?'

'What am I to tell her if I do?' countered Dorothy.

'That my husband has been in a fight? Don't you think it's best to keep the whole wretched business to ourselves?'

'I wish we could,' said her father, 'but I don't quite see how. Strictly speaking, we ought to have informed the police that an assault has been committed. Mr Tarrant has legitimate cause to bring a case. Perhaps he would like to do so. Perhaps he thinks that would be the best way of helping you in the long run, Dorothy, disagreeable as it would be. Am I right, Mr Tarrant? You have been considering it?'

Peter admitted that he had. 'That's why I wanted to be quite clear about Dorothy's position,' he added. 'I don't want there to be any danger of her being suspected of anything at all, and I don't see why she should be, in view of all the previous suicide attempts which will obviously have to come out. But it'll be a horrible strain for Dorothy, and it's not worth it unless it achieves its aim. Which is to get Gerry locked up and in proper care.'

'Would it do that?' enquired Mr Thorn of his daughter.

'It might. For about three months,' said Dorothy bitterly. 'And what then? But it's more likely that Gerry will win everyone's sympathy because of his unfaithful wife. Naturally he attacked his wife's lover. Who wouldn't? Naturally he often felt suicidal, knowing his wife was deceiving him . . . oh, what's the use of talking about it! It's hopeless. There's no way out. I shall just have to go on as before. I'm sorry I dragged you into it at all. Both of you. That must be Gerry.' She cocked her head on one side and listened. 'He's coming round. I'll have to go.'

After she had left the room Peter stood up. 'I suppose I'd better go too. Unless you think there's any point in my remaining here.'

'At the moment, no,' said Mr Thorn. 'We'd all better simmer down, I think. It's never wise to start discussing the possible long-term effect just after a crisis. But one always does it. I think I'll be able to persuade her to get him into hospital to recover from the concussion, at any rate, and that will give us a breathing space. Leave me a phone number where I can reach you.'

Peter wrote out a number.

'Thank you,' said Mr Thorn. 'And thank you for everything else.' He took the younger man's hand. 'I hope that cut won't trouble you for long. You've been a good friend to Dorothy. And to me. I'm grateful.'

Peter pressed the old man's hand gently and noticed again the extraordinary resemblance between father and daughter. Intensity, vitality – a similarity of character, not of outward appearance alone. It was all the more remarkable in the father because of his physical frailty. He made Peter think of a powerful engine that might easily shatter the feeble framework in which it was encased, if it weren't for the strength of mind and will controlling the engine to ensure that it did not run too fast.

'I hope we shall meet again in any case,' he said. 'I'm very glad that you are staying here with Dorothy.'

'Here I am and here I shall remain. If she tries to send me home it will bring on one of my attacks of breathlessness. That will settle the matter. Gerry is not the only one who can work that ploy.'

Peter laughed. 'Good luck. She's got her match in you. I love her, you know, Mr Thorn,' he added conversationally, 'but God knows what will become of it. Good night.'

CHAPTER XI

'Well, my love. You've news, I see.'

Mr Thorn was seated in a long garden chair on the lawn in front of Pond Cottage, half in and half out of the shade cast by the copper beech tree. It was Sunday afternoon. Gerry had been in hospital for three and a half days, during which time Dorothy had gone to work and seen a few patients at home, and Mr Thorn had done a little shopping and cooking, a fair amount of sitting in the garden and reading, and a very great deal of thinking. In the evenings they had watched television or listened to records. Very little had been said about either Gerry or Peter.

By Sunday morning Dorothy had begun to look more rested, physically at any rate. But now, on her return from visiting Gerry in hospital, she had about her that haunted look again. She plumped down on the grass beside her father's chair and leant against his knee.

'He's much better,' she said in a low voice. 'They want to discharge him on Wednesday.'

Mr Thorn took a few of his carefully controlled breaths before he replied. 'That'll be just a week. A week's not a bad breathing space. You're much better than you were.'

'Yes,' agreed Dorothy, and fell silent, plucking at blades of grass.

'Do you want to tell me about him?'

'There's not much to tell really. He's still very weak and seems rather dazed. Can't remember anything about how it happened. Or at any rate he pretends not to be able to remember. Very convenient, concussion. You can forget or remember just as you please. Gerry's going to make full use of it.'

'It's convenient for you too,' said Mr Thorn after a moment's thought. 'You don't want anybody to know that Gerry went for Peter with a knife and you don't want anyone to know that Peter knocked him out. Now whatever Gerry remembers, or decides to remember, nobody is going to believe it on his evidence alone.'

'Oh, he won't make any fuss publicly,' cried Dorothy. 'That's never been his way. He's always put on a beautiful public show. Even during his breakdown. He specializes in private emotional blackmail. And that's going to be worse than ever.'

'Different, perhaps. Not worse. Don't forget that I'm living here now. The presence of a third person will rather cramp his style.'

Dorothy twisted round to look up at her father's face. 'You can't stay here after Gerry comes home,' she said. 'I can't bear it. I won't have him tormenting you too.'

'Are you afraid he is going to go for me with a knife?'

'No. I don't think he will attack you. But he might attack me.'

'In that case I shall call the police.'

'I don't think he's going to attack me physically,' said Dorothy. 'He'll find other ways of getting at me. You can guess. I don't need to tell you. Please, Dad, I'm sure it will be worse if you stay here.'

'I am not going to leave you, so there's no point in saying any more. I am not afraid of a poor, sick, unbalanced mind. It's no good arguing, Dorothy. I am not to be shifted and that's an end to it.'

'An end to it! There's no end to it! And you promised me there would be, didn't you? And for a moment I believed you. Like a child. Never mind, darling.' She got up from the ground. 'It was lovely to be soothed and pretended to, just for once. Let's have some tea.'

'I promise you again,' said Mr Thorn, rising slowly from his chair, 'that this situation is not going to continue for very much longer.'

'Really? How is it to be stopped? Either Gerry or I must die. That's the only way out. He'll never leave me and I can't leave him. And he seems to be very good at not dying, in spite of everything. Perhaps I'd make a better job at suicide myself. I might well come to it. Is that what you were thinking of, Dad?'

And she pressed his arm affectionately, to show that she knew it wasn't, and to show that she was grateful to him for letting her talk and relieve her hopelessness in this manner.

'Think over what I suggested,' said Mr Thorn presently, 'about getting some resident domestic help. I'll meet half the cost. The more people you have here as buffers between Gerry and yourself, the better. I would suggest an attractive au pair girl. That might distract his attention and turn the tables a little. It would cheer me up too. Italian preferably. Limpid and languorous. None of your big beefy blondes.'

'You're a wicked old sinner, Dad,' said Dorothy. 'And it wouldn't work, you know. Gerry would never make love to her. I only wish he would. He'd nag her and make sarcastic remarks and drive the poor girl away.'

'Then I would bring her back again. Think it over,

Dorothy. Naturally whoever we get would have to be warned of his condition. That would be only fair. But some people would not mind. There's safety in numbers, you know. I'm a great believer in throwing in more and more factors when you've got what looks to be a hopeless situation. Stir it up a bit. Muddy the waters. When they clear again they could show quite a different pattern.'

'Yes, an even worse one,' said Dorothy, laughing. 'A glamorous Italian girl with a knife in her throat and Gerry swearing I did it out of jealousy. That's what you'd call stirring it up, I suppose.'

'Perhaps it will work the other way round. Perhaps the girl will murder him.'

'No such luck.' Suddenly Dorothy dropped her bantering manner and spoke in a muffled voice as she buried her head against her father's shoulder. 'If only I could just be sorry for him. If only we could talk about it and comfort each other . . . or if only we could really forget it . . . Oh God, if only I didn't hate him so!'

'Suppose,' said Mr Thorn presently, 'that a patient of yours was in the same position that you are, and asked your advice. What would you tell them to do?'

'I'd tell them not to give in to emotional blackmail.'

'Well, then.'

'It's different when it's yourself. If I walk out on Gerry and he kills himself . . . or if he carries out his threat and starts telling people about Irene . . .'

'Telling them what, my love?' asked Mr Thorn after waiting in vain for Dorothy to continue. 'What is there to tell? You lost your baby daughter. By a tragic accident. How can Gerry hurt you any more over it than you have been hurt already?'

Very gently Mr Thorn tried to turn Dorothy's face towards his own, but she pulled away.

'I'm talking nonsense, Dad. I'm sorry. Don't let's talk about Gerry any more. It only makes me feel feeble and sorry for myself.'

'Very well,' said Mr Thorn, and he did not mention Gerry again that evening, but he was more thoughtful than ever.

When Dorothy had left for the hospital the following morning, Mr Thorn dialled the number that Peter had given him.

'Is there any chance of your getting up to Hampstead this morning to look at the 'fridge?' he asked. 'It's very awkward to have it not functioning in this weather.'

'I'll try to get round between eleven and twelve,' was Peter's reply.

'That will do fine.'

Peter replaced the receiver. His friend and employer, Len Hardy, looking up from a complicated tax form over which he was frowning, asked: 'New customer?'

'Could be.'

'Big stuff? Or little nuisance jobs?'

'Too early to tell yet. I can fit it in on the way to the Heathfield Road job. See you, Len.'

When Peter got to Pond Cottage Mr Thorn had some iced drinks ready.

'The 'fridge has miraculously righted itself,' he said. 'I hope you didn't mind my employing that little subterfuge.'

'I don't much like telling lies to Len, but I suppose I must put up with it,' replied Peter. 'We usually tell each other about our friends and activities, but of course I haven't said a word about Dorothy.'

'It's difficult for you, I know,' said Mr Thorn sympathetically, 'but it would have been even worse if I'd tried to tell you over the phone. Gerry is coming home on Wednesday.'

'So soon? Surely Dorothy is in a position to – '

'Pull strings? I'm sure she is but she won't. Her argument is that it would only be postponing the inevitable and that Gerry might be easier to handle if he doesn't suspect he's being kept in hospital longer than he need be.'

'There's something in that, I suppose,' said Peter, staring gloomily at his tumbler. 'How is she?'

'A lot better than when you last saw her.'

'Is she going to do anything about him? Other than just grin and bear it, I mean.'

'I'm afraid not. I'm trying to think of minor ways to make her life more tolerable. I've a feeling she might agree to some sort of resident domestic help.'

'That's a good idea,' said Peter. 'Somebody like Mrs Oliver. She was frightfully upset about losing her. The more normal people she has about her the better she'll be. Look, Mr Thorn – '

'Bill, please.'

'Look, Bill, I know you'll be honest with me. Is there anything at all that I can do for Dorothy now? Or would it be better for her if I just slide out of her life completely?'

'My honest answer is that I simply don't know. I think it's probably better for you to keep away from the house for the time being. Gerry seems to have forgotten whom he hit or who hit him, but I don't think a meeting between you two would be very pleasant.'

'But does she want to see me at all?'

'I don't know that either.' Mr Thorn looked at the strained and anxious face opposite to him and relented. 'I don't know it for certain, but it's my guess that she does.'

Peter did not look much happier. 'I don't want to carry on an affair with another man's wife, whether he's a schizophrenic or not. Though if he were a normal person it would be easier. But as it is, she's never going to leave him, is she?'

Mr Thorn did not answer this question, but asked another instead. 'You want to get on in life, don't you, and your studies mean a lot to you?' Peter nodded without speaking. 'Dorothy was telling me you are doing an Open University degree,' went on Mr Thorn. 'It takes great strength of purpose to stick to the sort of programme you've set yourself. I hope you won't think I'm being patronizing when I say I admire it enormously. And so does Dorothy. It would be a tragedy if anything were to happen to make you give it all up. Especially after the sacrifices you've already made.'

'She's told you about Stella then,' said Peter, looking away. 'It wasn't a bad marriage. She was inclined to think me dull, which I am, and I was inclined to think her silly, but we rubbed along quite well until I started getting what she called big ideas. She couldn't bear to sit quiet while I was studying, and I grudged all the time spent going to the pub. We had a few frightful rows and then decided to part company for the rest of the year and see how we both felt after that.'

'Sad, but probably inevitable in the circumstances, and certainly very sensibly dealt with,' said Mr Thorn.

'Do I take it that it's unlikely you will ever come together again?'

'Very unlikely. I ran into her the other evening with her current boy-friend. They seemed to be very happy and well suited. We'll probably get divorced in the New Year.'

'So that's one problem solved,' said Mr Thorn. 'I wish Dorothy's troubles could be so easily dealt with, but I'm afraid they look like taking up a great deal of time with very little result. They are emotionally exhausting not only to herself but also to everyone connected with her. You can't spare that time and that emotion, can you, Peter, if you're to fulfil your ambitions?'

'Why don't you ask me straight out if I'd be willing to give up my studies and my future if I could have Dorothy?' Peter's tones were aggressive.

'That was to be my next question,' said Mr Thorn, unmoved. 'Let me phrase it another way. Suppose Dorothy were to agree to leave Gerry. Would you be willing to give up your plans in order – say – to emigrate to Australia and start again from scratch?'

'Of course I would! As if there'd be any question of it!' Peter stared angrily at Mr Thorn.

'H'm. I see.' Mr Thorn stroked his chin. 'But you wouldn't give it all up for your wife?'

'That was quite different. You can't compare Dorothy with Stella.'

'Dorothy has many faults, you know,' said Mr Thorn.

'Of course she has. Who hasn't? What does it matter?' Peter was sitting back listlessly now. 'I haven't a hope in any case, Gerry or no Gerry. Oh, she might fancy me for a little while. I think she probably does. But she'd never marry me. Dr Laver, consultant psychiatrist, and P. Tarrant, electrician. Can you see it? Sounds daft, doesn't it?'

'I don't see anything the matter with it,' said Mr Thorn sharply. 'You disappoint me, young man. I didn't expect this stupid sort of self-deprecation from you.'

'Sorry.' Peter got to his feet. 'But I can see it's hopeless. All the same, I'd like to know what happens to her. And if she really would like to see me . . .'

He left the sentence unfinished.

'We know where to find you,' said Dorothy's father. 'I promise you won't be left in the dark.'

CHAPTER XII

'Goodbye, Mrs Bertram,' said Dorothy. 'I hope you'll soon be feeling better.'

'Goodbye, Doctor.'

Dorothy stood at the window of the consulting-room and watched the small figure move slowly down the drive to where her daughter was waiting with the car. Mrs Bertram was wearing a very elegant blue silk summer coat and hat to match, and the car that her daughter was driving was a Bentley, but nevertheless there was something pathetic and forlorn about the old woman. What's the point of it all, if that's how one ends up, thought Dorothy. But at least that was the last patient of the day, and she could look forward to a quiet evening with her father.

Then she suddenly remembered that she had told that little runaway girl to come again. Nina Farrell. Another hopeless case. Would she turn up? Most probably not. The girl would never stick out the week in the hostel. She'd probably drifted half across London by this time. Or been picked up by the police. Or drowned herself. There was no possible way in which Nina Farrell could be salvaged. On the whole Dorothy hoped she would not come. Her own vitality was at such a low ebb that she had none to spare for giving hope to hopeless cases. She frowned when she saw the girl opening the gate, but irritation gave way to curiosity as she watched Nina come up the drive.

The girl was wearing the same jeans and tunic, but they didn't look quite so dirty, and she had washed and brushed her hair. She was walking slowly and carrying with great care what appeared to be some sort of square box. She looked up at the house and Dorothy hastily moved away from the window. The bell rang and Mr Thorn, who was coming into the hall at that moment, answered it. Dorothy remained behind the slightly open door of the consulting-room, curious to hear what sort of encounter there would be between her father and Nina.

'Good afternoon,' she heard her father say. 'What can I do for you?'

'Is Dr Laver in?' asked the girl. The voice, too, sounded stronger and rather more determined than Dorothy had remembered it.

'Is she expecting you?' countered Mr Thorn.

He's trying to protect me, thought Dorothy with affectionate amusement; he doesn't know she's a patient and he doesn't know what to make of her.

It was at that moment that the crazy idea first shot into her head.

'Yes, she is,' said Nina firmly. And then added, with the anxious note back in her voice: 'At least she told me to come.'

Dorothy reached for the door handle: it was time to intervene. But she paused again when she heard her father's next words.

'What have you got in that box? A hamster?'

'A hamster!' Nina was shrill with indignation, and indeed Mr Thorn had sounded rather as if he were humouring a child. 'It's a cake for Dr Laver,' Nina went on. 'I promised to make her one.'

So she did, thought Dorothy with a little click of the memory. How extraordinary! And what a long time ago it seems.

'Hullo, Nina,' she said, coming out into the hall. 'This is my father, Mr Thorn. Miss Nina Farrell. Is that for me?' She relieved the girl of the big cake-tin and Nina and Mr Thorn shook hands.

'What sort is it?' asked Dorothy, pulling at the lid of the tin. 'Coffee icing and walnuts. Super. Look.'

Mr Thorn examined the cake. 'A thoroughly professional job,' he said. 'It also happens to be my favourite. There's going to be some rivalry for the lion's share of this.'

'You take it,' said Dorothy handing him the tin, 'and we'll all have a slice in a minute or two. I want to talk to Nina for a little while first.'

'Yes, ma'am.' Mr Thorn made a little bow. 'My daughter's the boss here, you see,' he said to Nina, who looked at him uncertainly, not knowing whether she was meant to laugh or not.

'Well, Nina, how have you been?' asked Dorothy, motioning the girl to an armchair and sitting down herself in the chair by the desk. 'Have a cigarette?'

It was very unprofessional to welcome a patient in this way, as if she were a visitor to the family, but Dorothy had her own reasons for breaking all the rules.

Nina, it seemed, had not had too bad a week at all. Dorothy, as she listened, wished she could say the same. The trouble was, apparently, to find somewhere more permanent to live. They couldn't keep her any longer at the hostel because there were so many emergencies, worse than she was, to take in.

'What were you thinking of doing?' asked Dorothy.

'I don't know. Go back to a squat, I suppose.' Nina did not sound very enthusiastic at the prospect.

'Have you thought of trying to get a domestic job? You're obviously a good cook.'

'I like cooking,' Nina admitted cautiously.

'But not cleaning? Dusting and washing up and things like that?'

'Not very much.'

'I don't suppose anyone does. But it has to be done. Could you bear it, do you think, and could you bear living in a dull and quiet household with only middle-aged people?'

'I don't know,' said the girl. 'I've never tried.'

'No. Of course you haven't. Silly question. I'd better say straight out what I was thinking. My husband is coming out of hospital in a couple of days' time. My father whom you met just now isn't very strong. I have a full-time job and no help in the house. The cooking and shopping are the most important. We'd all help with the cleaning. There's a fair-sized sunny room on the top floor. You could have that and do what you liked with it. Fifteen pounds a week and all your food. It probably won't come to more than four or five hours' work a day but it's got to be the hours when we need you. Otherwise your time is free. Well? What about it, Nina?'

Dorothy had been watching the girl closely while she spoke. After the first blank astonishment there had been some signs of anxiety, followed by the familiar suspicious look. At the mention of cooking, however, a gleam of enthusiasm had come into the girl's eyes.

'I can do Chinese dishes,' she said when Dorothy had finished. 'We had a chef in one of the squats and he showed me how.'

'I like Chinese food, and so does my husband, but my father would probably rather have scrambled eggs. Does that mean you'd like to come, Nina?'

Nina opened her eyes very wide. 'D'you mean it? You don't really mean it, do you? Come here and live with *you*?'

'Is it so very awful a prospect?' Dorothy tried to speak lightly. The expression on the girl's face was quite frightening. 'Of course I mean it, Nina,' she said, hoping to ward off a violent outburst of emotion. 'I meant it when I told you to come and see me again, didn't I? It can't be a permanent solution, but it would help us both out for the time being. You need a home and I need someone to cook. I couldn't give you any formal treatment, but you could talk to me whenever you like and we would look around for a suitable job or training for you.'

The attempt to stem the threatened flood was unsuccessful. Dorothy gave a little cry as the girl flung herself upon her, clamped her arms around her neck, and cried as noisily as an infant in a tantrum. Dorothy's own arms tightened involuntarily about her and for a moment they clung to each other.

'There, that's enough,' said Dorothy, shaken and appalled by her own reaction to the girl's passion of gratitude and hope. She disengaged herself gently. 'How about that cake? My father will be longing to try it but he won't start till we come.'

After supper that evening, when Nina had gone off to fetch her few belongings, Dorothy and her father stared at each other.

'Don't say it,' she begged. 'It's too late. I can't let her down now. It was a sudden mad impulse and I just gave way to it.'

'I was joking, of course,' said Mr Thorn rather stiffly, 'about the glamorous au pair girl.'

'I know you were.'

'What I had in mind was a mature student working her way. Preferably somebody with nursing experience. Someone who would be a genuinely stabilizing influence in the house.'

'I know you did. It would have been a very good idea. Instead of which I take in a terribly disturbed child who's attempted suicide herself and is now clinging to me like a limpet because I stand for the mother who rejected her. And I'm clinging to her because . . .' Dorothy did not finish the sentence. She got up and came over to kiss her father. 'I'm barmy, I know I am,' she said. 'But it's partly your fault. First of all you brought me up to have a social conscience and secondly you said just now that it was a good idea to add a new factor when you'd got a seemingly insoluble problem. What's worrying me at the moment is that I didn't tell her about Gerry. I just said he was coming out of hospital.'

'It wouldn't make any difference if you'd told her there were ten homicidal maniacs living in the attic. She'd still want to come. You're going to have that girl with you for a very long time, Dorothy. And she's a lot younger than Gerry.'

'Oh well, at least she can cook. I had my suspicions about the cake, you know, but she certainly did make that risotto herself. It was delicious, wasn't it?'

Mr Thorn admitted that it was. Then he rubbed a hand over his eyes and said: 'I think I really must be getting old. Somehow I don't feel I want to hear any more about the problems of social misfits and suchlike.'

'Well, you can always go back to your flat, can't you?' said Dorothy mischievously. 'I'm not keeping you here against your will.'

Mr Thorn opened one eye. 'And miss all the drama? No, no. I'm seeing it through. What are Nina and Gerry going to make of each other. That's what I want to know.'

CHAPTER XIII

The crucial first meeting between Gerry Laver and Nina Farrell, rival claimants for Dorothy Laver's sole attention and care, could hardly have taken place in a less auspicious manner.

Dorothy had arranged with the authorities in the hospital block to which Gerry had been admitted that she would collect him herself at five o'clock and drive him home. On the way she would gently break to him the news about her father and Nina being in the house. But whether through some administrative muddle, or whether through Gerry's own machinations, he came out several hours earlier and took a taxi to Pond Cottage.

Nina and Mr Thorn had had lunch together and had shared a huge bowl of strawberries and cream, for which both of them had a great weakness. Conversation had consisted of information about the lives of late-twentieth-century squatters, supplied by Nina, and about the lives of early-twentieth-century unemployed labourers, supplied by Mr Thorn. Each listened with genuine interest to what the other had to say. Nina and Mr Thorn, after an initial slight awkwardness with each other, were now getting on very well indeed. They had washed up together and then Mr Thorn had gone for his usual little after-lunch stroll. Nina said she was going up to her room to get on with painting the woodwork her favourite shade of dark purple, but after the old man had gone she went back to the kitchen and took a big recipe book down from the shelf. She was thinking of making something very special for the homecoming of the husband of her beloved Dr Laver, and was glad to have the house to herself to cogitate about it in peace.

She sat cross-legged on the kitchen floor – a habit that was proving rather hard to break – opened the book at a luscious-looking coloured illustration, placed it on the floor in front of her, and then put her elbows on her knees and her chin in her hands and stared at the picture, deep in contemplation.

'Peppers,' she murmured to herself. 'There's two left. Paprika. Cream – I've left some over. Mushrooms – have we got any mushrooms?'

She got up and inspected the vegetable rack and then returned to her devotions. For what was possibly the first time in her life Nina Farrell was utterly absorbed and utterly happy.

When she heard the sound of the key in the front door Nina did not stir. The old man can't have gone very far, she said to herself, and thought no more of the matter. Then suddenly she raised her eyes from the book on the floor, pushed the hair back from her ears, and listened with her head tilted to one side, as alert and suspicious as a little wild animal. There was something about the sounds of movement going on in the hall that told Nina at once that this was not Mr Thorn returning from his walk. When the old man came into the house he always rubbed each shoe three times on the doormat, wet or fine. Nina was very quick to recognize little habits like this, and after barely a couple of days in their company, she had already noticed quite a lot of such little mannerisms in both Dorothy Laver and her father. When she particularly disliked somebody she would mimic these little habits, and she was quite a good mimic. But she had not the slightest desire to imitate either Dorothy Laver or William Thorn in any unkind way.

There was no sound of the scraping of shoes on the mat. Instead there were footsteps that sounded rather impatient and a strange male voice muttered: 'Where the hell has she got to?'

Nina's head shrank down deeper between her shoulders

and her apprehensive look intensified. In the kitchen doorway stood a tall man of about forty wearing a light lounge suit. He had a fine, Byronic-type head with thick brown hair, hazel eyes, and strong regular features except for the mouth, which was too small and had a petulant twist to it. It was turned up now, in what looked like a sneer, as he said in what Nina mentally described as a mean and uptight sort of voice: 'And who might you be?'

'I'm Nina,' she replied, and her own voice came out as a nervous squeak.

'Nina,' repeated Gerry Laver. 'Very brief. Very much to the point. But not particularly informative. What might you be doing here?'

'I'm the cook.'

Nina scrambled to her feet with some idea of feeling less at a disadvantage if she were standing up, but it was not much help because her head only came up to Gerry's shoulder. Gerry looked her up and down with what his pupils, during his schoolmastering years, had called the lingering Laver look. It had a remarkable capacity for making its object feel thoroughly contemptible in every way. Gerry at the height of his powers had been quite well liked by his colleagues because he kept order in class, was reliable and hardworking, and punctilious about administrative detail. But his pupils, although they learnt well and usually passed their exams, had hated and feared him.

Nina, subjected to this merciless scrutiny, went crimson and looked around like a hunted animal seeking a way to escape.

'I see. You are the cook. We appear to be making some

progress,' said Gerry. 'There are two aspects of your statement that puzzle me. My concept of a cook as a woman of a certain maturity and dignity is no doubt completely outmoded, but even in this enlightened era I confess I should have expected some lingering traces of those old-fashioned qualities. However. The second aspect is at the moment causing me rather greater concern. I appreciate that my memory is bound to be rather un-reliable as far as the events previous to my accident are concerned, but external evidence tells me that I have been absent from home for barely a week. I am almost sure that my household did not boast the services of a cook, nor, to my knowledge, was there any intention on the part of myself or my wife to seek such services. But it seems that I am mistaken. In which case the concussion from which I have been suffering must have been more severe than I have been led to believe. I find this rather disturbing. Do please try to stand still for a moment,' he concluded irritably, 'and kindly enlighten me about your presence in my house.'

Nina, who had been fidgeting about and twitching her face and hands all the time Gerry had been speaking, held on to the side of the kitchen table and made a great effort to control herself.

'I came to see Dr Laver for treatment,' she managed to say at last. 'I needed somewhere to live and she needed help in the house and I can cook quite well so she offered me the job.'

'I see,' said Gerry. 'Very interesting. Occupational therapy for a mental patient in the practitioner's own home. No doubt Dr Laver proposed it as some sort of scientific experiment.'

It looked for a moment as if he were about to embark on another long speech, but to Nina's immense relief he turned and left the room, only to return a moment later to say in a very offhand manner: 'Presumably Dr Laver will be home later and will fill in the necessary details herself. Meanwhile I am going up to my room to lie down and I should like some tea and biscuits brought up at half past four. I take it that is within the scope of your duties in my house?'

And he was gone before Nina had a chance to reply. A few moments later she heard the slight sound of a door opening and shutting on the floor above.

Nina let go of the kitchen table and slid down on to the floor beside the open cookbook. There she lay drumming on the tiles with her toes, banging with her fists, and whimpering and moaning uncontrollably.

Mr Thorn, coming in a few minutes later, heard sounds coming from the direction of the kitchen and went to investigate.

'Nina! My dear child! Whatever is the matter?'

Nina continued to writhe and moan.

Slowly and deliberately, conserving his strength and making sure he did not strain himself, Mr Thorn lowered himself on to his knees beside her, caught one of the flailing hands between his own and held it gently.

'You must get up, my dear,' he said, 'and come and tell me about it in the sitting-room. I cannot kneel like this any longer. I must sit down and rest.'

Nina stopped shuddering, rolled over, sat up, and turned on the old man a face so twisted and smeared with tears and fury that it was barely recognizable.

Mr Thorn got carefully to his feet. 'Come on. Let's

hear about it,' he said.

In the blue and white room he settled himself comfortably and told Nina to shut the door.

'Now,' he said, 'what's happened to upset you like this?'

'He's come home too early,' replied Nina, standing stiff and straight just inside the door and putting a deep tragic note into her voice. Then she came forward and beat upon the back of the settee with both hands and let out a stream of abuse against Gerry. It stopped as suddenly as it had begun and she put a finger to her mouth and bit on it and said: 'I'd forgotten you were a clergyman. I'm sorry.'

'Whatever does that matter?' said Mr Thorn impatiently, and added, half to himself: 'This is most unfortunate. Very unfortunate indeed.'

'You mean you don't mind me swearing?' Nina looked at him wide-eyed.

'I dare say you had provocation. But on the other hand it must have been quite a shock to Mr Laver to come home and find a strange girl in the kitchen. And people aren't exactly at their best when they've just come out of hospital and when they've had concussion. And quite apart from that, Mr Laver had a bad nervous breakdown not so very long ago. That also tends to make people rather difficult to get on with sometimes.'

Nina sat down to listen to him and did not interrupt, but she looked very unconvinced at this defence of Gerry.

'You must remember that he is a sick man,' concluded Mr Thorn.

'He's a nutter all right but there's no need to be like that,' said Nina.

'In a way, no. I agree with you. But on the other hand – '

'Look, Mr Thorn, I've seen nutcases. Lots of them. I'm one myself, aren't I?' Nina spoke with an air of great reasonableness. 'But there's loonies and loonies. They're all just people, aren't they? Some of them are bastards to start with and if they go barmy it only makes them more so. And others are all right and you can tell they are, even if they're washing their hands every five minutes or walking backwards because they're afraid of their shadow following them. It doesn't matter how daft people get. It shows through, what a person really is. That one up there – ' and she jerked her head over her shoulder – 'is one of the first sort. He's never had any sort of decent feelings at all. He'd be a rotten sort of character even if there was nothing the matter with him.'

She spoke with a quaint sort of primness that Mr Thorn found touching and even a little amusing, though in fact there was nothing in the situation to be amused about. He made a further effort to explain and defend Gerry's attitude, but it was not very convincing, even to himself. He had been very much struck by the girl's division of people into irreversible categories and by her forthright rejection of mental illness as an excuse for disagreeable behaviour.

'Nina,' he said, when it was obvious that nothing was going to make her feel more kindly disposed towards Gerry, 'do you really believe people ought to be judged as good or bad whatever their circumstances? However ill they are? However unlucky they have been in life?'

'Yes,' she said without hesitation.

'Then if somebody goes and bashes an old lady in the park and pleads that it's because he had a miserable childhood, you'd say it was no excuse for his behaviour?'

'Of course it's no excuse!' she cried vehemently. 'Lots of people have miserable childhoods but they don't go knocking other people about because of it.'

'Yes, yes. You're quite right, of course.' Mr Thorn was somewhat taken aback. 'But we have to try to understand it all the same. We have to try to be charitable. After all, even the law, a very blunt instrument at best, makes a distinction between those who are responsible for their actions and those who aren't.'

Mr Thorn was talking as much to himself as to Nina. He had found her remarks rather disturbing, particularly as coming from one who had herself had an atrociously unhappy childhood but who, so Dorothy assured him, had never committed any acts of violence against other people or other people's possessions. The Reverend William Thorn, MA, with a lifetime of ministering to the needs of the poor, the sick, the bewildered, and the outright bloody-minded behind him, found himself feeling curiously humble in the presence of this sixteen-year-old waif who had formed such strong moral judgements without the benefit of a good home, or a good example, or a decent education to support her.

'That one knows what he's doing all right,' said Nina, and again her eyes went upwards to indicate Gerry, presumably still quietly resting on the floor above.

'But what did he actually say to you to upset you so much?' asked Mr Thorn.

'It wasn't what was said. It was the way he said it.' And Nina, perhaps involuntarily, perhaps with deliberate malice, raised her eyebrows, looked down her nose, and tilted her head very slightly to one side as she spoke, in such unmistakable mimicry of Gerry's most supercilious manner that it gave Mr Thorn another little shock and almost made him smile. He was very hard put to it to find an answer. He had disliked his son-in-law from the very first, but had kept these feelings to himself in the face of Dorothy's evident infatuation with Gerry. Even when Gerry was at his best, Mr Thorn's charitable feelings towards him had been achieved only at the cost of much prayer and self-discipline. But since the revelation of what Dorothy had been going through, Mr Thorn had been rather neglecting these strenuous efforts to be fair to Gerry and had been letting his detestation of the man have its full fling.

He was in no position to preach to Nina, he reflected guiltily. And yet something had got to be done. And quickly, because Gerry would be waking up soon and Dorothy would be coming home. What Gerry would say and do to her could be guessed at but not prevented. Nina, however, was more malleable. Nina must be worked on at once.

'I know how you feel and I can imagine how it was,' said Mr Thorn. 'I've often felt like that myself as a matter of fact. But there's my daughter to be considered first and foremost. We have to keep quiet for her sake. It's an awful effort, but it's got to be done. You wouldn't want her to be made unhappy about it, would you, Nina?'

This appeal received a grudging assent. 'He wants me to take him up some tea at half past four,' added Nina.

'It's nearly that now. Hadn't you better go and make it?'

Suddenly Nina began to cry. 'I was going to make a goulash for dinner,' she wailed. 'It's too late to start now. It needs ages to simmer. And besides . . .'

There was no need for her to explain any further. It was only too obvious that the homecoming of the master of the house was not an occasion to be celebrated with special culinary efforts.

'Perhaps we could have it another day,' said Mr Thorn.

'Not for him! I'm not going to cook anything for him!'

'But you want to help my daughter, don't you?'

Nina's expression would have been laughable if there had been anything to laugh at in the situation. Adoration of Dorothy and hatred of Gerry fought with each other to produce an appearance of total confusion.

'Of course you do,' said Mr Thorn. 'So do I. That's why I am here. I have a flat of my own, you know, and I'd rather be living there. But it's better for my daughter to have other people in the house. Of course if you really can't stand it, we will have to find somewhere else for you to live and someone else to do the work here, but – '

He broke off. At the mention of leaving Dorothy, horror had taken precedence over all other emotions in Nina's face.

'In that case you will just have to come to terms with it,' said Dorothy's father firmly. 'Just as I've had to do. We're in the same boat, Nina, you and I. We've got the same problem. And that means we can help each other. Now you go and make that tea and take some upstairs and then bring the tray in here. Will you do that, please? For Dorothy and for me?'

'All right.' Nina got up despondently and left the room.

Mr Thorn lay back and shut his eyes. His body was

relaxed and he was breathing slowly and regularly. But the turmoil in his mind could not be stilled.

The new and unknown factor, he was saying to himself. And what a factor! Explosive, no less. Was it his fault? Was it Dorothy's? Ah well, he concluded, there was no turning back now.

CHAPTER XIV

The tension between Gerry and Nina electrified the whole house.

'It positively sizzles,' said Dorothy to Peter. 'It's a pity you can't come and de-fuse it.'

She was sitting in his most comfortable armchair and although she looked tired after the long afternoon session at hospital there was an air of almost desperate cheerfulness about her. It was the third time in the ten days since Gerry had come home that she had called in on Peter after work. He had only just got in himself and they relaxed in a companionable way.

'What part of your timetable is this coming out of?' she asked him teasingly. 'Or have you decided to allow yourself half an hour a day for sundries?'

'If we have some coffee it can count as shopping and eating, etc.,' said Peter in the same tone of voice. 'No. You sit there. I'm the host.'

He produced coffee and biscuits. Dorothy declined the latter.

'I daren't eat anything before dinner,' she said. 'I have to save up every bit of my capacity to do justice to Nina.

She counts every mouthful I take, like an over-anxious mother watching the progress of an underweight baby. I have to be careful not to gobble for fear she comes and pats my back to bring up the wind.'

'It's not doing you any harm, though,' said Peter, 'being fed properly. You don't look quite so hag-ridden as when I first saw you.'

'I don't know whether that's due to Nina's cooking or to the fact that for much of the time now I feel totally irresponsible. Everything seems to be completely out of control as far as my domestic life is concerned. I haven't the slightest doubt that something frightful is going to happen but I no longer feel as if I can do anything to prevent it. The boat's lost its rudder. Or rather the rudder has been taken over by two equally determined pairs of hands, pulling with equal force in totally opposite directions. I'm just the donkey doing the rowing.'

'As long as they don't tear you to pieces between them,' said Peter.

'There's a certain amount of that, of course, and some-times it is a bit harrowing. Meal times are the worst. But it's no worse than when I had Gerry to cope with on my own. You see I'm not there for a lot of the time. My poor father bears the brunt of it.'

'How is he standing up to it?'

'Pretty well on the whole. He had a little attack yester-day evening and Nina fussed over him like a mother hen.'

Dorothy had certainly spoken the truth when she said she was feeling irresponsible, thought Peter; she would never have referred so lightly to Mr Thorn's state of health two weeks ago. He was pleased but at the same time rather anxious: the change of mood was too sudden and too violent; it could so easily swing back again.

'Well, that's one comfort,' he said stolidly. 'That Nina and your father have made friends, I mean.'

'Oh, they're thick as thieves. They have long conversations about moral philosophy. Dad's quite taken with her. He can't decide whether she's going to turn into an actress or into some sort of missionary.'

'It sounds to me as if she ought to make a career out of catering.'

'I expect it will come to that in the end.' Dorothy got up. 'Well, I must go. Thanks for letting me come and natter, Peter.'

'You're welcome. Any time. Always.'

After she had gone Peter told himself that yet again she had managed to avoid saying anything specific about Gerry. Was this because Gerry was concentrating his forces on the battle with Nina and had little energy left to direct at his wife? It would be nice to believe this, but Peter was sceptical. There was no doubt, however, that for the time being at least, Dorothy's life might have been worse.

Fortified by this comforting reflection, Peter pushed aside the coffee cups, slit open the bulky envelope of study material that had arrived that morning, and tried to devote himself to the mysteries of the Open University foundation course in Mathematics, which he was taking concurrently with that in Technology. It was tough going and required every bit of his power of concentration, undisturbed by any speculation about what was going on at Pond Cottage, Middle Lane, Hampstead.

Meal times are the worst, Dorothy had said. The hour before dinner, in particular, was crackling with antici-

pation. Nina's loathing of Gerry had, among less fortunate
effects, that of spurring her on to ever more ambitious
efforts in the kitchen – a sort of flaunting of her own skill
and usefulness as opposed to Gerry's idle and pointless
existence. Sometimes these efforts were successful and
sometimes they were not. If Mr Thorn said that a dish
was over-seasoned for his taste, or that on medical advice
he would have to avoid it, Nina would accept his comment
without taking offence and would make a mental note
not to give it to him again. If something had gone so
disastrously wrong that even Dorothy, with all her concern
for Nina's feelings, felt unable to eat the offering, then
there were long and tearful apologies and a great deal of
comforting had to be done by Dorothy and her father.
Gerry, on these occasions, would take no part in the
proceedings, but would sit with a satisfied smile on his
face, watching and biding his time.

It was when Gerry, alone among those present, decided
to make some adverse comment on Nina's cooking that
the fireworks really began.

When Dorothy got home at about seven o'clock she
found what looked like an idyllic scene for a summer
evening. Gerry and her father were stretched out in
garden chairs near the copper beech tree, a table with
glasses and a jug between them, and a comfortable
scatter of books and newspapers on the grass by their
sides. Gerry had accepted Mr Thorn's presence in the
house with very little surprise and no protest: Nina was
the arch enemy.

Dorothy left the car in the drive and came to sit in the
vacant chair.

'It's been quite a day,' she said. 'Can we really be

going to have a good summer after all?'

'The long-range forecast,' said Mr Thorn, after glancing
at his paper, 'is for below average temperatures and
above average rainfall except in the north-west of Scotland.'

'Bad luck on Scotland,' said Dorothy lazily. 'It's
bound to be the other way round.'

'You are looking very weary, my dear,' said Gerry
who had been silently observing Dorothy up till now.
'Did you have a particularly exhausting session with
your lover?'

Mr Thorn's grip on his newspaper tightened involuntarily, but Dorothy appeared to be unmoved.

'Oh yes, frightfully exhausting,' she replied lightly.
'But then I took in six of them, you know, one after the
other, after I'd finished the afternoon clinic.'

Gerry's eyes narrowed. This was a new technique on
Dorothy's part and so far he had not found the perfect
answer to it. But that Dorothy found it an effort to
employ this method of dealing with him was shown by
the thoughtlessness of her next remark.

'I wonder what Nina's making for dinner,' she said.
'I'm ravenous.'

'For how long,' asked Gerry with an air of weary
resignation, 'are our digestions to be at the mercy of that
adolescent delinquent? I fear it cannot be much longer
before she decides to work off her grudge against society
in general and against the bourgeoisie in particular by
dropping a taste of arsenic in the soup. It did taste a
little odd last night, to say the least of it.'

This speech was not up to Gerry's usual standard of
needling Dorothy or anybody else he wanted to take it

out on, and Dorothy herself had no difficulty in simply ignoring it. But it got under Mr Thorn's skin to such an extent that he broke his rule of never rising to Gerry's baits.

'For somebody who has met with so little human affection and suffered so much from human neglect,' he said with spirit, 'Nina is remarkably free of any grudge against anybody.'

Gerry looked at first faintly surprised and then delighted. 'Well, well,' he said. 'So the child has a champion.'

Suddenly Dorothy could not bear to listen any longer. She jumped to her feet, cried, 'I want a wash,' and ran into the house. In the hall she met Nina, who was coming out of the kitchen to say that things had got a little delayed and would it be all right if they ate fifteen minutes later than usual.

'Good,' said Dorothy. 'That'll give me time for a bath. I'm feeling thoroughly hot and mucky.'

'You don't look it,' said Nina. 'You look lovely.'

The adoration in her voice was almost painful to hear. Dorothy said lightly, 'Thank you,' and was about to go upstairs when some impulse made her turn back. The girl ran towards her and for a moment they clung together as they had done on the occasion when Dorothy had suggested that Nina should come and live there.

I'm sure she knows, said Dorothy to herself as she ran the bath; there's some sort of telepathy that's told her I have lost a daughter, although of course I shall never tell her myself. And she's got an instinct about Gerry too. It's not only that she is competing with him for me. It's more than that. And Gerry knows too. How much longer will it be before one of us mentions Irene? Gerry must be thinking of her; he must. She would have been about Nina's age now. Did I take in Nina because I knew it would force Gerry and me to talk about Irene? I suppose that was it; I suppose that's why I feel better now, because I've taken some action at last, done something that is bound to force both Gerry and me into facing the truth together . . .

Dorothy's thoughts drifted on. It was quite true, as she had told Peter, that she was feeling oddly irresponsible. It was almost as if she was watching the whole domestic set-up, herself included, from the stance of a detached observer, curious to know the end of the drama but not personally involved in it.

CHAPTER XV

The meal was at first a very silent one. They ate in the dining area of the large kitchen and Dorothy thought she could detect a smell of fried onions, although none were present in the harmless but rather ordinary chicken dish and salad that Nina produced. Probably they had been in whatever it was that went wrong and had to be thrown away, thought Dorothy, and hoped Gerry would not come to the same conclusion and make a comment on it.

Gerry appeared to be eating somewhat absent-mindedly. His eyes were as often upon Dorothy, sitting opposite to him, as on his plate. When Nina got up to put a raspberry flan on the table, Gerry, still staring at Dorothy, said in a speculative manner: 'Curious. I never thought you would resurrect that dress again. It's so very much not your style. It needs a bit of youthful glamour to carry it off. Or if not glamour, at any rate a modicum of beauty and charm.'

The rather frilly summer dress did indeed look wrong on Dorothy, who needed simple, even austere clothes to achieve her odd flashes of something like beauty. She had only put it on because it was cool and comfortable and the first thing that had come to hand.

'Do I look like mutton dressed as lamb?' she said good-humouredly. 'I seem to be short of summer clothes. I'll have to get some more if the weather goes on like this.'

And she smiled at her father to show that this sort of thing did not worry her.

But it worried Nina, who was already upset by the failure of the sauce she had been attempting and who had indeed felt, when she and Dorothy had momentarily hugged each other, something of the older woman's deeply suppressed yearning and despair.

Gerry reached out for the sugar, which was at the corner of the table nearest Nina's seat. Without a word Nina suddenly bent over and bit his bare forearm.

It was not a very hard bite. As quickly as Nina's head had ducked it came up again and she stared, white-faced and cringing, at Dorothy. Gerry did not even trouble to move his arm or touch the spot. He picked up the sugar canister and sprinkled sugar over the raspberries before he began to eat. For a full minute there was silence. Then Gerry said conversationally: 'I was not aware, Dolly, that it came within the scope of the Hippocratic Oath, nor that it was accepted medical practice even today, to treat violent mental patients by giving them privileged positions in the practitioner's own home.'

'It isn't.' Dorothy's voice held such fury and menace that her father looked at her in alarm and Nina looked more terrified than ever. 'Except,' continued Dorothy with deadly clarity, 'when the violent mental patient happens to be the practitioner's own husband. In that case she has no choice.'

Gerry got up, came round the table, and hit her with considerable force across the side of the head. Dorothy gave an involuntary cry of pain. Nina shrieked and sprang at Gerry. Dorothy's father, instantly judging this to be an occasion when his own carefully conserved energies would have to be brought into action, jumped up and caught hold of Nina before she could either touch Gerry or Gerry her.

Nina struggled hard but Mr Thorn held her. To his great relief Gerry left the room. But Nina clearly wanted to run after him.

'No,' gasped Mr Thorn. 'It will do – no good.'

His breathing was becoming very laboured but he continued to hold Nina back. Dorothy, recovering from the shock of the blow and seeing his condition, cried: 'Stop that at once, Nina! Can't you see my father is ill? Help me to get him to bed. At once!'

The voice of authority had its effect, helped by the old man's rapidly increasing distress. Nina ceased to struggle and asked what she could do to help. The next two hours were very busy and very anxious. Mr Thorn's own doctor was summoned and agreed with Dorothy that it would be better not to risk moving the old man to hospital, although he would need constant care and attention. At that point Nina begged to be allowed to look after him. Dorothy surveyed her doubtfully.

'He must not be excited in any way,' said Dr Ferguson.

'I won't excite him. I'll keep him quiet. Truly I will!' cried Nina.

'All right,' said Dorothy at last. 'But I shall be here too. I shall take a few days' leave. You can start by sitting with him now, Nina, while I show Dr Ferguson out.'

When Dorothy came upstairs again after a few final words with Mr Thorn's doctor, she stood for a moment in the doorway of her father's room. The curtains were drawn across, but the short summer night had not yet begun and there was enough light to see that the old man was lying peacefully asleep, breathing lightly but evenly. The oxygen equipment stood at one side of the bed. At the other side Nina knelt with her eyes on the old man's face. Her elbows rested on the edge of the bed and her hands were clasped together as if she were praying. Dorothy silently withdrew, leaving the door slightly ajar. Then she went in search of Gerry.

He had not gone to bed, neither was he in the bathroom or in any of the spare bedrooms. Dorothy went downstairs and tried the door of the study. It did not open.

'Gerry,' she called softly. 'It's all right. My father is better now. The doctor has gone.'

There was no reply.

'Are you coming to bed?' she asked and then held her ear close to the door. There was not the slightest sound from within the room.

Dorothy rattled the doorhandle. 'Don't be silly,' she said in a harsh whisper, fearful that she might disturb her father on the floor above. 'I know you're there and I know you're all right. You wouldn't take an overdose of anything without making sure I could get at you to bring you round. Open the door, Gerry. This has gone on long enough.'

Dead silence followed this speech.

'All right then,' said Dorothy. 'Stay there. I shall go to bed.'

And she let go of the handle and stood still for a moment or two without speaking, to give the impression that she had indeed gone away. When this produced no reaction she began for the first time to be seriously anxious. Curiously enough, the anxiety no longer took the form of a struggle between her own desire to find Gerry dead and her fear of her own guilt if she were to do so. She was conscious only of great weariness and an intense reluctance to deal with any more emergencies tonight. For this reason she found herself positively hoping that he was alive and uninjured so that, medically at least, there would be nothing she need do. If he had harmed himself, she hoped it would simply be a case of a few sleeping tablets too many, which could be quickly dealt with by giving salt water as an emetic.

But if he was really in danger, which would mean all the fuss of an ambulance, or if he was dead, which would mean sending for Dr Ferguson again and perhaps for the police, Dorothy did not know how she would find the energy to cope with it.

Why not just go to bed?

She was almost able to do this, but not quite. The habit of years died very hard. She thought for a moment and then decided to try to get at Gerry through the window of the study, which he must surely have left open on so hot a night as this. She collected a small stepladder from the broom-cupboard and left the house by the back door, still taking care to make as little noise as possible, and grateful that her father's room was on the other side of the house.

There was no light coming from Gerry's study, but one of the casement windows was wide open and the curtains were drawn only half across. Dorothy stood on the third rung of the stepladder and leant on the sill.

'Gerry!' she called softly. 'Are you going to open the door now or do I have to climb in?'

There was no reply. She could see him dimly, sitting in the desk chair with his arms on the desk and his head buried in his arms. Whether or not he was breathing was impossible to tell in the near darkness.

Dorothy took a further step up the ladder and put one knee on the windowsill. It was possible to get in, although it would require an awkward manoeuvre, because the desk was pushed against the wall directly in front of the window, and she could not simply fling a leg over the sill and then drop down on to the floor. She would have to shuffle or crawl on to the desk on her knees, and if Gerry was alive and conscious and was simply playing with her, which was perfectly possible, then for a moment or two at least she would be in a very vulnerable position.

But there was no help for it. Dorothy got both knees on to the sill and crawled forwards on to the desk. She had turned round and was about to slide to the floor when a hand shot out and grabbed her ankle and a triumphant voice cried: 'Got you!'

For all her preparedness, Dorothy could not suppress a little scream.

'What the hell are you playing at?' she cried. 'Didn't

you hear me at the door?'

'Yes. I heard you.'

'Then why didn't you open it?'

Dorothy shook herself free and walked over to switch on the light. Gerry was lolling back in the desk chair, surveying her with an expression of great malevolence.

'Very interesting, that little experiment,' he said. 'It proves that it is perfectly possible for you to enter this room in an unorthodox manner. So that when my body is found it will not necessarily present the police with an insoluble locked room mystery. The murderer, having locked the door on the inside in order to suggest suicide, then made her way out of the room through the window. That is one point settled. The method? Ah, there's the rub. What method can be adopted that will point directly and exclusively to Dr Dorothy Laver? This is quite a problem. But we will find an answer, given patience and time, patience and time, patience and time...'

He continued to repeat the words, beating a little rhythm with one hand as if conducting an orchestra.

'Perhaps we could defer until the morning our discussion of the means whereby I am to be convicted of your murder,' said Dorothy. 'I think you'd better come and rest now.'

Her voice sounded calm and firm, the doctor dealing with a difficult and excitable patient. But in fact she was not at all confident of being able to manage him on her own as she had always done in the past. His whole pattern of behaviour had changed. He seemed less subtle and less cunning in his choice of disagreeable things to say, less in control of both his words and his actions.

Involuntarily Dorothy put a hand to her face: Gerry had never actually struck her before. He noticed her gesture, came and put an arm round her and stroked her hair.

'I'm sorry I hurt you, Dolly,' he said. 'That was naughty of me. But it was naughty of you too, wasn't it, to make such unkind remarks in front of other people. And now you've gone and made your father ill. All because you couldn't control your naughty tongue. Poor Bill. Suppose he should die? It will be your fault, won't it, Dolly? Naughty Dolly. Unlucky Dolly. She keeps losing people. And it's always her own fault. Her father . . . her daughter . . . and now her husband.'

Dorothy stiffened. Gerry continued to stroke her hair.

'And her husband, which won't be much loss,' he said. 'Everyone will say – that wretched man, making her life such a misery, such a burden to her, how good that she's free of him at last. But you won't be free, will you, my darling Dolly, because they'll know you killed me and even if you manage to get acquitted because you've made them believe it was an accident, it will still be a life sentence because you'll never forget, never forget, never forget . . .'

Again he went on repeating the words, this time to the rhythm of the movement of his hand over her hair. Dorothy pulled herself away with a jerk, backed towards the door, leant against it and felt for the handle and cried: 'We both killed Irene. Both of us, both of us, both of us . . .'

It seemed as if she, too, had to keep saying the same words over and over again. At last she managed to stop herself and stood clinging to the doorhandle and trembling uncontrollably. It's come at last, she thought; this is the end now. There is no more pretence. One of us has to admit to having killed our child. And one of us has to die.

As usual, having driven her to the verge of collapse, Gerry began to recover his own composure. In this respect it was just the same as it had always been. It was as if between them there was only enough calmness and sanity for one person. Whichever one of them possessed it was automatically depriving the other.

'That was certainly the intention that the coroner intended to convey,' said Gerry, and his voice had never sounded more schoolmasterly and precise. 'A tragic accident arising from a misunderstanding. Deep sympathy for the bereaved parents. Impossible to apportion blame, or indeed to blame anybody at all. Accidents will happen. It is the way of life.'

Dorothy tried to speak. Her mouth opened and shut but no words came. Her one short outburst had exhausted all her powers.

'A tragic accident arising from a misunderstanding, and deep sympathy for the bereaved parents,' repeated Gerry slowly and emphatically, as if he was trying to get a difficult point across to a not very intelligent pupil. 'That was the impression left by the inquest, and that was the story for public consumption thereafter. But you and I know that it was not true, don't we, Dolly? We know that you have always felt solely responsible for Irene's death, don't we? We know that you believe you killed Irene. Am I not right, Dorothy?'

'Yes, that's right,' muttered Dorothy. And then she added more firmly: 'I've always felt responsible because I believed you when you told me it was I who had made the mistake. It has only been in recent years . . .'

Her voice faded away.

'What have you been thinking in recent years?' asked Gerry in the same tones of weary patience.

Dorothy did not look at him because she did not want to see the expression in his eyes. She was becoming very frightened indeed but there was no drawing back now. She had gone too far.

'I have been wondering whether it wasn't you who was to blame,' she went on hurriedly. 'Whether it wasn't because you had killed Irene that you felt you had to kill yourself . . . whether you'd been torturing me all these years to try to stop me suspecting the truth.'

'Can I be hearing aright?' said Gerry in his most sarcastic manner. 'Me torturing you? What a very peculiar way to look at it. Which one of us has had an unbroken and successful career and has reached a position of considerable eminence in it? And which one of us has suffered a serious mental breakdown with severe residual symptoms in the form of suicidal impulses? I had rather been under the impression that the former description applied to my wife and the latter to myself. But in addition to losing my daughter through my wife's carelessness, in addition to allowing myself to be partially blamed, and in addition to suffering serious illness and the ruin of my career, it appears that I am also to be deprived of the one consolation left to me – that of knowing myself to be the more unfortunate of the two of us.'

Dorothy clamped her hands over her ears as if to shut out an intolerable noise.

'Stop it, stop it!' she cried. 'My mind is reeling.

Which of us is crazy – you or me?'

Gerry shrugged his shoulders, pulled the chair out from the desk, sat down, and took up a book that apparently he had been reading earlier.

Suddenly something snapped in Dorothy. She no longer possessed a controlling mind: she was all blind impulse. She rushed at Gerry, caught hold of his shoulders, and shook him hard.

'You killed her!' she screamed. 'It was you – you – you!'

Gerry caught her hands and held them down. 'My dear Dorothy,' he said, 'I really think you had better make an effort to control yourself. You might be overheard, which would be very embarrassing for you.'

'I don't care who hears!' cried Dorothy.

'Don't you? Do you really want your father and your daughter-substitute to suffer for your sins as well as yourself?'

Suddenly Dorothy stood quite still. 'You wouldn't – you couldn't – you wouldn't harm them,' she whispered.

'I have protected you all these years from the consequences of your criminal negligence,' said Gerry, 'at great cost to myself. I think it is time now to redress the balance and give myself a chance.'

Dorothy shut her eyes for a moment. Then she opened them again and said very quietly: 'Why don't you just kill me, Gerry, if that's what would make you happy? Go on. Strangle me.'

A cunning look came into his face. 'Ah no. That's what *you* want, isn't it? They'd get me if I did that, wouldn't they? You're determined to make me into a murderer one way or the other, aren't you, Doll, even if you have to die for it. No, no. That's not what I want.'

'Then what is?'

'I think we will have a reversal of roles for a change. We've had enough of the heroic Dr Laver and her mad husband. I think we will have the mad Dr Laver and her so very calm and coping husband.'

Again Dorothy shut her eyes. 'All right. If that's the way you want it,' she said softly.

CHAPTER XVI

Three days later Peter had a telephone call from Bill Thorn.

'Thank God you're there,' said the old man's voice when Peter lifted the receiver.

It was six-thirty in the evening, and Len Hardy had gone home. Peter had come into their combined office and workshop for a few minutes to collect some materials for a rewiring job that he was starting early the following morning.

'Are you all right?' he asked. The old man sounded very breathless.

'Yes. I've been ill but I'm much better now. Just give me a moment.'

Peter waited anxiously.

'I really am all right,' said Bill Thorn a moment later. 'That was a tactical silence – somebody passing by. Are you free this evening and if so can you come round to see Dorothy?'

'Of course. D'you mean come to Pond Cottage?'

'Yes. She's not feeling very well. Don't worry. Gerry

won't be here. Seven-thirty. Not earlier.'

'I'll be there,' promised Peter, and again there was a silence, which was broken eventually by Mr Thorn saying in a rather plaintive voice: 'I'm so sorry, my dear fellow, but I'm afraid I can't take on any locum jobs nowadays. Health isn't up to it. My preaching days are over. Glad you tracked me down, though. I'll be staying with my daughter a little longer and will get in touch with you when I go home. Perhaps we can meet for a chat some time. Goodbye.'

The line went dead. Peter, after the first bewildered moment, wondered whether he ought to have disguised his voice and pretended to be some clerical acquaintance of Bill Thorn's. It was obvious that the last sentences had been intended for the benefit of whoever was now overhearing the conversation.

But would Gerry be so easily taken in, wondered Peter. For surely it could only be Gerry who must not know that a call was being made to Peter. On the other hand, Bill had said that Gerry was not there. Where then could he be? And Dorothy was not feeling well. Was that Bill's tactful way of saying she was very ill? Had Gerry injured her in some way, and been committed to hospital himself?

With his mind swarming with questions, Peter finished his business, locked up the shop, and drove slowly in the direction of Hampstead, taking care not to arrive at Pond Cottage even half a minute too early. It seemed a long time before anybody came to answer the bell. The road was very quiet, almost uncannily so. There was a faint distant hum of traffic, and several streets away somebody was practising the flute, but otherwise blackbirds and thrushes held full sway. It was difficult to imagine a greater contrast to Victoria Avenue than this exclusive little leafy enclave, with its pink chestnut trees and white-painted balconies and shiny metal burglar alarms.

Peter had his own dream of an ideal home and every intention of trying to realize it; nevertheless he could not help wondering for a moment whether the semi-slum in which he was now living was not in some respects a healthier neighbourhood than the one where Dorothy lived and suffered. How much more domestic misery lay locked away in these discreetly luxurious homes?

His mind had slithered on to a ridiculously idealistic picture of himself and Dorothy in some superbly designed modern bungalow on the outskirts of a south coast town, when at last the door was opened.

'Ah. There you are. Come in here, please,' said Bill Thorn.

In the blue and white sitting-room Peter asked at once: 'Where's Dorothy?'

'In the consulting-room. She's using it as a bedroom and is resting there. You'll find her changed. Let me explain before you see her. We've plenty of time. Gerry is out all evening.'

Mr Thorn lowered himself slowly into a chair before continuing. 'I'm sorry,' he said. 'I can't hurry. I've been rather ill.'

He did indeed look more gaunt and frail than ever. Peter expressed concern. Bill Thorn waved it aside. 'I'll be all right,' he said. 'These turns are alarming but I soon recover. Until the final one comes, of course, but I don't think that will be just yet.'

And he proceeded to relate in detail the events leading up to his recent attack.

'At that point I was no longer able to take an active part in the proceedings,' he concluded. 'The following day I was also not very much aware of what was going on, although I know Dr Ferguson came a couple of times and I believe Nina scarcely left my room. No one could have had a better nurse. I saw nothing of Gerry and next to nothing of Dorothy. I believe I did think it odd that she only looked in to ask whether Nina was looking after me and didn't seem to want to attend to my needs herself.'

'That's not like Dorothy at all,' agreed Peter.

'No, but I thought perhaps she was doing it for Nina's sake – letting the girl see how well she could cope. It was another night and half a day before I had recovered enough to realize that something was very wrong.'

Mr Thorn paused for a moment to rest himself and Peter waited silently in wretched anxiety.

'Something must have happened between Gerry and Dorothy that night,' went on Bill at last, 'and I want you to find out what it was. She says nothing. In fact she does nothing – just lies on the couch all day. It was actually Gerry who rang the hospital to say she was ill and who asked them to make arrangements for someone else to see her private patients as well. It's years since he has been capable of such decisive action. He has also made it plain to me, quite politely, that I shall not be welcome here for much longer and as soon as I am completely recovered I am expected to go. While as for Nina – '

Again Mr Thorn had to take a little rest before continuing.

'I don't know what Gerry's intentions are with regard

to Nina. I imagine to get rid of her, but it may be that he is waiting until I am out of the way. Or he may be intending to make use of her in some way connected with Dorothy. At the moment he is completely ignoring her and she him. It's very odd but at least it's peaceful.'

'But what can have come over him?' cried Peter. 'Is he suddenly cured? Is it possible for that sort of condition suddenly to work itself out in this way?'

'I've no idea,' said Bill. 'Dorothy would know, but she's not in a fit state to ask. He certainly seems to be going through some sort of active phase, but whether it's permanent or not . . . I'm inclined to think not. There's something unnatural, almost hysterical, in it. I suppose Dorothy would call it the manic phase of a manic-depressive cycle. That's the jargon, isn't it? I expect he's had such fits before but I don't think they can have resulted in quite such a burst of activity. And they certainly have never had an effect like this on Dorothy. Nothing ever has. I have never seen her like this in my life. Even after her own grievous loss she never became as completely demoralized as this. She seems to have lost all will to live. I'm relying on you, Peter, to bring it back to her.'

'I can only do my best,' muttered Peter, getting to his feet.

Mr Thorn rose too. 'Yes, we will go to see her now. Nina is upstairs at the moment, but she'll bring some coffee later on.'

'And Gerry?'

'Gerry has gone out to dinner with Dorothy's old schoolfriend Pauline, who was at one time a friend of his. She is now a wealthy widow. An over-sweet lady. I don't trust her. Gerry phoned her the day after I became ill.

That is also something he has never done before, to my knowledge. She bustled round full of sympathy for everyone and terribly anxious to help. Very inquisitive. Very determined that Dorothy's nervous collapse should be made much of. Very keen to advise Gerry about what to do with her. I imagine this little dinner-party is to discuss the situation at Pond Cottage. Lots of sympathy for poor Gerry. God knows what they are cooking up between them. Or what he is telling her about Dorothy.'

Peter gave a short angry laugh. 'Telling Pauline he's got a mad wife, no doubt,' he said. 'I suppose he's trying to dump his neurosis on Dorothy.'

They moved to the door.

'It seems so, it seems so,' said Bill.

Peter glanced at him and for the first time that evening caught the full measure of the old man's distress.

'You think Gerry is seriously trying to make out that it is Dorothy who is out of her mind?' he asked.

Bill Thorn nodded. 'But it doesn't matter if he manages to convince Pauline. Or anyone else for that matter. That can be dealt with in due course. The essential thing is that he doesn't succeed in convincing Dorothy herself. That's where you come in. To find out exactly what has happened between them and to get it across to her that she is perfectly sane. She's not simply exhausted, Peter. She's very frightened indeed. That's not like her, and I want to know why.'

After the sunny blue and white room, Dorothy's consulting-room, with the long wall of books and the desk and the filing cabinet, looked austere and even sombre. It also looked to Peter rather larger than it had done on the evening when he had helped to carry Gerry in there. But that might have been because Dorothy herself seemed so small and shrunken. Cushions and pillows had been piled at one end of the couch and she was curled up against them. She was barelegged and was wearing a rather crumpled cotton dress. Her black hair was untidy and straggly, as if it had been dampened and was hanging in rat's tails, and her eyes were dull. A plain woman. Sick, weary, and defeated. Every little spark of that vitality that had so attracted Peter seemed to have been extinguished. Had he met her now for the first time he could have felt no stronger emotion than pity.

He felt pity now, but also fury at whoever or whatever had done this to her. If there was anything on earth he could do to restore Dorothy to her former self, he would do it, at whatever cost to himself or to anybody else.

Dorothy put down the evening paper and looked up at him.

'Hullo, Peter,' she said. 'I thought I heard your voice. Did my father ask you to come?'

She sounded very listless but quite normal. Peter felt immense relief. For a horrible moment he had feared that her mind had been so affected that she would not recognize him.

'He told me you weren't very well,' said Peter, coming to sit on the end of the couch. 'I hope you don't mind me coming to see you.'

'Not a bit. It's very kind of you,' said Dorothy formally. 'I'm sorry I can't entertain you in any way, but I'm almost too feeble to walk across the room. I seem to be having some sort of nervous collapse. Not what you'd expect of a psychiatrist. Funny, isn't it?'

'I suppose doctors can fall ill just like anybody else,' said Peter. 'Have you consulted anybody about it? Or are you prescribing for yourself?'

Dorothy did not reply to this direct. 'There's nothing much to be done,' she said vaguely. 'Just rest. Try not to worry. Try not to get over-excited.'

Peter asked several more questions about herself but she answered them all in the same uninformative manner. It seemed to him that she was deliberately spinning a web about herself, keeping him at bay. If that was the case then there must be some core of energy left in her, something of her own true self. But how was he to get through to it? The precious minutes were passing and he was getting nowhere.

'And what about you, Peter?' she asked presently. 'How is all the studying going?'

He began to tell her about the course in Electromagnetics and Electronics that he had chosen to do the following year and that he was looking forward to because there would be less of the theory and more of the practical work, with which he was always happier. Previously she would have been interested, but he could see now that she was not really listening. Her eyes were open but they were turned inwards.

'I think you're marvellous to work so hard,' she said. 'I'm sure you're going to get to the top one day.'

There was nothing of Dorothy's fervour and intelligence in the remark. It was as if she was playing the little woman, the ignorant female boosting the male ego, and it disgusted Peter so much that quite automatically, and without any planning, he did the best possible thing.

'Will you please stop that bloody silly act at once!' he said brutally. 'It's not surprising that you're worn out after all the strain you've been through, but because your body and mind and emotions need a rest doesn't mean that you have to take leave of your wits!'

Dorothy put her hands over her face and shrank back against the pillows.

'I don't see why having a nervous collapse should make people feeble-minded,' continued Peter in the same tone of voice. 'It didn't do it to Gerry. You said yourself that his intellect always continues to function, however crazy he is.'

'Gerry isn't crazy,' muttered Dorothy between her fingers. 'It's been all my fault.'

'Balls!' shouted Peter. 'Will you stop talking such rubbish?' He caught hold of her hands and held them away from her face. 'Now what's all this about? What's this hold over you that Gerry's got?'

Dorothy blinked and gave a little moan.

'I'm not going out of this house till you tell me,' said Peter. 'If Gerry comes back and tries to turn me out, then we'll have another fight, that's all. If he gets hold of a knife, then I'll grab one too.'

'A knife?' murmured Dorothy questioningly. The dull look had gone out of her eyes and she looked both startled and puzzled.

'Yes. A knife. Don't try to pretend you've forgotten. That crazy husband of yours went for me with a very sharp breadknife. If you look above my right eye you'll see the scar. You cleaned it and disinfected it yourself. Fortunately no stitches were required.'

Dorothy was shuddering and grimacing all the time that Peter was speaking. It was painful to watch, as if somebody was coming round out of an anaesthetic too soon. It was going to get worse, he had no doubt, but he could not turn back now: this sort of shock treatment was the only way.

'Yes,' she said at last. 'I remember.'

'And while we were sitting on Hampstead Heath you told me about all the times he had tried to kill himself. Remember?'

'Yes.'

'And then he got rid of Mrs Oliver. And he left you a letter saying he was going to commit suicide and make it look as if you had murdered him. You showed me the letter. And you showed it to your father. We both read it. It was not the letter of a sane man. Was it? Was it, Dorothy?'

He shook her a little and again she whispered an answer. 'No.'

'What happened the other night after your father had that attack?' went on Peter.

Dorothy made no reply.

'Did he threaten you that way again? Is that what you're afraid of?'

Peter waited but she still said nothing. 'You know what the best answer to that threat is, don't you, Dorothy? It's just to clear right out of here, isn't it? If you're nowhere near him, then there's no way you could be suspected of killing him. But he's not going to kill himself. You know he isn't. He's gone and taken up with Pauline. She wanted him in the first place. You told me so. Let

her have him. Let her take him on and the house too
and you come away with me, Dorothy. Now. At once.
Tonight.'

'No, no.' She was crying now. 'I'm so tired.'

'Yes, of course.' Peter laid her back against the cushions,
held her hand gently, and then hastened to retrieve his
error of tactics. He had let his anxiety to get her out of
this house at all costs run away with him and divert him
from the attempt to find out what had happened. He
believed that he had been making some progress and
hoped that it was not too late to regain the position.

'You'll rest soon,' he said, 'and you'll rest much better
when you've told me how Gerry is threatening you. I'm
not going away from here until you tell me. I mean that,
Dorothy. He hit you, didn't he? Your father told me. Is
that what's worrying you? Or has he threatened Nina?
Or your father? Or me?'

Peter persisted with each question until he got some
sort of response, even if it was only a slight movement of
the head that could not be interpreted as either a shake
or a nod, but that did at least show that she had heard his
question.

'Nina,' he said thoughtfully. 'Your taking in that girl
brought matters to a crisis. As if Gerry were a spoilt
child who could not bear to share you with another . . . a
spoilt child . . . a child . . . Dorothy,' he said, leaning
towards her and speaking very urgently, 'was there ever a
child?'

The spasm that contorted her face gave him the
answer. Bill Thorn's remark about her 'grievous loss'
came back to him and he knew he was getting to the
heart of the matter at last.

'When?' he asked. 'What happened?'

'Fifteen years ago. She died.' Dorothy was weeping now but her words were quite audible.

'I'm sorry,' said Peter very gently. 'How did it happen?'

'I killed her,' said Dorothy in the same clear low voice. 'I gave her an overdose of a drug.'

CHAPTER XVII

Peter managed to control his shock and say in steady, matter-of-fact tones: 'Now we're getting somewhere. How did you come to make such a mistake? And was Gerry there at the time?'

The story came out jerkily and disjointedly but it was not too difficult to piece it together into a coherent whole.

'Was it proved beyond all doubt that the drug was responsible for her death?' Peter asked.

'No doubt at all. A colleague of mine carried out the post-mortem.' Dorothy was now quite calm and still and hopeless; a witness for the defence knowing there was no way of avoiding a guilty verdict.

'But you didn't actually hold the cup for the child to drink from it?'

'No. Gerry did that. I'd been called to the telephone.'

'Then couldn't it have been Gerry who made the mistake about the dose?'

'No. I'd already prepared it. I'd measured out the drops from the bottle into the orange juice. The phone call came as I was doing it. I was rather expecting a call from a patient who was very disturbed and in danger of harming himself. Gerry answered the phone in the other room – we lived in a flat then. He came into the kitchen and said "Sounds like one of your dottier cases, Dolly". I hadn't qualified in psychological medicine then. I was still training. I got very anxious if a patient looked like coming to serious harm. I wasn't particularly bothered about Irene at that moment. She'd had this nasty chest trouble, but it was clearing up well. The medicine she was taking was effective and perfectly safe . . . in the correct doses. The orange juice was to make it more palatable, although in her case . . .'

Dorothy's voice faltered for the first time.

'She was a good little patient,' she said at last. 'Took everything given her without making a fuss, even if it didn't taste very nice.'

'So it was Gerry who actually gave the dose?' prompted Peter.

'Yes. He was quite good with her. We had a girl living in but it was her evening off.'

'It must have been a very tough time for you,' said Peter, 'doing a hard professional grind and with a young child to look after. Not to mention a husband who presumably made a lot of demands, even at that time.'

'It was my own choice,' said Dorothy. 'It's overworked professional women who kill their babies.'

'Nonsense.' Peter gave her a little shake. 'Snap out of that! If you were indeed responsible for measuring out too much of the drug, then it was nothing more than a most ghastly mistake, the sort of thing one does when thinking about too many things at once. But I'm not at all convinced that you were responsible. There are so many other possibilities. Couldn't Gerry have added the extra drops after you'd gone to answer the phone?'

'That's the story he told for the coroner. He said that he had understood me to say, as I went to the phone, that I hadn't put the drops in. When I gave my evidence I said that I had told Gerry I'd done the drops. They believed us, both of us. The verdict was accidental death. Everybody was very sympathetic.'

'Your father?'

'That's the version of the story that he knows. And my mother too. She was alive then. And everybody else. Everyone has always believed that is what happened. You are the first person who has ever heard the truth. Apart from Gerry.'

'I don't think I am hearing the truth now,' said Peter firmly. 'I believe the account that was given at the inquest was in fact the true one. I believe it is Gerry himself who has put this idea of your own guilt into you over the years. I've never learnt anything about psychology but that seems to make sense. He felt guilty himself. He couldn't stand it. And he was jealous of you. You were more successful in your career than he was in his. You were more brilliant in every way. He worked hard at making you believe you were solely responsible for the child's death. But the strain on him has been very great. He's forced a lie on you for all these years and now he is afraid you are going to reject that lie. So he has to force you into a collapse. If you give up fighting, then it lets him off. It proves his lie is true. There!' Peter finished triumphantly. 'How's that for a piece of subtle psychological analysis on the part of a plodding student of technology?'

'Pretty good.' Dorothy gave a wan smile. 'I should give it an alpha minus.'

It was a fleeting glimpse of the old Dorothy, and it gave Peter hope, although the hope faded again when she almost at once reverted to her obstinate, almost sullen manner.

'It's a pretty story but it isn't true,' she said. 'The truth is that I put the extra drops in myself.'

'How can you be so sure? It's a long time ago and it's terribly easy to be mistaken about pills and things.'

'Terribly easy. I was mistaken. My mind was on my patients, not on the child.'

Peter tried another tack. 'All right then. Let's suppose it was really you who made the mistake. You felt guilty, at any rate, you felt as if you had done it. But haven't you paid for it over and over again? Haven't you served your sentence? Fifteen years is a long time. Longer than anybody would get for manslaughter. Don't you think it's time you came out of prison now?'

Dorothy shook her head. 'I can't live with it any longer,' she muttered.

A new and horrible suspicion came into Peter's mind. Could it possibly be that Gerry was trying to drive it to the bitter end? To push Dorothy to suicide? He fought down the suspicion. Dorothy would never give in; she would never take that way out.

'Of course you can't live with it any longer,' he said robustly. 'Isn't that exactly what I am saying? You've been punished enough. It's time to call a halt. And the only way to do that is to get you away from Gerry.'

Again Dorothy shook her head.

'Good God, woman, haven't you any pride?' cried

Peter. 'How much longer do you want to act as whipping-girl?'

Dorothy began to cry again and Peter made a great effort to take a grip on himself. He stood up. 'I think I'd better go and tell your father,' he said. 'He knows better than I do how to manage you.'

'Don't tell my father!' Dorothy actually got up from the couch and clung to the table. She looked and sounded horrified.

'You ought to have told him about it ages ago,' said Peter. 'It would never have got to this point if you had.'

'I couldn't . . . it would have hurt him so much . . . he's been so proud of me . . . and my career.'

'When I see what a fool an intelligent person can be,' exclaimed Peter, 'it's almost enough to make me give up my academic ambitions.'

'You mustn't do that!' cried Dorothy.

'No, I mustn't, must I, or you'll be feeling guilty about that too. All right then. For the time being I won't tell your father that Gerry has been morally blackmailing you for years in this absolutely unspeakable manner. But I'll only keep quiet on one condition.'

Dorothy glanced at him apprehensively. She looked so pitiful that Peter ached to comfort her but he kept saying to himself: no, not yet. This is the only way.

'If I promise not to tell your father,' he said, 'will you promise in return that you will make every effort to keep yourself alive and to get well again?'

'I'm not well,' she muttered.

'No, you are not well, but there's no need to make yourself worse or to take any risks. You understand me, don't you? Yes, I see you do. I'm warning you, Dr

Dorothy Laver, if you go overdosing yourself or doing anything idiotic like that you'll be going to heaven or hell with the whole of my own life's misery on your conscience. You mean everything to me. I don't want to have to face my life without you. And what about your father? What about all your patients who depend so much on you? What about your friends? What about Nina? What help will it be for Irene who has long been dead if you take yourself away from Nina who is alive and desperately needs you?'

Peter had never been so worked up in his life. He was speaking with a passion and fervour that would have astonished anybody who had ever known him. Dorothy said nothing but he had the feeling that his appeal had struck home and would not be forgotten. Perhaps that was all he could expect at the moment; perhaps he had better leave it at that.

There was a knock at the door and he went to open it. The girl who came in carrying a tray looked almost as white and frightened as Dorothy did herself.

'You must be Nina,' said Peter. 'I'm Peter Tarrant and I've been telling Dorothy she's got to look after herself.'

Nina nodded vigorous approval as she poured out the coffee.

'Here's my address, Nina,' said Peter. 'Two addresses – my work and my home. And here's my work phone number. If I'm not there Mr Hardy will be and he'll know where I am. Here's my landlord's phone. He'll take a message or call me if it's a real emergency. I want you to get in touch with me immediately if anything happens here that you think I ought to know. Get me?'

'Yes,' said Nina.

'Even if Dorothy says you need not.'

'Yes,' said Nina again.

They both looked at Dorothy. She had sat down again and was slowly shaking her head.

'And keep close watch on her,' said Peter. 'Whatever happens. Whoever tries to stop you.'

'I am keeping watch!' cried Nina. 'I come and sleep down here when *he*'s gone to bed. In the other room. With the door open so I can hear.'

'Good girl. Thanks for the coffee.' Peter swallowed it in a couple of gulps. 'Goodbye, Dorothy. Good luck. See you again soon.'

He could not bear to look at her; he felt he had caused too much pain.

Bill Thorn was waiting anxiously in the blue and white room.

'She's told me about it,' said Peter. 'I've been bullying her horribly. I feel sick with myself.'

'It will pass,' said the old man. 'Well?'

'I promised not to tell you,' said Peter slowly. 'Actually it doesn't really matter very much what it is. She feels guilty about something in the past – whether rightly or wrongly I don't know – and Gerry's been playing on it all these years. Just recently he's been stepping up the blackmail, putting on the pressure to an intolerable degree. That's why she's cracked up.'

'The child,' said Bill Thorn promptly. 'It's obviously to do with the child's death.'

'You know about it?'

'She's never talked to me about it,' said Dorothy's father, 'but it's not been difficult to guess that she feels herself completely to blame. I suppose Gerry has been encouraging that belief in order to have a hold over her. Is that it, Peter?'

'I promised I wouldn't tell you,' said Peter.

'You haven't told me. I've guessed it. If it weren't that he is so obviously insane, that man would be an offence to humanity.'

'What's worrying me . . .' began Peter and then stopped.

'Yes?' Bill Thorn looked very alert.

'I hope I haven't made things worse for her,' said Peter. 'With Gerry, I mean. By forcing her to tell me about the child.'

'Go on,' said Mr Thorn grimly.

'If he finds out that she's told me it could drive him into drastic action.'

'Go on,' said Bill Thorn again.

Peter jumped up and began to walk excitedly about the room. 'Suppose – just suppose – that it was Gerry himself who killed the child. Perhaps by accident, perhaps on purpose. He came back to his right senses and panicked. How could he escape the consequences? By blaming Dorothy. Dorothy was young and overworked and worried and perhaps still rather deeply in love with him. At any rate she did not know then just what he was like. He conceived a masterstroke. Put it into Dorothy's mind that she had been to blame and at the same time Gerry would get rid of his own guilt and have a wonderful hold over Dorothy. And so he persuaded her that the death of the child was entirely her own doing, and she was the more easily persuaded when he very nobly agreed to share the blame himself. She certainly believed him at first. Perhaps she has believed him for a long time. But suppose she no longer believes him? Suppose she is willing to accuse him? Wouldn't you say she was in serious danger? Wouldn't you say that her only protection would be to play along with Gerry and pretend to him that she is still blaming herself? If she is weak and guilty she is no threat to him. But if she's strongminded enough to bring the whole truth out into the open . . . oh, my God, what have I done!' exclaimed Peter, stopping suddenly in his tracks and staring at Bill Thorn in horror. 'Bullying her into telling me!'

'You've probably saved her soul,' said Bill quietly.

'I reckon I've signed her death warrant!' cried Peter.

Bill got up and took him by the arm and gently forced him to sit down again. 'It's not going to help if we get into a panic ourselves,' he said. 'You may be right about Dorothy being in danger, but that is nothing new and it is certainly not your doing. She has been in danger from Gerry for years.'

'Not as badly as this.'

'Not as badly as this, but don't forget that she is not alone with Gerry. Nina and I are here too. I know what you're thinking. An old man and a young girl – what protection can they possibly be against a maniac? They can be a very good protection, my dear Peter, believe me.'

'If only she'd come away with me. Or if only I could stay here. I could hide in the garden – '

'It would be most unwise of you to stay on the premises. Look what happened last time. I swear to you, Peter, that I am going to get Dorothy away from Gerry. Not tonight. Tomorrow. I promise you. She will come to no harm tonight. I will keep watch on Gerry upstairs. Nina will keep watch on Dorothy down here.'

'But if he gets really violent – '

'He is still no match for the three of us. And he won't get violent. It will be done by subtlety if anything is to be done at all. Peter, you must go now. Please trust me.'

But when Peter was at the door Bill called him back again. 'I very nearly forgot. Could you show me how to work this gadget of Dorothy's? I want to record a radio programme. I'm afraid I'm a dreadful old duffer at this sort of thing.'

The gadget was a little tape-recorder.

'Dorothy has been using it to record interviews with patients for some research she has been doing,' said Mr Thorn. 'She always gets their permission, of course, and I know she is very careful to destroy all material that is not going to be used . . . thank you, Peter. Yes, I've got the hang of it now. Good night, my dear boy, and thank you again. I'll be in touch in the morning.'

After one last anxious glance at the closed door of the consulting-room, Peter left the house. He had never believed it possible that he could feel this overwhelming urge to take a fellow creature's life. If he were to run into Gerry now he would not be responsible for his actions; there would be no restraining himself. He had to admit that the old man was right to send him away, but it was terribly hard to go. He lingered for a moment or two in the drive, assessing the height of the consulting-room window from the ground and wondering whether to attempt a midnight abduction of Dorothy – willing or unwilling. Why hadn't her father persuaded her to come away now? Surely he would have been able to do so? What was he up to? Why the tape-recorder? Peter didn't believe for a moment that Bill simply wanted to record a radio programme. The old man was playing some deep game of his own, gambling with Dorothy's life.

By the time he had reached the van Peter had worked himself up into a state of great indignation against Dorothy's father. He switched on the engine and the lights and sat staring at the white gateposts of Pond Cottage, as he had done on another occasion not so very long ago. A car came slowly past the van, turned left in front of it, and paused for a moment before proceeding between the gateposts. The driver turned to look at Peter. His face was clearly visible in the remaining light of day, aided by the headlamps and the streetlamp. And Peter's face was equally visible to him.

If he gets out I am going to run him down, thought Peter, putting the van into gear and watching intently.

But Gerry did not get out. He drove on up the drive and round the corner of the house. Peter switched off the engine and the lights again and slumped back dejectedly in his seat. It seemed to him that he had done nothing but harm all round. He had shaken Dorothy out of the listless passivity in which alone she was safe from Gerry; he had not followed his own deep instinct to stay in the house regardless of Mr Thorn's wishes; and he had not got away in time to conceal his visit from Gerry.

One by one the lights in the windows of Pond Cottage went out, and Peter was still sitting in the van near to the gate. He could neither bring himself to go in nor to drive away. He cursed himself for his own bungling, and was tormented by thoughts of what Gerry might be saying or doing to his wife.

CHAPTER XVIII

'You know it's the only way,' said the low voice, very gently, very persuasively. 'You can't live with it any longer and it's so easy to end it all . . . easy to end it . . . easy to end it . . .'

Dorothy lay curled up under the bedclothes on the couch in the quiet room. The thick curtains were drawn across and no crack of light showed through them. The door was shut. The still darkness was infinitely soothing. Like the womb, like the tomb. She wanted nothing else; no light, no movement, no struggle. Just for the quiet and the rest and the darkness to go on and on, for the sleep that was on its way to her to last for ever.

She didn't know whether the voice was inside her own head or outside it. It felt like inside; it spoke her own thoughts.

'There's water and the bottle there. Within reach on the table. Very little effort. It will only take a few seconds. You've already had two of them. All you have to do is to reach out, empty the rest of them into your hand, lift the glass, lift your head, and swallow. Not much effort to make for everlasting peace. For freedom . . . for peace. Not much to do. It's so easy . . . so easy . . . so easy . . .'

The thoughts were hers and the desire was hers. Only somewhere there seemed to be a stubborn little nagging voice that was pulling in the opposite direction. This other voice was definitely not in herself; it was somewhere outside her, this voice that was so insistently trying to frustrate her own wishes. She wished it would go away, this other nagging voice, and leave her in peace with the thoughts that she wished to hear.

'It's so easy . . . just stretch out your hand . . . empty the bottle . . . so easy . . .'

The low comforting voice went on and on.

'All right,' said Dorothy, but whether she said it aloud or only in her own mind she did not know, 'I'll do it. I'll do it in a minute . . . I'll do it now.'

Her hand reached out, felt the edge of the table, found the bottle. Its lid felt very loose. The feeblest effort would set its contents free.

The comforting voice that spoke her own thoughts went on and on, encouraging her, helping her.

And then the lovely peace was shattered. There came a piercing, intolerable shaft of light; a scream followed by scuffling noises. All was glare and movement and angry voices.

Dorothy curled herself into a tight little ball and pulled the covers over her head. If only it would all go away, leave her in peace to listen to her comforter again, so that she could make just that last little effort.

It went away at last. The still darkness came back, the shouting and the scuffling died except for a distant muffled banging that disturbed her no more than the faint hum of traffic from the main road.

But the comforting voice had gone too.

Dorothy pulled the covers off her head, stretched her limbs, and then curled up again and waited to recapture the drift to endless oblivion.

It would not come.

She was hot and cold and hungry and cramped and

the screaming and the scuffling sounds went on and on inside her head. She moved the pillows and shifted her own position, but still there was no rest and no relief. She raised herself on one elbow but felt so giddy that she quickly lay down again. Thoughts and memories and images came in disconnected flashes. There was no clear reasoning; she did not try to work out what the scuffling and the screaming could have meant. Perhaps it had been a dream. Perhaps the comforting voice had been a dream. All she knew was that she was now awake, weak, giddy, feverish, but certainly awake, lying in bed on the ground floor of her own home, and that there was no regaining the lost paradise of nothingness. All the myriad aches and stabs of human consciousness were with her again and she wept for the peace of death that had been snatched from her.

Mr Thorn, standing in the darkness just inside the door of his room, waited until the shouting had died down and the slight creak of the bedroom door opposite to his own had come and gone. Then he made his way silently and very slowly down the thick carpeted staircase, holding on to the rail with one hand, and holding a little torch in the other. In the hall he paused for a moment or two to take careful breaths. There was a muffled thumping sound audible down here. It seemed to come from the back of the house, but Bill Thorn moved first to the door of the consulting-room, which was slightly ajar. The torchlight showed Dorothy curled up with her face to the wall and one arm flung outside the bedclothes.

'Are you all right?' asked Mr Thorn softly.

She stirred slightly and moaned. He could not tell whether she was asleep or not. He felt for the hand and held it a moment. The pulse seemed to be steady, the breathing even. He laid the hand back on the cover and flashed the little torch on to the bedside table. There was a glass of water standing there and near it a bottle nearly full of dark-coloured capsules. Bill thought for a moment and then drew out a handkerchief from the pocket of his dressing-gown, held it lightly round the bottle, and dropped them both into the pocket. Then he switched off the torch and stood still by the side of the couch for a while. Dorothy made no further sound, and her breathing remained steady, but the distant muffled thumping was still going on.

Mr Thorn came out into the hall. As he neared the kitchen he could hear faint cries for help. He shut the kitchen door behind him, walked across and opened the door that led to a small utility room, and said: 'Is that you, Nina? Where are you?'

'In the broom-cupboard,' came the stifled reply.

Mr Thorn turned the key of the broom-cupboard and Nina collapsed at his feet, lay there for a moment, and then picked herself up.

'Dorothy,' she cried hoarsely. 'Got to see to Dorothy.'

And she would have rushed off at once if Mr Thorn had not restrained her.

'Dorothy is all right. She's asleep. I've just been to look. What happened, Nina?'

'He was by her bed, whispering to her in the dark,' replied the girl. 'I thought I heard something. I went in and switched on the light. I couldn't get near Dorothy. I didn't even see her. He got hold of me and locked me in here. Are you quite sure she's all right? Hadn't I better go and see?'

It was clear that Nina's anxiety was not to be put at rest.

'Go and see for yourself,' said Mr Thorn. 'But don't wake her. Don't go too near her.'

After the girl had gone he lowered himself stiffly into a kitchen chair and put a hand on the outside of the dressing-gown pocket. There will be his fingerprints on the bottle, he said to himself, which won't prove anything but it will help a little, because these are Dorothy's sleeping pills and there was no need for him to be handling them. And then there's that little gadget. Bill Thorn glanced at his watch. I'm afraid it won't have anything much on it, because Peter said the tape would only run an hour. But one never knows. It might have picked up something. And Gerry is not to know when it was put in place. Bluff ought to be enough. It will take him by surprise to learn that I had thought of recording him. Even with all his cunning he would never suspect that of me. His highly-respected father-in-law to go bugging a room! Even in his own thoughts the old man used the phrase a little self-consciously. He was indeed very surprised at himself, but having made up his mind, he was going to shirk nothing, absolutely nothing. He had, in the last resort, his own life to give. Those who do not care whether they live or die, they are the strongest, he said to himself.

But Nina must be kept out of it. She was young and had everything to live for. Mr Thorn had no doubt that the girl would gladly put herself in front of an assassin's gun in order to protect Dorothy, but she must not be allowed to get into such a position. She had suffered enough violence already this evening.

'Well, my dear,' he said when Nina returned. 'Are you convinced now?'

'I suppose so,' said Nina reluctantly. 'But what was he doing there, whispering to her in the dark?'

'I don't know,' said Mr Thorn, 'but it can't have been anything to upset her. You can see she's come to no harm. Which is more than can be said of you, my poor child.'

He looked at the girl with concern. Nina did indeed look very battered and dishevelled.

'Oh, I'm all right,' she said impatiently. 'I can look after myself. And I'm not going to leave Dorothy alone. I'm going to stay in the consulting-room for the rest of the night. No one can stop me. I won't disturb her. I'll lie on the floor near the door.'

This was not quite what Bill Thorn had wanted, but he merely said: 'I don't think it is necessary, but if it would make you happier, then you do that. Perhaps you would warm me up some milk first, will you? And I'll look in on Dorothy again while you're doing it.'

I don't trust her not to go snooping around, he said to himself as he retrieved the tape-recorder from under the couch. She's much too bright and suspicious. I'll have to think up some means of keeping her out of the way when I tackle Gerry. Shall I do it tonight? No, I think it had better be tomorrow. He isn't likely to come out of his room again tonight. Not after all that rumpus. And having his behaviour to Nina to explain away.

Mr Thorn placed the little tape-recorder next to the radio in the sitting-room. My fingerprints are all over it, he said to himself, but that does not matter. It's the bottle I have to be careful about. The tape is merely for bluff. And in any case, with any luck this will not be a matter for the police. Not in that way, at any rate.

When he had drunk the warm milk he said to Nina: 'I think I will doss down on the settee in the sitting-room for the rest of the night. It's just as comfortable as a bed and I shall do very well there.'

Nina looked shocked. 'You ought to be in bed, in your state of health.'

'Of course I ought.' Mr Thorn smiled. 'But I'm not going to. I don't feel at all bad. Do I look as if I'm going to collapse on you again?'

Nina had to own that he did not. In fact he looked astonishingly spry for an old man who had recently been so ill and had been got out of his bed only a little while after retiring to it.

'I don't think Mr Laver will disturb us again,' said Mr Thorn. 'He will be rather ashamed of himself after losing his head and locking you up like that. If anything does happen, we are within call of each other and of Dorothy.'

He stood up, took the girl's hand, and pressed it to his lips. 'Thank you with all my heart, my dear little Nina, for being such a good watchdog for my daughter. May God bless you.'

The hours of darkness passed in silence. Outside Pond Cottage Peter dozed over the wheel of the van, hoping that Middle Lane was free of nocturnal wandering policemen who might wonder what he was doing there. And inside the house Dorothy stirred again and then once more cried herself to sleep, unaware that three guardian angels were watching over her.

CHAPTER XIX

When the early summer dawn came, it occurred to Peter that if he was not going to try to get into the house, it would be more sensible to be somewhere where Nina could reach him by telephone. He drove home, made tea, sat down at the table, opened his copy of Galbraith's *The New Industrial State*, which was a set book for his course, and stared at it uncomprehendingly. After an hour of this he shut the book up in disgust with himself and tried to sleep. By eight he was at the shop, quite certain that Nina had been trying to get in touch with him there and that something disastrous had happened to Dorothy. When Len came in at half past eight, Peter told him in great agitation that he was expecting a call any moment on a personal matter and asked Len to be sure to give the caller the number of the house where he would be working for the day. The owners had gone on holiday to escape the upheaval of rewiring and had given Peter the key and the run of the place.

He was struggling to get the fitted carpet in the dining-room out of the way without doing any damage to it when the telephone rang. It never occurred to him that it was more likely to be a call for the owners than for himself, so much had the affairs of Pond Cottage come to dominate his whole horizon and upset his normal balance. It was, in fact, Nina ringing from a call-box.

'Mr Thorn told me to ring you,' she said, 'to say to stay away from here. He says he's got everything under control and he'll let you know when to come. He wants me to keep out of the way too but I'm not going to. I'm going back. I won't interfere with him but I've got to be there.'

'But what's happening?' cried Peter in an agony of bewilderment. 'Hi – don't ring off.'

Nina, who appeared to think that her cryptic message provided an adequate report on events, had seemed about to do so.

'Here – give me the number of the box,' said Peter. 'I'll dial it and you won't have to keep putting coins in.'

She gave it and rang off and he dialled and waited in misery until she answered.

'Is Dorothy all right?' he asked immediately.

'I suppose so, but they don't seem to want her to wake up properly.'

'Who is "they"?' Peter was irritable and impatient until it occurred to him that Nina, too, might have had a very bad night and be feeling confused and afraid. 'Do you mean Mr Thorn?' he added more gently.

'Yes, and Dr Ferguson. He sent for him and they sent me out of the room but I overheard some of it. She's to stay asleep all morning. I think he's given her an injection of something. Her mind needs a very long rest, they said.'

Nina sounded very worried. Peter made an effort to console her. 'Look, if it's Dr Ferguson and her father, it must be all right. She was terribly tired, wasn't she, and couldn't rest properly. I don't suppose she's had a good night's sleep for months.'

'I suppose that's all it is but I wish they'd let me talk to her. I wish I knew what they were doing.'

'So do I,' groaned Peter.

'I wish she was having this rest somewhere else.'

'Me too. But I don't see how she can come to any harm, honestly. Dr Ferguson wouldn't allow it. What's Gerry Laver doing?'

'After he locked me in the broom-cupboard last night,' began Nina.

'Locked you in the broom-cupboard!' exclaimed Peter, with all his anxieties returning in full force.

Nina gave a hasty account of the events of the night as far as she knew them. 'What was he doing there, whispering to her in the dark?' she demanded as she had done of Mr Thorn. Peter's mind only went as far as subliminal suggestion or 'sleep learning', which he had been reading about recently with a view to trying to speed up his studies.

'What's he like this morning?' he asked. 'Gerry Laver, I mean.'

'Sort of funny. Doesn't say much. Looks sort of trapped. But nasty too.'

Peter didn't find this sketchy description at all comforting. A kind of simmering viciousness was all too characteristic of Gerry. But surely he couldn't actually do Dorothy any harm, not if she was lying there unconscious. Or could he? Presumably he could use a hypodermic and had access to drugs. Peter groaned again. What the hell was going on in that house? What was Bill Thorn up to?

He asked this last question aloud.

'Mr Thorn said he was going to talk to him seriously,' replied Nina, 'and that no one was to interrupt. I don't like it.'

'Neither do I,' said Peter.

'He'll kill the old man.'

'Oh no. I don't think so.' Belatedly Peter realized again how much Nina herself needed comforting. 'Mr Thorn can look after himself. But it might bring on another of his attacks. That's what is so worrying. I don't see how you can do anything to stop it, though.'

'I've got to go,' said Nina abruptly, and rang off, leaving Peter staring stupidly at his customer's telephone and wondering whether he ought to leave some money for the call.

Nina ran up the road from the call-box and in at the front door of Pond Cottage. Then she tiptoed into the consulting-room. It was cool and quiet and dim in there, with the curtains drawn against the morning sun. Nina stood looking down at Dorothy. They had said she was perfectly all right and only needed a very long sleep, but she looked very white and her breathing seemed scarcely to stir the bedcover. Nina could not help being afraid. She longed to put her arms round Dorothy and beg her not to desert her, to come back to life, but she dared not. Instead she stood twisting her hands together in unconscious imitation of Dorothy's own habitual gesture of tension and whispered her plea.

'Please get well, please get well. Don't go and leave me all alone again.'

Then she ran to the door of Gerry's study and put her ear to the keyhole. She would hear if there was any sound of a fight. If he hit the old man she was going to go in and do something about it: kick him where it hurt most. She would get it in first this time instead of being bundled ignominiously into the broom-cupboard.

But there was no sound of any violence, nor indeed of any movement at all from within the room. There was nothing but the old man's voice going on and on. Nina could hear it perfectly clearly.

'I am not condemning you,' he said. 'No one of us has any right to condemn another. And I realize that yours is a sickness of the mind rather than a crime. But the suffering it has caused has got to come to an end. It killed your own daughter – '

There was a pause, in which Nina, rapidly digesting this statement, could hear no sound from either of the two men in the room.

' – and last night it nearly killed mine,' continued the voice of Mr Thorn. 'Last night you made a deliberate attempt to induce Dorothy to kill herself by taking an excessive dose of her sleeping capsules. Dorothy is not a child whom you can easily induce to swallow a fatal dose when one of your mad fits of jealousy comes upon you. She would not ignorantly swallow a poison – at any rate not any poison known to chemistry. But you have been poisoning her nevertheless. Poisoning her mind for many years, persuading her that in a tragic moment when her own mind was overburdened with its respon-sibilities, she made a mistake and gave the wrong dosage to her own child.'

For a moment the old man's voice seemed to falter and then it went on again, more strongly than before. 'That is in the past. It is last night with which we are concerned at this moment. This is a very different matter. I have firm evidence of attempted murder. When Dorothy was totally exhausted in mind and body and longing only for rest you worked upon her to push her over the edge and you put the means of self-destruction within her grasp.'

'Well, well.' Gerry spoke at last. 'I never would have thought you capable of inventing such a curious story, Bill. However. Do go on. I am all agog to hear the end.'

The tones were as mocking as ever, but Nina believed she could detect some anxiety as well.

'I am not bluffing, I assure you,' continued Mr Thorn. 'I have evidence enough to warrant a police enquiry, at any rate.'

'Evidence! Come now, Bill, aren't you being just a teeny bit fanciful?'

'The bottle bearing your fingerprints, with the lid left very loose so that it would be easy for Dorothy to open it, is now locked up safely in Dr Ferguson's possession. The tape-recording of your voice – '

'Tape-recording?' Nina, feeling her own heart give a sudden jump, could almost hear Gerry's start from the other side of the closed door.

'Tape-recording,' repeated Mr Thorn firmly. 'This too is in safety – in possession of Dr Ferguson. It is not very clear, but it is none the less unmistakably your own voice. There will be witnesses to swear to that, I think.'

Gerry laughed, but not very convincingly. 'Really, Bill, this is too absurd. You don't know how to use a tape-recorder. You've often said so. And in any case a tape doesn't run for long.'

'I admit that I know very little about these electrical gadgets myself,' said Mr Thorn, 'and that is why I consulted an expert.'

'An expert?' Again there was a quick change in Gerry's voice and Nina heard the sound of movement in the room. 'An expert! That man!' There was menace in the voice now. 'He was here. I saw him. You've been plotting together. You'll pay for this.'

There came further sounds. Nina gripped the door-handle and drew a deep breath to prepare herself for the attack. But almost instantly her own grip relaxed. Mr Thorn's voice sounded as steady as ever and it seemed that he still had the situation well under control.

'If you make any attempt on my life or injure me in any way,' he said, 'that is certainly the end as far as you are concerned. And it won't be treatment in a mental hospital that I am proposing for you. It will be a prison sentence. If that is what you want, then go ahead. It is of no great consequence to me. I am old and sick and have not much longer to live in any case.'

After this there was a silence, lasting what seemed to Nina for a very long time. She held her breath. Then Mr Thorn said: 'I don't know whether your form of sickness of the mind can be cured. Science is able to do a lot nowadays and it may be that you can be helped. I hope so. I would like at any rate to give you the chance to try to heal yourself. I have been making enquiries and have made provisional arrangements for you to be taken into hospital at once.'

He paused once more and Nina thought she could hear some muttering sounds, but could distinguish no words.

'I have been able to do this,' went on Mr Thorn, 'without actually mentioning your attempt to kill Dorothy. This need not be made public and the evidence can remain unused provided you keep to certain conditions. They are two in number and very simple.'

The old man was speaking as calmly as ever. There was no malice in his voice; there might even have been a touch of compassion, but there was a quiet ruthlessness about it that made Nina shiver.

'The first condition is that you do not try to leave the hospital or to communicate with Dorothy in any way. The second is that you relieve Dorothy once and for all of her undeserved feelings of guilt about Irene by signing a statement that you were solely responsible for the death of the child. I have prepared such a document for you to sign. I do not call it a confession, because that implies free will and I do not think you were responsible for your actions when you gave that overdose to Irene. I believe that you were out of your mind. You will see that I have not written that it was done deliberately. That is not necessary for Dorothy's peace of mind. It is enough that she knows it was not her doing. After she has read the statement it will be destroyed. Nobody else will ever know of its existence. It is up to you, if you wish, before you sign it to add a rider asking her forgiveness. But the evidence of your last night's attempt will not be destroyed. It will be used if you refuse to sign this statement or if, having signed it, you refuse to remain in hospital. I will leave it with you now. I have another copy if this one should become damaged.'

Nina pressed her head more closely to the door. Again she thought she had heard Gerry say something, but could not hear what it was.

'It may be,' said Mr Thorn, and it seemed to Nina that his voice was at last beginning to show signs of tiring, 'that you will decide not to sign because you have some other plan of escape in your mind. I will not try to guess what that plan is. I will not try to frustrate your plan provided it causes no harm to Dorothy. It will be advisable, however, to come to a decision within the next few hours.'

After that came the distinct sound of a chair being moved back and Nina hastily retreated a couple of yards. The door of the study began to open and Nina made a dash for the kitchen. When Mr Thorn came in a few minutes later she was rushing about opening and shutting drawers and cupboards in a meaningless manner. If he suspected that she had been eavesdropping he gave no sign of it.

'This is the key to the consulting-room,' he said. 'I have taken the precaution of locking the door. There is very little likelihood that my daughter will wake for several hours yet, but I'd like you to keep this safe and go in every now and then to see how she is. Will you do that, please, Nina?'

'Yes,' said Nina taking the key and putting it into the pocket of her jeans. 'I'll keep it on me.'

She glanced up at him apprehensively. He looked just the same as before: an old man whom she had surprisingly come to like and respect, although normally she didn't have much use for old people. He talked in an interesting way and treated you as if you were interesting too. She felt that they were friends, but she would not have expected him to be a force to be reckoned with. After all, he was only a sick old man, and as such was to be cared for or put up with, according to your tastes. It was very difficult to picture him as the owner of the voice that she had heard from the other side of the study door – the voice of retribution. She was longing to ask him about Mr Laver but was afraid to do so. She would be sure to give away the fact that she had been eavesdropping at the door, and then the old man would talk to her in that awful way and she could not bear it.

'Are you all right?' she asked instead.

Mr Thorn smiled in his usual manner and Nina felt a little better.

'You are surprised that I'm not in a state of total collapse,' he said. 'I'll let you into a secret. I am pepped up – is that the phrase? – with some sort of wonder drug that keeps you going during an emergency. You'll probably know more about it than I do. Dr Ferguson was reluctant, but I explained how important it was that I should keep my strength up for the next few hours and in the end he allowed himself to be persuaded. The effects will wear off later on and I shall become very feeble and you will have to be very patient with me again. But I hope that by then we shall see more clearly what is to happen.'

'What is going to happen?' asked Nina in a frightened whisper.

'I don't know, my dear. It's in the lap of the gods. We must try to be patient.'

'Shall I – ' Nina broke off and then took the plunge: 'Shall I get Mr Laver some lunch?'

Mr Thorn considered the question. 'No, I think not,' he said at last. 'Have you got any leftovers in the 'fridge that he can come and get if he wants to?'

Nina reeled off an impressive list of cold meats and cheeses and various other delicacies.

'Then we'll leave it at that,' said Mr Thorn. 'I'm afraid I don't feel very hungry myself. This pep pill, perhaps. Or some other reason. But a cup of tea later on would be very welcome. I shall be in the sitting-room. I don't feel in quite the right mood for the garden. Do you know where the papers have got to?'

Nina found him the two daily papers that came into the house and he smiled and thanked her and settled down to read just as if he were any other harmless and kindly old gentleman who had nothing more in his mind than the news of the day and where to go for his walk and what was for dinner.

When Nina came out of the sitting-room she heard a door close on the floor above. There was no wind that day, and with Dorothy lying dead to the world and Mr Thorn sitting on the settee reading there was only one person who could have closed it. She ran back to Mr Thorn and cried in an excited whisper: 'He's gone upstairs!'

'Well, what of it?' He looked at her in mild reproach above his reading glasses. 'A man may move around his own house, mayn't he?'

'I thought you'd like to know,' said Nina.

Mr Thorn's look became rather more severe. 'Nina,' he said, 'have you been – '

But Nina had vanished, guessing what he was going to ask her.

CHAPTER XX

Nina looked in on Dorothy, saw that all was well, and then went to the kitchen and tried to amuse herself by planning meals, but without much success. She could not even keep still. Her mind was in a turmoil, going over and over the amazing things that she had overheard.

Dorothy's baby, and Gerry trying to kill Dorothy, and
Mr Thorn threatening Gerry . . . She came out into the
hall and stood listening, she did not know for what. Then,
becoming very bold, she opened the door of Gerry's study
and peeped inside. As she had expected, there was
nobody there, and she tiptoed over to the desk. The
urge to find out whether the 'confession' was lying there
and if so, whether he had signed it, was irresistible.

There was no sheet of paper lying on the blotter; only
the ballpoint pen that Gerry normally used. Nina leafed
through a couple of books and an educational journal
that were lying on the desk and then glanced around the
room. If he had signed it and put it into a book or into a
drawer she would have a long search. Perhaps it was in
the waste-paper basket. She squatted on the floor and
examined the contents. A few used envelopes, that was all.
The sound of running water in the house caused Nina to
leap to her feet and stand quivering for a moment behind
the study door. Then, drawn back as if by a magnet to
the desk, she bent more closely over the blotter. The
pressure of a ballpoint, used on a single sheet of paper,
would surely leave a mark on the blotter underneath.
The blotting-paper was barely used: Gerry was fastidious
about taking a clean sheet every morning, whether or
not he intended to do any writing that day. In the right-
hand bottom corner Nina believed she could discern the
faint imprint of a signature: Gerard F. Laver. Of course
this did not necessarily mean he had signed the confession: he might have been putting his name to some
quite unimportant document for all she knew. But it was
exciting to find this, all the same. And even more exciting
when she believed she could distinguish some further

marks underneath the signature, right at the lower edge of the blotter. These were less clear, however. She could make out a few letters, but no full word.

Nina stood up again and wondered what to do now. If Gerry had indeed signed the paper, then Mr Thorn ought to know at once. But how could Nina convey her information to Mr Thorn without letting on that she had been eavesdropping? How could she persuade the old man to go into the study? She stood by the desk, grimacing at the blotter, and for a moment she almost wished she had not listened in to the conversation at all, so great was the burden of the knowledge she had gained thereby, so overwhelming was her need to talk to somebody about it all. She thought of Peter, but was not sure whether he, too, might not blame her. In any case, she dared not telephone him from the house and she could not leave the house because it was her job to keep an eye on Dorothy.

As she stood there in increasingly agitated indecision, she once again heard the sound of running water. Somebody was using the downstairs cloakroom. Probably Mr Thorn. Terrified that he might step across the hall and find her in the study, Nina rushed out and along to the sitting-room. Mr Thorn was not there. He had evidently finished with the newspapers because they were lying folded on the coffee-table, and on top of them lay an open book. Nina picked it up. It had a pale green jacket similar to those on a row of books on one of the shelves in Dorothy's consulting-room. What's he reading medical books for, wondered Nina, and then she looked at the title: *Self-poisoning: an Investigation into Cases Treated in a Special Unit.*

Self-poisoning, muttered Nina to herself; I could tell

them something about that. And so could Gerry Laver.
She was about to replace the book on the table, open as
she had found it, when a few words caught her eye. 'This
widely used and convenient household remedy is by no
means without its dangers, and if the patient fails to
vomit within – '

That was all Nina had time to take in. She had put the
book back and was puffing up the cushions on the settee
when Mr Thorn came back into the room.

'Would you like your tea now?' asked Nina in the most
innocent of voices.

'Not just yet, thank you,' said Mr Thorn. 'In about
half an hour's time, if that is convenient to you.'

'All right.'

Mr Thorn settled himself comfortably on the settee
and picked up his book.

'Do you think it would be all right if I go and dust the
study now?' asked Nina.

Mr Thorn looked up and said severely: 'Have you any
particular reason for wanting to do it at this moment?'

'I just thought of it,' muttered Nina lamely, and once
more she fled from the room and took refuge in the
kitchen. All sorts of ideas were beginning to boil up in her
mind, and for all her histrionic powers, she did not feel
able to be with Mr Thorn in the same room without
giving some of them away. Could it possibly be true,
what she was beginning to suspect of him? Was it possible
that this nice kindly old man could look just the same as
ever and chat about cups of tea while all the time he was
relentlessly pushing another human being into suicide?
For Nina could not help but feel that this was Mr Thorn's
intention. This must be the 'other plan for escape' that

he had mentioned to Gerry, the plan that he himself
would not frustrate provided it did not harm Dorothy.
In other words, if Gerry chose to kill himself rather than
go to hospital or have his murderous attempt on Dorothy
made public, then Mr Thorn would not stop him. And
Dorothy, who might yet try to save his life in spite of
everything, was to be kept out of action until it was all
over.

It was appalling to think that this was in the old man's
mind, but Nina could see no other explanation for his
behaviour. The only thing that didn't quite seem to fit
was the book that he was reading. Self-poisoning cases.
People who had swallowed overdoses of drugs. He would
obviously be interested in this if that was his plan for
Gerry, but on the other hand why should he be reading
about first-aid methods? That rather looked as if he was
thinking of trying to save Gerry's life after all.

Nina, who had been sitting huddled up on the kitchen
stool, suddenly got to her feet and cried aloud: 'What
shall I do? Oh, whatever shall I do? Ought I to tell Mr
Thorn I know about it and beg him to stop Gerry killing
himself . . . ought I to try to stop him myself . . . ought I
to wake Dorothy . . .'

She began to run around the kitchen, beating her hands
against her head. Suppose Gerry had gone upstairs to
take his own life. She hated him; she wished him dead,
but all the same . . . You couldn't be in the same house
with someone trying to kill himself and not do anything
about it. Or could you? It was plain enough that Mr
Thorn could do just that. Why, it was scarcely better
than murder . . . an old man like that, a clergyman, a
man who cared so much about other people and was so

tolerant and so willing to forgive everything . . .

Fragments of one of the many discussions she had had with him came back to Nina's mind. They had been talking about the sacredness of life — plant, human and animal. 'Yes, I would shoot a rabid dog,' Mr Thorn had said. 'It is sad, because it is not the animal's fault, but it has to be done to protect others.'

'And if it's a human being who is running wild?' Nina had asked.

'The same applies,' he had answered. 'Although of course one should make every possible effort to render him harmless in some other way before taking such drastic action.'

Presumably, thought Nina, Mr Thorn thought of Gerry Laver as a rabid dog or a lunatic at large with a knife. She supposed that most people would agree that other people had to be protected. She'd agreed with it herself during their discussion. But to take the law into one's own hands like that . . . wasn't that a bit different?

Nina sat down on the stool again and covered her face with her hands.

'If only I didn't know anything about it,' she moaned. With all her heart she wished now that she had never listened at the study door, never seen what Mr Thorn was reading. It was a terrible thing to feel that you might have the responsibility for life or death in your hands.

Suddenly she could bear it no longer. If she were out of the house it would be less her responsibility. Even in the garden she would not feel quite so close to it. Ashamed of herself for her own cowardice, quite forgetting that she was supposed to be making tea, she gave way to the impulse to run away and hide until it was all over, whatever 'it' might be.

At the side of the house where the old coachhouse, now the garage, stood, there was a little shrubbery. Nina made her way there, sat down on the grass under a lilac bush, and hugged her knees. Then she tried to beat her mind into forgetfulness by repeating the same sentence over and over again. This method had sometimes worked in the past when she had been caught up in something terrifying that she didn't know how to cope with. It's nothing to do with you, she told herself, and went on telling herself this for a long time.

After a while she thought she would be more comfortable if she lay down, and she stretched herself out on the grass, still repeating her sentence. It began to have a hypnotic effect. She had had a sleepless night and many hours of great tension and anxiety. Her hands relaxed and the words of the sentence began to get jumbled up and then stopped coming altogether.

When Nina woke the sun had gone off the bushes and she was stiff and shivery. Her first thought was horror that she had forgotten to check whether Dorothy was all right. She fished for the key to the consulting-room and ran back into the house. All was exactly as she had left it. Dorothy was still asleep, Mr Thorn was still reading in the sitting-room and did not even look up when Nina put her head round the door. And there was still no sign of Gerry. It was as if time had stopped while she slept. But the hands of the clock had moved on. The electric clock over the kitchen door said half past three.

I can't bear it any longer, said Nina to herself: I don't care what happens. I shall have to go upstairs to see.

It was when she reached the foot of the stairs that she

heard the first faint groaning sounds. At first she thought it must be Dorothy, and hastily she unlocked the consulting-room door again and crept inside.

'Are you all right?' she whispered.

Dorothy woke, muttered something, and turned over again as if she was wanting to go back to sleep. She was not in any distress; the groans could not have come from her. Nina left the room, omitting this time to lock the door behind her. As she stood in the hall she heard the groaning again. She rushed into the sitting-room and caught hold of Mr Thorn by the arm.

'Please, please, we've got to do something. I can hear him. It's awful. Please can't we *do* something!'

Mr Thorn got to his feet. 'What is it, Nina? What do you want me to do?'

'Go and see if he's all right. It's awful. I can't bear it. He must be ill.'

Mr Thorn looked at her with pity. Nina looked almost more dishevelled and distraught than she had when she fell out of the broom-cupboard.

'All right,' he said. 'I will go up and see. Wait here.'

After what seemed another age she heard his voice again.

'Nina.'

He was standing at the turn of the stairs, calling her softly. She ran up towards him.

'Will you go and fetch a glass of warm water with salt in it – plenty of salt.'

'Salt water?' repeated Nina in a dazed manner.

'Yes. It's a quick way to rid the stomach of poison. I'll wait here for you.'

Nina returned with the glass. Her hand was trembling

so much that the water slopped over as she carried it.

'Thank you,' said Mr Thorn, taking it from her.

'Hadn't we better . . .' began Nina.

'Yes?' He turned to face her again.

'Hadn't we better phone Dr Ferguson?' she faltered.

Mr Thorn considered this for a moment. 'I doubt if there is any need for it,' he said eventually. 'And in any case I imagine Dr Ferguson is out on his rounds. But if you wish you may telephone his surgery and leave a message. Say that Mr Laver has swallowed four or five sleeping tablets and is still conscious and that I am giving warm salt water as an emetic. Will you give that message to the receptionist, please, Nina?'

'Yes,' said Nina softly.

She telephoned the surgery. Dr Ferguson was not there. She repeated the message and the receptionist promised to contact the doctor as soon as possible.

'Is it – is it all right giving him salt water?' asked Nina.

'Oh yes.' The voice the other end was brisk and confident. 'That's the standard first-aid treatment when the patient is still conscious. Once he's brought up the poison he'll be better.'

'But you will tell Dr Ferguson, won't you, as soon as you can?' begged Nina.

The voice promised that it would. Nina replaced the receiver, feeling only partially reassured. She would much rather have spoken to the elderly Scots doctor herself. He, at any rate, could be trusted not to do anything really wrong.

She ran upstairs and stood still on the half landing. There were sounds coming from the bedroom. She felt that she ought to go in but her feet would not take her.

Mr Thorn heard her and came out. She reported her conversation with the doctor's receptionist. Mr Thorn made no comment, but handed her the empty glass. 'Some more,' he said. 'It's not working yet.'

Nina fetched another glass of warm salt water and then another.

'Hasn't he been sick?' she whispered to Mr Thorn as she handed over the glass at the bedroom door.

The old man moved his head slowly from side to side before going back into the bedroom. Nina stood outside on the landing. The sentence she had read in the book on self-poisoning seemed to be burning itself into her mind.

'This widely used and convenient household remedy is not without its dangers, and if the patient does not quickly vomit . . .'

It was no good. She could not bear it any longer. She would have to go and find the book and read the rest of that sentence. And suppose it is to do with salt water, she asked herself as she ran downstairs, and suppose it says it is dangerous. What are you going to do then? Tell Mr Thorn to stop? Refuse to fetch any more? Go and wake Dorothy?

She found the book and the sentence, and was reading the relevant passage with increasing certainty and horror when the front doorbell rang. Nina did not answer it immediately: she was quickly coming to a resolution. It was her own fault that she knew what Mr Thorn was up to, and she was going to be punished for her eavesdropping by having to live with the knowledge for ever afterwards. Well, she would just have to endure it. She would have to live with her own conscience for always because she knew she could never give him away. Now that she knew for sure she would keep the secret and back him up, whatever happened. Just so long as Dorothy was not suspected. If Dorothy were to be suspected . . . but the last thing in the world that Mr Thorn would want was that. If Dorothy were suspected then he would certainly come forward to take the blame himself.

The bell rang again, loudly and impatiently. Nina reached the front door at the same time as Dorothy came out of the consulting-room in her nightgown, dazed with sleep.

'What's happening? What's the time?' she asked in a blurred voice.

Nina gave her a despairing look and the front doorbell rang yet again.

'All right, all right,' muttered Nina and pulled it open.

A short, plump, fair, well-dressed woman stood on the doorstep. She was red in the face and looked both anxious and bad-tempered.

'What on earth's going on here!' she exclaimed. And then with a little scream: 'Dolly! What's the matter with you?'

Dorothy had collapsed on to the chair that stood by the telephone table. 'Pauline,' she said faintly. 'What are you doing here?'

'Doing here?' The newcomer sounded increasingly indignant and alarmed. 'What am I doing here? I'm here because Gerry invited me. Didn't he tell you? He said you were feeling rather low and suggested I should come round at tea-time and stay the rest of the evening. I was rather under the impression that I might be able to be of some use. But he didn't tell me you were seriously ill. Hadn't you better be in bed?'

'I've been in bed. It's time I woke up,' said Dorothy.
She stood up, staggered a step or two forward, and then
said weakly: 'It's no good. I'll have to go back. Nina,
would you look after Pauline? Mrs Crofts. Get her some
tea or something. Where's Gerry?'

'He's upstairs, he's ill!' cried Nina. 'I keep trying to
tell you.' She had in fact been making efforts to whisper
into Dorothy's ear without the visitor hearing, but
Dorothy was not in a fit state to take notice of hints.

'Ill!' exclaimed Pauline. 'He wasn't ill last night.
What's the matter with him? What have you been doing?'
And she glared at Dorothy. 'Why didn't you tell me
before?' she demanded suspiciously.

'She didn't know,' cried Nina in a fury. 'She's been
asleep all day and only just woken up.'

Pauline took a deep breath and rolled her eyes upwards
before speaking. 'It looks to me as if you need someone
responsible to take charge here,' she said. 'You – whatever your name is.' And she turned to Nina. 'You'd better
help Dr Laver back to bed and I'll go upstairs and see
what I can do for Mr Laver. I suppose no one has thought
to send for a doctor?'

And she ran upstairs, still talking. Nina stared after her
and breathed deeply and rolled her eyes just as Pauline
had done. Then she turned to Dorothy.

'I must pull myself together,' said Dorothy. 'I'll be all
right in a minute . . . if you'd get my slippers and dressing-
gown . . . thanks, Nina . . . and make some tea. Strong.'

Clinging to Nina's arm, she walked to the kitchen and
sat down again. 'God, my head,' she groaned, holding it
between her hands as if that was the only way to keep it
in its place. 'It's splitting. What's the matter with Gerry?'

'I think he's swallowed . . .' began Nina as she switched on the electric kettle.

She was interrupted by the door of the kitchen being flung open. Pauline stood there holding an empty glass. 'Salt water!' she cried as she handed the glass to Nina with a dramatic gesture. 'Hurry up, girl! It's a matter of life or death.'

CHAPTER XXI

After Pauline had left the room with the replenished glass, Dorothy said to Nina: 'What's he done this time?'

She was still holding her head between her hands and looked on the point of collapse again.

'He's swallowed too many sleeping pills,' said Nina. 'Your father is looking after him and we've rung Dr Ferguson's surgery. He's coming as soon as he can.'

'Again,' muttered Dorothy. 'All that over again.' She leant forward and beat her head against the kitchen table. 'No, no, no,' she moaned.

Nina poured boiling water on to the tea-leaves. While Dorothy drank she put an arm round her protectively.

'Thanks,' said Dorothy. 'I feel better now. Honestly. I'll go up and see what's happening.'

At the foot of the stairs she was nearly knocked over by Pauline coming down in a frantic rush.

'He's worse! He's dying!' screamed Pauline. 'I'm phoning another doctor.'

Dorothy recovered her balance and went slowly upstairs, ignoring Pauline. Pauline turned over pages of the telephone directory, muttering to herself, and Nina, after a moment's uncertainty, followed Dorothy up-stairs.

In the big bedroom Gerry lay motionless with his eyes closed. Leaning back in an armchair and looking very white and exhausted sat Mr Thorn. Dorothy went first to him. 'Dad! Are you all right?' she asked anxiously.

He lifted his head and spoke faintly. 'Perfectly, my love. But I must rest now. I can't do any more.'

'No indeed. You've done more than enough already.'

Dorothy turned her attention to Gerry, examined him closely, looked at the bowl that had been put for him to use. She frowned and turned back to her father.

'Has he brought anything up?' she asked.

'No,' he murmured. 'Not yet.'

'How much salt water has he had?'

'I don't know. Quite a lot.'

'Five glasses full,' said Nina coming forward from the doorway where she had been hovering and looking down on Gerry with fear.

'Five glasses full!' repeated Dorothy in a voice full of alarm. 'We must get him to hospital at once. I'll phone for an ambulance.'

She picked up the receiver on the bedside telephone extension. Pauline's loud voice, arguing with a doctor's receptionist, became instantly audible.

Dorothy cut in. 'Will you clear the line, please. I want to get an ambulance.'

'Get off the line!' shouted Pauline. 'I'm dealing with this!'

'Make up your minds,' snapped the receptionist and replaced the receiver at her end.

'Please let me use the phone, Pauline,' said Dorothy in a very strained voice. 'This is urgent.'

'You're darn right it's urgent. Too urgent to trust you with. Get off!'

Dorothy put down the bedside extension in despair and looked around for Nina. But Nina had gone. Dorothy came downstairs to find her having a tug-of-war with Pauline over the telephone in the hall.

'Nina,' said Dorothy. 'Leave it alone.'

Reluctantly Nina abandoned the struggle, leaving Pauline holding the receiver with both hands.

'I've got to get Gerry to hospital,' said Dorothy with weary patience. 'If we don't get him in soon he could be dead.'

'Dead!' shrieked Pauline. 'That's what you want, isn't it? You want him to die – he told me so himself. You've killed him!'

'Shut up, you bloody old cow!' yelled Nina, beside herself with fury.

'Nina,' said Dorothy sharply, 'will you go to the call-box and dial emergency and ask for an ambulance? Give the address, then my name and title, and tell them I say it's very urgent.'

Nina rushed off obediently. Pauline stood clasping the telephone to her as if it were her most treasured possession. Dorothy passed her tongue over her lips as if preparing to speak, but said nothing, and after standing in silence for a moment she returned upstairs, leaving Pauline looking down at the telephone in her hand in a bemused manner.

'I wonder if I ought to go and look,' she muttered to herself.

Then she replaced the receiver, gave herself a little

shake, and appeared to come to a decision. Dorothy was unlikely to come down again until the ambulance arrived and the girl would be gone for several minutes so there would just be time.

'If anything should happen to me, Pauline,' Gerry had said over dinner the previous evening, 'I'd like you to have a look inside the folder in the bottom right-hand drawer of my desk if you get the opportunity.'

That had been all, but they had been talking about Dorothy and how peculiarly she was behaving, as if she wanted to get rid of Gerry. Hints had been dropped about another man. Pauline had to admit that it looked at the moment as if Dorothy was doing all she could to save Gerry's life, but all the same . . .

After a quick glance around to make quite sure that she was alone on the ground floor of the house, Pauline walked in a purposeful manner towards the study.

When Nina returned from her telephoning Pauline was nowhere to be seen, and if either Nina or Dorothy thought about her at all during the next hour, it was only to be thankful that she had taken herself out of the way. Mr Thorn was put to bed in his own room; Gerry was put into the ambulance and Dorothy followed in the car. In no time at all, so it seemed to Nina, she was back again.

'He died on the way,' she said in almost casual tones, and went straight upstairs to her father.

Nina, left standing alone in the hall, was suddenly overwhelmed by a terrible feeling of desolation.

It's all over, she said to herself; Dorothy doesn't need me any more; she only needs her father. And he doesn't need me either.

After all the tension and excitement and strain the

sense of anti-climax was intolerable. In all her lonely life, Nina had never felt quite so lonely before. Dorothy and her father would be consoling each other. There was no place for Nina; she was left out yet again.

But I know what the old man has done, she said to herself: I've got a hold over them. They'll have to keep me here. For a little while fear and resentment struggled with her love and gratitude. And then Dorothy came downstairs and put an arm round her.

'My father wants to see you,' she said. Her head drooped low over the girl's shoulder. 'He'll never get over this,' she added wretchedly.

Nina flung her arms round Dorothy and hugged her. All the desolation and the bitterness and the fear had vanished in a second. She was not going to be turned out: she was needed as much as ever.

'I'll get him well for you,' she said. 'I did last time, didn't I? You'll see.'

And she ran upstairs.

Mr Thorn was propped up high to ease his breathing. His eyes were closed and he lay white and still. Outwardly he looked just the same as he had looked half an hour ago, when Nina had left him to run downstairs to greet Dorothy. And yet Nina could sense the difference. He had decided to give up the struggle now. He was not going to make any more effort.

'Come,' said the old man raising one hand very slightly. 'Come and sit by me.'

Nina did so. His hand felt for hers and held it. It was he who was giving out strength and comfort to Nina; not Nina to him.

'You have taken a terrible burden of knowledge upon

yourself,' he said presently. 'And you will have to live with it all your life.'

Nina could not speak.

'I do not blame you. You were very tempted. Like Eve, perhaps.' And the faintest of smiles came over the old man's face.

Nina gave a sob.

'And without you things might have been very different,' he went on. 'So I have no right to scold.'

'I'm sorry,' muttered Nina. 'I only listened at the door because I was afraid he might hurt you. Truly.'

'I believe you, child.'

'But the book,' went on Nina. 'I looked at the book because I had to know.'

'Yes, my dear, we will say no more.' Mr Thorn was silent for a little while, conserving his strength. 'I am worried for you,' he said by and by. 'That is why I have mentioned it. Dorothy has no suspicion at all. She need never know anything.'

'I'll never, never – ' began Nina fervently.

'You will be very tempted,' broke in Mr Thorn, 'if you are ever angry with Dorothy and want to score over her. You see, I hope you will be lifelong friends, but it will be very hard for you, holding such a secret. Will you promise me something, Nina?'

'I can keep secrets,' she said.

'Indeed you can. Admirably. But that's not the promise. It is this. If the burden becomes too great for you, if you are ever tempted to use your knowledge to hurt Dorothy, then promise me you will tell Peter and nobody else.'

'I promise,' said Nina.

'Thank you.' The old man lay back with a little sigh

of relief. But a moment later he said: 'Don't go yet. There is something else. Let me catch my breath a little.'

Nina got up and began to prepare the oxygen, but he shook his head. 'Not necessary. Just a minute or two.'

She sat down again.

'I'm worried about that statement I wrote out for him to sign,' said Mr Thorn after a little while.

Nina interrupted to mention the marks on the blotter.

'Yes. He signed it. I gathered that when I was attending to him. But he wrote something else too – something harmful to Dorothy.'

'Oh no!'

'Oh yes. He could not bear that she should feel free of guilt. You must find that paper before she does, Nina, and use your judgement about whether to show it to her. Or ask Peter.'

'But where is it?'

'Somewhere in the study. You will have to look for it, Nina. I have not had the opportunity or the strength and it is too late now. Thank you, Nina.'

It was said quietly and calmly and without any particular sign of strain. Nina was silent, expecting him to say something more. To give her a further clue, perhaps, or to say that he was too tired to talk any longer tonight, or to ask her to fetch Dorothy.

But he said nothing more. For a minute or two she believed he was resting again and she was not unduly concerned. Then a suspicion came into her mind and she stood up and leant over him.

'Oh no, no, no!'

It was a stifled cry. She dropped down on to her knees, caught his hand and began to kiss it again and again, desperately, yearningly.

'You can't leave us – you can't leave us like this,' she cried between sobs. 'Not without seeing Dorothy again – not without speaking to her. You mustn't go – you mustn't go!'

There was no response from the still figure on the bed. Nina put his hand back on the bedspread and stood up. A moment later Dorothy came into the room and Nina turned on her a face streaming with tears. They clung together for a moment and then, holding hands, looked together down at the bed. William Thorn lay there as still as a marble effigy on a tomb; on his face was an expression of utter contentment and peace.

'Please, Nina,' said Dorothy in a strained voice. 'Will you do something for me? Peter will be coming soon. He was very anxious to see us all and I couldn't stop him. But I can't see him now. I must stay here. Will you explain to him when he comes? Tell him everything he wants to know.'

'Yes,' said Nina faintly.

'Thank you, Nina,' said Dorothy.

It was said in much the same tones as Mr Thorn had spoken his last words. With a little cry of distress the girl ran from the room. Peter, arriving shortly afterwards and expecting to have the not unwelcome task of comforting and supporting Dorothy, was confronted instead by a sixteen-year-old girl whom he could see at a glance was at the very end of her strength.

'Nina! What's happened? Where's Dorothy?'

For a nightmarish moment he believed that he was going to hear that Gerry's death had in some extra-ordinary way deprived Dorothy of her own sanity; that she had after all taken her own life.

'She's all right,' gasped Nina. 'She said to tell you – she's sorry – she can't come – down now.'

'She's not ill?' Peter's anxiety receded but did not entirely disappear.

'No. It's Mr Thorn. He's dead.'

Nina blurted it out and then burst into great hiccuping sobs. Automatically Peter put an arm round her. When she was a little calmer she was able to explain in more detail what had happened. Peter listened in a state of grief and shock not so very much different from Nina's own. But even while he was saying that naturally Dorothy wouldn't want to see him or anybody else just now, the chilly certainty was creeping over him that Dorothy was never to be his. She had turned to him in her hour of great bewilderment and fear, but she had not turned to him in her hour of grief. It was an omen: they would be friends and that was all.

So while Nina wept on his shoulder and Peter murmured soothing words, both of them were following up their own thoughts. When Peter said, 'It's a wonderful way to die, quickly and easily like that,' and Nina agreed, both of them were really thinking very different things.

Then Nina said: 'There's something I've got to tell you. It's very important. We'll have to do something about it at once.'

She found a handkerchief, blew her nose, wiped her face, and began to talk. Peter listened carefully to her somewhat incoherent story.

CHAPTER XXII

'Perhaps Mr Thorn was wrong and it isn't in here after all,' said Nina despondently after she and Peter had been searching the study for the best part of an hour.

'Well, at least it isn't in an obvious place where Dorothy can't help seeing it. I suppose that's some comfort,' he replied.

'What happens when people die?' asked Nina. 'I mean, what happens to things in their pockets.'

'They're handed over to the next-of-kin. I don't see how you can stop Dorothy seeing it if it was in his pocket. What about somewhere else in the house?'

'It's not in the bathroom,' said Nina, 'and if it was in the bedroom I should think Mr Thorn would have found it. He had plenty of time to look around. It can't be in the consulting-room because it was locked up and it can't be in the sitting-room because Mr Thorn was there, and I was in the kitchen.'

'The top floor?'

'He never goes up there. I mean, he never went up there. Gerry, I mean.' Nina corrected herself, gave a great yawn, and sat down suddenly in the chair at the desk.

'I think we'd better call it a day,' said Peter.

Nina did not reply. She was slumped low in the big leather-seated chair with her head drooping over the back. Her eyes were closed and she was fast asleep.

'Poor child,' murmured Peter, looking down on her. It

might have been Bill Thorn speaking. For a few minutes he looked around in a desultory manner at places which they had already searched and then he heard sounds of movement from the floor above. It sounded as if somebody was coming downstairs.

'I'd better go out of the back door,' he said to himself, 'if Dorothy doesn't want to see me now.'

The thought was no less painful than it had been when it first struck him.

The following morning, which was a Saturday, Peter was staring without comprehension at a page full of diagrams and calculations, when there was a knock at the door and his heart leapt. It sounded just like Dorothy's knock when she came to call on her way home from work. When he saw Nina standing there it was all he could do to control his disappointment.

'Dorothy sends her love,' said the girl as if she knew what he was feeling. 'She's much better this morning but terribly busy. One of the secretaries at the hospital is coming round to write letters and make phone calls and things. There's the funeral to arrange and lots of people to tell and all sorts of other things and there's the police.'

'The police,' repeated Peter, feeling alarmed in spite of himself. 'There'll have to be a post-mortem on Gerry, of course, but surely there's no question – '

He broke off. He saw that under Nina's determinedly bright manner the girl was very much afraid.

'They're coming to see Dorothy this morning,' she said. 'I suppose they'll want to see me too.'

'All you do is tell them the truth. Exactly what happened,' said Peter.

'I can't, I mustn't!' she cried, and yet again Peter felt that apprehensive little chill.

'Nina,' he said, 'has Dorothy done something that she doesn't want known? Is that why she wouldn't speak to me? Don't be afraid to tell me. I won't let her down.'

Nina shook her head violently. 'Not Dorothy,' she said.

'Then who?'

'Mr Thorn,' she replied and burst into tears.

'I'm awfully sorry,' she said after she had been revived with brandy and coffee, 'you'll think I do nothing but howl on you. That's the last time, honestly. But I'll have to tell you about it now. I don't think I can tell lies to the police without someone else knowing. There's something I didn't tell you last night. He said I could tell you if I had to but I didn't think it would be so soon. I didn't think I would be so feeble.'

'You're not feeble, Nina. That's the last thing you are.'

'Thanks,' she said, wiping her face. 'Well, here goes.'

After she had finished Peter said: 'I'm afraid you're going to have a tough time with the police enquiries and the inquest. But there's no need to tell any outright lie. All you have to do is not tell the full story. We'll go over it all again, with me asking questions and you answering them as you are going to do at the inquest. Ready?'

Nina was ready and performed very well.

'There you are, you see. There's nothing to it,' said Peter.

But privately he was very worried, and Nina had good reason in the days to come to be grateful for his coaching.

The day after Mr Thorn's funeral, when Dorothy and

Peter and Nina were having an evening meal together at Pond Cottage, Dorothy suddenly said, in the middle of a conversation about what to do with Gerry's books: 'I always used to have a good opinion of the police. But they're being so slow and stupid over Gerry's death that I'm beginning to revise it.'

Peter and Nina exchanged quick glances.

'I've answered the same questions a dozen times at least,' went on Dorothy. 'So has Nina. And if my poor father were still alive no doubt they would be pestering him to death too. Surely they know exactly what happened by now. The autopsy was clear enough.'

'I suppose they have to be very thorough,' said Peter uncertainly.

'Here's your pudding,' said Nina, putting a plate in front of him. 'Don't wait for us. Your television programme's coming on in a few minutes.'

'So it is. Thanks,' said Peter.

Nina was always very anxious that he should not miss any of the relevant Open University broadcasts and that he should keep strictly to his timetable of study; but Dorothy, who had once been so helpful and encouraging, now showed only a token interest in his work. Why should she do otherwise, he said to himself; she's mourning her father; her whole life has changed completely since Gerry's death; she is coming to terms with herself. But for all his sensible arguments, it still hurt, and Nina's enthusiastic interest was comforting.

After Peter had left the room Dorothy said to Nina: 'Why aren't the police satisfied? Can you think why?'

It was the question that Nina had been dreading, and she wished she had Peter's support and did not have to face it alone. She shook her head without speaking.

'It's horrible,' went on Dorothy. 'I feel as if Gerry is hitting back at me from beyond the grave.' She looked round the kitchen as if she expected Gerry to come into the room. 'He's haunting me,' she went on. 'I'll never be free of him.'

'You'll feel better after the inquest,' said Nina as soothingly as she could. 'It will soon be over.'

Dorothy did indeed look haunted. She went through the duties of each day in a businesslike manner, but when all demands had been met she returned to this tense and apprehensive state. It was as if she could not accustom herself to being without the menacing presence of Gerry, as if there was no way in which she could feel free.

'I feel as if he's planted a time-bomb,' she said to Nina, 'and that it will go off at the inquest. I can't tell you how I'm dreading it.'

Nina did not know how to reply. This was so very much her own and Peter's secret dread. For Gerry's confession had never turned up, and after going into all the possibilities again and again they had come to the very unpleasant conclusion that only one thing could have happened: somehow or other Pauline Crofts had got hold of it.

'If only we knew what he'd written, or what she's told the police!' Nina cried for the twentieth time when she was alone with Peter later that evening.

'He'll have written that Dorothy was to blame for his death,' said Peter.

'But they know she wasn't! Even if they don't believe me they must believe Dr Ferguson. She was asleep all morning. She couldn't possibly have done anything!'

'I suppose they're trying to find a loophole,' said Peter wearily.

'And in any case,' continued Nina, 'Pauline herself saw Dorothy come out of the consulting-room half asleep. So her own evidence lets Dorothy out, doesn't it?'

'Not necessarily, I'm afraid. Dorothy could have woken earlier and come out and doped Gerry and then gone back to sleep.'

'But I told them – '

'You were in the garden for quite a long time. You told them that. And Mr Thorn is dead. There was nobody else in the house.'

'But the consulting-room door was locked and I had the key!'

'Perhaps there was another key. Perhaps Mr Thorn let her out. Or even Gerry himself.'

'Peter!' Nina was indignant now. 'You can't possibly suspect that Dorothy – '

'Of course I don't. I'm only pointing out how people's minds might work if they didn't know as you and I do that she is completely innocent.'

'I could murder Pauline,' said Nina, grinding her teeth.

'So could I. But it would be too late. The damage is done.'

The inquest on the death of Gerard Laver attracted a considerable amount of attention and received wide coverage in the press. Not only did it make good human interest reading, but it was medically noteworthy too. Mr Laver had swallowed five of his sleeping tablets when the normal dose was two at the most, but death was not due to the drug. It had been caused by hypernatraemia, haemorrhaging resulting from too much salt in the bloodstream. It could have been avoided if the dead man's father-in-law, who administered the remedy, had been aware of its dangers. And it could have been avoided if the dead man's wife, who had been suffering from nervous exhaustion, had been called earlier to her husband's aid.

For Dr Dorothy Laver was fully aware of the dangers of this treatment for poisoning. The coroner was very interested indeed in her evidence, not because of any reflection on herself but because of its general implications. Dr Laver explained that she had come across a similar case in the course of her work, and that on a previous occasion when her husband had taken an overdose she had been very careful about using salt water as a remedy. There had been a certain amount written on the subject, she said, but she agreed that the risks were not widely known. Dr Ferguson, who had been called in but arrived too late, said that he himself was unaware of the danger. The coroner hoped that this case would alert people to the risks of this widely used household remedy.

When the question arose of whether any suicide note had been found, Peter and Nina held hands tightly and held their breath. No such note had come to light, replied the police sergeant. Nina and Peter looked across to where Pauline was sitting. She was staring straight ahead of her, very red in the face.

'What can have happened?' whispered Nina to Peter when it was all over and a verdict of death by misadventure had been recorded, with a rider to the effect that the dangers of administering salt water should be widely publicized. 'D'you think she never had the confession? Or didn't she tell the police about it after all?'

'Ssh,' he replied. 'Later.'

Dorothy had joined them. She looked tired but relieved. 'Well, that's that,' she said. 'Poor Nina. They did put you through it, didn't they? I'm beginning to think it was you whom they suspected of killing Gerry, and not me at all!'

She said this lightly but with an undertone of serious-ness. It seemed a good thought to encourage, and Peter and Nina did so.

'You know, Nina, I've suspected all along that you've been hiding something,' said Dorothy a little later when they were all three lingering in the garden at Pond Cottage, talking in the desultory manner of people who have gone through a dreaded ordeal and cannot quite make the transition back to their normal course of life.

'I haven't been hiding anything,' said Nina in so convincingly innocent a manner that Peter's admiration for her stirred afresh. 'I'd never dare to. I'm much too scared of the police. I'm a teenage delinquent, aren't I? Or I was until you rescued me.'

Dorothy smiled faintly. It was hardly a happy smile, but it held a promise that the sparkle might return to her one day. 'Dear Nina,' she said affectionately. 'We'll have to think about what you are going to do with your-self soon. Damn. There's the phone again.'

'I'll go,' said Nina.

But Dorothy was already running across the lawn. It was not the first time that she had so obviously avoided being alone with Peter. She needn't have bothered, he thought rather bitterly; I'll never say anything to embarrass her.

Nina, who noticed everything, had noticed this too, and as they walked slowly after Dorothy into the house, she tried to console him.

'I don't believe she'll ever marry again,' she said. 'I know I wouldn't – not after being married to Gerry. It'd put anyone off for life.'

'Thanks, Nina,' said Peter, accepting this speech in the spirit in which it was offered.

That's another of them, thought Nina. They all thank me. It would be nice if one of them would really love me too. Although I think perhaps the old man really did love me. Her eyes stung. She could not think of Mr Thorn without a gaping sense of loss.

'That was Pauline,' said Dorothy, putting down the telephone in a rather puzzled manner. 'She wants to come and see me. She says she meant to speak to me at the inquest but didn't get a chance. I suppose she wants to apologize for that ghastly business on the day Gerry died, and I must say it's about time too.'

Peter and Nina silently signalled their alarm to each other.

'When is she coming?' asked Nina.

'Now.' Dorothy looked at her watch. 'Better make her some coffee. I'm sick to death of chatting to people and offering them cups of coffee,' she added in a sudden spurt of irritation. 'I'd like to get right away from it all. All the social trivia. I'd like to do something tough and unsociable and mindless. I wonder if they'd take me on an Antarctic excursion or something like that if I brushed up my general medicine a bit.'

'But, Dorothy,' protested Nina, 'you'd never want to leave this house.'

'Yes, I would. I'm sick of this house. What's a house anyway? Something to fuss over. I'd rather be in an igloo in a blizzard and fighting with something worth while. Or I could get in touch with the World Health people and get them to send me to somewhere really tough. There's Pauline, damn her. I'll let her in.'

In the kitchen Nina said to Peter: 'We couldn't have stopped them meeting, could we?'

'No way,' he answered. 'But I'm beginning to wonder whether it matters all that much after all. I wonder whether we haven't been underestimating Dorothy, thinking she needs our protection. The way she was talking just now I reckon she can cope with anything.'

'I suppose,' said Nina slowly, 'she was never really herself while Gerry was alive. I suppose she's only just beginning to turn into her real self now.'

'I wonder whether she really will go and work in a disaster area,' said Peter. 'I should have thought Dorothy liked her comforts too much. Not that there's anything wrong with that,' he added hurriedly. 'I like them myself.'

'People change,' said Nina sadly.

Peter put a hand over hers. 'You're not to worry, Nina. Even if Dorothy does go off into the wilds you've still got me, for what that's worth. I won't desert you, Nina.'

'Never?'

'Never.'

'Thank you,' said Nina.

Some time later they heard the click of the front door.

'Now for it,' said Peter.

Dorothy came into the kitchen looking quite calm but still rather puzzled. She was holding in her hand a sheet of paper with handwriting on it.

'It's the most extraordinary thing,' she said. 'Peter – Nina – had either of you any idea of what my father was up to?'

They both shook their heads.

'Apparently he got Gerry to sign a confession saying that it was he who gave the overdose to Irene. I can't quite see how Gerry was persuaded to, except that Dad was awfully good at getting people to do what he wanted. Anyway, Pauline found it in the study and went off with it. She's got some story about Gerry telling her there was a document he wanted her to have in the event of his death. One of his idiocies, I suppose. Anyway, she says she hadn't realized quite how mad he was until she'd taken this home and had time to digest it properly, and then she was so shocked that she couldn't make up her mind what to do – whether to tell me or whether to tell the police or what. She says that in the end she did nothing, but decided during the inquest that I ought to have this. I'm really quite glad to know. I suppose it was after he signed this that Gerry went over the edge for the last time. Well, I'm off back to work now. Thank you, both of you. For everything.'

And she kissed first Nina and then Peter before she hurried away.

'Quite glad to know!' they exclaimed aloud almost in unison.

'What have we been worrying ourselves to death about?' said Peter.

'I don't trust that Pauline,' said Nina. 'I'm sure she said something to the police and only decided at the very last minute not to make trouble for Dorothy.'

'You're probably right, but at least her better feelings came out on top in the end and she suppressed anything really harmful. Look.' He held out the sheet of paper for Nina to inspect. 'The bottom edge is uneven. Something's been cut off.'

'Mr Thorn was right, then,' said Nina slowly. 'Gerry did write something. I wonder what it was.'

'I don't suppose anybody but Pauline will ever know,' said Peter.

RECENT CRIME CLUB TITLES

January – June 1978

JANUARY

Deep Pocket MICHAEL KENYON
Inspector Peckover, would-be poet, newly translated from vice squad to fraud squad, found little difference when he was precipitated into a world of bribes, blackmail, sex and murder, all described in Michael Kenyon's inimitably delightful style.

Judge Me Tomorrow HAMILTON JOBSON
Trevor Grant, insurance broker, tries to help someone suspected of murdering one of his clients and ends by planning to commit murder himself. Only then does he discover the extent to which he is already involved in crime.

One-Way Ticket HARTLEY HOWARD
New York private eye Glenn Bowman investigated the disappearance of one Danny Falkner, and found himself in a web of conspiracy where he could trust nobody – especially when he realized espionage might be involved.

FEBRUARY

An Uncertain Sound ROY LEWIS
How well can you know another person? When solicitor Frank Hales's practice ran into difficulties, he learnt a number of things about his partner. He also learnt a surprising number of things about himself and about his own wife.

Sunk Without Trace DOMINIC DEVINE
An illegitimate girl returns to her Scottish birthplace in search of her father. Instead she unearths skulduggery in local government – and then disappears. But not without trace – as several people discover to their cost.

A Pinch of Snuff REGINALD HILL
Inspector Pascoe's dentist believes he has witnessed a murder on film, but he has other worries when accused of assaulting a patient. Not so Pascoe, who finds himself going round a curiously circular track, alternately advised and abused by Superintendent Dalziel.

MARCH

The Foursome LIONEL BLACK
'Two's company and three's none' was certainly true when George Chapman kept wife and mistress under one roof. What happened when the uneasy threesome became an explosive foursome makes an absorbing drama of suburban sex and crime.

X Marks the Spot MICHAEL BUTTERWORTH
X marks the spot where Karl Marx reposes in Highgate Cemetery – or does he? When a one-handed ex-pickpocket decides to sell the bones behind the Iron Curtain at the same time as the Vatican is conducting discreet negotiations of its own, the reader is in for a treat.

Daylight Robbery MARTIN RUSSELL
The Canary Islands offered a perfect holiday setting for solitary Philip Lambert until he became involved in first abetting, then averting, a daylight robbery.

APRIL

Treasure Up in Smoke DAVID WILLIAMS
King Charles Island in the Caribbean was out of this 20th-century world – or so banker Mark Treasure thought when business took him there. But even this enchanted isle, blessed with a benevolent despot and a trade in very special cigars, was not exempt from murder.

Dutch Courage RITCHIE PERRY
Further escapades of the ebullient agent Philis, now involved in the Israeli-Arab conflict, and masterminded as usual by Pawson.

One of Us Must Die ANNA CLARKE
Dorothy Laver, married to a mentally sick husband, was slowly being driven mad by guilt in her past and by her husband's machinations in the present. Anna Clarke weaves a compelling suspense story in which one of the protagonists – but which? – must die.

MAY

Counterstroke ANDREW GARVE
A politician's wife is kidnapped and held to ransom against the release of a terrorist. An actor on the skids volunteers to impersonate the terrorist long enough to dupe the gang. A rash ploy or a deadly counterstroke?

Unruly Son ROBERT BARNARD
Best-selling novelist Oliver Fairleigh left the copyrights in his works to his wife and children. But there was something odd about who got which copyrights. And something decidedly odd about Oliver Fairleigh's death.

Last Will and Testament ELIZABETH FERRARS
Old Mrs Arliss died peacefully in her bed, believing that in her last will and testament she had done the right thing. Not everyone agreed with her, and to restore the status quo one person was prepared to kill.

JUNE

The Day of the Donkey Derby JOAN FLEMING
Expecting to meet his prospective daughter-in-law for the first time; summoned to attend a patient already dead; held captive because he refused to sign the death certificate; Dr Tom Lavenham had plenty of reason to remember the Day of the Donkey Derby.

Sleep in a Ditch MAISIE BIRMINGHAM
An unknown young man is found dead outside the East End Settlement which was the setting of *You Can Help Me*, and Kate Weatherley discovers that the Settlement is no protection against the past she thought she had shut out.

Garvey's Code ROGER BUSBY
Garvey – cussed, independent, disrespectful – hadn't risen higher than detective-constable because he insisted on believing it took a man, not a computer, to investigate the crimes of men. Was there still room for men like him in a modern force?

The Dark Pasture

JESSICA STIRLING

The
Dark Pasture

HODDER AND STOUGHTON
LONDON SYDNEY AUCKLAND TORONTO

To
John and Helen
of
Drumore

The
Asp Out of Eden

January

Four black toms, spawned from the same fierce queen, huddled by the byre wall, waiting with surly patience for their share of the morning's milk. By comparison the rest of Hazelrig's cats were brindled slugabeds. Eight or ten would be snuggled in the musty hay-loft and a lucky dozen curled on the rancid sheets of Hurley Pritchard's cot in the bothy by the sheep fank. No matter how cold the night, with the approach of dawn those four satanic males would be crouched against the wall, green eyes glinting in the spill of light from the milkhouse door, their hunger never quite sharp enough, though, to tempt them to thieve from the standing dishes. Fleck, the collie, was seldom far from Malcolm's heels, and Fleck was too cantankerous a brute to tolerate the presence of felines, especially on a bitter, tail-nipping January morning.

Besides, Mirrin thought, as she peered, yawning, from the kitchen window, there would be precious little milk to spare for cats in this season of dry teats. Malcolm, her eldest son, would be fortunate to draw more than a gallon or two from the handful of cows that still had a dribble in their bags. Though the beasts seemed content to be tethered indoors, sometimes Mirrin wondered if they nurtured a secret longing to feel the sun on their backs and sniff the warm wind, or if animals were blessed with total forgetfulness of the freedom of the high spring pastures.

In the byre a lantern glimmered.

Hurley was up and about. That was no surprise. Hurley was invariably first up. He prided himself on always beating the gaffer to the yard. Even Malcolm, full of the sap of youth, could

9

not catch the wee man napping. On the rare occasions when Hurley reeled home blotto from the Crosstrees pub and crashed on to his cot like a log, Malcolm would cock his ears and gloat and, next morning, would tumble out of bed especially early— only to find Hurley already clanking pails loud enough to waken the dead. And that, Malcolm would declare, just proved that it paid not to have a brain in your noddle or a care in the wide world.

Mirrin yawned again.

Faintly but clearly the hooter sounded from Blacklaw colliery down in the valley of the Sheenan, four miles to the west. It marked the end of the night's labours for half Houston Lamont's grimy wage-slaves and the beginning of a long day's toil for the 'change shift'. Accustomed to the irony of checking farm routines against the ugly wail of a pit klaxon, Mirrin realised that milking would soon be finished and Hurley ready to heave the churns into the dog-cart. By the time Malcolm had skimmed off the unsettled cream, ladled out sufficient for the family's needs and made his usual over-generous libation to the cats, there would hardly be enough milk left to justify a trip into town. But the early-morning ritual, essential in summer, had become sacrosanct.

As the year of 1896 began, Mirrin leaned heavily on Kate, her sister, and an hour's uninhibited conversation in the bakehouse kitchen in Kellock's Square off Main Street. In recent months, the daily jaunt offered Mirrin respite from the doubts and fears that crowded round Hazelrig like a flock of scolding crows.

If anything the Stalker family was more close-knit than ever. The sisters were still referred to as Alex Stalker's lassies, though both were married and their father had been dead these twenty years. Blacklaw was much altered since the great pit disaster of 1875, when sudden violent explosions in the seams had wiped out over a hundred men and brought terrible hardship to the village. That was just a fragment of history now, the mournful memory dimmed. In a strange way, Blacklaw miners were proud of 'their' tragedy, or perhaps, more properly, of having survived it.

Crossing from the window to the iron range, Mirrin lifted the kettle, tipped boiling water into a huge brown teapot, then, warned by a nose that her children claimed could smell burning before the fire was lit, shifted the porridge pot back from the cooking lid that flaring new coals had already licked red. She transferred the teapot to the deal table in the centre of the floor and covered it with a knitted cosy.

Bread was cut, butter patted on its board, jars of jam and jelly laid out, a wedge of ripe cheese trapped under an earthenware cover.Lamps on mantlepiece and dresser had been trimmed and, with the fire, transformed the big kitchen into a haven of warm yellow patterns and intimate shadows. The familiar room encompassed the woman and, for an instant, stirred again an awareness of a cherished security that, inexorably, seemed to be slipping from her grasp.

The empty kitchen held no threat. The source of her anxiety lurked behind the bedroom door. She glanced at it, almost furtively, knowing that he would have extinguished the lamp and would have latched the door from the inside. Shivering, she stepped round the table and crossed to the bedroom door in the alcove under the wedge of the stair.

"Tom?"

No answer.

Mirrin bit her lip. "Tom? Are you awake?"

Still no answer.

Tentatively she touched the latch. As she suspected the inside bolt had been shot, evidence of the gnawing influence of disease upon her husband.

"Your breakfast's on the table," Mirrin called.

Try as she would she could no longer feel pity for him. Turning away from the door, she pulled a shawl from a hook, went back across the kitchen and out through the hall into the yard.

Arctic morning air gripped her, a bitter invigorating cold. It was still dark, though the moon had not yet set across the copse of hazel and grey alder on the sealskin breast of the hillock above the Witchy burn. The roofs of byres and sheds were etched by hoar frost, cobbles silvered, puddles turned to steel. The snout of the yard pump dripped a long stalactite of bubbled ice that Hurley, when he came to water the calves, would chop off with an axe. Steam wisped from under the byre door, a welcome softness in the hard-edged morning.

Down at the end of the yard, the inmates of the stables conversed in an odd whinneying way, each courteously leaving pause for the other. Noss and Eriskay, the Shetland ponies, were perhaps speculating on which of them would be privileged to pull the dog-cart that day, the massive, passive dignified plough-hauling Clydesdales, Clay, Pharaoh and Derry, joining in with flurried snorts and snufflings. From the roofridge of the two-storey farmhouse, a mad hen and a lunatic duck, boon companions in stupidity, peered down into the yard. A black-back gull, renegade from the distant sea, carved circular designs against the cold silken sky above the house's smoking chimneypot.

Hazelrig farm was better stocked than most in Lanarkshire, rich by some steadings' standards. There was money in the bank and more in the chest under the gaffer's bed. Rent was paid in full each and every feein' day, May and November, counted out from Tom's green leather wallet in notes and big silver to the Duke's factor in the estates' main office in Sma' Hall in Hamilton. Eighteen years of thrift and discipline, of hard cooperative labour by husband and wife, aided in recent years by strong-growing sons, had kept the Armstrongs well fed and moderately well protected against the vicissitudes of weather, crop failure, cattle blight, depression, cheap American grain and fluctuating yield prices. Dairying remained Hazelrig's mainstay. Liquid milk, some cheese and salted butter, were all sold through Kate's husband's shop in Blacklaw. Thirty head of cows, a good seed bull, thirty-four blackface ewes and a sturdy ram, three draught horses and two ponies, a scatter of hens, ducks in the pond of the Witchy burn, the livestock was neatly balanced against the fodder reaped from the well-drained rigs of the farm's one hundred and forty-four acres—fifteen acres hay, twelve acres oats, six acres potatoes, four acres turnips; a garden too, and apple trees, raspberry canes, wild plums and gooseberries. Small sweet hazelnuts dropped in October for boys and squirrels to harvest. All told it was a fine fat steading, really, to have built up in a country with a notoriously wet climate, starved soil and a centuries-old legacy of over-exploitation and withering decay.

Eighteen years ago, almost to the day, Mirrin had come

riding into Hazelrig on a tinker's cartie. She had married the tink the following month in a quiet ceremony in Blacklaw kirk, married Tom Armstrong, a man she hardly knew. At the time he had seemed right for her. Had she, she wondered now, married the man or the life he'd offered? In eighteen years she had seldom had occasion to question her decision. Though her love for him had been dissipated by the arrival of three fine sons and a pretty little daughter, that had always seemed right and proper in the nature of things, and she had supposed the marriage deepened, made more satisfying, because of it. In eighteen years, she had never doubted Tom. She had married him for his vision, his patience, his humour, his strength, for the fact that he made no pretences. And she had never regretted it—until now.

The byre door opened. The toms crept forward. Malcolm was framed against the rectangle of amber light. A tapestry of straw, hay and hairy rumps was bound together by the fecund steam of dung troughs and cattle breath. He had not noticed her yet. Speculatively, she watched him as he grinned and lowered a battered tin feeding bowl. The cats rushed to it while the young man held Fleck back with his left hand, and told the dog to *Wheesht*. Physically he did not resemble Tom, or her father for that matter. He reminded her most of her brother James who had died in the pit disaster and whose widow and son presently lived in a house above the stables in Kellock's Square.

"I'm away now, Malcolm," Mirrin said.

He looked up, startled. "Before breakfast, Mam?"

"Ask Hurley t' load up."

"There's precious little milk for the Blacklaw bairns the day," the young man said. "I put a half by for us, an' made the rest up t' two gallons exact. Old Meggie's near dried out. It'll be pease brose for our puddin' come the end o' the month."

He was not usually quite so garrulous at this hour of the morning. Mirrin realised that he was embarrassed by her departure from routine—and aware of the reason for it.

Gripping the collie by the ruff, Malcolm moved aside to allow his brother Sandy to lug out a dumpy churn. Sandy shouldered it as if it was weightless. He was brown-haired like his brothers, and had a frank, open face peppered with permanent freckles that in summer grew so dark that it looked as if a cow had shaken a muddy hoof at him. Already he was tall, springing up to near six feet, and without the pubescent stringiness that weakened the younger colliers in the town. He was not as intelligent as Malcolm, but had inherited from his father a strain of quick humour, and his mother's hot temper.

Malcolm said, "Rope it in quick, Sandy, since Mam wants t' be off."

Mirrin said, "Breakfast's laid, ready for servin'. See that Davie and Kitten get up right away. Make sure they wash an' wrap up warm an' aren't late leavin' for school."

Davie, aged eleven, and Katherine—called Kitten—now approaching her sixth birthday, attended school in Crosstrees, a mile south down the brae. Malcolm and Sandy had received their schooling in Blacklaw, but it was no longer the seat of learning it had been in Dominie Guthrie's day. It was staffed now by a crew of stiff-necked spinsters under the rule of a headmaster who believed that the only possible benefit in educating working-class children was to dun them into accepting their humble place in God's scheme of things.

Crosstrees was a tiny rural hamlet that, in the past decade, had expanded into a trim village with a kirk, a pub, a new schoolhouse and twenty tithed cottages for workers on the oddly-named Neapolitan Horticultural Estate. Most mornings, Mirrin dropped her two youngest off at the road-end, saving them a half mile, but the day was dry if cold and the walk would do them no harm.

She said, "Sandy, would you bring Noss out, please."

Sandy was as good with horses as Malcolm was with cows. Within minutes, he had led the garron from the stable, backed her into the shafts of the dog-cart and hitched the leathers. Mirrin climbed up into the cart by the back step and closed the little gate behind her. The single churn took up very little space. In summer, the dog-cart was replaced by a box-cart and both ponies were used so laden was it with milk churns and cans.

Waterbuckets in hand, Hurley appeared at the byre door.

"Missus, Missus, bring us a ginger cake, eh?" he called, as Mirrin twitched the reins and nosed the pony round and out of the yard.

"I will, Hurley."

"Tottie scones for me," said Sandy.

Glancing back, Mirrin glimpsed Tom's face at the bedroom window sketched by the light of the candle he used in preference to the stronger flame of the oil lamp. He was scowling. She halted the pony and gestured to Malcolm, who came across the yard with obedient manly strides, boots ringing on the frosty cobbles.

"It seems your father's up," she said. "See that he eats somethin'."

"Aye, Mam," Malcolm said.

In her son's eyes she detected bewildered anxiety, as if he suspected that she might one day ask too much of him.

If only she could hold on to Hazelrig for another three or four years until Malcolm supplemented his theoretic knowledge of farming with more practical experience. Then what? Mirrin asked herself. Will I steal my son's life from him? Am I that selfish?

Malcolm patted the garron's rump. Mirrin snicked the rein, clopping the cart briskly past the window. She did not glance again at the face there, that peering self-pitying image that haunted Hazelrig like a phantom.

Drawing the shawl tighter over her head, she braced herself and rode on past the wall-end into the pale tarnished darkness between the fields. In a half hour or so she would be in the bakehouse kitchen and there, for a while, she would be allowed to share her elder sister's impregnable security.

If the worst came to the worst, Mirrin thought grimly, there would always be a place for her and her youngest children with Kate and Willie down in the mining town that she had struggled so hard to leave, back in Blacklaw where it had all started.

★　★　★

They were all there, Kellocks and Stalkers of three generations, packed into the long bustling kitchen that had once been no more than a cubby behind the bakehouse ovens. In 1883 Willie had had the kitchen extended so that it jutted out from the end of the yard and offered a panoramic view of the 'kingdom' that Willie Kellock, masterbaker, commanded—

from stables and van-sheds to the apartments on the second floor that he had had converted from haylofts to house Kate's relatives from Lancashire.

The kitchen was the hub of the Kellock-Stalker empire, a huge square room, warmed by the ovens through the wall and by a long Dandorelli kitchen stove on which a plentiful supply of hot food simmered throughout the day.

Flora Stalker, Mirrin and Kate's mother, had her own special parlour but she had long ago forsaken it as being too grand for the likes of her and settled instead for a wooden-armed rocking chair by the open grate. Her sewing and knitting baskets were shelved on an ebony chiffonier and a conical oil lamp gave her all the extra light she required for needlework. Approaching seventy, Flora had outlived most of her contemporaries. Willie was a year her senior, however, and, by the look of his rubicund cheeks and merry eyes, might well become Blacklaw's first recorded centenarian. Kate Stalker was his second wife. The twenty years age difference between them had not, as had been predicted at the time of their marriage, brought moral ruin and misery to either party.

Lily Dawson Stalker, James' widow, and her son Edward, were present too. Lily had finally grown tired of living at home in her parents' boarding-house in England and had returned to Blacklaw. For the past fifteen years she had helped in the bakehouse though Willie still insisted that baking was a man's trade and that no woman, even one as determined as Lily, would ever make a go of it.

Like his father before him, Edward Stalker was a Blacklaw collier, a strapping blue-eyed young man, inseparable from the other young fellow who, that January morning, was seated at the table in the Kellocks' kitchen tucking into a roll and bacon like a starvling.

Neill Campbell Stalker, almost nineteen years old, was known and accepted as 'Kate's lad'. Certainly he bore all the hallmarks of a Stalker grandson—brown hair, a straight nose and large chin. But Neill was not Kate's natural son. The facts of his birth and parentage were known only to his family, a secret that Stalker pride had held close for two decades. If Neill's real father had observed his son that day, still smeared with pit dust and eating in a manner that only uncouth miners would condone, he would have shuddered in disgust and told himself how fortunate he was to have got shot of the whole damned lot of them.

Though he had been informed as to the truth about his father and mother, Neill never raised the subject. From the day of his birth he had been looked after and cared for by Kate. He called her Ma, and Willie Kellock Pa, and thought of them in no other way. He was their child—and that was an end of it as far as Neill was concerned.

In the yard—known now to everyone in Blacklaw as Kellock's Square—a brightly-painted milkfloat and covered breadvan had been trundled from their stalls by Willie's assistant, a young man named Duncan Lennie. Duncan had been rejected for pit work because of a crippled leg and, like several other lame ducks, had been taken on as Kellock's 'apprentice' to tide him over. In the front corner of the yard, the shop was already open. Two girls from large families—in need of extra shillings and the 'treat' of cheap bread—were serving a crowd of colliers.

Mirrin slotted the dog-cart out of the way and, leaving Duncan to fetch down the churn, made straight for the door of the two-up, two-down house and the corridor that led into the kitchen.

Kate was in process of lugging hot water from a huge copper pan out to the tin baths in a side shed in the yard. There, as soon as the meal was over, Edward and Neill would sluice the pit dirt from their bodies before wearily making for their beds.

"Is it that late already?" Kate asked, as Mirrin entered the room.

"No, love, it's me that's early," Mirrin explained.

Kate glanced over at Lily who was breaking eggs into a bowl to prepare a batter pudding for that night's dinner.

Lily brushed a strand of hair from her pretty face, and said, "You'll not have had your mornin' cuppa, then."

"I could do with one, right enough," said Mirrin.

"And a fresh roll?"

"Aye, why not," said Mirrin seating herself at the table opposite her nephews.

17

Edward winked. "You'll be gettin' fat, Auntie Mirrin."

"Not me. Farmers' wives work too hard for fat t' stick—not like you idle miners lyin' on your backs all night long, tap-tappin' at a wee bit o' slag now and then for the foreman t'hear."

"Hoh," said Neill, reaching for a second roll. "Maybe that's how it was in your day, Auntie, but if y'don't fill your darg nowadays, then it's Lamont himsel' that'll come down after you an' hammer your nut on the wall."

"Or Thrush," said Edward. "Man, I'd rather face up t'Lamont than Thrush any day."

"An' when did either of you ever have t'face up t'the owner or the manager?" said Mirrin. "They don't even know the likes o'you exist."

"That's what you think," said Edward. "I'm tellin' you, Auntie, Thrush has a big blackboard in his house wi' every young collier's name chalked on it, an' . . . ."

"That story's so old it's growin' whiskers," Mirrin interrupted.

"Even your grandpa used t'tell that one," said Flora Stalker from her rocking chair by the fire. "Only it was a man called Donald Wyld was manager in those days."

"An' a fine man he was," said Mirrin. "I'll grant you that, you pair, when you're discussin' how grim things are now—Wyld was ten times more fair than your precious Sydney Thrush."

"Here we go again," said Willie Kellock, appearing in the door that led from the bakehouse. "Pits, an' colliers an' times gone by. Every mornin' when you come through that door, Mirrin Stalker, it's a signal for a trip int' the past."

Mirrin laughed. Relaxation was taking hold of her, easing the strain of living with Tom, of trying to be kind to a man who had become a stranger to her.

As if reading her daughter's thoughts, Flora said, "An' how's Tom today, Mirrin?"

"He's fine, Mam."

"Is there any improvement?"

"Aye. It seems a bit better with him," Mirrin lied.

Willie said, "Has he finished ploughin' the long field?"

"The ground's been too hard," Mirrin said.

"Well, there's time yet, I suppose." Though he had no

farming experience, Willie's contact with millers and conversations with his brother-in-law had made him an armchair expert in steading management. "But I'd have thought the frost would be out o' the ground by ten these mornin's for . . ."

"Willie," Kate warned, "leave Hazelrig business t'Hazelrig folk."

"What? Aye. Oh, aye. Excuse me, Mirrin."

"Can Hurley no' plough?" Neill asked.

"Hurley's furrows are as kinked as cats' tails," said Mirrin. "But Malcolm's learnin' the knack. Perhaps he'll run over those last rigs today or tomorrow."

"Farmers," said Edward again, with mock scorn.

"What farmers need," said Neill, ingenuously, "is a more active labour union."

"Enough of that kind of talk," said Kate.

"What's wrong wi' unions?" Neill demanded, compounding his error with bridling persistence.

"You promised me you'd have nothin' t'do with Rob Ewing's daft schemes," said Kate.

"Rob Ewing's no' the union," said Edward, reluctantly entering into the developing argument.

"Anyhow, it's a miner's duty t'attend the meetin's," said Neill. "An' Rob's our unofficial representative on the Miners' Federation. He gets all the reports from England, an' . . ."

Mirrin clicked down her teacup. "If ever there's mischief brewin' then you can be sure Rob Ewing's behind it."

"He's the miners' *friend*," said Neill, stoutly. "I mean, Auntie Mirrin, y'can't sit there an' tell me that Rob hasn't done a power o' good for Blacklaw colliers. All he's feared of is that the present-day miner won't have the guts o' the older generation—like my Grandda—an' that they'll give up the struggle before the battle's half won."

Kate was disturbed by Rob Ewing's influence on the young men. She had no patience at all with militant union politics that, as always, ran rife in Blacklaw in spite of all that Sydney Thrush and Houston Lamont could do to suppress them. Politics were like a species of weed that would not be eradicated, stronger than ever now, much stronger than in Mirrin's youth when she had stood on a box at the street corner and invoked rebellion with all her might. She had not entirely lost sympathy with the ardent enthusiasm, and naivety, of young miners who sought to make the world a better place. Twenty years ago it had all been a wee bit of a joke—though the participants took it seriously enough—but now, with organisation and administration, the Movement was much more than inflamed rebellion against local injustice promoted by amateurs.

Though she understood their ardour, she was not prevented from carrying on the argument as vehemently as if she was one of Thrush's Tory bosses. "Rob Ewing did most of his fightin' in the public house. He was no union hero, I tell you."

Kate shook her head. She put down the cauldron of hot water. Her sense of fair play would not let such a calumny pass, not when it affected a long-time neighbour and friend like Rob.

She said, "I may not agree with him now, Mirrin, but you've no right t'condemn Rob for keepin' in the background. He stood up with the best o' them when anythin' important was at stake. Besides, he had his plate full with poor Eileen, an' his Dad and Mam. It was no fun for him t'have t'watch his father, wife an' mother die, like that, one after another."

Over the rim of her teacup Flora Stalker studied her eldest daughter intently. Kate never forsook her allegiance to old friends; not like Mirrin who, it seemed, wavered now in her loyalties like smoke in the wind.

Unaware of the harsh, and not altogether accurate, opinion that her mother held of her, Mirrin grudgingly capitulated. "I suppose you're right. I never envied Rob those miserable years nursin' the dyin'. It's a pity, in a way, that old Callum never lived t'see his son in such a strong position, or the end of the fight comin' nearer."

"None o' us will live t'see the end o' that particular struggle," said Lily.

"Maybe *we* will, Neill an' me," said Edward. "Ma, I keep tellin' you that things've changed since the old days. We're united enough, organised enough . . ."

"An' ugly enough," said Mirrin.

Willie and Flora laughed. It was a deliberate puncture, a quip designed to let the steam out of the conversation. But Edward Stalker frowned and, planting his elbows on the table, wagged a buttery knife in his aunt's direction. "Aye, pass it off wi' a joke, if y'like. That's what undermined the miners' cause in the past—levity an' indifference. But . . ."

Lily's hands closed on her son's hair. She had moved stealthily, and nobody had noticed how close she had come to a striking position. She hauled her son from the table and steered him through from the kitchen into the yard and the washing shed.

Everybody grinned at the youngster's shouts of "Haw, Mammy. Mammy, naw."

Neill grinned too, smugly, until he noticed Kate slipping round behind him, then he was up in pretended panic, calling, "I'll go quiet. I will. Here, Mam, give's a chance."

Mirrin swivelled quickly and stuck her legs out between the table and a big pine dresser and refused to let her nephew pass. Willie blocked the other exit, and, within a moment, Neill Campbell Stalker was rendered helpless. His ear pinched between Kate's finger and thumb, he too was dragged, protesting loudly, out to the cold wash shed.

When the boys had gone and the kitchen had quietened down again, Willie returned to the bakehouse and Lily to her morning's routine of stocking the breadvan for its rounds, leaving the sisters and their mother alone.

The ebullience that the young men had engendered drained quickly from Mirrin. She no longer felt safe here. There would be questions now, questions that she did not want to have to answer. In a vain attempt to forestall Kate's inquiries, Mirrin hastily gathered the breakfast dishes from the table and carried them to the sink at the back of the kitchen.

It was Flora, not Kate, who stopped her, staring up from her rocking chair with eagle-like concentration.

"You're not yourself, Mirrin," Flora said. "What's wrong?"

"Nothin'."

Flora turned in the chair, stout iron springs creaking. Mirrin rattled crockery into the sink and twirled the brass tap that fed a stream of warm water from a small boiler built into a cavity behind the cooking range.

"Did you talk t'Tom again?" Kate asked.

"Aye," said Mirrin, curtly.

"An' what did he say?"

"What he always says these days—not a blessed word."

"Does he not see . . . ?" Flora began, then bit off the sentence, embarrassed by the irony of her choice of phrase.

"He does *not* see," said Mirrin. "He won't *listen* t'me. He won't *answer* me."

Kate put her hand on Mirrin's shoulder.

Mirrin brushed the kindly gesture aside. "I'm *sick* tryin' to talk t'him. *I'm sick of him.*"

"Now, Mirrin, now," Flora reprimanded. "It must be terrible for an active man like your Tom t'be . . ."

"I know. I know," Mirrin clenched her fists. "Don't think I haven't tried. Two years I've tried. But it's up t'him now."

"What d'you mean?" Kate asked.

"I appreciate how bad it must be for him. I understand that better than any of you," Mirrin said, bitterly. "But he won't *fight*, won't *try* any more. He's lost all hope. *All* hope."

Turning again to the grate, Flora nodded.

That was the root of it. Kate and she had suspected it. It was an attitude that they could understand. With her patience and infinite capacity for kindness, Kate might have contrived to sustain pity for many years. But Mirrin was not like Kate, and Flora, old now as she was, could clearly remember the family's struggle for survival, and the part that Mirrin had played in it. What would have happened to the Stalkers—to Drew and to Betsy, as well as Kate—if Mirrin had meekly accepted the lot that circumstances had dealt to them?

Flora had never much cared for Tom Armstrong. She had never understood the bond between the tink—she still thought of him as that—and her Mirrin. But she had not shown her mistrust in any way at all, disguising it completely over the years.

Mirrin said, "*You* understand that, Mam, don't you?"

"Aye," said Flora. "I think I do."

"What would you do?" Mirrin asked, not pleading so much as demanding. If was fine for the family to heap pity on her husband—God knows he deserved it—but nobody spared a thought for her, for the decisions that she must make, struck off from the man whose strength had been her strength for almost two decades. Their marriage had seemed like a tall strong tree and, in her mind, could be as strong again, made stronger still by Tom's affliction.

And then she would hear a voice in her that said, "Aye, but you don't have to live with it."

And her own voice answering, "Aye, but I do."

She acknowledged that there was no escape for him but, out of desperate selfishness, she blamed him for denying her escape. His silence, his rock-like refusal to redeem what he could from the years remaining to him—and they might be many— had alienated her, not only from Tom but from her sons and daughter too. Now, it seemed, the process was eating into her relationship with Kate and Mam and all the others whom she cared about and loved. In a strange perverted way, Mirrin imagined that her husband had been waiting for this opportunity throughout their life together, waiting for an excuse to rid himself of the hard grind of caring for the land, for his children, for her. Logically of course, she knew that that was a fallacy that her anger had flowered. But it was the one dream that she cherished above all others at that fearful period in her life, the belief that he had always been unworthy of her, that her determination and zest had cloaked his weakness all along.

Once more it appeared that Mam had read her mind.

Flora sighed. "In spite of what you think, Mirrin, Tom still needs you."

"Then why, *why* will he not tell me so?"

"Because," Flora said, "he fears so much that you no longer need him."

Such sagacity and insight caught Mirrin by surprise. She thought of her mother still as a woman who had failed to cope with the tragedies in her own life, who had gleaned her strength from her family. A residue of that arrogance was still in Mirrin, a subtle scorn for a woman who had been beaten down by disaster. Now she saw how wrong she'd been.

Mirrin leaned against the edge of the sink.

Kate was close by her, torn between her desire to offer sympathy and the cautious need to avoid meddling. Mirrin wept, not with frustration, not in a great show of troubled conscience letting the tears come naturally, as if her conceit had been pricked by that one perceptive sentence. She wept now, without shame, for herself, having no need to pretend that her grief was for Tom and Tom alone.

In her turn, Kate was thinking of her own man, an old man who, though he seemed in the pink, might die this year, or next, just because of his age. Kate had reconciled herself to the passage of years and the inevitable shrinking of the future's bright array. Now she acknowledged that what she had once thought she wanted was what she had, lacking only the impossible assurance that life would endure unchanged forever.

How much harder it must be on Mirrin, who, when young, had loved and been loved by other men, important men, men full of honour, yet passionate in their desire. All wives, at some time, felt trapped by their choices, suffered doubt over that dusty, one-summer's day decision by which they had picked the man for them. It was easier for the rest, Kate told herself, easy to shut out grand dreams when all was well and the world comfortable. How much more difficult it must be for Mirrin, though, who was handsome, and still young, and had tasted varieties of joy and sorrow that lay far from the hodden-grey experiences that were the lot of most Blacklaw girls, past, present and, probably, future.

"There, love; there," Kate said, soothingly.

Mirrin wiped her nose on the back of her hand—a childish gesture that made her, fleetingly, tomboyish again. She sniffed, tried to grin and seem jaunty. Bravado did not quite come off now.

"Better?" Flora asked.

"Aye, Mam; better," Mirrin answered.

Outside, in the square, the young men had emerged from the wash shed. Their loins were draped in towels, like the slaves in the Egyptian Palace, and their clean muscular bodies steamed in the cold winter air as they ran, barefoot, across the cobbles, Edward heading into the jeers of the colliers by the shop door to dive up the outside staircase to his room above the stable, Neill barging through the bakehouse hall and on down the corridor into the house proper. Soon, both would be wrapped warm in bed, feet planted against the stone 'pigs' that their Mams had put in to cosset their lads and spoil them a bit.

The moon had waned now. The Square had slipped into a pre-dawn darkness that made the shop windows seem yellow as gold and the gas-lamps across the main street like gilded crowns spun with silver filigree. The kitchen was full of the smell of the bread that Willie had just taken from the ovens, overlaid by spices and the savoury aroma of bacon fat still sizzling in the pan on the hob.

"Here, Mirrin, I'll make us a fresh pot o'tea," Kate said. "Sit yourself down."

"No, I'd better get back. I promised Malcolm I wouldn't be long."

After kissing her mother, Mirrin went into the hall, calling out to her nephew, "Sleep tight, Neill, an' don't give cheek t'the foreman." The already-sleepy reply floated down to her from an upstairs bedroom, "I'll do that, Auntie Mirrin."

The sound of Neill's voice made her think of her own sons; how well the whole bunch of Stalker grandchildren had turned out. Malcolm and Sandy were farmer's lads, as she'd once been a collier's daughter, packed with confidence in their skills, undaunted by the problems that tomorrow might bring.

Today's milk churn had been removed from the dog-cart, replaced by yesterday's empties. Noss had been fed a wee nibble of hay. Mirrin unhitched the rein from the posting rail and climbed up into the cart. She waved to Lily who was toting a tray of crusty loaves to the breadvan, then hesitated as Kate came running from the house.

Kate handed her up a brown paper bag. "Gingerbread an' tottie scones."

"They'd have skinned me back at Hazelrig if I'd forgotten their teabreak," said Mirrin.

Kate did not release her just yet. Hand on Mirrin's arm, she looked up solemnly at her sister. "Mirrin, promise me that you won't give up on Tom."

"No, love, there's no fear of that."

"After all . . ."

"I know," said Mirrin, patiently. "After all, he's near enough blind."

"There's nothin' you, nor any of us, can really do about it, Mirrin," said Kate.

Mirrin's mouth set into a determined line. "You're wrong, Kate," she said, "There is. Something that Tom can do for himself—only he won't."

Bewildered, Kate asked, "What?"

"Later," Mirrin said. "I'll tell you later—or maybe I won't tell you at all."

She touched the tip of the little whip to Noss's rump and nosed the pony forward, navigated between milk-float and breadvan, out through the wide arched gate past the baker's shop.

"Ho there, Mirrin," a collier called jovially, though she could not identify him in the shadow. "How's it goin' with you?"

"It's goin' fine," she shouted and, flicking the whip, trotted Noss into Main Street and set her nose for the Hazelrig road.

*   *   *

The change in Tom Armstrong's voice, like the deterioration in his appearance, was not wholly attributable to the passage of years. Heavier, thicker in shoulders and neck, with grey sprinkled liberally through his dark hair, pain and melancholy had slackened the planes of his face and etched deep furrows down each side of his mouth, cutting away the last traces of his roguish smile. Steel-rimmed spectacles, made to special prescription in Glasgow, pinched the bridge of his nose. With the nervous impatience of a man who cannot accept the inadequacy of optical lenses, he had developed the habit of punching and worrying the glasses with his forefinger so that the flesh of his nose was calloused and the tiny veins on his cheeks broken, like those of a typical souse. Drink was not Tom's downfall, though. His condition could not be blamed on any avoidable indulgence. It was a stroke of evil luck, haphazard and cruel. His diseased eyes were protected by coloured lenses. The laughter-lines that had once webbed the corners had been strained into ugly grooves by peering, to add to the other changes in his compact and graceful appearance. Even his gestures had altered; they too seemed clumsy, splenetic and coarsely demanding, like his voice.

26

When Mirrin returned, it was daybreak, and Tom had emerged from his self-imposed imprisonment in the chill back bedroom.

There was no life in the yard, except the ubiquitous cats and a half dozen hens that had wandered through a broken pipe from their run round the back of the byre. The old byre door stood open. Mirrin could tell by the pungent odour that Malcolm had broken open the crust of a dungheap and would be out ploughing the stuff into next spring's oatfield. Though the day had not lived up to its promise, and cloud kept out the sun, it was likely that Sandy and Hurley would be up on the end march repairing a hedge that had been damaged in a wild November gale. She put away the pony, dragged the light dog-cart into its shed, laid the two churns out by the milk-house door and then, carrying the bag of Kellock's best baking, went into the house.

It surprised her to find Tom in the kitchen. In the mood he'd been in since Christmas, she might have expected him to take to his heels at the first sound of her arrival, to be immured in that gloomy room where, God knows why, he seemed to find himself most comfortable.

But Tom was up and dressed, though he had not put his boots on. He was lying back in the huge wooden chair with a cushion under his head and his stockinged feet planted on the knob of the drying rail at the end of the stove. The empty porridge pot had been pushed to one side. The table was littered with the breakfast dishes.

Mirrin said nothing.

Tom did not stir. The position of his head was a telltale, however, and she could feel his listening. In this mixture of lamplight and daylight, like as not he would only be able to see her as a blurred shape on the narrow horizon of his vision.

Noisily she piled the dishes and took them out of the main kitchen into the scullery. The scullery formed a double-wedge with the 'dunny', a stone and plaster-lathe glory hole where scraps of metal, wire, sound timber and general bric-à-brac were stored. There was no fancy boiler-heated water in Hazelrig, alas, and Mirrin put the dishes and pots into the stone sink and then returned to bring the kettle from the hob. The kettle was three parts empty. Just yesterday, she had berated Tom for not at least doing that chore for her. Today she held her tongue.

She went out into the yard and filled the kettle at the pump, clanking away at the handle as hard as she could. When she got back indoors, her husband had moved nothing but his head. His face was turned pointedly from the centre of the room, lifted with haughty aloofness so that his profile made a perfect intaglio in the lamplight and seemed to be nobly cut into the corn-coloured material of the cushion.

For an unguarded moment, Mirrin experienced anger at his posing, then, in the instant following, suffered a heartbreaking memory of Tom as he had been on the day they first met at the Lanark Hiring Fair, in his gypsy's leather waistcoat, cocky and raffish, his flop-brimmed hat trimmed with tinkling coins and small medallions. He did not look at all like one of the travellin' folk now, not even one of the tribes' elders, more like a conceited clod-farmer nursing a bad hangover.

In the beginning, Mirrin had agonised over Tom's failing sight, and been buoyed up by hopes of a complete cure. But months had passed with no improvement under the Hamilton doctor's treatment, and two prolonged stays in the Glasgow Ophthalmic Institution had finally put paid to the optimistic pretence that Tom's sight might be miraculously restored. Marginal improvements had gone, eager questions, minor triumphs of returning vision that had soon proved to be but temporary reversals in a pattern of steady decline.

At first Tom had made a joke of his failing eyesight. Very quickly, however, the disease had passed beyond that stage. Farm work was affected, then relationships. The children had become cowed in his presence as though fearing that their natural good spirits would be an affront to their father's affliction.

For a year, including Tom's two periods in hospital, Malcolm had tended the steading. For a year, Tom had doled out advice, issued commands, become more and more bullying in his attitudes until, in the back end of '95, he had reached a base level of retreat from all involvement that seemed, to him, a suitable life-style for a blind man.

28

"What time is it?" he growled.

"Look at the clock."

"Are y'mockin' me, woman?"

"Stand up, put your hand on the mantel's edge, open the clock glass and feel the hands wi' your fingers."

"Bitch."

"What time d'you think it is, then?"

"How would I know?"

"Go t'the window. You can still make out daylight."

"You don't know what I can make out—or can't."

"I only know what you care t'tell me, Tom—in respect o'your sight, that is."

"You've been damned quiet this mornin'. Where were you at breakfast, then?"

"In Blacklaw. I went early."

"Gabblin' t'those idle . . ."

Mirrin interrupted. She spoke calmly, in a voice low enough to prompt him to sit up and pull his head from the pillow. "When d'you intend t'finish the ploughin'?"

He barked with laughter, a harsh condemnation of her stupidity.

"So that's what they were sayin' in Blacklaw this mornin', was it? Sayin' that it's time the ploughin' was done. Well, they can take a trot up here any time they like an' get on wi' it—an' if they want t'know the secrets o' the straight furrow, they can sight on the posts."

"You've a lot t'say for yourself all of a sudden," Mirrin remarked. "But you've said nothin' yet I want t'hear."

"*You* want t'hear," he exclaimed. "What about me?"

"What about you?" said Mirrin.

"Nobody cares a spit what a blind man says."

"Those that love you," said Mirrin, cautious and seemingly casual, "don't give a button whether y'can see or not."

"Oh, aye, that's hell of a bloody decent o'them."

"It's got nothin' t'do with decency. It's just the way it is."

"Make me a fresh pot. The last cup was cold."

"Make it yourself."

"So that's the way o'it," he murmured.

29

"That's the way of it," Mirrin agreed. "I'm not runnin' after you, Tom. I'm done wi' that."

"Strikin' me off—at forty; well, well."

"Just lettin' you strike yourself off, that's all. It's clear that's what y'want. I've enough, more than enough, t'keep me busy. I've a farm t'run—without your help. If y'won't lift a finger t'help me, or yourself, then . . ."

Swaying, he leapt to his feet. He steadied himself quickly by bracing his right foot against the side of the hearth.

"Aye, so the truth's out at last. You can't be bothered nursin' me. Next thing it'll be another man you'll be after."

"I don't want another man. I just want the one I had."

"Even if he's blind?"

"Drownin' in self-pity may drag you to an early grave, Tom, but I'm damned if you'll take me with you. Stop thinkin' what y'*can't* do, an' start thinkin' what y'*can* do. You can walk out that door an' lead a horse up t'the high field for a start. You can see well enough for that an' don't tell me y'can't."

"Today, aye, maybe today—but what about next week . . ."

"I'm not talkin' about next week."

"Damn it, the bloody cuddy can see more'n I can."

"Maybe because the cuddy's got more brains."

He crabbed along the front of the range.

Mirrin watched him intently, muscles tensed to grab for him if he stumbled or put his hands down on the hot parts of the metal. Though his vision was severely restricted, he could still make out colour and shape and, when he forgot himself, travelled across the room with assurance. He left the range, got to the window and, stooping, peered out.

"What time *is* it?"

"A quarter t'nine."

"Hah."

"If the cloud keeps down," said Mirrin, conversationally, "we might even have a sprinkle o'snow."

He did not respond. He put his palm to the glass and rubbed it, peered again, then turned, as Mirrin, carrying the kettle full of hot water, passed him on her way into the scullery.

"*You* did this," he said. "You did it to me."

Mirrin stopped in amazement. "What?"

"It was you kept buildin' up my hopes. For near on two bloody years. If you left me t'myself I'd have come t'terms with it, learned t'accept it. Aye, but you couldn't leave me be, Mirrin. Doctors, an' specialists, an' oculists, an' infirmaries. An' you chantin' away at me that it would be all right. Those soft voices tellin' me, 'Everything will be perfectly fine, Mr. Armstrong.' Christ, woman, how can I believe anythin' after lies o'that magnitude."

Mirrin went on into the scullery, stowed the kettle safe at the back of the draining board, then came out again.

"Where *are* you?"

"I'm here, I'm here," she said.

He said, "I think y'did it deliberately."

"Of course I did it deliberately."

"To torment me?" he said. "Or t'give yourself an opportunity t'scout round for another chap?"

"Tom," she said, "I'd rather have you wi' half an eye than the whole of . . . of the damned Northrigg back shift. We need you, me an' the children."

"Aye, t'amuse you. T'laugh at."

"To farm Hazelrig," she said. "If you'd agree to another operation . . ."

"I won't do it, Mirrin. Not again. Enough. Oh, Christ, Mirrin, *enough*."

"You're afraid, Tom, aren't you?"

"Aye, I'm scared t'death. Another operation: another failure. *Blindness, for bloody sure. Blindness for good an' all.*"

"Better go through to the bedroom."

"This's *my* kitchen. I won't be shut out o'it."

"I've work t'do. You'll only be in the way."

"Mirrin, what's this you're sayin'?"

"I'll help you, will I? I'll help y'back t'bed," she said, unctuously.

"Mirrin, listen. I'll not stand for this treatment."

"Then go an' lie down."

"Y'heartless *bitch*." He aimed a swipe at her with his open fist. She stepped back, caught his wrist and pulled it, drawing him to her. With finger and thumb, she snared his spectacles and whipped them from his face. He winced and jerked his

31

head away, not from the light, but from her. There was little enough to see, a receding of the pupils, a certain discolouration.

"You'll not be needin' these, Tom—in the dark."

"Give them back."

"I'll put them by the bed."

"I'm not goin' t'bed. *I'll* decide what *I'll* do."

"Suit yourself." Mirrin hooked the spectacles into the pocket of his waistcoat and released him, pushing past him.

"Where the hell're you goin'?"

"T'make the beds."

"Mirrin, what . . . what about me?"

"*You* decide what *you'll* do."

She left him, went out of the kitchen and along the narrow corridor and upstairs into Kitten's room. Closet-like, it was compressed between the larger bedrooms, its attic window facing down into the yard not out across the pastures and the Witchy burn. The bed was small and sturdy, yet dainty, like Kitten herself. A ragged doll lay neatly on the pillow, bedclothes pulled up to its chin. On the little dresser was a ball of brightly coloured cloth, and two picture books.

Respectfully Mirrin removed the doll, sat it on the dresser, opened one of the picture books—Bible stories for the very young—and placed it before the doll, so that she might say to Kitten, on the child's return from school, that Dolly Daisy had been very good all day.

Then she sat on the end of the bed, trembling.

Below, through the floorboards, she could hear Tom moving, heavy-footed, but not unsure. She could not interpret the sounds. The trembling eased and finally ceased. She heard the yard door clack open and click shut again.

She got up and stood by the window. Leaning on the dresser she looked down into the yard.

He had his heavy tweed jacket on, a woollen scarf knotted in the collar of his shirt. His boots were laced and tied tightly with a leather knot, ends dangling down his calfs. She watched him make his way across the yard, peering through his glasses, hands doggedly clenched by his sides. He reached the stable door, and felt his way along the wall to the bar. He tipped the bar and pulled the door open, his leg back and braced to keep the huge Clydesdale—Derry—checked within her stall. He latched the door to its hook, then went in and, a moment later, led out the mare. It dwarfed him completely yet he held himself close to her swelling flanks, halter rope, shortened, twisted in his fist. He was gentle enough with the animal, a docile beast, the best of the three plough-horses. Holding Derry, he groped for the hook and, without much difficulty, secured the stable door behind him.

Leading the mare, yet led by her, in curious mutual dependence, he set off out of the yard and down the lane that would take him to the high field, passing quickly out of Mirrin's sight.

The woman sat on the bed again, hands folded in her lap.

The victory of her will over his meant nothing.

She had sacrificed much of her dwindling stock of trust to goad him into action. How much more must she give, at the risk of alienating him forever, to drive him to a decision to agree to one last major operation within the gloomy precincts of the Ophthalmic Institution.

What he had said was true; she *had* offered him a surfeit of hope. Her optimism had lifted him and spurred him forward— and, in that, she had played him false. But now, this morning, he had reacted against the role that he had cast for himself. That initial reaction might auger well for the future.

Sighing, Mirrin clapped her hands on her thighs and pushed herself to her feet.

Compared to this present trouble, most past crises now seemed insignificant. But it was not the present, or the un-certain future that held the greatest threat to Mirrin Armstrong's security. Already the seeds of tragedy that would ensnare her before the summer was spent, were germinating, sullen and silent, deep in the buried past.

*   *   *

The robing room in Edinburgh's Parliament House was crowded with advocates preparing themselves for the ten o'clock call to court. Top hats and white ties were *de rigueur* and the steep slopes of the Mound that led up from Princes Street had the appearance of a Greenland icefloe as the throng of legal gentlemen in penguin suits legged it towards the Court of Session, Mecca of the Scottish Bar.

In that era, late in the century, the Court had reached a peak of prosperity and efficiency and Outer and Inner Houses were presided over by a worthy collection of judges. It is true that there was some evidence of incompatibility between justice and bickering ambition in the Second Division, but Second Division matters were of little moment now to Mr. Andrew Stalker, Q.C., who had long ago shed connection with more lowly orders.

In the lofty black-beamed hall where Scottish Parliaments had once fretted over the destiny of the nation, counsels, clerks and agents hustled across the warped floorboards and clustered, on that cold January day, round the three huge carved fireplaces to warm their hands and haunches and, stealthily forsaking dignity, to lightly toast the chilly parchment of their wigs. It was hardly a solemn scene, though the setting, magnificent in its antiquity and embellished by rows of grim portraits and even grimmer statues, still dourly resisted merriment. Camaraderie conquered all, however, for the court-houses were like clubrooms to the lawyers who daily met there to argue cases before their lordships.

On that particular morning more attention than usual was being paid to the entrance hall. A number of young acolytes, those without briefs of their own, and a flock of reporters were eagerly awaiting the arrival of the day's Top o' the Bill. When Stalker was 'up' junior members of the bar invariably packed the reporters' box to listen and to learn from this master of the strategic arts.

The case before the Inner House had more than academic interest, however. Staggering sums of money and hints of a velvet scandal were involved; divorce settlements between members of the nobility were great draws for the public.

Who better then to conduct the arguments for the Lady Lavinia Torquil than Mr. Andrew Stalker? Who better to represent Sir Ramsay Torquil, than Mr. Hector Mellish, Stalker's only rival for the *ex-officio* title of Most Brilliant Young Prodigy of the Scots Bar, and his deadly enemy both in and out of court? Who better to occupy the judgment seat than Lord McSherry, that learned feudalist whose knowledge of the law was tempered only by his inordinate respect for 'property' and a Calvinistic loathing of 'dalliance, sir, dalliance'?

In two days of expositions and harangues there had already been several witty exchanges between Bench and Bar. For example, after one lengthy submission, larded with best Latin, concerning *jus relicti*, alimentary life-rents and hairsplitting definitions of Marriage Contract Acquirenda, Lord McSherry had sternly rebuked Advocate Stalker for 'clouding the issue with an excess of clarity'.

Behind the jural arras, loomed the dangerous and saturnine figure of Frederick Ashpont, ironmaster, Lady Lavinia's lover. He had his beady eye on the Mineral Lease Rights to the portion of the Earl's West Stirlingshire estates claimed by Lady Lavinia as her due in settlement. Obviously Ashpont hoped to acquire the former by continuing to curry favour with the latter.

Stalker did his best to keep Ashpont's name out of discussions. Lest that tactic fail, however, he was prepared to introduce the names of two dainty sprites that Daniel Horn, Stalker's trusted clerk, had wooed out of their provincial retreat. Wispy as chiffon, these two bourgeois châtelaines, sisters no less, had frequently given succour to the noble Earl during the course of his visits to their father's mansion in Dumbarton. What was more, the young ladies now seemed willing to admit the extent of their mutual indiscretions by means of sworn depositions, though what pressure Horn had exerted on the pair to make public confession the lesser of two evils Andrew Stalker did not dare enquire.

Naturally, nobody had yet been informed of the existence of the Dunbartonshire dollies—excepting Mr. Hector Mellish, Q.C. He could certainly be counted upon to keep the information locked under his wig. As Mr. Stalker had privately explained to Mr. Mellish in the precincts of the Advocates' Convenience, late yesterday evening, it wouldn't do for the *whole* sordid mess to come to light, would it? Wouldn't do to make a *moral* issue out of a clear case of *law*, would it? Particularly with McSherry sitting up there like the Lord God Almighty ready to hand judgment to the *least* sinful of the parties. Both he and Mr. Mellish knew who *that* party would be, didn't they? Two sisters taken at one bedding *more* than equalled 'dalliance' with a *mere* ironmaster in terms of wickedness and eternal damnation, did they not?

With this assessment, Mr. Mellish angrily concurred. It was therefore tacitly agreed that battle would henceforth be joined on the field of Law, and Law alone. Ashpont would not be mentioned, and the Dunbartonshire 'indiscretions' would be permitted to retain their public reputations intact.

On the field of Law, and Law alone, Mr. Stalker could surely be counted upon to outfox Mr. Mellish. By dusk, Lady Lavinia would have won her claim for settlement. In due course, Mr. Ashpont would receive his mineral rights at a nominal sum, and, in addition to his provident fee, Mr. Stalker would acquire, through a seedy little agent in a run-down Glasgow office, a block of stock in the Ashpont Mining & Smelting Company.

Though the Torquil case was virtually cut and dried and the macers of the Division might have saved themselves the effort of belling it, Mellish would go through the rigmarole of fighting a rearguard action and Stalker would dazzle the occupants of the reporters' box with his caustic analyses; after all, only the two Advocates knew that the case was over, and they were by profession committed to follow through the formal rites of jurisprudence.

So, the Children of the Bar and newspaper reporters eagerly awaited Stalker's arrival that morning and cast speculative glances at the big brown leather case that Horn, following tradition, had dumped on the seat by the east wall an hour ago. Now Stalker would be pulling up the Mound from his chambers in stately Moray Place, his team of sombre stallions slipping and scraping, hauling to Court the handsome old barouche that was the Advocate's one piece of ostentation.

Stalker was rich, Stalker was famous, and Stalker—though admired even by his enemies—was not well liked. There was still a sinister mystery to him, not only in the paucity of details about his origins and background, but in the rapid manner of his ascent to power. True, he had no wife, no children and no dependent relatives to hamper him. True, his beautiful twin sister Elizabeth had married into McAlmond stock. True,

Stalker had been shrewd enough to serve his so-called 'off years' devilling for Patrick Lauder who was more renowned than Stalker even now. And true, he worked harder than any other legal man in Scotland. Even so, intangible and sourceless, the air of mystery remained.

Somehow, at a mere thirty-six, Stalker seemed to attract only the fattest briefs. He had hewn out no particular area of specialisation and had trained himself to plead all across the board with equal assurance. He was thoroughly competent to speak in shipping and commercial matters, in interpretations of wills, property disputes, divorces, patent wrangles, railway rates, land purchase, maritime collision cases, conveyancing and trusts. He was also proficient in Criminal Law, having appeared for the defence in seven trials for embezzlement, four for fraud, and three for murder, winning the verdict in all fourteen instances.

All his briefs, including the capital charges, had brought him generous reward. One of the pithy sayings that did the rounds of Edinburgh's clubs claimed 'that ne'er a tide ebbed in Leith dock but Neptune left a fee for Stalker'. Certainly he performed one feat of legerdemain that gained him his colleagues' respect. Somehow he managed to sidestep the Scottish Rules of Court that stipulated that 'no advocate without good cause shall refuse to act for any person tendering reasonable fee under pain of deprivation of his office of advocate'. Stalker had never yet made plea for a poor man; the betting was that he never would.

To see Mr. Andrew Stalker, Q.C., step from his barouche, already portly and pompous and aged far beyond his years, no man in the capital, or out of it, would have guessed that the Advocate had fathered a son, or that the aforesaid son was, at that very hour, sprawled in bed in Kellock's Square in the mining town of Blacklaw, Lanarkshire, sleeping off a hard night's labour in the dank, dark seams of a coal pit.

Apart from the fact that Mr. Andrew Stalker was regarded as rather a 'neutered Tom', it was difficult to visualise him taking time off from his relentless pursuit of legal excellence and power to woo and win a lady. Arithmetic would have further bewildered interested parties by proving that Mr.

Stalker's one act of folly had occurred so far back into his youth as to make him little more than a boy at the time. And the mother? Well, the mother had been a poor serving lass, lost in the city and near starving, and had conveniently died at the birth.

Nobody, apart from Elizabeth, knew of the intimate connection between Mr. Andrew Stalker, Member of the Faculty, and the grubby face-worker, Neill Campbell Stalker, of Blacklaw. Nobody, apart from Elizabeth, even knew that Andrew had relatives still living in Scotland; all contact between the twins and their kinfolk had been broken many years ago. Quite naturally, Elizabeth, wife to Fraser McAlmond of the respected firm of solicitors, Sprott, McAlmond and Sprott, mother of McAlmond's heirs, and darling of the whole McAlmond clan—plus a dozen notorious Edinburgh rakes— had no desire to unveil her brother's secret or admit to the faintest connection with a class that she despised.

The four-wheeled carriage lurched as Stalker climbed down at the steps of the Parliament House. He was dressed in sober black, a close-nap topper planted square on his sparse and prematurely greying hair, a scarf of white cashmere wool wrapped round his jowls, grey gloves covering his hands. His rotund contours carried no impression of well-fed jollity but transmitted a strange aura of decay, like certain types of tree fungus, smooth but unhealthy. By rights, Stalker's life-style should have whittled him to the bone, made him spare and brittle like so many of his brethren. In spite of his insatiable capacity for work, however, he abdured all forms of physical exercise and indulged a large, if unselective, appetite. Sacks of fat under his eyes were stained with ineradicable fatigue, as if his corpulent body was obliged to absorb all the punishments imposed by his schedule and leave his brain ever quick, alert and incisive.

It had been said that elevation to the Bench was inevitable, since Stalker already possessed features appropriate to a hanging judge. It had also been said, in the columns of Advocate McCrindle's weekly column in the *Scotsman*, under the *nom-de-plume* 'Mayfly', that Mr. Andrew Stalker was 'a pearl dissolved in vinegar'; and a verse in the latest collection of

Ballads of Bench and Bar immortalised him further, concluding, 'And he's the Deil's braw siller tongue, the Asp out o' Eden— Stalker, Q.C.'

All of which was true.

But if you were a plaintiff who could afford his price, then the sight of Andrew Stalker's stony face and glaucous eye was immensely comforting, and you cared not whether he looked thirty-six or fifty-six but thought his appearance ideally suited to such a wily practitioner and were damned glad to have him pleading your case.

Nipping nimbly out of the far door of the carriage, Daniel Horn, the Advocate's clerk, reached the Courts' heavy oak portal before his master was half up the steps. Horn held the door open as the Advocate sailed past, then fell in behind.

Horn was tall and dessicated and haggard of gizzard, but he had a glint in his eye and a crooked smile that still took in the innocent and unwary. Twenty years or more senior to Stalker, he moved with a spryness that the master would never be able to emulate. He was subservient without being humble, tactful without being mealymouthed, and as loyal as a tiger fed twice a day. Cruelly, and never in print, Horn was referred to by the inner caucus as 'that old whoremonger', the reflection on Stalker being quite intentional. Horn had clerked for the Advocate since the very first day that Stalker's brass plaque had appeared on the railings of his old lodgings in Northumberland Street. Without a qualm he had abandoned his first master, the ailing solicitor Gow Havershaw, to follow his fortunes with the younger, brighter man. Havershaw had died soon after, quite unmourned. Oddly, the active parts of Havershaw's business had drifted to Sprott, McAlmond and Sprott, a wee bit of extra hand-washing that Horn accomplished without even rolling up his sleeves.

It was three minutes to ten o'clock when Stalker entered the long hall. Instantly, on his appearance, the law students and reporters rushed for the door to Court Number One. Plucking up his brief case as he passed, Stalker sailed directly into the robing room without acknowledging the optimistic 'Good-mornings' from the loungers who remained by the fires. His robe and wig were out of the stuff bag in a twinkling and he was helped into them by Horn even as he crossed out of the robing room once more and walked the dozen steps to the door of the court. Out of nowhere—or so it seemed—Horn had acquired a Pisan tower of mouldy legal tomes, each bristling with paper markers, the volumes having been culled in advance from the Advocates' Library and stowed away under the boot-bench in the ante-chamber.

Stalker had less than sixty seconds to be at the table on the far side of the Bar before Lord McSherry made his grand entrance. It displeased him greatly, then, to be checked in flight by a slender youth wrapped, like a miniature guardsman, in a huge royal-blue greatcoat topped off with a gilt-encrusted cap. The youth was not abashed by the Advocate, nor should he be, for the youth knew himself to be an emissary of the one person in the city, perhaps in the whole country, that the Advocate feared—Drew's twin sister, Elizabeth.

Impudently the youth placed his palm upon the Stalker belly, pressing him back from the door.

"Here you, boy," Horn growled, then focused long enough to identify the livery of Elizabeth's pantry-boy in his more familiar role as messenger-about-town.

Between gloved finger and thumb the lad held up two identical mauve envelopes.

"Wath ma lady's complamants," he intoned, giving his rote performance, since he had no other. "Fram the Mastrass Elizabeth McAlmond. Ah am anstracted nat ta await a ra-ply."

Stalker glared at the missives. He sucked in a long shuddering breath then, rudely brushing the boy aside, said, "Take them, Daniel, take them," and hurried on into court.

An hour passed before Andrew Stalker had an opportunity to investigate his correspondence, an hour of vigorous cut-and-thrust, not with Mellish but with his Lordship. It seemed that McSherry had twigged the Advocates' barter, and was hell-bent on 'digging up the bodies' for himself, presumably to allow an opportunity for delivering one of his droning sermons on moral turpitude and the downfall of Christian society. Neither Mellish nor Stalker would permit him ingress, however. Stalker carried the ball for a while until Mellish marshalled a long digression on Forfeited Rights *Ex Lege* and launched himself into it as if it was Sir Ramsay Torquil's neck and not just his face that he had been commissioned to save.

With a ruler Stalker slit open the first letter. It was penned in green ink on lavender paper watermarked with the monogram of the McAlmonds of Pearsehill. Like the tarted-up messenger, the wording of the missive had a Regency ring to it, a frilly outmoded style that Elizabeth revelled in and that made her brother heartily sick, Andrew being very much a man of his times.

The letter reminded him—as if he needed reminding—of the dinner party that evening, and claimed that she and Fraser were so much looking forward to having him join them in celebration of their twelfth wedding anniversary. It also warned that urgent business would not be accepted as an excuse. Stalker glanced over the letter, grunting. Damn it all, he'd already ordered an appropriate present, a pair of silver wine-coolers from Luis of Princes Street, and had no intention of missing the occasion.

He slit open the second letter.

In the same breathless sort of prose in which she'd served the reminder, Elizabeth informed her brother that she intended to run away with her lover and spend a whole week in London with him, and would he—her own dear kinsman—make an excuse to Fraser to account for her absence.

Stalker groaned, covered the noise with a cough and, folding the letter passed it to Horn who was sitting attentively behind him.

Horn scanned it, leaned forward and whispered. "Again?"

Cupping his hand to his mouth, Stalker leaned back. "It couldn't be the truth, Daniel, could it?"

"What d'you think, sir?"

"I think . . . I think you'd better spot off and pay the bitch a call."

"Surely it's hardly necessary. She's just inventin' again, t'keep you dancin'."

"This lover . . . ?"

"There *is* no lover, Drew."

"How can you be sure, Daniel?"

"Take m'word for it, it's all just foolish womanly nonsense."

Stalker tugged his robe around him and sat forward again,

41

leaning his elbow on the table and staring vacantly up at McSherry's sour face. For once, he did not believe Daniel. He knew his sister of old; she was flighty, crafty, irresponsible and fiendishly cunning—a paradox unto herself. He did not understand her motives, and her methods were sleek, bordering on the vicious now and then. Besides, he had proof.

What the hell did she want of him?

Hand to his lips, he slowly craned back in his chair.

"Best go, Daniel."

Resignedly, the clerk nodded. "Very well, sir."

"Tell her . . . tell her . . .'

"Tell her t'wait until tomorrow?" Horn suggested.

"Yes," Mr. Andrew Stalker said. "Tell her anything you like."

Making no noise at all, Horn slipped from the clerks' bench and exited through the rear door of the courtroom.

Stalker sat back and tried to concentrate on Mellish's intricate phrases—overblown bumble, most of it—then became aware of Lady Lavinia's eyes upon him. Turning his head, he returned her scrutiny.

The Lady gave him a faint enigmatic smile. Perhaps she supposed that the famous Advocate was succumbing at last to her charms. Pshaw! They were all the same, every last one of them. For a fleeting, irrational moment, he had half a mind to sell the harlot to the other side; Mellish would love that. Then he thought again of Elizabeth, and quailed at the prospect of crossing any of that sex, McAlmond or Torquil.

Women: damn and devil them all!

* * *

Time had laid its mark on Edith Lamont and her husband. Beneath the latest bell skirts and leg o'mutton blouses, Edith had run to fat. Though her hair, thanks to frequent applications of Coston's Best Tint, retained much of its colour, her florid skin had taken on the papery texture of a withering leaf. Houston, on the other hand, had changed in less obvious ways. He had become more spare but his back was ramrod straight which gave him a military bearing that suited his broad shoulders and luxuriant white hair.

Wednesday luncheon was almost over for another week. The Lamonts stood in the hall of their mansion, within a sheltering circle of oaks on the knoll above Blacklaw, bidding their guests farewell. Held by a uniformed maid, the door opened to a view of a gravelled drive, along which three carriages growled, their iron wheels hardly denting the frosty surface.

"A very pleasant lunch, Edith, as always."

"I do envy you your cook; such a way with beef."

"Look in at my Glasgow office, Houston; Monday, if you will."

'We'll take a bite at the club."

"Excellent."

Wednesday luncheons stood in lieu of dinner parties, social occasions that Houston detested. In any case early afternoon seemed a more reasonable time to discuss business and exchange industrial gossip than late evening.

At the lunch table that particular afternoon, the subject that had occupied the gentlemen—and ladies, too—had been disquieting figures recently issued by the Trades' Office, figures proving that the marked increase in the quantities of non-phosphoric ore being imported into Britain from the Continent was no mere scaremonger's rumour.

Later, over brandy, Sir William Wintrup, had casually raised the subject of labour-management relations. Realising at once that Sir William was fishing for information on the disposition of Blacklaw's militants, Houston parried the questions and turned them over to Edith. Ten or twelve years ago Edith would have waxed lyrical about the advantages of 'private' police forces and the necessary curbing of the so-called 'freedom to work' movement, claiming that it really meant freedom to be idle at the owners' expense. Mellowed by experience, however, she reassured Sir William that, though all was not calm in Blacklaw, no immediate stoppage was envisaged to curtail production.

Edith Lamont was not the only wife who took a keen interest in business affairs. Of the four women who sat at table only young Lady Clelland, second wife of the ageing Baronet and a vapid little creature with nothing but her prettiness and youth to commend her, was bored by chat of tonnages and gross production and all the sundry jargon of commerce and industry. Edith enjoyed the luncheon parties. They gave her an opportunity of showing off the splendours of Strathmore, one of the finest of all mansions built not on old family inheritances but raised up, by acumen, ambition and the proper exercise of power. Now that she was older, she no longer cared to court the aristocracy. In fact she much preferred to patronise less wealthy members of her own class, the new industrial gentry.

Edith remained in the hall while Houston courteously escorted the ladies to the carriages. Only young Lady Clelland lingered behind, her hand on Edith's sleeve. "Now, Edith, you *will* remember to donate something to my church bazaar on the 29th, won't you? It needn't be anything too grand, just a little trifle for the auctions? I really wouldn't want the manse roof coming in on our handsome young minister; he's such a pet lamb."

Church bazaar, indeed! Edith felt contempt for the child. There was no gain, no power to be had in organising church bazaars. Did poor Lottie Clelland hope to make the Baronet's workers love her for such trivial charity? There wasn't a collier in Scotland who wouldn't take the charity, snigger behind the Lady's back, and immediately return to plotting disruptive action.

Personally she had long since given up pandering to Houston's people. However, she smiled condescendingly and charitably informed Lottie Clelland that of course she would donate some little thing, never fear—then handed the girl over to Houston to see out to the waiting carriage.

Had she ever been *quite* as silly as Lottie? Objectively, Edith did not suppose that she had. Not even when her marriage had been threatened by Houston's mad sister, and that collier's slut, Mirrin Stalker. Between them, they had turned her husband's mind to jelly and driven him to the brink of self-destruction. Edith prided herself that it was only her innate strength that had redeemed him and set his feet once more upon a righteous path. Mercifully Dorothy Lamont had died. And Mirrin Stalker, well, she'd found her own low level by marrying a clodhopping farmer, to breed and milk cows on a miserable steading out in Crosstrees direction.

44

Rarely now did such angry thoughts stray into Edith Lamont's head. She crowded them out with business. If her husband was 'Master of Blacklaw' then assuredly she was its mistress. After all, it was by her efforts, aided by Sydney Thrush, that the pit had been saved from bankruptcy. At a most crucial time in Blacklaw's history, Houston had simply turned his back on the colliery, on Strathmore, on her, had renounced all his obligations to chase the length of the country after that Stalker girl.

But that was all long, long ago. In the intervening years, Houston had been almost all that she could have wished for in a partner. She had completely forgiven him.

Chaffering horses pulled the three-carriage procession away down the gravel towards the gates. Houston returned. The housemaid closed the door behind him.

The coalmaster walked across the hall and entered his study. Edith followed him. The study was no longer the male sanctuary it had once been. She was as familiar with its document cabinets and hard leather chairs as Houston was. He poured himself a whisky from the decanter on the side table, then, turning, asked, "Do you wish to speak with me, Edith?"

"Merely to enquire why Sydney was not invited today?"

"Thrush and Willie Wintrup rub each other the wrong way," Lamont said.

"But Sydney is our partner, Houston. Sometimes, I feel that you don't give him his proper place."

Lamont studied her over the rim of the glass. She bore his scrutiny, confident in the knowledge that his temper was banked down like a furnace. She fluffed a crease out of the lace of her day dress.

"Thrush is in his proper place," Lamont said, "at the Eastlagg pithead."

Edith shrugged. "What has Wintrup heard, do you think?"

"Wild rumours, that's all."

"About possible strike action?"

"God in heaven," Lamont said. "Will the day never come when I can hew coal out of the ground without being plagued by threats of strikes? Are they blind, deaf and dumb, those stupid miners? Can't they see that they have rich pickings here?

45

We are one of the few pits in Lanarkshire on full production."

"It's this talk of a national stoppage," said Edith. "It makes them feel important. An illusion, of course."

"It was no illusion in the English pits, last year," said her husband, replenishing his glass. "Three and a half months without a nugget of coal being taken from the ground, anywhere."

"That can't happen here."

"Edith, Edith; don't be naive. It most certainly can happen here. If pressure goes on in Fife and Midlothian then the Blacklaw colliers will support their so-called 'brothers', even though the district situations are not parallel. They won't hesitate. And we, this time, may be the losers."

Edith nodded. Unfortunately, it was quite true. The capital commitment of Lamont enterprises, spread into many industrial securities, would not stand the strain of loss of primary revenue for long. The gross tonnage was contracted so far in advance, and the revenue from it in turn contracted, that financial flexibility had been sacrificed to growth. Besides, the Continentals were standing, as always, in the wings. If native coal production ceased, the Germans and the Dutch would be only too willing to satisfy the markets with their imports. Even so, she was less pessimistic than Houston. She retained a firm belief in the bondage of fear. Fear was a hard taskmaster. Miners had long memories for suffering. While they might give vocal support to their political leaders by packing meetings convened in the yard, the big Co-op hall or at the back of The Lantern, they seldom failed to report on the dot for their shifts, to dig their daily quota and stuff nineteen or twenty shillings into their pockets without a sign of rebellion.

"Houston, have you concrete evidence that Blacklaw is heading towards a strike?"

"Thrush is gathering evidence."

"He said nothing to me."

"I told . . . asked him not to mention it. I know how much you worry."

"I worry no more than you do, my dear."

"Thrush tells me that applications for affiliation with the United Miners' Federation of Great Britain have gone out from

46

a dozen districts in Fife, Lanarkshire and the Lothians."

"From Blacklaw?" Edith asked.

"Not yet; not as a separate entity. Blacklaw's representatives voted for affiliation at district level, though, that much I did hear."

"That was a secret ballot, was it not?"

"Few secrets are safe from Thrush."

"I see," Edith said. "What do you wish me to do?"

"Visit some of your friends in Glasgow," Lamont said. "As you used to do."

"Ah, yes," said Edith. "You wish me to make light of the situation."

"Gossip is as important as a balance sheet when it comes to decision-making," Lamont said. "Will you do it?"

"Of course," Edith said. "I'll write tomorrow to Lady Traynor; she still gives those tedious soirées every month. I can begin there."

"You know what to do?"

"Yes, Houston."

"Thrush," said Lamont, "will be travelling to London tomorrow. Ostensibly, he will attend the Commons as my observer during the first reading of the Safety in Pits Bill."

"But?"

"He may find time to dine with a friend'."

"Friend—in London—Sydney?"

Lamont smiled. "Not a lady-friend, Edith. A valuable contact in the Miners' Federation, a gentleman rather too fond of feathering his own nest."

"Presumably the information that Sydney brings back will determine our policy for the next half year."

"Longer," Lamont told her. "Much longer."

"Is Sydney dining with us tonight?"

"Yes. Will you inform cook, please?"

"Eight o'clock?"

"Seven," Lamont said. "I don't want to make a night of it; you know how Thrush is when he gets the bit between his teeth."

"Seven, then," Edith said.

She left her husband in the study and crossed into the drawing-room at the rear of the house. There she rang the bell

47

to summon Mrs. Dickson, the latest in a long line of house-keepers to govern the general running of Strathmore. She told the woman that Mr. Thrush would be joining them for dinner and itemised the menu; she knew the kind of fare that Sydney enjoyed. When the Dickson woman had gone, Edith rose restlessly from the Sheraton sofa, from which, like a queen on her throne, she invariably delivered her domestic instructions.

The luncheon, and her discussion with Houston, had excited her. She did not altogether relish the prospect of making a grand tour of Glasgow's salons and drawing-room teaparties, but she could see the sense in it. The mineral-source fraternity was a tightly-knit group. Anything that she yielded up would be passed on to all interested parties within days. Besides, she would also be able to take 'the barometric pressure', as Houston termed it, of the markets, and deduce the degree of uncertainty that pertained in respect of the Coal-owners' Association's promises to allied trades and industries.

Ten years ago, none of this would have been possible. Women, then, were regarded as ornaments. The business of the city was conducted in male preserves, in clubs and offices. It was possible now for a woman, if she were determined enough, to forge a career for herself in one of the professions, though Edith would not have approved had she encountered one of that coterie of young 'independent' women.

Moving nearer to the French-tiled grate, Edith saw that the fire had burned quite low, and that a fragment of soot, round as a ball, adhered to the lip of the grate. She recalled the old superstition that a sootball forecast a visitor. How had it been when she was a child? Tell off the names of the days of the week and clap your hands; on the day of the week when the soot ball . . . Oh, she could not remember the whole nursery ritual now.

Times changed so much. She enjoyed participation in the process of change and felt privileged—yes, actually privileged—to be of an age to straddle nineteenth and twentieth centuries. If he had lived, her son would have been in the prime of his manhood now. She could not imagine him grown. He remained framed in recollection like a portrait, fair head upon a pillow, eyes closed, red lips slightly parted—in death, not in life—a child unfulfilled—so many, many years ago now, when love had still been possible.

Caught on an invisible draught, the sootball fled upwards.

"Thursday," Edith murmured, counting the days in spite of herself.

She did not believe that the prophecy would come true; yet the propsect of surprise pleased her.

Whether a mysterious visitor came or not, at least she would see Sydney tonight. In his way, Sydney Thrush was her lover, her cherished secret, the source and receptacle of fondness, affinity and respect that every woman, high or low, must have to help her through the difficult years when the promises of her youth have all been betrayed.

★   ★   ★

"Sir, I believe that Madame is dressing."

Andrew Stalker did not demean himself by answering the flunkey. He surrendered his overcoat, scarf and silk hat into the footman's hands, first placing on the oval hall table a large parcel containing a brace of silver wine-coolers, his gift to the supposedly 'happy couple'. The fact that Betsy—he still thought of her by that name—and Fraser had remained pledged to each other for a dozen years was testimony to Betsy's cleverness, or Fraser's stupidity; Drew could not decide which. Of course, the young matron, doyenne of Edinburgh society, much admired for her infectious gaiety in this stuffy city, did not play her flirtatious games with everyone.

There was nothing 'silly' about Betsy Stalker. Her brother was at a loss to understand why she would perpetrate such nerve-racking demands upon his time and attention. In this case, he did not exercise sufficient objectivity to realise that Betsy had simply adopted the best method of defence—attack —against his ruthless, self-centred ambition. Drew had what he wanted from her—connection with the McAlmond family. The fact that she had not been at all unwilling to become Fraser's wife had nothing to do with it. Drew had highhandedly assumed that she was there to be used, as he had used Kate and Mirrin, Dominie Guthrie, Gow Havershaw, and, indeed, every person with whom he had ever come into contact.

Many years ago Betsy had decided that she was not a chattel, not a checker on the board for her brother, however successful he considered himself, to move at will.

Though Betsy had loved Fraser once, after her fashion, and still cared for him to some degree, her husband had gradually drifted into a genteel Edinburgh stuffiness so bound by the mores of fashion and his family that he was afraid to blow his nose without first giving 'due regard' to the consequences of his action. In short, the handsome young dandy had become dull.

Apparently Drew knew nothing of her discontentment. And Betsy remained an enigma, a sore thorn in his flesh.

Ponderously he made his way up the curving staircase to the first floor of the opulent residence in Grantham Square. Three floors, servants' attics, stables at the rear; an ideal town-house for a successful solicitor and his family. A fluttery maidservant endeavoured to hinder the legal leviathan's progress, chirping that 'the mistress' was not prepared to receive callers. Drew Stalker scowled and brushed the girl aside. In spite of Daniel Horn's assurances that 'there was nothin' wrong with Betsy, that she was just teasin' him again', Drew was nervous. Why the devil *should* she tease him after all he had done for her? Bringing her from a shop in Hamilton, giving her everything she'd ever dreamed about—a high place in society, wealth, a loving husband? Though he did not expect thanks, he did feel entitled to a modicum of respect.

Reaching the first-floor corridor he walked along it to Betsy's 'boudoir', knocked, and, without awaiting an answer, entered.

Another maid—French, supposedly— babbled incomprehensibly and shoo-ed him with a feather fan as if he was an offending insect.

God, how ridiculous! Often in the past he'd seen Betsy in curling-papers and cotton shift, looking like a trull. Now she was modestly clad in a peignoir of Chinese silk with a turban of Turkish fine stuff wrapped round her pretty head to protect her coiffeur. And this gibbering maid considered it 'indelicate'!

The room was hardly typical of ladies' dressings in Edinburgh. Even in private, feminine inclinations were expected to be tempered by sobriety. Betsy, however, steadfastly refused to live 'in a furnished pulpit or a quilted deed box'. Consequently, she had modelled her suite on the Moorish fashion that was sweeping the salons of London's outrageously *avant garde* hostesses. Even Drew, who disapproved of lavishness, had to admit that the boudoir was tastefully 'all of a piece'. Apart from aesthetic considerations he knew to the penny how much it had cost Fraser and could not separate price from result.

Mauve and silver wall-hangings blended round chairs like spun sugar and a vanity table like a fairy coach. Each inch of fabric and foot of material had been chosen to harmonise and create for Betsy an elegant dream-in-reality.

Reluctantly, Drew acknowledged that the occupant was still pretty enough to benefit from such an Arabian Nights setting.

In the mirror, Betsy's eyes widened childlishly.

"Andrew, you're early."

"Ask the maid to leave, Elizabeth."

"Why, Andrew?"

"You know da . . . perfectly well."

"*Berthe, il faut que tu laisses maintenant, s'il te plait.*"

"*Oui, Madame.*"

"*Je t'enverrai chercher quand j'ai besoin de toi encore.*"

"*Oui, Madame.*"

Scowling blackly at the male intruder of whom, at the best of times, she did not approve, the maid left.

Betsy lifted a heavy lead-glass bottle from a nest on the wing of the vanity table, extracted a glass rod from it and sniffed the rod delicately. As if inspired, she smiled and glanced over her shoulder, holding the perfume stick like a wand.

"Did Lavinia win her case?"

"Of course," Drew said.

"How much?"

"McSherry conceded her full entitlement to the land; that was all she wanted."

"Hm," said Betsy. "I think that would have satisfied me, too."

Going forward, heavy as a pachyderm in that delicate room, Drew tossed the letter onto the table. "What does this mean?"

"Just what it says."

"And what, pray, is this . . . lover's name?"

"I'm not one to kiss and tell, Drew. It isn't becoming to a lady."

"According to Daniel . . ."

"Ah, yes, the Book of Daniel; what secrets that must contain."

"Do not be snippy with me, Betsy."

"Now, is that your stern manner, or your flash-of-ire manner, or your . . . ?"

"You *have* no lover."

"Do I not now?"

"According to Da . . . Horn assures me that you . . ."

"Did you bring an anniversary gift?"

"The wine-coolers from Luis."

"Oh, really, Drew, you shouldn't have gone to such expense. After all it's just a small occasion."

"Are you mad, Betsy? Are you really mad?" Plucking up the letter, Drew shook it at her. "This is a dangerous thing to do. Suppose that it fell into the wrong hands."

"That's why I sent Alphonse."

"Alphonse?"

"My little herald."

"Dear God," Drew moaned in despair. "That urchin's name is Peter. *Peter*. Not, *not* Alphonse. He's no more French than, than I am."

"Thank you for the wine-coolers. Fraser has coveted them for so long. Where are they?"

"In the hall. Betsy, I demand t'be told why you continue to harass me with such stupid letters?"

"I just want you to be prepared."

"Prepared? Prepared for what?"

"To protect your name and reputation."

"Surely I'm not seriously to suppose that you ever for a moment intend to run off with a . . . a lover."

"Perhaps."

"Tonight?"

She turned back to the mirror, touched her eyebrow with her fingertip, the glass rod held out at an angle. "No, not tonight. I changed my mind about tonight."

"Pshaw."

"I never could pronounce that word, Drew. You must teach me. *Psstawww*. It's *so* expressive."

If, at that moment, Betsy had not been arrested by her own prettiness, she might have detected in her brother a disturbing withdrawal from bantering contest. Though his seriousness was deadly, it showed in his expression hardly at all. Indeed, only she might have noticed it, only she might have understood its meaning and, quick as a firefly, have snuffed out her artificial brightness of manner.

Drew stepped back from the dressing-table, lifted one of the flimsy chairs from a corner and fitted it under his backside. Carefully he lowered his weight into it and leaned his elbow on his thigh. In a step-roll evening-dress coat, with squared shoulders and silk facings, stomach contained within its tailored fashion-waist, he looked imposingly sartorial. His hair was pommaded, strands laid across the scoop from brow to crown, crosshatched across the balding crown itself. Wig irons had puffed the hair above his ears to disguise his flabby jowls. His toilet had been effected by Corby, his valet, while the master gobbled up a couple of veal cutlets and a half bottle of marsala, in the hour after court adjourned.

Out of habit, Drew extracted a slim gold watch from his pocket and checked the time. He must allow his twin a further half hour to complete her dressing and five minutes to make a gracious descent into the reception room. Therefore, he had fifteen minutes in which to present his evidence, evidence that he—without Daniel's assistance—had been systematically accumulating for some time.

He said, "It occurs to me, Betsy, that you must take me for a fool."

"Not at all, Drew. I have every respect for your intellect." She glanced at his reflection in the mirror, and, sensing at last the change in his attitude, elected to control her teasing tongue.

"I am assured by my clerk, who, as you know, performs investigative as well as administrative functions," Drew went on, "that these outrageous 'confessions' of yours are founded on no more than a whimsical urge to taunt

53

me; that they are, in effect, baseless. But I know otherwise."

"I'm not a jury member, Drew," Betsy said. "You don't have to lecture me."

"I make no apology for my formal style of address," Drew said. "It may serve to prepare you for certain proceedings that might arise in the near future."

"Proceedings?"

"Divorce proceedings."

"Drew, don't joke with me, please."

"Hear me out." Raising his forefinger to his lips as if she was a juvenile witness who required mime as well as explanation, Drew said, "It has long puzzled me that you should so blatantly flout all the laws—I used that word in context and do not intend it to be confused with mere convention—the laws, I say, of decent society, and should openly and unashamedly boast of your promiscuity to me."

"You, after all, *are* my own dear brother."

"Some eighteen months ago," Drew went on, remorselessly, "on receiving four such nonsensical epistles in the course of a single month, and a negative report on their veracity, it became obvious to me that you were either mentally deranged or were engaged upon a game so devious that you had succeeded in deluding the best efforts of my clerk, a fellow not easily deceived. Now, Betsy, I know that you are not mad, and I cannot believe that you would torment me simply out of malice. Seeking a purpose behind this wayward mischief-making, and recognising that your deviousness equals my own in many respects, it occurred to me that you might be serving a double function in discharging such a rash of self-condemnatory correspondence."

"Please, Drew, speak plainly."

"Plainly? Very well, if that's what you wish," Drew said. "Plainly, you *were* having affairs. Plainly, you still *are* having affairs. Plainly, you wish to keep me 'primed' in case something misfires and your wickedness is discovered."

Slightly abashed, Betsy said, "I lied. Truly, I lied. I just wanted to see how you'd react. The letters mean nothing."

Drew said, "To give him the benefit of the doubt, Horn may have ignored circumstantial evidence. He may, as is his wont, have sought only positive proof, sifting the chaff of rumour from hard grains of truth."

"Come to the point, for heavens' sake."

"The point is that I can name many of your lovers."

"How silly!"

"I have no servants' testimony, no cab-drivers' depositions, or hotel clerks' statements. The lack of such positive proof only attests to your discretion, Betsy, not your innocence."

"I wish I'd never . . ."

"I wish that too," said Drew. "Most fervently I wish it. However, let me disclose just a few of the facts that I have discovered—concerning Jonathan Douglas, and three 'incidents' at the Haddington Inn, during the autumn of 1894; concerning Mr. Robert Carter, and several assignations at his apartments in Lauriston Place, not a quarter of a mile from here, during his residence in Edinburgh in the early spring of 1893."

"I . . . I've never *heard* of these gentlemen."

"Come now, Betsy, it was I who introduced you to Carter in the first place, at dinner in my house in the January term."

"Oh, that Mr. Carter?"

"Yes, *that* Mr. Carter."

"But you don't suppose that I would . . . ?"

"Have you also conveniently forgotten Ainslie Whitesmith, James Younger, Ronald Baker, and Crawford McColl?"

"Drew, you don't *understand!*"

"I understand that Fraser is my friend as well as my brother-in-law; that my dear nieces—your children, Betsy—are not deserving of a mother who is worse than a street whore in satisfying her degraded appetite for sexual congress."

"How dare you talk to . . ."

"I assume that you are still rational enough to recognise the dreadful risks you run in conducting these sordid affairs. You must be only too well aware that the slightest hint of adultery to any of the Pearsehill McAlmonds, or to Fraser himself, will ruin not only you but me."

"That . . . that's why I wrote to you, Drew."

"To warn me?" Drew demanded. "I don't believe you."

Blue eyes swam with tears. A corner of her turban had

worked loose and now pathetically draped her forehead. The glass perfume rod tinkled to the table top. In an instant, before Drew could prevent it, Betsy had flung herself from the stool to the carpet at her brother's feet.

The Advocate was completely taken aback by the astonishing transformation in his sister. He had supposed that she would remain brazen and defiant to the last. Now, suddenly, she was sprawled on the floor in a most unseemly position, clutching at his knees, her small hand seeking his large hand.

Drew rocked back; he detested physical contact of any sort. But her anguish softened him. Tentatively and jerkily he stroked her arm.

"Why *did* you tell me, Betsy?" He had already formulated an answer, on the evidence of her despairing contrition.

"To *force* you to help me, Drew. To bring you here as you have come tonight, to berate me, *to make me stop*."

Gently, he asked, "Why? Tell me *why* you risked so much for so little?"

"I . . . I don't know. I was a fool."

"Yes," Drew agreed. "You were. And what of the future?"

"It's over. I swear it's over. You haven't let me down, Drew. I knew you wouldn't fail me."

"And this letter—the one you sent today—to whom does it refer?"

"Nobody."

"Betsy?"

"Nobody that you know, I swear. Nobody of the least consequence."

"Have you . . . have you committed 'an act' with this fellow?"

"No, Drew. No."

"I must have the truth."

"It is the truth."

"Yet you gaily threaten to trot off to London with him."

"Only to, to sting you into helping me."

"You could have had my help at any time, for the asking."

"How *could* I, Drew? How *could* I bring myself to confess to you face-to-face . . ."

"Instead you devised this cruel game."

"I did not mean to distress you so."

Rackingly she wept again clinging to his knees, much to his embarrassment. At length, as tenderly as possible, Drew detached her arms, lifted her head from his lap and got to his feet. He hoisted her up by the wrists. Her head hung in shame, cheeks flushed with remorse.

"There must be no more of it," he told her gruffly. "No more liaisons of any kind; no more ridiculous letters to me."

"I'm sorry. I'm sorry."

"We have far too much to lose. Do you want to wind up back in that town, with those people?"

She knew what he meant. There was no need to be explicit. It was the ultimate threat, reminder of how far they had climbed together and how slippery was the slope that might carry them back to Blacklaw.

"No," she sobbed. "That's the last thing I want."

"Then I will say nothing to anyone on this occasion," Drew promised her. "I'll give you this, you've been more discreet than I would have believed possible, Betsy."

"How did, did you . . . ?"

"I guessed," Drew said, smugly. "I have no real evidence apart from the dates of your letters, and a knowledge of the type of man that you might decide was suitable. However, I'm glad that it's out in the open, that you have told me everything. No more of it. Do you swear?"

"I swear."

"And this current chap; no more of him?"

"Oh, no, no more of him," Betsy said.

"Then mop your eyes and wash your face. I'll send in your Frenchie in a few minutes to help you dress."

"Oh, Drew, my dearest. I don't know what I'd do without you."

Disentangling himself, Drew struck a paternal pose, flabby chin tucked into his collar, hands crossed behind his back. "Now, now," he muttered. "That's enough, quite enough."

Standing on toetip, Betsy rewarded him for his understanding by kissing him on the brow, cheek and chin. He really believed that *she* was relieved to have discharged herself of the truth. Certainly *he* was relieved that no permanent harm had been done to his reputation by her folly.

When Drew departed, leaving her to repair the damage wrought by the performance, Betsy smiled at her reflection in the gilded mirror then winked, reverting to the forward little counterhand of twenty years back, to the girl she'd been when she'd selected her first lover from Dalzells' Emporium's wealthy customers. She had come close to falling in love with that gentleman. But she had been too hungry for advancement in those days to toss her heart away, too eager to reach her goal of a position in Edinburgh society. Now, having achieved that pinnacle, she was bored with the summit and, being bored, was vulnerable. Last autumn, almost in spite of herself, she had fallen deeply in love. Only prudence and guile had kept her free from ridicule, and had maintained her unblemished position, and her lover's, in capital society.

Drew was really the major threat. It had been her lover's idea to continue to confuse Drew. The strategy gave every appearance of having had the desired effect. For all his reputation for winkling the truth from practised liars, it seemed that Advocate Stalker had been thoroughly hoodwinked by his sister's act. As she dabbed Aimant's Peach Blossom powder on her nose, Betsy giggled. It might be possible, one day, to tell her brother how he had been deceived and—more to the point —to divulge the name of the man who had planned the duplicity. If ever that day came, Betsy thought, Drew would drop with apoplexy; or, and the thought sobered her just a little, strike her dead on the spot.

Adultery was bad enough in her brother's book; adultery between his sister and a fellow advocate would be the worst sin imaginable. No, Betsy decided, her brother must never discover the source of the fire beneath the smoke. Fire was one element that Drew could not be expected to handle with equanimity.

At ten minutes to eight o'clock, Mrs. Elizabeth McAlmond descended the beautifully curved staircase into the main hallway of her house in view of the guests assembled in the reception room. She was flattered when her husband gave her applause, more flattered still when her brother joined in the ovation. She was most flattered of all however, by the quiet conspiratorial smile on her lover's face when he wished her a formal good evening, a smile that assured her that her ardour had, at long last, found its match.

*　　*　　*

Blacklaw's new Cooperative Society hall already bore the scars of five riotous weddings, ten Lodge concerts and a dozen mass meetings. The management had posted notices to the effect that 'All Damage Must be Paid for', 'Spitting is Forbidden', and 'Alcoholic Beveridges are not to be Consumed on the Premises', injunctions endorsed by the presence of stewards who, that Wednesday night, paraded among the wooden benches and did their best to protect the fabric.

"Here you, McGuigan; lie off the wall."

"Get your bloody pit boots down from the seat."

"Come down from that ledge."

But the Co-op representatives, minor figures in the panoply of authority, only provided targets for the miners' rough humour.

The Stalker lads, Neill and Edward, arrived early. They had switched shifts for the event. Indeed it was a thin night crew that had gone below, many colliers having ignored Thrush's warning that 'any fit man not signing on for work on the evening of January 11th will be suspended for the period of one week'. It was seriously doubted if Thrush would uphold his threat, though he might pick a dozen or so names at random to stand as an example. Solidarity was the watchword, however, and the meeting promised to be one that no conscientious collier could afford to miss.

On the platform at the end of the hall, were three chairs and a table draped with green cloth. A water jug, three glasses and a sickly fern in a blue pot stood on the table. At eight o'clock exactly, Pat Marshall and Dick Thoms lead the guest of honour through from the room at the back. To thunderous cheers, handclapping and piercing whistles, the three men climbed onto the deck.

Though he had been the prime mover in persuading Leslie Dutton to visit Lanarkshire, Rob Ewing was not in evidence. Since his wife's death, Rob had thrown himself into the colliers' struggle with bitter, vengeful cunning. Not for Rob heated demonstrations at colliery gates, impromptu assemblies in the Lantern's yard, half bricks pitched through the windows of manager's offices. Schoolboy retaliation was a thing of the past, wide open defiance of punitive work systems something to be avoided. The rowdiest of Blacklaw's militants had been 'eased out'—a euphemistic phrase meaning that they had been paid off by the management. Though outspoken in his youth, Rob had learned the wisdom of fighting the system from within. Now he kept a public profile so low that even the wily Thrush could not invent a plausible excuse to discharge him.

Discreetly arranged by Ewing and funded from the district 'contingency chest', Dutton's visit was intended to bring speedy consolidation of Blacklaw's miners and prime them to support the imminent national strike through hell and high water.

Rob was present, of course. He stood quietly at the back of the crowded hall, arms folded across his chest, heavy-set, thick jowled, his skin coarse and pitted. Though he wore a tight shiny blue suit, and a tie was screwed into the collar of his shirt, he looked brutish. Hatred for the coalmaster and his toadying managers, Thrush in particular, seeped out of Rob's pores like the rank odour of sweat.

Pat Marshall got to his feet, glanced from the platform, found Ewing's eye, received a terse nod and raised his hand for silence.

"Are we, are we ready t' begin, my friends?"

The hubbub was slow to subside.

Pat shouted, "Brothers, gentlemen, please; have a wee bit of respect for our guest."

The noise dwindled into expectant silence.

Only when he had total attention, did Marshall say, "I'd be grateful if all doors were locked."

Rob had told him to say that. The gesture of secrecy drew the miners together.

Marshall said, "Without more ado, friends, I'd like you t'give a real Blacklaw welcome t' Mr. Leslie Dutton of the United Federation of Mineworkers. Mr. Dutton, as most of you know, is Chief General Secretary of the U.F.M., an' a very busy man. I'm sure I speak for all of you when I say how grateful we are t'him for givin' up his time t'journey here from London t'speak t'us t'night."

Marshall sat down. Leslie Dutton got to his feet.

The applause was respectful, if a shade restrained. Dutton was an Englishman, and Blacklaw lads were suspicious of the English; in addition, they were a little put out by Dutton's appearance. He was a sleek fellow, dressed in a style usually associated with higher ranks of management—dark suit, pin-collar, shoes instead of boots. When he spoke his accent was an unfamiliar brogue sanded to a strange mincing tone.

For the first seven or eight minutes Dutton outlined the victory of the English miners in the great lock-out of August, '95 and the final triumph of the passing of the Eight-Hours Bill. "Unity, the reduction of the individual's role to make it subservient to that of the mass, that was our principal weapon, that was what gained us our triumph. An army that fights on a divided front is an army that fails. You've seen that 'ere, chaps, in Scotland. I'm sure you 'ave."

"We've seen it; aye, an' experienced it," somebody shouted from the body of the hall. He was backed by a roar of agreement.

Dutton's oratory, like the man, was sly and persuasive. At least he had their attention now.

"Pits that took the fight as personal and tried to go it alone— we don't know what 'appened to them."

There was bewilderment at this statement.

Stretching his neck, his white face mean and vicious, Dutton called out, "But we can guess, can't we?"

"*Aye: aye, we can guess.*"

"They were *made* to retreat, to turn against each other. *Management skulduggery*, that's what done it."

More angry shouts of agreement.

Dutton did not raise his voice, though he picked up the tempo now, pronouncing each word precisely. "You know without being told what 'appened in East Fife, in pits not a day's tramp from 'ere. Redundancies, cut-backs, sackings. The bosses went through the paysheets with a curry-comb." He hesitated, then punched out the question, "*And. For. What?*"

Intelligible answers were swallowed up in a mighty stamping

of feet, a clamour so loud that it seemed as if it might lift the roof off the new hall.

Dutton raised his hands in a gesture that they all understood, a messianic pose that, of all the muscular orators they had seen, Dutton was judged to do best.

"I'll tell you for why," he shouted, loud and crisp. "Because men wanted a living wage. *A. Living. Wage.*"

He let them shout back at him, leap up, thud their fists on the benches. It was not a phrase that Dutton would have used of his own accord; Ewing had fed it to him. In spite of its banality, it seemed to have the desired effect.

"*Better conditions. Job Security. The stranglehold of the owners and their bloody lickspittles, broken.*" For a minute or so Dutton felt himself lifted by the colliers' response to his clichés, then pulled himself together. Ewing hadn't invited him just to make another stirring speech. "In England, in some districts, we achieved our demands. In England. In some places. But in others, where there was calculated division, we failed. *Are you Scotch lads not better than the English?*"

"That we are. We'll show the bastards."

"We're the wee boys."

"We'll not crack."

He had them in the palm of his white hand now. He kept them aloft with rallying calls and promises, Nationalism and old saws. But in between, they listened as he fed them facts, less pallatable, perhaps, requiring intelligence as well as gut response. He told them how the power structure operated, spoke of organisations, opposing factions and legislation open to every man with a vote. He ran them through a rogues' gallery of parliamentary opponents and their heroic counterparts within the union movement. At the end of an hour-long address, he concluded, "Applications for affiliations to the United Federation of Mineworkers are pouring in from all over Great Britain, including Scotland. It's the considered opinion of the executives that all districts in Scotland should band together into one home federation, so that affiliation could be granted them under their own leaders. Nothing is to be gained by holding back. Nothing is to be won by disunity. We—Englishmen, Welshmen and Scots—must act in unity against the greater divisions in the society in which we live, endeavouring to bridge the gulf between profit-hungry classes and slaves. Slaves? Yes, slaves some of us are, and slaves we will all remain, unless we fight the bosses with their own weapons—the weapons of unity, law, organisation, and solidarity."

Dutton sat down in a storm of approval. He had moved them. He had appealed to their nationalism and flattered them by seeming to address them as intelligent individuals.

For the next hour the meeting was given over to questions, to vociferous requests for more information on the benefits Blacklaw colliers might receive in future dealings with employers, Lamont in particular. Briefed in advance, Dutton impressed them with his knowledge of the history and current state of Blacklaw pits, and his acquaintance with Lamont's foibles as an employer.

Shortly after ten-thirty, the meeting was adjourned. Colliers crowded round the exit doors. Neill and Edward Stalker loitered on the bench, discussing the relevance of the speech to their own youthful predicament.

Neill said, "For my money, he spoke a lot o'sense. I can't understand why we never got ourselves t'gether before, here in Blacklaw."

Edward said, "Ach, we all like t'be cock o'the walk on our own middens. When managements swell up an' get over-large they collapse. Happens t'unions too, I suppose."

Neill frowned. "What the hell d'you mean, Edward?"

Edward said, "Dutton doesn't have the look of a collier t'me."

"They can't all be as good lookin' as us," said Neill.

"Sure, Dutton's got brains. But *he's* up there, 'an *we're* down here. When we're crawlin' along the seam t'morrow he'll be dinin' in some posh hotel—just like a coalmaster."

"Stop moanin'." Neill dug his cousin in the ribs. "Somebody's got t'pass the word. I'll bet Dutton's done his time at the face."

"I don't doubt it," Edward said. "All I'm sayin' is that it's interestin' t'learn that there's different classes o'colliers too."

"God, you're like an old woman, bletherin' away." Neill did not take the point behind Edward's observations. "See, yonder's

Rob Ewing. Ask him. He'll explain it t'you in one syllable."

"Not him," said Edward. "He'll be away back t'the parlour in the Lantern wi' the toffs."

"Toffs?" Neil shouted. "Come on! Y'can hardly class Dutton as a toff. Anyhow, it doesn't look t'me like Rob Ewing's goin' anywhere."

To the boys' surprise, Rob pushed himself away from the wall as they approached the tail of the queue. "What did you think of it, lads?"

"Grand," Neill's eyes shone with pilgrim enthusiasm. "Grand."

"An' you, Edward?"

"He's got reservations," Neill said, before Edward could answer. "He didn't like it 'cause Dutton wore a collar an' tie."

Rob nodded. "Rather have him flung out o'hotels because he wore black overalls?"

"Well . . ." Edward shrugged.

"Bein' respectably dressed isn't treachery," Rob declared. "Anyhow, the way Mr. Dutton looks has nothin' t'do with the way he performs or what he says."

"Just what I told him," put in Neill, vindicated.

"What about Dutton's concept o' affiliation?" said Rob. "D'you approve?"

"It's the only course open to us," Edward admitted.

"Good." Rob put his scarred hands on the boys' shoulders and steered them through the corridor into the cold street.

Knots of miners hung about, buzzing with speculation over the Englishman's speech. Rob grunted in reply to acknowledgments as he strolled past. At any moment the young Stalkers expected him to break from their company. But he did not. He continued to walk with him, a hand on each of their shoulders, until they were clear of the hall and on the corner of Main Street.

Edward said, "When it's all set up, this Scottish Union Committee, you'll have a place on it, will y'not, Rob?"

Rob shook his head. "Not me."

"We thought you'd put in for the job o' District Representative," Neill said, ingenuously.

"Maybe I'll accept a delegate seat. But I'm not even sure I

want that," Rob said. "I see you've been discussin' the matter between you?"

"Well . . . aye," Neill admitted.

Shrewdly, Edward held his tongue. Three years older than his cousin, he was less easily swayed. In Ewing's withdrawnness he recognised a kind of ambition that was not entirely honourable. Neill was more emotional in his response. In Rob Ewing he saw not only a self-effacing leader, but also a man who had sacrificed personal happiness. He pitied Rob, with his haggard face and unsmiling eyes, threadbare jacket and patched trousers, his empty house.

Impulsively, Neill said, "Come on back t' the Square, Rob, for a bite o'supper."

"No, no," Rob protested. "I . . . can't."

Edward said, "Have you a meetin' arranged wi' Mr. Dutton?"

"Dutton's been on his feet since Sunday," Rob said. "He's probably in his bed by now."

"Come on, then," Edward said. "Kate and m'Ma will be glad t'see you."

"If you're sure it'll not put them out," Rob said, reluctantly, and allowed the Stalker lads to lead him down the short slope of upper Main Street and into Kellock's Square.

*　　*　　*

Kate was alone in the big kitchen when the boys clattered in. She viewed the unexpected visitor with surprise and, perhaps, apprehension. Close friends at one time, changing circumstances had opened a gulf between them. She could barely recall when she had last had prolonged conversation with Rob Ewing. He had been so withdrawn, so strangely defensive, that even Kate did not dare invade his privacy.

"Good evening, Rob," she said, quietly.

"I told him you'd be glad t'see him," said Neill.

"Rob's always welcome here."

Edward peeped through the half-open door into the bakehouse. "Where's Ma, Gran, an' Willie?"

"Gone t'their beds," said Kate. "You pair may not realise it, but its pushin' eleven o'clock."

"Och, the night," Neill announced, sitting himself in his grandmother's chair and propping his heels on the hob, "is' young. Pull up a chair, Rob. Edward an' me are just burstin' with questions."

"You'll be burstin' with a clip in the lug if you don't take your hoofs off the stove an' wash your hands before I serve supper," said Kate. "You too, Edward."

"Wash, wash, wash," Neill said. "You'd think we were dirty tinks, the way y'go on about washin', Mam."

"Do as your mother says," Rob told them; he glanced at Kate. For a moment there was a hint of the old humour in his eye. "You'll be wantin' me t'scrub myself too, like as not?"

"Visitors are excused," Kate said.

Obeying the 'sanitary code', the young men trouped off to Neill's room to find jug and basin. The instant they had gone, Rob said, "I'll not be stayin', Kate."

"Why ever not?"

"I just dropped in t'see how you all were."

"Well enough," Kate said.

She wondered if he had sensed her wariness, if that was the reason for his hasty departure.

She said, "Did the man from London turn up?"

"Aye," Rob said.

"An' the meetin' was successful?"

"Oh, aye." His tone was defensive.

Kate said, "Why won't you stay, Rob? What have we done t' annoy you?"

"I just don't feel like talkin' politics," Rob said. "Not in this house."

"This house?" said Kate. "I thought Neill an' Edward were staunch supporters o' the union cause."

"It's not the lads," Rob said. "It's you."

Kate nodded. She infused tea into the pot but did not take it to the table, putting it instead on the edge of the range to keep warm. She had known all along that Rob did not approve of her indifference to the colliers' struggle. Perhaps he equated the signs of comfortable affluence in this house with aims and principles that smacked too much of the capitalist ethic. The boys—well, they were still fair game, Kate supposed, being colliers, Stalkers, and young.

She tested him out. "I assume y'mean that we don't encourage them enough; Neill and Edward?"

"From what I hear, you're never done runnin' down me an' my objectives."

"Not you, Rob; there's never an ill word said in this house against old friends."

"Not even by your Mirrin?"

"Not in my presence."

"Or . . . or Lily?"

Aye, Kate thought, Rob would not have been so quick off his mark if Lily had still been up. Of them all, Lily was the only one who spoke up in favour of militancy. Lily had a soft spot for Mr. Rob Ewing.

Kate said, "I've been hearin' promises all my life, Rob; bosses' promises, and promises o' union men. I just can't set any store by them now. Besides, what good will it do for Blacklaw miners t'be tied t'the coat-tails o' a bunch of English radicals?"

"Not tied—united," Rob said, sourly.

"I may not say much about all this," Kate told him, "but I do keep abreast o'what's goin' on. When the almighty Federation starts layin' down the law to coalmasters about standard wages an' basic conditions, sooner or later your high ideals are goin' t'be reduced by bargaining and concessions. It doesn't need a fortune-teller t'predict where that will leave the workin' miner."

She had not intended to be so outspoken, or so harsh. It was true what he said, to a point. Politics could not be ignored in any Stalker residence. She had inherited the curse of concern from her father and brothers.

Rob shifted awkwardly to the door.

"I'd better go," he said.

"Stay, if you like."

"No."

"Well, Rob, let me ask you one last question."

"What?"

"If short-time redundancies *are* t'be the order o' the day, are they likelier t' be imposed on colliers in England, or in Blacklaw?"

"That's a trick question Kate, and not worthy o'you."

"Meanin' you can't answer?"

"Not . . . not in a word."

Neill came bustling back into the kitchen, hair plastered down over his temples, water dripping from the lobes of his ears. He was amicable and eager as a puppy. But he stopped at once by the door, grin crimping into a frown, as he saw his mother and Rob Ewing engrossed in an apparently bitter quarrel.

Kate said, "I want you t'keep them out o'it, Rob."

"Who?" he asked, jeeringly. "The colliers?"

"Neill . . ."

"Mam, don't say . . ." the young man murmured.

". . . an' Edward."

"They're big lads; old enough t' have minds o' their own," Rob said.

"Please Rob," Kate begged.

"I'm doin' nothin' t'harm them."

"Rob, don't listen t' . . ." Neill tried to interrupt.

"I *know* what drives you, Rob," Kate said. "Is that why you're so shy o'callin' at this house—because you know that I can see right through you?"

"What drives me is . . ." Rob began.

"Hatred," Kate said. "Hatred for Houston Lamont."

"I suppose you'd have me lick the bastard's boots," Rob snapped, "like you Stalkers did."

At that second, Edward stepped into the kitchen. Jaw gaping, eyes popping with amazement, Neill held his cousin back with his shoulder.

"You shouldn't have said that, Rob." Kate spoke in a whisper.

"I'll take nothin' back."

"Then you'd better go."

"Right." Deliberately he hesitated, peering past Kate's flushed face to the young men by the door. "I'll see you two tomorrow."

"Aye, Rob," Neill answered.

Edward said nothing, not meeting Rob's challenge.

The colliers' leader nodded curtly, and went out, closing the yard door behind him. The woman, her son and nephew listened to the sound of his boots stumping away over the cobbles. Kate turned. There were tears in her eyes, though she held them back and kept herself in shadow by the dresser.

"Sit down, you two, if y' want fed."

Subdued, but curious, Neill and Edward made their way to the table and pulled out chairs.

After a couple of minutes of leaden silence, Neill asked, "Mam, what did Rob mean by that—about Stalkers lickin' Lamont's boots?"

"Nothin'," Kate said. "He meant nothin'."

"But Mam . . .?"

"Shut your mouth, daftie," Edward growled.

"But . . .?"

"Rob's just jealous," Edward said.

"Jealous?" said Neill. "Jealous of what?"

"Us," said Edward.

"Aye," said Neill, in sudden comprehension, "I do believe you're right."

Kate clanked a plate of buttered bread onto the table. "I don't want you talkin' about it," she snapped. "Eat your supper an' get off t'bed."

For once there was no rebellion.

As they walked to the pit next afternoon, Neill and Edward would discuss the strange quarrel in confidence between themselves. But that Wednesday night, they had sense enough to let well alone. Perhaps instinct told them that Kate was frightened that harm would come to them, that disaster and hardship would cull the new breed of Blacklaw miner as it had taken its toll of the old.

However, even Kate, for all her experience, could not have guessed that Rob Ewing had already spun the web that would bring her son—Drew's son—into peril of his life.

February

February, when at last it came, was even more inhospitable than January had been. All thought of spring was lost in the icy fields of Hazelrig. Hurley, however, brought home cheerful tales of crocuses and snowdrops braving the blast in the sheltered dells of the Neapolitan and, one dinner time, produced a spray of willow catkins to prove that he and Mother Nature had not lost faith in each other or in the eventual defeat of winter.

For Mirrin it was a grim time; cobbles stippled with snow pellets, mud like pig-iron, and the pump frozen down to its roots, so bad that even Hurley could not free the crank. Falling back on an age-old solution, Malcolm lugged water from a hole axed in the Witchy burn, pail upon pail slopping on the yoke to water the young stock and keep Mirrin's sinks and boilers full. Byres and sheds, stone and timber alike, creaked, and the land creaked too, then, when the frost bit deeper, fell silent, calcified by ice in every sinew.

Thaws were instant things, too brief to give much hope, an hour's wet slick upon the surfaces, a fresh layer of varnish on the one before, set hard as tortoiseshell by dusk. The sheep suffered little for they were hardy beasts and soon learned to eat the oat sheaves strung for them on posts. Sandy kept a weather eye on the lambing ewes, however, streaming the flock past him, for early warning of disease. Some days his father would stand by him, leaning on a carved crook, straining to discern the woolly blurrs or, snaring a ewe, squinting at the parts of her through his steel-rimmed spectacles, and pointing out to the boy what signs to look for. There was no milk now in any of the cows. Calves were mash fed. Morning trips to Blacklaw ceased. Mirrin could no longer contrive a legitimate excuse for them. Two weeks went past with no contact between farm and town, between Mirrin and Kate. Hazelrig seemed isolated, more cut off than any island croft. Malcolm and Sandy took advantage of the dearth of work, and had themselves a jaunt to Hamilton. Kitten had a cough, Davie a wheeze, and Tom, driven further in on himself, veered between black moods and guilty idleness when only food and the warm range comforted him.

One Wednesday, last in the short month, Kate tramped into the yard, bringing a basket of scones and cakes. She did not stay long. Tom was down that afternoon, complaining about the fact that the boys had 'slunk off' to Hamilton once more in search of a bargain bicycle.

But there was news from Kate, disturbing news. The sisters stole a minute in the yard to talk. They were an odd-looking pair of scarecrows in heavy tweed coats, hand-knitted tammies, mile-long scarves twined round their throats and chests and pinned securely at the breast.

Almost as soon as they were alone, Kate said, "You'll have heard the big talk about affiliation with the English Union?"

"Is that still a prime topic?"

"An' likely to remain so," Kate said.

"Is Rob Ewing stirrin' things up?"

"Worse than ever," said Kate.

"We'll it won't last long," Mirrin was largely indifferent to colliers' problems now. "I suppose Willie's worried about the loss of trade if there is a strike."

"D'you think there will be a strike, Mirrin?"

"I'm sure of it. Rob'll not rest happy 'til he's brought Blacklaw grindin' to a halt," Mirrin said. "You know more of what's goin' on that I do, these days."

"But you were always better versed in politics than me," Kate said. "Some things are still beyond my understandin'."

"Aye, daft things," said Mirrin. "Like colliers."

Suddenly Kate blurted out, "I'm frightin'."

"Frightened? But there's no scarcity o' money, is there?

71

I mean, Willie can surely find Neill an' Edward some useful work t'do while the strike lasts. You'll not be desperate for their wages t'put food in your mouths?"

"You an' I learned how t'cope with that sort o'hardship long since," Kate said. "This is different, Mirrin. If there's a strike now, it'll mean fightin'; men bein' maimed, maybe even killed. There were four deaths last year, y'know."

"Aye, I heard; up in Garphinn," said Mirrin "But Edward and Neill are sensible. They'll not be involved."

"Rob Ewing will involve them. He'll involve us all, if he can. Even Lily's worried."

"I thought she was a union sympathiser."

"Och, she pays lip-service t'strike action but, when it comes t'it, she's as worried as I am."

"Look," Mirrin said. "There's nothin' you can do—except trust t'the boys' good sense. They're both Stalkers, an' anythin' but stupid. If there's real fightin', they'll soon make themselves scarce."

"I hope you're right."

"Of course, I'm right," said Mirrin, forcing a grin. "I'm always right."

"Or think you are," said Kate. "But what about Tom? Is he always as surly as that, Mirrin?"

"He's screwin' up his courage t'go int' hospital for another operation. He knows this will be his last hope. He's reluctant t' commit himself in case it fails."

Kate nodded understandingly. "I suppose there's nothin' you can say or do that'll make him hurry his decision?"

"I've done all I can," said Mirrin. "What's more he hates me for it."

"Y'know, Mirrin, if the shoe had been on the other foot," Kate said, "maybe we could have put up with it better; you in Blacklaw, an' me up here."

"Never," Mirrin said. "Whatever happens t'Tom, I'll never regret havin' picked this life."

Kate looked around the yard. "It's too bleak for me," she said. "Though right now I think I'd swop my lot for yours if it would keep Neill out o'Blacklaw colliery."

"What's Lamont doin' about the strike?"

"Watchin', waitin'. He'll make his move when the time comes," Kate said. "Mirrin, do you ever see him now?"

"I haven't so much as clapped an eye on him for years. Strange, isn't it, an' Strathmore lyin' just six miles over the hill. But then Houston's not the sort t'waste his time wanderin' country lanes and fields."

"Do you still think of him fondly, Mirrin?"

"I think of the way he used t'be when there was still hope for him."

"How do you find the gall t'pity the wealthiest man in the county, next t' the Duke himself?"

"Don't forget, Kate, I know what Houston Lamont sacrificed to get that wealth."

"Your—love?"

Mirrin laughed, ruefully. "Not that; that was never worth as much as he thought. No, he was bred to a hard trade. He married a hard wife, and in consequence he had t'be hard too— even if it was contrary to his nature."

"He's hard now, all right."

"I wonder," said Mirrin.

She was still thinking about Houston Lamont after Kate left, hurrying to get back to the warmth of her own kitchen before dusk and bone-gnawing cold came down from the east. Besides, Kate knew if she was still at Hazelrig when Kitten and Davie returned from school she would be stuck there all evening. Kitten would not let her go, and she could refuse the pretty wee girl nothing, being as soft an auntie as she was firm a mother.

So Kate went. And Tom came out of the house, wrapped up well. Unasked, he replenished the cribs with hay and helped Hurley quarter turnips for the sheep. Just before nightfall Kitten and Davie returned from school. Mirrin gave them hot broth to warm them, and let them help her prepare tea to keep them occupied and out of the yard. Then it was Malcolm and Sandy stalking in from Hamilton, having caught the bus along the main road and hoofed it up from Crosstrees. Though the bicycle hunt had not been successful they were full of high spirits. Tom shouted and generally let them know what he thought of such gallivanting when there was a farm to be run,

shouting that he was still the gaffer and they were employed
hands. Was he paying them so damned much that they could
flit off to squander money on any toy that took their fancy?
He was still grumbling when the family sat down to eat.

And the cold came down; worse that night, Sandy said.
Anxious about the cats, Hurley went away to the bothy as
soon as he had cleared the last scrap of suet pudding from
the dish. He would stoke up his stove and make the place
ready to accommodate every feline in the county that needed a
warm bed. Tom continued to grumble, focusing his ill-
temper on Hurley now. He muttered about that dirty stinkin'
useless cratur and talked about payin' the halfwit off come the
end o'the term. Nobody took him seriously. Hurley was more
needed now that ever, if Hazelrig was to be kept up to the best
mark. Then, growling and complaining, Tom settled into his
chair by the fire, reached for his tobacco tin and, with paper
and shag held up to his eyes, rolled a thin brown cigarette
for himself, smoked it, and fell asleep.

Mirrin put the children to bed; Kitten first, dreamy,
dawdling Davie next, while Malcolm and Sandy took a turn
about the outbuildings with a lantern apiece, checking, in
particular, the hen-run since this hungry weather drove foxes
from the woods and made them daring.

Finally, shortly after nine, Mirrin found herself alone in the
kitchen with her snoring husband.

The fire had burned hard on the inside of the grate, leaving
a crust of dross stretched across the bars. When at last the
dross caved in, a shower of crackling sparks flew upwards,
wakening Tom with a start.

Hands balling into fists on the arms of the chair, he jerked
bolt upright. "What is it? What's that?"

"Only the fire, Tom," Mirrin said. "It's all right."

"What time is it?"

"Close to ten o'clock."

She went to him, kneeling by the chair, and closed her
fingers on his fist. "Did y'have a bad dream, Tom?"

"No. I just . . ." He hesitated. "The only time I see things
clear is when I shut my eyes. Now isn't that damned funny?"

"An' what do y' see?"

His fingers slackened. Mirrin twined them in her own, shifting her breast against his knees. He sighed and relaxed into the cushions.

"Tell me, Tom, what d'you see so clearly?" she coaxed.

"Us."

"Go on."

"In the fields, in Ayrshire, when we were young. I can see the Arran mountains so vivid, green forests and shadows thick as paint, so that if y'could just reach out across the sea you could bring off the colours on your palm, still wet an' sticky-like."

"What else?"

Spectacles slipping on his nose, he frowned, staring at the grate, at the hot whorls of the coals. The image was often fragmented, so he had explained in an effort to make her understand his disease, into a diffuse mosaic of colours.

"I was remembering a beach at Valparaiso, where I went when I was at sea. I came up from below at dawn, an' there it was; the colours . . ." He laughed, softly, for the first time in months. "I can't tell y'what they were like." His hand shifted from her grasp and touched her hair. "Are y'tired, Mirrin?"

"A bit."

"Talk t'me; not about my damned eyes. Talk about somethin' else."

"The tinkers came through Crosstrees on Sunday," Mirrin said.

"Which tribe?"

"Patersons," Mirrin said. "They were in a bad way. The laird let them put up two nights in his nice new barn at Ingleford."

"They must've been in a sorry state indeed for the laird t'do that."

"They've moved on t'Glasgow, I hear."

"Aye, it's the frost," said Tom. "It's lasted too long."

"There was only a dozen o'them. But, I heard they had three sick bairns."

"Aye."

"D'you ever miss the road, Tom?"

"Never."

75

"I thought y'did."

"I miss bein' young," he said. "You loved me then, flower, didn't you?"

"I love you more now," Mirrin said.

"You're just sayin' that."

"I mean it."

For a moment she thought she had somehow offended him, that his mood was about to pendulum again, that he was about to push her away as if suspecting her of deception, of loving not him but the ghost of the man he was. Instead, he chuckled and lifted her onto his knees.

"By God, Mirrin, you're not as light as y'were twenty years ago."

"Aye, but there's more of you t'sit on," Mirrin said.

He closed his arms about her. His fingers traced the outline of her cheek and brows down to her lips.

She pressed closer against him.

After a minute, not speaking, she lead him across the kitchen into the bedroom under the stairs. Later she would return to smoor the coals, fix the fire-guard and set out oatmeal to steep for the morning. Now, though, she would not break this spell of tenderness.

Imprisoned so long within himself, tortured by pain, loneliness and dread, Tom's passion expanded into a frenzy that at first roused similar responses in Mirrin. He clung to her desperately, caressing her naked body in the ice-cold room then, fumbling off his own clothing, pulled her roughly into bed. Huddling close to her, with unusual greed he took her suddenly. He burrowed his face into her breasts, fingers knotted in her thick hair. Their intercourse was completed without endearment.

Once he had told her that blindness was the quietest disease of all; it disturbed no one by its coming. In the darkness of the cold bedroom, sight or the lack of it did not matter. Mirrin would have welcomed a sign of tender hesitation to tone the passion down, to bring them together as once they had been together, humorously, playfully, with lust a pleasure shared and loving more than the fulfilment of needs that could not be fulfilled, in bed or out of it, by man and woman.

Gradually, Tom's arms loosened about her. His weight shifted. He did not break contact with her body, though, and held himself against her, trapping warmth between them, his face against her hair.

"Is that what y'wanted?" he asked.

"Uh?"

"Is that what y'needed? Aye, I don't need eyes for that, do I?"

"Tom. No."

"You'll not need t'look elsewhere, not for that anyhow."

"*Tom.*" She drew herself away from him. Sitting upright against the wooden headboard, the air of the room was like ice on her bare skin.

"Aye," he muttered, lying back and catching the blankets to him, "that's one thing y'can't do for yourself, Mrs. Armstrong, is it not?"

Mirrin covered her face with her forearm, pressing her mouth into the soft flesh to hold back her sobs.

"Is it not?" His hand clutched her thigh.

With every ounce of will in her, she controlled herself, saying, "Aye, Tom."

He chuckled. "So I'm still worth my feed, am I not?"

"Yes, yes."

"Come on down here."

"I . . . I've t'smoor the fire an' put up the guard yet?"

"Do it later."

"I'd best do it now."

"What's wrong?"

"Nothin's wrong," Mirrin said. "I just don't want t'have t'get up again. We . . . we can take our time, next time."

Dragging his hand across her belly, he released her. She slid from the bed, and, pulling a woolen robe from the closet, groped towards the door.

"Mirrin?"

In the light from the half-open door she could see him clearly and, she guessed, he could make her out too. He was propped on his elbow, his face broken into ridges of shadow and pale polished flesh, eye-sockets dark, hair rumpled and feathery. Shoulders, arms and chest were thick with muscle.

Simultaneously, Mirrin experienced desire and a revulsion at the interpretations that he would surely put upon her need of him.

"I'm here, Tom."

"The operation; the new Glasgow doctor; I've been givin' it thought."

She tried not to shout, saying quietly, "An' what have you decided?"

"I've decided t'hell with it."

Expecting remonstration, he paused.

She said nothing at all, though she did not move from the rectangle of light from the door. She felt as if he was spying on her.

He said, "Y'hear me? No more knives. No more drugs, or bloody bandages. I'm blind, an' that's that."

"Is that your decision?"

"It is."

She remained mute.

"Mirrin?"

"I'm here."

"What d'you intend t'do about it?"

"Me?" she said. "I'll do whatever you decide is best Tom."

"I've told you what I've decided."

"I mean the rest of it."

"Rest of what?"

"The rest o'the decisions you'll have t'make now—about the future o'Hazelrig; about Malcolm an' Sandy; Davie, even Kitten. An' about me."

"That's got nothin' t'do with it."

"Are you not still head o'this house?"

"Aye, but . . ."

"But?"

"*I can't see.*"

"You can *think*, though, can't you? So think about us, your wife, your sons, an' the farm that keeps us in bread."

"Mirrin?"

"I'll be back in a minute."

She moved out of the light, passing into and through it to the kitchen. Her skirt still lay by the fire on a bundle of patched undergarments. She picked them up and shook out the goblin-like woollen socks that were standard wear in winter. She put them on.

"Mirrin?"

"I won't be long."

Gently, she closed the bedroom door and clicked the latch. If he wanted her, for any purpose, he must come for her now— and she understood him well enough to question if he would tear himself from bed.

Outside the yard was visible, lit not by moonlight, but by the hoary breath of frost, still falling, still sifting down to bristle roofs and rigs.

She was defeated, beaten, driven too far even for tears.

She extinguished two lamps, trimmed the third and set it on the mantel's edge to shed yellow light around her chair. She raked out, then re-built the fire and, because she was chilled, opened the oven door and shifted the chair to allow her to stick her feet into the side oven. The kettle, with water still in it, she elbowed onto the cooking ring.

Slumped deep in the chair, legs stretched out, feet thawing in the oven, a delicious warmth soon spread up through her. Here she was—Tom Dandy's flower, the Country Rose, Songbird of the North, Mirrin Stalker Armstrong, thickened a little, her fine fair belly marred by stretch-marks and more ample than it was, with her feet stuck in the oven. The scars were nothing, badges of honour, like soldiers wore, aye, and colliers.

When the coal caught and the fire was bright and the kettle purled steam, she made herself cocoa, thick and sweet, in a tall beaker, and sat down again.

It was very quiet. She guessed that Tom had fallen asleep. On the boards upstairs she heard Fleck whimper, the thud-thud of his strong tail, and Malcolm, in a drowsy voice, not even out of sleep, tell the collie, '*Wheesht, lad. Wheeeesht*'. All the tiny noises of the house became hers exclusively, familiar but inconstant.

"Damn the tink," Mirrin sighed. "I'm stuck with him."

And with myself too, she thought.

Maybe that was the worst of it.

Acceptance, not resignation.

About midnight, sleepy at last, she returned to bed.

*   *   *

"Good morning, Houston."

It was the coalmaster's mansion, and the coalmaster's study, but Sydney Thrush had enjoyed the privilege of free access for many years now, though he was careful not to abuse it. Once or twice, he had arrived early enough to test out Lamont's chair, a massive antique that looked—and felt—as if it had been cobbled up from horsecollars. Thrush had savoured briefly not only the throne but the power that went with it as overlord of Blacklaw and all its leases. Though Edith and he were full partners, Houston retained a fifty-one per cent controlling interest in the companies that traded under the Blacklaw Colliery banner.

That Thursday morning, however, Thrush found the coalmaster already in the study. Puffy eyes and the quantity of tobacco smoke in the room attested to the fact that Lamont had been 'at it'—whatever 'it' might be—for hours. A tray with a coffee pot upon it and an empty cup helped set the manager on his guard. Lamont was already halfway through the day.

Thrush had hardly changed. Early in life he had reached a state of middle-age and, finding it comfortable, had settled there. Unlike Drew Stalker, however, Thrush had not been undermined by the stresses of his profession. He relished stress. To him the management of Lamont's enterprises was more vocation than job. He was still as he had been when Lamont first employed him, at Edith's insistence, back in the year 1876—smooth, clean-shaven, with skin like porcelain, and a head as bald as an enamel basin. His manner was less sly— he had learned to disguise that quality rather well—and he was not so unctuous, as he had been then when he had plotted to oust Donald Wyld from the manager's position and tried to wrest ownership from Lamont himself. In that ultimate treachery Sydney Thrush had failed. Only Lamont's urgent need of a man without a shred of conscience had brought him back into the fold.

Going to the hearth, Thrush leaned over the railing and poked up the coals. "God, but it's cold."

"How's the machinery standing up to this frost?" Lamont asked.

"Well, I made a tour this morning, after I got back." Thrush had just returned from his second trip to London within a month. "The cables are showing strain. I've marked a dozen or so for replacement. And, would you believe, the bogie lines have warped, six sections, over in the dump behind Pit Three. Apart from that—all's well."

"I heard there was a problem with the chute dross," said Lamont, who had visited the pitheads regularly in Thrush's absence.

"Frost freezing it solid?" said Thrush.

"What can we do about it?"

"Lard the chutes with crude oil."

"Ah," said Lamont. "Yes."

"Pickers and sorters hate it, of course. But to hell with them. It's better than losing a couple of hours hacking the stuff out every morning."

"What if the oil freezes?"

"We'll run a steam hose down the underside of the chutes; the oil melts and gives us some kind of flow."

Lamont nodded. He hadn't thought of that, nor had his engineers who had come up with a clumsy scheme involving two big traction engines. He gave Thrush no praise. Nor did he offer him refreshment. No doubt Edith would attend to such hospitable gestures as soon as business was concluded.

"What happened in London?" he asked.

"It was not so easy as I had anticipated to acquire further detailed information. My contact was apprehensive."

"Understandably," said Lamont.

"I did, however, obtain something to recompense us for the expense of the trip," Thrush said. "It would appear that the United Federation is no mere ragbag association. An alarming number of Liberals are throwing their political weight behind it."

"Who?"

"Jervision, Edwards, Ray Williams, Scatliff . . ."

"I could have learned that from *The Times*."

"Ah, but did you know, Houston, that the young Baron Waites, Lord Lugton and Harold Ennion are also backing it—with capital? They are highly influential men, as well as very rich. They will, I fear, soon declare themselves, now that the U.F.M. has gained respectability."

Lamont said, "Gamblers, that's all."

"Well, some union negotiations in England proved successful," Thrush reminded the coalmaster. "In the past twenty months, the U.F.M. pressed for and got pay rises totalling forty per cent over the 1888 basis."

"How long did that flush last? By the end of last year the very pits that had supposed themselves to be absolutely secure were fighting tooth and nail for a share of the market. What happened to big wages then?"

"As you say, Houston, but . . ."

"English owners may not have achieved the twenty-five per cent wage cut they wanted. On the other hand, the damned colliers were out of work for seventeen weeks. It remains to be seen just what a Conciliation board will do for them. No, Sydney, the average collier wants *work*, and the average collier, however militant, must be thoroughly well aware that his European brothers are hewing coal more efficiently and more cheaply than he is."

"The Federation blames bad management and under-investment in modern equipment," Thrush reminded him.

"The old whipping-boy. There's no arguing with facts and figures. America, sixteen *million* tons up on Britain in output: Germany, Silesia, France—all up. It's the same tale in steel, pig-iron and wrought-iron."

Thrush made a small humming noise in his nose. It was on the tip of his tongue to remind Lamont that, whatever the output ratios in comparison with foreign fields, the fact remained that profits taken from Scottish pits had grown steadily over the decade and had reached an unprecedented peak in the previous year, due mainly to the great lock-out in England.

"Colliers don't give much thought to figures, Houston.

Besides, the leaders of the U.F.M. have sheaves of facts of their own."

"Did you discover how much backing the Federation has here in Lanarkshire?"

"Enough," said Thrush. "The word is that they can close *all* our pits on twenty-four hours' notice."

"That's just an idle boast."

"Well, I think—actually, perhaps, they can."

"No," Lamont said. "Whatever the Federation might become in future, at present it hasn't the power to threaten us."

"My assessment suggests otherwise."

Competing fiercely for a shrinking slice of the market in spite of the national boom in engineering and metal production, the only course open to any coalmaster who continued to demand high profits, was to reduce wages. Put at its simplest, that was the bone of contention between owners and workers. The owners shouted about 'competition from abroad' and falling output, but the figures, those of them that became public, told a different story, one of profiteering and greed.

"And just what *is* your assessment, Sydney?" asked Lamont.

"I really do think that there will be a strike."

"Balderdash."

"Houston," said Thrush, mildly, "there's seems to be very little purpose in my cultivating high-level 'friends' in the Union if you intend to ignore judgments based on their information."

Lamont rapped his knuckles on the desk. He had been taken to task—rightly, as it happened. He glowered at his manager.

"Very well; what if there is a strike, or a lock-out? It won't last long."

"It lasted seventeen weeks in England," Thrush reminded him.

"It won't last a week here."

"Houston, really!"

"I'd give it a month, at most."

"How long can Blacklaw Collieries stand complete closure of all its pits?" Thrush knew the answer to the day.

"Seven weeks, at most."

"Yes," said Thrush. "Seven weeks, at the *very* most."

"Then we simply cannot allow it to happen."

"I agree we must prevent prolongation of any national strike action," Thrush said. "We must plan to undermine the so-called 'solidarity' that is the Federation's watchword."

"Do you have something in mind?"

"Of course," Thrush said. "For the time being, Houston, I would strongly advise against expansion."

Lamont's head shot up. "You, Thrush, you have always pushed *for* expansion. Opening up the Claypark field was your idea. Draining the old Inchpit field, too; look what that cost us."

"We made our profit," said Thrush. "This is not a *volte face*, Houston. But for the present I recommend caution. We're overextended."

"Fifty bee-hive coke ovens ordered for Carlneuk—again, on your recommendation."

"Carlneuk coal has the best coking properties in Scotland."

"Yes, yes, Thrush, I admit that."

"Houston, as General Manager and a Director of the Blacklaw Colleries Company, I am only too well aware of our commitments. If there is no prolongation of strike action, and no serious interruption to production in our major fields, then we will emerge as one of the most efficient companies in the country. But if there is a shut-down, and if it lasts for any length of time, then either we secure a rapid settlement with U.F.M. leaders—which means backing down from the twenty-five per cent wage reduction agreed by the Coalmasters' Association—or we . . ." He hesisted.

"Say it Thrush."

"We risk going bust."

"That's baldly stated."

"It's a bald fact, Houston."

"And what is the solution?"

"Obviously we endeavour to prevent extended closure."

"I won't capitulate with miners, nor their damned Federation."

"Of course not. We must stand firm," said Thrush. "Might I suggest that, as an emergency measure, taking into account our paucity of immediate financial reserves, we endeavour to call in more capital."

"How much can *you* subscribe?"

"Not much."

"Nor can I; nor can Edith."

"I know, we have all sunk our funds in expansion," said Thrush. "On the other hand, we are a large company now, with many assets. I think it may be desirable to form a limited liability company."

"And give away control of Blacklaw?"

Thrush tutted. "Certainly not. But the scheme has merit, Houston. It doesn't mean that we—you—need sacrifice power. We would require the written acquiescence of the ground landlords. They, I'm sure, would not stand in our way, provided that we, the partners, remained personally liable to implement obligations under the respective leases."

"I'm not for this, Sydney. I'm not for any of it."

"The present situation just proves how vulnerable we are to short-term interruptions. Extending the list of shareholders would buffer us against a strike, and any foreseeable mishaps in the future."

Lamont pursed his lips. "How can we float stock on the eve of a strike threat, in a declining market?"

"The slump in market trading is only temporary."

"Who would be willing to buy stock?"

"A holding in the Blacklaw Company would, I'm sure, prove an attractive proposition."

"What does Edith have to say to all this?"

"I've no idea," said Thrush, innocently. "I haven't spoken with her on the subject. Mrs. Lamont isn't, as you know, an accountant."

Lamont continued to rap his knuckles on the desk for a moment, an impatient, irritable drumming that rattled the ink bottles in their silver frame. Thrush knew that he had come up with a proposal that had caught the owner off guard. That had been his intention.

"Let me leave it with you, Houston," he said.

"I take it that you have compiled a report?"

"Of course," said Thrush. "It's rather rough-hewn, I'm afraid. I prepared it hurriedly during the train journey last night."

Opening his briefcase, he produced a folder of brown card fixed in the left corner with a brass octopus clip. He put it on the blotting-pad directly in front of Lamont.

"How long do we have, Sydney?" Lamont asked.

"No Union action will be taken until the weather warms up. May or later, I would imagine. The executive seem to be gearing for a summer campaign, now that domestic coal sales are less important than they used to be."

"Yes," Lamont said. "That gives us a full quarter to prepare."

"It's not long," said Thrush. "Not if we decide to float a block of shares, as a precaution."

"Come tomorrow," Lamont said. "Tomorrow evening, I'll give you my decision."

"Certainly, Houston." Thrush lifted his briefcase and made his way to the door. "I assume that you will inform your wife of my proposals?"

"Yes." Lamont was already engrossed in the contents of the brown card file. "I'll inform her."

Thrush said good-morning. He received no reply.

Closing the heavy oak door behind him, he left the coalmaster to wrestle with this latest problem, the result of a year's careful planning on the manager's part. Lamont was old now. He did not look it, perhaps, but his brain was not so agile as it had once been. Radical expansion of the Blacklaw Company must be made to seem inevitable, not a loss, but a gain, to Houston Lamont. The first broad financial outline, clipped in the brown file, had been doctored to lay the foundation to that end. The strike, when it came, would surely clinch matters.

Jauntily, Thrush crossed the hall and entered Edith's domain, the huge sequestered morning-room that overlooked the rolling lawns of the east gardens, sugared now with crystals of unmelted frost. A cheery fire burned high in the grate under a decorated mantelpiece. The light from the many tall windows seemed pleasantly coloured by the flames.

Edith looked attractive in her tailored costume, skirt close to her figure and flared at her ankles, calf shoes, round-toed, peeping out. Her hair was brushed back in a Greek-style coil. The tint of it seemed even darker than he remembered. She was smiling at him in a most welcoming manner and had the tall silver teapot in her hand, ready to pour at his command.

"Tea, Sydney?" she asked, as soon as he entered the room.

"Indeed, indeed; yes."

"You must be famished."

"Indeed, indeed, yes, I am." He behaved like a suitor of twenty when he was alone with Edith Lamont; a little bit of a pose, actually. She enjoyed it and, to be perfectly honest, he enjoyed her reciprocal posings, girlish and, in terms of any sort of final romantic consummation, ridiculous. This, however, was the relationship they had built for themselves on a bedrock of mutual ambition, and it proved highly satisfactory to both parties.

She gestured at the silver cakestand, though it was early in the day for its appearance. Individual trays held a selection of custard and icing pastries, a weakness of Thrush's almost amounting to a vice. Thrush seated himself on the edge of the tub chair in front of the hearth.

Edith poured tea into a china cup, added a precise measure of milk and a generous helping of sugar, even stirred it for him and held out cup and saucer.

Their eyes met across the little table.

"Did you put it to him, dear?" the woman asked.

"I did."

"And?"

"I do believe," said Thrush, "that he'll agree to it."

"Sell stock, you mean?"

"Of course," said Thrush. "To be sure, if there's a strike he'll have to."

"And we will buy it back through the fellow in Glasgow."

Thrush glanced quickly at the morning-room door then, reaching, lightly patted Edith on the cheek. "Quite right, my love."

"Sydney, dare I say it?"

"Permit me to say it for you; in a year or less, we will control Blacklaw Collieries."

"You and I?"

"Just you and I, together."

"And Houston?"

"Houston," Thrush told her, patting her cheek again, "will

be in no sort of position to argue. Thereafter he must do exactly as we dictate."

Edith giggled, and offered the manager the cakestand intact. "Have a pastry, my dear."

"Thank you, Edith," he said. "I do believe I will."

*　　*　　*

Veering to the south, the wind increased in volume over Friday night and, by dawn, blew warm. Gradually the ground unlocked its odours, a pot-pourri of decaying leaves and dung, spiced with a green hint of growth for, even on that first morning of the thaw, seeds and tubers stirred in the sleeping soil.

By noon, with the sun warm upon the fields, the land ran with surface water. The burns shed ice, and loose ice tinkled and chuckled in drains and ditches. A heron stalked the pool of the Witchy burn, scaring the ducks. Sensing spring, the cattle lowed and bellowed and were thrawn until Hurley lead them to the pond to drink. The pump belched water of its own accord, and Mirrin, sleeves rolled up and arms red, attacked the mound of dirty wash that had accumulated during the stiff six weeks' frost. Soon the lines were bent with flapping linen, pants and knickers dancing skittishly with socks and shirts, big white bedsheets cracking like mainsails above the glistening grass of the drying green.

Cats coiled sensuously on the cobblestones. Sheep grazed in broken ranks, heads down, shadows short and passive as they nibbled the wisps across the breadth of the home pasture. Hurley and Sandy mucked out the byre and swept the sheds. Inspired by the weather, Malcolm took Clay and Pharaoh and the heavy plough out to the rigs to do the best he could with the last length of deep ploughing. Davie, the dreamer, with a little spade, scraped the hen roost and Kitten, clothes pegs in her mouth, hung handkerchiefs on a low rope strung between apple trees. Dinner was a bowl of soup and hunks of bread and cheese, then it was out again for all of them, bar Tom, to take advantage of the sun.

Lost amid the quickening pace of farm work, Tom sulked in his chair and barked at Mirrin as she heaved tubs and scrubbing boards and cargoes of hot water about. She was too preoccupied to take much notice of his complaints, however, and whistled and sang jaunty songs as she worked. At dinner break Malcolm sought his Da's advice on ploughing style. But Tom was mad that the lad had even tackled it and gave him the rough edge of his tongue, so that Malcolm went back to the three-mile field, shaking his head sadly.

It was coming on towards that ten-minute spell when day changes into dusk, when Tom emerged from the house and, with the long crook tapping, pecked his way clear of the fank and set off across the downward slope of the apple garth towards the path to the ploughing field. Once clear of the buildings, he walked faster, touching the posts now and then with the crook, not to guide him, but merely as a gesture, practice perhaps for that day when the aqueous fluid would drown his sight completely.

He had gone a dozen paces or so onto the path when he heard her calling, her voice lifted hopefully, gladly. Since he was never cruel to her, he stopped and looked back.

"Kitten?"

"Where are y'goin', Daddy?"

"Out t'the ploughin'."

"Can I come?"

He hesitated. He thought that he could make out the blot of her bright blue coat against the fence, but the colours blurred that brilliant evening, for the sun was westering low, beams slanting across his spectacles.

"Please, Daddy?"

"Aye, come on then."

She would slip through the fence, quick as a wee rabbit. He could make out the movement of blue, then saw her for a moment as she swam through tongues of shadow cast by the apple trees, saw her quite clearly, oddly undistorted. He felt pain in his eyes, stabbing, put there of a sudden by that other greater pain as he realised what pleasure he would lose in not being able to see her at all. He would never see her grown, or half grown, transformed from child into girl, girl into woman, with her corn-coloured hair and her clear brown eyes, like Mirrin's.

89

She came eagerly to him. He peered down and saw her face, centred, again only for a moment, in an uneven focal spot where the fluid—the aqueous humour—that had built up behind the iris did not seem so thickly congealed.

Dr. McVicar, in Hamilton, had explained it all to him, had shown him large coloured diagrams to help him understand the disease. But Dr. McVicar could give no reasons for its insidious onset, the failure of the fluid to be reabsorbed by the cornea. Glasgow specialists had gone through it all again, in plainer language. Even the experts, however, could not say why glaucoma should have attacked him.

"The gutter, as we'll call it, is very narrow in both eyes, Mr. Armstrong," Graham, an Ophthalmic specialist, had told him. "It would seem that the body is producing more aqueous humour than the pores in the eye can cope with. On the other hand, it may be that there is obstruction in these tiny filters."

It was all very well knowing what the causes *might* be; even Graham had never quite decided between one and the other, and Graham had put the knife in each eyeball in turn.

Tom cast Graham's failures from his mind.

The discomfort and inactivity of the post-operative period had made him wildly restless. He remembered that restlessness, like a maddening itch in all his nerves, and how he had drained himself of will-power lying motionless in bed to speed the healing.

"Daddy?" Kitten put her hand into his. Her fingers were cold. She wormed them into his big hard palm. "Can y'see today, Daddy?"

None of the others in the family, not even Davie, would have dared ask that question. Tom could no more be offended with his daughter, however, than he could lose his temper with a recalcitrant lamb.

"A bit," he told her. "I can see a bit."

He would have lifted her into his arms but he was afraid of stumbling. Besides, he was respectful of her dislike of being carried now; she thought herself too grown up for that. She still loved sitting on his lap, though, hanging onto him like, just like a kitten, while Sandy or Davie read her a story from one of their 'grown-up' books, stories about dogs or horses, usually, or sometimes about Jesus and his Apostles.

"What are y'goin' out for?" she asked.

"T'see how Malcolm's gettin' on."

"I'll take you."

"Na-na," Tom said. "I'll take *you*, flower, that's what Daddies do when it's a long walk."

"I can see Clay, an' Fairy. I can see Malcolm. The birds are havin' a feed."

"Aye," Tom said. "The birds'll be hungry after the cold spell."

He could hear them. Indeed, he had heard them long before Kitten remarked their presence. With the gradual sharpening of aural perception, he could even make out their individual cries, tell gull from rook and rook from peewit, starling from thrush, too, which was much less easy. He could hear many other things—the leathery creak of the horses and the *dint-dant* of the share striking a stone. Behind the approaching work-sounds, was the fleet wind in the saplings and whippy young willows. Far away, he caught the *whumph* and iron chatter of a steam puffer hauling Lamont's laden trucks. He could smell the tarry reek of a coking oven, though God knows how that came to him all the way from Craigneuk. Imagination, perhaps, enriched the experiences that his four hale senses picked up. When he reached the fence that separated the springy turf from the moist crumble of the oatfield, he even fancied that he could see the furrows filing away before him, filled at this cooling hour, with umber shadow. Then, with the ache in his pupils increasing, he made out the huge Clydesdale stallions pulling, with their heads up, and the cheesy slice of soil, too shallow, paring back from the blade.

It was a treat to hold the scene in all its familiarity for ten or twelve seconds. If he had been alone he would have stopped and kept it still. But Kitten pulled him eagerly on, calling out to her brother to tell him they were coming. All Tom chose to remember from the sight he'd seen, were errors—mis-strapped harnesses, the fact that the boy had let the horses' heads up so that they were shanking the plough that way and this, the blade set too steep for soil that was unevenly thawed.

He reached his son, yelling.

"Y'great thick-lugged buggerahell."

Kitten's hand had gone from his. He did not think of the child, or of anything much except that the furrows would not be as straight as they would have been if he'd had the handling. Goaded by envy and deep-seated fear of being outstripped by the youth, he roared again. "Keep the brutes' hard down or you'll wander int' the bloody burn an' break their bloody necks."

The strong ammoniac smell and rasping of the horses told him how close he was to them. He shouted, *"Give me that damned plough."*

"Take it then." Angrily, but not defiantly, Malcolm answered.

"Have I not taught y'how t'set? Have y'not been told often enough?"

"Seems I haven't."

"Aye, I know how long you'll bloody last in that fancy Kilmarnock Dairy School y'want t'attend; about ten bloody minutes."

"I'm not there yet."

"Look," Tom raged. *"Here's how its done."*

The plough was an Uddingston swing model, stilts adjusted to allow the ploughman to walk comfortably in the bottom of the cut furrow. The twist of the mould-board laid the slice neatly up on its edge. But ploughs were sensitive implements and the young man had not yet acquired the knack of setting. Snapping the bolt ring, Tom furiously adjusted it. Malcolm watched. He did not resent instruction, only his father's attitude.

Scared by her father's outburst, Kitten stood silently some yards away. Sensitive to antagonism and a hostile atmosphere, the big horses chaffed restlessly, and caused Tom to yell and curse them.

"You'll . . ." Malcolm blurted out.

"I'll what?"

"Upset them."

"Ach, what d'*you* know about it?"

"Enough," said Malcolm.

"You've a bloody lot t'learn, I'll tell you."

"Aye, an' I'm in no danger o'learnin' it here."

"Eh?"

"You heard me, Da," Malcolm said. "There's nothin' wrong wi' your lugs."

"Think I can't teach you a thing or two still, d'you now?"

"In this mood o'yours, aye, that's what I think."

"*Then get out.*"

"What?"

"Go on; *get out.* Away an' find yoursel' a place in yon fancy Dairy School you're ay bletherin' about."

"I would an' all," said Malcolm, "if things were . . ."

"*Say it.*"

"It's not for your sake I stay here; it's for Ma."

"Is it, indeed!"

"She needs me."

"She needs *nobody*," said Tom.

"That's enough, Dad," Malcolm warned. "Rant an' rave at the rest o'us if y'must, but keep your ugly tongue off Ma. I'll not stand for that."

"Christ!" Tom exploded. "*Now* we know how the land lies."

His shout caused the Clydesdales to rear a little and pull at the plough. Malcolm reined them, mouthing soothing phrases.

"I'd . . . I'd better get this rig done," the young man said.

"You'll do what I tell you t'do."

"An' what's that?"

"*Get out,*" Tom bawled again.

"Think what you're sayin', Da."

"I've thought, an' I *know* what I'm sayin'. I want y'out o'this field, an' off this farm before dark."

"Ach, away an' don't be daft."

Fist clenched, arm quick in the air. Tom swung, Malcolm had no time to duck. The back of his father's fist struck him on his side of the jaw with a loud *thwack* and, caught off balance by the unexpected blow, he staggered, tripped and sat down in the furrow. He sat quite still, head hung, for a moment, then leapt to his feet. Hands bunched loosely, like a boxer, Tom extended his arms.

"I'll not strike a blindman," Malcolm said.

"Try it. Go on, *try it*. Blind'r not, I'm more than a match for you."

Tom aimed another swipe at his son. Malcolm stepped to one side. Catching his father's forearm, he snapped it down and smothered the attack by drawing the man to him. He was taller than his Da, and quicker. He pinned Tom's arms to his side, and thrust his face close to his father's.

"Tell me again," he seethed. "Go on, Da. Say it right t'my face."

"Get t'hell."

"If y'mean it—*say it*."

"Get off Hazelrig. I've no further need o'you."

"Right."

Turning, Malcolm walked away.

Tom's mouth opened. He swung around, momentarily helpless. He was at a loss to know how to redeem the situation, how to apologise, when every grain of pride in his body screamed that what he had done was right. He could see the horses, humped and huge, brown earth, the green of the pasture, with a weave to it like tweed. He could even make out the mobile blot of his son's body, diminishing out of his range of vision.

"Malcolm," he bawled. "Malcolm."

"What?" from ten or twenty yards away.

"What about the horses?"

"You're such an independent old bugger, you fetch them in."

"Malcolm, a ploughman never leaves . . ."

"I'm no ploughman; not *your* bloody ploughman, anyhow."

"*Malcolm?*" Tom bent forward, face fiery with fear and rage. "*Malcolm.*"

There was no answer, only a swirling medley of bird-cries, pierced by the razorish shrieks of blackbacks and the derisive crawing of rooks. A tumbling gust of wind tossed the trees. The stallions stamped and snorted.

"*Come back here, y'bugger!*"

The rigs were noisy, as Tom waited, for his son's reassuring reply.

It did not come.

Shivering, he knelt and felt for the plough hooks and uncoupled the Clydesdales. Clay and Pharaoh knew this series of motions well and stood motionless, realising that the day's work was done, that they would soon be home in their stalls with hay to munch.

Tom did not converse with the team.

His eyes were smarting, swimming and smarting. He was thinking, not of his son, but of his wife, of the row there would be when he got back to the yard. God, if it hadn't been for the team, he would not have gone back at all, at least not sober. He would have picked his way across the low pasture to the road and gone on down, somehow, to Crosstrees and drank himself sick, making that most vulgar of all escapes for a man who knows that he is wrong but is too stiff with pride to admit it. But he could not abandon the team, not with dark coming down fast now and the wind turning snell on his cheeks. He took his time, though.

His fingers were not devoid of nimbleness and he was not totally without sight. When he forgot the degree of vision that had been lost and concentrated on using what remained, he could struggle along well enough. None of that was foremost in his thoughts, however. He hung back during the trek across the oatfield and through the gate to the track that would take him up into the yard. It was coming dark, the sweep of the east wind bringing night in. He absorbed the sounds of the night's approach—the flight of rooks from the feeding ground to the nests in the pines that ribbed the march with the Duke's leasing fields away to the north, the flock going overhead, low and solemn, weary, craw-craw-crawing now. He could see his breath cloud before his mouth, and the steady swaying of the horses, Pharaoh leading Clay.

Mirrin would sort it out. Malcolm would not leave. He would surrender to his mother's need of him. Mirrin would allow her husband to salvage his pride and, in a day or two perhaps, he would come out of his black mood and would have a crack with the boy and make it all right again.

Mirrin would act as peacemaker.

Aye; Mirrin still needed them both.

Nursing self-pity and rehearsing his demands upon their tolerance in gestures not words—it was safer to keep his mouth shut under the circumstances—Tom brought the team to the rear of the byre and round into the yard.

The walls still held some light. He could see them clear enough, black-painted doors and green-painted drains giving him a geometry of planes and angles that he could follow like a plan without groping and stumbling. He strode into the yard just as he had done in the old days, only without his jovial yell to let her know that he was home and hungry, without the children running to him, and . . .

The thought wriggled into his mind like a worm.

He checked the horses outside the stable.

Off to his left he could discern light, yellow as butter, the shape of it as Mirrin came out to him, stepping quickly, her rage tamped down.

Aye, Mirrin would stand no nonsense. He must hold his tongue. The thought niggled and wormed into him. He would have asked at once, but there was too much else going on.

"What's wrong with you?" She snapped. "Have you gone mad, Tom Armstrong? What's the meanin' o'this, tellin' our Malcolm t'pack his bags? If you think I can . . ."

Then, even as Tom tightened his facial muscles to indicate that he would not be lectured like a naughty bairn, Davie's voice piped up, shrill, querulous and surprised.

"Da," the little boy said, "where's Kitten?"

*　　*　　*

The spirit of uncertainty that hung over the mineral trades in Scotland in that February month was nowhere in evidence in Glasgow. Steaming full ahead, the manufacturing city was in no doubt of its directive, to put the nation's money to good and pious use by turning a profit on every conceivable article of trade.

Across the chasm of Stockwell Street, virtually obliterating the carbonous façade of adjacent blocks, hoardings advertised Malloch's Glass & Mirrors, Mitchell's 'Prize Crop', Hubbard's Celebrated Rusks, Challenge Whisky, and the Colosseum's Great Apodeictical Developmental & Alteration Reduction Sale. Even the window of George Arnold Craddick's little office, on the fourth floor of the Saint Kentigern Property Insurance

Company building, was partly hidden behind the dusty gilt M of a sign touting Thomson's Glove-Fitting Corsets.

Mr. George Arnold Craddick might have stood as a model for Glove-Fitting Corsets. He had a shape that many a dowager would have envied, waist narrow, chest and bottom prominent. Heavy gingery sidewhiskers framed a depressed nose, like that of a spoonbill, and quick minnow-like eyes of a strange silvery-blue colour. His trim waist notwithstanding, he was well into his fifties. Of course, he kept himself sound in wind and limb by training with the Glasgow Police harriers on Saturday afternoons, and swimming in the Merchants' House Bathing Club pond two evenings in the week. During the course of the working day he kept up his strength by partaking of six or eight cups of pure beef tea, brewed for him by his secretary, who resided, like a mouse, behind the wainscot—in a tiny cupboard office—and was summoned by rapping the skirting with the heel of the shoe.

Mr. Craddick eschewed heavy wines, beers, spirits, tobacco, cotton underwear, sweetmeats and confections. He ate quantities of green vegetables with every meal except breakfast, that being composed of a Finnan haddock lightly poached in milk and a slice of oat bread. Mr. Craddick wore a light woollen garment beneath his waistcoat in the winter months, and did not feel the cold. As the fire in the office hearth was miserably inadequate. Mr. Sydney Thrush did feel the cold, or rather the dampness, for the Glasgow air was composed of a fine sifting rain that stained the rooftops, canvas awnings and the horses' coats in the street below.

Shoppers thronged the bazaar lanes, and the five p.m. hiatus of cabs, carts, omnibuses and horse-trams was building up to its nightly jamboree—total congestion—which usually took place around six. A tripe cart, delivering supplies to His Lordship's Larder in St. Enoch's Square had locked wheels with a tiny van labelled Webster's Unique Shirts. Offal vendor and gents' couturier were furiously belabouring each other with their whips and bellowing for the other to *"Back up, back up,"*, a manoeuvre that had been impossible for three minutes or more.

Mr. Craddick did not notice the bedlam.

Mr. Thrush did.

He was obliged to raise his voice, to make it less suave and more demanding than he would have wished.

Mr. Thrush had great respect for Mr. Craddick, and did not intend to seem bullying in any way.

"Mr. Craddick," said Mr. Thrush. "I trust that I have made myself clear on every point?"

"Indeed you have, Mr. Thrush."

"I assume that you will undertake the necessary action to secure the three equal blocks of stock and will be prepared to make purchase without impediment within a day of receiving my notification?"

"I will require documents of implementation and leasing fee rights."

"You will have them, Mr. Craddick, very soon."

"Then the legal technicalities will present no problem, Mr. Thrush."

Technicalities were Mr. Craddick's speciality. He excelled in manipulating technicalities, though he was not exactly a lawyer. He also excelled in accountancy, though not exactly an accountant, and in stockbroking, though not exactly a stock-broker—and in behaviour bordering on the criminal, though he ran, literally, with the Deputy Chief Constable and swam, literally, with an ex-Lord Provost, and had an impeccable record as a benefactor to widows and orphans. Mr. Craddick was an agent, and it is best to let it go at that, without further libellous embellishment.

"You will, then, personally take purchase of all shares offered for sale?" said Thrush.

"In the Blacklaw Collieries Company, yes."

"And, after a decent interval, you will re-sell the full stock to me?"

"At the original price, plus ten per cent of the total sum involved," said Mr. Craddick, from his chair behind his tall counting-house desk.

From a chair on a lower plain, Mr. Thrush said, "You may only have to carry the stock for a week or two, you know."

"In which time it may ascend in value."

"Or descend," Thrush reminded him.

"One month: ten per cent," said Craddick.

"Mr. Craddick," said Thrush, "I apologise for asking such an indelicate question," he glanced around the shabby office, "but do you, personally, and in effect, actually have the where-withal to do this deal?"

"I am notoriously reliable." Craddick said. "Have you ever found me otherwise?"

"Oh no, certainly not, never anything but most reliable."

"Mr. Thrush, sir, such wee bits of dealing are well within my scope. I have, in fact, performed many such transactions."

"Yes, quite," said Thrush. "I'm sure you have."

"If you require controlling interest in the Blacklaw Collieries Company, then I'll get it for you. It'll cost you ten per cent of the quotation on the stock sold; no more, no less."

"I am . . ." Thrush once more was at a loss for words. He did not wish to seem weak in front of the robust Mr. Craddick. It was perfectly true that Craddick had performed many 'wee bits of dealing' for him over the years, all without hitch. But with Lamont's Company almost within his grasp, Sydney Thrush could not quell his anxiety.

"You don't trust me?" said Craddick, sympathetically. "Ne'er mind; I trust you, Mr. Thrush, and that's enough to be goin' on with, surely?"

"Of course I trust you, my good chap," Thrush said, rising.

Craddick undoubtedly had a reputation, in certain circles— very closed circles—for a selective kind of honesty. He had been recommended to Thrush by the chief clerk of the costing office of the Bowhouse Locomotive Engineering Works, who, it seemed, had heard good things of Craddick from Galloway McFadyen, clerk to the firm of underwriters, Brayne, Bradman & Angus, who, though Thrush didn't know it, had been fed the message by a certain Balfour Sprott, solicitor, of Edinburgh. Where Sprott got it from only God, and Andrew Stalker, knew, and they had sealed up their lips like tombs, in the manner of the ruling caste.

Mr. Craddick descended from his tall chair and moved round the polished corner of his tall desk. With a trace of reverence, he shook Sydney Thrush by the hand.

"I trust you, Mr. Thrush," Craddick said, in a husky tone, "because I would not dare do otherwise."

Thrush raised one eyebrow. "How is that, Mr. Craddick?"

"Any man, sir, who can contrive a scheme as patient and as thorough as you have done, is not a man I would be o'er keen to cross in the matter of business."

"Most kind, Mr. Craddick. Most kind."

Leaning a little closer to Thrush, as he opened the office door, Mr. Craddick confided, "I wish I had your deftness, sir, *and* your acumen. I envy you, Mr. Thrush. I positively *envy* you."

Thrush made a little puffing sound, like a steam-tug. Bowing graciously, he shook Mr. Craddick's hand once more and took himself out into the long, gloomy corridor that would lead to the stairs to the street. He was thinking, "It'll work: it *will* work. Lord in heaven: it's going to *happen*, at last."

And Mr. Craddick, quietly closing the office door, thought, *"Fool!"*

*   *   *

"God, Da, I'm sorry," Malcolm said. "I thought she'd stayed wi' you."

"Aye, an' I thought she'd gone home wi' you," said Tom, grimly. "This is no time t'parcel out blame." He felt detached, the panic in him balled to a brittle lump in his gut; he would not let it break, not until she had been found.

At the rear of the byre, Sandy was calling, *"Kitten— Catherine—Kitten, where are you?"* Hurley, who had keen eyesight, had taken himself to the fence at the fank to scan the fields. Moist and chill, dusk gathered thickly in the hollows. Mirrin ran after Hurley, crying, "Can you see her? Is she there?"

Tom put his hand on his son's arm. "Put the horses away first, Malcolm, then get Fleck an' search the glen behind the ploughin', over int' Butt's woods."

"But why did she wander off? It's no' like her."

"Our shoutin' frightened her," said Tom. "Davie?"

"Aye, Da'."

"Is there someplace she'd go t'hide, someplace special?"

"I can't think o' one, Da."

"Try, son."

"The hay-loft?"

"Look there." Tom did not really think that the child had returned at all to the farm precincts. "Look well, mind—an' in the apple wood. There's light enough. Then come back here t'me, an' we'll take a lantern an' we'll go out together. You'll need t'be my eyes."

"Aye, Da'." The boy hurried off towards the hay-loft, calling his sister's name.

Malcolm put the Clydesdales into the stable, being hasty with them. Running, Mirrin returned from the fank. "Tom, there's no sign o'her. Oh, God, Tom, an' it's near dark."

"We'll find her."

"Tom, what happened?"

"Not now, Mirrin," Tom said. "Fetch out four or five lamps."

"Should I ride down t' John Butt's steadin' an' get him t'help us search?" Mirrin interrupted.

"Not yet," Tom said. "Kitten's sensible enough t'make her way in now that dark's comin'. If she's not back b'six . . ."

"Six? Tom, she'll perish wi' cold."

"Mirrin," he warned. "Just hold t'gether, woman."

"Aye, Tom." Mirrin choked back mounting panic.

"Remember the evenin' Sandy took the huff 'cause I skelped him; he ran away?"

"Aye, but that was summer."

"He made a bee-line for his Aunt Kate's."

"D'you think Kitten could've gone there?"

"It's likely," said Tom.

"Would she know the way?"

"She's upset," said Tom. "But she's no toddler. She could travel fast enough."

"It's so near dark."

"She'd strike for the road, perhaps, in which case we'll easily find her—get Sandy out on the pony, down int' Blacklaw if needs be—or she'd head up t'wards the ridge, straight over ont' the old stock track through the top o' McClure's land. It's my guess that's the way she'd go."

"Perhaps she's not headed for Kate's at all."

"Light the lanterns, Mirrin."

"Oh, God! Oh, God!"

"Do as I say. One for Malcolm. He'll take Fleck up t'the glen an' the woods. One for Hurley. He'll take the field track t'Crosstrees."

"I'll get the dog-cart ready."

"Aye, for Sandy. Put a lantern on it."

"An' you?"

"Davie an' I will search the ridge an' the stock track. We'll all be back here in an hour or so." Tom put his hand on Mirrin's cheek. "If we haven't found her by then we'll turn out the neighbours."

Davie returned. "She's no' in the loft, Da."

"Then you an' me'd best get started. We're goin' over the ridge by the back route t'Blacklaw. Fetch a lantern from your Mam."

They knew what to do. He had dispersed them sensibly. Trembling, he leaned against the stable wall. Deliberately he had chosen the back route for himself. Kitten had a half hour's start, but the hill was steep. The dark would make no difference to him. The boy would have the lantern to light his steps. What Tom had not revealed was his fear of the morass of old shale tips, slurry heaps and gravel pits that lay on the ridge's north-facing slopes. If Kitten angled off the ridge too soon she could not avoid that dangerous region. It had happened before; children up from the village—broken limbs, broken heads. Ten years ago there had been a drowning in the porous gravel pits. He had not reminded Mirrin of it. He suspected that the memory was vivid in her mind too.

Malcolm emerged from the stable just as Hurley and Sandy converged in the yard.

"No sign o' the wee lass, gaffer," Hurley said.

"The missus'll give y'a lantern," said Tom. "She'll tell you both what t'do. Davie?"

Anxious, yet eager too, the boy came. The episode seemed like an adventure, the real hazard to his sister lost in the heat of activity. He carried a big tin storm lantern hooked to a short pole.

"Give me your hand, son, an' don't let go," Tom told him.

Mirrin called, "Tom, please find her."

"We'll find her, love," he called back. "She'll not be so far away. Keep the supper hot. We'll all be needin' a good feed when we get back; Kitten too."

Father and youngest son rounded the farm house, climbed the stile over the wall of the long field and set out across the rising pasture. Startled sheep rose and loped away from the light. Davie's hand was tight in Tom's, the boy dragging him on, yet having to run, now and then, to keep up with the man's strides.

Tom shouted, "*Kitten!*" He counted twenty paces, shouted again, "*Kitten!*" Holding his breath, he listened for a reply.

An owl in the hazels by the burn, on Malcolm's search beat, *yyyeeeeeeekkked*. Fleck gave out a gutteral bark. Peering into the twilight, Tom thought he could just make out Malcolm's lantern heading across the ploughed field towards the glen. Though he could see very little beyond the patch of grass under the dancing spot of the lantern, he knew instinctively where he was. Nudging Davie, he steered a course along the crest of the ridge to the fence at the end of the march, over it onto the steeper, stonier ground of McClure's neglected grazings.

"*Kitten!*" For the fiftieth time, he called her name.

"I can see the lights o' the pit now, Da."

"Aye, son. Keep a close eye on the ground in front o'us. We'll go slower. Careful not t'fall int' any holes."

"Da, this is where y'told us not t'come, isn't it?"

"That's right, Davie."

Sounds were divided by distance. Tom could hear the seeping of the earth around him, muffled, sibilant and hostile, the ashy yield of changing strata as he picked down from the open hill; hear too, distant and hollow, the clangings and clankings of the colliery, the metallic chirp of cables and couplings on the winding gear; then the wind was baffled, the din of industry blocked, dropping away from his ear as shale hillocks and skeletal undergrowth closed round him.

He stopped.

"*Kitten? Kitten?*" He shouted at the top of his lungs.

A dog barked in McClure's ramshackle steading on the edge of Blacklaw.

"Listen, Davie, listen."

"*Kitten!*"

"No, son. I'll shout, you listen. *Kitten?*"

Another owl: a dog bark: the plash of drainage water brought on by a windy gust. The last sound made Tom's gut clench. Even Davie was aware of the seriousness of the situation. All the adventure had gone out of it. If Kitten had navigated through this raddled zone, then she would surely have made it down into town, into Kellock's Square. He would search here though, search thoroughly. He had to be sure that she was elsewhere, not—Dear Jesus—not face down in a soot hole, drowned in a grey suppurating gravel pit.

"*Kitten: Kitten: Kitten: Kitten.*"

"Da, *sh-ssshhh.*" Davie punched him urgently on the side.

Heart beating furiously, Tom stooped. "What is it, son?" he whispered, sensing Davie's alertness.

"I heard . . ." the boy began. "*Listen,* Da."

Tom closed his eyes and concentrated all his senses, straining against the distractions of the bustling wind, the colliery, the farms.

"*Kit-ten?*"

"*There: hear it?*"

Tom heard it; a plaintive cry, halfway between a shriek and an intelligible call.

"*Daaaaaaaaaady.*"

"Where, Davie?"

"That way, over there, Da."

"Aye, that's what I thought, too," Tom said. "Now, don't run; walk as fast as y'can, keepin' hold o'my hand."

They crabbed across the breast of the hillside, ripping through wiry bramble and gorse, skirting sour, crumbling fissures where frost had melted into lentic rivers of rusty mud that cascaded over rotting cliffs and eroded precipices—all the litter of old mines and pits shrouded by hardy growths, traps for the unwary.

Tom checked the boy's eager progress, reining him in. The lantern bobbed on its pole, jerking speckles of light into the grotesque landscape. Tom thought that the sounds came from the gravel trenches, the 'digs', where, even now, colliery road-menders occasionally stole filling for the tracks that carried carts and bogies round the skein of the workings. It was filthy gravel now, though in its day the pits had yielded a tidy sum to old McClure. Young McClure did not care enough to charge a fee.

Tom shouted Kitten's name. This time her reply was clearly audible. The stark terror in the voice made him swear under his breath.

"Son, I think she's down in one o'the gravel pits."

A tumulus of shale-streaked mud brought boy and man to their hands and knees. Surrendering to panic at last, Tom clawed his way up it. Kitten's shrieks dragged him on. He could see—not much, but enough— of that crater-wall to dig into until he reached its rim. Shouting incessantly, he stared blindly down into the pit below.

Hard on his father's heels, in spite of the awkward burden of the lantern-pole, Davie blundered against Tom's warning arm.

"She's down there, Da, in the mud. She's stuck."

"Daddy's here, Kitten: Daddy's here," Tom called, then said, "How far out is she, Davie?"

"Not far. I could reach her, I think."

"No. You'll stay here. How far?"

"Six'r eight big steps. I can see where she fell down an' rolled. There's holes in the mud."

"How deep's she in?"

"T'her waist, Da."

"Kitten," Tom said. "Don't move, Kitten. Da'll get y'out in just a minute."

"Daddy, don't go away, Daddy."

"No, no, no," said Tom. "Just keep still, love. Keep still."

He told Davie to hold the lantern pole steady, then, feet first, belly to the slope, lowered himself over the rim of the crater and slid his body down the greasy, rasping slope. Strangely, he could see the scores and gullies in the stuff clearly. He did not look round or down, groping with his feet for a first contact with the porridge-like mud. The child was not in immediate danger of drowning. The mixture, unlike quicksand, would have a base. But she was undoubtedly stuck fast, and the February night was cold. If he had not had the luck of the devil, he might not have found her at all. In an hour or two, she would have died of exposure. Recognition of what might have been tormented him more than reality. He slid himself into the water. It was thicker than liquid, more viscous than mud, a coarse broth-like substance that thinned in its consistency only when he pushed himself further from the bank. It consumed his knees, then his thighs. He wallowed towards the cries that Kitten made to guide him. Below the melt, the ground was like kneaded dough, sucking and clinging to his boots. It required considerable effort to thrust through to the child, more effort still to pluck her from the pit's grasp.

She was weaker than her cries indicated. She clung to him like a monkey, knees around his waist. He could just see her face and hair in the spill of light from the lantern twenty feet or so up the almost vertical wall of the hole. The cold clasping substance had bagged the air out of his clothing and his garments clung to him like sheets of ice. Cold ate into his flesh, sapping his strength, even in the few brief minutes of his immersion. He understood Kitten's weakness. She had been closer to death than he had imagined. He must get her to a warm fire, find her something hot to drink—and very soon.

The greasy wall of clay-coloured mud rejected him. He rolled down into the soup again, twisting to keep the child in his arms clear of it. She said nothing, she did not even gasp or sob, but clung to him mutely, cramping his actions, as he crept out of the pond again.

He looked up towards the lantern glow.

"Davie," he said. "I want you t'take the lantern off the pole an' lower the pole down t'me. Don't stand up. Lie on your stomach an' stretch the pole down an' we'll see if I can reach it."

"Aye, Da."

It only took the boy a moment to unhook the lantern and do as his father asked. He steered the end of the pole towards Tom's palm, but it was too short. He told his father that it wouldn't reach. Tom told him to slither it down. When he had the pole, the man jabbed it deep into the wall and, using his right arm, muscled himself up until he could tuck the prop under his armpit.

"Kitten," he said, gently. "Go round ont' Daddy's back, like a coalbag, a wee coalbag. Kitten, can y'hear me?"

She seemed to be asleep. Her lethargy was worrying.

Tom patted her cheek and shifted her weight. She stirred. Once more he told her what he wanted her to do. Listlessly, she shrugged herself round and, with a heave, Tom finally got her onto his back. When he pressed his body against the granular mud, the burden seemed to help him find, not purchase, but adhesion. Using his left hand, he twisted the pole until it came free, then, transferring it to his right hand, he leaned back far enough to plunge it deep into the mud again, three feet above him.

Once more he levered himself upward, once more freed the pole, once more drove it in like a dagger and, thus, in a series of wriggling, awkward motions came close enough to sling his elbow over the lip of the pit and, with a final surge of strength, pull himself and the child up and out of the crater.

Kitten tumbled away from him, and lay still.

"Da? Da? Look't her!" Davie exclaimed, in awe.

"Now, listen t'me son," Tom gasped. "She's very, very cold. We'll need t'get help. Hazelrig's nearest, I think. Fish up the pole—it's just there— an' hook it t' my belt. Aye, hook it firm t'the buckle. Hold the lantern. Be careful not t'burn your knuckles. God's sake, son don't drop the light whatever y'do."

He did not repeat the orders. He was obliged to trust his son now, trust him to be sensible and proficient, to act the man.

Stripping off his jacket and woollen waistcoat, which, at least, was partly dry, Tom fumbled with the buttons of his daughter's coat and peeled it from her. She stirred and whimpered a little. Her skin was like ice, her breathing shallow. Using the waistcoat, Tom chaffed her limbs with it, then fitted the garment over her head and wrapped it around her. He got to his knees, lifted her and pressed her against his undershirt. Except for his legs and feet, he was not cold himself, though the wind seemed like a whetted scythe. He contrived to get the jacket buttoned over the child, drawing her bare legs around him so that she was slung tight and snug from his chest. He wrapped his arms around her and rubbed and patted her vigorously while Davie, who had retrieved the pole, bent before him and attached the lantern clip to his belt.

"Got it, Da."

Tom rose to his feet. He staggered a little, regained his balance and, for an instant, thanked God that his affliction had not affected his stamina. He was strong enough; he had more than enough in reserve.

"Lead us," he said. "Go on, son. Don't rush it. Lead us out o'this hellish place, up t'the ridge."

"Right." Davie sounded just like Malcolm at that moment, the same note of determined assurance in his voice.

Tom saw the lantern lift and cross his range of vision, passing into and out of view. Then it appeared, oddly starred, a great slender cruciform shape, that congealed into a blob of bright light just ahead of him. A tug on his belt tweaked him into motion. He gave himself over to the boy's guidance, following the lad, trusting him.

It took twenty minutes to reach open grassland on the crest of the ridge. Kitten was warmer now and making tiny sobbing sounds in her throat. Tom talked to her, cheering her, still rubbing the jacket against her.

"Fence, Da. It's our field, I think," Davie said.

"Aye, son." Tom touched the wire with his left hand and climbed over it, carefully. The boy unhooked the pole.

Tom stumbled, then straightened, his son's hand anxiously upon his arm, helping him. Kitten began to cry loudly, perhaps with the numbness tingling from her legs. Tom gulped air, sensing the direction of the wind, strong and steady and to his right. Though he could see little—there was no moonlight and the stars were faint—he knew at last where he was and carried a vivid picture of the land in his mind's eye.

"Take the light, Davie. Go on ahead, quick as you can. It's a straight half mile t'the dyke, the one at the back o'the farm. Bring Malcolm and Sandy, an' a couple o'blankets. Tell your Mam t'put on hot water for a bath an' get Kitten's bed heated."

"Right," said the boy again and ran quickly out of Tom's sight.

Then there was only darkness, not a dead and vapid darkness however, not one that threatened him. It would have been near as dark even if he'd had full sight in both eyes.

Left hand extended, he measured out a step and started forward, heading for home.

Walking upright, the child secure in the crook of one arm, he was only a few yards short of the dyke when the others came out to meet him.

"Mam," Kitten whimpered. "Mam."

"You're all right now, love. You're safe home."

"Daddy found me," Kitten said. "Daddy's not angry."

"Aye, love; Daddy found you," Mirrin said.

★　　★　　★

It was late when Mirrin came to bed. Bathed and fed, Tom had been there for an hour, lying on his back staring at the pool of light that the single candle cast on the ceiling.

"How is she?" he asked.

"She'll be all right after a good night's sleep."

"Take her int' Hamilton t'morrow. See the doctor."

"Aye, maybe I'd better," said Mirrin, lying on her back too. "To be on the safe side."

Tom said, "Another hour . . ."

"Don't."

"It was my fault."

Mirrin did not contradict him.

Tom said, "I didn't mean it—about Malcolm. Mirrin, he'll not leave, will he? We need him here, for a while at least."

"Tell him that, Tom. Tell him you need him."

"Aye, I will. First thing tomorrow," Tom said. "An', Mirrin—when you're in Hamilton, ask McVicar t' make me a written appointment at the Ophthalmic."

Mirrin said nothing for a moment, then asked, "Why, Tom?"

"If there's one chance in a thousand o' regainin' my sight," Tom said, "then I'd better take it."

"But . . ."

"One chance might be enough."

"Tom. Oh, Tom." She turned and put her arms about him, holding him tightly, while, outside, the wind sighed across the roofs of Hazelrig.

PART TWO

The Rights of Man

July

———

Long before the tragedy, Kate was conscious of the quickening tempo of everyday life. It was not just symptomatic of her age; the pace of events seemed to be powered by the sheer energy of the century that was thundering to a close, an era whose weight and velocity would drive it on to unimaginable marvels in the century to come. In the baker's shop, on the communal drying greens between the colliers' rows, mixed with the trivial gossip of the town, there was speculation as to what Utopian dreams of peace, prosperity and equality would be made real when the twentieth century got underway. Somehow, Kate did not believe that the next decade would bring much improvement in the workers' lot, though she had escaped the despair that went with submission to the system. She could not even begin to describe that 'system' in words: it was as diffuse as the 'movement' that Rob Ewing, and the Stalker lads, clattered on about. For all that, Kate Kellock, thoroughly content with her husband, her house and her adopted son, was uncommonly on edge throughout that spring and early summer.

Perhaps it was Mirrin's anxiety about Tom's operation, due in July, that sparked the fuse of concern over the stability of her own small empire. Perhaps it was the chronic tension in the town, in the whole country, in fact, over the U.F.M.'s collision course with the Coal-owners Association. Whatever the reason, Kate felt that life was rapidly becoming more fragmented, broken up, like hard toffee on a tray, into lumps, splinters and grains, that its shape, its wholesome regularity, would never be recovered, in this century or the next.

There was talk now, talk, talk, talk: meetings, covert quarrels, scuffles in the pub, shouts at the street corner, grim *tête-à-têtes* in the shadow of the gate of Kellock's Square—a taut, furtive, suspicious season. Nobody was immune.

The West of Scotland Coal-owners' demand for a twenty-five per cent wage reduction had rocked an industry geared to hard knocks. Hot heads regarded the bosses' action as another turn on the screw and, stalking out of the cages, left the pit hooters to wail over deserted yards. By May, 30,000 men were idle in Scotland—938 of them in Blacklaw Company pits. Making useful capital of the figures, Rob Ewing was all over town—though hardly ever seen—posting notices of meetings and broadsheets giving detailed news of what was happening in other districts. One sheet, copies of which appeared overnight in every one of Lamont's holdings in Lanarkshire, intimated that a report on the Scottish situation had been received by the executive of the U.F.M. in London and, in bold, blotchy print, announced in the next paragraph that the owners had refused to meet the miners' representatives.

"A strike, that's what we need here. A strike."

"That's what we want."

"All across the bloody country."

"A strike."

"Nothing else for it."

"I say we wait t'hear what word comes up from London."

"London: I wouldn't piss on London."

"We've got a voice in parliament, have we not?"

"Aye, a voice that speaks *their* bloody language, no' ours."

"That's unfair."

"What's no' unfair, I ask you?"

"A strike's fair."

"Aye, a strike's the *only* answer."

Rob Ewing made it known that a national ballot was in progress. He advised that no action be taken until the results of that ballot were known.

"Piss on you, too, Rob Ewin'."

"Naw, naw: Rob's one o'us."

"Aye, while it suits him."

"Say that again, an' I'll bash your bloody mouth."

"Calm down: calm down."

"I'm for doin' as Rob says: who's with me?"

"I am. I'll tak' Rob's word."

"An' me."

"I'll side wi' Rob—for the time bein'."

"Piss on Rob Ewin'."

"Throw that bastard out."

Though it was summer now, and the weather fair, the women in the towns knew that any strike action at local level would immediately dry up the supplies of domestic coal and make the feeding of kitchen stoves and ranges difficult, cooking a problem. They took to conserving what stocks they had, and children were dispatched with buckets and zinc baths to salvage nuggets of dross tramped into the weeds between the pits and the railway sidings.

"Willie, you'll have t'take precautions," Flora Stalker counselled the baker.

"Aye, Flora: I've been through this sort of thing before," Willie answered. "Strikes mean hungry mouths, an' hungry folk have little respect for law an' order."

"What d'you mean, dear?" Kate asked.

"Break-ins, theft, lootin'," said Willie. "I've endured strikes before now."

Flora said, "You'll have ordered shutters."

"I have," said Willie. "An' a set o' iron bars for the back windows."

"Willie, are y'serious?" asked Kate. "I've never known lootin' an' riotin' in Blacklaw before."

"It's not just Blacklaw," Willie explained. "It's the whole country—Northrigg, Eastlagg, Craigneuk, Inchpit, Cansk, Ironford—all o'them swarmin' with starvin' colliers, their womenfolk an' bairns. No, no, Kate, m'love; this time it'll be a dirty struggle against an enemy without a face."

"How d'you mean?" The vision made Kate shudder.

"It'll not just be Blacklaw versus Lamont."

"It's Lamont that Rob Ewing aims t'bring down."

Willie shook his head. "Lamont's just Rob's private target. This strike is no isolated local stramash; this strike means changes, big, important changes in a whole manner o' thinkin'."

Agitatedly, Kate said, "Well, that's as maybe. But what can we do about it?"

Punch-like nose almost meeting his chin, Willie smiled tightly, "So long as I've got flour, water an' fire, I'll feed as many as I can."

"That's the stuff," Lily Stalker said.

"You're as bad as they are," Kate snapped accusingly at her sister-in-law. "You shouldn't be encouragin' them."

Lily looked bewildered. "Encouragin' who?"

"My Neill an' your Edward."

Lily shook her head. "So that's what's got you all fired up, is it? The boys. Well, Kate, not you, not me, an' not the Queen's Own Highlanders can stop them bein' men."

"You call it manly t'fight?"

"There's been no fightin' yet," said Lily, calmly. "An' maybe there never will be."

"Aye, an' if there is," said Flora, "then it's my opinion that our pair o'heroes will come scuttlin' home cryin' for their Mams."

"Like as not." Willie wrapped his arm round Kate's broad waist and hugged her. "Maybe it'll all just fizzle out."

"No," Lily said. "That it will not do, Willie."

"We've little cause t'worry, anyhow," the baker said. "Now if I was a coalmaster instead o'a baker, if my name was not Kellock but Lamont, I *would* be sweatin' right now."

"Lamont; sweat?" said Lily. "He'll have somethin' planned t'save his fine mansion from ruin."

"Like as not, like as not," said Willie, amicably. "But I'd swop all his brass for my wee wife; that's one thing the mighty man hasn't got—a wife like mine."

Such speculative conversations were not confined to colliers' rows. Flensed of their niceties, eight or ten pieces of dialogue exchanged between the partners of Blacklaw Collieries Company stood like tablets to mark the progress of impending crisis.

"Thrush, when's this damned meeting set for?"

"The twenty-ninth of May."

"And the policy of the U.F.M.?"

116

"No secret there: they have pledged support to any district that resists wage reductions."

"Injury to one is injury to all," Lamont had quoted.

"We'll look to ourselves; never fear."

"I've been thinking about your recommendation."

"Which recommendation, Houston?" Thrush had said.

"Selling stock. Three equal blocks, you suggested, I believe."

"That's right."

"When the findings of this Executive Committee are made public," Lamont had said, "then we will consider taking such drastic action."

"That might be too late, you know."

"I won't do it unless I have to."

"Of course."

In the first week in June a ballot had been taken among Scottish mine-workers. The results showed that 25,617 men were eager for strike action, and that 14,490 deluded souls were not. A majority of 11,127 was decisive enough, however, and on Tuesday, June 26th, for the first time, strike notices were posted in every Scottish colliery.

"So—it's happened, has it?"

"Regrettably, yes," Thrush had said.

"I suppose now you'll advocate that I sell stock to supply ready cash?"

"I've already given my advice, Houston."

"What do you say, Edith?"

"I am not in favour of limited liability companies as a rule," said Edith, primly, "but, under the extreme circumstances, I recommend that we do not delay too long. As I told you, Houston, the feeling in Glasgow is that the Association will not win this battle. If the tide turns against us before we put the stock to market, then we will not receive its true worth."

"Thank you, Edith."

"Well, Houston?"

Lamont had hesitated, then answered. "No, I will not sell."

"But the purchasers are there, Houston," Thrush had said. "They have been discreetly broached, and . . ."

"Nothing wrong with the list," Lamont had agreed. "But I

do not want dilettantes dabbling in my trade, creaming profit from my company."

"Our company, Houston," his wife had reminded him.

"What the devil do Pumpherson, Gladding and the Earl of Rowanbrook know about coalmining? *Nothing*."

"But they have money, Houston; and we need money to keep our Company holdings intact, our programme of expansion mov . . ."

"I shouldn't have listened to you, Sydney. Programme of expansion! More expenditure!"

"It's too late to disagree, Houston," Thrush had said. "What shall I tell the agents of the interested parties?"

"Tell them to wait."

"Until the price of our shares plummets?"

"That will not happen."

"Or until we are squeezed into a corner?"

"I trust my friends," Lamont had said. "The Blacklaw Collieries Company will *not* be 'squeezed', Sydney, I assure you of that."

"We wait, then?"

"Yes, we wait."

All the better, Sydney Thrush had told himself, for that was the strategy he had planned. Only when Messrs. Pumpherson and Gladding, and the Earl of Rowanbrook, had taken cold feet—in six or eight weeks—would the situation become desperate enough to persuade Houston to deal with an agent, with George Arnold Craddick.

But Thrush was wrong in his estimate. It did not take six weeks to bring Lamont to heel. It took exactly one month and, in the short run, though he did not know it, it was not Thrush who sprung the trap.

*　　*　　*

Sipping mocha chocolate spiced with Black Hart rum, Daniel Horn propped his feet on the footstool and made out of his bony thighs a support for a pad of lined foolscap. Pinned to the left corner of the pad was a list of companies. Adjacent to each name a number and a figure in pounds and shillings was printed.

Eighteen hours had passed since union men had tacked strike notices to doors and gates of collieries up and down Scotland. The miners' strike did not seem relevant to anything that might be happening in Moray Place, Edinburgh. Here domestic coal supplies had been secured weeks ago by diligent housekeepers, and peripheral nuisances planned for well in advance. The several stockmarketeers who resided in Moray's stately mansions, had discreetly shifted their investments to import companies and commodities less combustible than coal. Besides, it was high summer and the city was stuffy enough without fires. It would be all over, this silly strike, before autumn nipped the air.

In the hearth in Advocate Stalker's office—which was also his study and general living room—a small fire kept the temperature even. In addition to a library of some three thousand volumes, there were four winged leather armchairs and a huge studded sofa that had come from the sale of effects of the Such-and-Such Club which had gone into liquidation following the embezzlement of lying funds by its honorary treasurer. There were several long tables, of the refectory type, a rolltop desk, and a sturdy trolley from which the Advocate ate his meals.

In shirt-sleeves, waistcoat unbuttoned, Andrew Stalker had just removed a deed-box from a slot behind a calf-bound set of *Hakluyt's Voyages*. He put the box on one of the tables and opened it with a key from the ring chained to his hip pocket button. He took out a notebook bound in liquorice-coloured linen and carrying that, and nothing else, seated himself, with a contented sigh, in an armchair opposite his clerk.

Heavy moss-green drapes were drawn against a soft summer twilight that lingered like a blush in the western skies. Even as Drew crossed his knees and opened the notebook, a dozen clocks within the house, and fifty more across the city, declared the hour of eleven.

"Ready, Daniel?"

"Ready."

"Each letter will form, as it were, a pair. The first letter of each pair will be sent to Mr. Houston Lamont of the Blacklaw Collieries Company."

"At his home address?"

"Strathmore, Blacklaw, Lanarkshire," Drew said. "The first

letter of each pair—that is, the letter to Lamont—will be transcribed by a different hand. I assume that you have enough clerks on call, Daniel?"

"More than enough."

"The second letter in each pair will be transcribed by our Mrs. Arbuthnot in her impeccable copperplate, on my paper. The collection will be brought to this house, by Mrs. Arbuthnot personally, not later than six o'clock tomorrow evening. You will collect the other letters and bring them here too at that hour. I will then sign one of each pair and you will post them by the first mail on Wednesday morning."

"Clear." Daniel tore off the top sheet and dropped it to the carpet. His pencil remained poised.

"The first letter to Lamont, as follows; 'Dear Mr. Lamont, it is with considerable regret that we must insist upon payment for the low-caste forgings completed by our company, Shoreness Foundries Ltd., and delivered to your pit at Eastlagg on October 27th, of last year. We sincerely apologise for calling in this bill, but under the circumstances, and with regard to the state of the national industries, we have no alternative but to press for immediate payment, that is, within fourteen days.' The signature block, Daniel, will be that of James Forsyth, Chief Accountant, Shoreness Foundries Ltd."

"And Forsyth will sign it?"

"Of course he will."

Daniel nodded, scribbled the signature block, and ticked off the first name on his company list. Fronted by Mr. Craddick of Stockwell Street, Glasgow, Drew Stalker was a majority stockholder in Shoreness Foundries.

"Second letter, to Forsyth of Shoreness, as follows: 'Dear Mr. Forsyth, I have been informed by my agent, George Arnold Craddick, that Blacklaw Collieries Company are in default of payment of a bill for low-caste forgings, to the sum of nine-hundred and seven pounds and nine shillings, this debit outstanding since October last. I enclose herewith a letter of demand to Blacklaw Collieries. I would be grateful if you would sign it and despatch it at once. As majority stockholder in your company—a fact that can be verified by application to Mr. Craddick—I am of the opinion that the stability of the

Blacklaw Collieries Company must, in the light of the current national miners' strike, be seriously questioned. I urge you most strongly to comply with my wishes that the debit be paid within two weeks. If this bill is not met, you will take steps to instigate court action for its recovery, not later than Thursday, July 15th. In all matters relevant to the redemption of this sum I will be spoken for by Mr. Craddick who will continue to represent me, as in the past, at board meetings of the Shoreness Foundries Company. I would be obliged if my connection with your company be held in strict confidence.' My signature block, Daniel."

"Hmmm," Horn said. "So you're comin' out of hidin', Drew."

"Company secretaries are seldom fools, Daniel. Though I have not revealed myself to them before, I'm quite certain that none of them will break my confidence and reveal my name. Otherwise, they run the risk of becoming abruptly un-employed."

Daniel tore two more sheets from the foolscap pad, gliding them down to the carpet too. He licked the pencil and waited for further dictation.

Drew thumbed over a page of the black-backed notebook. "Ah, yes, Globe & District Glass Company. One hundred and forty-six pounds owing. A letter to Lamont, as follows: 'Sir, with reference to our Invoice No. 405, for August'— August, Good Lord—'for the sum of . . .'"

Thoroughly enjoying himself, Drew Stalker occupied Daniel Horn for the next three hours, pausing only to drink a dish of tea and to allow Daniel to refresh himself with more chocolate.

It was after two o'clock before Daniel knelt on the carpet, gathered up the scattered sheets and arranged them carefully in matching order, those for Mrs. Arbuthnot on the left, those for the assorted clerks on the right. He put the bundles into separate folders and slid the folders into his document satchel.

Leaning back in his chair, Drew lit a sticky brown cheroot, a domestic indulgence, since the brand was too cheap for a man of his distinction to smoke in public.

"That'll do the trick, I'm thinkin'," Daniel said.

"Yes: demands amounting to seven thousand pounds will worry even our Mr. Lamont."

"Enough to induce him t'sell stock?"

"That rogue Thrush has done that job for us," Drew said. "Or my judgment of character isn't what it should be."

"Craddick confirmed, didn't he?"

"He did."

Daniel drank the dregs of the chocolate from the cup and ran them round in his mouth with an odd chewing motion. He swallowed. "I'm loathed t'believe that this is all it was ever for?"

Frowning, Drew glanced up at his clerk. "I beg your pardon?"

"The goad, the spur. Ambition," Horn said, with a quirky smile that indicated that he meant no offence. "Was it just to take vengeance on Lamont that you drove yourself so damned hard?"

With a guttural bark of laughter, Drew said, "Is that what you think? Well, old friend, you have erred for once. No, no. No, no, no. I bear no animosity towards my former patron. I simply want a share in the Blacklaw company because it's the most progressive enterprise in Scotland. Properly managed, it can fuel my engines, stoke my ships, keep my furnaces glowing."

"That's very near poetic."

"A mere statement of fact, Daniel. I do not intend to practise law for ever. In eight years, perhaps ten, I will withdraw from the Bar."

"You'll be a judge by then."

"Perhaps. What is relative at present, however, is that Lamont will be obliged to sell stock. Thrush intends to purchase it back from our friend Craddick for himself. But, after the sale is made, Mr. Craddick will experience a change of heart. Quite naturally, there will be nothing on paper, nothing legally binding. Mr. Craddick will be registered as the purchaser, and Mr. Craddick, under law, will be entitled to sell or keep the stock as he wishes."

"And he'll sell."

"To me."

"That sister o'yours in Blacklaw, she'll have a fit when she finds out."

"What sister?"

"The bonnie one."

"I have no sister in Blacklaw," Drew said sharply. "My only near relative is Elizabeth. In any case, nobody will know that I have a stake in Blacklaw Collieries. Until such times as I can acquire more stock, Craddick will act for me. Lamont is not a young man, Daniel. If I'm patient, I may eventually own Blacklaw Collieries."

Grinning wolfishly, sharing in the devouring ambition of his master, Horn said, "Aye, Drew, that's what you have over most of them; your youth."

"Thank God my youth is no longer held against me."

"Tell me," Horn said, "what is it you're really after?"

"I . . . I don't know," Drew said. "I have no *ultimate* objective."

"You should marry an' settle down."

"And be cuckolded, like Fraser McAlmond," Drew said, quickly.

"He's not bein' . . ."

"Daniel, I realise that your motives are probably altruistic. But I am not a little boy now. I do not need that kind of protection. My sister has had several affairs; not mere harmless flirtations—though God knows there's no such thing in Edinburgh as a harmless flirtation. Elizabeth has hazarded her marriage on many occassions."

"I found no proof, Drew."

"But I did."

"Oh?" Horn waited for the sky to fall. But it didn't.

Gazing into the embers of the fire, Drew said, "So, Daniel, poor Fraser is a cuckold, and I do not wish to follow his example."

"If you'll excuse me sayin' so, perhaps you'd make a wiser choice than he did when it came to takin' a wife."

"Probably," Drew said. "Most probably. But a man never knows what he's got in that bag until he returns home with it; by that time, it's too late."

"There is a young lady . . ." Daniel Horn began in the

persuasive voice he used when making a suggestion that he expected would be rebuffed.

True to form, Drew pushed himself out of the armchair, and made an expressive gesture of the right arm, as if to cast women in general and Daniel's 'young lady' behind him, like a legion of demons. "No, Daniel. Whoever she may be, I'm not interested."

"You don't know what you're missing, Drew."

Wagging his finger, but smiling still, Drew said, "Ah, no, Daniel. Ah, no. I *do* know what I'm missing, and I prefer to be without it, thank you."

"Instead of *billets amoureuse*," Horn said, "you write these." He touched the satchel of letters with his toe.

"Infinitely more profitable," Drew said. "And more fun. Now, be on your way. We have an early case, remember."

"Goodnight, Drew."

"Goodnight, Daniel."

Toting the satchel, the clerk saw himself out of the silent house. Corby, the valet, and Mrs. Whitby, cook and house-keeper, had retired to bed long since. Upstairs a brace of maids would be huddled together in an iron bedstead, hugging each other perhaps, not for warmth but for companionship. Horn thought fleetingly of the girls as he quietly closed the front door and went down the steps to the pavement. He had found both girls a position as a reward for favours—not sexual in this case—granted. One of them, Audrey, was pretty as a china-doll and the other, Mairi, was a nice wee highland lass, sturdy, flaxon and ripe.

Sighing, Horn clipped across the road and headed round the railings of the gardens, making towards his apartment in a tenement behind Charlotte Square, not far distant. He had never lodged with his master, though Drew had suggested it several times. He preferred to retain some vestige of privacy. He was scrupulously careful, however, to do nothing that would endanger his reputation and, by reflection, might bring disrepute to Advocate Stalker. God knows, between them they had quite enough skeletons hidden in the closet—Drew with his bastard son and disreputable sisters stuck away in Blacklaw; he with his private 'deals, and his 'annuity', as he liked to call it, from dear Elizabeth McAlmond's current lover, a tidy sum in hush-money that had swelled his personal nest-egg considerably.

Aye, Drew was right: chastity was a small price to pay for profit.

Consoled by that thought, Daniel Horn turned into George Street and strode on home, swinging the heavy leather satchel by its thong.

★   ★   ★

The feud between John Reissberg Wolfe, founder of the Ophthalmic Institution, and the staff of the Glasgow Eye Infirmary delayed Tom's operation. In a fit of pique, Wolfe had dropped from public view, leaving the Institution in charge of Acting Surgeon Francis Horatio Napier. Dr. McVicar, Tom's local G.P., had once attended a series of lectures given by Dr. Napier and was not unduly impressed. For better or worse, it was McVicar's opinion that Tom had better hold off 'going to the knife' until a certain doctor Frank Parfitt joined the Ophthalmic's staff, an event promised for the early summer. According to McVicar, Parfitt was the most skilled surgeon of his day. He had qualified in London, M.B., M.R.C.S., had undertaken advanced studies in Gottigen, Berlin and Paris and had gained vast clinical experience in Moorfields and Bart's. In addition he had written the only really worthwhile monograph—so McVicar claimed—on the causes of Glaucoma Simplex. If any man could cure Tom's malady then, said McVicar, it was Frank Parfitt.

Encouraged, Tom continued courses of drug treatment at McVicar's hands in preparation for the day when Parfitt would take up his post at the Institution in West Regent Street, Glasgow. Steeled in his resolve to go through with it, Tom pulled out of his depression and occupied himself with Hazelrig during the busy seasons of spring and early summer. Making the best of his remaining sight, he gave much practical advice to his sons and, in general, attended to the farm's overall management as efficiently as possible.

Lambing was accomplished during a spell of placid weather. The drop was good, the incidence of live births high. The cows plopped out a dozen sturdy calves, five of them heifers. In May and June the daily milk yield was higher than ever before. Profits from milk sales, produce and the marketing of slink calves were put away in the bank, though Malcolm and Sandy were rewarded by the present of a brand new Leyton bicycle complete with a clockwork bell and carbide dusk-lamp. So busy were they with farm chores, however, that they had precious little time for joy-riding.

As shearing time approached—a task that Tom could easily undertake—so also came a letter direct from the great Dr. Parfitt setting an appointment for examination in the Ophthalmic Institution. Since nobody could be spared in the morning, Tom went to Glasgow accompanied by Davie.

Lean, brusque and youthful, Parfitt crackled with an electric energy that seemed at odds with a man whose skill required manual dexterity.

Tom was not impressed by the new medico.

"He's o'er young," he told Mirrin later.

"Better than some old dodderer." Mirrin sensed that her husband's courage was waning.

"Didn't seem t'have much time for me," Tom said.

"He's a busy man. More patients on the books than you."

"Aye, but when he examined me, he never took more than a minute or two at each instrument." Tom fancied himself an expert in routine ophthalmic examination. "He didn't seem t'think much o' Dr. Graham's diagnosis, or the fact that Graham'd done an iridectomy on me."

"Any other complaints?"

"It'll not be a general anaesthetic. Parfitt doesn't believe in them."

"That's all t'the good," said Mirrin, encouragingly.

"An' I'll only be inside for three or four days."

"Even better," said Mirrin. "How did he rate your chances o' complete recovery?"

"He wouldn't say anythin' about that," Tom said. "Listen, I'm wonderin' if I'm wise goin' ahead with this. I can see well enough for some things, an' I'm needed for the shearin'. The sheep'll not wait for my eyes. Anyhow, there's been no recent deterioration, an' . . ."

Mirrin sighed and put her arms about her husband's shoulders. "When?"

"July eighteenth. I'm t'report at ten in the mornin'."

"Then we'll be there, you an' me, Tom Armstrong."

★   ★   ★

Though Mirrin had not been much affected, the national strike had gripped Blacklaw in an iron fist. The town, like all towns and pit villages throughout the country, was indeed under siege. Colliers with the stamp of determination on their faces positioned themselves at the gates. Others deployed themselves in the streets, in furtive-looking gangs, berating those few who, treating the strike as an unwelcome holiday, got on with chores that had piled up over the winter.

Working with U.F.M. Scottish representative, Arthur Webb, Rob Ewing established headquarters in a vacant shop in Eastlagg, from which source he distributed news. The most heartening item was that in four days the number of men to join the 'movement' had risen to seventy thousand. No miner doubted the statistics, and jubilation greeted the appearance of the broadsheet. One useful episode occurred in the Albion Colliery in South Wales on the eve of the strike, an explosion that wiped out almost two hundred men. Strike and Disaster shared the national headlines for a couple of days.

"That'll make them see."

"It's a God-send."

"Well, I wouldn't put it like that."

"Did y'read this?"

"What?"

"Coal Strike is an Attack on the Nation'."

"An attack on the pockets o'the capitalists, that's what they really mean."

"But is it? That's what I'd like t'know. How bad will it hurt their profits?"

"It'll hurt," Rob Ewing had assured them.

As usual, Rob's assessment was accurate. His prediction was borne out during the next fortnight by glaring headlines in the Scottish press reporting that business had practically come to a standstill in the Forth and Clyde valley, and mordant prophecies that orders in hand in the General Shipping Terminus would, within the week, sink to the lowest figure ever recorded.

"Where will it end?" Kate asked.

Lily and she were in the biggest of the sheds, scalding cloths that had been used that morning. Neill and Edward were on picket duty at the colliery's main gate.

"Where it ended before, no doubt," said Flora Stalker as she brought in a bundle of cloths. "With the men crawlin' back t'work when they can't listen any longer t'their bairns wailin' from hunger."

Lily's round with the bread van had been cancelled for the duration of the strike. There were no hordes of hungry men to muster round the van at the shifts' end now and the baker was shrewd enough not to advertise temptation. In fact, with the strike less than a month old, some of the grasshoppers in the village had run right out of cash and were already looking starved. Gangs were poaching rabbits in the surrounding fields, and farmers—including the Armstrongs— were taking extra good care of their hens. In a month, they would probably be obliged to protect their sheep and calves too, for the sight of meat free on the hoof was a lure to desperate men. Good-hearted Willie Kellock had posted a notice in the bakeshop window stating that credit, to a reasonable figure, would be made available to families in want, and he liberally gave away misshapes and pan-ends to any child that looked hungry enough.

During this period, Mirrin's contribution to the miners' struggle took the form of a daily trip to Blacklaw to deliver milk at a reduced rate and to give over for distribution an occasional basket of winter-shrivelled turnips. It wasn't meanness that prevented the Armstrongs from being more generous; agricultural economy was too precariously balanced to be upset by gestures.

Try as they would, the colliers could not take the broad view. They knew that they were part of a larger movement, of a huge and potentially powerful force capable of tipping governments. But, in their hearts, they were as they had always been, brothers only in an attack on Houston Lamont's heartlessness and greed. He was their bogey-man, their target. His name stood for all the owners and managers in the country.

The family apart, nobody spared a thought for Tom Armstrong's plight. The Armstrongs were a different class and, to the colliers, lucky to have an income that did not depend on Lamont's whims.

As for the high and mighty Mr. Lamont, it was told in the towns by the gardeners that he was entirely unperturbed by the huroo and spent his days in the sun-bathed garden whacking a golf ball with a mashie or, more expertly, clicking round the croquet green with a bloody mallet. Playing games while his workers starved.

Sydney Thrush and Edith were not deceived by Houston's apparent indifference to the turbulent events beyond the walls of Strathmore. They knew that he was brooding on the first defeats of the campaign. The open-air exercises were a sign of it, hobbies that he indulged only when he found the study claustrophobic. Another man, a gentler man, might have pondered on his problems while trimming roses, but with Houston stick and ball were, perhaps, symbolic. He was out on the lawn when Thrush found him, two days before the strike caused all the gates to be locked.

"Houston, have you considered my proposal?"

Lamont lifted the golf club to his shoulder and chopped viciously at the gutta-percha ball, flaking a divot from the smooth lawn. Thrumming, the ball flew into the rhododendron shrubs, shaking down a shower of mauve petals. Fishing another ball from his pocket, Lamont dropped it on the grass and arranged the lie with the sole of his shoe.

"No." He squared for the shot.

"Edith tells me that some of our creditors . . . ?"

"Edith talks out of turn."

"Houston, I feel I have the right to know if our Company's being squeezed."

Lamont waggled the mashie, drew it back, then checked its arc. He glanced round at Thrush. "What d'you know of this?"

"Of . . . what?"

"The squeeze, as you call it?"

"Only that some of our creditors . . ."

"It's deliberate." Lamont seemed to weigh up Thrush and, deciding that it was too far-fetched to ascribe blame to his partner in this instance, brought the golf club to rest across his shoulders. Clasping the shank with his left hand and bending the wood across his back, he said, "I suppose if I told you that I suspect a plot, you'd think I was suffering from delusions?"

"Quite the contrary."

"I don't know who," Lamont said, "but somebody is trying to break us. I don't mean Ewing and his Union backers. I mean, somebody is trying to compel us to liquidate, for commercial reasons."

"Houston, it's time we had an official board meeting. This afternoon would suit me."

"Very well."

"How much has been called in?"

"Over four thousand pounds."

"Dear God!" Thrush exclaimed.

"We will meet for lunch, and go into session immediately after."

"This is serious, very serious," Thrush said. "Why wasn't I informed before now."

"You were informed. Edith informed you."

"But not of the extent, the degree, the sum, the . . ."

Lamont released the club, swishing it down with his right hand and chipping the ball across the lawn towards the kitchens. "Don't they realise that the more they try to hound me, the more I will resist?"

"They?"

"The ironmasters—Fleming, like as not, and that buzzard Torrington will be leading the pack."

"Yes, coalmaster." Thrush hid his delight. "Fleming and Torrington are just the sort to attack you at this time."

"So they think that my pit will remain closed, do they? that Lamont's collieries will stay dry for the duration of this damned strike."

"But . . .?"

"We'll see about that." Lamont tossed the club away and, grasping his partner's elbow, steered him towards the French doors that opened directly into the boardroom on the wing of the mansion. "If it proves possible to break the will of the strikers in my pits, to have them back at work in a week or so, then I believe that I can raise enough wind to cover pressing debts."

"That's . . . impossible," said Thrush. "This 'solidarity' that they talk of, it has the whole damned lot of them in thrall. No, sir, the only feasible means of keeping the company afloat is to sell off stock to a suitable partner."

"And who would you suggest?"

"Well, under the circumstances, I would hesitate to sell to any one on the short list, to our so-called friends. My suggestion would be to make up a package of stock that would be acceptable to an agent, to sell, say, seven per cent equally from our own holdings, and incorporate the agent as a temporary partner on the clear understanding that we will recover the stock from him at a higher rate—say, ten per cent over the purchase figure—within six months."

"No agent would touch that kind of deal."

"I think it might be possible to find one who will."

"And nobody need know of it?"

"Nobody: only the three of us, and the agent."

"Seven per cent each?"

"Equally; thereby leaving you with the majority holding as at present."

"But this agent, he would hold twenty-one per cent?"

"Not hold," said Thrush; "carry."

"Supposing he elected to take an active part in our affairs and refused to sell the stock back to us in six months. Supposing we could not, even then, afford to buy," Lamont said. "This agent would hold more shares than you or Edith."

"True," Thrush admitted. "But collectively Edith and I would retain more authority than he would. And the three of us together would still own seventy-nine per cent of Blacklaw Collieries."

"Do you actually know of a trustworthy agent?"

"No, but I believe it might be possible to locate one."

"Then do it," Lamont said.

"Sell, you mean?"

131

"No, merely make the necessary arrangements for sale."

"Houston, as I've explained a dozen times before, delay can only mean . . ."

"Wait," Lamont said, "until after the eighteenth of the month."

"The eighteenth?" said Thrush, puzzled and fretful. "What significance has that particular date?"

"It seems that your spies in the U.F.M. have not been feeding you the right kind of information, Thrush," Lamont told him. "As it happens, on the eighteenth Blacklaw will be treated to a rally lead by Arthur Webb."

"Webb's meetings are commonplace," said Thrush. "What's so . . .?"

"Sydney." Lamont gripped his arm again as they approached the shadow of the house close to the French doors. "Sydney, for once you have been less than efficient."

"Really, Houston; really. What more could I do? This strike is so deeply rooted. I'm—yes, I admit it—I'm flummoxed."

"I'm not," said Lamont and led Thrush indoors to pour him a glass of sherry before lunch.

Try as they would, however, neither Sydney Thrush nor Edith could persuade Lamont to divulge what special event he had arranged for July 18th, and why it had so miraculously restored his good spirits.

*　　*　　*

Lily was first to see the blacklegs debouch from special coaches uncoupled from the Glasgow train at remote Claypark Halt. She had gone round by a dirt road to deliver buttermilk to the Claypark school-teacher. Hunger was already rife there, for the Claypark community was made up largely of lowpaid coal-sorters and surface workers who had no reserve to fall back on and who, within the caste system that had evolved over the past ten years, held a relatively humble place in the Movement itself. It was rare for a passenger train to stop at Claypark and Lily, curious and suspicious, drew up the pony-trap in the lee of a thorn hedge that flanked the station.

They were blacklegs all right, roving Irish navvies, North

of England professionals, and Scottish trash. Jeering voices
rose loud on the warm morning air, horseplay and oafish
catcalling as the gangers sorted the men into ragged marching
order. They all had the insolent swagger of rogues who
survived by strength of arm, and reaped fat wages from doing
things that no decent man would do. Lily knew the breed
only too well. She had seen them at work in coaltowns
before, and storming the mill-yards in her father's town in
Lancashire. They were evil men who flouted every moral
tenet, yet remained protected by authority and the law.

As if to demonstrate the absolute legality of their trade,
the crew were accompanied by a dozen burly policemen who,
in spite of the July heat, were wrapped in thick winter coats,
the usual armour for a stone-fight.

It was no coincidence that the strike-breakers had turned
up this morning. Lily had no doubt as to their destination.
Webb and Rob Ewing were scheduled to hold one of their
'solidarity' rallies at the picket line outside Blacklaw colliery.
Edward had told her. Her son, it seemed, was apprehensive
about Lamont's passivity and Thrush's apparent acceptance
of the shut-down. So far there had been no evictions, no show
of force by the owners, none of the hundred-and-one
retaliatory tricks that Lamont's work-force had expected.
Thrush had hardly shown his face near the pits since the
strike began.

Kleeking up the pony, Lily steered the trap away from
Claypark Halt and headed along the track to Blacklaw, giving
the animal a touch of the crop when she was out of sight of
the station.

Fifteen minutes later she was on the outskirts of Blacklaw.
Sitting high in the seat, she drove the trap as fast as she
dared over rutted cobbles down the long bleak stretch behind
the colliery wall. The winding towers loomed motionless above
her, the whole place possessed of an unusual silence that now
seemed menacing. Clattering, the trap rounded the corner into
Benburn Street and, with children shouting and running
before and behind, turned the curve round the town's
tenements and headed along towards the main pit gate.

The picket line was made up of a dozen miners. Some

were playing pitch-and-toss against the wall, using metal slugs in lieu of coins; others were huddled round a pair of whippets, sleek, lean handsome dogs, so clean and graceful among the lumpy miners. It was an old man's watch that morning.

Neill and Edward were not present.

Lily reined the pony. The trap slewed across the road. The men looked up and one, Jim Prester, came over to her.

"Are y'sellin' food, Lily? We've no money t'buy."

"Strike-breakers," Lily pointed across the pit territory. "Marshallin' down at Claypark Halt. A rough crowd lookin' for trouble, backed by special constables."

"Jesus," Prester said.

"Where's Rob Ewing? I thought there was a meetin' here."

"No' for an hour yet, Lily."

"Send word down the town." The man seemed at a loss to know what to do in this crisis situation. "I'll find Rob. Where's my lad?"

"They were here, the pair o'them, 'til a wee while ago. They must've walked down t'the brig at Poulter's burn t'meet Rob. He's got Webb wi'him, y'know."

"Damn Webb." Lily flicked the reins and urged the pony on again, sweeping left into the top of Main Street and trotting down towards the lane by the kirk. She had heard that Rob had lodged Arthur Webb in a house over by Eastlagg; it seemed rational that they would come over the narrow wooden bridge. Odd, though, to think of a man of Webb's status walking, not riding, to a meeting.

She drove the trap on. In her were mixed emotions—apprehension and fear but also tingling excitement at the prospect of what the brave colliers would do to those bully-boys. It was as if she had taken over Mirrin's mantel of involvement. She could quite understand now what had stimulated her sister-in-law back in the old days.

Braking the pony on the hill, she tucked the trap in by the kirkyard wall. Behind that wall, in mellow graves screened by ramblers, lay Alex and Douglas Stalker, and her husband James. Though she was not an imaginative person, Lily was aware of the encouraging presence of the dead. She tethered the pony to the gate and hurried on foot through the rows that backed the lane out into the field path that lead to the Poulter's burn.

She was a quarter of a mile along the path beyond the brig when the first savage shout went up from the direction of the pitgate. She knew then that she had missed Rob, missed Neill and Edward, and that, much more quickly than she would have supposed, strikers and blacklegs had met in combat in the streets of Blacklaw.

★   ★   ★

There were eight in the party who nipped into The Lantern's back room for a pint of beer—Rob and Webb, four solemn members of the district strike committee, and Neill Kellock, and Edward Stalker. The youngsters had met up with the officials in the kirk lane and, tagging along behind their hero, Rob, had drifted into conversation with Arthur Webb and a man called Morris from Redhill Pit on the far side of Hamilton. It was a low-key, relaxed discussion. There was no hint of belligerence among the committee men, only weary determination. Trouble was not anticipated.

The purposes of the rally were to spread the latest news on the progress of the strike, to show the Blacklaw miners that they were not forgotten by their leaders and, most important of all, to pull them out of their homes and band them together to boost morale. Rob had mounted eighteen such meetings throughout the district in the past eleven days. Like the conscientious trooper that he was, Webb had dutifully supplied the oratory at them all. Rob was not 'a platform man'. Indeed, he took no obvious part in any of the proceedings and, in spite of what local colliers supposed, held no official post.

Those refreshing pints of beer, however, were to cost the Union dear.

It did not occur to the messengers sent out from the pit gate that anyone would be in the back room of The Lantern at that hour of the morning, much less the speaker's party. Jim Prester had issued no specific instructions to search for Rob.

It was twenty minutes after ten when the six men and two youngsters came out of the side door into The Lantern's yard and, looking towards Main Street, first noticed the running figures.

Webb said, "What's their rush, Rob?"

"We're not due 'til eleven are we?" Morris checked his pocket watch.

"Listen," Neill said. "What's that?"

Rob clumped ahead of the others, walking with hands on hips, a strange gait. When he reached the end of the yard, he snapped out his right hand and plucked a young collier seemingly out of the air, lifting him bodily in mid-stride and swinging him to a halt against the stone gatepost.

"What's up?"

"Blacklegs. Backed by the bloody polis," the youth gasped. "Christ, Rob, they've caught us on the hop."

"Where are they?"

"They're attackin' the main gate, right now."

"How many on the picket line?"

"Can't say.

"On your way, then."

Rob returned to the group. "It's Lamont," he informed them. "He's hired himself a gang, backed by the riot squad by the sound o'it."

"Are they into the colliery yet?" asked Morris.

"They're endeavourin' to take the main gate."

Webb nodded. "Once they're inside an' have gear operatin', we're in trouble, Rob. I've seen this tactic used before. The law plainly states that we cannot prevent an owner hewin' coal on his own property."

"So that's why they've struck the main gate an' not gone sneakin' through the railway sidings," said Rob. "It's a manoeuvre calculated t'force attention on Blacklaw. Lamont's tellin' the country that he won't sit back an' let the strike take its course."

"Why are we standin' here yappin'?" Neill asked.

Ignoring the young man, Rob said, "Arthur, what do you advise?"

Webb looked pained. "Listen, Rob, I can't afford t'become involved. I'm sorry, but violence—my condoning violence— won't help us at all in other areas. It'll give the newspaper men somethin' positive t'use in arguments against our cause."

"That won't stop *us*, Mr. Webb," Neill declared.

"I should be up there, y'know," said Rob.

"Rob, if you'll heed my advice, you'll hold off 'til the first onslaught is over," Webb advised. "After that you must salvage what y'can out of the situation."

Rob glanced uncertainly at the other committee members who hung back in the yard. "Mr. Morris, what d'you say?"

"I'm afraid Mr. Webb's right, Rob."

"My God," Neill cried. "What's this? Are y'*all* showin' the white feather?"

"Shut your damned stupid mouth." Catching his cousin by the shoulder, Edward spun him away from the committee members who, occupied with the larger issues at stake, spared the brawling youngsters hardly a second glance.

Struggling, Neill shouted, "Let me go, y'bastard."

"You an' me—we're goin' home." Twisting, Edward tried to place a headlock on his cousin but he was shy of hurting the younger man. In an instant, Neill was free of him, darting into Main Street, shouting, "*You go on, then, back t'your Mammy.*"

"Neill, listen t'me."

Too late: Neill had already been carried away by a surge of six or eight miners pounding up the pavement.

There were ferocious shouts, whistlings, the sound of sledge-hammers smashing wood.

Rob ran out onto the pavement, Edward by his side.

"Christ, they're breakin' down the wee gate," Edward said. "Why haven't they got a key?"

"Because there are no managers on the spot," Rob told him.

Edward raised his fists to a level with his shoulders. His fair skin was suffused with blood, a high feverish flush of frustration. "What'll I do?"

Though his mind was occupied with ethical and tactical problems of his own, Rob slapped the young man a stinging blow on the rump, and told him, "Get up there an' make sure nothin' happens t'Neill."

That was all the excuse that Edward needed. He raced away like a whippet towards the phalanx of colliers that ebbed and flowed on the upper corner of Main Street. Behind him, Rob Ewing turned his back on the fighting.

Webb touched his sleeve consolingly. "There, Rob. I know how hard it is for you. I've been through it. But believe me, it's the best thing. You'll destroy your authority as an organiser if you get sucked int' a brawl."

"We haven't even got fifty men there yet," said Rob, seethingly.

"Aye, but your boys'll fight, won't they?"

"They'll fight," Rob said.

But the fight, such as it was, was short-lived, lasting only five or six minutes. The first three or four minutes involved a stalling action by the morning's picket-line. In spite of Lily's warning, nobody had expected the paid blacklegs to arrive from Claypark so quickly. They had doubled along like a platoon of Grenadiers, using speed not stealth to achieve their ends. They intended to take Blacklaw in short order with a sure-fire, all-out, two-pronged attack.

Twenty of the youngest and fittest of the hirelings arrived first. They were accompanied by two constables on horseback, and dispersed the pickets almost immediately, felling one man, a sixty-year-old, who was too slow to get out of their way.

Sledge-hammers were striking the wee door before the old collier hit the cobbles. There was no crowd to oppose the gang. Coming from the main stem of the town and out of the tenements, the colliers arrived in small groups, lacking the weight needed to form organised opposition and minus a leader to give them instructions. Incensed by the criminal injustice of the attack, however, a dozen or so flung themselves unarmed into the ranks of blacklegs who had strung themselves out to protect the hammermen. Two colliers—one, the biggest man in Blacklaw, Peter Ree—carried a thrust through the ranks and, as Neill arrived, set hands on one of the hammermen. Ree wrenched the short-shafted sledge from the Irish scab. Swinging away from a blow aimed at his head Ree went in under the arc, lifting his huge, powerful frame so that the scab, who was no lightweight himself, was raised on his right shoulder, then jerked back and down like a coalsack, left arm snapping with a sound like a rifle shot. The scab screamed and writhed on the cobbles. Almost casually, Ree kicked him in the ribs.

Peeling inwards, the broken rank directed itself upon Ree and his companion, a wild red haired bachelor named Grogan.

Neill Kellock was no hero, and certainly no leader. By sheer chance, he happened to be on the fringe of a pressing heap of colliers who, in those few seconds, had piled up from the town. Seeing Grogan fall under the flailing clubs of the blacklegs, they swarmed involuntarily forward. Neill found himself propelled over an estuary of empty cobbles towards the thick of the fight. For a moment he was filled with fear and horror. Digging in his heels, he tried to hold back. But the press was too much for him and, driven like a piece of flotsam on a wave, he rammed smack into the back of a scab who was thrashing away at Grogan.

Out of the corner of his eye—so Neill later claimed—he saw dark blue uniforms career around the corner and mass behind the horsemen. Somebody was yelling, *"Copper down. Copper down."* But no member of the constabulary had, at that juncture, entered the ferocious hub of the fighting close to the area of the wee door.

Neill had fought before, collecting his share of black eyes and jelly noses, but only in scraps where a nebulous line of decency had been drawn. Never before had he been hurled into the storm-centre of a barbarous riot. Coming hard against the blackleg, Neill stumbled. He caught at the man's upraised arm, a defensive gesture, designed only to stop himself pitching headlong into the middle of the circle where Grogan, knees hunched to his belly, head tucked into chest, was doing his best to deflect the rain of blows. The blackleg's reaction to Neill's attack was seasoned by many fights. Driving up with his knee, he was round on Neill before the boy could release his grasp. Only an automatic response on Neill's part prevented serious injury. Stepping back, he cocked his right hip and took the numbing blow on his thigh. Pain clinched it. Timidity turned to anger and anger exploded into rage, shooting a charge of energy into his bloodstream.

Connecting square with the blunt jaw as the man, out of balance, swung across him, he downed the scab with a single jab of his fist. He had a fleeting, gratifying glimpse of the man's eyes rolling, his mouth gaping, his spittle flecked with blood, then the head itself snapped away until it seemed that it must screw right round like a squat metal top. The force carried the man's shoulders, chest, torso, thighs and finally feet off in a flinching parabola as if he had been flung from the rim of a spinning wheel.

A pack of colliers swarmed past Neill to block the second wave of blacklegs.

Urged on by gangers, the special constables, whose job it was to protect 'innocent' strike-breakers, came clattering behind the skittish glossy-brown horses that swerved to scatter scuffling men and disrupt the fist fighting.

Still fired by rage, Neill leapt over Grogan's body and, as the wee door's hinges cracked, grabbed the nearest hammerman by the waist and dragged him back from the gate. There was no hope now of preventing entry to the yard, though the door was small in relation to the towering gate and the smashed frame had jammed so that only one man at a time could squeeze through. Waltzing round the startled hammerman, Neill caught the first entrant with his leg half through the aperture. Hugging the thigh, the boy wrestled and hauled him out again, ripping his chest on a jagged spar so that he plopped out bawling in pain and sprinkling droplets of bright red blood around him.

The hammerman aimed his sledge at Neill's shoulder; he knew better than to go for the head with a ten-pound weight of iron. The edge of the iron skinned the boy's arm as neatly as a flensing knife. Neill hardly noticed. He was possessed of a demon, a prancing ranting devil that had found an outlet for its fury. Come what may, he decided that no dirty blackleg bastard would enter that yard while he stood to prevent it. But the hammerman, equally determined, came again, shaft in both fists, like a rifle at the port. By sheer brute force he ran Neill back into the timbers so hard that the gate rattled its massive bolts and, for an instant, even seemed to yield.

To keep himself from being throttled, Neill also gripped the shaft. He saw the scab's swart features, eyes glinting with triumph, as he drove his full weight into the ash-wood length.

Gaining an inch of clearance, Neill wriggled and dropped. His boots entangled the blackleg's ankles so that the man swayed and, with Neill seated on the stones, tripped and sprawled back. He had sense enough to release his hold on the shaft or, for sure, he would have broken his spine. Recoiling into the gate, Neill executed a frantic Cossack-dance and, still with the ten-pound sledge like a pikestaff in his hands, leapt to his feet once more.

It was then that the police, in a figure of five, approached from his right. Furious still but beginning to come off the boil, the boy moved forward and, with a careless sweep of his arms, cast the hammer aside.

The square block-iron head struck Special Constable Ronald a glancing blow on the temple. His lips pursed at the contact. His brows shot up. His eyes widened with astonishment as if the dignity of the law had been flouted by nothing more damaging than a splatter of mud or a piece of soft fruit. Constable Ronald gave a croak of surprise and buckled. Knees bent, he eased into a squatting position from which he jack-knifed abruptly onto his belly and, according to a doctor's report, thereupon died.

Neill Stalker, of course, did not realise that Constable Ronald was dead. He did not resist when four other officers bore him to the ground and, a minute later, carried him bodily from the scene.

★   ★   ★

Kate did not know that a riot had started. Though only a couple of hundred yards from the pit-gates, Kellock's Square was a backwater. Besides she had been occupied in helping Duncan Lennie scrape out the sponging oven, a fussy kind of job, requiring thoroughness and careful applications of the soda solution that Willie mixed to his own formula. To Duncan fell the actual arm work with a wire brush. The scratching of bristles in the cavernous oven obliterated the sounds outside in the square.

The 'riot' lasted only six or seven minutes all told. The convergence on Kellock's Square of Lily, Rob Ewing, Edward and, a little later, of Constable Munro from Northrigg, happened so quickly that at first Kate suspected some kind of conspiracy between her relatives and friends. Numbed by the magnitude of their tidings, she begged them to tell her the whole truth, to confess that Neill was in fact dead.

Helping her sister-in-law to a chair in the kitchen, Lily said, "There, there, Kate. Neill's all right. He's fine."

"Where . . . where is he?"

"They took him to Hamilton," Edward said.

"Hamilton?"

"There has t'be an enquiry," Rob said.

"What are you sayin', Rob?" Kate pushed herself from the armchair. "What's happened t'him?"

"I told you," Rob said. "There was . . . an accident. A policeman was killed."

"What's that got t'do with Neill?"

"He was there," Rob said.

Willie and Lily tried to make her sit down again but she would have none of it. Of them all she knew that Rob Ewing would tell her the truth. She craved his directness.

"*Tell me.*"

"A special constable, one of the Hamilton force, was killed by a blow," Rob said. "Neill was involved in the fight. He's been arrested."

"How was the man killed?"

"By a blow t'the head."

"Then it wasn't my Neill."

"From . . . from something thrown; a hammer."

"Did *you* see it, Rob? Did you *see* him do it?" Kate cried.

From the corner of the kitchen, Edward spoke out. "I did."

Lily was on him. "You did? An' what were you doin' there?"

The young man—so like James—came out of the shadow. Warm July sunlight laid a shaft of gold across half the room. The Dandorelli cooking range gleamed. Pots steamed on the simmering ring, cooking a dinner that would not be eaten now.

"Aunt Kate," Edward said. "I saw it."

"Then tell me that he didn't do it?"

"Neill did it," Edward said. "He threw the hammer."

"But not intentionally, surely not intentionally?" Willie said.

"I don't know," said Edward. "But he threw it. I saw him."

"An' . . . an' . . . a man . . . is dead." Kate staggered. Lily caught her as she sank back and eased her into the armchair.

At that moment, Constable Munro, an acquaintance of the Kellocks, knocked on the door and tentatively entered the kitchen. He did not relish this job, the more so as his loyalty was divided. He felt sorry for Kate Kellock, very sorry indeed. But he had no sympathy at all for the hot-headed young rebel who had brutally slain a comrade. Trapped in this unpleasant situation, Munro formally delivered himself of his information.

". . . and will be brought to court tomorrow morning and formally charged. Until that time he will be detained in Hamilton police cells."

"What *is* the charge?" Rob asked.

"I am not empowered . . ."

"For God's sake, Munro," Rob shouted.

"Murder," Munro said, glancing at Kate. "The charge will be one of murder."

"In that case," Rob Ewing said, "Mr. Shallop, the Union's lawyer, will appear for the boy. An' by God, Munro, he'll have him out before you know it."

Bridling, Munro drew himself up, all sympathy for the family gone. The Stalkers had always been thick with Rob Ewing, and he had always been a pernicious influence on the peace of the district.

"We'll see about that, Rob Ewing. We'll see about that."

"You'll need witnesses to prove intention."

"Those we will have, believe me," Munro grated. "Why, there's a witness right there. You, Edward Stalker, you saw it."

"No," Edward said, without hesitation. "I saw nothing."

At that, Kate burst into a flood of tears.

★   ★   ★

At ten minutes to ten o'clock, Mirrin and Tom had entered the big square gloomy building of the Institution in Glasgow.

It was raining, a fine gossamer summer rain that caressed Tom's face and, unnoticed, turned the lenses of his glasses opaque. In such soft weather, the city seemed more ominous than ever. Carrying the valise that held the few items her husband would require during his three or four days' stay, Mirrin escorted Tom through the swing doors. She kept up a stream of chatter about how grand a place it was and what miracles of healing had been accomplished there and how fine a doctor Parfitt must be if old McVicar was impressed.

They were greeted by the Matron, a plump, whey-faced, prissy woman. Conducted in a little side room that smelled of beeswax polish and roses, the formalities of reception were brief.

"Will I be able t'see my husband tonight?" Mirrin asked.

"Seven o'clock." Matron pressed an electrical bell on the wall.

"Will that be after the . . . the operation?" Tom asked.

"Three o'clock," Matron said, like a talking chronometer.

A Clinical Assistant appeared. Though he wore the traditional black morning suit under his white linen coat Mirrin noticed that the hems of his trousers were frayed. Matron said not a word to the Clinical Assistant, whose age, Mirrin guessed, was not more than twenty-three or four. The woman handed him a buff cardboard folder.

The Assistant glanced inside, then smiled reassuringly at Tom.

"This way, Mr. Armstrong. Here, let me take your bag."

"I can manage."

Tom turned and kissed Mirrin briefly on the cheek. Any further demonstration of affection was stifled by the Matron's presence.

"Tell Malcolm," Tom said, "t'cut close an' firm, an' not be slack about whettin' the shears. He's t'leave the three marked . . ."

"You told him all that at breakfast, Tom."

"Aye, aye; so I did."

"This way, Mr. Armstrong. You'll be back near your flock in a week or so," the Clinical Assistant said.

Mirrin followed. She noted the way the young man walked close to Tom, shoulders touching, leading him. She must remember that technique for guiding the blind.

She heard their voices echoing in the corridor. "So you're a farmer, Mr. Armstrong? I've spent a wheen of summers on my uncle's croft on the Isle of Mull."

"Sheep?" Tom asked.

"And cattle."

The voices diminished. Mirrin loitered in the long linoleumed corridor, gazing down to the blank doors at the end. In the light from the street door and three tall windows the polished linoleum was like ice. Tom and the assistant rounded a corner and disappeared.

Behind her, Matron said, "Seven o'clock, Mrs. Armstrong."

"Thank you." Mirrin went out into West Regent Street in a lonely daze.

Throughout the remainder of the morning she wandered the Glasgow streets, listlessly window-shopping. She had no heart for it. Indeed, for many years now she had abjured the city. It held no excitements for her, only a remembrance of other large cities through which she had passed in her youth. Those memories were not particularly happy ones, now that she thought of it; Leeds, with its foul mills, Liverpool with its miles of docks. No worse than Glasgow, but no better.

She lunched at Miss Ancroft's, a pleasant restaurant much frequented by spinster ladies and widows. From the table she looked over busy Buchanan Street at its junction with St. Vincent Street, at the lunch-hour throng in business suits, at women in long skirts and white blouses. As the sun broke through the thin cloud and sparkled on the stone façades, she thought with longing of Hazelrig's flowing hayfields and cropped pastures.

At three o'clock, the hour scheduled for Tom's ordeal, Mirrin found herself in the Saltmarket near the river. Her feet hurt, for she was not used to pavements. She was dewed with perspiration, her hat band pressed wetly against her forehead. The Saltmarket was no place to be on a summer's afternoon. It reeked of the river, of close-packed tenements, of a thousand-and-one food shops hardly wider than fish barrels, crammed together along the gutters. At three o'clock, Mirrin stopped her aimless wandering. She stood by the kerb, looking up over the noisy morraine of carts, cabs and omnibuses at a hexagonal clock with gothic hands that graced the front of a Weathercoat shop.

She could not imagine what Tom must be experiencing now, conscious, blind, and laid out on his back. She could not imagine what he must be thinking as tiny steel knives probed his eyes. She felt helpless and forlorn in that hostile street in a city that seemed so far from home.

Impulsively she turned from the direction of the Clyde and headed back towards George Square and the hill that would lead her up to West Regent Street, just to be closer to him.

At that precise moment she heard the cry.

The accent was alien, the words broken into five gutteral syllables. For all that it was unmistakable. She turned again, this way and that, searching for the source of the sound.

"Black-a-law Strike-ah. Black-a-law Strike-ah."

The newsvendor was toddling down from the inner city, heavy canvas sack slung round his shoulder. Small and stunted he wore an unbuttoned waistcoat over a collarless grey shirt. On his head was a split straw hat. The big flapping news-sheet taped across his chest like a heraldic shield had ten words printed on it.

Mirrin stared. Still shouting the latest news, the dwarf stopped in front of a seedman's store and set up his pitch. When the vendor straightened, Mirrin was standing by him offering him a coin. He looked at her for a moment, jaws peppered with stubble, his eye quick, then, champing his brown teeth into a grin, said, "They done it now, they miners. No' much in this edition. Aye, it'll b' the morn afore the truth's out."

Mouth dry, heart pounding, Mirrin drew away from the man and, with fists clenched on the paper, scanned the headline. The item was embellished by a crude drawing of a collier with fist raised, hatred stamped on his brutish face.

Until that instant, Mirrin had failed to grasp the magnitude of the events that rocked her home town. Somehow, though she had absorbed all the gossip, it's significance had passed her like thistledown, events that five or ten or twenty years ago would have totally involved her and would have roused her to activity.

Kate had said nothing at all that morning; nor had Lily. The women's conversation had been confined to light and in-consequential questions about the farm. Of course, they knew she had troubles enough of her own. Even so, she should not have forgotten, not completely, that Blacklaw, Carlneuk, Eastlagg, Northrigg, Claypark, Inchpit, all Lamont's collieries, every pit, mine and digging in Scotland, in fact, was in a virtual state of siege.

She focused on the printed report, trying hard to grasp this latest threat. As she read, her features hardened in shock at the account of the doings in Blacklaw that morning, at the horrifying catalogue of riot, violence, and death.

★　　★　　★

At three-thirty on Wednesday afternoon, the main gate of Blacklaw Colliery was thrown open. In front of scattered crowds gathered by the tenements and broad corners of Main Street, Lamont took possession. Short of recourse to physical attack the colliers had no means of pulling Blacklaw back into the national shut-down. Liberals, Irish Members, Unionists and Conservatives might lobby to argue the rights of the common man, the Trades Union Congress might behave as if it was already an arm of the parliamentary system, but the truth was that an owner like Houston Lamont was still master of his own midden. The national press might print Lamont's name a thousand times in the months to come; men and women who had never clapped an eye on his sombre figure might talk of him as if they were privileged to be part of his inner circle, but the person the colliers saw ride through the gates of a pit under strike was still the old bogey man, the *bête noire*, that they had known for thirty years. History may be a matter of the recording of decisions but the decisions that Lamont arrived at were not so cut and dried as to make comprehensible reading. His strategy, from that day on, was like a river that progresses beyond the source of its energy and dissipates itself in a morass of stubborn resistance to logic and good order.

A half hour after Lamont's arrival Thrush rushed into the pit in a hired fly. For once his dress was not that of a drawing-room engineer. In a light-check Cheviot tweed suit, round crown felt hat tipped back from his face, he had the appearance of a person thoroughly harassed by circumstances beyond his control.

The gate was guarded by two grim special constables. Of Ronald's death-spot there was no visible sign, no chalk mark or rope barricade, not even a stain of blood. Inside the yard, blacklegs busied themselves with the maintenance of machinery. The sudden startling *whuuuuum-whum-whum* of a shunting engine welcomed Thrush to Blacklaw. He hopped out of the fly, flung money at the driver and hurried up the wooden steps onto the porch of the long low wooden block that still served as the manager's office.

Lamont waited inside, seated on a tall stool, one elbow resting on the desk lid, his left foot stretched for balance. He was dressed in an unfussy square-shouldered frock-coat and, to Thrush's surprise, was smoking a cigarette. With him was Dunlop, oldest manager in employment. Dunlop was a notorious 'company man'. One glance was sufficient to tell Thrush that Dunlop had again thrown in his hand with the owner. There had been few occasions in the past when Dunlop's role of henchman had promised more notoriety.

Thrush said, "Must we have him here?"

Dunlop looked hurt. He made a gesture in Lamont's direction as if to relinquish his fate to that divine judgment.

Lamont said, "What did you discover?"

Thrush said, "It's Stalker. Neill Stalker. He's being held in the police cells in Hamilton and will be brought to court to-morrow morning. It is quite clear that the charge will be one of homicide with malice aforethought. It wasn't, was it?"

"The police are bringing the charge, not me."

"From what I gather, the Special was struck with a hammer that one of the new labour force was using to break into the yard."

"What's wrong with you, Sydney?" Lamont asked. "I thought you'd be delighted at this turn of events."

"A man's dead."

"Apart from that."

"Stalker's surely not to blame."

"He struck the constable down, didn't he?"

"With provocation, in self-defence."

"Not as I saw it, Mr. Thrush," Davie Dunlop said.

"Where were you?"

"Watchin' from the tenement close."

"And that's what Dunlop will report to the police?" said Thrush.

"Of course."

"You claim that this isn't your case, Houston. Legally, I realise that it isn't, but morally . . ."

"Morally, Stalker is guilty. He killed a police officer, a man who was only doing his duty, by throwing a ten-pound hammer at his head. That, it seems to me, is clear indication of an intention to kill. However, I'm not concerned with that argument," Lamont said. "I'm more concerned with keeping Blacklaw pit in production."

"How?"

"By employing outside labour."

"It takes three hundred men to fetch coal out of the ground in any worthwhile quantity."

"I know that as well as you do," Lamont said. "I've hired a full squad."

"You mean," said Thrush, incredulously, "you mean, you've amassed a blackleg force of *three hundred* men?"

"The majority should arrive tomorrow."

"Houston, you'll start a riot."

"No, I've had my riot. It's over."

"The colliers won't stand for it."

"Then, perhaps, they will find more of their number in jail, along with the Stalker boy."

"I see," said Thrush. "*He's* your scapegoat."

"I did not intend that blood be shed," said Lamont. "On the other hand, Sydney, I did not shrink from the possibility as, in this instance, you seem to have done. Why did it not occur to *you* to bring in a blackleg force?"

"It did," Thrush said. "I rejected the idea as being too, well, dangerous; too inflammatory. And so it has proved."

"A collier has cold-bloodedly murdered an officer of the law," said Lamont. "He will be charged with that murder and, in due course, brought to trial."

"And found guilty of manslaughter—at worst."

"I think not," said Lamont. "I intend to cooperate with the police to the fullest extent. I believe that Stalker is guilty, and I will certainly marshal as much evidence as the police deem necessary to help them to prove their case. In the interim . . ."

"Ah, yes," said Thrush. "I thought there would be an interim."

"In the interim, with the help of my loyal managers, I will conduct the business of Blacklaw pit. I will hew coal, draw coal, transport coal, and *sell* coal."

"The wage of a single blackleg," Thrush said, "comes to more than that of three employed miners."

"I will pay it," said Lamont.

"And Eastlegg, and Northrigg, and the other pits?"

"There too, early next week. I will claim my legal entitlement to work the seams. I doubt if there will be more than token resistance."

"You're talking about hiring a thousand men?"

"A thousand men, Sydney, or more."

"Where will they live, eat, sleep?"

"In huts, in tents. They may lodge in Glasgow, if they wish. I will hire trains for them, if need be."

"Good for you, sir," chipped in Dunlop.

"Thank you, Dunlop," Lamont said.

"The Scottish County Unions will . . ." Thrush shrugged, helplessly.

"There are thirty-one thousand pit workers in Lanarkshire," said Lamont. "Individually only three thousand belong to the U.F.M. That isn't *real* strength. When they see their jobs being done by others, they'll come skulking back quick enough. When they pick up a newspaper and read that one of their precious brothers is being tried for his neck for murdering a policeman in a pit riot, they'll think twice before they lift a stone or a club, or even raise their voices. And if they do, in my bailiwick, on my policies, then they will have soldiers to contend with."

"The militia?" Now Thrush was really dumbfounded. "You would bring in the soldiers, Houston? It was tried in Wales, you know, and all it did there was consolidate public opinion in favour of the colliers' cause."

"I will have soldiers, if I need them. I have a murder to drag in front of newspaper reporters, a wanton brutal killing to win me public sympathy."

Thrush leaned against the edge of the sloping desk. Behind him an oillamp blazed; the windows of the managers' office, small and dirty, admitted little light.

"Aye, sir, that'll teach them what side their bread's buttered on," said Dunlop.

Thrush collected himself. He could see force in Lamont's arguments, admire the simple ruthlessness of the scheme, but there was nothing subtle about it, and its heartlessness disturbed even Sydney Thrush. He had not imagined Lamont capable of such vindictiveness. How long, he wondered, had this hatred of the colliers been festering in his master. Lamont had always looked after them reasonably well; he was fairly generous when it came to repairing houses and paying compensation for injuries and certain illnesses. He did not subscribe to the social welfare of the townships over which he held sway, but he was a better boss than most when all was said and done. At the time of the great debate about the Eight Hours Bill he had given the appearance of being left of centre in his sentiments. Had it all been a cloak, a disguise? Was Lamont, at last, showing the effects of too much power and too much worry? The altruism that, for a minute or so, diluted Thrush's selfishness, vanished. He began to plot his course of action, to turn the unexpected event to his own benefit as Lamont had so rapidly turned it to his.

"If you intend to pay a thousand casual workers, Houston, then you will need to tap a cash reserve that, to the best of my knowledge is not available." Thrush hooked his thumb in Dunlop's direction. The manager was all ears, not even trying to hide his delight in being made privy to such confidential secrets.

"We'll talk of that later, Sydney," said Lamont. "In the meantime, Dunlop, I would be grateful if you would find a dozen reliable witnesses to the killing. Colliers, not men from management or casual outside workers. Blacklaw colliers."

"Dunlop, perhaps I may assist you in . . . ah, tracing the witnesses," said Thrush, quick to realise Lamont's intention.

"Aye, it's not likely they'll offer themselves voluntarily," said Dunlop. "But I know them, an' there's ways and means t'make them tell the truth."

"It must *be* the truth, though," said Thrush. "It must be what they saw, or *think* they saw."

"That might not be t'our advantage, Mr. Thrush."

"Advantage, Dunlop?" said Thrush. "I'm talking about justice under the law. What did *you* see?"

"An unprovoked attack on a polis officer wi' a hammer. Stalker flung it straight at the constable."

"How far off was the constable?"

"Ten or fifteen yards."

"Ten?"

"Aye, ten."

"Not eight, or seven?"

"Well!"

"Seven yards is twenty-one feet, Mr. Dunlop," Lamont said. "To throw a ten-pound sledge-hammer that distance with any accuracy would require a very great deal of physical strength and determination."

"Aye, maybe it *was* closer."

"Then it could have been four or five yards, could it not?"

"I would say, Mr. Thrush, that it *was* five yards; not more than that."

"Other witnesses will be willing to corroborate your account, I'm sure?" said Thrush. "Now, Dunlop, I want you to think before you answer: who did you notice among the crowd, what miners?"

"Pat Lennox."

"Go on."

"The two McMurdo brothers, Silverdale, Bob Kerr, Bob Ward, Harold Jones, George and Bill Watson, some of the Williamses, Henderson, Joe McLaren, an' Tam Scott, an' . . ."

"Henderson," said Thrush. "Henderson might put truth before loyalty, I'm sure. If he's approached tactfully."

Dunlop winked. "I ken what y'mean, Mr. Thrush."

"Then get along with you," said Lamont.

Sunlight, thick with dust, formed a seemingly solid rectangle. The distant timpany of trucks was constant now and the cries of the casual labourers' foremen. Most of the blacklegs were skilled. Hard as granite and embittered by ill-luck they sustained a real or imagined sense of injustice that had struck them from the register of honest employees and sent them to join the outcast gangs. It was a legion with whom few coalmasters cared to acknowledge alliance, a threat to all small county strikes, and one that was seldom called into play. Now Lamont, without thought for reputation, had apparently invited every last labouring rogue in Scotland and the North of England to converge on the Blacklaw area with the promise of pound for pence, the dirty wage required to make them keep faith with his capitalist ideal. For hard cash he would buy their muscle, their loyalty and their vicious disregard for the system that had rejected them.

"How will you finance this venture, Houston?" said Thrush the moment the door closed behind Dunlop. "It might break us, you know, if we hew out less than we pay in wages."

"Economics have nothing to do with it," said Lamont. "It's principle that's involved now, Sydney. Believe it or not, I am a man of principle."

"Principles will not stuff a wage packet."

"Sell the stock."

"Seven per cent from each of our holdings?"

"Yes. Sell it as quickly and as shrewdly as you can. I want no hint of the sale to reach the open market. Did you contact a trustworthy agent?"

"I did, Houston."

"Then sell."

"What if that's not enough?"

"If more's required," said Lamont, calmly lighting himself another cigarette, "then I'll put Strathmore on the market."

*   *   *

Clad in a short stiffish green shift, Tom lay prone upon a coffin-shaped table, head buttressed by two leather pillows enveloped in white linen slips. The table was adjustable for height and rake, relative to the light shed from the tall windows of the operating ward on the second floor of the Institution. As he began his surgical preparations and the lecture that, apparently, went with them, Frank Parfitt fiddled with the iron wheel that raised and lowered the table. The motion imparted an odd sensation of weightlessness to the patient. No drug, apart from a five per cent solution of cocaine injected into the conjunctival sac, had been administered. Dr. Parfitt was scornful of general anaesthesias. He had warned Tom that he would suffer some discomfort, however, and, during the actual incisions, pain. With all the authority of a man who has never been on the receiving end of a blade, Parfitt assured Tom that the pain would not be excessive and that a 'big, strong chap like you will certainly be able to grin and bear it'.

What disconcerted Tom more than the prospect of pain was the fact that Parfitt's operation on *his* eyes had been chosen as the subject for a demonstration to ophthalmic students. A dozen students clustered eagerly around the table peering into the patient's face every time Parfitt made a move.

Tom felt like a show-beast; worse, since he could not demonstrate displeasure by tossing his horns or kicking up his hoofs. He had to lie still as a corpse, only winking his eyes to keep the corneas moist, with all those fleshy blobs bobbing in and out of range; had, too, to hear in graphic detail every item of the progress that was being made, though the high-flown medical phrases bore no relation to the pricks and stings and uncomfortable sensations that he felt in his eyes.

He listened to every word, though, for he had nothing else upon which to fix his attention. Besides, he was a man, not a sheep. The doctor's voice was perfectly audible in spite of the gauze mask over his mouth. Tom could smell the sterilising fluids that had been used—benzine, oxycyanide solution, iodoform powder. He did not like any of the smells and, coupled with his nervousness, they made him gag a little.

"Steady now, Mr. Armstrong," Parfitt commanded.

The surgeon's face loomed large as he examined Tom's eyeballs through an optical lens.

"As has been explained to you, gentlemen, in respect of our patient's condition, we are dealing with Glaucoma Simplex in primary form. A non-congestive affliction. According to my predecessor's notes, it is of no discernible cause, and certainly not rooted in congenital anomaly. I myself question if this case —indeed any case—is caused by nervous irritation of the secretory fibres due to inflammation of the chorioid or the ciliary body."

The hanging shape, like a hallowe'en lantern, receded from Tom's sight. He was left with a sheet of light, the mottled texture of parchment. Parfitt's voice came from below the level of his feet, or so it seemed. He was tempted to lift his head to catch the lecture better. As if sensing this motion before it was made, young Hibbert—the affable Clinical Assistant—touched Tom's breastbone with his forefinger, holding him down.

Parfitt went on, "Surgery has been performed on both eyes on two previous occasions in this Institution, by my predecessor. Healing in both cases was complete but the effectiveness of the operations in permanently alleviating the condition has proved very disappointing. In both cases, the operation was that of simple iridectomy with the intention of releasing the aqueous via a filtration scar. In neither operation did the surgeon attempt to create a cystoid scar by cutting out a portion of each sclera and forming a thin cicatrix." Parfitt paused. Even Tom, lost in the river of medical terms, sensed Parfitt's implied criticism of his predecessor, Dr. Graham.

For no reason Tom thought of Mirrin, an idle flash, like a lantern-slide briefly exposed within his brain. He saw her eagerly stooped over a white bull-calf, first ever born on Hazelrig, on a vast cold starry February night in the steaming byre stall, Mirrin bent over the long jelly-streaked wee beast, her fingers plucking the stuff from nostrils and mouth, the smile coming to her lips as she felt the calf's blubbery snort of breath for the first time.

"It is my belief that Mr. Armstrong's condition can effectively be relieved and his sight restored by performing a sclerectomy, by trephining the sclera in other words. In this case the present remaining field of vision is just large enough to suggest that the operation might increase it without the usual early intussusception that carries it beyond the point of fixation."

Tom listened, Mirrin, the calf, the past wiped from his

thoughts. It was becoming increasingly difficult to associate that dry English voice with his future. So far, Parfitt had not touched his eyes. It relieved him to learn that Parfitt did not require the use of hellish spring devices to jam his lids wide open during the operation. Though the eyeballs would be fixed by using toothed forceps, Parfitt had assured Tom that he would not suffer the acute discomfort that he had done on previous occasions. The Assistant, Hibbert, was very skilled. He would simply hold the lids apart with his fingers, thus, Parfitt said, avoiding any pressure on the eyeball.

"*Pince ciseaux*—these—scissors," said Parfitt, "will enable me to divide the conjunctiva five millimeters above the cornea and in a direction concentric with it. I will then prolong the incision downward at both ends as far as the corneal margin, forming a conjunctival flap with its base at the upper limbus. I think we'll begin, Hibbert, if you will hold the lid of the right eye."

Tom stiffened as huge club-like fingers loomed over his brow, but he felt nothing, truly nothing, not even the imaginary nick of the glittering scissors that he glimpsed for a split-second before Parfitt's hand blotted out light completely from his right eye. He could discern the side of Parfitt's head, sprigs of hair, the pink earlobe, very clearly indeed with his left eye. Though he had been warned to expect pain, there was none.

After several minutes, still bent over Tom's face, Parfitt, in slower tempo, said, "I . . . am . . . now in process of dissecting off the flap as . . . far . . . as . . . the limbus. I . . . will . . . now . . . carry . . . the dissection . . . somewhat beyond by undermining the limbus and the superficial layers of the cornea."

God. Striving to instruct his quailing, unfeeling flesh, Tom spoke to himself. His voice seemed to boom in the occipital cavities, as if he had a head cold; *God, is it me he's talkin' about?* What would Kitten make of all this? He thought of her because the cuts, as he imagined them, were dainty and miniature, like the stitching on a dolly's dress, like the tiny fine blonde hairs on his daughter's neck when seen against sunlight. Then he thought of rowan berries, and drops of blood, pure and heavy and frightening.

Parfitt's head was raised, showing Tom a chin and the pores

of a throat lightly dusted with talcum to cool the shaving-razor strokes. "I have now exposed the real junction of the cornea and the sclera."

"Doctor Parfitt," said a deep Fifeshire voice, "what is that implement you have just taken up?"

"Ah, yes," said Parfitt. "Naturally, it's unfamiliar to you. Elliot's trephining tool. A steel tube. Inferior sharp edge of one and half millimeters diameter. Set on the eye so that the tube's opening lies half on the cornea, half on the sclera, I will revolve the trephine between finger and thumb and—well, bore—bore into the sclera. Gradually, of course. When I feel no resistance, penetration is complete. On withdrawal of the trephine the excised disc of sclera comes with it, leaving a narrow coloboma to the pupillary margin. Note that the instrument does not enter the anterior chamber, though the fistulising effect is much more permanent than with ordinary iridectomy and, indeed, it is an easier operation to perform."

That much Tom understood: a hole bored into his eye.

He would hardly be likely to miss the part that was taken away.

What he would miss would be a similar excision from his store of memories. A desperate kind of dullness came over him as Parfitt concluded the operation on his right eyeball. He had no interest at all in it. He was more concerned with the restlessness in his ankles and an itch that had developed in his big toe. What a joke! He could take off the toe himself with a sickle and never miss it. Never miss it. But that grain of pus-like substance—how minute it must be—perhaps he would miss that after all.

What if Parfitt's hand slipped.

No, he could not even make himself nervous with that inane thought. In spite of himself, he trusted the doctor's skill.

At length, Parfitt said, "I have replaced the conjunctival flap in its former site. It will soon become adherent without suturing. Before I proceed to his left eye, you may ask questions."

"Sir," said a light, very proper, vowel-rolling sort of voice, "I have heard that Elliot's trephining has the disadvantage of giving rise to late infection. Is this so, in your experience?"

"No, Mr. Stewart, this is not so, in my experience," said Parfitt curtly.

"Panophthalmitis, or irido-cyclitis can lead to total destruction of sight," said the same voice, autocratically.

Tom swallowed the sticky spittle in his mouth.

Hibbert patted his cheek with his forefinger and, with his mouth close to Tom's ear, whispered, "Don't listen to his blethers."

"I commend your knowledge of the subject, Mr. Stewart," said Parfitt. "But this is not a length of wood I'm punching holes in."

"Sir?"

"Discussion of possible complications should not take place in the operating room, Mr. Stewart," Parfitt said. "Besides, the risk of such esoteric infections is absolutely minimal. Now, Hibbert, if you will prepare the left eye perhaps I may complete the operation without further interruption. We will take this matter up again, Mr. Stewart, at Tuesday class."

"Yes, sir," Stewart said, without a trace of contrition.

Total destruction of sight. It had finally been said. It had been brought into the very operating room. The words echoed in Tom's head throughout the rest of the hour. Did Stewart know what he was talking about? Did he know more than Parfitt? 'This is not a length of wood.' Parfitt did not want him to learn the truth.

Tom squirmed. Politely but firmly, Parfitt told him to hold still.

By four o'clock, it was all over, and Tom was back in a strange bed in a small lonely ward on the south side of the building. He could see nothing now; a pledget of sterilised gauze had been placed over his eyes and a latticed frame with padded patches taped, like a mask, across his face. He lay on his back, a thin hard pillow under his neck, and stared at utter blackness. His eyes pricked and smarted. He paid not the slightest attention to the discomfort. Already he had descended into a state of adjustment, despondently reconciling himself to blindness. The effort represented escape from the torment of uncertainty that he must, realistically, endure for the next several months. Very well, he *would* believe the snobbishsounding young student. Infection *would* set it. His optic nerves *would* rot. He would never see *anything* again.

That was the way of it, the end of it.

He really *was* blind now.

He curled his fingers into fists where they lay on his chest on top of the light blanket.

Outside, Glasgow hummed with summer sounds.

He did not sleep.

He was still lying motionless in a wallow of self-pity at seven o'clock when Mirrin brought him the news. After that, to his immense relief, he had something else to think about and there were minutes, many accumulated minutes, during the next few days when he did not think of himself at all.

★　★　★

Dusk was falling across the town of Hamilton. Neill marked changes of light on the far wall of the corridor by standing at his cell door and raising himself on his fingertips. The action hurt his bruised arm and nipped the bandage under his armpit and he soon returned to the bed. The cell was thirteen feet by seven feet by nine. The ceiling and half the height of the walls were limewashed. A dado of dull brown rose four feet from the floor, and the outer wall, which faced onto a gloomy niche adjacent to the police stables, was patched with cement. The window was high. Neill could not see out of it without balancing himself like an acrobat between the bed-end and the halfmoon-shaped shelf on which were a Bible, a cup and a tin plate. On one panel of the door was a placard outlining the rights of prisoners on remand, together with the scale of charges for additional comforts. A warning, in blacker type, stated that it was a prisoner's duty to obtain legal advice and to ensure the attendance of witnesses at trial, though how this trick could be managed from within a police cell was more than Neill could imagine.

Strangely, the young man was not distraught. He had a natural curiosity that, mingled with shock, initially deadened him to fear and shame. In no uncertain manner he had been informed that he had killed a police special constable, a man with a wife and two small children. The policemen with whom he had come into contact did everything in their power to fan his guilt. But he did not feel guilty. Horse-sense inured him to the tortures of emotion, plus a belief that he, as well as Constable Ronald, was the victim of a devious plan to break the national strike. By promoting himself to martyr's status Neill succeeded in creating the belief that Rob and the U.F.M. lawyer, Mr. Shallop, would protect him from Lamont's machinations. Knowing that there was nothing he could do, he relied on his brothers to guide him safe through the shoals of law and have him back home in a week or two.

Shallop, a wiry little man with a soft Border accent, had questioned him closely. Shallop had also tried to make him understand that the process of law would take time, that he must be patient. Apparently, Shallop would make his first bid to have him discharged the very next morning when the case appeared on charge. But Shallop was not optimistic about obtaining a release at that stage.

"I'm sorry about Constable Ronald," Neill had said, without a great deal of contrition. "But I just never saw him."

"You simply threw the weapon away?"

"It wasn't a weapon, it was a hammer," Neill had said.

"Aye, lad, that's a good point."

Shallop's interrogation had lasted over an hour during which he had made copious notes. At the end of it, he had encouraged Neill, playing shrewdly on the young man's self-created image, telling him that his mates would be proud of him, that it would all come right for him in the long run.

"What about m'job, though?" Neill had said.

"Lamont'll not have you back," Rob had told him. "But we look after our own. We'll find you other employment, never fear."

"Did y'see the fight, Rob?"

"Some of it."

"I kept the blacklegs out."

"Aye."

"Pity they got in after all."

"Aye."

"It won't break the strike, will it?"

"No, Neill. No, it won't break the strike," Rob had lied.

It was dusk before the stimulation of the day's events began to wear off and the young man slipped inevitably into loneliness and depression. As the smart of tears came to his eyes he remembered Shallop's parting words, *You are guilty of no crime. You are innocent until the Crown proves you guilty. Remember that, Neill, you are not yet a criminal.* It did not seem to help. His mother's arrival only served to release the negative feelings that had swelled in him during that half hour of twilight when the rest of the world was free to go home to its supper and its bed.

When Neill saw Kate's face, he knew.

When Neill saw the kitbag that Willie had brought, he knew.

When Neill saw the change of clothing, the books and magazines, the extra warm blankets, and the foodstuffs, he knew that Rob and Shallop had told his parents that the first appeal to legal sanity would be made in vain and that he, on the morrow, would be remanded to a higher court for judgment, that his confinement—innocent though he was—would be a long one.

He thought not of Blacklaw but of Hazelrig, how he would miss the harvest there, how the high summer would wane and autumn come and he would still be here, locked up in this dingy narrow place. The weeks stretched suddenly to an eternity, and his faith in Shallop, the U.F.M., Rob Ewing and the nebulous figures of justice splashed away like water from a holed bucket. When his mother entered the miserable cell, Neill threw himself into her arms and dissolved in uncontrollable weeping.

*   *   *

It was dark now, and soft. Bats flittered between the trees that arched over the back road to Blacklaw, a half-mile stretch that had not been robbed of its rural character by the spread of industry. Below the cart, the slope dropped sharply to a stagnant lake in which the last pinky flecks of the long-set sun were caught. Scents of wildflowers and flowering weeds were heavier than the burning gases from the smelting wastes seeping from the chimney just over the brow. Kate clung to her husband in a pose that, under other circumstances, would have suggested romance, not a need born from grief and despair.

Steering the horse with the reins in his left hand, the baker hugged Kate to him, cradling her head to his shoulder. Sobs still racked her, though the full flood of her anguish had passed.

"Kate, Kate," Willie crooned. "He'll be all right. He didn't mean t'kill that poor chap."

"It's . . . not . . . not that, Willie; though that's on my conscience too."

"What then, love?"

"That . . . that place."

"It'll only be a month or so 'til the trial, so Shallop says."

"Shallop! I don't trust him any more than I trust Rob Ewing."

"Is that no' a wee bit harsh, Kate?"

She raised her head, hair spilling from under her Sunday hat. "Could they not just be content."

"Hm?" said Willie. "Who?"

"Ewing; the miners."

Cautiously, Willie said, "It's precious little they have t'be content with, Kate."

"You too?"

"Now, now, dear," said Willie. "It'll not help t'blame me, or Rob for that matter."

"But Neill did kill that man."

"It was an act o' God," said Willie.

"What . . . what if he's found guilty an' convicted. Oh, Willie, what if . . ."

"Shallop says there's no chance o' that happenin'. A good lawyer'll sweep away the Crown case in no time. At worst, it'll be a manslaughter charge."

The baker realised at once that he should not, at this stage, have passed on Shallop's confidences to his wife.

"Manslaughter?" Kate pushed herself away from him. "An' what sort of prison sentence does that carry?"

"Not . . . well, maybe just a year or two."

"An' Neill will be branded a criminal for the rest o' his life."

"Acquittal's the most likely verdict."

"How can you be sure?"

"Nobody can be sure. I'm doin' everythin' I can," said Willie. "Neill won't lack for money, nor for friends."

"Friends, aye, like the friends who deserted him, left him to carry the blame," Kate said. "He'll have no friends when the time comes, you'll see."

Willie chose his words with care. "Maybe not, but at least he'll have his family."

That quietened her. He had not expected rancour from his wife. In all the years he had known her she had never been less than generous to others, in attitude as well as deed. If there had been a bright side, then Kate had searched for it. Sometimes, he had supposed her gullible, almost naive.

"He's not your flesh an' blood Willie."

Hurt, Willie resisted pointing out that Neill was not her flesh and blood either. He said, "Maybe not, dear, but it was me that helped you raise him, an' we'll have t'stand together by him now."

"If Lamont stood by him . . ."

"It was Lamont who brought in the 'specials'."

"Lamont could not have known that it would lead t'a man's death," Kate said.

Perplexed by this latest turn of thought, Willie said, "I don't see what Lamont can do t'help, even if he was so inclined."

"He could speak up for Neill. They'd listen t'him. He's a powerful man in Lanarkshire. If he spoke up for Neill, then surely there'd be no case t'answer."

"Well . . ." said Willie, dubiously.

"If Houston Lamont said that Neill did not do it, then everybody would support Neill, an' the police would have t'release him."

"Kate, don't build up your hopes. Lamont won't do it. Don't y'see; Neill's his . . . his enemy."

"Lamont could be made t'change his mind," Kate said.

"No, no, dear. No."

She was sitting upright now, tucking her hair neatly beneath her hat again, her head cocked in a manner that indicated not contemplation but decision. The cart rolled out of the trees and the built-up crescent of cottage rows and industrial warehouses that crowded round Claypark became visible across the railway tracks. Gently Willie urged the horse onto the crest of the hill that overlooked Blacklaw. Kate sat back against the cord-padded seat, hands folded in her lap. At that moment, she reminded

Willie of her mother, Flora; the same dour, stubborn posture.

"Mirrin could do it," she declared.

"Do . . . do what, Kate?"

"Talk t'Lamont," Kate said. "Mirrin could make him change his mind."

"Oh, now, Kate, you've no right t'ask Mirrin."

"She's my sister, Willie."

"Even so, at this time, in view of what's happened . . ."

"Mirrin will do it."

Though more troubled than ever, the baker had sense enough not to argue.

"After all," Kate added. "She's done it before."

★　　★　　★

"No, Kate," Mirrin said. "That's too much t'ask."

"Don't you care what happens t'Neill?"

"Of course I care. I'll do anythin' I can . . ."

"Then go an' speak t'Houston Lamont."

"I've no influence over him."

"You have," said Kate flatly. "If y'exerted yourself y'could make him change his mind."

"Willie," Mirrin said. "Can you not make her see reason?"

Willie shook his head.

It was well after eleven o'clock in the Kellock's kitchen. Lily had met Mirrin's train at Hamilton and had informed her of the details of the day's dramatic events. Mirrin's mind was still full of Tom; the turmoil caused by conflicting loyalties made her snappish. She should have been home, at the farm, looking after her family. It had not yet occurred to her quite how grave Neill's position might be. Lily had given no indication of Kate's intention; she had not known of it in advance. Lily had not seen Kate since mid-afternoon. In Willie's absence, it had fallen on Lily, assisted by Edward, to keep the bakehouse and its attendant businesses running.

Now the family were gathered in council and any vacillation in Kate's attitude had gone. Bitter, forceful and to the point, it was as if she blamed them—Mirrin, Lily and Edward—for promoting the incidents that had put her son behind bars.

Tom had predicted as much. He had talked hardly at all of

the operation and had evinced no great concern for his future. He had lain on his back with the mask over his face and his hand in Mirrin's for the whole of the evening visiting and talked of nothing but Edward, Neill, Kate and Willie. Lifted out of himself, he had eagerly seized on this drama to relieve the monotony of self-pity.

Mirrin remembered his warning. "Watch out for your sister, Mirrin. She'll throw blame where she can."

"Kate's not like that."

"She's a Stalker."

"An' what's that supposed t'mean?"

"She'll need t'find somethin' t'fight, an' the law's a poor target, I'm thinkin'."

"I've . . . I've too much t'do t'become involved."

"Get away with you, Mirrin," Tom had told her. "I don't mean that for a minute."

"Ach, the poor lad," Mirrin had said, and Tom had squeezed her hand to comfort her, a strange reversal in their roles. She had watched his mouth, seeking there an expression of his feelings. She had noted how calm he seemed, the harsh lines of strain smoothed a little, as if the surgeon's knife had removed a source of pain from his body. Normally she would have questioned him about his condition, but Tom would have none of it. Instead he had led her through an hour's discussion of the news, squeezing out each droplet of information that the evening newspapers contained. His objective assessment had been valuable. Though she was not aware of it at the time, it had helped prepare Mirrin for this family gathering.

Edward had been sent up to Hazelrig to carry the news to Malcolm, to tell him that his mother would be late returning. Kate had thought of that. Normally it would have seemed like a thoughtful act, but tonight Mirrin suspected that Kate had deliberately got her nephew out of the way, as if the sight of him—at liberty—offended her.

After fifteen minutes of conversation concerning Neill's courage and the conditions in Hamilton police cells, Kate suddenly blurted out, "You must go t'Lamont, Mirrin, an' tell him t'speak out in Neill's favour. That way we might get the case dismissed."

The hostility that had floated in the air since Mirrin's arrival now took definite shape: Lamont, Houston Lamont, that distinguished-looking gentleman industrialist, her former lover. At long last he had reached his influence into the very heart of the Stalker clan. Had he changed their relationships one to the other, or was it, Mirrin wondered, just the passage of years, the natural divisions of responsibility and affection that occur in all families?

Mirrin thought, "Aye, Kate has confused me with the girl I once was, though she sees me every day and accepts me as Tom Armstrong's wife. But now I am to be her sister again, not as I am, but as she thinks I was eighteen years ago, with the strength to do all the things that she was never able to bring herself to do."

That's what Tom had tried to put into words.

The bond between Mirrin and her husband was suddenly re-established in this new, puzzling arithmetic that linked past and future, sister and sister, mother and son, and now, unpredictably, husband and wife. Once more the time had come, Mirrin thought, to take sides. A modicum of prosperity had brought them out of the primitive circle of work and worry, had given them an opportunity to think of other, more human things. But Tom's blindness, and Neill's arrest had dragged them backwards. Harbours and anchorages that had served two decades ago, would not serve now. How could she make Kate understand that life was so much more complex than she remembered it to be?

She looked closely at her sister's face. In the eyes was a hardness that went beyond determination.

Once more Mirrin refused to consider a personal appeal to Lamont.

Kate's lips compressed. Her brows made a dark scowling furrow in her forehead.

"I see," she snapped. "I'm glad that's out. I'm glad that's been said."

"Kate, listen . . ." Mirrin began.

There was no point in arguing.

Hunched in her chair, thick chin bunched against her left shoulder as she watched her daughters and restrained herself from intervening in an explosive situation, even Flora seemed to radiate the suspicion that Mirrin was heartless.

Mirrin sensed that Willie was on her side. Tacitly he acknowledged that any attitude she might adopt in relation to Neill's innocence or guilt was bound to be construed as wrong.

She had put the family before her own happiness many times in the past. She had come close to sacrificing her future for them. Now she had no future left to sacrifice—or precious little of it. Perhaps Lily, too, understood that much.

Mirrin said, "When does Neill appear in court?"

Kate shook her head, and made a long, impatient whining sound. Kate turned her back and—for some reason—reached the big poker from the side of the grate and rattled it against the drop-trap of the Dandorelli before plunging it into the heart of the coals between the bars. She left it there, her hand on the staghorn handle as on a sword.

"Willie?" Mirrin appealed to the baker. He shrugged again, apologetically. He knew how bad this whole business was and, what's more, how much worse it was liable to become.

"Tomorrow morning, Mirrin," he answered.

"This Union lawyer, is he good enough t'be goin' on with?"

"I think so," Willie said, uncertainly.

Mirrin glanced at Lily who was seated in shadow at the far end of the supper table holding a cup in both hands and sipping from it from time to time, though the tea it contained must have turned cold long since.

"Will I come down?" Mirrin asked. "Do y'want me in court?"

"Don't ask me," said Lily.

Kate rounded on her. "If it had been your boy, you'd have answered quick enough. But, oh, no. Your Edward wouldn't do anythin' like that."

Lily sipped tea and stared at the pattern of the cloth.

Kate said, "I suppose since the Union got him int' it you'll all stand idly back an' wait for the damned Union t'get him out of it?"

Mirrin said, "There's no point t'be served by this discussion Kate. Nothin' can be done t'night. It's late, an' we're all exhausted."

"That's right, walk out on me."

Flora said, "Will y'not try, Mirrin?"

"Try what, for God's sake?"

"Your friend Lamont."

Hastily, Willie said, "It'll do no good. There's nothin' t'be gained from such a move at this stage. Lamont couldn't stop Neill bein' charged an' committed t'trial even if he wanted to."

Addressing herself exclusively to Willie, Mirrin said, "Is there anythin' I can send down for the boy? Milk? Vegetables?"

"We'll see t'all that, Mirrin, thanks," Willie said.

"If it's money . . ."

"Keep your money, Mirrin," Kate snapped.

Willie sighed. "You'd better go, Mirrin," he whispered. "She's . . . she's not herself at all."

"Small wonder," Mirrin said.

Picking up her hat from the sideboard, with a nod to Lily and Flora, she went out into the corridor. Willie followed her. He had the restrained manner of a mourner who must check his own sorrow to comfort others.

At the door to the yard, he put his hand on Mirrin's shoulder. The woman turned and embraced the elderly baker. "How bad *is* it?"

"With Kate, y'mean?"

"Aye."

"She just doesn't comprehend what's happened. She doesn't understand how it can have happened t'her son."

Mirrin said, "An' with Neill?"

"He's young enough t'be resilient."

"He killed a man, though."

"He did," said Willie. "But it really was an accident."

"As long as Neill himself continues t'believe that," said Mirrin, "then like as not he'll weather the storm."

"Aye, but it'll be a hell of a long storm, Mirrin," said Willie. "I've said nothin' t'Kate yet, but it seems t'me that if Lamont deliberately mounted that take-over on Blacklaw to demonstrate t'his creditors that he's strong, then this bloody development will suit him just fine."

"What's that you're sayin', Willie?"

"Just that Kate, for all the wrong reasons, may have put her finger on the one aspect o'this case that'll make it a major issue."

"I still don't grasp . . ."

"Class war," said Willie. "Not at the pithead or in the bloody Cooperative hall, Mirrin, but in the High Court."

"That's what Tom said."

Willie touched his hand to his brow in a tapping gesture of self-reprimand. "All this put it out m'head. How *is* Tom? What happened at the operation?"

"He's fine," said Mirrin. "I mean it, Willie. He's fine. Whether the operation will succeed in restorin' his sight or not, well, that's another matter. But just havin' it over an' done with has fairly settled him."

"I tell you, Mirrin, I wish Tom Armstrong was here," Willie said.

"What could he do?"

"He's got a head on his shoulders," Willie said. "An' he's neither a union man nor blood-kin. I could use his advice, I'll tell you."

"Advice?" said Mirrin. "I think you'll have plenty o'that, Willie, whether he's in Hazelrig or in bed in Glasgow."

*   *   *

One of the Duke's managers called for Hazelrig's fleeces before eight on Thursday morning. Mirrin greeted him in the yard and invited him to join the family for breakfast. But the depute claimed that he had too many calls to make to stay. Collecting wool from tenant farms—at a decent price—to haul to Burroch Mills, another of the Duke's many thriving enterprises, seemed to have become an urgent job. The depute had never been in much of a hurry before; it cost Mirrin only a couple of minutes to realise that the man was embarrassed.

"You'll have heard about my nephew, Mr. Millar?"

Millar leapt onto the plank seat. Seven bundles, three fleeces to a bundle, looked lost in the empty box-cart. Beyond the cart was Malcolm, listening, beyond him, Sandy listening too. In the doorway of the kitchen Davie balanced on one leg, one shoe on, the other off.

"Sorry I was t'hear it," said Millar quickly. "It's a nasty turn-up for the colliers' cause."

"A nasty turn-up for Neill Stalker an' his family too."

"Quite so. Quite so. I feel for you all."

"Comes from gettin' mixed up with union politics." Mirrin baited the trap.

"Exactly what I was sayin' m'self last night in the pub," Millar confessed, not realising that he had been trapped. "Not that there isn't sympathy for the lad. He's just the tool o' unscrupulous factions."

"Is *that* what they're sayin' down the county?"

"Words t'that effect." Millar snatched the whip from its stump, to administer a slap to the horse's rump then he paused and gazed at Mirrin, speculatively. "I'll be frank, Mrs. Armstrong, most o' the chaps I drink with, farmers, are o'the opinion that your nephew was in the wrong."

"Constable Ronald's death was pure accident."

"Accidents don't just happen," Millar said. "The boy was there t'fight. If he hadn't been there—fightin'—then poor Constable Ronald would still be alive t'keep his bairns fed."

"Do any o'your wise friends know what the fight was about?"

Though still anxious to be clear of Hazelrig and on his way to safer ground, Millar did her the courtesy of giving her a considered answer. "In basic terms, it's about the right o'the common man t' withhold his labour."

"Too glib, Mr. Millar."

"Too one-sided, maybe, Mrs. Armstrong," Millar admitted. "But it'll not seem glib when that issue is given shape by the judges. It'll not be a simple test o'justice, then, believe me, not a question o'whether a young boy killed a Special Constable or not. It'll be a question o'the use o'power, an' the misuse o'power."

"I see you an' your friends have already given the subject a good maulin'."

"I wish your nephew no harm."

"Glad t'hear it, Mr. Millar."

"But I'd be less than honest if I pretended to approve o'what he did, or his reasons for doin' it."

"I appreciate your honesty, Mr. Millar," said Mirrin. "Now, since you're in a hurry, I'll not be keepin' you further."

"Goodbye, Malcolm." Millar was a popular man and did not like ill-feeling.

Malcolm raised his hand in farewell as Millar steered the cart out of the yard.

"Tell Tom we hope he's back in harness soon," Millar shouted above the rumble of the wheels.

Malcolm nodded and waved again, then strode over to join his mother who was staring thoughtfully after the departing vehicle.

The young man's shirt and melton trousers smelled strongly of sheep grease. Two or three washings would be required to remove the odour. Sandy joined them. He wore a faded canvas overall with bib and braces. He had removed his shirt, leaving his chest and shoulders bare. His skin was freckled.

Sandy said, "What's bitin' old Millar?"

"Neill," Malcolm told his brother. "An' Millar's only the first taste o'it. Is that not right, mother?"

"I'm afraid you've struck it, Malcolm. Your cousin'll have very few supporters now."

"But Neill never . . ." Sandy shrugged. To be truthful, it all seemed a little beyond his sphere of concern. He lived from day to day, thinking ahead only in terms dictated by the demands of the land and the beasts that lived on the land. His attitude was little different from that of the miners, who concerned themselves intimately only with the township and little else.

Mirrin said, "Come in an' we'll have breakfast together. I want a word with you pair."

At the mention of the word breakfast, as if summoned by a soundless bell, Hurley appeared from the cow-house where he had been doctoring a cow with a swollen udder. The byres were empty now, clean and cool, while the herd grazed the pastures.

When the family were seated round the table, Mirrin dished out porridge, bread and a bowl of boiled eggs. Davie attended to Kitten. Sensing the mood of his elders, he kept her quiet by reading to her from a coloured rag-book that Sandy had brought from town last week. Mirrin knew that Davie was listening with both ears and taking it all in. It was an unsettling time for the younger children, particularly as they did not have the routine of school to give their lives a fixed point. She was thankful they were such a harmonious bunch. It had been bad enough with Tom's illness to contend with but this latest event was more difficult for the bairns to understand.

She wasted no time in coming to the point.

"There 's sure t'be a lot o'this," she said. "As I told you last night, it's difficult for us t'realise that Neill's famous—or soon will be."

"Famous, Mam?" said Sandy.

"I mean, your poor cousin will become the centre of a controversy. It's not his fault. Killin' that Special wasn't his fault. It could've happened t'anybody at the picket line yesterday."

"We'll stand by him, Mam," said Sandy.

"It's better," said Mirrin, "not t'put yourselves in a position whereby y' have t'stand by him. In other words, I want y'to keep yourselves t'yourselves for a while."

"Easy enough," said Sandy. "We've plenty t'do here. But what about the market?"

"Hurley an' I'll go t'the market when we have to," Malcolm said. "How long will this hostility last, mother?"

He called her mother only when he was very serious about anything. Mirrin answered, "Until after the trial."

"When'll that be?"

"I'm told it could be delayed as long as three or four months."

Malcolm puffed out his cheeks and shook his head. "Poor Neill, stuck away in jail through the best part o'the year."

"I've got a penny I'll give t'Neill," Kitten suddenly announced.

"Well, love, Neill won't need your penny, but y'could do him a wee drawin'," Mirrin suggested. "He'd like that."

"Like I did for Daddy?"

"Just the same."

"Is Neill sick, like Daddy?" Kitten asked.

"Aye," Malcolm said. "But Auntie Kate'll go t'visit him. Neill's in an Institution too."

"Same as Daddy?"

"Not the same one," Davie said and, to shut his sister up, scooped chopped egg from the cup and weaved the spoon towards her mouth, making a game of it.

Mirrin and Malcolm were silent for a moment, looking at the youngest boy, surprised at his perception. Only Hurley ate with his usual appetite, though even he was subdued by an awareness of a drama he did not in the least understand.

Speaking in a low voice, Malcolm said, "Will there be victimisation?"

"It's possible."

"Will we be affected?"

"We might have trouble sellin' our milk."

"That's no real threat," said Malcolm. "We can turn it int' cheese, if the worst comes t'the worst. It'll mean a loss o'turnover, but I think we can weather that."

"Your father'll have somethin' t'say about it."

Sandy asked, "How soon will he be out?"

"Monday, at the latest," said Mirrin. "But he'll have t'rest a lot for a month or so, to ensure that the eyes heal up."

"An' then?" Sandy persisted.

"Nobody knows," said Mirrin.

Malcolm said, "Mother, you know we can handle the day t'day runnin' o'Hazelrig. We've proved it."

"I know that, son."

"But . . . well, I need Da's cooperation. I need his advice about so many things."

"You'll get it."

Malcolm grunted sceptically. "There's another thing, what if the Duke won't accept Da as tenant any longer."

"We've ten years o'the lease t'run."

"But what," said Malcolm, "if the Duke makes Da's lack o'sight an excuse for cancellin' the lease."

"An excuse?"

"If this court case involvin' Neill is as important as you say, an' if Lamont is set against Neill, then pressure could be brought t'bear on us, through the Duke."

"I hadn't thought o'that," said Mirrin.

"The Duke's ay been very fair," Sandy remarked.

"Aye, but Lamont has influence even at that level," Malcolm said.

Mirrin said, "Your Aunt wants me t'go an' talk t'Houston Lamont."

"You?" Sandy said.

Malcolm, who had gleaned a good deal of information on his mother's early history from various sources, kept silent, studying her closely from the corner of his eye.

"I used t'work at Strathmore," Mirrin said.

"Aunt Kate told us," Sandy said. "You were a housekeeper."

"Will you do as Aunt Kate wants?" said Malcolm.

"I . . . I don't think I should," said Mirrin.

"Lamont wouldn't even let y'in the door, Mam," said Sandy. "Not even for auld lang syne."

She looked across the table at her big flaxen-haired son, wondering at the innocence of him. It was on the tip of her tongue to impress him by assuring him that she still had enough appeal to gain a hearing from the coalmaster. But that would open her to too many difficult questions.

"What does Kate expect y'to do?" said Malcolm. "It's little enough Lamont could accomplish. He wouldn't be able t'get Neill off scot-free, not now the police have him."

"I don't quite know what Kate expects," said Mirrin.

"You're goin' t'see father tonight, are y'not?"

"Of course."

"Then ask father's advice."

She realised that Malcolm was testing her. Perhaps he had heard too many stories about her past to be entirely sure of her responses. He was of an age now when he could begin to separate her from the kitchen and the farm, to think of her as an individual. Perhaps somebody had remarked that she was still a good-looker. Did her son suppose that there was any attraction left in Houston Lamont, though? How could she tell? Like so many of the relationships in the Stalker family, this tenuous mother-son thing was not constant but shifting.

"That," Mirrin said, "is just what I'll do."

"The milk's ready." Hurley rose from the table. "It'll no'

keep fresh, this hot weather, missus. Gaffer wouldn't leave it sittin' in the cartie.''

"Right, Hurley," said Mirrin.

"Let me take the delivery down t'the Square this mornin', mother," said Malcolm.

Mirrin was relieved. Until then she had not realised just how much trepidation had been building up in her, and why she'd put off departure. The truth was that she did not want to face up to Kate.

Malcolm said, "I feel I should show my face, y'know. I'd like t'say how sorry I am that this's happened."

"Kate'll appreciate that," Mirrin assured him.

The young man stood up, wiping his mouth with his wrist. "I'll shave, wash an' change, then. I'll only be ten minutes."

"Don't make yourself too grand, Malcolm," Mirrin said. "After all it's not a funeral."

"In some ways it's worse than a funeral. I wish Da was here."

"I'll tell him," said Mirrin, "t'hurry home."

"Any special message for Kate?" the young man said.

"No," Mirrin replied. "Just give her my love—though she may not thank y'for it."

The sun was high and the morning settled, before Malcolm drove off in the laden milk cart. Kitten wanted to go with him to see her aunts, uncle and Gran'ma, but Mirrin told her that they were all very, very busy that morning. Davie persuaded his sister to go with him instead to count the tiny seedling apples in the orchard, an offer that made her feel very grown up since she had only lately learned how to count at all.

As she cleared and washed the breakfast dishes, Mirrin thought over all that had been said. She was glad of Malcolm's advice. He was sensible and pragmatic, like his father. He would never have got himself into such a desperate scrape as Neill had done. Following that line of thought, she realised, however, that Sandy might be capable of such impulsive stupidity, given the wrong set of circumstances. That brought Kate's anguish into clearer focus. Mirrin felt a pang of guilt and, almost at the same instant, the desire to be free of their problems. How volatile she was under the set pattern, how contradictory her moods. Just a couple of months ago, she had yearned for the security to be found in Kellock's Square, the closeness of her blood kin. Now the reverse was true. Kellock's Square held the threat, and Hazelrig, even without Tom, had become a sanctuary from involvement. She could not deny Kate aid. But involvement with Houston Lamont, particularly now that Tom . . . Sternly, Mirrin checked the taunting notion.

Hand buried in the big porridge pot, bristle scourer in her fist, she paused. Across the yard one of the sleek black toms was courting a faded grey queen, oldest of all Hazelrig's cats. Mirrin watched their fascinating ritual, that mingling of sensual coyness and spitting aggression. Instinct dictated the form of courtship. She had seen lust in men run a similar course, but she had never been foolish enough to equate it with the infinite pleasure of loving nor had the men she had known most intimately. Houston's love had been too intense to endure, not his sexual hunger. And Tom? Virile though he was in every way, he had a gentleness that showed as consideration. These past years, she had taken his good qualities so much for granted. Not until he had changed, had she realised how much he had contibuted to her contentment.

That was the word.

Contentment.

The cat bristled and leapt at the queen who, elderly though she was, whisked up from her sprawling concubine-like pose and met the male's strike with unsheathed claws. There was a yowl and a *screeee-scrrrrrrrah*, and the pair were off, female after male, like two streaks, down the length of the wall and around the corner. There was no gentleness in that.

Vigorously Mirrin screwed the brush into the corners of the pot and worked hard to drive away the dangerous thoughts that were collecting. She had to prepare herself for involvements of an unwelcome sort, away from Hazelrig.

First, however, she must bring the matter up with Tom.

She had a feeling that she could predict just what he'd say.

The decision, as usual, would be hers.

*   *   *

"Tom," Mirrin said. "Neill's been committed for trial and

refused bail because of the grave nature of the charge."

"Murder?" Tom was propped on his elbow. She had brought him an egg custard and, with the bowl in her lap, was feeding it to him with a spoon. She had tucked a napkin round his neck. He looked more like an invalid than ever, with the thick, ugly mask across his face. He was eager, though, to involve himself in the Blacklaw drama, more eager than Mirrin.

"Aye. It seems there was nothin' the U.F.M. lawyer could do at this stage."

"An' Kate?" Tom asked. "How is she?"

"She wants me t'go an' see Houston Lamont, t'intercede on Neill's behalf."

"It'll do no good."

"I've told her that."

"Will y'go?"

"I don't want to."

"Aye, go," said Tom. "It'll help find out how the land really lies."

"But Tom . . ."

"Nothin' t'be frightened of, Mirrin,"

"I'm not frightened, not exactly."

"Is it what I'll think?"

"I've never kept anythin' from you, Tom."

"In spite o'the rough time I've given you this past year?" Tom held his mouth out like a fledgling for more of the thick sweet custard. He sighed as Mirrin fed him a spoonful, and swallowed. "No, m'flower, I've never doubted your loyalty, not in m'heart. I may have said wicked things, but that was just blethers. If Kate wants you t'talk t'Lamont, then do it. Nobody else stands a chance o'gettin' within earshot."

"Yes, Tom," Mirrin said.

"But," Tom propped himself higher, staring sightlessly at his wife's face. "But, there's somethin' else that should be done, somebody else that y'should go an' see."

"Who?"

"Your brother."

"Drew?"

"It's as plain as the nose on your face that there's no man

in Scotland better qualified, or better placed, t'get Neill out o'the jail without a blemish t'his name."

"Kate won't stand for it."

"If it's t'save Neill's neck, you might be surprised whàt Kate'll stand for," said Tom. "Has nobody mentioned your brother, yet?"

"You don't *know* him, Tom."

Tom brushed the protest aside. "Listen, Neill Stalker is *his* son. I can't believe this brother o'your's is such an ogre that he doesn't have a grain o'humanity in him somewhere."

"What are you suggestin'?"

"From what I've read in the newspapers, Andrew Stalker is considered t'be the best advocate in Scotland."

"For that reason if for no other, Tom, Drew can't stand up an' admit that Neill's his son. He can't afford t'be connected with Neill."

"What is he then, a wee tin god? Sometimes I wonder how you an' your sister got through this life." Tom hoisted himself into a sitting position, cautiously holding the mask with his fingertips. "Listen, Neill's sure t'be sent for trial in Edinburgh. That's the whole intention behind chargin' him with a capital crime. They'll never make it hold water, but by God they'll create enough stink about violent, brutal miners in the process. An' what they *might* make stick is a manslaughter charge."

"That's what Willie said."

"Manslaughter, if he's found guilty, could put the boy behind bars for fifteen years. *Fifteen years,* Mirrin."

"That would break our Kate's heart."

"So it's acquittal, or nothin'," said Tom. "Am I right?"

"You're right."

"An' that means employin' the services of an expert lawyer. Make no mistake, the Crown'll have some haughty, snotty advocate t'present its case. What'll Neill have—a U.F.M. lawyer, briefed by another U.F.M. lawyer. Apart from which, even that'll cost money."

"Willie has money."

"Willie has breadcrumbs," said Tom.

It was clear to Mirrin that her husband had had the morning

edition of the *Glasgow Herald* read out to him, had assimilated the wealth of details given therein and had applied his mind to the problems all that day.

"Willie's few bawbees," Tom went on, "will hardly pay the solicitors' fee never mind hire a decent advocate."

"The Union . . ."

"Believe me," said Tom, "when it comes right down to it, the Union won't toss away their limited resources on a murderer."

"I can't believe that Rob would . . ."

"Rob Ewing? He's shrewd enough t'know how the land lies," said Tom. "If Neill had been responsible for the death of a dirty blackleg, then, maybe, the Union would have felt the case worthy o'defendin'. But it was a Special Constable, a police officer, that got killed. Now what sort of case can the Union make against that? They wont back one raw young miner, against the weight o'public opinion. They won't sacrifice their support for Neill's neck."

"So," said Mirrin, "it's up t'us, as usual?"

"Call on Lamont," Tom advised. "Then take the train t'Edinburgh an' seek out your brother."

"After twenty years?"

"Your brother never got t'be an advocate at the Scottish bar by ignorin' the facts," said Tom. "An' the bald facts are that his son will shortly appear in the high Court o'Edinburgh, an' that some smart newspaper reporter is bound to trace the connection."

"I see," said Mirrin. "If Drew can't remain out, then he'd better come all the way in."

"Tell him that, Mirrin," Tom said.

"Kate won't like it. She despises Drew."

"T'hell with Kate," Tom said. "If she wants her son saved then she can't afford t'be fussy."

★   ★   ★

On the other side of the country, Edinburgh's socialites, those that were left in the summer city, dined and wined and danced, oblivious to the issues that were beginning to amass on the horizon. After all, the fate of a collier was of little concern to them. So cut off from the tide of national affairs was Mrs. Elizabeth McAlmond that a full day passed before she was made aware, by her husband, of the turn of events in Blacklaw. She was careful to parry Fraser's jocular suggestion that Neill Stalker might be a long-lost cousin. During the course of the morning, just to be on the safe side, Betsy sent her Frenchie to acquire a copy of the *Hamilton Gazette* from the station magazine stall and, as she'd suspected, therein discovered all the details that had been edited from the national dailies.

She was neither dismayed nor shocked to learn that the young collier presently under lock and key in Hamilton was her nephew. Armed with the newspaper, she coolly made preparations to take herself round to Drew's that very evening. Indeed, she had another pressing engagement and Fraser was aware that she would not be at home for dinner. Betsy sometimes thought that he was rather glad to have her out of the way so that he could spend an hour in the company of his daughters and then take his dinner in peace. Later, perhaps, he would toddle round to his club, a remnant of his 'inflamed' youth. The club was the preserve of many such gentlemen, few of whom had retained that early spark and, burdened by wives, a quiver of children, and by 'reputation' had sunk into a miasmic middle-age enlivened only by bawdy talk and, in season, an occasional descent on somebody's grouse moor for a day's shootin'.

Corby, Drew's valet, was engaged in cooking a light repast for his master who was expected early from his labours at the Parliament house. Corby was a majestically built highlander whose beard, shaped like a trenching tool, hung from a fine eagle's beak of a nose. If he had been younger Betsy might have found him attractive. In sole charge of the household, Corby did not instruct the maid to show the lady into the parlour. Instead, he permitted her to wait in the 'office' where, to Betsy's surprise, an oil cooking stove had been set up together with plates and cutlery. In a white shirt, black waistcoat and stock collar, Corby had the appearance of a conjurer. Apparently, he was preparing to whip up a savoury omelette to keep his master appeased until dinner time.

Only minutes passed before the Advocate and his clerk trudged in from court. Drew was less than delighted to see his sister. Horn took the master's summer overcoat, fine suede gloves and cane and removed them, presumably to some other, more suitable apartment in the house. Seating himself by the embroidered screen that stood in front of the hearth, Drew removed his shoes and put on a pair of morocco slippers.

Silently, Corby dispensed two glasses of sherry and carried them on a wooden tray, offering one to Betsy the other to Drew.

"I take it, Elizabeth," said Drew, "that you will not be staying long?"

"Only a few minutes, alas."

"Then, Corby," said Drew, "I will delay the omelette, if that's possible, until twenty minutes to six."

"As y'wish, suur," Corby said.

Forsaking the cooking dishes, the valet discreetly left sister and brother alone.

"I think I can deduce why you've come," said Drew.

"I thought this might interest you." Betsy took the copy of the *Hamilton Gazette* from her ample handbag and passed it to her brother. He did not even glance at it, though portions of the headlines were visible—COLLIER, MILITANT, MURDER.

"I've read it."

"And?" said Betsy.

"It's nothing to me."

The woman marvelled. Throughout her life she had devoted herself exclusively to consideration of her own affairs, yet her twin's singlemindedness never ceased to surprise her. How assiduously he must have tamped down the recollection of the squalid little episode that had resulted in his fathering a son.

"There's no doubt, Drew. The collier in custody is your son."

"Perhaps . . . not."

"Drew, for heaven's sake, at least face facts. The age is right. The report refers to tearful mother, Mrs. Kate Kellock. She married some dreadful fellow in trade, a shopkeeper, if I remember correctly."

"Kellock was, and is, a baker," said Drew, sipping sherry. "He owns a substantial property in Blacklaw, a house, stable yard and shop; all bought and paid for. He has acted as the young man's father."

"How long have you known all this?"

"Not long. I made discreet enquiries just yesterday."

"And the condemned youth is . . . ?"

"The youth is not condemned yet," Drew interrupted. "Any fool of a lawyer should be able to get him off, at least from the capital charge."

"Is that really the truth, Drew?"

"There *is* no murder charge there, not that I can detect on the weight of the hysterical evidence printed in the journals. Conviction for manslaughter is the most the Crown might hope for."

"Manslaughter?" To Betsy it sounded worse than murder.

"That's what it was. Mitigation? Justification? Defence of the Person? All possible defences. But, I fear, manslaughter could be shaped into an impressive enough charge, and given emotive overtones."

"What do you intend to do about it?"

"Absolutely nothing."

"He's your child!"

"Upon whom I haven't clapped eyes since he was less than one day old. This militant collier is not my son, Betsy. I am not his father. William Kellock is his father."

"Potentially it's a scandal, Drew, a secret that won't keep." His composure, his ostrich-like attitude, appalled her. She had no way of knowing that her brother had been shaken by the news, and that, if Daniel Horn had not braced him, he would have tumbled down in the street with the newspaper in his hand. "Somebody is bound to discover the connection between you and this person."

"I shall deny it."

"Denial will not be enough," said Betsy, "What if she comes here?"

"Who?"

"Kate."

"I doubt if it will cross her mind."

"It may well cross Mirrin's mind, though."

"Yes, I'll grant you that," Drew said.

"What if she does?"

"I shan't be here."

"What?"

"I'm leaving for New York next Friday, a week from today."

"*What?*"

"I shall be away for six months; on holiday."

"You devil, Drew."

Drew finished his sherry. "Does that answer all your questions, Betsy? Does that make you feel a little more secure?"

She stared at him, her pretty, sensual lips parted in astonishment, then hooking upward into a smile. "Much more secure," she said. "And to ensure that gossip doesn't reach my way, I too will sojourn abroad throughout the winter."

"If you can persuade Fraser to take you."

"Fraser," she said, with a tinkling laugh. "He may not be able to tear himself away from his cronies in the Morningside Club."

"In which case . . ."

"I will go alone—with the children. To Italy, I think. It's warm in Italy. Lady Glencross went to . . ."

"One scandal at a time is quite enough, Betsy."

"What do you mean?"

Drew got to his feet. "The trial is unlikely to fit into the August calendar. It may even be November before it comes before the Bench. You must remain out of Scotland from October until March."

"I'm sure that can be arranged."

"What reason will you give for wintering abroad?"

Betsy lifted her lace handkerchief and manufactured a tiny ladylike cough then, with round sad eyes, peered up at her brother and batted her lids. "My health," she said.

★　　★　　★

On Saturday afternoon in the graveyard of Sholton Kirk, east of Hamilton, Constable Ronald was buried with due ceremony and pomp and a great deal more attention than he had ever gained in life. Though nobody was aware of it there was a little too much emphasis on the emotional trappings of the funeral and not quite enough on the practical aspects that the law required.

In the picturesque environs of Sholton kirkyard there gathered contingents of policemen, solid and sweltering in their blue uniforms, and almost as many journalists. This official band was swollen by sightseers, not all of whom were motivated by genuine respect for the cause in which Constable Ronald, according to the press, had given his life. They came from Glasgow by horse-bus, from Edinburgh by train, and, by carts and flys, from many towns and villages, large and small, in the nether wards of Lanarkshire. Perhaps they hoped that the barbarous law of the lynch-rope would be revived there and then. Indeed, if it had been left to that huge crowd, which, after an hour or so hanging about Sholton's streets, seemed to acquire a will of its own, the Hamilton Police cells would have been stormed and the Murderer Stalker lugged to the top of Ravens Brae and strung up willy-nilly from the ash-tree there.

Naturally there were very few miners on view at Sholton and those common labourers who, at first glance, might have been mistaken for brethren, got themselves out of the village double quick lest that first glance was all the brooding crowd was willing to accord to them.

As it happened there was no demonstration.

The Glasgow police pipe-band played. Pipe-Major McCrimmond squeezed out a lament as the coffin was lowered. The plaintive sound of the pipes brought tears to all eyes. The sorrow of the young constable's widow, his mother, sisters and friends was real enough, a dark, rich, mourning core amid the stiff, grey conniving solemnity of the throng. When the service was over, there was a general wending off in the direction of local pubs and hotels, and Hamilton, four miles off, had quite a gala day since it was already playing host to several hundred off-shift blacklegs and their camp-followers. There were those—numbering a hundred or more—who crowned the outing by walking round the side road that backed onto the Police Station. Peering up, shinning up even, the younger ones, stared hopefully at six barred windows—three of which were the muster-room—in the hope of catching sight of the evil visage of Stalker. All in all, given the short period between the killing and the funeral, it was a remarkably satisfactory turnout for the county's bigots and diehard establishmentarians and a very enjoyable jamboree for all members of the public who fancied themselves a cut above the working-class.

Houston Lamont and his wife Edith attended, accompanied by Sydney Thrush and his sister Anna, in a very dignified landau drawn by coal-black horses. The Deputy Sheriff of the County turned up, as did the Chief Constable of Lanarkshire and the Assistant Chief Constables of Glasgow and Midlothian. Edith and Anna wept when the pipes played and, later, at Thrush's personal instigation, a fund was set up for the widow and orphans, and twenty-eight pounds and some shillings cajoled from the dispersing crowd.

Affecting though it all was, perhaps the most touching sounds of all—which could not quite be heard in distant Sholton—were the creak of the winding cables, the rumble of coal in the shutes and the *wheeping* of shunters dragging laden trucks to the mainline. As they returned from Hamilton, it was that melody that brought a lump to the throat and wetted the eyes, not only of Edith but of Sydney Thrush.

For the time being, there was little more that either Lamont or Thrush could do in the matter of Neill Campbell Stalker. The 'witnesses' had been found. During a long, secret meeting, their 'reliability' had been established, and their 'loyalty' assured. In due course, when a high lord had been appointed to look after the prosecution of the accused, the names of the witnesses would be passed to the proper authority. In the meantime, Thrush and Lamont were quite busy enough recruiting colliers from the hordes of casual, money-hungry labourers who trooped to the pay-desks in the managers' offices in Eastlagg, Northrigg and Blacklaw.

In the three other pits that Lamont had elected to put back into operation—all in the heartland of strike territory—no opposition at all had been encountered from the local miners. Picket-lines had simply dissolved on the appearance of Mr. Thrush, the resident manager, two special constables and four grim-faced blackleg gangers.

It was even easier than Lamont had expected to hew coal from his pits. The costs, though, were staggering and the wage-bill promised to keep the pits in the red, at least until slackers, incompetents and thieves were weeded out. On Monday, however, Thrush had promised the sale of company stock, an immediate infusion of ready cash that would ease the pressures from those unknown enemies in commercial and industrial regions. The threatened court actions had not been brought forward. Lamont had written personally to the companies that had called in the bills, berating them for their lack of faith in the viability of his business. To those letters he had received no replies at all. He did not suppose that the bills had been put aside, however, and was quite prepared for the institution of proceedings in the small debt courts. Selling Blacklaw Company stock, even in such careful proportions, was not at all to his liking. On the other hand it gave him intense satisfaction to have the only operating pits in the whole of Scotland and to have received, discreetly, the acclaim of several fellow-members of the Coal-owners Association who, though applauding his stand, were not yet willing to emulate his ruthlessly expensive tactics.

It was tea-time before the landau reached Blacklaw. Edith would have had Sydney and Anna stay on for dinner but Sydney had work to do. It was no mere excuse; the Saturday shift of hired labour had to be supervised. Drink was the bugbear; an accident at one of the pits at this stage would do Lamont's credibility no good at all. Anna, however, accepted Edith's invitation to take tea, a silver plate and china cup ritual that Lamont could not abide.

After conversing with Thrush on the steps of Strathmore, Lamont bid his manager goodbye and turned to enter the house.

Strathmore's apron lawns had been extended in recent years. The circle of oaks that stood like a bastion between mansion and town had been thinned to give the grounds the same neatness as the architecture of the house. Wings that Lamont had added to the original mansion were baronial rather than Grecian, but the Scottish style went well with the pillars that flanked the wide stone portico.

Though it was July, and only five o'clock, already there was a deepening of shadows among the trees. The soft crescent shade of the hill that sheltered the mansion from the rear crept nearer to the edge of the lawn. The flowerbeds seemed heavy, almost ominously so, the colours oily in changing weather. Rain, Lamont thought. There's rain about. Pausing on the steps, he turned and glanced at the sky to the west which, sure enough, was layered with cloud. Even as he paused, a chill little wind cavorted with the heads of the roses and chrysanthemums, and dipped one of the heavy oak boughs with a nodding motion that made the leaves flicker pale in the slant of the sun.

She was coming across the lawn towards him. For a split second, Lamont did not trust the evidence of his eyes. He glanced off, dartingly, to his left. Sitting upright in the quick, one-horse gig Thrush was bowling off through the gates. He had seen nothing. The door of the mansion had been closed behind the women, but a maid, or the damned housekeeper, would be lurking in the hall to take his hat and gloves when he entered. He dared to look again across the lawn, half expecting that the vision would have vanished, leaving only the sorrow of its insubstantiality in his mind, a sign that he was again driving himself into a state of nervous stress. But the vision was real enough. She was still there, walking rapidly across the grass through rich light and richer shadow, seeming to extract from the atmosphere of the waning afternoon a similar quality of sadness, a beautiful remissness, as if she, like the summer's day, had reached a zenith beyond which lay only decline.

At the gate, the gig had gone.

Lamont listened : no sound at all came from within the house.

No longer, he discovered, did he feel relaxed with her. Irritation came over him. Over the years, he had seen her from time to time, riding in that farm cart protected by rattling milk churns, or walking, with a graceful feminine swing to her hips. He had marvelled at how little she had changed, in spite of the hardships that she must endure scraping a living out of the land at Hazelrig, in spite of having given birth to four children, in spite . . .

"Mr. Lamont? May I speak with you, please?"

Across the width of the gravel drive, was Mirrin Stalker. For one fleeting moment, he experienced an ache of longing. The scars that loving her had inflicted on his heart pained him. Her face was weather-tanned, her hat worn without style, a knitted tammy, not a Sunday best bonnet such as she had worn the very first time she'd come to this house. In a way, now that he thought of it, he had half expected her. It was the first word that she had addressed to him in almost eighteen years, but he did not suppose that it was friendship or sentiment that had brought her here. He knew perfectly well what her purpose was.

"Yes," he said, standing above her on the step. "What do you want?"

He could not invite her into the house. Indeed, he did not want to. Strathmore now was no place for a woman like Mirrin; an exhibition hall for Edith's trophies, a mausoleum, too vast and ornate. Objects that Mirrin had known within the mansion's walls were gone, tossed out, donated to charity sales or consigned to attics and cellars. Outside, in the gilded garden, at least he could retain a faint memory of a civilised past and restrain the anger that was an evitable part of his response to her.

"Mr. Lamont—Houston—I think you can surmise why I'm here."

Surmise—a formal word; she was keeping him at distance. Perhaps there was anger in her. Perhaps she too, would have preferred to leave the past intact, and resented the circumstances that had jolted them together in conflict. They seemed fated to be in conflicts not of their own making, enmity generated by his wife, by her family and, in large measure, by the divisive structure of Blacklaw.

"It concerns that young miner, your sister's son, I take it?" he said.

"My sister, Kate Kellock, has asked me to speak t'you, Houston, about the possibility of . . ."

Regarding him with a puzzled frown, she hesitated. Her bewilderment was hard to understand. Had he changed so much that she could find *nothing* in him now except the lacquered shell of the man she had once held in her arms? It could not just be age, for she too was older and must surely have made subtle adjustments at the very first moment of their meeting.

She said, "Will you speak on the boy's behalf?"

"Speak? To whom?"

"The authorities, the police," said Mirrin, "whoever y'do speak to on such matters?"

"I see. You require a character reference for a violent delinquent who struck down a police officer under my employ?" Lamont spoke more harshly than he had intended. "Is that what you wish from me?"

"Your intervention might make it easier on him."

"I have no means of 'intervening', as you put it," Lamont said. "More important, perhaps, I have no *wish* to intervene. I believe that the culprit should be treated by the law, as lightly or severely as the evidence merits."

"He's only young, Houston, hardly more than a boy."

"Nineteen is no boy," Lamont said. "If I recall, your brother was a graduate of the Faculty of Law at nineteen— among other things."

Mirrin put her hands on her hips in a pose that had once indicated an impending hurricane of temper or indignation. Now, though, her tone was mild, not meek but tolerant. "He did not mean to kill anyone. It was accidental."

"But kill he did," said Lamont. "Surely, Mirrin, you must appreciate the implications of the crime—whether accident or homicide—the implications of permitting physical retaliation against a legal . . ."

"Please," Mirrin said. "Please, Houston, don't make a speech. I've come here to ask for a favour."

"I'll grant you no more favours, Mirrin."

"Houston," she said. "What if Neill was *my* son?"

The question caught the coalmaster off-guard. It was not relevant. It referred to other more personal issues and drew the skein of ethics and morality, law and commerce down to the hypothesis he had dwelled on, almost to the point of madness, twenty years ago. He did not, however, suspect her of trickery.

"I know that the Stalker boy is *not* your son, Mirrin."

"If he was, Houston, would you do as I ask?"

"No, Mirrin. My answer would be the same."

She did not know what to do with her hands. This manifestation of a lifetime's activity was bound to show up he supposed, with an ailing husband, a growing family and the farm, to keep her free from the travail of thought. Only ladies, like Edith, really learned how to be motionless, to keep their hands in repose, like waxworks dressed for a dull tableau. Mirrin had never aspired to be that kind of lady, though there had once been in her a fineness of spirit that, he realised, had mellowed into resignation. No longer boisterous, no longer extravagantly outspoken, Mirrin hid her hands in her pockets and let a single unwavering stare say it all.

The urge to justify himself rose unbidden. In the past he had sometimes felt compelled to make her understand that her code was so much simpler than his. But that division was broken too now. The century had itself become expansive and complex, drawing farmer and collier, housewife and lady, clerk and coalmaster into the same intricate web. Obviously Mirrin had been quicker to sense that fundamental change than any of her contemporaries, though he doubted if she was capable of expressing it in words. In the narrower sphere, the changes that the years had brought to each of them, a man nearing sixty, a woman nearing forty, needed no justification, no explanation. They were facts, sad, inescapable facts. Mirrin recognised what he had become, and knew the reasons for it.

"I thank you for your time, Houston. And for your honesty," Mirrin said. "I'll detain you no longer."

Lamont kept his lips sealed. All that he could have expressed was regret and, so imprecise had his purposes become, he could not even claim to regret the direction in which he had been driven, could not be sure that it was not of his choosing as well as his making. The precarious imbalances of his prime had steadied, making him stubborn as well as proud.

Inclining his head, he bowed in acknowledgment that neither of them had anything left to bargain with.

Mirrin turned and went off down the gravel drive towards the town without another word.

And Houston entered his mansion to take tea with his wife.

*　　*　　*

"There now, I said your Mama would hear you."
Betsy McAlmond paused in the doorway of her daughters'

room and, prompted by the remark, assumed an expression of mild censure. Her thoughts had been involved in other matters and she had heard nothing at all from the bright corner room. Recognising in the governess's words an oblique appeal to higher authority, however, Betsy dutifully raised her eyebrows and said in a shocked voice, "Indeed I did hear you. From the very end of the corridor."

The look on her daughter's face told her immediately that she was wrong. Ten-year-old Roberta took it upon herself to defend her younger sister and, with childish haughtiness, enlightened her mother. "You did not hear a single thing, Mama. Please do not pretend that you did, just because of some chance remark that Miss Millicent makes."

Roberta's precociousness was not matched by seven-year-old Lisbeth. "Mama, Mama, we were just singing our song, the French one we're learning for Caroline Tate's birthday party. Miss Millicent peeped out to see when you left your room, and then said that you would h . . . h . . : h . . . hear . . ." In spite of her superficial aplomb—which came, Fraser would have said, from being absolutely certain that the world of the nursery was blessed by justice—Lisbeth could not prevent her under-lip trembling.

Betsy dropped to her knees and pulled both children to her. They were such pretty little girls, delicate without being weak. Best Bone China, Fraser called them. Betsy loved them dearly, though in a manner more distracted than Fraser's. He spent a great deal of time with them, scorning the traditional image of the remote, godlike paterfamilias and, when they were younger, had even crawled about the crapet of the nursery with them, behaving like a clown. It was their influence, Betsy felt, that had tamed the last lingering inclination to riotousness in Fraser McAlmond. His daughters had become his conscience, God help the poor mites. In addition, the charm of the little girls had caused their McAlmond grandparents to forgive Betsy for not yet bearing a son. She would not conceive another child now, no matter how strenuously her mother-in-law urged her to try. The thought of a third disfiguring pregnancy filled her with horror. Besides, it would spoil her fun, the fun of being head-over-heels in love, really and truly, wildly in love. The

experience was new to her; she had been too calculating in her
'teens to entertain the sweet pain of adolescent romance. Now,
she would make up for it, not with a simpering laddie but with
a tyrannical bachelor whose passion more than matched her
own.

She had never found it easy to communicate with her
daughters. Desirous of making amends, but mindful of the
time, she hugged them and said brightly, "I am truly sorry,
my dears, but I'll make it up to you, I promise. Tomorrow
evening, you may give a special performance . . ."

"In the music room?" put in Roberta, who was as much a
bargainer as her mother.

"In the music room, certainly," said Betsy. "We will light
the candles for the occasion . . ."

"And invite Papa?" said Lisbeth.

"If he does not have an engagement, Papa will be there too.
Miss Millicent will arrange it." Betsy glanced up at the young
governess, who nodded assent. "You will be announced by
Mister Gillies, just as if you were performing on a real concert
platform."

"And will you wear one of your special pretty dresses?"
Lisbeth had recovered; her eyes shone.

"Of course I shall," said Betsy.

Miss Millicent, a thin pallid girl, clasped her hands as though
it was she who was to be given this famous treat. "Now, isn't
your Mama kind?" she declared.

"Yes," said Roberta, drily. "Thank you, Mama."

With kisses for each of them and exhortations to be good
girls, Betsy left the room and resumed her course for the head
of the stairs. She was arrested by Roberta's voice, its childish
clarity not entirely muffled, coming after her. "I am *not* ungrate-
ful, Miss Millicent. I *did* say thank you to Mama. But you *know*
how Mama forgets her promises."

Irritated, Betsy shook her head and, pulling on her gloves
with sharp little tugs, continued on her way downstairs.

In the library Fraser looked up from his chair by the fire.
He insisted on a fire in the library even in the height of summer
for that corner of the mansion caught sunlight only in the
morning.

"Fraser," Betsy said, without preamble. "You and I must soon have a lengthy discussion about Roberta."

"Roberta? What's wrong with her?" Fraser threw his newspaper aside and made to push himself to his feet. He wore a velvet jacket over a starched dinner shirt, and a pair of morocco slippers that Drew had given him.

"Nothing," said Betsy, "is wrong with her that a good boarding-school wouldn't cure."

"Elizabeth, we've been into all this before," Fraser sighed and settled back into his winged chair. "I really do not feel that girl children should be, on principle, separated from the domestic environment. If they had been boys, well . . ."

Still fussing with her gloves, Betsy stooped over his chair, "I find it extremely disconcerting for a child of ten to be permitted to say exactly what she thinks."

"Do you?" said Fraser. "I find it rather refreshing. I wish I had the courage to do it."

At that moment he seemed to become aware that his wife was dressed for an outing. He craned against the leather wing of the chair to survey her. His profile, against the lamp, was as handsome as ever, but there was a self-satisfied blandness built into every expression that robbed him of attractiveness for the opposite sex. None of Betsy's women-friends, not even the most outrageous, ever hinted that they envied her or considered Fraser attractive. He was dull, dull as soda-water.

"That," Fraser remarked, mildly, "is a deuced smart outfit for a miserable charity concert."

"The charity concert is next week," said Betsy. "Tonight, I am dining with Mrs. Fountain."

"Mrs. Fountain? Do I know her?"

"You would hardly be likely to know a widow who lives in Portobello and is concerned about the morals of fisher-wives?"

"Lord, Lord! Another all-female 'emancipated' evening!"

"We women," said Betsy, "are capable of looking after our own affairs, you know."

She kissed him, leaning over the back of the chair, then, before he could enquire further as to the nature of the dinner and Mrs. Fountain's 'connections', Betsy was off towards the library doors.

Fraser called, "Will you be late?"

"Probably," his wife answered.

*   *   *

The quilt was composed of patches of coarse tweed in shades of misty blue and brown. The fabric tickled her delicate skin and rasped against her French silk underwear, a scant frilled tunic that came only to her thighs and revealed more than it hid. Not for the first time Betsy thought that the bed was like a heatherbank. The impression was increased by straight unvarnished bed posts that rose like pines to the moulded cornices of a dark blue plaster ceiling. A cheval glass reflected light from a single gas-mantel, a colour like mulled ale. Head propped on hand, limbs arranged in Classical pose—Venus by Tintoretto—Betsy surveyed herself in the mirror. She also studied her lover, Patrick Lauder, as, without pomp, he untied the cord of his robe and stripped it from his body.

In the effete society that the couple inhabited during daylight hours, Lauder's nakedness would have shocked not only women but some men. Unclothed, Lauder did not at all resemble a cultured gentleman but rather some hairy clansman who had escaped the imprisonment of stony corries and bleak moors. Muscular thighs, hard torso, deep chest and bulging shoulders, devoid of robes, capes and tapered tailoring, gave evidence of enormous physical strength. Along with several dozen other fillies, Mrs. Elizabeth McAlmond was privvy to the secret of Lauder's charismatic power, the source of the bull-like aggression that could, if need be, make judges as well as juries quail.

It flattered Betsy to be desired by such a man. He had status, wealth and fame second to none. He was so self-possessed, so lionised that merely bagging him for a soirée or dinner party was considered a great coupe. Above all else, in natural state he was so challenging, so incredibly masculine that Betsy felt more feminine and beautiful than ever.

The hour was now a little after ten. Of course, Betsy had dined with Mrs. Fountain in her shoebox house in Portobello but had made an early departure. Travelling by hired cab, in a lather of anticipation, she had hastened back to Lauder's terraced house in Brunton Street where, as usual, Patrick had made ample preparation for her visit. The man-servant who looked after the premises had laid a cold supper on a table by the fire and had discreetly quit the house for the night. Built in the shadow of the castle hill, the terrace rooms were furnished with ponderous highland-style pieces, embellished by portraits of horses and hounds and mounted trophies of silvery salmon and startled pheasants, while in the hallway were herds of antlered stags' heads and a huge stuffed grizzly bear, an animal that Lauder claimed to have shot during a trip to the Rockies.

On an ancestral Sutherland estate, Lauder retained a secluded manorial lodge. When not intimidating judges or pursuing the fair ladies of Edinburgh, he would invariably be found in the company of lairds and ghillies stalking beasts over barren hillsides or waist deep in freezing torrents flicking flies at fish. Not surprisingly, Patrick Lauder remained a bachelor. In fact, it was rumoured that his father had remained a bachelor too. Such disreputable backgrounds were considered frightfully colourful —provided they were Highland. No Lowlander could have supported Lauder's legacy of scandal and survived in polite God-fearing society, let alone have carved out an illustrious career as an advocate.

Betsy supposed this man to be in love with her.

True, his need of her was palpable. For all her coolness and experience, however, Betsy misinterpreted her lover's ardour. Giddiness had overwhelmed her under the onslaught of Lauder's personality. She attributed a similar giddiness to him. But Lauder's promises were no more permanent than smoke-rings. He took her and entertained her for pleasure—his pleasure. Connivings and schemings, shy assignations, the nosegays of romance, were a small price to pay for bagging such delicious game.

He came to her now and lay by her, hands stroking her silken belly. She purred, then groaned and rolled against him, hands about his shoulders, nails digging into his skin. If she had a fault, it was her greed. In Lauder's book, insatiability was not a serious defect. He laughed and pushed her away from him. Pinning her to the patchwork with his arm, his fingers plucked at the pearl buttons that ran up the front of her slip. With finger and thumb he flipped the garment open. He put his mouth against her breasts.

Betsy's head jerked, hair tossing across her face so that she looked up at the ceiling now through fern-like fronds. As he brought her dexterously to a peak, she stretched her arms to their fullest extent and gripped the thick bedposts. Pulling against them, her fine beautiful body was drawn taut, bowed to meet him.

He made love to her for an hour then, almost inconsequentially, found his own release. During love-making, they spoke of nothing but their actions, using the strange, throaty, unromantic language that Lauder coaxed from her, a compound of the remembered speech of colliers in all its crudity and directness, as intense a stimulus as touch.

Later, washed and dressed, the couple sat at table by the low fire. Lauder cracked a bottle of iced wine, served Betsy with slices of cold meats, boiled beetroot and button mushrooms basted in vinaigrette. She ate hungrily, with one eye to the clock. She must be home by midnight; a self-imposed curfew. If Fraser had gone to the club, she would be back before him. If he had stayed at home all evening, he would still be awake. She knew that he would not suffer suspicion or anxiety until after midnight and, ingenuously, she did not want to disturb his peace of mind.

Dressed in a robe, and nothing else, Lauder sat cross-kneed across the table from her. He ate even more voraciously than she did, laying slices of meat and onion on slabs of buttered bread which he devoured in three huge bites.

"I am going to Italy, Patrick," Betsy said, without preliminary.

Lauder stopped chewing. "Italy?"

"Ravenna, perhaps, or Milano."

"When?"

"In two or three weeks; a month at most."

"Is this your husband's idea?"

Betsy laughed. "Of course not, silly. It's my idea. I prefer to be out of Edinburgh this winter. I'm tired of fog, snow and rain."

"Surely you will not go alone?"

"I trust not."

Nonchalantly Lauder buttered a fourth slice of bread. He drank a glass of wine at one swallow, his eyes wary in his swarthy face.

He said, "Ah, you'll be taking the children."

"They will be at school, an academy for boarders."

"And Fraser?"

"He has his practice to attend to."

"He'll never let you go unchaperoned."

"Fraser," said Betsy, "is my concern. Besides, Patrick, I shan't be alone—you will be with me."

"Hoh, will I now?"

"For part of the time, at least."

"So that's your plan?"

"We can be together for as long as you wish, Patrick."

"The Italian idyll," Lauder said. "Is that to be the name of the next chapter? Followed, no doubt by divorce, re-marriage and exile."

"Patrick?" A querulous note entered Betsy's voice. She reached across the table to take his hand but he lifted the sandwich in two fists. Her fingers remained outstretched in empty air. "Patrick, I thought that you would *welcome* an opportunity to be with me."

"Italy is not my dish of tea," he said.

"It need not be Italy."

"Elizabeth," Lauder chewed thoughtfully, "it is altogether an impractical suggestion. I cannot scamper off in midwinter. I have cases, clients to consider."

"A month, Patrick; you could manage a month, at the midwinter term."

"I do not much care for Europe."

"Then we could go to . . ."

"Canada? America? Peru?" Lauder said sarcastically. "No, my sweetheart, if you elect to trot off in search of sunshine then you must reconcile yourself to being without my company."

"But you . . . you . . . promised me that . . ."

"Promised you? What did I ever promise you, Elizabeth?"

"That one day, we would . . ."

"Now, now, Elizabeth. Am I likely to make a statement that

I do not intend to support? No, my sweetheart, I made no promises of any kind. If you suppose that I did, then that day-dreaming nature of yours has concocted it out of nothing at all."

"Patrick, *please*, listen. Why can we not meet in Europe, in, say, December? What's to prevent it? You have no wife . . ."

"But you have a husband. And children. And a brother."

"Do you not think that we could manage to be discreet?"

"It's not a question of being discreet," Lauder retorted. "It's a question of being busy."

"I do not understand."

"I have umpteen briefs laid out for my attention," Lauder said. "Good God, you're married to a solicitor and your damned brother is an advocate. Have you not yet learned that we are chained to the courts during the three seasons?"

"If you *wanted* to, Patrick, you would find a way."

"Very well, Elizabeth. Since you force me, I will admit that I *don't* want to."

"But . . . but you . . . do love me."

"You are the most beautiful woman I have ever slept with."

Betsy leapt to her feet. "Don't butter me up, Patrick Lauder. You love me. You know you do. Why won't you admit it?"

"There's nothing *to* admit."

"You do *not* love me?"

"Yes, Elizabeth. Yes, I love you. But you must appreciate my position."

"That isn't good enough, Patrick."

"Sweetheart," he muttered, rising to take her in his arms. "Why *must* you go off on this impulsive trip to Italy? Edinburgh isn't so bad. Court closes in three days. If you can contrive to be free we will go off together then."

Betsy's expression changed to one of radiant hope.

"Run . . . run off?"

Lauder laughed. "Hardly that," he said. "I meant that we might take two or three days' holiday together. I know of a cottage in the Borders where . . ."

"I will *not* be treated like a common whore," Betsy cried. Though distraught, she was astute enough to realise that she had created a sham. It was over. In that single instant, it was all over. Belief in her beauty and power over men collapsed with a sudden, painful implosion. Somehow, she had gulled herself into believing that Lauder was an honest man who would not spin her along with lies, as she, in her time, had spun others along. "I want you for my own, Patrick. And I shall have you."

He reached for her but she flirted away towards the bed. "Don't be a fool."

"Oh, yes, I've been a fool," she cried; "a fool ever to imagine that you were capable of affection, let alone love."

"You got what you wanted—a thrilling hour on your back two or three times a week."

"*How dare you. How dare you say that.*"

"Keep your voice down, please."

"*I will not.* What right have you to talk to me, Elizabeth McAlmond, like that. My father-in-law owns more land than you . . ."

"Stupid bitch!" Lauder snarled. "What a stupid class-ridden little upstart you are! I thought you had a certain style, but it seems that breeding will out in the end."

"What . . . what . . ." Betsy was speechless. Perspiration, not tears, stained her face. She would not weep, not until she had privacy to let her heart break—and heal again.

"What—what—what?" Lauder mimicked. "What gave you the notion that I would ever stoop—aye, stoop—to trading my reputation for a jumped-up collier's brat?"

Reeling, Betsy clutched the bedpost, pressing herself against it, as if she feared that this half-naked man might be transformed into the horned god before her eyes.

"How did you . . . ?" she gasped.

"Find out? I've known for months. Not only that," Lauder went on remorselessly, "I'm fully aware of your reason for fleeing Scotland this autumn. Your dear brother advised it, didn't he?"

"No, Patrick. Drew does not know."

"I didn't think he would be brass-necked enough to stand up and be counted as the father of a young killer." Lauder did not allow her to search for words, to frame denials or embark on involved lies. He knew the truth. More to protect himself from her dangerous designs on his freedom than out of malice, he threw truth at her in handfuls, like salt. "Yes, Elizabeth, I am only too well aware of what you were—as well as what you are. I do not embark lightly on any affair. I study my quarry, you see, habits *and* background. Hector Mellish informed me of your humble origins. What's more, Hector Mellish told me that this Stalker fellow is your nephew, your brother's bastard."

"Mellish couldn't possibly know that."

"He's suspected something of the sort for years, apparently. He has a long memory for exploitable facts," said Lauder. "He vividly remembers the events of twenty years ago, that period when your brother was lambent with ambition and the pair of you hellbent on shedding your grubby origins. Was that not the way of it—Betsy?"

She sprang from the bedpost and raked him with her nails. He was too quick for her, too strong. He pulled her against him, holding her arms spread. As his robe flapped open, she saw to her astonishment, to her horror, that her baiting had stimulated him once more. He laughed and forced her head against his chest, then, tweaked it back to kiss her fiercely on the mouth. "You are *common*, Mrs. McAlmond. You are extraordinary, yes, but you are *common as clay*. I like that. I prefer that, *that earthiness*."

"*Leave me. Let me go. You . . . you vile animal.*"

"I am not the animal. You are the animal, a bitch in heat. It was not enough for you to achieve rank, respect and honour among your peers. You had to flaunt your deception over us in every conceivable manner. Am I not right?"

"*Patrick, I warn you.*"

Forcibly he pulled her dress from her shoulders. Tearing lace fastenings and hooks, he hauled it down until her arms were pinned. "Warn me of what? There's nothing you can do to harm me, my sweetheart. You *dare* not tell, *dare* not 'clipe' on me, not even to your dear brother. He is more of a prig than you are, though, I fancy, less of a hypocrite. Perhaps he learned his lesson early. Now I will teach you *your* lesson, Mrs. McAlmond. Lie on the edge of the bed."

"*No, Patrick, for the love of heaven.*"

Even as she spoke, she was lifted and thrust down, neck and spine twisted against the edge of the mattress. As he loomed closer, his intention was abundantly clear. She felt shame more than revulsion, shame that he should regard her as natural prey simply because she was a collier's child, through an accident of birth. As he thrust himself to her, she let out a long wailing cry, that Lauder choked off. He had no thought now for her pleasure. Ruthlessly he forced her to do what he commanded. Demeaned, brutalised and humbled, she was eventually instructed to gather up her clothes and be on her way. She stumbled from his apartment by the kitchen door, to sneak through the streets and slink into her husband's house like any tupenny harlot.

Later that night when she lay trembling in bed, bathed, perfumed, groomed and alone in the privacy of her silly, frilly Arabian Nights' sanctuary, what made her weep so inconsolably was not what Lauder had done or what he knew of her past but the inescapable fact that she could devise no means of gaining her revenge.

★   ★   ★

It rained all morning but, in early afternoon, the sun came out and bathed the fields round Hazelrig. Bruised cloud loomed over the Lothians and the colours of the land were sombrely beautiful. Tom was not aware of the threat that rain would return. He enjoyed the warm scents of the ripening earth, the feeling of openness that deprivation of sight did not impair. Though his eyes pricked and sweated under the metal mask he was more or less at ease. Accompanied by Mirrin he had returned that morning from Glasgow. The train ride had not been much fun; four days in bed in the Ophthalmic had rendered him vulnerable to noise. He flinched and started involuntarily, though Mirrin's arm was tight in his, as she lead him across the bustling station concourse and helped him into the angular darkness of the compartment. In motion, in a strange environment, without light, he had felt raw and exposed, as infirm as a damned old cripple. Not until the rhythm of the train had soothed him and he discovered that arrival at Hamilton was not quite so much of a nightmare did he begin to settle a little and, with resolution, come to terms with how he would pass the three week period under the mask.

Though Parfitt had advised him to rest, Tom rejected Mirrin's cosseting. He dozed in the kitchen chair for a half hour after dinner then, calling Davie and Kitten to him, told his wife that he would take a turn up the road. He wanted out into the air for a sweet breath—and that was that.

With Davie to guide him, Kitten's hand in his, and Fleck sniffing and nosing round, he got himself out of the yard. Rebuffing Hurley's offer of a ride in the trap, he walked fairly steadily, though at funeral pace, up the road.

Coming to terms, that's what the process involved. The healing of his mind and spirit was important now and, with his in-laws' problem to turn to when waves of despair approached, he undertook the adjustment that would be needed to endure a sightless period.

The sun offered comfort. The sounds of birds, the voices of lambs, quite grown now but still voluble, the lowing of beasts, the drone of insects, and all the sundry smells: it was a world he had always loved. He ran out of energy quickly though, and asked Davie to help him to the side of the road on the breast of the hill by the tree stump. The tree, an elm, had been blown down in a gale eighteen months ago. The sawyer from Crosstrees had ripped it up and carted the lumps away. But the stump was still there, moss-grown and brambled, a natural seat. Mirrin had given him a packet of Prize Crop cigarettes since he was not up to the frustration of trying to roll his own yet—though he would get around to that too in time. He put one in his mouth and, with slow precision, lit a match and guided it in cupped hands to the tip of the cigarette. Inhaling, he blew out smoke, and stuck the match into the grass to make sure that it would not cause fire. Aye, there were a host of new tricks to be learned. Parfitt had been hopeful that he would regain fifty or sixty per cent vision. Figures meant little to Tom. He wanted to see enough to work, that was all. It was surprising how many adjustments he had already made over the past couple of years.

"Well now," he said. "Isn't it grand t'be home again."

Ingenuously Kitten said, "When will the doctor give you your eyes back Daddy?"

Tom laughed. "He hasn't taken them away, flower, just tried to make them better. I have t'wear this mask t'keep out the light; the light makes them very sore."

"Does it hurt much?" Davie too was curious.

Tom told his son that the pain wasn't by any means severe and then, because the boy was obviously interested, explained what had been done to his eyes and something about the wonders of medicine. They had been seated there on the tree stump for some ten minutes when Davie announced, "Here's a trap comin'. It's Uncle Willie, an' Lily."

Almost as the boy spoke, Tom caught the sound of hoofs and wheels.

Not without vanity, he wondered how he would appear to Willie and Lily, seated there on the stump with the mask strapped over his nose. He turned his face towards the approaching sound.

"By Gum, you're up an' about early for a sick man, Tom," Willie called, with forced cheerfulness.

It was comforting to hear the baker's voice. Tom could imagine just how Kellock looked. There was no strain as there would have been with a stranger.

"Goin' up t'the farm, then?" asked Tom.

"I heard you were due home t'day," Willie said. "I expected t'find you stretched out in bed, lookin' all pale an' wan."

"Ach, I've had enough o'beds," Tom said, "though I'll not be balin' hay or steerin' bullocks this while yet."

"Was the operation successful, Tom?" Lily asked.

"We'll have t'wait a month or two t'find that out."

Willie said, "Tom, it looks very pleasant on that stump. I think I'll sit with you for a while."

"Come on, Kit; you too, Davie," said Lily. "I'll give y'a hurl back t'the farm. There's a sugar cake here for each of you an' I'm dyin' for a cup o'tea."

Kitten was eager, but Davie, having taken on responsibility for his father, said, "Will I come back an' help you home, Da'?"

"Thanks, son, but Willie can do it. Off y'go. Tell Mam t'keep the kettle singin'," Tom said.

As soon as Lily and the children were gone, Willie wasted no time in coming to the point.

"I'm glad I got you alone, Tom."

"I'm glad y'came, Willie," Tom assured him.

"It seems selfish o'us t'burden you at this time . . ."

"You'll have heard that Mirrin visited Lamont, an' wrung no change at all out o'him."

"No more than I expected."

"What was Kate's reaction?"

"Anger," said Willie. "I'm worried about her. She's changed so much since the arrest."

Tom groped for the baker's hand.

It was not a gesture he would have made if he had been sighted. It was too soft, too unmanly, that grip. But he could not offer comfort with a glance now and needed to make contact with Kellock, a man he much respected and admired.

"I understand, Willie."

Willie gave a rasping sigh. His stoicism was only skin deep. He too suffered over Neill's imprisonment. He did not release Tom's hand; he was not embarrassed by the gesture of friendship. "She's aged ten years this last four days."

"What of Neill?"

"He's dumped, but otherwise in good health. He spends his time eatin' the food we take him, an' readin'."

"I take it he's not fully aware o'the seriousness o'the situation?"

"He's young," said Willie. "It's best that way."

Tom nodded, released the baker's hand, fumbled for his cigarette packet and offered it to Willie. Willie did not usually smoke, except an occasional puff at a pipe after meals. Today, though, he accepted the Prize Crop and the men went through the ritual of lighting up. The sun had gone behind cloud: Tom was aware of it. Automatically he inclined his head, as if to scan the sky for signs of weather change.

He said, "It has t'be the brother, Willie. You'll have t'send for Drew Stalker."

"I know it."

"Kate can't refuse."

"In her present condition who knows what she'll do," said Willie. "It's not so much Kate that worries me as what that young man himself'll say."

"D'you think he'll refuse?"

"I'm positive he'll refuse," said Willie. "You've met him?"

"Never had that pleasure."

"It's no pleasure," said Willie.

"He'll need persuadin'," said Tom.

"An' that means Mirrin?"

"Aye."

"Will she go?"

"I'm sure she will," said Tom.

"Can you spare her at this time?"

"We'll manage fine here," said Tom. "Malcolm's capable o'fryin' ham. It'll only be for a day or two at most."

"Y'know I wouldn't ask this of you or of Mirrin," said Willie, "but I can see no other path for us t'follow."

"The risk, I think, is yours."

Willie nodded, then, remembering that Tom was blind, said, "I know exactly what y'mean."

"Puttin' Neill an' his father together, in the public eye. It might mean . . ."

"Who knows what it'll mean," said Willie.

"Change o'some sort, maybe drastic changes."

"That's not somethin' we can avoid now." Willie laughed, ruefully, not bitterly. "What did we get ourselves into, you an' I, marryin' those Stalkers?"

"God knows." Tom put out his arm and let Willie help him to his feet. "Come on, we'd better get back. It takes me a while, an' I'm thinkin' it'll rain soon."

"When will Mirrin go t'Edinburgh?"

"Tomorrow," Tom said.

★　　★　　★

Thrush strode into the drawing room of Strathmore without pausing to divest himself of his dripping yellow oilskins. He looked, thought Edith, like a lifeboat captain returned from an errand of mercy upon the briny deep. The double-lock heavy leather bag in his right fist, she assumed, contained the spoils of his sortie. Knocking back the oilskin hat, Thrush kneeled on the Afghanistan rug between Houston and Edith and, glancing first at one and then the other, twisted the catches with his thumbs and let the locks spring up. He pulled open the bag, prising its jaws wide and, sitting back on his heels, said, "There you are, Houston, ten thousand pounds in cash."

"In cash?" Lamont peered curiously at the treasure. Even the coalmaster had never seen that amount in hard currency before. "Why not a banker's order or a straight-forward cheque?"

"That isn't how Mr. Craddick works." Thrush lifted out a bundle of ten-pound notes and weighed it in his hand like a brick. "It is one of his foibles that I respect; he deals, where possible, in cash."

Edith flounced out her skirt, bent her knees and, supported on her hands, looked into the depths of the bag like a child into a goldfish pond. "Ten thousand pounds."

Thrush said, "Houston, I suggest that we deposit this sum in five separate accounts, with checking facilities, and pay our creditors from separate sources, thus avoiding too much interest on the part of 'other parties', shall we say?"

"An excellent idea, Sydney," Edith agreed.

Lamont said, "Edith, get up, please. It isn't seemly for a woman of your age to be crawling on the carpet."

"What if we cashed in all our stocks." said Edith. "How large a bag would it take to carry that profit in cash?"

"A cart," said Thrush, joining in her game. "A large hay-wagon, perhaps."

"Nonsense." Stiffly, Lamont slid forward from his chair and knelt over the bag. "In ten pound notes, two canvas sacks would carry our entire worth."

"I disagree," said Thrush. "Besides, what fun it would be to collect it in sovereigns, nice, heavy, old-fashioned sovereigns and shovel them into a bunker somewhere."

"I fear that the sound of all that clinking would bring our colliers swarming in a pack like rats," said Edith.

Tiring suddenly of this stupid speculation, Lamont pushed himself up. Hands behind his coat-tails, he stood looking down imperiously at Thrush and his dumpy wife.

"The point is entirely moot," he said. "I never think of the Blacklaw Company in cash terms. Our stock means land, coal, machinery and men."

"But this." Thrush waved his hand over the bag. "This is what we need right now."

Lamont moved away, as if he feared contamination from the

banknotes. Thrush got to his feet and began stripping off his oilskins.

Lamont said, "We will do as you suggest, Sydney; put enough into assorted banking accounts to pay our debts. The balance we will place in my safe to meet immediate wage-bills."

"And we will be solvent again, thank the Lord," said Edith.

"We will *appear* to be solvent again," the coalmaster corrected "which, my dear, is quite a different thing."

"Do not be so pessimistic, Houston," Edith said. "I'm sure that your strategy will pay off. I'm sure this strike is effectively broken, and that, within the month, our colliers will be back at work."

"At a cut wage, too," Lamont said.

Thrush jerked his head in the coalmaster's direction, his mouth open to interject a comment. He thought better of it, however, and merely nodded. "Is that what you plan, Houston?"

"You don't imagine *I* intend to pay for this squalid interruption out of profits, do you?" Lamont retorted. "No, Sydney, Edith, no, no. I will blackleg it as long as I have to, and when my colliers do elect to return they will come back on *my* terms."

"I . . ." Thrush began, but Edith tugged the tail of his jacket, indicating that he should hold his tongue.

It was injudicious of Lamont to play the tyrant now. The strike had been symptomatic of labour unrest throughout Britain. Though Lamont had broken the union hold in the Blacklaw area, strike action continued in all other major coalfields. It could still find a foothold here in Blacklaw too, Thrush thought, particularly if Lamont insisted in squeezing advantage from his victory. What would happen when the blacklegs had been paid off and drifted out of the district? What would happen when there were no more hired 'specials' on patrol, and the hang-fire threat of military intervention was removed? Would there be sabotage, annoying acts of retaliation, time-consuming, money-burning 'accidents' both above and below ground? Thrush had been through all that before; he knew how much production could be lost by a broken cable, a tilted trough, a cutter with striped gears, by a derailed truck. Though he had no respect at all for miners, he had enough common sense not to push them too far, not to kick them when they were down.

Houston, who had once professed loyalty of a sort to his parishioners, seemed wilfully set against them now. Edith had told him that the Stalker woman had called at Strathmore. Thrush wondered if the mysterious visit of Mirrin Stalker—concerning whose purpose Houston would divulge no information—might have softened the coalmaster's jagged edges just a little. It seemed to have had just the opposite effect. Still that, as Edith's tug upon his coat-tail had reminded him, might be advantageous in the longer term. His personal dealing would, with luck, reduce Houston to the status of frustrated bystander at board meetings of his own company. Such a pass, when it came—and what could prevent it, really—would be sweet.

Returning to the bag, Houston stooped and lifted it, grunting a little. "We'll count it in the office, Sydney."

"It's all there, I assure you."

"We'll count it, nonetheless."

"By all means, Houston."

Opening the drawing-room door, Lamont went out into the hall carrying the bag. Thrush would have followed him immediately, if Edith had not clasped his hand in hers. "Did it go well, my darling?" she whispered.

With a furtive glance in the direction of the open door, Thrush whipped round and planted a kiss on Mrs. Lamont's cheek, murmuring, as he pulled back, "In three months or less, dearest Edith, you and I will have Blacklaw for our very own."

*   *   *

"Good of you to come, Craddick," Andrew Stalker said.

"Not at all, not at all. Enjoyed the breather."

"Will you stay the night? I can offer you my guest bedroom."

"Must get back, Mr. Stalker; last train."

"Then I will not detain you."

"Here we are, sir."

Drew took the documents, shaking Craddick's hand as he

did so, as if to seal a treatise. If they had been caught in that position by a camera, the plate would have suggested a diplomatic occasion. But, naturally, there was no camera; no other person, not even Horn, was present in the chambers. Though he had not expected it, Drew experienced a charge of satisfaction at the touch of the documents, tangible proof that he had become part owner of the pit that had claimed his father's and brothers' lives.

He did not believe that Blacklaw had made him what he was. He did not regard his background as either handicap or advantage, or as the wheel on which he had been shaped. But the feeling was deep in him, ingrained, multifaceted and complex. The sigh as he closed his fingers on the stock documents unwittingly revealed it.

Craddick gave him a hearty hand-shake. "My cheque, I take it, will be forthcoming shortly."

"I'll let you have it now."

"No, no. No need for that, Mr. Stalker. The weekend will do."

"How did you pay Thrush?"

"Cash."

"He asked for cash?"

"It's how I reckoned he'd like it."

"And he smelled no fish?"

"Not a whiff. Dazzled by his own cleverness is our Mr. Thrush."

"Good," said Drew. "It's how I wish it at this stage."

Craddick said, "I take it that you will not tarry o'er long before making your presence felt?"

"On the contrary," said Drew. "It will be six or eight months before I have the opportunity to attend a Blacklaw Company meeting in person."

Craddick pulled an enquiring face.

"I am about to leave Scotland for America," Drew explained.

"Oh, that's a new one," Craddick said.

"Partly a holiday," said Drew. "Partly business."

"America," said Craddick. "Aye, I've often thought what an excellent place that would be, in all its diversity, for a go-ahead fellow like yourself. Is it mineral rights you're investigatin', may I ask?"

"Possibly," said Drew. "More likely engineering."

"Six months." Craddick glanced at his hunter as if to check the exact period of his partner's absence. "That takes us through most of the autumn and winter court terms."

"Quite," said Drew.

Craddick nodded. "This country, I sometimes think, is going to the doggies, though it is unfashionable to voice that opinion."

"I will be embarking on the first leg of my journey—that is, boarding the London express train—one week from today. I have already cancelled or re-directed my calendar of briefs, pleading ill-health. I would appreciate it if you would continue, in my absence, to act for me on your own initiative, or, if necessary, to consult with Daniel Horn on any matters pertaining to the more central aspects of my business."

"That I will do," Craddick promised.

"But no more purchases, not at present."

"One question, Mr. Stalker, if I might put it without giving offence?"

"Put it by all means. I've no secrets from you, Mr. Craddick."

"My question—will those Blacklaw shares really pay off?"

"I gather that you consider them a dubious risk."

"In the circumstances, that isn't for me to say."

Drew smiled faintly and, wagging the shares, told the agent, "The Blacklaw Company will pay off handsomely, Mr. Craddick. I'll see to it that it does."

"That's what I thought," Craddick said. "Good luck on your voyages, Mr. Stalker."

"Thank you," the Advocate said.

*   *   *

Stirred to action by rumour, Edward followed the trail from a starting point at the now abandoned 'headquarters' with its heaps of stale broadsheets and smudged posters. He asked miners gathered on corners and in close-mouths, quizzed barkeeps in outlying public houses until he found a blackleg who was too soused to be cautious, and who gave him a precise direction.

Walking with shoulders hunched against the sifting twilight rain, big-looking in his pilot's coat, winged collar spread, fists deep in the patch pockets, Edward tramped from Blacklaw to Northrigg and entered a long straggling street of broken cobbles flanked by merchants' haulage yards. At length, a half mile or more along that godforsaken highway, he found the dingy island-like building at the corner of Patton & Smithvale's and the public house called, with more truth than imagination, The Cage.

It was not a haunt of miners or foundry workers, of corn-dealers, knackers or any of the legitimate tradesmen that survived in the wilderness beyond Patton's weeping brick wall. The community was a day-time one, made up of burly domestic coal-merchants who grafted for profit and put away more liquor at a dinner-time than the average miner could afford to consume in a week. More of a backwater than an oasis, The Cage had no regular evening clientele. The bar was zinc-topped, the round tables scratched. One brand of beer was pumped up through a warped coil that caused it to gurgle gaseously from the taps. Three cheap whiskies were stocked and a single gin kept especially for the retired preacher who lived in one of the hinterland tenements and played the cornet each Sunday evening in the kirkless square as if to inform the Lord that he was still alive and unwavering in his faith.

Jutting out his hand, Edward Stalker pushed the scrolled door so that it flew inwards. Gaslight made a sickly aura over the fly-blown mirror behind the bar and the young collier saw their faces in it, serious and conspiratorial, Rob with a pint to his mouth and Davy Dunlop with a nip of whisky.

Two old men sat in a corner by a scrap fire. Three haulers, none of them young, were propped on a bench in the alcove, mute with drink. It was the ideal spot for a rendezvous, and it must have startled Rob Ewing to be confronted by Edward that far out of Blacklaw, and have put the fear of death in Dunlop, who was capable of feeling threatened even in his own water-closet.

Standing in the doorway, Edward shouted, "So it's true, Ewing."

Rob brought up his pint pot and drank. Though he appeared to be calm, his knuckles were white.

"You'd better come in, Edward," Rob said.

The haulers were trying to focus on this loud stranger, the worthies by the fire champing on their clay pipes and staring as if General Booth in person had just marched into their sanctuary.

Stalking forward, Edward said, "You *are* sellin' us out t'Lamont."

"Friendly drink," Dunop muttered. "Friendly drink, that's all."

"Shut your bloody mouth," Edward said.

Rob put down the pot. "Listen, son . . ."

"I want no grease from you, Ewing," Edward told him.

"Time I was away home," said Dunlop. "Sarah, the daughter, she worries if . . ."

Hardly seeming to move, Edward's right hand caught Dunlop's bowler by the brim, and yanked it down over the wee man's fat red face.

"What d'you want, Edward?" Rob asked, imperturbably.

"I want t'know what the hell you're doin' consortin' in secret wi' that piece o'slime."

"Union business."

"You're sellin' my cousin out."

"Is that all you think o'me?"

"Jack Gower told me you'd been seen wi' Dunlop."

"What's it got t'do wi' Jack Gower?" said Rob. "I'm not answerable t'him—nor t'you for that matter. I'll drink where I like an' wi' who I like."

"Tell me one thing," Edward said. "Has this got t'do with our Neill?"

"A murd . . ." Dunlop began, squaring his hat.

Edward punched him in the throat. The manager reeled back, gurgling. Edward shouted, "I know what *you've* been up to, Dunlop. You've been *bribin' witnesses.*"

"Careful, Edward." Rob shifted his weight.

Even when angry, Edward had none of Neill's indifference

212

to consequences. Besides, there was no centre of argument.
Obviously, as the rumour had suggested, Rob Ewing and
Lamont's inner clan, the managers, were doing business—not
Union business either. From Jack Gower, a man who spoke his
mind, Edward had heard how Dunlop had tried to wheedle an
old collier named Orrinsmith into giving evidence against Neill.
How many others had already been got at in that way? Edward's
first thought had been to inform Rob. But Rob, it transpired,
had also been consorting with Dunlop. All afternoon, Edward
had walked the streets picking up gossip. He had said nothing
at home, not even to Willie. It was his business. The rumours
tallied with Rob's attitude to the murder, and the jailing of
Neill. Brooding, Edward transferred some of his own guilt at
being a party to the riot to Rob who, the more he thought of it,
was just the sort of embittered man who, in the tradition of
turncoats, might be persuaded to name his price.

"D'you want your thrashin' outside?" Edward asked.

"I won't fight wi' you, Edward."

"Too lily-livered?"

"I've no cause."

"Is Neill's neck not cause enough?"

"This's not what you think, son."

"If it wasn't for you, Rob Ewing, my cousin would be free."

"I'm not t'blame."

"Outside."

Dunlop was leaning against the counter. The barman relieved
him of a shilling before giving him another nip of whisky to
swab his aching throat.

"Listen, Edward . . ." Rob began.

"I'm sick t'bloody death listenin' t'you."

"It's a conspiracy."

"Right." Loose-knuckled, Edward's fist struck Rob's mouth
in a slapping punch. Blood welled at once from the split skin
of the lower lip. Rob did nothing, did not even raise his arms
to defend himself. Edward struck him again, the same sort
of blow and blood flowed thickly into the stubble of Rob's
chin.

The publican had been summoned from his parlour upstairs.
He stood in the curtained doorway at the back of the bar while

the barman, a stooped gnome of sixty or more, gaped and would not, as urged, step in to break up the fight.

"Outside, then" Rob said softly.

As Edward turned, Rob lunged at the young man, snapped his strong arms under Edward's armpits, locked his fingers in a vice across his nape, doubled him over, and trotted him, like a 'special', straight across the room, out through the swing door into the rain-slicked street. The manoeuvre was so fast, so powerful, that Edward could not retaliate. He was in motion before he realised that Rob had outsmarted him. Not until he was flung forward onto the cobbles did he have an opportunity to gather his wits and consider a counter-attack. Even then, Rob was too quick for him. Projecting him forward with a boot planted squarely on the base of his spine, Rob followed him and, as he pitched and sprawled on the cobbles, dropped and pinned him to the stones, a knee on each shoulder, one big hand on his neck.

Leaning, Rob hissed into Edward's ear. "You damned hot-head. You're as daft as your bloody cousin. I thought you had more sense. Now you've queered it."

"Queered your bloody sell-out," Edward gasped.

"Dunlop wasn't bribin' *me;* I was bloody bribin' *him*—aye, wi' Union funds."

"Wha . . . ?"

Cheek plastered to the ground, Edward cocked his head to squint back at Ewing. Anger was scored into his gaunt features, making his eyes fiery. "Y'wouldn't trust me. None o'you would trust me. Well, son, I'm not deaf, nor am I thick as *you* seem t'be. I guessed what Lamont would do, an' who he'd use t'do it. He wants witnesses primed an' ready. An', by God, he's got them."

Slackening his hold, Rob allowed Edward to turn his head. The young miner was round-eyed with horror, more at the foolishness of his own behaviour than at Rob's information. All doubt vanished.

Rob climbed off. "Get up." He hauled Edward to his feet.

"Rob, I . . . I don't know what t'say."

"Ach, I don't know either," said Rob. "What's become of us in Blacklaw? I was your father's best pal. We were as close as you an' Neill are. I was there the day your Da' died, burned and broken a thousand feet underground, all because Lamont was too gluttonous for profit t'heed our warning about fire damp."

Rob shook his head, and put his hand on the young man's shoulder. "You're like him in many ways, Edward, only maybe without so much laughter in you."

"There's damn all t'laugh about."

"True," Rob agreed.

"What about Dunlop?"

"That's blown; he'll go sneakin' away t'tell Lamont. The courtship's over. He knows we're scuppered."

"Is Lamont really bribin' witnesses?"

"In a way," said Rob. "Cleverly."

They walked back along the cobbled street. Behind them, in the doorway of The Cage, the publican watched them go with relief. No damage had been done. So remote was the public house that the inevitable crowd that mustered whenever a fight was in the offing had failed to materialise. Only the two old codgers stood by the entrance, puffing on their pipes, disappointed that no punch-up had occurred to break the monotony of life under Patton & Smithvale's wall.

"Can Lamont not be brought t'book for it?" asked Edward.

"In spite o'Dunlop's ham-fisted approach," Rob answered, "Lamont's too clever t'fall into a trap. He's only tacklin' those that really were at the pit-gate. He's not gettin' them t'invent lies, just bend the truth int'a suitable shape."

"Suitable—for him?" said Edward. "Hell, Rob, what's he got against us Stalkers?"

"He knows our time is comin'—I mean the working-man's time. He knows that him an' his like will be brought up by justice, that new parliamentary laws will eventually protect us against criminal neglect, and greed."

"Aye, but when?"

"Ten years, twenty years. I'll maybe not see it happen, Edward, but I think you will."

"In the meantime . . . ?"

"In the meantime there's your cousin in Hamilton cells on a capital charge," Rob said. "An' there's Lamont doin' his best t'see that the charge sticks. You asked about Lamont an' the Stalkers—did y'know, Edward, that your Aunt Mirrin and Lamont were . . . friends."

"I've heard stories, most o'them none too savoury," Edward said. "But I've always liked Mirrin, an' it strikes me that if there *was* anythin' between her an' Houston Lamont then it was a long time ago when both she an' the coalmaster were different folk."

"We were all different folk," said Rob. "That's one thing that you youngsters have over us—you have no past t'measure life against. You're better off without it, believe me. I near married Mirrin m'self."

"Kate told me you were sweet on her when you were young."

"But," said Rob, avoiding the obvious line of the conversation, "that's all water under the Sheenan brig now. It was Lamont I was after, an' it's Lamont I failed t'get."

"But, Rob," said Edward, "you always claimed there was no personal feud between you an' the boss. I've heard y'tell my mother that a dozen times or more. You certainly convinced me."

Rob said, "I hate that man. I hate him, his wife, his manager, his pits, his property; all that he stands for. He's the idol I'd like t'overthrow. It's more difficult now, since he broke the strike."

"Blacklegs," said Edward bitterly. "Only Lamont would have the bloody gall t'employ a whole workforce o'blackleg labour. He must be payin' out more than he's pullin' in."

"I'm sure o'that," said Rob. "But how long can the colliers stand back an' watch their jobs bein' done, coal being hauled, while they starve?"

"What about sabotage?" Edward was perfectly serious. He was well enough read in labour literature to appreciate the value of well planned, well executed acts of destruction. "Lamont's stretched as far as he can go, Rob. I'm not one o' the dafties that suppose him t'have a bottomless purse. Could we not make it even rougher for him?"

"It's what I'd have put forward myself," said Rob. "But Lamont has a nap hand—your cousin. While he has Neill in jail an' a trial pending, what sort o'direct action can we take against him? God, if we start slicing cables an' layin' explosives down in the seams—an' we could organise that easy enough—it would reflect so badly on us, an' on Neill, that any picked jury who didn't happen t'be miners would hang the lad on principle."

"So that's Lamont's purpose in keepin' in thick with the law, in helpin' them build up a case against Neill."

"Neill is Lamont's insurance policy," said Rob.

They had emerged from the long empty street now. Across the crook of the Poulter's burn, beyond a massive iron sewer pipe, they could see Northrigg and Blacklaw, the lights bleary in the July rain, rain so fine it fell like dew upon the nap of the men's jackets and their hair.

"I suppose you'll be headin' home now, Rob?"

"Aye."

"Then I'll walk with you."

Not speaking, the men angled west by waste ground and crossed the burn by an iron bridge that rang dully under their heels. A narrow macadam walk brought them out into Northrigg's main street. The town was subdued. An empty hay cart rumbled in a lane. Far down, the pub gave out a drone of sound, tobacco smoke hazed moistly about the cheery red lantern above its doors. Smells of cooking hung faintly in the air, mingled with the brown odour of coal fires. A child cried loud and sore in the ground floor room of a tenement.

"It used t'be all cottages here," Rob said.

"The boss can pack more folk int' one place wi' tenements," said Edward, grimly. "They call that kind o'thinkin' 'economics'."

Walking more quickly, they crossed the main street and went through a back lane towards Blacklaw, not far off.

Rob said, "Have y'calmed down?"

"I never lost m'head," said Edward. "But do y'not think I was justified in bein' suspicious?"

"Maybe," said Rob. "But it's no' like you t'be violent."

"What d'they say—violence breeds violence," Edward said. "I'm sick wi'worry in case the bloody lawyers find a means o' contrivin' a verdict o'guilty against Neill."

"It worries me too," said Rob. "The law's Lamont's law,

drawn up by his kind t'protect his kind. An' there's nothin'
I can do about it."

"I know," said Edward.

"Aye, but d'your aunts know."

"My aunts? What does it matter what they think?"

"It matters a lot t'me," said Rob. "Strange as it may seem,
your family is all I've got left."

Edward glanced at him in surprise. It had not occurred to
him before that the friendships and loyalties of the past were so
strong, strong enough to endure the erosion of the changing
times. He regretted his attack on Rob Ewing now, but he was
wary of sentiment.

"How's the split lip?" he asked.

"I've had worse hurts in my day," said Rob.

Edward nodded. "Come on," he said. "Let's hurry home
before this bloody rain gets worse."

★　　★　　★

Not least among the thoughts that occupied Mirrin during
the train ride from Hamilton was consideration of the changes
that she would find in her brother and sister. She remembered
them as little more than children, Drew scrawny and scraped
down, Betsy, pretty, slender and pert, with bouncing ringlets.
In dress at least, Mirrin had not changed much. Out of the
wardrobe had come her 'Sunday best', a tailored coat and fancy
bonnet that she had bought when she was a music hall star.
Stored in a dry chest they were still in perfect condition. It
was all she had by way of finery. There had never been enough
in the farm purse to squander on fancy clothes.

Unlike Glasgow, Edinburgh thrilled Mirrin as the majestic
architecture of the capital unfolded beside the railroad track. She
was less thrilled by her reception at Waverley Station, however.
After due consideration, Tom had suggested that she had
better not arrive entirely unannounced. Consequently a special
delivery letter had been sent, informing Drew that his sister
would call upon him at his chambers at eleven-thirty on
Wednesday.

Waverley Station was big and grand. Sunlight streamed
through glass to sharpen the angular façades. Mirrin reached

the ticket gate and went through it. She carried a small bandbox in which were her overnight clothes, just in case Drew was 'too busy' to see her that day. If that happened she would take a room in a boarding house and wait her brother out, a campaign that Tom and Willie had devised between them. Though Mirrin did not protest, it occurred to her that Drew, and Betsy, might simply refuse to entertain her, make her 'whistle' for her interview. They were quite capable of it. It transpired, however, that she had misjudged them. As she passed through the ticket gate, a man detached himself from the crowd collected in the concourse. With a nod of welcome, he took off his hat and touched Mirrin's arm. He seemed faintly familiar, a dessicated, lantern-jawed individual with scornful, calculating eyes. She had met him only once but he was too striking a character to forget.

"Mrs. Armstrong?"

"Yes."

"I'm Daniel Horn. I have the honour t'be your brother's clerk."

"Is my brother not in Edinburgh?" Mirrin's nervousness surfaced in the question. She imagined Horn steering her back onto the Hamilton train.

"He is in Edinburgh, ma'am. He has asked me t'accompany you to the place where he is, in your sister's company as it happens."

"I gather he got my letter?"

"Late last night," said Horn.

"How . . . how is my brother?"

"He's fine," Horn said. "Permit me to take your luggage."

"Thank you." Mirrin handed over the bandbox.

Past book kiosks, tobacco stalls and the upright tents of tea and coffee sellers and vendors of ice-cold 'fizz', Horn led her across the station. Tall hats and Empire skirts were everywhere. Knots of holiday-makers, some elegant, some red-faced and harassed, clustered by the booking office grills. Up a steep staircase, across an iron bridge above the rails, Horn guided her, to an upper level above which a strip of blue sky was visible at the top of a flight of broad stone steps. There were shops by the sides of the steps. Children—ragged children—

clustered about the doors; bootblacks, sellers of matches and 'genuine shepherds' crooks', posies of flowers, pills and potions against every summer ailment known to man. Edinburgh too had changed; the snooty Victorian city had finally swept its hucksters underground.

Horn did not guide her up the steps. Abruptly he turned along a short passage at the end of which was a handsome glass-panelled door. Behind the door, at the foot of a tall building, was a plushly carpeted staircase and a foyer guarded by two porters in hotel livery. As Horn held the door for Mirrin, the porters stepped forward. Horn brushed them aside. He was thoroughly at home in this mysterious entranceway. In his treatment of the hotel staff, was a wry high-handed brusqueness that defined the clerk's status precisely.

"This way, ma'am."

An interior staircase ascended from the foyer by means of a series of landings. Cumbersome landscape paintings hung over each landing. A luxuriant rubber plant, in a Chinese pot large enough to hold a family wash, sprouted up the flock wall, reaching its leaves towards slotted windows. Windows revealed glimpses of the station's inner secrets, sidings, roofs, the outer reaches of platforms and, from the fourth landing, permitted a perfect view of the dipping skyline of the Royal Mile. Horn gave Mirrin no opportunity to play the tourist; nor had she the inclination. Her stomach was tight with nervousness. This overture to her meeting with Drew, made by way of back doors and staircases, smacked of a secret assignation. A plaque on the wall told her that she was within the precincts of the Portland Northern Hotel, site of many famous balls and receptions, the frequent lodging of dukes and earls. The knowledge did not make her feel grand, only apprehensive. From a corridor on the fourth landing, a door opened into an anteroom—the Kenilworth Lounge. Seated at a table by the window were Drew and Betsy.

Horn held the door open. Gathering herself, Mirrin went through it into the compact lounge.

"Mrs. Armstrong, your sister," Horn announced.

At once Drew got to his feet.

"Thank you, Daniel," he said. "Ask the waiter to bring tea

and coffee, and some buttered muffins—with jam—then you may leave us."

"Enjoy your visit, Mrs. Armstrong," Horn said, with a sloping grin, and putting the bandbox on the carpet by the door, slid away again, like a lizard.

The door *paaaaaphed* shut beind him.

Coming forward, Drew offered Mirrin his hand.

Though careful to hide her shock, Mirrin could hardly believe that this was her brother. He looked ten years her senior, like no member of the family she could recall, not even a boozy blacksheep of an uncle who had visited them when they were children. A tailored dark grey frock coat and four-in-hand tie could not disguise his portliness.

Mirrin shook his hand. Stiff and formal, the greeting, together with his first words, set the tone of his reception. "I would like to say that it is good to see you, Mirrin, but under the circumstances I think that would be inappropriate, do you not?"

Betsy got to her feet now. Her manner was still as quick and effusive as ever. Her brightness was at least a pleasing affectation. She had put on a little weight too, but it improved her. She wore a blue boucle suit and a hat like an inverted flower trough and as she moved to greet Mirrin, wafted a fragrant and expensive perfume.

"Mirrin, my dearest Mirrin. How well you look, how radiant with health."

The women embraced. Immediately conscious of Betsy's lack of feeling, Mirrin realised that she could never hope to recapture the affection she had once felt towards her sister. Too much had happened; too much had not been shared.

"What of your children? *Four* children. Goodness, how four children must try your patience, Mirrin. Do they keep good health?"

"They're well, thanks," said Mirrin.

"I have two. Did you know? Daughters. Pretty, bright little things. But, oh, how irksome they can be. Don't you find that?"

Sensing a widening of the fissure between Betsy and Mirrin even at that early stage, Drew pulled out chairs. Seconds later, before awkwardness could break into words again, a waiter brought in a trolley and dispensed tea and coffee. On Drew's specific instruction, the waiter actually split and buttered four of the floury yellow muffins. After offering the muffins to his sisters, both of whom refused, Drew helped himself and, during the first few minutes of conversation, put away three. It crossed Mirrin's mind that this greed—for greed it seemed to be—was a quality that her brother shared with Sydney Thrush. Perhaps the deprivations of younger days had to be compensated for at every possible opportunity in later life. Though Betsy encouraged Mirrin to chat casually of her family, the farm and her husband, and gave a breathless account of her own domestic bliss, Mirrin was too aware of Drew's severity to be at ease. She said nothing at all about Tom's blindness, nor did she mention Kate.

Four or five ineffectual, embarrassing minutes went past before Drew considered that courtesy had been served.

"Mirrin."

The sisters looked at him immediately.

The framing was apposite—the window with its view of Edinburgh's Princes Street, monuments gilded by sunlight, Drew's profile against it; an artificial but evocative composition.

"It takes little intelligence to deduce why you have asked to see me after so many years," Drew said. "No doubt it concerns Kate's son."

Mirrin resisted. It was Betsy who said, "*Your* son, Drew."

"The Stalker boy." Drew wriggled nicely out of verbal commitment.

Mirrin said, "Kate—we—have nobody else t'turn to. Kate doesn't even know I'm here."

"Does she still resent me?"

"Aye," Mirrin answered. "But it would be the height of folly, Drew, not t'approach you—at least t'get advice."

"It's a capital charge," said Drew. "From the little I've read of the case, the boy seems to have killed a special police constable by dint of striking the constable on the forehead with a hammer."

"He was throwing the hammer away," said Mirrin. "He didn't intend t'kill anyone. You've my word on that, Drew."

"Were you an eye-witness?"

"No, but . . ."

"Then your word is worth nothing in a court of law."

"Drew, Neill's incapable of . . ."

"Oh, yes, yes, of course he is," Drew interrupted. "The point is that sufficient evidence exists for the Crown to demand the ultimate penalty with *some* hope of success."

"It's a . . . well, a political move, I suppose you'd call it. Lamont's usin' Neill t'keep his colliers in check."

"I question if it's that simple, Mirrin."

Betsy said, "If it is that simple no doubt the lawyers will devise ingenious ways of making it seem more complex."

"Betsy, please." Drew's patience was ill-disguised.

Mirrin said, "According t'Willie—Kate's husband—an' to my husband, it's a trumped up charge that's bound t'be reduced t'manslaughter before the trial's far gone."

"Perhaps," said Drew. "Lacking plausible evidence I cannot commit myself on the strengths or weaknesses in the prosecution's case. A hammer is clearly a deadly weapon; a riot at a pit-gate is clearly a setting conducive to violence."

"On both sides," Betsy put in.

"Please, Betsy," said Drew again, with less patience this time. "I am endeavouring to clarify the legal position, in some small way, to allow Mirrin to carry back to Blacklaw accurate information."

"Drew," said Betsy, "I imagine that Mirrin requires more than the benefit of top-of-the-head advice."

"Does he, the boy, have a legal representative?"

"Mr. Shallop, solicitor for the United Federation of Miners."

"I've heard of Shallop. He's well out of his depth."

"That's part of the reason I'm here," said Mirrin. "We need t'find a good lawyer, the very best lawyer."

"First you need a solicitor," said Drew. "In addition you must retain a pleader, that is, a member of the bar; an advocate."

"We must have the best available," said Mirrin.

"For the best the costs will be very high," said Drew.

He turned his eye on Betsy, as if to forestall interruption. She scowled at him, shaking her head so that the flowers on her hat bobbed and expressed her irritation in a fetchingly feminine manner.

"In all, in a case of this significance, legal costs may reach fifteen hundred guineas."

Mirrin gasped. She had considered Willie's prediction of five hundred pounds excessive. "Fifteen *hundred*?"

"Guineas," said Drew.

"We can't afford that, nor near it."

"Doesn't Kellock have property?"

"Aye, but . . ."

"What is it worth?"

"The business, with goodwill, might fetch . . . I don't know, seven or eight hundred pounds."

"Say, eight." Drew produced a plump-barrelled fountain pen from his vest pocket and a small shell-backed writing tablet. In minute figures he marked the sum at the top of a page. "Eight hundred; now what can you raise, Mirrin?"

"Nothin' like the sum you mentioned."

"Is your farm leased?"

"We're tenants of the Duke."

"You won't have any trouble from him," said Drew. "Old Teddy certainly won't toe the Tory line and terminate your lease because you are connected with a labour scandal. On the contrary. The Duke's no lover of the new-money class. He would prefer to support an honest bondsman any day of the week."

"Besides, I am well acquainted with the Duchess," put in Betsy; a statement of fact. "We can ensure that no pressure of *that* sort is brought to bear upon you and your husband, Mirrin."

"That's a weight off my mind," Mirrin said.

"Now." Drew tapped the end of the pen against his teeth. "Can you estimate the value of your stock?"

"Drew," Mirrin declared, "you can't expect us to sell our stock. The farm's our sole means of makin' a livin'. No more can Willie Kellock sell up his bakery. What would we all live on, then?"

Drew sighed loudly. He poured tea and drank it. He rattled the cup into the saucer—a signal of displeasure, mannerisms that Betsy identified as parts of his courtroom technique.

Drew's pen remained poised. "How much do you want from me?" he enquired. "I warn you, Mirrin, I will not foot the whole bill. I expect some sort of sacrifice from you, all of you."

Mirrin's eyes widened in disbelief.

"I will pay half." Betsy cupped her gloved hand over Mirrin's wrist. "At least Fraser, my husband, will."

"Deuced if I know why I should," said Drew, "but I will guarantee the other half."

Mirrin said, "Is it just a matter of money? Is that enough t'purchase Neill's freedom?"

"The higher the fee, the better the service," said Drew. "Naturally, that is not the principle, but it does tend to be the practice of legal representation in Scotland."

"And who is the best lawy . . . I mean, advocate?" asked Mirrin.

"Patrick Lauder."

"No," snapped Betsy. "*Not Lauder.*"

"Without the shadow of a doubt, Patrick is the finest advocate, *vis-à-vis* obtaining a verdict for his client, in the country. If you can get him, Lauder is your man."

"Emphatically not, Drew," said Betsy. "*Anyone* but Lauder."

"What do you have against Patrick, Betsy? I thought you liked him. Lord knows he favours you; attends your dinner parties, does he not?"

Like strangers, the pair had a web of reference that excluded Mirrin. Dinner parties, clients, thousand guinea fees, great advocates; now Mirrin understood just how much her brother and sister had changed. In this remote society they were intrinsic, comfortable. She could understand why there had been no contact over the years. After all, apart from a bucketful of shared memories, the Blacklaw Stalkers and the twins had nothing in common. She wondered how she would have fitted into this society if she had chosen to follow a stage career. Now, she must admit, she could not make the butterfly change that would allow her ingress into Edinburgh's upper crust. She had lost adaptability. She might not be a typical farmer's wife, but clearly she was not of this breed, and never would be, no matter how adroitly she played the part.

"Betsy," Mirrin said, "if this Patrick Lauder is the best . . . ?"

With shocking vehemence, Betsy blurted out, "He is evil."

"Betsy," said Drew, "did Lauder in some way offend you?"

Mirrin watched Betsy gain control of herself. It was obvious to her, as an outsider, that Lauder had hurt Betsy deeply; that meant that she had been in love with him. Recalling the amours of Betsy's young womanhood Mirrin could, with fair accuracy, speculate on the relationship. Oddly, Drew seemed to be blind to it.

Stepping in, Mirrin said, "I imagine he'd cost too much anyhow."

But the twins were intent upon each other. It was to Drew that Betsy explained herself. "Patrick Lauder, my innocent brother, would not defend a collier for all the gold in the Bank of England. In case you'd failed to notice, Lauder is an arrant snob."

"He would do it for me," said Drew.

"He would *not* do it for you," retorted Betsy.

"What other advocate is there?" asked Mirrin.

"Next to Lauder," said Drew, promptly, "there is Mansfield, or William Argyll, or Kinnemouth; all very excellent pleaders."

"Where do you rank yourself, Drew?" asked Betsy.

"I am . . ." Drew's chin tilted. There was fierce arrogance in his eyes. He fought to modify an outright declaration of his worth. "Kinnemouth has more experience in the Criminal Courts than I do."

"Betsy?" Mirrin enquired.

Betsy too was filled with misgivings. It was obvious that Mirrin had travelled to Edinburgh expressly to ask Drew to defend her nephew.

"Unfortunately, Mirrin, neither Drew nor I will be in Scotland this autumn or winter. We are both—separately—passing the winter abroad."

"I have business in America," said Drew.

"And I have made arrangements to visit Italy."

"I see," said Mirrin. "Aye, it had crossed my mind that the pair o'you just might be 'winterin' abroad'."

Drew sighed again. "Mirrin, I know what's in your mind. I *cannot* defend the boy, your nephew."

"Your son."

226

"Yes, quite. Precisely. Very well—my son. It is by reason of the fact that he *is* my son that I am deprived of the opportunity of defending him."

"You mean, you'd have t'admit fatherhood."

"Not necessarily," said Drew.

"It would be bound to leak out," said Betsy. "The insatiable curiosity of newspaper reporters would uncover the truth."

"Not to mention the thoroughness of the defence counsel and his cohorts," Drew interrupted. "No, it is impossible. Personal involvement? Absolutely impossible."

Betsy said, "Frank Kinnemouth would do it, Drew. He would defend, if you approached him."

"What if," said Mirrin, "I were to offer you a brief, Drew?"

"You can't," said Drew. "A solicitor must be found. He might offer me a brief on your behalf. He would, of course, have to be conversant with . . . ah, *all* the facts of the case. That being so he would surely recommend another reputable advocate."

"Is that how it's done," said Mirrin.

"Believe me, Mirrin," said Betsy, "Andrew would fight the defence case for you, for Kate, if it was possible."

Mirrin turned her eyes on Drew. "Would you?"

"No," Drew said. "No, Mirrin. Even if there were no regulations to prevent it, I would not associate myself with this case. Elizabeth and I will both be out of Edinburgh. Even in our absence the gossip will be unwholesome enough." Fanning the fingers of his right hand, like a parrot's poll, he said, "To save wasteful discussion let me state categorically that I will not defend him. I will not directly associate myself with the case, nor will I remain in Edinburgh during the course of the trial. What I will do is arrange through a reputable solicitor—one whose discretion I trust—the briefing of an advocate of high standing whose sympathy is with the labourite cause. I will also meet a half share of the costs."

It was on the tip of Mirrin's tongue to tell him to eat his money. She wanted to withdraw at once from that room, from that city, let Rob Ewing's man Shallop do the best he could. It's what Kate, in her fury, would have done. But that was the very reason that Kate had not been sent to plead her fosterson's case. Below the table, Mirrin gripped her thighs, fingers digging into the material of her skirt as if to force herself to remain in the chair. She kept her voice low. "Will that be enough, Drew, t'ensure a verdict in Neill's favour?"

"It should be," Drew said. "Kinnemouth really is an excellent pleader in criminal trials. He has defended a dozen or so murderers over the years, usually successfully."

"Usually?"

"No advocate can guarantee acquittal."

"How many acquittals've you won in the past ten years?"

"I have had my failures."

"But few, Drew, very few," said Mirrin. "Am I not right?"

Drew's mouth was drawn tight, his chin creased. "The boy will not hang, Mirrin, that much I promise."

"But he may go to prison."

"I confess that that *is* a possibility. I refuse to make rash statements at this stage."

Mirrin rose and crossed to the window behind Betsy's chair. A fine film of dust coated the outside of the glass. She could both look down onto the clamour of Princes Street and, at the same time, watch the pale reflections of her sister and brother behind her. She noted the quick, anxious glance they exchanged. In her youth, she would have raged at them for their selfishness. But she was mature now, as they were—too mature, perhaps, for her to cope with. She could not hold out, particularly if it was true that the law did not allow an advocate to defend his kin. I must salvage what I can, she told herself. I didn't come here to ruin him. It isn't revenge, it's help we're after. I must do what's best for Neill's future and stifle my own malice, all the old, outmoded feelings. Kate did not raise Neill out of duty; she did it out of love. It will not do, Mirrin thought, to destroy the boy's chance from pride and anger. They are different from us, Drew and Betsy; we have no real call on them now.

Turning, she said, "I'm grateful t'you for your advice, Drew. I'm sure any solicitor you employ on our behalf will be fine, an' that any advocate briefed by that solicitor will do the best possible job."

"That's . . . that's eminently sensible of you, Mirrin," Drew said; not even he was able to hide his relief.

"If you can afford it without hardship," Mirrin said, "then I accept your generous offer."

"Good, yes, good." Drew got to his feet, a faint smile at the corner of his lips, a glint of gratitude in his eyes. "I admit that I thought you might try to . . . to . . ."

"To blackmail us," said Betsy. "You may speak openly to Mirrin, Drew. It was our great fear that you would force us— Drew *and* I—to be associated with this case. Such an association would ruin us, Mirrin. I do not exaggerate. It would ruin us both, completely."

"You too, Betsy?" said Mirrin. "Surely you'd be safe from waggin' tongues."

Betsy shook her head. "You do not understand how society works, Mirrin. Without doubt, we would be ostracised. Oh, Fraser would stand by me, but his family might not. It's so large, so influential, you see."

Drew said, "Will you stay in Edinburgh overnight, Mirrin?"

"If it's important."

"I will make arrangements through my clerk for you to be introduced to Mr. Dana of Dana, McConnor and Cree. He will interview you tomorrow and suggest a suitable advocate, probably Kinnemouth."

"When I return from Italy, Mirrin," said Betsy, "you really must come and visit; in the spring perhaps. I'm sure my girls would like it very much, not to mention Fraser."

"Aye, in the spring," said Mirrin.

"Where are you staying?" Drew asked.

"I haven't got a place yet."

"Then stay here, in the Portland. It's very good, I'm told."

"Too grand for me, Drew."

"Hm. Suit yourself, Mirrin. My clerk will know of some comfortable lodging, I'm sure."

"I won't see you again, then?" Mirrin asked.

"It's better if we do not meet," Drew answered.

"In case we're spotted?" said Mirrin, with a faint trace of irony. "Aye, we must be careful."

"I'm so glad that you understand," said Drew. "Now, I really must hasten to make those arrangements."

"Do come again, Mirrin," said Betsy, kissing her effusively on the cheek; "under happier circumstances."

Drew gave her a formal bow and opened the door for Betsy who, with a wiggling wave of the hand, sailed out, leaving behind that expensive fragrance of Continental perfume, like an insult.

"Drew," said Mirrin, just as her brother turned to leave.

He glanced back.

"You got off bloody lightly," Mirrin said.

The hooded eyes blinked and then, with complete sincerity and conviction, Andrew Stalker said, "I know I did."

*   *   *

Meetings were comparatively rare between Patrick Lauder and Daniel Horn, but, when summoned, Horn was skilful in contriving to enter Lauder's house unseen. Not even Lauder's servants knew who came and went through the kitchens in the hours after eight o'clock for Lauder picked his domestics from men and women who were too respectful to be curious.

Horn opened the conversation in the lawyer's chambers, rooms gloomier than Stalker's and not quite free from spillage of fur, feather and fin from the living quarters among the orderly rows of journals and the ebony furniture.

"I'm glad you summoned me, sir. I have information to impart."

"You first, then," Lauder said.

"Perhaps you have heard of the case of a young miner accused of murdering a special constable durin' a strike riot in the town of Blacklaw in Lanarkshire."

"I have heard of it." Lauder wore evening dress. His hat, cane and cape were laid over a chair as if he had newly returned from dining or, as proved to be the case, was about to hurry off to a late engagement.

Horn said, "The accused's name is Neill Campbell Stalker. He is a relative of Andrew Stalker and, in consequence, of Mrs. Elizabeth McAlmond."

"What sort of relative?" Lauder asked, as if he knew nothing at all of the matter.

"I'm not certain," Horn lied. "Nephew, or cousin."

"What is this to me, Horn?"

"Your . . . friendship with Mrs. McAlmond may be in jeopardy," said Horn. "After all it would not be seemly for a man in your position t'be . . ."

Lauder interrupted. "One reason that I've sought this meeting, Horn, is to inform you that my friendship with Mrs. McAlmond is over."

"Oh."

"The second reason touches upon the matter you have just raised," said Lauder.

"In what way?"

"The Lord Advocate, this very evening, has appointed me to act for the Crown, as Advocate-Depute, in the Blacklaw case."

"Ah," said Horn. "Then I have further intelligence that may be of worth t'you, sir."

"What?"

"Stalker's sister arrived this mornin' from Blacklaw t'seek Andrew's advice."

"Did she not seek his involvement?"

Horn grinned. "He would not give that commitment. He will, however, make the arrangements, an' cover the costs. I'm to approach Kinnemouth."

"Who will be the agent—McAlmond?"

"No," said Horn. "Dana."

"Stalker intends to keep his nose completely out of it."

"He intends t'leave for America early next week."

"That," said Lauder, "is most unfortunate."

"He couldn't have hoped t'defend his . . . relative."

"As there is precedent," said Lauder, "it is possible that dispensation might have been made by the Faculty."

"The last thing Andrew wants," said Horn, "is t'become involved in a public scandal."

"And Mrs. McAlmond?"

"She'll not be over-keen on acknowledgin' connection with a family of common colliers, especially when one o'them is in the dock on a murder charge."

"You will not, Horn, inform your master of the Lord Advocate's choice of Crown counsel. It will come out very soon, of course, but let it take its own course."

"I take it, sir, you'd prefer my master not t'be involved in the defence; that you'd rather he was out of the country?"

Lauder shrugged. "If he stays, I shall ruin him."

"What do you require of me, then?" said Horn.

"I require that you keep me thoroughly informed of what goes on in that direction."

"Why is it so important t' you, Mr. Lauder?"

"It is not important," Lauder said, "merely part of the sport."

Horn said, "Part of makin' certain that it's you an' not Andrew Stalker who finds favour with the Faculty when the appointment o' Solicitor-General falls vacant—or is it the Lord-Advocate's post that you're chasin'?"

"I have nothig to fear from Stalker in that direction," said Lauder. "He is too young, yet, for either post."

"Aye," Horn said, "but you have already been passed over have you not, Mr. Lauder?"

"I will not be passed over this time."

"*If* you obtain a conviction for the Crown."

"Come now, Horn, you know that has nothing to do with it."

"Your reputation's against you."

"And Stalker's is not?" said Lauder, suppressing anger.

"His record's unblemished, his reputation untarnished."

"It will not be so for much longer, I assure you."

"So, you're askin' me to keep a watchin' brief—just to be on the safe side?"

"You will be paid."

"Thank you, Mr. Lauder," said Horn with a nod. His mouth was caught up, showing yellow teeth. He looked more vulpine than ever. "I'll not require t'be paid."

Lauder glowered suspiciously.

"I'm not a man of much principle an' certainly I've precious few scruples," Horn said. "But I'll not be involved in this travesty."

"Travesty?"

"I've spied, aye, an' pandered, an' done a multitude of wicked things in my day," said Horn, still grinning, as if he found this sudden attack of conscience amusing. "But I will not be a party t'duplicity in which burnin' ambition is matched against a man's life."

"The Stalker boy is not likely to hang."

"I see; you're not pressing for murder?"

"He is charged with murder," said Lauder. "Naturally, I am not yet in command of all the facts, but, even if I do persuade the jury to bring home a verdict of guilty, an Appeal court, under the circumstances . . ."

"Mr. Lauder," said Horn, loudly and firmly, "do not blether."

"Horn, I warn you to be careful."

"There's nothin' you can do t'harm me, sir," Horn told the advocate. "I know far too much about you."

Lauder licked his upper lip. "By the same token, Horn, there's little you can do to injure me."

"I'll keep my mouth shut about what's past."

"And about the payments you've received from me, no doubt," Lauder said.

"But I'll do no more so-called work for you, Mr. Lauder."

"What are you up to now, Horn?" Lauder demanded.

"Up to?" Horn looked startled. "I'm up to nothin' more sinister, for once, than drawin' the line. That's all it is, Mr. Lauder, drawin' the line."

"The leopard does not change its spots."

"I'm no leopard, nor even a lion," Horn said. "An' at times like this, I thank God for it."

"Very well," Lauder said. "If you wish to ruin yourself, Horn, I won't stop you."

"That's my choice."

"I ask only that you do not impart to Stalker the information I have given you tonight."

"I won't have to," Horn said. "It'll be all over town by tomorrow."

★　　★　　★

Though the Lammas term in law had not begun, the populace of Edinburgh and areas appropriate to the hearing of pleadings, criminal and civil, had in such matters excelled themselves that summer. The library and halls of the Faculty building were busy throughout the holiday period. Tanned and relaxed

233

by random adventures on the promenades of fashionable resorts, upon the breast of the ocean or on the golf links, writers, clerks, solicitors and advocates convened among the stacks in a manner that seemed at once solemn and casual or, seeking refreshment, met under the stone arches of the hall where tea and coffee were served.

Much occupied in re-arranging his calendar, it was here that Advocate Stalker came in search of Advocate Kinnemouth hoping to persuade that worthy pleader to stand in for him, not only on a half dozen rewarding briefs but in the defence of one, Neill Campbell Stalker—now isn't that a coincidence—in the Martinmas term beginning on the 11th of November. Though the bulk of the work incurred by the imminent trip to America was left to Stalker's clerk and to the solicitors' firm of Sprott, McAlmond and Sprott, conscience prompted the Advocate to explain to Kinnemouth in person what was what and why America called.

It was on Thursday morning then that Stalker and Hector Mellish met and shook the monumental edifices of courtesy, and the gothic ornaments of the legal tower. After their chance encounter in the sunlit, mote-filled, kirk-like hall, whose acoustics carried much of the conversation into every corner, the issues became simpler. Even those whose business was based on obfuscation could not regard the case of the Crown versus Neill Campbell Stalker as other than a deadly duel between princes of the Scottish bar, and thereafter followed each legalistic trick with the avidity of sweetie-wives poring over the reports in the *Northern Echo*.

While Mirrin slept fitfully in a stuffy bedroom in the Ninian Guest House in Eastbrae Place, and Betsy moaned under the influence of a dank dream of Italian lakes, and Daniel Horn sat with his feet on his mantelshelf sipping rum and wondering what it would be like to live with a conscience, Advocate Andrew Stalker tossed and turned in his bachelor bed in agonies of indecision. In his waking moments, which were frequent, he found that he was thinking of the streets of Blacklaw and picturing to himself the son he had disowned. Caught on the forks of this nocturnal dilemma, he lay on his back with his hands on his belly and carefully reviewed his future in the light of several opposing sets of circumstances. It did not occur to Drew, however, even in that sweaty and unpleasant reverie, that he would finally be knobbled by impetuosity and regress to the condition of a schoolboy who cannot let an insult go past without retaliation. He was not prepared for atavism.

Mellish was already ensconced by the door of the coffee-room, seated at a rectangular table with a coffee-pot and cup on straw mats on the polished wood. With him was a Writer to the Signet, a mild youngish man with a lank moustache and jug-handle ears. Advocate Mellish was dressed in a lightweight suit that, in the opinion of traditionalists was more appropriate to the bandstand than the hall of the Faculty of Advocates. Mellish had grown more slender. His indolent manners had quickened, perhaps through association with Lauder or, as some said, by his need to catch his good-lady wife, daughter of Professor Lossie, without her Bible and Anglican Prayerbook. A mysterious inconsistency of character had led Mellish to the altar with Prudence Lossie. She brought no wealth, beauty or charm as her dowry, only a bargeful of respectability and ingress into a circle of true scholars and celebrated *literati*. What Mellish sought there, no man could explain. Eventually, it was suggested—and accepted—that Mellish had married Miss Lossie just to please his father and ensure that, though he might bask in Lauder's professional brilliance, he would not be caught in the shadows of Lauder's unsavoury reputation.

The tight nap of his hair, his small close-nap moustache and the elegance of his clothes made Hector Mellish seem devilish handsome. Considering the proclivities of his temperament, he was hard pushed to remain a paragon. More to protect himself than anything, he had fathered three sons in three years, a record of virility that gave even the most ardent of adultresses pause, and permitted Hector to escape from an excess of temptation. Without doubt his career was his life—and his life was his career, arranged like a stepladder with a seat in the House of Lords on the uppermost rung.

Exactly what passed between Mellish and Stalker by way of introducing the subject that was to ignite like gunpowder, only the mimsy Writer to the Signet could say. Apparently he was so intimidated by association with public scandal that he elected to say nothing at all, not even when mobbed by half the journalists in Edinburgh and wooed with eloquence and port by legal gossips. The truth was that the mild young W.S. hadn't quite caught the first exchanges between the advocates. He had seen Stalker enter, pause to survey the hall as if in search of an acquaintance, seen Mellish stare at Stalker, Stalker flick his eye over Mellish and make to go on down the central aisle; had seen Mellish, with a rapid gesture, pluck his cane from the table and lay it out to form a barricade against which Stalker's stomach came to rest.

The conversation that the W.S. missed, went as follows.

"I hear tales that you are surrendering to the inevitable and quitting the law, Stalker?"

"Damned if you do, Mellish."

"Fleeing to the Americas?"

"Damned if it's any of your business."

"Bad breeding always comes out in the end, Stalker."

"I've no notion of what you mean."

Pricked now, the Writer's ears caught the rest of it. In fact thirty or so tea-drinking members were treated to a hearing so strident had the advocates' voices become.

"Your son—remanded on charge of murder."

"My son? God, that's slander, Mellish."

"Neill Campbell Stalker."

"Never heard of him."

"Typical that you should not only fail to acknowledge him but that you should abandon him in his hour of need."

"Attendance at melodramas has softened your brain, Mellish. I have no son."

"No wife, certainly. But you *do* have a son. I have a notarised copy of his birth record. Also, purely for its curio value, I have obtained a notarised copy of a death certificate issued on one, Heather Campbell, of . . ."

"What does this have to do with you, Mellish?" Stalker had turned even more cheesy than usual. His eyeballs were the colour of sea-washed glass. "*Just what the hell does it have to do with you?*"

"I am proud of my profession. I do not wish to see it infiltrated, yes, in-fil-trated by low-born scum like you. That is what you are, Stalker, and the case may very well prove it."

"The case is none of my concern."

"No, of course, you will be hiding in America."

"Mellish . . ."

"While Patrick and I make sure that the hangman removes that 'little embarrassment' from your life for good and all."

"Lauder . . . and . . . and *you*, Mellish?"

"Patrick received the appointment from the Lord-Advocate last night."

"But the Lord Advocate, or the Solicitor-General . . ."

"For reasons of their own, they do not wish to lead the case for the Crown. That honour, that exquisite privilege, has been accorded to Patrick, who will be assisted in counsel by me."

"You bastard, Mellish."

"I am not the bastard, Stalker; the bastard will be in the dock."

"Kinnemouth will . . ."

"Oh, it's Kinnemouth who will act as your shield, is it? Poor Kinnemouth, I hope he knows what he's getting into. We will make mincemeat of Kinnemouth, I think."

"I . . . I . . . I cannot def . . ."

"There is precedent," Mellish said.

Stalker was still leaning against the cane, left hand closed lightly upon it. He lifted it now and twisted it and wrenched it away from Mellish, much to the chagrin of the members. Witnessed by all of those present in the long hall, the act had a quality of violence that took it out of the realms of feud. Though it was not designed specifically to draw attention, Stalker's next action—that of throwing the cane up the length of the floor—had that effect.

"There *is* precedent, Stalker," Mellish repeated, following the flight of his best morning cane with his eyes, then flicking his gaze suddenly back to the granite face of his enemy. "So, that being the case, you have no excuse but cowardice."

"*I need no excuse,*" Stalker cried. "*I will defend him.*"

"Then you will lose everything—including the case."

"*Every damned thing, Mellish, but not the case.*"

Mellish got suddenly to his feet. They were of a height,

Stalker and he, but his slenderness made him seem taller, and younger. "It cannot remain in the closet now."

"*Then let it come out.*"

"As the trial will be set for the Martinmas term, you must weather three months of prying and ridicule."

"*And you, sir, had better guard your tongue, yes, and your reputation.*"

"My reputation is not in jeopardy. This wild miner is not *my* son."

"No, Mellish," Stalker said. "He is mine."

"And you *will* defend him?"

"*Yes, I will defend him.*"

*   *   *

The letters that Daniel Horn delivered shortly after noon on that Thursday towards the end of July appeared to have been penned by a person in the grip of madness. The dashing characters were larger than Drew's normal hand and the lines on the white sheets listed badly until the signature—*Stalker, Q.C.*—slid off the bottom right-hand corner as if trying to avoid association with the text.

The first letter Horn delivered to Mrs. Armstrong who was listlessly partaking of soup in the dining room of the Ninian Guest House and just beginning to wonder if her brother had abandoned her completely. Mirrin read the letter, glanced up at Horn, then, pausing only to gather her hat from her room, left with the clerk for Betsy's house.

In the McAlmonds' town house, Horn, who had had the benefit of verbal instruction from his master, was punctilious in the discharge of his duties. First, he found Fraser McAlmond, asked that gentleman, who had a napkin already tucked into his collar and a piece of pork chop on the end of his fork, to step immediately into the library and there handed over Drew's lengthy missive. Next, he escorted Elizabeth from the dining room into the morning room, closed the door, and, before Elizabeth could put on an effusive act of amazement at finding her sister there, planted the envelope in her hand and told her bluntly, "Read this."

Elizabeth read.

238

Elizabeth let out a cry.

Elizabeth did not even pretend to swoon.

Abruptly Elizabeth was transformed into a vixen.

"Do you know what this letter says, Daniel?"

"In substance."

"Lauder and Mellish are to form the Crown counsel in the prosecution of . . . of . . . the miner."

"That 's official," said Horn.

"And Drew has agreed to defend?" said Betsy. "*Why? For heaven's sake, why?*"

"I think he lost his temper," said Horn.

"Betsy, will it change things for you so very . . ." Mirrin began, but at that instant Fraser, still wearing his bib, burst into the morning room.

"Oh, you have a guest." He came to a halt and bit back his tirade like the gentleman he was. "If the lady would please excuse us."

"My sister, Mirrin," said Betsy.

"We met once, Mr. McAlmond," Mirrin said.

"I remember it clearly." Fraser hesitated, then, putting the pieces together, nodded and said, "I take it that *you* have persuaded your brother to assume the burden of this case."

"No," Mirrin said. "I asked, but he refused."

"Seems he's changed his mind, Mr. McAlmond," Horn said.

"Elizabeth, Andrew has requested that we—that is, Sprott, McAlmond and Sprott—act as agents. I wonder if he realises what that will mean?"

"Are you capable?" Betsy demanded. "Are you *good* enough?"

"He says that the . . . the accused is his son? Surely he means nephew, cousin, something other than . . . ?"

"He means *his son*," said Betsy grimly. "Just that."

"Good Lord!"

"What's more," said Betsy, "you will do it, Fraser, and you will see to it that Innis and Balfour Sprott do it too. You must all stand by Andrew at this time."

"You *wish* him to acknowledge . . . ?" Fraser began.

"You forget, Fraser," said Betsy, "what we are—all of us,

Drew, myself, my sisters, and the poor prisoner in the dock. We are *working class*. You've always known it. And when it comes down to bedrock, as it has now, we are loyal to our kind."

"That," said Fraser, "is not exclusively a working-class virtue. Yes, of course we will serve as agents."

"Thank God," said Mirrin. "Thank God."

"Thank Hector Mellish would be more appropriate," Horn said.

Fraser turned to the clerk. "Where is Andrew now?"

"Gone to Hamilton."

"To Hamilton?" said Mirrin. "What for?"

"To interview his client," said Horn.

★   ★   ★

When the heavy steel-hinged door of the Hamilton police cell grated open, Neill swung his legs from the cot and shot guiltily to his feet. Involuntarily, he groped for the starched collar that his Mam had brought and insisted that he wear at all times. In a big blue cardboard box with *Groves Gentlemen's Outfitter* printed on it, she had also brought in a spanking-new broadcloth waistcoat, matching trousers, and a Norfolk-style jacket that was presently draped over the end of the bed. The cuffs of the new linen shirt reached to the middle of his palms and, with collar properly fastened and butterfly tie in place, the young prisoner would have presented a picture of Sunday School respectability. But the stranger had arrived suddenly and caught Neill unprepared to receive visitors. His waistcoat was unbuttoned, his new brown boots at attention by the stool, and his wrinkled rubber braces and darned stockings created an impression of disarming ingenuousness.

Neill stared at the man who, without a word, snapped gloved fingers and imperiously gestured to the policeman to close the cell door.

As soon as the lock clacked, the man said, "You don't recognise me, do you?"

"No, sir."

The stranger's tone was haughty but, under the larding of round vowels, Neill detected traces of a flat Lanarkshire accent.

In his nervousness, he assumed that this was some lackey from the Fiscal's office come to question him further. He made a half-hearted attempt to tack the collar to the yoke of his shirt then, flustered, dropped the object to the bed and contented himself by fumbling with his waistcoat buttons.

"My name is Stalker—Andrew Stalker."

My God, Neill thought, before he could help himself; he's my Da, an' I'm taller than him. Immediately, his nervousness ebbed. He had expected to be awed, to be moved, by a meeting with his father. Sometimes, though not often, he had fastened on the possibility of such an encounter, and allowed his mind to dwell on how he would cope with the imposing personality of the famous advocate. But he had imagined his father as mute, dignified and immobile, like the statue of Provost Thompson in Hamilton town square, dressed in leaden legal robes and twice life-size. It threw him off balance to be confronted by this grey, whey-skinned, balding, barrel-gutted person. Though the lawyer's frock coat and silk hat were top-drawer trappings, they did not quite seem to belong to him. It was as if he had hired them for the occasion or, Neill thought, as if *his* Mam had bought them special to keep him neat for the public.

"Do you not know who I am?"

"Aye," said Neill. "You're m'father."

"It's my intention to act as your defence counsel."

"What about Mr. Shallop?"

Though his social intercourse had been limited to the rough-and-tumble of the pit community and the bustling family kitchen, behind the man's dry approach Neill recognised an uncertain quality that indicated that his father too had contemplated such a meeting. He felt a pang of guilty sorrow that it had come about in this dismal confinement. For an instant, he felt demeaned; then, in the lawyer's clinical, detached approach, the young man found a manner to emulate.

As his father embarked on an answer to his question, Neill straightened his shoulders, hooked his thumbs into the pockets of his waistcoat and listened with grave attention.

"Mr. Shallop is not an advocate. He is a solicitor and I doubt if he has much experience in criminal cases," Drew said. "With your permission, I propose that the papers in the case be handled by the Edinburgh firm of Sprott, McAlmond and Sprott. McAlmond is your uncle by marriage, the husband of my twin sister, Elizabeth."

"What'll Mr. McAlmond do with these papers?"

"He will present them in the form of a brief, to an advocate. The function of an advocate is simply to plead your case in court; that is, to convince a jury that you are not guilty of the crimes wherewith you are charged."

"You're an advocate," Neill said.

"Indeed, I am an advocate of some standing."

"Who sent for you, Mr. Stalker?"

"Mirrin."

"Aye, I didn't think it would be Mam."

"I will tell you something, young man," said Drew, "and I will not repeat it. Your present situation is sufficiently grave to override any petty squabbles that may have infected our family in the past."

"Go on, Mr. Stalker."

"I have no knowledge of or interest in what you may have been told about me. It is obvious, however, that Kate, your . . . your 'Mam', did not keep you in the dark about your parentage."

"She told me all she thought was right."

Drew hesitated. His familiarity with police cells was not extensive, though this one seemed more comfortable, if that was the word, than many he had visited in the course of his duties. For all that, he would have welcomed more space and more furniture, a larger setting within which he might have found a remote stance. It was harrowing to have to look squarely into his son's eyes, to find curiosity there, an honest interest with no hint of humility or esteem. At least, there was no apparent resentment: for that he must be thankful. He was grateful to Kate for bringing up the boy so well. Fleetingly, Drew tried to raise an image of how Neill might have turned out if he had had all the advantages of wealth to succour him through childhood and youth. But the advocate's imagination was cramped by reality and projected only visions of the reeking slum in which Heather Campbell had lived and died, extending those hellish recollections into a squalid drama of disease, starvation, beggary, theft and punishment, with his son condemned from birth to suffer the abject deprivations of poverty.

Not that: no. I would not have permitted *that* to happen to my own flesh and blood, Drew told himself. If there had been no Kate to take the baby off my hands, I would not have abandoned him. But his self-assurances were not convincing. He could still recall the feverish ambition of his young manhood and knew in his heart that he would have been rid of the infant—somehow.

The copperplate phrases of the law courts became thick and jagged on his tongue. He cleared his throat, holding the knuckle of his forefinger politely to his lips, then said, "Although I am your natural father, I am first and foremost an advocate of the city of Edinburgh. You, young man, are presently a prisoner on remand. Consequently, you will not refer to me as anything other than Mr. Stalker, in my presence or out of it."

"Right you are, Mr. Stalker."

In vain, Drew sought for sly insolence in the obedient agreement. There was none. Neill was a Stalker, with more than his share of the outspoken frankness that was the family's hallmark. With a start, Drew realised that he did not now class Betsy—or himself—with the rest of them. They were the exceptions. They were seldom frank, and slyness of various persuasions was integral to their position in society. He wondered, almost for the first time, at the quirk of heredity that had produced him, that had set him so far apart from his kinfolk.

He said, "I will defend you against the charges to the limit of my professional ability, Neill, but I will not endure recriminations, bitterness or hindrance from you or any member of your family."

The young man said nothing. His dark blue eyes were quizzical. He was handsome and, though a little gauche, not lacking in intellect. Drew experienced an unexpected flood of pride in his son and with it, by a peculiar transference, suddenly found it easier to keep emotion at a safe distance. A subtle rapport had been established. Now he could concentrate on Neill Campbell Stalker, a client at risk.

Quickening the tempo of the conversation, Drew said brusquely, "If your plight was not so dire, I would not be here;

nor would I re-establish contact with you or any of your kin in this part of the country. I want to be clear on that score."

"Are you tellin' me, Mr. Stalker, that this is duty an' not kindness?"

"In a nutshell. I am glad to see that you are not wanting in perception."

"You're not what I thought you'd be like."

"That's besides the point. Will you accept Sprott, McAlmond and Sprott as agents? If you do, they will officially approach my clerk with a brief and I will officially accept. That's the procedure. It needs only your agreement to put it into effect."

"I suppose I should talk t'Mam first, or t'Willie."

"Neill, I appreciate your uncertainty. I believe, however, that Willie Kellock was in part responsible for persuading your Aunt Mirrin to approach me."

"Mr. Stalker, I can't help thinkin' o'Willie and Kate as my Ma and Da."

"That's as it should be."

"I must talk t'them before givin' you an answer."

"Caution and loyalty are, I suppose, admirable qualities. One wishes, however, that you had displayed more of one and less of the other outside Blacklaw pit on July eighteenth."

"I . . . I . . . lost my head. I was hoppin' mad at them blacklegs."

"And at the intervention of the police?"

"Horses; they had bloody horses, even. There was only a dozen old men on the picket line that mornin'."

"So, you threw a hammer at Constable Ronald to redress the balance?"

"I threw the hammer *away*."

"At Constable Ronald?"

"I didn't even see him."

"To whom did the hammer belong?"

"One o'the blacklegs; he was breakin' down the wee door with it. I grabbed it off him, then threw it away."

"The blackleg, you did not strike him or at him with the hammer?"

"I'm not daft. God, it could've killed him."

"Are you comfortable here?"

244

"What d'you think, Mr. Stalker?"

"Quite. However, are you as comfortable as can be expected?"

"Aye, I suppose so. Ma an' Da bring me food. They pay for extra comforts."

"If you do agree to engage my services, I wish to have you transferred to Calton prison in the City of Edinburgh as soon as possible."

"That's a long way from Blacklaw."

"It is more convenient for me. I will see to it that you have every possible luxury that regulations allow."

"Can you not come here?"

"Certainly not. It's important that the case be prepared thoroughly. In essence, Neill, the charge is simplicity itself. I fear, however, that the prosecution counsel will complicate it with many factors that I would prefer to keep out of court."

"The rights an' wrongs o' strike action?"

"Among other things. It will be my task to predict every manoeuvre that the prosecution will make and to devise suitable legal ripostes. The Crown will endeavour to prove that you deliberately threw that hammer as the constable with—as the phrase has it—malice, either expressly or by implication."

"It was an accident, a pure, bloody accident."

"As your counsel, I cannot risk pleading accident as a sole defence. Accident would leave us open to conviction on the reduced charge of manslaughter and that, young man, means several long weary years of hard-labour. No, I must prepare our defence strategy skilfully, with a degree of flexibility, so that I may take advantage of ill-defined areas in the matter of the burden of proof. Do you wish me to explain?"

"Aye. I like t'know just what's goin' on. It . . . it helps t' understand."

"Put simply, it is the duty of the prosecution to prove a prisoner's guilt. In a murder case the Crown is obligated to prove that death resulted from a voluntary action of the accused, accompanied by malice. If this evidence is given, as it will be, then the counsel of the accused may show, by evidence or examination of the circumstances outlined by the Crown, that the action that caused death was unintentional or provoked."

"It doesn't sound very simple t'me, Mr. Stalker."

"Even so that is the principle that will govern the trial. If the Crown fail to prove all points, then we will gain acquittal. Unfortunately, however, in spite of any ruling that the judge may lay down in his directions to the jury, it is the jury that must bring home the verdict."

"When will I appear in court?"

"Not until November. I could press for an earlier trial but I prefer not to."

"Oh God, am I t'be stuck in jail 'til November?"

"Better that you endure an extra eight or ten weeks as a prisoner on remand—as an innocent person, may I remind you —than rush to a judgment that may result in a conviction."

"I see. We're waitin' 'til the strike situation cools down."

"Exactly."

"There's sense in that."

"That also provides another valid reason for requesting your transfer to Edinburgh. Hamilton will attract the wrong sort of attention, will become, perhaps, a storm-centre."

"I never realised I was that important."

"You, young man, are *not* that important. Why, if you had downed this policeman in a public-house brawl, you would have received hardly a jot of attention. But you committed the action at the gate of a pit under strike, and that makes it important as an issue of interpretation of rights."

"Aye, wi' my neck at stake."

"I am not particularly interested in political machinations. I am concerned only with having you acquitted."

"I was right t'go t'the aid of my comrades; I'll not let you say otherwise."

"I have no time for argument. Later—perhaps—we may enter a discussion as to the merits of militancy . . ."

"We weren't militants."

". . . but not at this juncture. I must return to Edinburgh shortly. If you do agree, with your parental guardians' consent, to approach McAlmond and Sprott, then we will have more opportunity to talk. If I am to defend you, Neill, I must know you. The Crown will attempt to portray you as an evil, or at best misguided, fellow capable of brutal disregard for the sanctity of life."

"But *you* don't think that, Mr. Stalker?"

"No, I do not think that."

"Mr. Stalker?"

"Yes."

"I'm . . . I'm . . . grateful."

*   *   *

A Stalker stood by the gate of the yard. On top of the dyke a surly-looking dog was poised, growling in its throat. Drew reined on the hired rig's reins and the pony slowed obediently. Already, on the last leg of his approach, he had begun to evaluate the farm's worth and the worthiness of its tenant. He saw the place not as the average townie might see it, as picturesque and pleasantly sited, but as reckonable property. Suppressing the emotions that the interview had stirred—particularly that last ironic statement, 'I'm grateful'—Drew adopted his most chillingly superior manner. When the young man—so like his memory of his brother James—stepped out and, with his hand on the dog's ruff, aimiably enquired, "An' what can we do for you?", Drew snapped back, "Are you the tenant of this property?"

"No, that's my father."

"What's your name?"

"Malcolm Stalker. An' yours?"

"Andrew Stalker. I'm your uncle, young man. I wish to speak with your father if he's at home."

"Andrew—mother's brother? From Edinburgh?"

"*Is* your father at home?"

"Bring the pony in this way." Malcolm pushed the dog gently off the wall, saying "Go'ay, Fleck; go'ay."

Not being the best of drivers, Drew allowed his nephew to take the check-rein and lead the pony through the gate and down a narrow avenue into the farmyard.

The walls were freshly painted, the drains in a good state of repair. There was none of the disgusting mess and litter that Drew associated with steadings. He could see the byre, cool and clean, its big door roped open. Apart from a haze of midges floating in the late afternoon air there were no clouds of noxious insects. He had had a brief once involving the inheritance of a steading, and his one visit there had been quite nauseating. Hazelrig, Mirrin's husband's farm, was quite different. Still haughty, though, Drew did not relax his guard. As he climbed awkwardly from the trap, Malcolm said, "I thought my mother had gone t'see you in Edinburgh. Did y'miss her?"

"We met," said Drew. "Yesterday. I take it you know why I'm here?"

"Because of Neill," said Malcolm. "But did y'not come back with Mam?"

"It is not yet exactly settled that I will—or will be allowed to—undertake the defence of your cousin. However, it is a matter of some urgency that I explore the broad outlines of the case and its circumstances."

"Mam doesn't know you're here then?"

"Here. No."

"What can we do for you? We're not directly involved."

"As I indicated, I wish to speak with your father."

"Did y'know he's been sick?"

"I heard something to that effect. Are you telling me that I cannot talk with him?"

"He's restin'."

Relenting a little, Drew said, "I won't keep him long, nor will I tire him."

"Come on int' the house."

Still standing by the trap in the yard, Drew became aware of a boy and a pretty little girl watching him from the doorway of a hayloft some ten or twelve feet above the cobbles.

As they walked towards the farmhouse door, Malcolm said, "Those are my sister an' brother, Katherine an' David. There's another hulkin' brute out in the fields; Sandy."

"Do you help your father on a permanent basis?"

"Aye."

"Do you enjoy farm labouring?"

"Aye."

The house had the familiar smell of cooking food, far from unwelcoming. It reminded Drew of his Mam's kitchen, cluttered and warm, in the colliers' row in Main Street. He had despised it at the time, its cramped lack of privacy. But now there was pardonable nostalgia, a softness in the recollection.

The Hazelrig kitchen was much larger, of course; neater too. On first entering, his quick eye was drawn to shared mementoes —a stone jar on the end of the mantelshelf, a particularly ugly cut-glass vase, a small wooden cradle with a doll in it, items sacked from the ruins of the tithed cottage, from the debris of the past. He had been right to plunge immediately into this dreaded contact, this meeting with the past. If he had delayed, even a day or two, he might have shirked the responsibility.

Though the day was sultry, the inevitable fire smoked in the range. In a chair by the fire sat a man. At first it seemed to be an old codger, like a done-in, burned-out face-worker dumped there to die, one of the shamans of the Blacklaw that endured in Drew's memory. But when his nephew spoke and the man grunted and rose, Drew saw the mask and realised that the fellow was neither old nor crippled but blind. He had been dozing and was not quite awake yet.

"Da, this is Mam's brother, Andrew."

"Don't get up, Mr. Armstrong."

"Is Mirrin with you?" Armstrong asked.

"She is still in Edinburgh. Possibly on her way back by now."

Tom Armstrong nodded as if he understood this odd situation and, with his left hand on the arm of the chair, stretched out his right in Drew's general direction.

The men shook hands.

"I believe you were instrumental in sending Mirrin to seek my advice," Drew began.

"First," said Tom, "let me offer you hospitality. Will y' take a glass of whisky?"

"Tea," Drew said. "Tea would be more refreshing at this hour, thank you."

"Malcolm, make us a brew—an' bring some oatcakes an' cheese."

"Local cheese?" Drew asked.

"Made right here on Hazelrig."

Drew glanced at his nephew. "I'd like that."

While the young man went about preparing tea, Tom and Drew settled in the armchairs by the hearth.

"If the family and the young fellow agree," Drew said, without preliminaries, "then I will act as his counsel."

249

"Can I ask why you're doin' this?"

"It's . . . my duty."

"Are y'not reluctant t'become involved?"

"Of course," Drew replied, "I would have preferred it not to have happened."

"That's not what I asked," said Tom.

Drew studied the farmer. He appeared lumpish yet his forthrightness appealed to the advocate. He had never been curious as to the sort of men that his sisters had married, assuming that they would be in no way uncommon. But Armstrong, even without his sight, had an aura of strength that suggested that Mirrin had chosen well.

"I have committed myself," said Drew. "Therefore I will do everything possible to secure Neill's release. I will 'put my back into it', Mr. Armstrong."

"Under the circumstances, it might be better if y'called me Tom. We are, after all, brothers-in-law."

"Very well, Tom."

"The next question is, can y'get the lad off?"

"I can certainly save his neck," said Drew. "But keeping him out of prison will be much more difficult."

"Is a trial date set?"

"November."

"Who'll prosecute?"

"Patrick Lauder and Hector Mellish."

"I've heard tell o'Lauder."

"A brilliant advocate," Drew said. "I served my apprenticeship under him. I know his methods and his styles better than anyone."

"Does Lauder know he'll be against you?"

"Not yet," said Drew. "In fact, the first thing I must do is to ascertain that the Faculty will give me a dispensation to act in this case at all."

Tom's head was cocked, the movement exaggerated as so many of his gestures had become. "Because o'the relationship between you an' Neill?"

"Yes. I will be obliged to admit that relationship to a special committee of the Faculty."

"An' you'll do this?"

"I will."

"That takes courage."

Drew sighed. "Courage? Hardly. It will take a certain bold-
ness and a good deal of forensic skill to convince the Faculty
that I am fit to counsel my own son. On the other hand, I'm
informed that there is precedent in the law, and I will exploit
that for all its worth."

"The scandal will hurt you, though?"

"Edinburgh, Tom, is a city founded on scandal; trivial
gossip most of it."

"Won't you be . . . ruined?"

If that question had been asked within the solemn rooms of
an Edinburgh mansion, or in the chambers of the Parliament
House he would have answered glumly. But here, in this tidy
farm, speaking to a farmer, the reply had to be geared to a
different set of values. "I will not be ruined, as you mean it."

"But your career will be affected?" Tom persisted.

"I see that you want the truth," Drew said. "I have no wish
to appear a martyr, but, yes, my career will be affected. From
now on the higher offices of the law will remain closed to me."

"An' your income?"

"That, Tom, is quite safe and assured."

Malcolm who had been listening to his father's interrogation
of the advocate, produced cups of tea, plates of oatcakes and
wedges of pale cheese, giving one to his father and the other to
his uncle. He seated himself in the corner behind the big table
and continued to listen attentively. Drew ate hungrily, declaring
that he had seldom tasted cheese of such flavour and texture.
He watched Tom's hands, the thick fingers breaking up the
food, feeding it into his mouth.

He said, "How soon will you be able to see again?"

"In a month or two—if the operation's a success," Tom
replied, then steered the conversation back to the less painful
topic of his nephew's trial. "I take it, Andrew, that you've come
here with a purpose?"

"I have visited the young man in Hamilton police station,"
Drew said. "It is now my intention to call upon Kate. I assume
that you are aware that Kate and I have not been on speaking
terms, not even remotely, these last eighteen years."

"Mirrin told me," Tom answered.

"To be frank," Drew said, "I do not wish to arrive alone on Kate's doorstep. I am rather afraid that her . . . dislike of me may cancel out her good sense and that she may refuse to let me intervene."

"Do y'want me to come with you?"

"If you feel able."

"Och, aye, I'm able enough," said Tom. "When do y'want t' go?"

"As soon as possible."

"I've the feelin' we might find Mirrin there too by this time," Tom said.

"It's strange," said Drew, "I am nervous of my relatives, many of whom I've never met or can barely remember."

"I can understand that," said Tom.

"There is one more point," Drew said, "I will require Kate's permission to have Neill transferred to Calton prison in Edinburgh."

"For handiness?" said Tom. "Or is it that you don't think Hamilton's the best place for him?"

"Both," said Drew. "Kate will consider this a slight, I think."

"In her present mood, I reckon she might," Tom agreed. "But her husband's a sensible individual. Willie Kellock'll back you up."

"I appreciate your assistance, Tom."

"Well, it's better than sittin' here starin' at nothin'," Tom said. "We'll leave right now if that suits."

"Perfectly," Drew said.

"You'll have t'drive the trap," Tom said.

*   *   *

Kellock's kitchen had the tense atmosphere of a cabinet room on the eve of war. After greetings had been exchanged, and Tom had taken it upon himself to introduce Drew to Edward and Willie, Lily sorted out chairs, and the whole family, including Mirrin, took places round the kitchen table. The parlour wasn't large enough to hold the clan. Besides, Kate was still in a state of angry shock at Drew's sudden re-entrance into her life and harboured the suspicion that the rest of the family had somehow tricked her. Fully aware of Kate's reaction, Mirrin murmured a few words to her by way of explanation, trying to make her understand that Drew, for all his haughtiness, was making a bigger sacrifice than any of them by agreeing to stand as counsel for Neill.

"*His* son," said Kate, darting a glance over her shoulder at the portly, pompous and out-of-place figure of her brother. "It shouldn't be a sacrifice t'save his son's life."

"Pull yourself t'gether Kate," said Mirrin.

"I'm not goin' t'make a scene. I wouldn't give him that satisfaction."

"I've seen how he lives," said Mirrin. "You've got my word on it Kate, he's a very important man."

"Not t'me, Mirrin. Never t'me."

"Aye, but he's important t'us, Kate, if we want Neill freed."

"Any lawyer would've . . ."

"Never," said Mirrin, sharply. "Accordin' t'Betsy this man Lauder is more than a match for any advocate. He might even prove too clever for our Drew."

"That wouldn't be difficult."

"Kate, for God's sake," Mirrin hissed. "He can hear you."

"I don't care. Have you forgotten what we did for him, an' how he treated us in return?"

"No, I haven't forgotten," said Mirrin. "But since then we've gone our separate ways, and time helps t'heal . . ."

"I don't want t'hear any more from you, Mirrin. He's here, an' I don't suppose there's much I can do about it."

"You're not yourself, love."

"Let's just hear what the 'great man' proposes t'do."

In deference, Willie had ceded his chair at the head of the table to the Advocate. On Drew's right sat Mirrin and Tom, then Kate, with Lily, Edward and Willie opposite them. Flora sat down the table from her son. That the old woman was much affected by Drew's arrival was plain to see. She spoke to him with a mixture of pride and deference and obviously considered that he should be accorded more respect than the family were inclined to offer.

"He's lookin' real well. Isn't he, Kate?" Flora said, several times in fact.

It was inevitable that a quarter of an hour was given over to plastering the cracks that the years had opened up. Drew hid his impatience. He would have preferred to treat them—all of them—as clients, to keep them at a safe distance. Already he was dismayed to find himself warming towards Tom Armstrong and Willie Kellock, though his animosity towards Kate, and his wariness in respect of Mirrin, were undiminished. Though Edward and Lily kept in the background, Drew sized them up too. He could not associate them with the broken-hearted girl and the little toddler who had gone off to England in the wake of the pit disaster. Lily seemed very tough now, and Edward, a real Stalker, had a quiet watchfulness that kept Drew on his guard. Dutifully, however, he let his mother question him concerning his success, telling her, as briefly as possible, of Betsy's children and about the house he lived in. It would have been possible to impress his mother by boasting of his friends. How she would have loved to learn that her son dined regularly with Lords and Dukes and Earls. But Drew knew that his sisters, Kate in particular, would regard such information as another sign of arrogance and snobbishness, so he held his tongue and toned down the details of his life-style.

Inevitably, it was Kate who steered the conversation back to the subject on hand. "Since you've condescended t'come an' see us," she said, "I take it y'intend t'help the lad?"

Drew explained that if Kate wished he would act as counsel for Neill.

"It's got nothing t'do with me, has it?" Kate answered.

"You are his . . . parental guardian," said Drew.

"What's the law on that, then?" Kate said. "Who's got the final say in what's good for him—me, or his *real* father."

It was a shrewd question. The law itself gave precious few guidelines, judging each case by its merits and, to keep the Bar in business, swamped such issues with portfolios of precedents and cross references.

Drew said, "Under the circumstances, the law would probably uphold your right to . . ."

Kate cut him short. "If it had been left t'me, Drew, you wouldn't have been told, let alone sent for."

"Very well, Kate," Drew said. "Let me put it to you in this

manner—Neill Campbell Stalker is less my son than he is yours. I regard him not as my son but as my nephew. I would do the same for my nephew, would I not, as I am being asked to do for my son?"

Kate frowned.

Drew said, "Let us assume that it was that handsome lad of Mirrin's—Malcolm—who had fallen foul of the law. If Mirrin asked for my assistance on his behalf I would give it."

Kate said, "It's not the same. You wouldn't have to admit that you'd spawned a . . ."

"Kate, really, that's enough," Willie said.

"I understand your bitterness," said Drew. "Neill is, however, a fine young man, and . . ."

"You've seen him?"

"I called at Hamilton police station today."

"You an' he met?"

"Yes," said Drew. "We met."

In spite of herself, Kate could not resist putting the question, "What . . . what did y'really think of him?"

Drew hesitated, then said, "He is more of a man than I could have made of him, Kate."

Willie put his arm around his wife's shoulders as she wept.

Embarrassed, Drew bridged his hands on the table and looked at them, waiting until Kate's spasm of grief had passed. Keeping his voice dry now, he outlined the essence of the prosecution's case against Neill and explained that he wished to have the young man transferred to Edinburgh.

Softened, Kate put up no argument.

Drew gave a shortened account of his interview with Neill and the gist of his findings to that point.

"Eye-witnesses, and their evidence," he concluded, "will be crucial to the Crown's case. I do not believe that Neill threw the weapon in malice. But throw it he did. It would be wrong of me to over-simplify the matter. The law is very unsure of itself in the allocation of responsibility. In the end, I fear, Neill's fate may hinge on the credibility of the *presentation* of the evidence to the jury, on the *plausibility* of the counsels, and on the *bias* of the judge in his direction to the jury."

"Bias?" Lily said. "I thought judges were impartial?"

"The judge's summing-up will cover all salient points of law," said Drew. "It must do so or it would not be valid. But the slant, the tone, will be coloured by the Lordship's own prejudices."

Edward, who had been silent until that moment, leaned forward now, saying, "The Crown'll have their 'reliable' witnesses, Mr. Stalker. Houston Lamont's makin' damned sure o' that."

"Explain, please." Drew jerked round to face the young man and fixed him with his courtroom stare.

Edward told Drew of Dunlop's 'bribing' of witnesses and, taking it further, made it clear to his aunts that Lamont was being devilish clever about it.

Drew said, "I quite understand how it works, Edward. I know Lamont of old, remember. How is he putting pressure on the colliers to speak out against their own kind?"

"Threat o'evictions," Edward said. "Threat o'the loss o' jobs."

"Can Ewing's famous Union do nothin' t'prevent it?" asked Tom.

"I don't know," said Edward. "Maybe. Rob's aware o'the situation."

Drew took his watch from his pocket and glanced at it. "I must leave soon for Hamilton. It is imperative that I catch the last train to Edinburgh tonight. Edward, we need witnesses of our own, men who are not afraid to stand up in court and swear under oath to the truth of what they saw, who are not afraid of Lamont and who will not be cowed or brow-beaten by bullying lawyers and a possibly hostile judge."

"Men who still bear the scars o'blacklegs' clubs, for instance?" Edward asked.

"Ideal."

"Peter Ree, an' Shaun Grogan; that's a pair t'start with."

"God, who'd believe them?" said Lily.

"Others?" Drew prompted.

"There's Rob Ewing—an' there's me."

"What did you see?" asked Drew.

"I saw Neill struck on the shoulder wi' the hammer. I saw

256

him pull the hammer from the blackleg an' throw it away."

"Neill was struck by a blow from the same hammer as killed the constable?" said Drew. "I did not know that. That is useful information."

"Rob saw it too. He says he didn't, but I know he did."

"Rob would make an impressive witness," said Lily.

Drew took out the tablet and the fountain pen and, even as he pushed himself to his feet, wrote down the names—Ree, Grogan and Ewing.

"Thank you, Edward," he said.

"Must y'go, son? It's awful late," Flora said.

Drew kissed his mother on the cheek. "I have business in Edinburgh early tomorrow morning."

"You'll be back, though?" the woman asked.

"I'll be back," Drew promised and, accompanied by Mirrin and Willie, went out into the yard to the hired rig.

As he climbed laboriously onto the padded seat, Mirrin put her hand on his arm. "I'd like t'thank you, Drew."

"No thanks are necessary."

"Betsy told me about Lauder, and the lawyer called Mellish. It's not just for Neill's sake, or Kate's, that you're doin' this, is it?"

"No," Drew said. "As you might have expected, Mirrin, my motives are selfish."

The woman grinned up at him. "That," she said, "makes me feel a whole lot better."

"I thought it might comfort you," said Drew, without expression, "to be assured that some things never change."

"I don't care why you're doing it," said Mirrin, "so long as you get Neill off."

"Justice for the miners?" Drew said. "Hm?"

"Why not?"

"Why not, indeed."

★　　★　　★

Reaching the upstairs room which she shared with her husband Kate crossed to the large wardrobe with its double mirror doors and took from it a dark cloth coat and hat. Dressed, shoes changed, she moved quietly down stairs again and, reassured by murmurous voices from behind the closed door of the kitchen, let herself from the house. She hurried round the side of the yard and out of Kellock's Square into Main Street. The sky was soft and dark overhead, the air warm. There was no lingering afterglow, though, and she guessed that rain was coming. It hardly mattered; her destination was close at hand.

In response to Kate's knocking, Rob Ewing opened the door of his cottage. His cheeks were flushed, his eyes heavy. For a moment, Kate thought that he had been boozing, then she realised that she had wakened him from sleep. He had been dozing in the rickety chair by the fire. He still wore his coarse work trousers and heavy shirt, but his feet were bare and his jaw dark with stubble.

"God," he said, rubbing his face with his hand. "It's you, Kate. I thought it was the bloody polis by the racket. What's wrong?"

Without answering, Kate pushed past him into the tiny lobby. Ingrained good manners caused her to delay there until the miner closed the outside door and squeezed past her into the kitchen cum living room of the narrow house. Shivering a little, Kate surveyed the empty, rusting range, its puny fire hidden beneath mounds of ashes. The room was damp, peeling and neglected. She recognised a rose-patterned wallpaper that had been hung at the time of Rob's marriage to Eileen McMasters.

"It's miserable in here, Rob," she said. "Don't y'even keep the place heated?"

"I'm not that often at home." He brushed dust off a wooden chair with a rag that had been lying on the untidy table. "Here, sit down. I take it that y'didn't drag yourself out o'your kitchen just t'berate me for slovenly housekeepin'?"

He knelt by the grate and, with sticks from an iron bucket, quickly built up the fire. Kate's anger had ebbed in the face of the lonely squalor of Rob's surroundings. As he prodded sticks into the flames, Rob glanced round at her, puzzled that she should be here after so long a time. When the wood caught with a heartening crackle, he stood up and dusted his palms on his trousers.

"It takes no great insight," Rob said, "t'guess that this concerns Neill."

"My brother's been brought from Edinburgh," Kate said. "Drew?"

"He'll appear for Neill in court, in November."

"Good God," Rob exclaimed.

"We can do without the services o' your Union man, thanks."

"Is that why y'came tonight, Kate, t'flaunt your marvellous brother over our Union lawyer?"

"The Union's of no interest t'me."

"Kate, Kate; how you've changed."

"*You* can say t'*me*. Look at this place; your Mam would've been ashamed."

"My Mam's long dead an' buried," Rob said. "I've nobody t'fuss about, except myself. An' I don't give a tuppenny damn how the place looks."

"We need witnesses, for the trial."

"Aye, so your Drew's come back t'the fold t'do his duty, has he?" Rob said. "An' already he's got you dancin'."

"Edward says Lamont's preparin' witnesses for the police."

"Right."

"Will you go int' the witness box an' speak for Neill?"

"Did Drew send you?"

"I came off my own bat."

"I can do nothin'."

"Y'mean you won't."

"Edward'll tell you—if you'll give him the chance—I wasn't even there."

"You were, Rob; at the end. You say y'didn't see it, but you did."

"What reason would I have for lyin'?"

"That's what I'm here t'find out."

He tried to brush aside her probing questions. "I was with Webb an' the committee. I saw nothin'."

"Will y' not go int' the witness box on Neill's behalf?"

"No."

"What are you afraid of?"

"Nothin'. I just can't help, that's all."

"Are you afraid o'Houston Lamont?"

"That'll be the bloody day," said Rob.

"You could say *somethin'*; it wouldn't have t'be the whole truth."

"Listen, Kate," said Rob, "they'll no' hang him."

"They've got him, an', at best, they'll lock him away for five or ten years. I don't know if I could bear that."

"Seems you've got no faith in your brother."

"Precious little," said Kate. "If they want Neill, then they'll surely get him."

"You're talkin' as if he was some . . . some sacrificial victim."

"The police have witnesses who'll swear Neill struck that man on purpose. Why, Rob? Why should anybody tell a lie that could ruin my Neill's life?"

"Ach, it's politics, lass, that's all; the same old dirty story. Politics can so twist a man he'd swear t' a lie on his mother's grave."

"I still don't understand."

"You never did, Kate," said Rob. "I don't know if I can explain it. Strikin' colliers mean trouble, an' vast loss o'profits. Neill's a scapegoat. They'll use him just the way they've used the rest o'us for a hundred years an' more—to their own ends."

Kate was unmoving. Tears were not far away.

She said, "An will *you* make him a scapegoat for another reason, Rob, for the sake o' the solidarity o' the Union?"

"I won't play the bosses' game," said Rob. "I won't lie in the box, under oath. Once we, the workers, start lyin' an' cheatin' too we become no better than the unscrupulous class we serve."

"A boy's freedom traded for an ideal," said Kate. "Is that your idea of a fair exchange?"

"Your father would have understood."

"Leave my father out o' it, Rob. He's been dead these twenty years. Besides he would hardly recognise Blacklaw, or Blacklaw's colliers the way they are now."

"An' would he recognise his son?" said Rob. "Has Drew turned out as your father hoped he would?"

"Drew," said Kate, "is not like us, Rob."

"Right," said Rob. "He was corrupted early."

Kate broke in with violent impatience. "Will you not speak

for him, Rob? Will y'not help counter the lies that Lamont's lickspittles'll parade in court?"

Rob shook his head. "I'm fond o'the lad, Kate, an' I suffer from the knowledge that by involving him in pit politics I might've helped put him where he is. But I will *not* sell out the one bloody thing I've got left—*my integrity.*"

"You traitor, Rob Ewing," Kate said. "You dirty traitor."

He sat forward. His voice was thick. "I'm leavin' Blacklaw, Kate. Not, not now, that would be too much like runnin' away. But afterwards—I'm leavin' this damned country that stinks like a corpse moulderin' in its own rotten juices."

"An' good riddance," Kate said.

Moving with the exaggerated carefulness of a person who is not sure that her legs will bear her, she walked to the door.

She heard Rob's groan of despair. Her automatic response, even now, was to return to the kitchen and comfort him. She steeled herself. She must be as hard as the rest of them, as selfish. If Neill's arrest had taught her nothing else, it had taught her that only selfishness paid. She could not afford the luxury of soothing the guilt and self-recrimination that tortured Rob Ewing. She could no longer afford to be merciful, to anyone at all.

★   ★   ★

Before July was out, the strike was broken. A conference of the U.F.M. held in Edinburgh dealt with conciliation in the form of amendments, resolutions and revised terms and, at the end of it, it seemed that some kind of new policy had been forged. Only the militant colliers of Fife remained out and that hardly mattered in Blacklaw.

Blacklegs had kept the wheels greased and the seams propped and drained. The miners went down on the first shift to a pit that, when all was said and done, had not choked on its own dross because they had withdrawn their labour. Rob Ewing returned to work with the others, chastened, silent, and more withdrawn than ever.

One wet night towards the end of that month, Lily Stalker encountered him on his way to the start of the back-shift.

"Rob?" The baggy hood of her waterproof cape muffled her voice. "Rob?"

Rob stopped. Groups of workmates avoided him, and he walked alone. Rain fell loudly. At first he could not make out the shapeless little figure by the kirkyard wall and thought that it was Kate come to badger him again, then he recognised the gentle eyes and younger face of Lily.

"What's up, Lily? What's happened now?"

It was the pattern of the poor's thinking to equate surprise with unpleasantness.

"I just wanted to . . . t'see you."

"Who sent you?"

"Nobody sent me," Lily said. "Come on, I'll walk you up t'the gate."

"Are y'not feared you'll be compromised?"

"Huh!"

They began to walk side by side towards the pit.

"Kate tells me you're leavin'?"

"Aye, in a month or two."

"Why?"

"There's nothin' here for me."

"Are you sure o'that?"

"I'm sure."

"Then Blacklaw will lose it's last good man."

"Lily, for God's sake," said Rob. "Don't be daft, woman!"

"I mean it."

"I've never heard y'talk this way before."

"I never felt I had that much t'say. You've made yourself the fightin' man o'Blacklaw, Rob, an' that was enough. But it's not enough now. Consider yourself."

"It's t'protect myself I'm leavin'."

She looked up at him, her face not much larger than a child's within the hood. Shadows made smudges under her eyes and a fine tracery of lines showed at the corners of her mouth. It seemed to Rob that he had never seen her before. She was Lily Stalker all right, and he had known her almost as long as he could recall, but unaccountably he wanted to put out his hand and brush the drops of rain from her brow. The emotion startled him. What was this now, that was coming out of the wicked clouds of loss and betrayal?

"If you need a friend, Rob . . ." she said.

"Go on home, Lily."

"I really mean it."

"I know you do."

She watched him walk across the cobbled street towards the black pit gates. He paused, and waved to her. She waved back, then, gathering the skirt of her cape in one hand, she turned and ran down the rain-soaked street as lightly as a girl.

*   *   *

Lightness was a quality conspicuously absent from Betsy McAlmond. Fraser was not an unreasonable man, but he was tied to his family and bound in his affections to his comrades. The taint of finding himself married to a collier's daughter and the risk of having his humiliation exposed on the front page of every newspaper in Scotland was difficult for him to stomach. Wakened from his comfortable slumber, he stormed and raged at his wife.

"Why have you done this to me?"

"I did nothing, Fraser. Please keep your voice down, you will waken the children."

"In my house, I will raise my voice to any pitch that I please."

"You sound like a hysterical fishwife."

"Fishwife? Good God, Elizabeth, I am married to somebody no better than a fishwife, it seems."

"You never gave one thought to my lineage, or lack of it, before now. Why, suddenly, should it become important?"

"I am wholly dependent upon the goodwill of respectable people," said Fraser.

"For what?"

"My income."

"Your income! Lord; your father could afford to give you an annuity that would keep you handsomely in style."

"I would not accept it. Besides, my father is unlikely to view this scandal in a forgiving spirit. It's just as well that he spends most of his time in London these days fussing with his railway stocks. As it is, he'll probably cut us completely out of his will."

"Oh, I don't care. At least your mother isn't a snob. She'll stand by us."

"Elizabeth, the newspaper reporters will probe and pry until

263

they dig up your connection with this . . . this bastard miner. Look, why don't you leave Edinburgh? Winter abroad?"

"Hah," said Elizabeth. "Don't you suppose that that was the first thing to cross my mind? Why, I had it all planned. I even asked . . ." She bit off the sentence.

"Who did you ask? Not me, not your husband."

"I asked Andrew, if you must know. At that juncture he was contemplating taking a long 'vacation' too."

"Why didn't you go? Why didn't you both clear out of Edinburgh?"

"Andrew changed his mind."

"I do not understand your attitude, Elizabeth. You're taking this impetuous act of self-destruction on Andrew's part so calmly. Have you not tried to persuade him to give up the case?"

"It's too late for that. Besides, I . . . I feel sorry for the boy."

"I find that very difficult to swallow, Elizabeth."

"Well, I admit that I would have preferred Drew to keep out of it, but he's gone into it, and I . . . I feel obliged to stay in Edinburgh and support him."

"Thus obliging me to support him too?"

"You must act according to your conscience, Fraser."

"There's more, much more to all this than you've admitted. I'm not stupid enough to be taken in by all this talk of 'conscience'. You are afraid of something, Elizabeth, and that is why you have meekly accepted Drew's astonishing decision."

"The boy is my own flesh and blood. There is a bond there. Don't pretend that you were ignorant of my background when you asked me to be your wife."

She had sidetracked him, she hoped, from the issue that had made him suspicious. It was true what Fraser said; she *had* been inclined to fly into a rage at Drew's impetuous championing of the miner. The fact that he was her nephew meant nothing. But she was also afraid of what might leak out in her absence if she had continued with her plan to winter on the Continent.

"I admit that I did suspect that you were of humbler origins than you . . . But, no; no, that's not material now."

"You will act as agents, won't you?"

"That depends on Innis and Balfour."

"Don't hive all the responsibility onto them."

"We must meet to discuss it."

"You, none of you, would be where you are now if it wasn't for my brother."

"Really, Elizabeth, I am at a loss to understand why you are so vehemently in support of your brother. He intends to expose his past to ridicule and, by reflection, hold the McAlmond family up to public scorn."

"The McAlmond family are the last of my concerns. The young man is my nephew. He also happens to be innocent of the crime with which he is charged."

"How do *you* know?"

"Drew says so."

"Your eagerness for Andrew to defend wouldn't have anything to do with the fact that Lauder is the Crown counsel, would it?"

"That matters not to me."

"Oh, so you are no longer infatuated with that gentleman?"

"Fraser, I . . ."

"I suppose he spurned your silly advances and you now wish to see him defeated, no matter what the cost?"

"How *can* you think that of me?"

"I have had many years of practice, Elizabeth. I understand you better than you think I do. This is a destructive whim, a grand gesture of personal spite?"

"The boy is . . ."

"Innocent: innocent: I know," said Fraser. "Lord, the boy may be the only innocent person involved in this entire mess."

"Drew will convince you."

"I'm not at all sure that we need convincing."

"We?"

"The Sprotts too are bound to be involved."

"Fraser, I beg of you . . ."

"Don't beg, Elizabeth; that's a working-class trait, and I abhor it."

"What will you do, Fraser? What *will* you do?"

"Stand by you, of course," Fraser said. "Faithfulness, alas, is the predominant trait of my class."

"Darling . . ."

"Not now, Elizabeth, *please*."

After lengthy discussion, the three partners of the solicitors' firm of Sprott, McAlmond and Sprott, elected to support the gentleman who had buttered their bread for a couple of decades, under the proviso that the Faculty of Advocates and other guardians of law accepted Stalker's right to defend his son.

★　　★　　★

In state and in secret the law lords met within the maze of halls, rooms and corridors of the Faculty of Advocates. They wore no robes, for the hearing was binding only in its formal declensions and there were no members of the public present to impress. If any of the six learned gentlemen seated round the polished table still wished that he was on holiday and released from the burdens of decision-making, he gave no sign of it. Only Blaven, Dean of the Faculty, displayed enthusiasm for the originality of the petitioner's claim, however. Blaven was a noted humourist, a pixie-like fifty-year-old with a crest of silver hair brushed back from a domed forehead and a pair of pince-nez that he balanced on the tip of his nose like a typical Dickensian eccentric. In displaying eagerness for argument, Blaven was the exception. The other lords, Watson, McAndrew, Vincent-Evans, Darlton and Forbes Adsett, the Lord Advocate, upon whose final word the granting of the petition lay, were all suitably grave though, on that muggy day, they sweated a little round the collars and Darlton frequently mopped his brow with a huge red polka-dot handkerchief that might have been filched from a ploughman.

Blaven conducted the proceedings. Adsett, in his quick shrill falsetto, put questions concerning the need and nature of the advocate's strange plea. Before the members of the committee were folios copied from Stalker's original request, substantiated by a weight of argument, in document and reference to document, that he had diligently marshalled. Boiled down, the entire interview might have been summarised in a dozen exchanges, more personal than forensic. "Mr. Stalker, you cite as precedent the case of the Crown versus Nicholl, 1788. In that instance, the father, a member of this Faculty, defended his son against a charge of rape on the circuit court in Inverness."

Blaven smiled to himself at the inopportune phraseology. Adsett, who was leaning forward, did not, of course, note the Dean's reaction.

"That is correct," Stalker said.

"Father defending son," said Adsett, "does not preclude the general statue of impartiality in respect of kin defending kin."

Stalker said, "The case, and the decision of this Faculty, is unequivocal. Advocate Nicholl could hardly have been considered impartial."

Very old now and inclined to impatience, Watson grumbled, "Seems to me it does."

Adsett peered down the table. "What does?"

"Indicates precedent," said Watson.

"You also cite the case of the murder of Thomas Hunter in the Stewartrie of Galloway in 1699, and his defence by his brother, Advocate William Mahaffey Hunter."

"Unequivocal," Watson said. "Quite unequivocal."

"But," said Vincent-Evans, "not done."

"Sirs," said Stalker, "is it not indigenous to the French model of justice upon which our own system of law is immutably founded that principle is more to be considered than precedent?"

"True, we are the envy of our English colleagues in that respect," said Blaven, "and often praised in the House of Lords for our respect for the civility and not the severity of our Scottish laws."

"I would, sirs, also ask you to consider the position of the family, and the statute that allows them to select as counsel any registered member of the profession."

"Are there not," said Darlton, almost teasingly, "enough advocates to choose from, Mr. Stalker, that they must choose you?"

"Not enough good advocates, my Lord," said Stalker.

"That smacks of conceit, Mr. Stalker," Adsett said.

"I make, your Lordship, only a factual statement, as objectively as possible."

"The fact remains that you are closely related to the accused," said Adsett.

"I am his natural father."

"So we are to understand. Have you proof of this relationship?" McAndrew asked.

"Documentary proof? I have none extant."

"How long since you consorted with the boy?"

"Apart from visiting him in Hamilton cells last week, I have not seen or communicated with him since the very day he was born."

"Might one enquire where the child's . . . the boy's mother is?" asked Blaven.

"She died," Stalker said, "in her first child-birth."

"You were not...ah, married to the woman?" said McAndrew.

"No, your Lordship. I was not married to the woman. I did not know that the woman was with child until the afternoon of her labour," he lied, convincingly. He had known of Heather's pregnancy in advance.

"But it seems that you knew her well enough to . . ." Watson made a swaying motion with his closed fist, a gesture too expressive for the prudish Adsett who murmured that there was no need to be offensive.

Blaven was smiling again.

Stalker's face was totally impassive, betraying no flicker of emotion.

He said, "As you are now no doubt aware, gentlemen, I came from a mining family—colliers—in the then village of Blacklaw in Lanarkshire. My father will not be known to you. He was severely injured in a major disaster in the pit and died soon after. I was fifteen years old. My sisters, aided in part by the coalmaster, scraped enough money together to send me to Edinburgh to study law in accordance with my father's wish."

"Our law school is generous, Mr. Stalker," said Blaven. "It makes no discrimination between classes."

"In theory, no, Dean Blaven," Stalker said. "But the law does not put food in a student's belly, and the human frame is not designed to survive on mere words."

"You are not the first poor boy to enter the Faculty of Advocates," Adsett said.

"And I hope that I shall not be the last," Stalker said. "To give relevance to this explanation, out of sheer necessity I shared room and board with the mother of the accused."

"You mean bed and board," said Watson.

"Yes, *bed* and board; one bed, one blanket, and crusts."

"Mr. Stalker," said Adsett, "we are not a jury. Sentiment has no place here."

"On the contrary," said Blaven. "It is my opinion that Advocate Stalker is correct in outlining the facts of the boy's parentage for us. Sentiment is close to being a Christian virtue after all. I for one am relieved to learn the exact circumstances from the Advocate's own lips. Your sister took the baby and raised it as her own?"

"Yes."

"Why did you not bring the child here to Edinburgh, once you had established yourself and could afford to do so?" asked Darlton.

"He was, I supposed, happy in Blacklaw."

"You supposed?"

"My sister and her husband provided a secure and loving home," said Stalker.

"You had no contact with them?" McAndrew said.

"None, directly. I heard news of them indirectly, through my sister. Our worlds did not join at any point. I felt that it would be unfair to the boy to uproot him from his natural environment."

"And to deny him the opportunity of a sound education, perhaps of following your footsteps?" said Adsett.

"The function of advocacy is not to make a man happy," said Stalker. "It is a vocation, and a harsh one at that. I had no time to examine my motives closely. He did not need me."

"But he needs you now?" said Dean Blaven.

"He needs my skill, my training, my experience."

"And none other will do?" said Adsett.

"None other will do—for me," Stalker said.

Even Adsett was silent for a moment.

At length, Blaven said, "It concerns us that you may bring

dishonour upon your profession by the admission that you have fathered a bastard child."

"It need not be publicly admitted," Stalker said.

"It will leak out," said Vincent-Evans. "Nothing can prevent it."

"It will remain speculation," Stalker said, "if I am granted the dispensation of the Faculty in consideration of the unusual circumstances of the case. If the point is not taken to legal ruling, that is, to the House, then many rumours will be quelled."

"And if you are not granted the dispensation?" Blaven asked.

"It will be necessary for me to associate myself with the defence without the definitions of my membership of this Faculty."

"Do I detect a threat there, Mr. Stalker?" said Darlton.

"I have no desire to take this case, no wish to involve myself in the causes that lie behind it," Stalker said. "But my sense of duty, honed by twenty years as a practitioner in Scottish courts of law, allows me no other honourable course."

"In other words," said Blaven, "you wish us to grant you a non-precedential dispensation in view of the rare circumstances, taking into account that there are past precedents for our action?"

"Yes."

"In short," Blaven added, "to allow you to be an advocate *in lieu* of being a father?"

"Yes, Dean Blaven, that is the fundamental principle that I would wish the Faculty, and the Lord Advocate, to apply."

"You may leave us, Mr. Stalker," Adsett said.

Two hours and eighteen minutes later, by the clock in the library, a clerk was sent to fetch Advocate Stalker back into the meeting chamber where, drily, Adsett informed him that he was permitted to act as counsel on behalf of the accused, Neill Campbell Stalker. There were no strings. Privately, Blaven wished him luck, and Advocate Stalker left the building to return to his chambers.

Twenty-four hours later, manacled to a police sergeant, Neill Campbell Stalker was transferred from Hamilton Police cells to the chill and foreboding precincts of Edinburgh's Calton Prison, there to await his trial come Martinmas term.

PART THREE

The
Lords of the Dance

November

Fatigue caught up with Andrew Stalker three days before the trial. Even he could not fight forever the effects of a twenty-hour working day while parrying the bickering attempts of press reporters to wring from him some sort of confession.

In the weeks immediately following Neill's transfer to Calton Jail, Drew devoted himself exclusively to the Stalker affair. He realised that he must prepare the groundwork before the public caught wind of scandal. Already he had to contend with witnesses whose credibility was seriously affected by all that they had read. As July drifted into August, Drew concentrated upon the legal writ, almost, if not quite, to the exclusion of the personalities in the case. Fraser McAlmond and the aristocratic Sprotts prudently persuaded Drew not to rely too heavily on forensic argument. Lauder and Mellish would spread emotionalism, like mustard on a saveloy, all over case law, and Drew would be made to seem naught but a carping pedant. Frank Kinnemouth was the book expert, Innes Sprott declared, let him earn his fee by getting on with it.

As depositions piled up, and the list of witnesses thinned, the tenor of the case changed in Drew's mind. He began to lose confidence in his own inviolability. Lauder had several trump cards in his hand—colliers willing to swear on oath that they had seen an act of murder, clear as day. All in all there would be a short list of witnesses, nothing like the forty or fifty that trailed nervously into the box in most murder trials. The inventory of physical evidence was also ludicrously short.

Indeed, it might have been reduced simply to the hammer as far as Drew could see.

By the end of August, he had prepared the essence of his case. On his list of sympathetic witnesses the name of Robert Ewing did not appear. That diehard had put an ideal of justice before loyalty to friends. In spite of all that Lily, Mirrin and Edward could say or do, Mr. Ewing remained adamant.

Throughout September, Drew busied himself with other cases, leaving the finishing of the Stalker brief to Fraser and the industrious Daniel Horn. Planning—much more than day-dreaming escapes from unpleasant reality—protected Drew against the infuriating attacks that began to appear about this time. Bedroom frolics were hinted at in yellow press journals. Two caricatures, at least, were not only obscene but libellous. Drew ignored them, as he ignored reporters' prying questions.

"*Sub judice,*" he declared, "*Sub judice,*" not once but a hundred times. He turned down all invitations to dinner, to luncheon, to meetings, and kept a distinctly low profile even in court. Fretting, harassed, and a little unsure of himself, Drew refused to let his emotions show. During the hot summer, the warm wet autumn and the sharp clear days of early winter, Stalker, Q.C., became more and more impassive. In 'Mayfly's' weekly snippet in the *Scotsman* he was described now as 'that perambulating pillar of granite,' a phrase that caught on in Edinburgh wineshop society and led to a crop of not terribly humorous jokes about 'chips off the old block'.

The morning had been taken up in a consultation with Frank Kinnemouth and Fraser. Fraser had called off early, however, to accompany Betsy and the children to the McAlmond estate in Perthshire where, thanks to the understanding of Lady Isobel, they would gain respite from the city's tensions. Kinnemouth too had a domestic engagement and, by four o'clock, Drew found himself alone.

Sifting up from the Forth, fog lay like salt wash in the wynds and vennels, rimed the dun leaves of the poplars in the private parks and, as night came, crystallised on the ledges of the buildings in Moray Place. Standing by the window of his chambers, Drew stared at the bleak scene. There was no object in it to trigger his memory of Blacklaw; even in such dismal weather, Edinburgh had a style far removed from that of the pit village, but he was so exhausted that he could not censor out the ghosts that stalked the lofty battlements of his mind, to cry out to him that of all the Stalkers, *he* was the one who had failed. Mirrin's fine sons and pretty little daughter had brought that home to him. Even Kate, in her fortress of affection in Kellock's Square, was better off than he was. At least Kate had known twenty years of happiness. All he had was his pride, his power, and his profession.

Unaware of the strain he had placed on himself, he was surprised to find that his hands were shaking. He held them out before him, watching with remote and critical interest. Surely the trembling was exaggerated? He was not a doddering old man yet; yet he was shrewd enough to recognise the warning. Naturally, his first response was to close his fists. The shaking ascended into his arms. Clinical detachment fled. Pain cut across his chest.

It was nothing! Imagination! Indigestion! Could it be his heart? Good God, no! Most certainly it could not be his heart. Leaning his sweating brow against the cold glass, he willed the chest pains to pass. Obediently, they did so, though the shaking in his limbs did not abate. Steeling himself, he walked slowly from the window to the armchair and seated himself.

After a moment, he shouted, "Daniel? Daniel?"

He waited; one minute, two minutes—then yelled again.

Daniel Horn did not appear.

Stretching, Drew cranked the handle that would sound an appropriate bell in the servants' quarters, shouting, quite irrationally, "Corby. Corby. Corby."

The simple action of winding the bell wire relieved the physical spasm, but the lack of response from the depths of the house frightened him inordinately. He did not dare shift from the chair, fearing that he might fall down and die there, alone in that gloomy book-lined vault.

The door opened. He lolled his head against the wing of the chair and stared into the mirk.

"Heather?" he said, first curiously, then in wonderment. "Is that—Heather?"

"No, sir. It's Mairi."

"Heather, I . . ."

Shyly the girl came forward. An entity of black and white, her face seemed to float in the grey air, a pretty, youthful face that he identified with that of Neill's mother, a secret image held in his brain for two decades. A sweet almost swooning relief possessed him. He sank back, saying, "It's all right."

The girl said, "Is there something you'll be wanting, sir?"

"Where is Corby?"

"Gone out t'the shops, sir."

"Come closer."

Afraid now, the girl drifted around Drew's chair in a half circle, staring at him as if *he* was the ghost. Drew studied her; no calculation, nothing but wistfulness, in his heart.

"Where are you from?" he asked.

"From Skye, sir."

"Do you like it here?"

"Aye, sir."

"Your . . . your family; your mother and father, do you not miss them?"

"They're dead, sir."

"Ah," Drew said, nodding.

"Are, are you not well, sir?"

"No, Mairi, I'm fine," Drew said. "But you may fetch me a glass of whisky. The cabinet in the dining room is unlocked."

"Will I be lightin' the lamps, Mr. Stalker?"

"There's no need. Bring me the whisky, Mairi. And my coat and hat."

"Aye, sir. Will you be going out? It's a terrible raw afternoon."

"That won't matter, Mairi," Drew said and, with a smile, dismissed her.

Twenty minutes later, with whisky warming his blood, he left Moray Place and, on foot, set off through the fog for Calton Jail.

*   *   *

"One stoup of wine per day," Drew said; "a ration still permitted under the regulations of this ancient institution.

Besides, I've squared it with the warder. Here, pass me your cup."

"I'm not much used t'wine, Mr. Stalker."

"It'll take the chill out of your bones, Neill."

"What'll you drink from?"

"We'll share the cup."

"Hardly seems right t'be drinkin' wine out of a bashed tin mug."

"Beggars," said Drew, "can't be choosers."

"You're right. By God, it's warmin'. What kind o'wine is it?"

"Claret."

"That's what the toffs drink."

"Try one of these."

"Looks like liquorice stick."

"It's only a cheap cheroot," said Drew. "Quite assuredly not the kind 'toffs' smoke."

"Bit stronger than a roll-your-own," said Neill.

"Smoke it slowly," said Drew. "The advantage of a cheroot is its strength. Economically speaking it lasts long."

"I see what y'mean."

"Are you nervous?" said Drew. "About Tuesday?"

"Aye, a bit," Neill said. "What's up, Mr. Stalker?"

"Up? Oh, nothing's up."

"I thought . . . seein' you here this time of a Saturday night . . ."

"I just happened to be passing, that's all."

"Ma an' Da' . . . Willie . . . they'll be here t'morrow. I had a letter from them, an' another from Malcolm, Aunt Mirrin's boy."

"A fine young fellow."

"He's a real pal."

"He seems settled to farming."

"It's in his blood, I suppose. That's what comes from havin' a tinker for a father."

"Quite."

"Is it really all right, then?"

"Neill, I have nothing to say about the trial. We've been through it all thoroughly. Please, talk of something else."

"What?"

"When you are free, what will you do?"

"Back t'the grind at the coal-face, I suppose."

"Have you ever considered enrolling in college?"

"College? Me! God, I haven't got the brains for it."

"A technical college, perhaps?"

"An' what would I gain from that?"

"Education—and opportunity."

"College," said Neill. "It's a thought."

"A worthwhile thought," said Drew. "You may imagine that you work hard, but digging coal is no labour at all compared with the hours of sheer slog that a student has to put in."

"An' at the end o'it all?"

"A managerial post."

"In a pit?"

"Foundry, engineering company, what you will."

"Aye, it really *is* a thought."

"I can help."

"I think we could manage it on our own."

"Now, now, young man, don't be so proud."

"It's not that, Mr. Stalker. It's Ma."

"She wants what's best for you."

"Does she?"

"Of course she does. She may not like me, Neill, but she is not daft enough, shall we say, to deny you opportunity."

"Ma's not like you think, Mr. Stalker. She's kind an' generous."

"I know that even better than you do."

"Aye, I keep forgettin' . . ."

"Think it over, Neill. Since Lamont won't have you back, college offers a good alternative to leaving Blacklaw in search of a miserable pit job in another district."

"Management; aye," said the young man. "It is a thought t'be weighed. Edward's the bright one, though."

Drew hesitated, then said, "It would be no hardship to me to see to it that the pair of you receive a technical education, equipping you for a proper career in industry."

"It would take time, an' money."

278

"I was the recipient of much generosity," said Drew. "I had the coalmaster himself as my patron."

"So I heard."

"You sound disapproving."

"Well . . . Lamont's no' who I'd pick for a patron."

"It was that or give up my dream."

"Your dream t'get shot o'Blacklaw."

"Is that what your mother, what Kate told you?"

"I don't blame you. It was harder in those days. Maybe I'd've wanted out an' all."

"But you *are* happy, are you not? I mean, you have been happy in Blacklaw?"

"Contended wi' my lot—isn't that the popular phrase, Mr. Stalker?" Neill said. "I'm a workin' chap; that says it all."

"In yourself, though, you were not unhappy."

"I've always been loved, Mr. Stalker."

"Yes," Drew said, quietly. "I envy you that."

"What was she like?"

"Who?"

"My real mother, what was she like?"

"Just . . . just a girl."

"Did y'not love her?"

"I think," said Drew, "that the allocation of love in our family was unfairly made, used up on Mirrin, Kate and my elder brothers. When it came to my turn, there was precious little left." Neill waited patiently for a straight answer. "Your mother loved me, Neill. I know that now. But I did not want to acknowledge it then."

"Why not?"

"Because it would have meant giving up too much of myself. I was niggardly, mean, with my emotions. I never knew how to cope with them, only how to suppress them."

"Is that why y'didn't marry her?"

"I was only seventeen years old."

"That doesn't sound like a proper excuse, Mr. Stalker."

"And I was too ambitious, too hungry for success," Drew said. "When you are older, perhaps you will understand."

"I'm older now than you were when y'fathered me."

"That's true," Drew conceded.

"Tell me about her."

Drew licked his upper lip. "She was a highland girl, from Inverness, an orphan. She was kind to me when I was in need of kindness. But I . . . I took what I wanted from her, and then discarded her. I regret it now, bitterly regret it."

"With everythin' you've got," Neill said, "you can afford t'indulge in a bit o'regret."

"That's a cruel remark," Drew said. "But, I suppose, it's no more than I deserve. Listen; I can't change the past. I cannot change what I am. Your mother, Neill, was innocent in her loyalty. I was never innocent: *never*. I was bred to be different, raised to do great things with my life. It was dinned into me from the time I could toddle. My father, in his way, was as ambitious as I am, and I was made the instrument of his ambition."

"Mam says he would have approved o'you, an' what you're doin' for us."

"Yes," said Drew. "Old Alex Stalker was a great one for the grand gesture. Kate's absolutely right. He would have applauded any action that smacked of martyrdom."

"I don't think there's much danger o'you becomin' a martyr."

"I don't believe in the value of needless self-sacrifice."

"An' yet you'll risk your reputation by takin' my part in court."

"I do that only out of selfishness."

Neill said nothing for a moment then with a gentle but impulsive gesture he reached out and gripped his father's hand. "Let everybody else think that, but I know different."

"What . . . what do you mean?"

"I think you're doin' it just for her."

"Mirrin, do you mean, or Kate?"

Neill shook his head. His father's alarm was considerable, as if he feared that the boy had stumbled on some profound truth that would consummate in an exposure of weakness. Drew doubted his own motives and had grown cautious of his reactions to this young man. The strange incident of the afternoon had increased his suspicions of himself. Unless he was very careful he would find himself divided, not just in loyalties, but in character, and that would not serve any of them well at this time. He regretted the question and put up his hand to rub it from the air, but Neill had already answered.

"Not Mirrin, or Kate. I mean, I think you're doin' all this for m'mother, my *real* mother; for peace o'mind."

Drew covered his face with his hand. He was moved by the boy's innocence, an echo of Heather Campbell's unoffending honesty, quite different from the Stalkers whose probity and candour were often tinged with cruelty or, at least, a quality of intentional hurt. There was little of that in Neill; not even the insult of this charge against him could curdle his spirit and turn him sour against society. For an unguarded moment, Drew was filled with optimism for the future and, hurrying after that flicker of hope, the sad realisation that he had gone too far ever to return to a meeting ground where men like Neill and women like Mirrin and Advocates of the Bar, like monuments of granite, could meet as equals. In his weariness, he broke a little, embarrassing his son.

For a minute, Neill did nothing then, with a sigh, he tentatively patted the lawyer's shoulder. "There, there, Mr. Stalker."

Drew got to his feet, hand still to his face.

"But is it not true?" Neill persisted, looking up.

"Yes, son," Drew said, thickly. "It probably is."

Neill pushed himself to his feet too, standing close to the haggard-eyed man. "I thought so," he said. "But don't worry, Mr. Stalker, I'll not tell a soul."

Drew gave a mirthless chuckle. "Tell whoever you wish, Neill. Nobody in the wide world would believe you."

"Until Tuesday," Neill said.

*　　*　　*

Saturday in Glasgow was not much different from Saturday in Edinburgh. The salt-tint in the capital's foggy air was replaced by buffalo brown, a granular colour indigenous to the Clyde valley and responsible for the rasping resonance of the natives' bronchial coughs and wheezes. There were no hackers in Dr. Parfitt's rooms, however, only an elderly minister with a clerical-grey patch over his left eye, and a portly young woman with the darkest spectacles that Mirrin had ever seen. Mirrin did not have to sit long with them, though, for the enlightened

Dr. Parfitt summoned her into the ophthalmic consulting room along with Tom and allowed her to watch the extensive tests that he conducted on her husband's eyes.

The consulting room was like the cabin of a ship, long, narrow and wood-panelled. A porthole on the right wall admitted daylight, augmented by a variety of shaded lamps that cast beams weak and strong upon the subject. On the wall were reading charts and two long ribbons of silk-like material containing all the colours of the rainbow and labelled 'Hirsch's Spectrographic Tester'. There was also an ophthalmoscope, which Parfitt used at great length, and other instruments including an oddly-patterned curtain on a frame that the doctor appeared to activate by the use of a wax candle on a little tin tray. This candle he carried about in front of Tom who sat bolt upright on a padded wooden stool and answered Parfitt's questions in monosyllabic negatives.

"Can you see, here?"

"No."

"Here?"

"No."

"Here, Mr. Armstrong?"

"No."

"Nothing?"

"Back a bit, where you were, Doctor."

"There?"

"A glimmer, just a glimmer, that's all."

"I don't understand it."

Parfitt seated himself on a swivel chair, put the candle down on a table and pinched out the flame with finger and thumb. A plume of acrid smoke coiled up to the ceiling. Parfitt looked, Mirrin thought, puzzled, angry and impatient.

"Mr. Armstrong, this is the third examination I have made of your eyes and, frankly, I cannot understand why sight is absent."

"I'm not lyin' about it."

"No, no, of course you're not." Parfitt slapped his hands on his thighs, cocked his head and gave Tom scrutiny. Tom remained seated, erect from the waist, face turned towards the Alphabet Reading Chart left of Parfitt's corner. "But, to every objective test, your eyes appear to respond perfectly. Healing of the surgical wounds is complete and there is no apparent erosion of the optic nerves."

"What about the aqueous?" Tom asked.

"Flow would seem to be adequate. Pain?"

"Not much."

"Sensitive to light?"

"Well, we haven't had much sun lately, but no, Doctor, I can hardly make out light at all."

"Not even in the left eye?"

"More so in it than in the right."

"You see, Mr. Armstrong, if I were to examine your eyes as they now are and base my prognosis upon the physical evidence alone I would say that you have restored vision."

"But I don't have any vision."

"I know."

"You're tryin' t'tell me that the operation wasn't a success, that I'm blind. Right, Doctor?"

"I'm not telling you that at all, Mr. Armstrong."

Mirrin said, "Pardon me, Doctor Parfitt, but is there a chance yet that sight will return?"

"Yes, of course," said Parfitt.

"But *will* it?" said Tom.

"I really don't know. That is the truth, Mr. Armstrong."

"So, what do I do now?"

"Hope for the best," said Parfitt.

"An' prepare for the worst?"

"Any change can only be for the better, can it not?"

"Aye. That's true."

"Good-day to you, Mr. Armstrong, Mrs. Armstrong."

"Good-day, Doctor Parfitt." Tom shook Parfitt's hand. "An' thanks for doin' your best."

"I'm only sorry . . ." Parfitt shrugged. "Come and see me again early in January. Make an appointment by letter, if you will."

"Aye, Doctor," Tom said.

As they walked slowly down the stairs in the fashionable tiled close, Mirrin said, "You've no intention o'goin' back, have you?"

"If y'ask me, it was never on in the first place."

"He's always seemed like such a good doctor."

"I don't doubt it," said Tom.

"There's another step at the foot o'the handrail."

"Right; got it."

Mirrin pushed the outside door with her shoulder and arm in arm the couple cautiously descended half a dozen steps to the pavement.

"God, but it's foggy."

"Aye, I can taste it. Keep yourself well wrapped, Mirrin."

"What'll we do?"

"Get out o' Glasgow as quick as we can."

"You're not keen t'stay for tea?"

"I'd rather get home."

"I hope the trains aren't held up."

"Hope not," said Tom. "Did y'buy a poke of sweets for the bairns?"

"I did," said Mirrin. "All the bairns; you included."

"Where are we?"

"Goin' up t'wards Charin' Cross. It's quite a walk, Tom. Will I look for a hack?"

"No, no, just step it out a bit, an' keep a tight grip on my arm."

"The pavement's crowded."

"We'll manage, lass."

"Tom?"

"Aye?"

"What'll we do now?"

"Mrs. McLaren'll come in for three or four days. We'll be fine wi' her."

"I don't mean durin' the trial; I mean—after."

"If the lads'll stay," said Tom, "we'll carry on as best as we can. They're the lords o'the dance now, Mirrin. We're done, you an' I."

"Havers, Tom Armstrong," Mirrin said. "I'm anythin' but done, an' the way you're shovin' yourself up this damned street I say there's life in you yet."

"What a bloody racket," Tom said. "Deafen you, so the city would."

"We'll be home soon enough," Mirrin told him.

She supported his weight on her arm. It was no mere gesture of courtesy this linking of arms now. He needed a guide and, already, had developed a sympathetic sense of navigation, matching the length of her stride and, though it took effort, pitching himself forward into—into what? she wondered; into a black soup? In contrast to his self-pitying phase of last winter he no longer complained. In fact, she was hard put to it to wrest from him any information concerning his condition, except in as much as it affected their future. Since he had been unable to burn off his considerable energies in work about the farm, it seemed to Mirrin that he had become more sympathetic to the problems of his family at a personal level, more interested and somehow gentler. It was as if he had finally found enough time to think.

"I wish," he said, cocking his head so that she could hear him above the clatter of the horse traffic. "I wish I'd been left with somethin'."

"Tom, you've got us."

"No, no, flower, I don't mean that. I mean, just a *wee* bit o'sight, enough t'see the shape o'your face, or the colour o'Kitten's hair."

"Maybe it'll come back."

"No; not now."

There was no chance for them to be maudlin, not bashing up Bath Street on a busy Saturday evening, with street lamps already vanishing in waxy-brown fog, crossings already manned by policemen with big bottle-eyed carbide lanterns and, as they turned down Renfield Street hill, trotting out with streaming red flares to keep traffic flowing.

"What a stink," Tom said. "That's tar burnin'."

"Fog-flares," Mirrin shouted.

Tom laughed. "That's what bein' blind is like, Mirrin, in the early stages, like livin' in a real pea-souper. I never thought t'tell y' that before."

"Tom?"

"What, love?"

"When I'm away in Edinburgh . . ."

"Aye."

"Talk t'Malcolm an' Sandy."

"I intend to. I've no desire t'see our bonnie boys slouch away in the huff."

"Is Hazelrig big enough t'support us all?"

"It has so far."

"Even when the boys get married, an' father bairns o'their own?"

"They're only lads yet, Mirrin."

"Lords o'the dance, Tom, as you said. Before y'know it, they'll be the next generation."

"Right enough, Mirrin; it'll no' be long before some sonsy wee filly catches Malcolm's eye. I suppose in time he'll need a place o'his own."

"What then, Tom?"

"By God, woman, y'pick strange places t'ask questions like that."

"Have y'got an answer?"

"Ach, hell, time'll provide its own answers. Just let's get through this week, eh?" Tom pulled her tighter, almost tugging her from her feet. "One bad thing at a time, Mirrin."

"The trouble with life," Mirrin said, "is that the bad things all happen at once."

"It could be worse. At least we've got each other."

"What?" Mirrin shouted as the current of heavy drays and horse-drawn 'buses that jammed St. Vincent Street surged into the flood that poured heedlessly down Renfield. "I missed that."

Tom pulled her closer still.

They stopped. She could see him against the gaslight of a milliner's shop-window, his heavy face attentive and, oddly, touched by amusement. He drew her to him until her breast was pressed against his chest. Reaching, he invited her kiss. She gave it, her lips to his. Two girls in gay bonnets and outlandish Bolero jackets paused, giggled and made barking sounds at the practically senile couple bussing away like mad there on the street corner.

"At least we've got each other," Tom said.

"I heard you that time, Tom Dandy."

★　　★　　★

286

THE TRIAL

of

NEILL CAMPBELL STALKER

From Tuesday 11th November, 1896 to Thursday 12th
November (inclusive)

First Day—the Court met at 10.45

Judge Presiding
THE LORD JUSTICE-CLERK (McSherry)

Counsel for the Crown
Patrick Lauder, Esq.,
Hector R. Mellish, Esq.,
(Advocates-Depute)

Agent
J. Morton Peebles, W.S.

Counsel for the Panel
Andrew Stalker, Esq.,
Francis Kinnemouth, Esq.,
(Advocates)

Agents
Messrs. Sprott, McAlmond & Sprott, S.S.C.

Tuesday, 11th November, was one of those days on which it seemed that all the colour had been sucked out of the world. Leaden skies rested on iron roofs and, on a lower plane, people and traffic swam in a gelatinous haze.

The High Court of Justiciary stood in Parliament Square, some distance back from busy High Street's motley tenements. Most days the court square was given over to a few straggling figures in black and to flocks of questing grey pigeons. On this day, however, the forecourts and pavements were packed with citizens hopeful of gaining admittance, their interest fanned by the highly-coloured reports that had appeared in the press and by the personalities of the advocates. Lauder was famous, Stalker hardly less so, and this was the first time the pair had met in legal combat.

The doors of the court building were opened at nine o'clock and the throng ushered through, officers and policemen acting as bastions.

At a minute to ten-forty-five, the trap in front of the dock opened and the prisoner, flanked by two uniformed officers, came up from the cells. Dressed in a suit of sober tweed, his fair hair wetted and brushed back from his brow, he looked appallingly young. He was composed—almost too composed. He did not bow his head and fix his eyes on the line of blunt iron stud-spikes along the front of the dock. On the contrary, he scanned the steep row of faces that swayed forward in the public gallery and, catching sight of a friend, gave a quick— some thought wicked—smile. Och, the brazen, bare-faced, rebellious, young tyke! Grannies in the gallery immediately condemned him to hang by the neck until dead. Others, grocers and merchants, senior clerks and their bosomy wives, con- sidered how much like their assistants he looked with that same insubordinate expression stamped on his sly features. Look at the eyes of him. Cares nothing for nobody. Cut your throat as quick as wink. Good luck to you, Patrick Lauder. Do your duty this day and rid our society of such dangerous influences.

Promptly at the hour appointed, in a sweep of robes, the Lord Justice-Clerk, McSherry, lumbered to his seat upon the bench. The fraternity of lawyers was again impressed by his lordship's bearing. He was no 'whisker', no brisk trotter of a judge who got to the bench in double-march time. He moved with the solemnity of a cardinal—the analogy would have riven his Protestant soul—and appeared to embody not so much impartial justice as a gaudy, theatrical grandeur that flowered but rarely in Scottish affairs. He did not even glance at the prisoner, though the prisoner followed his lordship with his eyes as if—the same malicious tongues said—he was calculatin' how much dynamite it would take t'blow the old boy up.

In the well, raised eight or ten inches by a hollow-sounding dais, advocates and agents gathered amid a fuss of papers.

In the public gallery, Betsy had procured a front seat. Near the back crushed against a wall that had already begun to 'sweat' with condensation, sat Willie and Kate Kellock, and Mirrin.

The proceedings began.

The indictment was read.

"Neill Campbell Stalker, now or lately prisoner in the prison of Edinburgh, you are indicted and accused at the instance of the Right Honourable Forbes Adsett, Her Majesty's Advocate for Her Majesty's interest: that albeit, by the laws of this and every well-governed realm, murder is a crime of an heinous nature, and severely punishable; yet true it is and of verity, that you, the said Neill Campbell Stalker, are guilty of the said crime, actor, or art and part; in so far, as on the 18th day of July, in this present year, in the public thoroughfare adjoining the entrance to the colliery of the Blacklaw Colliery Company, Lanarkshire, you did wickedly and feloniously participate in riotous behaviour and, in the course of rioting, did with malice and due knowledge of consequence seek to murder or to grievously do harm to Constable Allan James Ronald of the Hamilton Constabulary who was acting in accordance with his duties; and, by aiming and striking with a hammer, did cause injury to Constable Ronald and, in result, did cause him to die."

There was more; a carefully-wrought rigmarole that laid down snares for the accused just in case he should wriggle out of the main charge of murder.

The indictment concluded, "All which, or part thereof, being found proven by the verdict of an assize, or admitted by the judicial confession of you the said Neill Campbell Stalker, before the Lord Justice-Clerk and Lord Commissioners of Justiciary, you the said Neill Campbell Stalker ought to be punished with the pains of law, to deter others from committing the like crimes in all times coming."

On the calling of the diet, Mr. Kinnemouth, for the panel, took objection to that part of the indictment in which there was an averment of malice and due knowledge of consequence. He did not, he said, dispute the right of the Crown to give notice to the accused that it was their intention to prove malice and due knowledge of consequence, but, if he might refer to the case of H.M. Advocate versus Robert Robertson McLellan, reported in Arkley's Justiciary Reports, page 137, 9th March, 1844, the objection there was taken by the accused that there was no specification of the act of malice or due knowledge of consequence and the judgment of the Court was to the effect that it did not fall upon the prosecutor to give articulate notice of such knowledge of consequence under standing rules of riotous behaviour.

At the request of the Court counsel read the terms of the indictment in the case referred to.

Challenged by the Lord Justice-Clerk as to whether the proving of malice and knowledge of consequence was a main issue, Mr. Kinnemouth then read an extract from the leading opinion in the case previously cited by him, and submitted that the set of facts which was in contemplation of the bench in a case of that kind was not on the face of it sufficient to induce his lordship to stretch the practice of the Court. Counsel concluded by submitting that the averment of evincing malice and knowledge of consequence should be thrown out of the indictment altogether and that, with regard to the rest, the latitude taken by the prosecution was too great.

Advocate-Depute Mellish, for the prosecution, said in reply that it was apprehended by the prosecution that the question would arise as to definition of malice and knowledge of consequence whenever a witness was examined in regard to it. The weight of facts or evidence so adduced was a question for the consideration of the jury, under the direction of the judge. He might frankly tell his learned friends on the other side that it was without reluctance that these allegations had been inserted

into the indictment, and that the details in question of statement and deduction from evidence were by no means mere
excrescences but were main issues.

Mr. Kinnemouth, for the panel, said that after what had
fallen from the Advocate-Depute there was little use in discussing the legal question at this stage. Though he did not anticipate
that either throughout the trial or at the end of it, would it be
necessary for those who represented the prisoner to make any
reflections whatever on the manner in which the Crown had
conducted the case, if this matter was not to be inquired into,
perhaps the better way for his lordship, after what the Advocate-
Depute had said, would be to allow counsel for the panel to
raise the objection again, if it should be deemed necessary to
do so in the course of the inquiry.

The Lord Justice-Clerk said that he thought that that would
be a proper course, within bounds.

After consultation with his colleague, Mr. Kinnemouth
accepted the indictment without deletion at this stage.

The libel having then been found relevant to infer the pains
of law, the prisoner was called upon to plead and replied in a
clear and firm tone, "Not guilty, my Lord."

A jury of fifteen men was then balloted for and empanelled,
and the trial proceeded.

*   *   *

"Look at them," Drew said. "Precisely what one would have
expected."

"Interchangeable with every other jury I've ever seen in
criminal court," said Kinnemouth.

"Kirk elders, mock-modest citizens, to a man. I doubt if any
one of them has ever gone short of dinner in his life."

"I'm rather sorry we did not make more of the 'malice'
inclusion. Did I retreat too easily?"

"No," Drew said. "That was the best we could expect. It
makes our intention in that respect known."

The first prosecution witness was the Reverend Matthew
Laird, presently resident in the parish of Blacklaw. He was an
elderly thin-faced spook of a man, who intoned the oath in his
pulpit voice.

Lauder did not choose to make the first sally.

Advocate Mellish did the honours once more. "You are Matthew Laird, Minister of the Church of Scotland?"

"I am."

"You serve the people of Blacklaw, do you not?"

"I do—for the past eleven years."

"So, Minister," said Mellish, "in the process of your pastoral duties you have come to know the good, hard-working people of Blacklaw well?"

"I have."

"You share their burdens and sorrows, and sympathise with them in the many vicissitudes that result from their harsh conditions of service?"

"I do so," Laird said.

"What is your opinion of them, sir?"

Laird put his hands on the edge of the witness box and, vibrating with conviction, declared, "There is not, on the face of this earth, a body of men, or of women, more visited by misfortune, or subjected to more oppression than are the collier folk. It requires to be said, sir, that not all their suffering follows as a natural result of the work that they do for their daily bread, but is visited upon them by the inhuman pressures put upon them by those who seek the dross of monetary gain."

Colliers in the gallery nudged each other and exchanged glances of approval. Others, more perspicacious, waited for the sting.

Drew stuck his tongue in his cheek. Pyrotechnics had started early: probably Mellish's idea. He too waited. The murmur in the courtroom quickly subsided.

Thoughtfully, Mellish said, "And would you, Minister, consider these inhuman pressures to be contributory to the strike action that was in effect at the time of the crime of which the accused stands charged?"

"Unquestionably."

"For what reasons, Minister?"

"Wages were being cut, men paid off, evictions announced arbitrarily, the whole legacy of cruel industrial slavery was still in evidence. What recourse is left for desperate men but to withhold their labour?"

"The situation was truly desperate?"

"It was, sir."

Old Laird was not known for his labour sympathies. Even the most naive of the colliers in the gallery began to smell a rat.

Conversationally, shoulder to the witness, Mellish said, "A desperate situation, Minister. Yes, and, when constables appeared in the thoroughfare at the pit-gate, what would be more natural than riot and bloodshed, that a hot-blooded young man might strike out with any weapon available against representatives of the authority by whom he felt oppressed."

"That is not what I said, sir."

"Oh, what did you say, Minister?"

"I do not approve of violence."

"Have you communicated this to your parishioners?"

"Where possible."

"But they did not heed you?"

"They are not all of my flock."

"Is the accused of your flock?"

"His mother . . ."

"I did not ask about his mother. Is the accused a member of your flock?"

"He attended my Sunday School until three or four years ago, then . . . No, sir, I could not call him a member of my flock."

"He attended Sunday School?"

"He did."

"For how long?"

"Oh, ten years, I would say."

"An attentive boy, not dull of hearing or wanting in the wit to understand the teachings of the laws of Christ?"

"Not at all: a very quick-minded little chap, as I recall."

"Minister, refresh my memory, please," said Mellish. "What is the text of the sixth commandment?"

"Thou shalt not kill."

"It does not say, Thou shalt not kill *except* when seeking higher wages, does it?"

"No."

"It does not say, Thou shalt not kill, *except* when challenged by constables during a strike, does it?"

"No, sir."

"It says plainly, and without qualification, *Thou shalt not kill*."

"It does."

"And the accused, Minister, when did he abandon Sunday School, when did he drift away from the Church?"

"He would be about sixteen."

"And working?"

"Yes, at the pit."

"Something, some other form of teaching, some other philosophy, perhaps, replaced the doctrines of the Christian Church in his heart and mind?"

"I would say that is possible."

"Possible?"

"Probable."

"Do you have any knowledge of what that philosophy might be?"

"No, I do not."

"Unionism?"

"Your lordship," Drew climbed to his feet; "that is patently an example of counsel leading the witness."

"I agree," said McSherry.

Mellish nodded. "Very well, Minister. Let me ask you, in conclusion, how many of your parishioners—no, how many of your congregation—attend kirk services with regularity?"

"Two hundred, or more."

"It is not, then, a heathen town?" said Mellish. "It is not a town where the Gospel remains unknown?"

"I would hope not," said Laird.

"How many of your congregation were involved in the bloody riot that took place on Wednesday, eighteenth of July, Minister?"

"None."

"Surely, Minister, not even you can be sure of that?" said Mellish. "None at all?"

"Not one, sir. I am sure of it."

"So," said Mellish, "the actions that took place in Blacklaw prior to and during the morning in question were not, in effect, carried out by men in communion with the kirk, by men to whom the harshness and hardships of life might be eased by the consolations and the *practical* recourses suggested by the Bible?"

"Happily, I would say that is the case," Laird answered.

"But by men who—some of them—dwelled in knowledge of the difference between good and evil, who elected to put material gain before all else, and to *kill* for it."

"M'Lord," Drew shouted.

McSherry nodded and, leaning forward, gently suggested that counsel might care to put the question in another form.

"I will withdraw it, m'lord," said Mellish. "It has, in effect, been answered already. Thank you, Minister."

Stalker was already on his feet. He passed Mellish, their robes wafting together in the passing and, before the Advocate-Depute could even turn around, addressed himself in cross-examination to the witness.

"Involvement, Reverend Laird?" Drew rapped out. "What is your definition of the word 'involvement'?"

"I . . . I do not understand the question," the Minister said.

The Lord Justice-Clerk, to whom much of the sentiment led out by Counsellor Mellish had been obliquely directed, was not so sunk in morality that he could not appreciate a fine point of counter-attack. Mellish's handling had been a shade clumsy. He took it upon himself to explain to the witness.

"You answered Crown to the effect that none of your regular congregation were 'involved' in the riot. Advocate Stalker is questioning your interpretation of that word."

"Thank you, m'lord," said Stalker.

"None of them were engaged in the fighting, that is what I meant," said the witness.

"Present at the riot itself?"

"Yes."

"But 'being present' is not at all the same as being 'involved', is it?" Stalker did not await the witness's confirmation but went on at a great lick. "How many Roman Catholics do you number in your congregation?"

"None, of course. I am a minister ordained by the Church of Scotland."

"How many Jews?"

"Really, that should be . . ."

"How many, sir?"

"None."

"So, by the so-called logic of supposition that my learned friend has wished upon you, Reverend Laird, one might feasibly draw the conclusion that the riot was conducted by Catholics and Jews."

"I said nothing of the sort."

"I know you did not," said Stalker. "I wish you to make it clear to the members of the jury, however, that there is no equation between a man's *kirk* connection and his social behaviour."

"But," said Laird, sticking to his guns, "I believe there is a connection."

"In theology, certainly," said Stalker. "In direct application to the Blacklaw riot, no."

"Well . . ." Laird was confused.

"You are acquainted with the accused?" Stalker asked.

"I do not know him well."

"He was a member of your Sunday School class for ten years, yet you do not know him well? Have you formed no opinion of his character—his character, sir—in that ten years' period."

"Of course, I . . ."

"What was your impression of the boy, the youth?"

"Ordinary. Intelligent."

"Given to violence?" Stalker snapped. "A bully?"

"I cannot say . . ."

"Yes, or no, please."

"No."

"Ordinary, yet with a mind of his own?" Drew said. "Now, apart from the Church, what, would you say, Reverend Laird, is the main influence upon a growing lad?"

"Companions."

"More important, perhaps, than companions."

"Ah, you mean the home background?"

"I do sir. Would you, as an experienced pastor, concur with that belief?"

"Indeed, indeed, I would."

"Now, Minister, you have informed the court that you do

296

not know Neill Stalker very well, that he is not currently a member of your congregation. On the other hand, I think that you do know his parents well, and have known them for the whole period of your tenure of the Blacklaw kirk. Am I correct?"

"His parents?" said Laird.

Drew was prepared. He side-stepped, saying, "His parental guardians, Mr. and Mrs. William Kellock."

"I know them."

"What is your opinion of them?"

"They are," Laird hesitated. "They are honest hard-working people."

"God-fearing?"

"Without doubt."

"Christians?"

"Certainly."

"And yet they produce a cold-blooded murderer—or so the learned counsellor for the Crown would imply."

"It is not unknown," Laird said.

"It is not my place to argue with you, Minister," Drew said, mildly. "Nor is it my intention to follow the Crown lead and explore the character of the accused within a frame of reference so broad as to be worthless. Since you are here, however, and since Mr. Mellish has already treated us, by proxy, to a lesson in Scripture, might I ask you to quote for the court the first few verses of the sixth chapter of the first epistle of Paul the Apostle to Timothy?"

"First Timothy, six?" Reverend Laird turned his eyes to the ceiling or beyond, as if in search of Divine guidance. At length, he said, "Off-hand, sir, I cannot quote those particular verses verbatim."

"We must have it verbatim," Stalker said. "If you will allow me—'Let as many servants as are under the yoke count their own masters worthy of all honour, that the name of God and *His* doctrine be not blasphemed'."

Lofty on the bench, McSherry put his palm to his mouth and coughed, covering his smile. He could have quoted the whole Scriptural passage, if required.

Stalker went on, his voice strong, "'And they that have believing masters, let them not despise them, because they are brethren; but rather do them service, because they are faithful and beloved, partakers of the benefit. These things teach and exhort'."

The Minister dipped his head in agreement. But Advocate Stalker wasn't finished. He completed the quotation in a crackling tone. "'If any man teach otherwise and consent not to wholesome words, even the words of our Lord Jesus Christ, and to the doctrine which is according to godliness, he is proud, knowing nothing, but doting about questions and strifes of words, whereof cometh envy, strife, railings, evil surmises, perverse disputations of men of corrupt minds, and destitute of the truth, supposing that gain is godliness: from such withdraw thyself'."

"Sir, I hope that you do not imply . . ." Laird blustered.

Drew cut him short. "*I imply nothing*. I am not in the business of implication." He wheeled away. "Thank you, Reverend Laird."

Then, before Lauder or Mellish could raise an objection or question the relevance of the question, Drew whirled round again. "What is the name of your Session Clerk?"

"David Dunlop," Laird answered, automatically.

"What is his employment?"

"Manager in Blacklaw pit."

"Ah, yes," Drew said.

He returned to the counsels' table without another word, leaving the fifteen good men of the jury wondering what the devil that final question signified.

*   *   *

Next to the stand, the Crown summoned three members of the Hamilton Constabulary. In turn, each policeman recounted the background to the riot from an official point of view, said a few—rather maudlin—words about Constable Ronald's devotion to duty, identified the hammer, identified the accused as the thrower of the hammer, gave the opinion that the act of throwing had been deliberate, and, on a large white card on a painter's easel that Lauder had brought into court, assisted a court artist to compose an accurate map of the Blacklaw Colliery Company's home pit. All just show: the plan was moderately useful but it could easily have been prepared before the commencement of the trial. Still leading the prosecution's interrogation, Mellish did not invite detail as to the accused's precise actions. Again, he preferred broad effect.

Drew left the coppers strictly alone. He knew the breed, knew that they would retract little and change even less. They felt the full weight of justice on their side, and the shadow of their dead pal hovering, like an avenging angel, nearby. No, Drew did not want to cross-examine such dour, adamant and prejudiced men. He let them, all three, leave the box unchallenged.

But the Police Surgeon, Dr. Nicholson, was a different type. On the conclusion of the surgeon's dry and factual evidence— he stated that the hammer caused the fatal blow to Constable Ronald's skull—Advocate Stalker got once more to his feet. Walking round the long cloth-draped table on which the items of evidence were laid out, for a full minute he said nothing.

"Do you wish to cross-examine this witness, Mr. Stalker?" McSherry asked testily.

Drew did not answer the judge. By now he had circum-navigated the table and gravitated towards the witness box. He was frowning, looking down at the floor, frowning. He leaned his left elbow on the rail of the box and brought his head round slowly to look straight into the dessicated features of Police Surgeon Nicholson who, in spite of himself, blinked behind his glasses.

"I see no skull," the Advocate declared.

"Skull?"

"Taken from the cadaver of the deceased?"

"I was not asked to remove the skull."

"You did not consider it necessary?"

"The cause of death was clear. Haematoma of the cranial . . ."

The Advocate interrupted. "Your evidence has been perfectly lucid, Doctor. I do not wish to impugn the medical facts that you have given us."

Nicholson relaxed.

"But," said Stalker, "I ask again, where is the skull?"

Lauder got slowly to his feet. Nicholson had glanced over at him, puzzled.

"Learned counsel for the panel knew that the skull had not been listed as evidence, m'lord," Lauder said, lazily. "If he had wished it, he might have requested it through an exhumation order."

"That is correct, Mr. Stalker," McSherry endorsed. "Let us hear no more of the skull, unless it is, in some manner, pertinent to your defence. Is it?"

"Not the skull, m'lord, but the *reason* behind the *absence* of the skull; the reason why no detailed post mortem examination was made in the hours after death. Such is the practice in all cases of murder, and the agreement of the next-of-kin is not required. Why was no dissection made in this particular instance?"

"I . . . I did not deem it necessary," said Nicholson.

"Oh, *you* did not deem it necessary, Doctor."

"I received no request from the authorities."

"So, *they* did not deem it necessary."

McSherry said, "What is your point, Mr. Stalker?"

"My point, m'lord, is that certain assumptions were already, even at that early stage, gaining credence and official endorsement."

Sanctioned by the bench, Nicholson told counsel, "I am in absolutely no doubt whatsoever, sir, that the blow which killed Constable Ronald was delivered by the hammer on the table."

"Not another like it?"

"Really, sir," Nicholson blustered in exasperation.

"You say that the blow killed the deceased?"

"Instantly."

"You are on oath, Doctor."

"*Instantly*, I say, and *instantly* I mean, sir. I am sufficiently experienced to recognise a lethal head wound when I see one."

"That is not in question."

"What *is* in question?" the Lord Justice-Clerk demanded.

"What is in question, m'lord, is the reason why no post mortem examination was called for or, indeed, made."

"Counsellor Stalker . . ." McSherry began.

Drew went on, "Was it, then, such a *clear* case of murder, of premeditated assault upon the person of the Special Constable, that no evidence was needed?"

"Put your questions to the witness, Advocate, do not harangue the jury, or the bench," McSherry said.

"Doctor," said Drew, "when does murder become murder?"

"I am no lawyer."

"You are a medical expert who has served the authorities for twenty years. You have written learned papers on evidence, in medical journals, you . . ."

"It would be simpler to answer the question, Doctor," McSherry said.

"At the moment of death," Nicholson said.

"Murder becomes murder at the moment of death of the victim?"

"It does."

"But, Doctor, there are occasions when the discovery of murder is delayed, often much delayed. Is that not correct?"

"That is correct."

"Under what circumstances?"

Nicholson puffed out his lower lip and wagged his hand as if to say that they were too numerous to itemise.

"One or two will do," Drew prompted.

"Delay in discovering the body."

"And another?"

"Uncertainty as to the extent of the violence done to the victim—as in certain instances of poisoning."

"There was no delay in discovering the body of Constable Ronald?"

"Of course not."

"In realising that his death had been caused by a violent blow to the head?"

"No."

"In acquiring the weapon?"

"It was there on the . . ."

"In pouncing on the alleged murderer?"

"That was not my . . ."

"We have heard that from the three police witnesses who have just been in the box."

"*Mister* Stalker." McSherry beckoned.

Calmly, Drew approached the bench. Drawing his red robes over his shoulders so that they appeared like the wrinkled skin of a strange par-boiled animal, the judge leaned down. "Advocate Stalker, I am dismayed that a man of your experience and repute should badger not only a witness but, by reflection, disgrace the dignity of this court. If it does not cease forthwith, I will be obliged to reprimand you."

"M'lord, I apologise for offending the dignity of the court," said Drew, *sotto voce*. "But the issues in this case are not clear."

"They seem perfectly clear to me."

"I am afraid, m'lord, that they will seem much less so before many more of the Crown's witnesses have passed through the witness-box."

"What do you mean?"

"If you will indulge me," Drew said, "I will not dwell much longer on such . . . soggy ground."

Scowling, McSherry told him, "See to it that you don't, or I will exercise my power to have you censured."

Returning to his stance by the witness box, Drew paused then, cheerfully, said, "Now, Doctor Nicholson, it seems that we have a dead man, a weapon, and a person apprehended by the police. When did you examine him?"

"Some twenty-five minutes after death. I was summoned directly from my home, which is on the Blacklaw side of Hamilton."

"A fortuitous circumstance," said Drew. "But you misunderstand me. I have not made myself clear, I see. When did you examine the *accused*?"

Nicholson blinked. "I did not examine the accused."

"Ah!"

"The accused was in custody. I was not called upon, in my capacity as Police Surgeon, to attend him."

"So it was not you who dressed Neill Stalker's wounds?"

"I . . . no."

"And you are unable to give expert medical opinion as to whether or not the wounds sustained by the accused were caused by the same or a similar weapon as that which struck down and killed Constable Ronald?"

"I am . . . No."

"In your capacity as Police Surgeon, Doctor Nicholson, it

would seem that your services were not wholly exercised on the day in question. When did you draft your report?"

"Later that evening."

"It was a simple medical report, not the result of a post mortem examination as is commonly recognised."

"I thought I had made that clear."

"Not quite, Doctor."

"It was a post mortem report, though I did not conduct an internal examination of the deceased by dissection."

"You are sufficiently expert to categorically state that a hammer blow was the cause of the constable's death?"

"I am. And I do."

"But you cannot categorically state whether the wounds received by the accused were caused by the same hammer?"

"As I told you, sir, *I did not examine the accused.*"

"We have, then, Doctor, a causal relationship between the deceased and the hammer?"

"If you mean it killed him, yes."

"But the hammer did *not* kill him; a hammer is a block of iron and a length of wood. It has no volition of its own."

"Really! a *blow* from the hammer is what I meant; *that* is the causal relationship."

"Yet no such causal relationship exists between the hammer and the accused?"

"Medically-speaking, I cannot answer that."

"If I told you that the fatal blow to Constable Ronald had been caused by a stone, would you believe me?"

"No, I would not."

"No doubt, you can prove otherwise—indeed, have proved otherwise—by medical evidence based on examination of the body?"

"Yes."

"Would it not then have seemed reasonable to you, Doctor Nicholson, as a man versed in the processes of the law in relation to murder, to have examined also the accused in an endeavour to complete the triangle?"

"Triangle?"

"Relating the deceased, the accused and the weapon."

"It is not for me to say."

"I ask you only, if it would have been reasonable so to do?"

"Yes, it would have been reasonable. But . . ."

"But it was not done?"

"No."

"Thank you, Doctor Nicholson."

★　　★　　★

The final witness of the morning's session was one Brendan Rahilly who described himself as a trained winding gear operator presently employed as a casual labourer. Skilfully, Patrick Lauder steered Rahilly through his evidence. The labourer was articulate and made positive statements. He wore a tweed suit, had a tie in his clean collar and his hair had been trimmed for the occasion.

Though the fact was not made known, Rahilly had received a certain sum of money in lieu of wages lost by his agreement to travel to Edinburgh and appear for the Crown. The sum had been paid over to him in The Nettle public house in Leith by a man he had never seen before or since. Guided by Lauder, Rahilly provided the court with the first coherent account of the advent of the blacklegs—for that, of course, is what Rahilly was. He told of his employment by an agent acting on behalf of Houston Lamont through an exchange in Glasgow, the marshalling of the 'casual labour force' and the ride to Blacklaw by train. He told of an orderly march to the pit, and a stormy reception by furious colliers. He explained how casual labourers who, he admitted, were not unused to such manoeuvres, made directly for the 'small gate' to get themselves into the safety of the pit enclosure. There being no manager present, and the matter being of some urgency, tools were used to effect an entry through the small door.

"Why did you not wait the arrival of a manager with a key?" asked Lauder.

"It was too dangerous, sir. The miners was in an ugly mood."

"You might have considered retreat to a near-by field, might you not?"

Rahilly shook his head. "Best t'get on wit'it, that's the motto. If we'd hung about in the vicinity, it would've been all the worst when it came t'it, sir."

"All the worse?" asked McSherry.

"Ay, sir, we came peaceable, but we came quick. If we'd have waited, the miners would've gathered a big force, an' we're not ones for the fightin'. We wanted int' the pit, that's how it was, t'be gettin' on wit' our work an' earn our wages."

"What happened next, Mr. Rahilly?" Lauder prompted.

Rahilly unfolded a story of a fight at the pit-gate, spoke of the accused's part in it, and the throwing of the hammer at the constable. Carefully, Lauder shored up the blackleg's evidence by astute questions, forestalling obvious points of attack by defence counsel.

No, Rahilly and his companions bore no animosity towards the miners; had they not been miners themselves once, living ordered lives in towns like Blacklaw until hard times caught up with them? Had he himself not a wife and five children back in Sligo, living on his father's homestead, and did he not send them money regular? Sure, and it was hard for colliers. He and his mates had every sympathy with them and what they were striking for. But he did not believe that a man should stop another man from working, if that was what he chose to do. Though he missed his homeland, his wife and his babes, it was the price he paid to put bread in their mouths, sir. He did not regret it, because it was his choice. Having thus established that Rahilly was no scoundrel but a man enterprising enough to support his family—by analogy, stamping all blacklegs as decent, creditable folk—Lauder led back to the crux of the labourer's evidence.

"Now, Mr. Rahilly, once more, I would be grateful if you would tell the court precisely what you saw and what you did a few minutes before the Special Constable met with his death."

"Sure, sir, an' it was just like I said. I was breaking the lock on the sma' door o'the pit-gate, where we saw on the plan there, when up comes the young chap, him there in the dock, an' leaps on me back."

"Did you retaliate? Think carefully before you answer."

"I did retaliate, sir. He was fightin' mad an' not like t'be calmed down just be talkin' t'him. He gript the hammer I was usin' at the time an' pult it off me like he was goin' t'hit me wit' it."

"But he didn't hit you with it?"

"No, sir. We had a bit o' a scuffle, like, nothin' fierce, though. An' he pusht me down . . ."

"Pushed, not punched?"

"Just a push, like, an' a trip wit' the feet. I wasn't for puttin' up me fists wit' him, I can tell ye, sir. I fell on the ground."

"And then, Mr. Rahilly?"

"The lad . . ."

"The accused, you mean?"

"Ay, the accused, he came like t'close wit' me again, but, just then, the Specials came runnin' up an' he turnt towards them instead."

"He turned towards them?"

"He did that, sir."

"Go on, please."

"I was sittin' just by him on the ground. He had the hammer . . ."

"The hammer you had been using on the small door?"

"The same; he swung it an' flung it an' it struck the young cop . . . constable on the side o'the head, a glancin' blow, y'might say."

"He turned, and he *saw* the policeman approaching; he aimed, he drew back his arm, and he *deliberately* threw the ten-pound short sledge hammer—that one there on the table—at the constable."

"He did."

"The weapon, in consequence of being thrown by the accused, forthwith struck the constable on the head?"

"That's correct, sir."

"How far away from the constable was the accused?"

"Well, the constables was approachin' fast, but when the accused let the hammer go, like, it would be no more'n four yards."

"Twelve feet. Is it, in your experience, possible to throw a short sledge hammer that distance with accuracy."

"It's an easy matter. I've enjoined in competitions, sir, for the throwin' o'the short sledge when men have hit the mark at twenty *yards*."

"I see. I take it, Mr. Rahilly, that this contest was not

between Irish giants?" The question raised some laughter. "But between ordinary mortals, like you, or I, or the accused?"

"Just ordinary fellahs, sir."

"And then, Mr. Rahilly, the constable fell to the ground and did not move again; is that correct?"

"That's correct, sir."

Shortly thereafter, Lauder yielded up his witness to cross-examination, but the Lord Justice-Clerk called the lunch recess and the court was adjourned until two o'clock.

Drew avoided his relatives. Only Betsy was likely to be brash enough to try to break into the inner circle to speak with him. Drew ate in the little 'club' round the corner from the court, making sure that he had a corner table and that he and Frank Kinnemouth were undisturbed. They talked strategy between mouthfuls, did not imbibe wine or any liquid containing alcohol and were back in ample time for the court's re-call.

To the spectators' surprise, Frank Kinnemouth conducted the cross-examination of Brendan Rahilly, and did not, in any way at all, press the witness or cast doubts upon his testimony.

In all, Kinnemouth asked Rahilly fourteen quiet questions. The answers seemed only to confirm the prosecution's assertion that Neill Stalker had, with malice and knowledge of consequence, hurled the hammer at the copper.

Kinnemouth concluded, "Did you, Mr. Rahilly, in the course of your struggle against the small door of the pit-gate, consciously strike the accused with your fist?"

"I did not, sir. Maybe wit' me arm or the flat o'me hand, but not wit' a closed fist, sir."

"Did you strike him with the hammer?"

"That I did not."

"You did wrestle for the hammer, however?"

"Only for a second'r two."

"Fiercely?"

"Pullin' an' tuggin', like."

"You did not wish to relinquish the hammer to the accused?"

"'Twas me own hammer, sir."

"I see. The accused was not then injured by you?"

"Not t'me knowledge, sir."

Rahilly was excused but, at Advocate Stalker's request, was

asked to remain in court against the necessity of his being required for further examination.

There followed, in sequence, Alfred Muir, Frederick Walsh, and a distinguished, well-spoken Irishman, Patrick John O'Shea. Each of the three gave an almost identical account to Rahilly's. All that emerged from their evidence was that the accused was one of only three 'real fiery' assailants. It was admitted that the other two 'real fiery' colliers had been knocked down, mainly for their own good and to protect the safety of the casual labourers. The fist-fighting that had been taking place on the periphery was, said the blacklegs, 'not serious'.

Drew let the first two labourers go without cross-examining. However, when Patrick John O'Shea had delivered himself of his sworn testimony, Drew got to his feet and, wrapping his robes about him like a bat's wings, walked straight to a spot below the box and, looking directly at the tall, silver-haired Celt, plunged into a crossfire of question and rapid reply.

"How long have you been a casual labourer, Mr. O'Shea?"

"Nigh-on thirty years."

"Do you find the work rewarding?"

"I do, sir."

"Do you enjoy it?"

"I do, sir."

"You are not just a 'casual labourer', are you, Mr. O'Shea?"

"I have trainin' in many trades, most o'them connected wit' minin'."

"You are a foreman, a 'ganger' as I believe it's called, are you not?"

"I am."

"It is part of your function to organise the labour forces that are employed to run mines and pits that, for one reason or another, have no employed work-force?"

"That is true, but it is not allers a pit or a mine, no, nor a works that ha'n't got an employed force."

"How many strike-bound pits have you worked in during the last three years?"

"Three or four."

"Come now, Mr. O'Shea! You are no mere 'thick-ear', are you? You have told us that you are a foreman. I cannot believe

that you do not know *exactly* how many strike-bound pits you
have worked in the past three years."

O'Shea did not blink. "Eight."

"Oh."

"Maybe nine, it was."

"Or perhaps twenty, or twenty-three. Is it true, Mr. O'Shea,
that you have not been employed as a foreman of casual labour
in anything other than a strike-bound pit or mine in the course
of the last three years?"

"That isn't true."

"Very well: a strike-bound pit, mine or mill."

O'Shea hesitated long enough for McSherry to prod him.
"Answer the question, Mr. O'Shea."

"In the last three years, no."

"You have not managed a crew or gang of casual labourers
employed in anything other than a strike-bound pit, mine or
mill? Answer me with a yes or a no."

"I have not," said O'Shea, wilfully.

"In addition to acting in the capacity of foreman to casual
labour forces, Mr. O'Shea, are you not also in large part
responsible for recruiting the casual labour required by the
owners of pits, mines and mills?"

"I know . . . many o' the boys, sir."

"Are you, Mr. O'Shea, a recruiter?"

"I have helped out managers, aye."

"*Are you a recruiter?*"

"Aye."

Over by the prosecution's table, Mellish leaned across and
murmured to Lauder. But Lauder knew better than to lodge
an objection which, at this stage, would only draw the jury's
attention to the importance of Stalker's questioning.

Drew said, "How many men were you asked to furnish for
'casual work' at the Blacklaw pits?"

"Eighty."

"Can a large pit be effectively operated by eighty 'casual
labourers'?"

"Most o' the men I recruit are colliery trained."

"Answer my question."

"Blacklaw pit can be opened wit' eighty men."

"I said, can it be *operated effectively*?"

"T'full capacity, no."

"Was it not, later in the week of July fifteenth, part of your function as a recruiter to find another three hundred men for the same employer?"

O'Shea turned to the judge. He seemed calm enough but his cheeks were flushed. "M'lord, d'I have t'reveal these facts? Part o'me job is discretion."

"You are under oath, Mr. O'Shea," McSherry told him. "Besides, I feel that the answer is quite relevant."

"I was asked t'find more men."

"How many?"

"Three hundred."

"Is that not an inordinately large number?"

"More'n usual, ay."

"But you found them?"

"I did what I could."

"And these 'casual labourers' were employed in the pits belonging to Blacklaw colliery?"

"They were."

"At great cost?"

"Fair wages, I'd call it."

"Hm," said Drew. "Who employed you?"

"I . . . I don't know his name."

"I think that you do."

"Mr. Sykes."

"Mr. Sykes: who is Mr. Sykes?"

"A gen'leman I know in Glasgow."

"How long were you in prison in Porthcawl?"

"I was never . . ."

"I advise you to be careful, Mr. O'Shea," said the judge quickly.

"One year," O'Shea answered.

"I do not feel," said Lauder, loudly, "that the history of this witness is material, m'lord."

"No, no, let him answer that question," said McSherry. "I will stop counsel when materiality is infringed. Mr. O'Shea, may I ask what your offence was?"

"Is it obliged I am t'tell?"

"Perhaps not obliged," said McSherry sweetly, "but advised."

"Assault."

"Assault on a collier during a strike-breaking action in the Aberpeny pit," said Drew.

"No, counsel, that is enough," McSherry told him. "You need not answer that, Mr. O'Shea."

But O'Shea had already blurted out, "Self-defence, it was bloody self-defence."

Advocate Stalker walked away from the box to let the witness compose himself. He returned.

"Is Mr. Sykes an agent for the Blacklaw Colliery Company's owners?"

"He's an agent, that's all I know."

"Come now, Mr. O'Shea, you did not undertake to employ three hundred . . ."

"Eighty, it were only eighty at first."

"Very well, eighty men, for Mr. Sykes. I assume that Mr. Sykes does not own mineral lease rights, and does not operate a pit?"

"It was for the Blacklaw Company."

"At last, Mr. O'Shea. Now, what were your instructions?"

"T'find eighty casual labourers wit' pit experience."

"Small men, front-seam men?"

"That wasn't told t'me."

"So, what kind of men did you employ?"

"What I could find."

"Fighters, Mr. O'Shea, scrappers, bully-boys . . ."

"*Mr. Stalker, that is enough,*" McSherry called out.

"Yes, m'lord; I agree, that is enough."

At the defence table, Drew appeared to calm himself. He had not lost his temper, not one inch of it. But his performance was excellent and the difficulty with which he restored himself to control was equally impressive. Holding the robe tightly around him, as if to contain his wrath, he advanced once more on O'Shea.

"Eighty men, protected by a group of Special Constables from Hamilton, arrived at Claypark Halt railway station from

Glasgow, then *ran* the three miles to Blacklaw colliery. Is that correct?"

"We didn't exactly run."

"Mr. O'Shea," said Drew, "do you wish to put this court to the bother of calling five witnesses who saw your squad of labourers *running* along the Blacklaw road?"

"We allers move fast—t'save trouble."

"Yes, yes," Drew said. "And do you always travel armed? No, I retract that question, with apologies, Mr. O'Shea. Let me ask you instead, do you always travel with your tools—your axe-handles, your sledge hammers, your long, lead-weighted clubs?"

"Implements o'our trade."

"Very useful, no doubt," said Drew then, abruptly, dismissed the man. "I have no further questions."

As a forerunner to the following morning's 'clinchers', the Crown next introduced two Blacklaw colliers. The trial stiffened its spine.

The colliers were not known to Drew. He could not even recall having heard their names. Edward had informed him that neither man had been long in Lamont's employ. In turn each spoke of the hardships of the miner's life, enumerated the number of his children and then, flicked across the pool like trout that have exhausted themselves in the current, Lauder landed each neatly enough by extracting an admission that the Blacklaw Company was fairly generous to its employees, that the tied houses were kept in good repair by the owners and that the 'darg', the day's pay, was higher than in other fields.

"But you still felt that there was reason to strike?"

"No, sir, if it had been left 'me, I would not've done so."

"Why then *did* you strike?"

"Everybody was doin' it."

"I see, you simply followed the flock."

"Aye, sir."

"Who led this flock?"

"The Union's representatives told us it was good for us."

"Naturally, you trusted the advice of these men, even against your better judgment and personal inclinations?"

"Aye, sir."

"Do you feel that you have gained benefit from the strike action?"

"No, sir."

"If the United Federation of Miners called another strike action tomorrow, would you withhold your labour again?"

"I would not, sir."

"Oh, why not?"

"Somebody else might get killed."

It was late afternoon before Lauder extracted the last of the evidence from his 'tame' colliers. Lights in the courtroom had been lit, making the gilt bright, bringing out the rich royal blues and reds, but also emphasising the shadows in the arches of the roofs and, by accenting the dark windows, made the proceedings seem ominous. The jurors had become restless. Drew's examination of the colliers was close to being perfunctory. He did not probe into the motivations. He did not question the colliers' accounts of the riot or the murder and, at five-fifteen o'clock, dismissed the second of the pair and allowed the Lord Justice-Clerk to adjourn the court until the following morning.

★   ★   ★

Kate refused to accept Betsy's invitation to dinner at the McAlmond house. She excused herself by saying that she was very tired. Not that Betsy minded. On the contrary, she was considerably relieved not to have to entertain her stern, grief-ridden and reproving eldest sister. All in all the family dinner party had been foisted upon her by Fraser's sense of 'the done thing'. She was happy enough to have it fizzle out.

When it came to it, the Stalkers did not seem in the least inclined to seek solace in each other's company that night. After visiting Neill, Kate and Willie returned to their boarding house and retired to bed before nine. Mirrin too went to bed early and only Drew was left up late to engage in lacklustre conversation with his cohorts—Daniel, Fraser, and Balfour Sprott.

"It does not appear to be going too badly, Andrew." Sprott said, for the umpteenth time, as if seeking reassurance that his impression of the trial was accurate.

"Not well, though, Balfour," said Fraser.

Horn said, "It's the colliers' evidence that was damagin'."

Seated in the big chair in his chambers, sipping port, Drew grunted. "Tomorrow Lauder will present more of the same."

"When will he finish?" Fraser asked.

"I would think by lunch," said Drew

"It will be possible to refute much of the Crown evidence when you bring on your witnesses, will it not?" Balfour Sprott asked.

"I trust so," said Drew.

Horn said, "It strikes me that Lauder doesn't have near enough for a conviction o'murder."

"He will go for manslaughter," said Fraser. "In his address to the jury I'm sure he will press more strongly for the lesser charge, thereby absolving the jurors from hanging such a young man."

"And making the Crown appear inclined to clemency," said Drew. "Yes, that's what he'll do."

"Manslaughter," said Balfour. "That's not so bad. What'll old McSherry dish out for manslaughter?"

"One never knows with McSherry," said Drew. "I have the impression that he does not approve of Lauder any more than he approves of me."

"It might," said Fraser, "be worth the risk."

"Risk?"

"Appealing for a lesser conviction."

Drew sat upright and glared at his brother-in-law. "I will not compromise, Fraser."

"You may antagonise McSherry by your inflexibility," said Balfour. "It may go worse with the boy."

"I intend to have him acquitted," said Drew. "All along, gentlemen, I've intended that thing and no other."

"But d'you have the strength of evidence, Drew?" said Horn, who did not believe that he did. "D'you have the kind o'witnesses who'll refute those eye-witnesses who say they saw the lad aim and throw the hammer?"

"It isn't refutation that will win the day," said Drew. "It is my ability to convince the court that Neill is innocent of a larger crime."

"Larger crime than murder?" said Balfour Sprott.

"The crime of ingratitude," said Drew.

"Good Lord," said Fraser. "How perceptive of you, Andrew. Ingratitude! Of course, they might find him guilty for sheer ingratitude to his employer."

"For darin' t'bite the hand that fed him," said Horn. "Aye, I've seen long jail sentences handed out for less."

"It is not how the jury will balance the evidence, but how they will react emotionally to the idea of allowing a young buck to challenge the established order of things," said Drew. "The death of that poor Special Constable—who, remember, was doing it for extra payment—is by way of being a side issue."

"Not in law," said Fraser.

"No, not in law, but in judgment. The jury will hand down a verdict of guilty on the lesser charge of manslaughter. McSherry will direct them towards that decision with his usual thoroughness—then he, McSherry, will slap a sentence of ten years or more on Neill just to prove that servants must know their places."

"Feudal! God, how feudal!" said Balfour. "I am glad that our business has little or nothing to do with criminals."

"You prefer property to human lives?" said Drew. "Yes, you have always confused the value of one over the other, Balfour, ever since we were at college together. It is the harlot mentality."

"I'm not sure I like that remark," said Balfour.

"And who am I to talk of the harlot mentality?" said Drew, rising. "You have my apology, Balfour. I am a trifle tired."

Solicitously, the three friends left the Advocate soon after and Drew, alone in his chambers, went to his deed box behind the bookcases and took out the papers that, if he dared use them, would give him victory.

*　　*　　*

On Wednesday, the case against Neill Campbell Stalker swung in favour of the Crown. The evidence was not particularly sensational. There were no incredible revelations, no major surprises. Aided by Mellish, Lauder was at his trickiest. The jury were clearly impressed and thoroughly out of sympathy with the accused's motives. The colliers clinched it, a parade of men just like the accused, a balanced, harmonious quartet who gave evidence that, except in manner of delivery, was so 'pat', so neatly dovetailed that any lawyer worth his salt could see that they had been coached. The Lord Justice-Clerk was far too downy a bird to be taken in. He made a note to advise the jury not to put too much weight on the colliers' unanimous agreement that Neill Campbell Stalker had deliberately thrown the hammer at the policeman *before* the policeman had reached him.

All hope of proving a defence of direct provocation was gone. Only the more subtle issue of indirect provocation remained. But Drew was leery of trying to bring it out in case he got into a political debate that—if McSherry allowed it— would simply alienate the jury further. Part of the problem lay in the youth of the accused. He had none of the charismatic mystery that shrouded many murderers and gave the jury members a focal point for their impressions. This role the Advocates in the case fulfilled. Drew was aware that Lauder had it over him in that respect.

He allowed Kinnemouth to cross-examine the morning's first witnesses and, as he had suspected, found them adamant. Lamont—or was it Thrush—had chosen well.

Then Dunlop was brought to the stand.

With pompous virtue, Dunlop told his version of the events of that morning, how he had seen, from a vantage point in a tenement close-mouth only thirty yards from the scene, the whole sorry business, including the accused acting "like a ravin' madman".

Lauder corrected him. "You do not mean that he was not in full possession of his mental faculties, Mr. Dunlop?"

"What? Oh, no, no. He knew what he was doin', sir. It was just . . . just a . . . ."

"Common figure of speech?" McSherry suggested.

"That's right, your worship."

"But he was angry?" said Lauder.

"Very angry."

"Did you see the accused being struck?"

"I did not, apart, maybe, from a few . . . er, light blows durin' his scuffle with the man at the gate."

"To gain possession of the hammer?"

"That's right."

"Did he see the policemen coming?"

"He could hardly have missed them."

"Are you sure that the accused was fully aware of the arrival of the Special Constables?"

"He looked at them."

"You saw him look at them?"

"I did."

"*Before* he threw the hammer?"

"Yes, sir."

When Drew took over the witness, he did not allow him to escape unscathed. He knew Dunlop of old, and Dunlop knew him. Oddly, there was no fear in the manager, rather scorn for the Advocate as if he suspected that Drew was out of his depth here, was a charlatan, and that he, Dunlop, was still more important. After all *he* was a pit manager and Stalker was only the son of a dirty face-worker; nothing could change that.

In spite of his slyness, Dunlop was stupid, but Drew, by omission, failed to prepare the correct atmosphere for the demolition of Dunlop's credibility, and soon found himself reduced to carping on minor points; that cut no ice at all with jury, or judge. Mellish smiled fatuously. It was tempting at that moment to throw away the pop-guns of civility and discretion and roll out the cannon that would blow Dunlop and all the rest of them away.

Floundering, Drew bit his lip and fought the temptation.

Even at that point, he had decided what he must do. He would save Dunlop for tomorrow.

Only a handful of his questions made Dunlop stutter and flush a little.

"When were you approached by the police to give testimony as an eye-witness, Mr. Dunlop?"

"I . . . what? I was asked that night; aye, that night."

"You were asked; you did not volunteer the information you had in your possession?"

"I didn't know that the boy had been charged."

Drew raised an eyebrow. "You did not know? Yet you had seen him commit what appeared to be a deliberately violent act, had—according to your evidence—seen him throw a heavy weapon at Constable Ronald, and knew, very soon after, that Constable Ronald was dead. Is that not so?"

"Aye, but . . ."

"You had also seen Neill Campbell Stalker apprehended, had you not?"

"Aye."

"*Only* Neill Campbell Stalker—no other arrests were made?"

"I never saw any."

"Yet you did not volunteer information?"

For some reason, McSherry intervened. "Perhaps, Mr. Dunlop was not aware of the procedure for giving a statement to the police."

"I was just about t'say that, your worship," said Dunlop, with relief.

"What did you do *after* the riot?" Drew asked.

"I . . . I talked t'friends for a while, then went down t'my daughter's house an'had my dinner."

"Had your dinner?"

"I was hungry."

"Quite. You had your dinner before you reported to Mr. Thrush?"

"I . . . I did not report t' Mr. Thrush."

"To Mr. Lamont then?"

"I didn't . . . well, I did later. I mean, I was the manager on the spot."

"After you spoke to Mr. Lamont, you gave a statement to the police in Hamilton?"

"I can't . . ."

"Oh, that *is* the order of things, Mr. Dunlop. I have the logged entry of the time of your arrival—unasked—at Hamilton Police Station, and a copy of your statement."

"Well, in that case, aye, that's what happened."

"Now, Mr. Dunlop, you watched the whole incident, from the first appearance of the casual labour force, from the close-mouth of a tenement some thirty yards from the pit gate?"

"Aye."

"Did you know beforehand that a casual labour force had been hired to enter and operate Blacklaw pit?"

"No, I did not."

"According to previous testimony, that of Mr. Rahilly and Mr. O'Shea, there were no managers present during the riot. Yet, it transpires, *you* were in a close-mouth a mere thirty yards away."

"There was nothin' I could do."

"You could have opened the small gate, thus saving damage to the property. Why did you not go forward and open the gate?"

"I . . . I didn't have a key on me."

"To my recollection, you live only three or four minutes walk from the pit-gate. Did you not have a key at home?"

"Aye."

"Surely you could have gone home and returned with the small-gate key?"

"I never thought."

"You never thought. Not even when the labourers attacked the gate to smash it down with a sledge hammer?"

"It all happened so quick."

"Too quickly for your reason to function, Mr. Dunlop, but not, it seems, for powers of observation so acute that you noted every detail of the 'quick' events that took place."

"I didn't go for the key," said Dunlop, "'cause I'd no intention o'breakin' the picket line. Managers aren't pop'lar in time o'strike."

"Understandably. However, the picket line was broken by that time, and the pit was about to . . ."

McSherry intervened again. "I think we have heard enough of that, Advocate. The witness is not a young man and I feel that he was perhaps prudent to keep away."

"Thank you, m'lord," said Drew, with a trace of irony.

Soon after he let Dunlop go.

The last witness for the prosecution's case was David Henderson, collier, of Blacklaw, an exact contemporary of Andrew Stalker, advocate, of Edinburgh. They had shared the same schoolroom where Henderson had been a bully, and Drew one of his victims. For all that, Drew felt a pang of sympathy, almost of remorse, when Henderson walked down the aisle into the witness box. The man was stooped and worn, stretched as if a fist had kneaded his body like dry clay and then knuckled him impatiently down: back injury, or rheumatism, Drew thought, against which Henderson struggled to hew his quota of coal from the deep seams, in pain or discomfort. The whole of the man's history was in his face, in the sullen glowering half-afraid eyes. There was no fight in Henderson now, only despair and bitterness accumulated from too many defeats. It was to Drew, at the defence table, that Henderson gave attention while he took the oath, glowering from under thatched brows, surly and unsure of himself—if not his purpose—in this majesterial setting.

To cap his case, to spike the testimony of Stalker's witnesses in advance, Lauder extracted from the stumbling, mumbling Henderson the background story of the strike in Blacklaw. Cleverly, Lauder portrayed the collier as a victim of a movement that he did not understand and that involved him in a cause of which he did not approve. Principles were less important than bread, Henderson seemed to say, not by his statements but by his very presence in court. His truculence and uncertainty were assets. He was a primitive figure, archetype of the miner, the kind of man too close to the earth to bear responsibility for himself. He needed food, a job, shelter. He needed to be looked after, to be freed from responsibility. He needed a boss and a system. A pit-lamp gave him light. A pick-axe gave him bread. The coalmaster painted his house for him and kept it warm and watertight. That, so Lauder implied, was all this man required from life. The power-hungry troublemakers of the U.F.M. should not be allowed to use him like a sacrificial goat.

Much—almost all—of Lauder's score was implicit, but the effect was plain enough. He mightily impressed the jury. Here was a man born only to work, a man too simple to lie. Henderson gave his evidence in a language, unfamiliar to the jury. With patience and no condescension, Lauder translated for them, coaxing from Henderson a clear account of what had happened that morning in Blacklaw, an account of the revenge of a thwarted self-seeking upstart, and the doing of the act of murder.

When Lauder finished, it was almost one o'clock and the Lord Justice-Clerk was anxious to be off for lunch.

"We will, I think, hold the witness for cross-examination until after recess," McSherry said to Advocate Stalker, already gathering his papers and rising.

Drew got to his feet.

"M'lord," he called, causing McSherry to stop half-risen and give him attention. Murmurous sounds in the courtroom ceased. Those who had been pushing to get out of the public gallery pushed now to get back in.

"M'lord, with the court's permission," Drew said, "I do not wish to cross-examine this witness."

"The court's permission is not necessary," said the judge. "It is your right to waive examination, as you know."

"I do, however, wish the witness Henderson to be re-empanelled," said Drew, "and to be added to the list of witnesses to appear for the defence."

"He will be hostile, will he not?" asked McSherry.

"He will, sir."

The court was suddenly in uproar and Henderson, who had stepped down from the witness box, hovered by the advocates' table as if he might suddenly have to run to Lauder for protection.

Seeking to recall to mind the exact procedure, McSherry said, "This is a somewhat unusual request."

"It is, however, quite procedural," put in Advocate Kinnemouth, ready to cite chapter and verse.

"Yes, yes: quite procedural," said McSherry. "Will you require the witness Henderson to be called this afternoon?"

"Tomorrow morning," Drew said.

McSherry nodded, stooped and audibly told his clerk, "See that it is done."

So Henderson was taken off to be fed, and the court broke up to eat luncheon and prattle about what Stalker had up his sleeve.

*   *   *

What Advocate Stalker had up his sleeve he did not reveal. He was not to be found that lunch-hour, not by his twin sister or his relatives who, no less curious than the laity, had relaxed their attitude sufficiently to wish to speak with him. Not even Neill, as he ate beef and potatoes in a cell below the court-house, could imagine what possible use Mr. Stalker intended to make of Henderson, a man that Neill had long abhorred. He was still wondering when, at ten minutes to two-thirty, Mr. Stalker appeared in his cell, already robed and looking, so Neill imagined, determined.

"How are you?" Drew asked, brusquely.

"I'm fine. Sore wi' sittin', though."

"I have no doubt, Neill, that you are curious as to how I intend to conduct the defence portion of this trial?"

"I'll admit it," said Neill. "But y'seem t'be doin' fine, so far."

"I wish that were true," said Drew. "We have not the time to go into the fluctuations of the thing here and now. I want, however, to warn you, Neill, that, on this afternoon's showing, it may strike you that I am not the advocate that I am cracked up to be, and that my promise to have you acquitted was a groundless boast. I will not visit you tonight. We meet in court again tomorrow morning on what will be the final day of the trial and, for you, the day of the jury's decision."

"It seems, Mr. Stalker," said Drew, "that you're none too happy."

"As it stands, Neill, I would be less than honest if I said that, so far, Lauder has convinced the jury that you are guilty of murder. I will soften the effect of his case, of course, but, at best, he will have you for manslaughter."

"Am I t'prepare myself for prison?"

"Prepare yourself for release, Neill," Drew said. "I may be down, but, believe me, I am by no means out."

"About Henderson; what can you . . .?"

Drew put his fingers to his lips. "Sssshhh."

Obediently Neill said no more.

Still standing, Drew told the young man, "I have decided *not* to call you into the witness box."

"But I thought . . ."

"Ssshhh. If I put you in the box, Lauder, or Mellish, will reduce the benefit of your denial of malice and knowledge of consequence, by making you seem confused. Believe me, Neill, Lauder is quite capable of making you doubt your own evidence. Once you are *seen* to be confused then your denials will be thrown into doubt and you will begin to seem like a liar. I will not risk that."

"How else can I tell the jury it was an accident, that I never saw that policeman at all?"

"I will say it, or have it said," Drew explained. "So far, your relationship with me has been kept out of court. Mellish has made no attempt to attack us on that score. He holds it like a threat over me, however. Interestingly, the prosecution did not summon either Sydney Thrush or Houston Lamont to the stand. That is shrewd."

"Maybe they wouldn't come."

"If they were summoned to appear, under law they cannot refuse. No, they were not summoned. They have been kept out of it. Lauder and Mellish, no doubt after considerable discussion, have patently elected to rely on the evidence of working-class witnesses. If I had Lamont here, I might wring too much of the truth out of him. Lauder will not risk that. The fact that he has pleaded the Crown case in such a manner indicates to me the direction that his address will take. I must remove his props —not just a few of them; all of them. He will say to the jury that you must be judged on the actions of a single morning."

"An' what'll you say, Mr. Stalker?"

"I'll tell them the truth, that you are no more guilty than they are, that the guilty ones are not in the dock, nor even in court."

"I'm beginnin' to understand."

"I doubt that, young man," said Drew.

*   *   *

Police Sergeant Lewis, first witness for the defence, might have been classed as hostile. There was nothing contentious in Advocate Stalker's questions, however, and the Sergeant, however much he disapproved of being a defence aid in the case against the young villain, had no choice but to answer honestly and without prevarication.

By diligent questioning of Sergeant Lewis, Drew brought

into the court matters that had been skirted by the defence. Cautiously he built up facts on the process whereby the appointed officers of the law could be bought by private parties and obliged to protect gangs of men who were, at best, of suspect character. Close to the end Lauder wearily interjected an enquiry as to the relevance of such material, asking if Advocate Stalker intended to prove provocation. The question was relayed to counsel for the panel by the Lord Justice-Clerk who received the reply that Advocate Stalker did not intend to prove provocation. After a short, vigorous exchange between the counsels, McSherry instructed Stalker to continue with his witness.

Mellish cross-examined, but gained nothing.

The Sergeant's evidence, though seemingly dry, was instructive to the jury and grew important in the minds of these serious gentlemen as the afternoon progressed.

Second witness for the defence was a collier, sixty-one-year-old Matthew Bald. After stating that he had been employed in Blacklaw colliery for forty-seven years, Bald placed himself in the picket-line on the morning of July 18th. He told an energetic tale of watching the 'blacklegs'—he was corrected at once by counsel—storming round the corner.

"And then what happened, Mr. Bald?"

"I got m'arm broke."

"In what circumstances?"

"I got hit wi' a club."

"While you were trying to prevent the casual labourers reaching the gate."

"Naw, naw. I knew I was far too auld for fightin', but I couldn't get out the road fast enough."

"One of the labourers struck you with a club?"

"Aye, an' broke m'arm."

"Did nobody else see this occurrence?"

"Aye, they all bloody saw it."

"Mr. Bald," McSherry warned, mildly.

"Who saw it, do you know?" Drew asked.

"Henderson was right by me when it happened. Christ, he picked me up."

A groundswell of sympathy rose in court, particularly in the public gallery. McSherry's reprimand—"Do not blaspheme in my court, Mr. Bald,"—was lost in it.

Raising his voice, Drew said, "Do you mean David Henderson?"

"Aye, Davy bloody Henderson."

Drew glanced quickly at McSherry. The judge contented himself with a savage scowl and did not rob the statement of effect by intervention.

"Let me ask you this, Mr. Bald," said Drew, "so that we might be quite clear on the point; you did not in any way at all endeavour to fight with or to impede the progress of the column of labourers?"

"I did not."

"And yet, because *you* did not move rapidly enough out of *their* way, one of them struck you with a club in a manner sufficiently forceful as to break your arm."

Bald held up his left arm: it was still crooked. "Aye, this arm."

Drew let Bald go. He counted on Mellish, in cross-examination, enquiring about the exact nature of the breakage. He received from the witness's own hand, a certificate from Dr. Thomson of Blacklaw attesting that the arm had been broken by a blow and set by him on the afternoon of July 18th in his consulting room in Main Street.

"Why was that not recorded as evidence?" Mellish demanded.

Drew answered, "I did not doubt the witness's word enough to *ask* whether he had such a certificate."

Thereupon the certificate was taken as evidence, though, McSherry said, he could not quite comprehend its validity to the case.

*   *   *

Unlike the majority of Crown witnesses, the witnesses for the defence were vehement and too impassioned to have much regard for the dignity of the court. Consequently, they were frequently reprimanded by the Lord Justice-Clerk, as they unfolded their particularised accounts of riot and crime.

The strongman, Peter Ree, frankly admitted that he had 'waded in' at 'them dirty, money-grubbin' black scabs'. He told how he had been beaten, and at Stalker's invitation, showed the court scars on his cheeks and neck. To judge from the expressions on the faces of the jury, however, they did not have much sympathy for Mr. Ree, and doubted that he had received the scars in honourable combat.

If the jury's doubts about Ree were hidden behind glumness, their disapproval of Shaun Grogan was more obvious.

Grogan was his usual wild Irish self. Even Advocate Stalker could barely prevent him from disgracing himself by the use of gutter language. It was difficult to credit that such a fiery, muscular bundle might have been in serious danger of losing his life—as he claimed—had not 'the youngster'—that is, the accused—'pitched in an' pulled off the buggers'. Obviously Mr. Grogan was incensed. Apart from admitting dislike of the bosses and professing loyalty to 'all workin' brothers, an' the Union', Grogan proved just a shade too hot for Advocate Lauder, and he was dismissed fairly rapidly from cross-examination.

Edward Stalker, cousin to the accused, was much cooler. A handsome level-headed and well enough spoken fellow, his appearance perked up the jury and took some of the embarrassment out of the air. He answered questions carefully and gave a great deal of consideration to those that seemed most important. He told the court how he had been with his cousin in the public house—"Were you drinking heavily?", "We had one half glass of mild ale each; it was a very warm mornin'."—and went on through the argument with his cousin to that moment when Neill had left him. He explained that he had followed Neill and had seen his cousin being struck with the hammer, wrest the hammer from his attacker and throw the hammer away.

"He did not look first, merely threw it away?"

"I think he was dazed."

"That is speculation," said Advocate Stalker before Mellish could open his mouth. "On the other hand, it is the truth as you saw it. You believed him to be dazed as a result of the blow he had received from the labourer, labourer Rahilly that would be."

"Aye," said Edward. "To me, he appeared t'be dazed. He was swayin' an' staggerin'."

"He did not appear to see the approaching policemen?"

"No."

"But the court has received the impression that the constables were almost at his elbow, is that not so?"

"They were runnin' fast but when Neill flung away the hammer the nearest was still twenty yards away."

"*Twenty yards?* Are you sure?"

"Aye, not less than twenty yards. I'd swear to it."

"You *have* sworn to it, young man," the judge put in.

"It was twenty yards," said Edward adamantly.

"That being the case," said Drew, "I take it that the hammer was not thrown over-arm, like this." He demonstrated.

"No, it was like this," said Edward, using a swinging action to discard the invisible hammer.

"Where—in what direction—was the accused facing?"

"T'wards the top o' Main Street."

Edward was then brought the plan of the area and duly pointed out his recollection of the disposition of the participants. After that, Drew lead him over several other aspects of the case and, soon after, relinquished his nephew to Lauder's inquisition.

"You are cousin to the accused, are you not?"

"Aye, sir, I am."

"Am I also correct in thinking that Advocate Stalker is your uncle?"

"He is."

Lauder let the muttering around the court die down. It was the first time that Stalker's kinship to the accused had been brought out.

"Are you on friendly terms with the accused?"

"We're pals."

"You live in the same house?"

"Aye, we do."

"You are concerned about him, I take it?"

"Aye, sir."

Lauder did not push that line; to go further would have invoked a strenuous objection by the defence. He moved on to the core of Edward's testimony and sought to cast doubt on its veracity by obliquely suggesting that Edward's prejudice in favour of his cousin made him untrustworthy. Edward was staunch and unwavering, however, and eventually, having shaken him not at all, Lauder released him from the witness stand.

Frank Kinnemouth whispered to Drew, "Well, that did us a bit of good, I'd say."

Drew nodded. It was now five minutes past five. He did not want to call another witness. He prayed that Daniel had done everything he had requested, and that the Lord Justice-Clerk would postpone the proceedings until morning.

As if reading his mind, McSherry summoned him forward.

"You have only one further witness to call; Henderson. Do you wish to proceed tonight, Mr. Stalker?"

"Might I suggest, m'lord, that the jury is becoming a little fatigued and lacking in attention."

McSherry was suitably impassive. "Adjournment is then in order."

Thereupon the clerk announced that court would meet next day at ten o'clock, and without ceremony the judge departed. Almost simultaneously, Drew shot out of the courtroom like a scalded cat and, to his relief, found Daniel waiting in the robing chamber.

As he stripped off his robe and wig and slid into the topcoat that Horn held out for him, Drew said, "Is she there?"

"Waitin' in a hansom outside the library steps."

"Where's my valise?"

"Here."

"Excellent," said Drew.

"Might I ask where you're off to in such a hurry, Drew?"

"I'm off to Waverley Station to catch the five-thirty train."

"Where to?"

"Blacklaw," Drew told him, and hurried out.

Two minutes later, he emerged from the door of the library building, skipped across the pavement, dived into the waiting cab and slumped breathlessly onto the seat beside Mirrin.

*　　*　　*

To be so suddenly returned to Blacklaw was disorienting. It seemed that Drew had taken power over time and space and that she had been whisked instantaneously from the august courtroom into dirty, friendly Lanarkshire. The Edinburgh train dropped them at Hamilton station at ten minutes to seven. Another hired cab lifted them at once and carried them along the main road to Blacklaw. It was a sour moonless November night. The landscape that Mirrin glimpsed through the cab window seemed warped and hostile. It was even more disconcerting to be there in her brother's company. During the past two days she had become increasingly alienated from him, and in the light of his performance in court, regarded him as a stranger, a man too clever to be understood by the likes of her.

Awe and admiration were given ungrudgingly by Mirrin and Willie. Only Kate, who did not understand the intricacies of argument, continued to be disparaging, saying, "Aye, he was always full o' hot air, was our Drew."

Now he was leading her through the darkness on a journey that, however short, would bring them together to that well-spring from which everything had flooded forth. Drew had told her only that he was going to call on Houston Lamont and that he required her support. Mirrin sensed what lay behind his command. He was challenging her as once she had challenged him, as if to say, "You involved me, now I will involve you." But the quality of involvement had altered. She could see herself at last for what she was, what she would remain until time caught up with her and drew her back to the earth in the Blacklaw kirkyard, or maybe to the sweeter soil of Crosstrees. They were not the men and women that she would have envisaged growing up from Alex Stalker's bairns. Oddly, though, they had come to fulfill the destiny that her father had predicted.

Now Drew might go as an equal into the coalmaster's mansion to speak for the colliers, though what his 'silver tongue' would say that would impress Lamont, she could not imagine. It did not occur to Mirrin that the special language that Drew had learned to speak was not the language of law but the language of money.

As the hired cab clipped through the gates of Strathmore, she had a vision of them all, like Tom, moving across a dark pasture, hands groping to seek contact, senses closed to all but the most blatant experiences, each of them swimming in an eternal night, touching and parting, parting and touching, on across the field towards a dark and unknown destination.

Mirrin wakened from a half-sleep as the driver reined the cab to a halt.

Drew got out and helped her down.

Bowling scatters of scrappy oak leaves, gusts of wind blew across the lawns, fresh, moist and cold after Edinburgh. Lit only by hooded lamps within the arch of the collonade, the mansion seemed insubstantial and dreamlike. Drew paid the driver a guinea and instructed him to wait. He carried his valise in his left hand, took her arm, wrapping her elbow into the sleeve of his heavy topcoat, and escorted her across the gravel and up the steps.

Drew's imperious knocking upon the front door soon brought a maid-servant. She knew gentry when she saw it and did not keep them waiting on the step. In the hallway, he handed the girl his hat and gloves and overcoat before giving her his name and, with a regal flick of the hand, sent her off to inform her master that Mr. Andrew Stalker and Mrs. Armstrong wished to speak with him on a matter of urgency.

Too many years had passed for Mirrin to retain much bitterness towards the Lamonts. Even so, it gave her a certain satisfaction to observe the confusion that Drew's unannounced arrival incurred. She watched that little cockatoo, Edith, hurry along a short corridor, not daring to look up at her guests, saw Houston emerge from the study buttoning his collar and vest. He gathered himself slowly, back to them, then, stiffening his spine, turned and approached. He did not offer his hand.

"Mr. Stalker," he said, "may I ask what brings you here?"

"Business, Mr. Lamont."

"Has there been a verdict on your . . . nephew?"

"The verdict will be delivered tomorrow," Drew said. "My business with you is not unrelated to that verdict."

"I have already told your . . . Mirrin that I have nothing to say on that score, that I will not interfere."

"I would not deign to trouble you," said Drew, "on a matter that was not of intimate concern to you, something as trivial, relatively speaking, as the future of a collier brat."

"You still have a sharp tongue, I see."

"Perhaps, but I have learned a *certain* amount of decorum, Mr. Lamont. I prefer not to discuss the future of the Blacklaw Colliery Company while standing in a hallway."

"The . . . *my* company?"

"Not in the hallway."

"Come this way." Lamont lead them into the drawing room where Edith nervously waited by the fireplace. She glared at Drew, then smirked slightly at the sight of Mirrin's old-fashioned dress.

"Please, take a seat by the fire, Mirrin," said Lamont with an effort at politeness. "You, Mr. Stalker, the armchair if you wish."

Edith remained standing. Houston made no introductions, nor did he offer refreshment. Standing too, he looked down at Drew. "I think I'm beginning to understand."

"That," said Drew, in his flat, dead voice, "will perhaps save explanation. My time is precious, Mr. Lamont."

"Come to it, then."

"I wish you to agree to travel to Edinburgh and enter the witness box in the high court tomorrow morning at ten o'clock."

"For what purpose?"

"To speak for the accused, to answer my questions with solemn truth."

"And in exchange," said Lamont, "you will not badger me for paltry sums due to companies in which you have a holding; is that the nature of the transaction?"

"That is *not* the nature of the transaction."

"Houston, what does he mean?" Edith asked.

Lamont indicated that she should keep silent. He did not take his eyes from Drew. "I know that you are a wealthy man, Mr. Stalker. I am now convinced that it was you who instigated the financial pressure put upon my company in the summer of this year."

"I am a wealthy man, Mr. Lamont; just a little more wealthy since you were 'persuaded' to pay your debts."

"All my debts are paid."

"All?"

"All that concern you," said Lamont.

331

"I doubt that," said Drew. "Our relationship is not that of debtor and creditor, sir. We are partners."

Edith gave a gasp of horror and put her lace handkerchief to her lips, the theatrical gesture made real by the sudden flush of colour to her cheeks. In contrast Houston Lamont's complexion drained to a livid white in which his eyes seemed brittle.

It was Edith who spoke first. "Leave, leave this house at once, sir. How, how dare you compare yourself to, to my husband."

"Partners in fact, in the Blacklaw Colliery Company," said Drew ignoring Edith entirely.

Lamont groped behind him, found the arm of a chair and guided himself into it. "Thrush sold *you* the stock?"

"I am the owner of the stock, sir, yes," said Drew. "I confess to finding part ownership of the colliery in which my father and brothers met their deaths and in which my sisters worked their fingers to the bone decidedly satisfying. I am not impervious to . . . sentiment, shall we say?"

Lamont turned his head. "Edith, what do you know of this?"

"He's lying. He must be lying."

Reaching down, Drew opened the valise and, as the couple and Mirrin watched, extracted the stock documents and held them out to the coalmaster. Lamont took them and inspected them in a casual manner.

To Mirrin's astonishment, he smiled and glanced at her. "First it is a job, Mirrin, then the tenure of a narrow house, next the patronage of your brother."

"I knew nothing of this, Houston, believe me."

Lamont continued to smile. "I have deceived myself. I have allowed myself to be deceived." He stroked the sheaf of documents across his palm. "I chased the wrong fox, did I not?"

"Houston, do not talk this way." Edith jerked forward from the hearth rug and tore the documents from his grasp to check for herself.

"I would appreciate it, Stalker, if you'd tell me precisely how you came by this stock?" Lamont said.

"It's not difficult to understand," said Drew. "I wanted a stake in the Blacklaw Company for commercial purposes: not ownership, merely a stake to obtain favourable tenders for my other mineral concerns."

"Why Blacklaw?"

"The company was progressive and in a phase of expansion," said Drew. "To cut it short, Thrush sold the stock to an agent on a short-term agreement."

"I knew of that. I sanctioned it."

"Did you also know that Thrush offered to buy the stock back—for himself?"

"I believe you," said Lamont. "That is just what Thrush might try."

"In which case, you would no longer have had controlling interest. Majority rule would have been shared in tandem by Thrush and your wife."

"Yes, I see it now. I would have had forty-forty per cent to their joint holding of fifty-six."

"Houston, don't listen to . . ." Edith began.

"Be quiet."

Drew said, "But the agent, Arnold Craddick, was *my* agent. He gained control of the stock for me. I am now a stockholder in your company with a right to share profits and attend all meetings."

"I would welcome that," said Lamont. "Truly, Stalker, I would welcome that. But, from what you've said, you now wish to trade your stock in exchange for the truth."

"Exactly," said Drew. "Strange as it may seem, sir, I am of the opinion that you are, and always have been, a man of honour, that you have acted only in your own interests when provoked to do so by changing times, and by others less scrupulous than you are. I am not here for revenge. You must be clear on that. I am here to ask you, in exchange for almost ten thousand poundsworth of stock, to be honourable once more—in the witness box, tomorrow."

"Do you admit that the boy is your son?" said Lamont.

"I do."

"It seems that you have developed some sense of honour too, Stalker."

"Only because I have been driven to it," Drew said, unsmiling.

"It's a generous bribe," Lamont said, getting to his feet. "I'd be a fool to refuse it."

"Houston, Houston, you *cannot*, you *dare* not appear in public." Edith clutched his arm. Firmly, but without anger, he detached her fingers and brushed aside her protest.

"I must warn you, sir," said Drew, "that I will not ride lightly on my questions, and that you will be under oath."

"If I had a son of my own," Lamont said, "I would ride lightly on no man who threatened him. *Do* I threaten him, Stalker?"

"You do."

"I will appear." Lamont nodded. "I have always been a fool. Perhaps now I should be a wise fool. What do you say, Mirrin?"

"You were many things but never a fool, Houston," Mirrin said.

"Only over you, you . . . you *slut*," Edith shouted.

Lamont ignored his wife completely. Taking Mirrin's arm he escorted her across the vast room towards the door. Chittering with rage and indignation Edith trailed them. Drew followed.

"Drew's son," Houston said. "Do you remember, Mirrin, when I thought that it was your son, perhaps my son?"

"Aye, you were a fool that summer, Houston, I'll admit."

"I should never have given in to the Stalkers, you know, not one inch."

"Do you regret it?"

"Certainly," Houston said.

She glanced at him, anticipating a softening of humour in his eyes. But there was no sign of it. With sadness in her heart Mirrin realised that he meant it. At last, at long, long last, they had finally parted.

"You're not doin' this for us at all, are you?"

He shook his head. "Only for myself, for my company."

"An' ten thousand pounds."

"It's a fair price for what's left of my pride."

"Goodbye, Houston."

"Mirrin." He lifted her hand and kissed it as if she was a lady. She knew that her knuckles would feel rough to his lips, that in the touch he would recognise the hard strength of a farm wife.

334

Releasing her, he shook Drew's hand, personally opened the door and showed the couple out into the darkness.

★　　★　　★

As the waiting cab started up, Mirrin sat back in the corner, her face in shadow.

"That was cruel of you, Drew."

"To take you along, you mean? No, Mirrin; that was the price you had to pay."

"All it cost *you* was money."

"Hah," said Drew. "There you are wrong, Mirrin. It cost me, and will cost me, much more than that. Besides, do not scorn a sacrifice that involves money. God knows, there were times when money was the most important thing in our lives."

"Not to me, Drew; there was always somethin' more important."

"All right, all right, Mirrin, please don't deliver one of your homespun sermons. I am in no mood for it tonight."

Mirrin said, "Did you really *want* the Blacklaw company?"

"Of course I did."

"You gave it up very easily?"

"Lamont bit quicker than I had anticipated," Drew said.

"Drew, what will happen tomorrow?"

"Oh, we will win an acquittal."

"In spite of Lauder."

"I told you, an acquittal. Neill will go free."

"An' then?"

She could see his face shaped by the light from the gas-lamp at the bottom corner of Main Street as the cab clipped past and out onto the Hamilton Road.

"You will go back to your farm," Drew said, "and worry about the future."

"And what about you?"

"I will take myself off on holiday," Drew said.

"You still despise us, don't you?"

"Mirrin, when will you understand that we are kindred, you and I? It is not something that you should forget."

"Just Alex Stalker's bairns."

"And always will be, no matter how old we become."

335

"Where're we goin' now?"

"Straight back to Edinburgh," Drew told her. "We both need a good night's sleep."

* * *

Houston Lamont was not the only surprise witness that Advocate Stalker added to his list come morning. When Drew descended to the small austere dining-room for breakfast, prompt at seven-thirty, he discovered to his amazement that Corby was standing guard over a visitor. It took Drew a moment to recognise the man; he wore a suit of sorts, had stuffed a tie into the collar of a clean but patched shirt, and had licked his hair down flat with pommade.

"Rob Ewing," said Drew.

The years had taken their toll of Ewing too. It gave Drew a peculiar satisfaction to detect signs of premature ageing in the Stalkers' former friend. Rob's seamed features put his own maturity into perspective. Lonely, Drew recognised the other's loneliness and responded to it.

"The fellow begged t'be let in, sir," Corby apologised. "He indicated that his business has relevance t'the trial."

"Thank you, Corby," Drew said. "Please bring some extra eggs and rashers, and put out another place setting."

"I've eaten," Rob Ewing growled.

Clearly, the rapport that Drew had fleetingly imagined was an illusion and had no matching response in Ewing. It occurred to him, then, that Rob must regard him as 'an enemy', a class-traitor, one of the 'professional parasites' that marched with the forces of the landed gentry and the bosses in the wars between the classes. His own concept of such social movements was, he realised, rather dated and naive. Rob's antagonism was probably more personal. He had heard whispers that Rob himself had been condemned as a judas of sorts by his own disciples. No doubt Mirrin and Kate and Lily had been harping at him to show the flag for Neill. On the other hand, Drew thought, perhaps Ewing had some clever trick up his sleeve and intended to use the witness box as a platform.

"Then you can eat again," Drew said.

While Corby set the extra place, brought in the hot-dish and put it on the sideboard servery, the collier and the advocate

336

eyed each other uncertainly. In the brief pause, Drew's instinct told him that what he sensed from Ewing was not resentment as such, but hostile respect.

"Shall I serve, sir?"

"No, Corby. I'll do it. You may leave us."

"Thank you, sir. Good luck in court."

"Thank you, Corby," Drew said.

"Servants," said Rob, when Corby had left. "You, wi' servants t'chase after you. It's seems all wrong."

"Disapprove if you like, Rob," Drew said, "but, please, disapprove while we eat. I have several matters to attend before leaving for court at nine-thirty."

Nudging the collier before him, Drew uncapped the dishes and served out bacon and fried eggs. He carried his plate to the table and motioned Rob to join him. Only when they were both seated and Ewing had actually eaten a mouthful or two, did Drew say, "It strikes me that you have come here to offer yourself as a witness on the boy's behalf."

"If you'll allow it."

"What can you contribute?"

"Lamont bribed Dunlop. I'll swear t'that in court."

"Have you proof?"

"Names, that's all; nothin' on paper."

"Will you talk about the Union, if I ask you?"

"Aye."

"Who else did Lamont bribe—Henderson?"

"Aye."

"I thought so," said Drew. "I take it you haven't been in court these last two days?"

"I was workin' on the day shift."

"But you have read the newspaper reports?"

"That's partly what prompted me t'come here."

"It seems that loyalty's a contagious disease," said Drew.

"I couldn't let the lad stew," said Rob.

"You left it long enough, though."

"It was yesterday before I made up m'mind."

"Better late than never," said Drew.

"I thought you'd have a Latin phrase t'cover it."

"No, no Latin. What I do have is Lamont."

Drew watched the miner's reaction. His surprise was genuine. "What? Where?"

"He too has 'decided' to speak up for Neill."

"Ach, you'll get nothin' but a pack o'lies from him."

"I think not." Drew poured tea from a silver pot. "Not this time."

"An oath'll no' stop him from lyin'."

"There you're wrong, Rob. For all his stubbornness and cunning, one thing that Lamont will respect is an oath. He'll tell the truth. It's going to be quite a day for the truth, one way or the other."

"The papers say there's little hope of gettin' Neill off scot-free."

"The damned papers say more than they should," Drew said. "I'm surprised they don't hang him from Canongate steeple flag-pole and be done with it."

"Can I . . . can I . . . help?"

"Of course," Drew glanced at the slim black clock in the corner. "Eat up, then we'll go to the study and I will ask you one or two questions in advance."

"Is that allowed?" Rob said. "I want t'keep it all above board."

"Rob, you would never have qualified as a lawyer."

*   *   *

"It appears to me, Mr. Stalker, that you are composing your client's defence as you go along," said McSherry, tartly.

"The witnesses would not come forward, sir," Drew explained.

"Until you pressured them?"

"Certainly not, sir. I would not even demand their presence here on court order. Apart from Henderson and Dunlop ... ."

"*And* Dunlop."

"Apart from hostile witnesses, there has been apprehension concerning the effects of the trial on reputations. I did not actively solicit the cooperation of Mr. Lamont or of Mr. Ewing."

"They are volunteers."

"Yes, m'Lord."

"Then," McSherry sighed, "we had better hear them, I suppose."

Ten minutes after the meeting in chambers, the court convened. Mr. David Dunlop was dredged up from his place in the public gallery and, with much trepidation, was sworn in again, having been dismissed on the previous day.

Drew wasted neither Dunlop's time nor his own.

"How long have you known the Stalker family, Mr. Dunlop?"

"Who d'you mean?"

"The Stalkers of Blacklaw—father, mother, sisters, sons and grandsons: how long?"

"All m'life, near enough."

"Are they a family given to disorderly behaviour?"

"Well, y'know, that depends what y'mean."

"Drunkenness?"

"No, no, not that," Dunlop, sweating, admitted.

"Fighting, brawling?"

"Well, not that I can recall."

"Yes, or no?"

"No."

"Violence of any sort?"

"Old Alex, he had a bit o'a red temper."

"But he was not a violent man in his habits?"

"I can't . . . no, you're right. He wasn't."

"And his sons, and his daughters."

Sweat poured down Dunlop's face. His eyes bulged out with the pressures of indecision. Nobody had told him what to say or what not to say. He was devilled by the malicious gossip that was packed into his mind and he resisted it only for a moment. Then it was too much for him and blurted out. "*You're* Alex's son, Drew Stalker, an' I know you well enough."

Nobody in court had been oblivious to the fact that the Advocate for the panel was related to the accused in some way, but it seemed shocking, as ⹁evelations go, to have it dragged from this puffy, pompous little manager.

Drew was onto Dunlop in a flash. "When did you approach the witness Henderson?"

"What . . . eh! I never . . ."

"On whose behalf did you offer him money?"

"Money? Listen, I had nothin' t'do with that."

"With what, Mr. Dunlop? How much did you pay Henderson to tell lies in this court?"

Lauder was on his feet instantly. "That is a monstrous accusation, m'lord: quite monstrous! I object most strongly."

McSherry said, "Are you accusing this witness of perjury, and of bribing Crown witnesses, Mr. Stalker?"

"M'lord," said Drew, calmly. "I crave the court's indulgence."

"Those are serious accusations, sir, and the court has been indulgent enough with counsel for the panel."

"M'lord," said Drew, "I ask only that the witness be allowed an opportunity to *deny* that he gave David Henderson a sum of money, on behalf of a third party, to appear in this court and deliver testimony weighted against my client."

Dunlop put a hand to his throat, as if to break the grip of an invisible fist.

McSherry hesitated. "I feel that . . . It is the court's opinion, Mr. Dunlop, that you had better deny the charges that Advocate Stalker has levelled against you."

Lauder and Mellish were both on their feet, protesting loudly. McSherry waved them into silence. The whole court was silent now, a hall filled with no sound but the faint rumble of traffic on distant streets.

"Do you deny, sir, that you bribed the witness Henderson on behalf of a third party?" said Drew, remorselessly.

"I . . . I . . . It had nothin' t'do with me. I was just doin' my job. I got nothin' out o'it. It wasn't my idea." Dunlop's head whipped this way and that, staring, pop-eyed, from judge to counsel, helplessly seeking a friendly face in the gallery, somebody who, by wink or nod, would instruct him what to do. In the absence of a saviour he did what he had always done best— he talked. "It wasn't what you said, Stalker. All I did was t'tell Henderson he'd better step forward an' tell the truth."

"The truth?" Drew said, quietly.

"Aye, we all know Neill Stalker's one o'Rob Ewing's lickspittles. Rob Ewing bloody-well put him up t'it. Got the right man, too. Bad blood. She's not even his nat'ral mother. God knows who his father is. There's been talk since the day he was born, an' I'll tell you . . ."

"That's enough, Mr. Dunlop," said McSherry.

"They said it might even be you, yoursel', Drew Stalker. Aye, I've heard that. But it can't be or you'd no' be allowed t' . . ."

"Dunlop, control yourself. *That is enough*," McSherry thundered.

Panting, sweat dripping from his brow Dunlop sagged against the stand aghast at his own outburst. His mouth opened and closed, but no noises came from him. He was empty of words, publicly stripped of deceptions, all the lies and conniving half-truths sucked out of him.

"That is all I require of this witness," Drew said.

"Do you wish to cross-examine, Mr. Lauder?"

Lauder and Mellish consulted for a moment, then Lauder said, "No, m'lord. The Crown feels that this witness has been subjected to enough harassment."

Dunlop was dismissed. Assisted by a clerk of the court, he reeled almost drunkenly from the side door of the court.

Rob Ewing's name was called. The collier appeared, climbed stiffly into the witness box and took the oath in a clipped tone that only those who knew him could define as nervous.

Quickly Drew identified the witness and established his intimate connection with the United Federation of Miners, then lead Rob through a potted account of Blacklaw colliery's strife-torn history.

Mellish objected. "Is this necessary, m'lord?"

Without a word, McSherry deferred the question to Drew, who answered, "M'lord, it is the intention of the defence to show provocation, not in the simple form generally recognised but, through the evidence of new witnesses, to demonstrate that the accused was the unwitting victim of circumstances that put him in an untenable position. It is also the contention of the defence that Neill Campbell Stalker did *not* respond as any ordinary person might have responded but, in fact, showed considerable *restraint*; that witnesses for the Crown have in-accurately presented testimony that denies accident, or, at least, suggests malicious negligence on the part of the accused."

The Lord Justice-Clerk considered Drew's statement for fully a minute, made several notes on his record then, glumly, nodded.

"You may continue."

To Rob, Drew said, "To the best of your knowledge, Mr. Ewing, has the work-force in Blacklaw colliery made a habit of engaging in sabotage or violent retaliation to policies of the coalmaster that displeased them?"

"Only a han'ful o'isolated minor incidents that had nothin' t'do with the U.F.M."

"Or your instructions, Mr. Ewing?"

"I don't believe violence solves anthin'. The best way t'shake the bosses out o'their complacency is t'organise an' unite, t'force legislation through talks an' legitimate demands."

"And by withholding labour?"

"If driven t'it, aye."

"Very well, Mr. Ewing. Now, whether one disagrees with your objectives or not, on the strength of your statement, one cannot disapprove of your means of achieving your ends. On the day in question, July eighteenth, what was planned?"

"A rally at the pit-gate. Mr. Arthur Webb was comin' t'talk about the National Strike."

"How many pickets were manning the approach to the gate?"

"Twelve."

"Big, strong men, no doubt?"

"Mostly men nearin' retirement. It was a quiet time."

"Twelve men, not so young in years," said Drew. "Where were you?"

"I had walked over from Mr. Webb's lodgin' accompanied b' Mr. Webb, a party o' four officials, Edward Stalker, an' the accused."

"You were, I believe, refreshing yourselves in The Lantern public house when you first received an intimation that a gang of casual labourers had descended on the pit-gate?"

"That's true."

"Why did you not rush to your colleagues' aid?"

"I have a wider responsibility," said Rob. "I could not afford t'be seen condonin' violence."

"Not even under such extreme provocation, out of a sense of

loyalty to your friends, to those old men on the picket-line."

"I . . . I was restrained," said Rob.

"Physically?"

"Prevailed upon t'stay out o'it."

"By Mr. Webb?"

"Aye."

"But the accused was not so bound."

"His cousin Edward tried t'persuade him not t'go."

"But Neill was angry?"

"Aye, he was angry."

"Were you not angry?"

"Of course I was angry. I was seethin' mad."

"You, however, are a mature man, and have no doubt seen violence done in strikes before. How many previous strike actions had the accused been involved in?"

"None."

"Are you sure, Mr. Ewing?"

"The lad's only nineteen. He's worked in Blacklaw since he was fourteen, no place else. He'd never even seen a blackleg before."

"So, out of loyalty to his comrades in the picket-line, and unaware of what to expect, the accused ran uphill to the pit."

"Aye, he did."

"The boy's grandfather was killed in a pit disaster, was he not?"

"Died as a result o'it."

"And his uncles?"

"Both of them."

"So he knew of the hazards, the dangers and the hardships of the trade?" said Drew. "Before he decided to become a miner?"

"Aye, he'd heard all the tales."

"His parental guardian is a baker, quite a prosperous baker, is he not?"

"Well, comfortably off, I'd say. His bakin' business does well."

"I wonder Mr. Ewing, why young Neill Stalker did not go into the baking trade?"

McSherry glanced towards the Crown advocates but neither

raised a protest. Leaning forward on the bench, McSherry urged Rob, saying, "Answer the question as honestly as you can, Mr. Ewing."

"Because he's a miner," Rob said. "Because . . . because bein' a miner is somethin' that gets in the blood."

"Go on," Drew said softly.

"Ach, d'you think that Blacklaw colliery belongs t'the coalmaster? On paper, maybe. But every collier knows that it belongs t'the folk who live in the narrow houses. It's *their* sweat, *their* blood that greases the wheels. It's *their* history that's written on the walls o' the splint-seams. Whoever takes the money, whoever reaps the bloody profit, Blacklaw is *our* pit. None o'us own it, no more than Houston Lamont owns it. We're all owned *by* it, are part o'it, as it's part o'us."

Rob stopped abruptly, abashed by his own vehement outburst.

"But profit is important?" said Drew.

Licking his lower lip, more cautious now, Rob said, "Profit—but not exploitation. When he . . ."

"Who?"

". . . the coalmaster loses touch, disregards us an' our stake in the future o'the pit, then we must do what we can t'retrieve it."

"Bringing in a casual work-force, at double the standard wage, is not playing fair; is that it, Mr. Ewing?"

"That's it."

"So, on the eighteenth day of July, you and your fellow miners saw your pit being unfairly attacked. You, Mr. Ewing, as a mature and responsible leader of the mining community, exercised restraint and curbed your anger. But Neill Campbell Stalker, who *chose* that trade in that pit, may I remind the court, is younger and more impetuous. He rushed to his colleagues' aid."

"I tried t'talk him out o'it."

"But words were not enough?"

"No."

"It would seem that words were not enough for the partners of the Blacklaw Colliery Company either," said Drew; "or they would have endeavoured to reach a settlement of the strike

344

through the negotiating boards of the Federation. However, be that as it may, Neill Stalker went to defend his job, his wage and his whole way of living."

"I doubt if any o'those things were in his mind," said Rob. "He went t'defend *his* pit."

"Speculation," said Lauder.

McSherry ignored the protest. Lauder did not repeat it.

Drew said, "When you arrived at the pit-gate, what did you see?"

"Colliers on the ground, beaten down. Grogan and Ree among them."

"Where was the accused?"

"At the gate, tryin' t'prevent the bla . . . labourers enterin'. He was struck wi' a hammer, on the shoulder, an' wrestled for the hammer t'prevent himself bein' struck again. He got the hammer an' staggered back from the gate an' threw the hammer away."

"*Threw* it away?"

"Aye. The first rank o' police specials were comin' towards the gate at the double. Neill never saw them."

"How can you be certain of that?"

"He was too dazed t'see them. They were well off t'his right."

"How far off was Constable Ronald when the hammer struck him?"

"About twenty yards."

"Mr. Ewing, what is Neill Stalker's attitude to you?"

"I . . ."

"No need to be modest."

"He respects me."

"And your principles?"

"Aye."

"Presumably he was aware that you do not encourage the use of violence?"

"He'd be daft if he wasn't."

Shortly after, Drew turned Rob over to Lauder. But the prosecution could make no impression upon the collier's statement that the accused had thrown the hammer while the police were still twenty yards away. After trying various subtle ruses to persuade Rob to alter his story, Lauder gave up and Rob stepped thankfully down from the witness box.

Henderson had been 'kept cool' in the witness room. He was afraid; he had no guidelines to help him now and, like Dunlop before him, did not trust his own wit to see him through the ordeal. He carried his secrets churlishly, trying hard to nurse derision for Stalker, the 'bloody wee swot'. But Stalker was here, in a different element entirely, conversing with learned lords, attired in shoes and breeks that cost enough to keep the Henderson family alive for a couple of months. So, as he was escorted to the stand once more, Henderson was more than ever aware that he was cut off from Blacklaw, that this was not the equivalent of the school playground, that the word was law here not a clenched fist.

It disconcerted Henderson even more when Drew approached him gently. His first question was full of sympathy. "I notice that you have a bit of a stoop, Mr. Henderson. Now what causes that—rheumatism, or an injury?"

"Rheumatics."

"Getting worse every winter?"

"I can cope wi' it."

"No doubt, no doubt. How many of a family do you have?"

"Five."

"Wife living?"

"Aye."

"You also support your elderly mother, do you not?"

"Aye."

"You live in a tied house; that is, tied to the job at Blacklaw pit and owned by Houston Lamont?"

"Everybody does."

"Everybody in Blacklaw," said Drew. "With very few exceptions. I know all about tied houses, Mr. Henderson."

"Aye."

"What will you do in three years or four, when your back seizes up and you can no longer dig coal from the seams?"

"It'll maybe no' happen."

"Come now, Mr. Henderson," said Drew, "you know as well as I do that the day will come, probably not too far into the future, when you will not be able to get into the cage let alone crawl along a seam."

"I'll get a surface job."

"Will you? But surely it's seam workers that are required in Blacklaw. Lord, if every crippled collier was given a surface job—light work—the payroll would be as long as the army list."

"I'll manage. I'm no' grumblin'."

"M'lord," Lauder interrupted. "I see absolutely no point in this line of questioning."

"Mr. Stalker?" said McSherry.

"Very well, I'll come to the point," said Drew. "Mr. Henderson, you are a face worker suffering from a progressive disease. You live in a house that is tied to the job. You have four children under the age of ten, a wife and an elderly relative who all rely on your wage for their food and shelter, is that correct?"

Henderson nodded. Was Stalker crowing over him?

"You are vulnerable, Mr. Henderson. My point is that *you are vulnerable*," Drew said, then raced on. "Being vulnerable means that you must do what you can to survive. Oh, yes, Mr. Henderson, I understand how it is only too well. Now, sir, let me ask you—and you are under oath—what did Mr. Dunlop offer you as an inducement to deliver prepared testimony here in this court?"

"I never've nothin' t'do wi' Dunlop."

"Did you not meet Mr. Dunlop in a public house called The Cage, a quiet public house some four miles from Blacklaw?"

"I . . ."

McSherry said sternly, "On your oath, Mr. Henderson."

"What if I did?"

"Is it usual for colliers to drink with managerial staff?"

Henderson was struck dumb.

"Very well," said Drew. "The court may be assured that it is *not* common for miners and managers to drink together."

"On whose authority is that statement made?" Mellish asked, then to the Lord Justice-Clerk, said, "On whose authority, m'lord?"

"On *my* authority, learned counsel," said Drew. "I speak for the moment not as an advocate but as the son of a collier, as a person *raised* in Blacklaw."

McSherry rapped his gavel three times and order was called for in the court.

"I am not ashamed of it," Drew said.

"Continue with your witness, counsellor," McSherry advised.

"Willingly," Drew said. "Now, Mr. Henderson, did you drink or at least meet with Mr. Dunlop in The Cage public house between the middle and end of July of this year? Yes, or no."

"Aye."

For a fleeting instant Drew remembered Henderson as he had been, rabbity features twisted viciously, as he pommelled and pinched Drew in the playground. He had left that recollection far behind, along with many other things. Now it was with him, not goading him into triumph but bringing regret, the realisation that Henderson had never had a chance.

"Please, Henderson, a little louder."

"Aye, I met wi' Dunlop."

"What was the offer?"

"I don't know what y'mean."

"Was it the promise of a light surface job, of extended lease of the narrow house?"

Henderson hung his head.

"Was it money?"

"He . . . He said we'd be evicted if I didn't come here an' tell what I saw at the riot."

"Who said?"

"Dunlop."

"But Dunlop has no power of eviction."

"He's a bloody boss, i'n't he?"

"You must have known that he spoke for a higher authority."

"He was backed b'Thrush," said Henderson. "An' by Lamont hi'sel'."

"You mean the partners in the company that owned Blacklaw?"

"Fine well y'know it, Drew Stalker."

"Whose name did Dunlop use?" said Drew.

348

"Lamont's."

"Now, what did he want you to say?"

"It wasn't so much diff'r'nt from what I saw. But I never thought Neill pitched yon hammer at the copper. I never thought that. I was *told* what t'think."

"Yes," said Drew. "You were told what to think. Go on, please, Henderson."

"Neill never saw the coppers. He never saw anythin'. He'd got hit wi' the hammer hisel' an' had got it away from the blackleg. He just . . ." Henderson made a sweeping underarm motion. "Just flung it from'm, hard, like, an' it went int' the front row o' the coppers. They were runnin' like hell t'help the dirty blacklegs. Not t'help *us*. T'help the *blacklegs*. That's how I saw it happen. Dunlop told me I was wrong. He told me what I was t'say I'd seen, an' told me Mr. Lamont ordered me t'come forward an' offer m'sel' as a witness."

"And you did," said Drew. "Who can blame you, Henderson?"

"Aye, it's no' like it was, is it?" Henderson said, nodding.

"Thank you," Drew said. "You have been . . . most helpful."

"Aye," Henderson said.

As Henderson was lead down, Drew addressed the bench.

"M'lord, in view of Mr. Henderson's cooperative attitude when summoned as a witness in defence of the accused, may I suggest that no further action is taken in respect of the possible charge of perjury. I take it that the Crown does not wish to press on this matter?"

Lauder shook his head. He looked black and sullen now. He was already beaten, and knew it, though the extent to which Stalker intended to go to remove the last shred of doubt as to Neill Campbell Stalker's innocence not even Lauder could imagine.

"I will make a record of your suggestion, counsellor," said McSherry, "and will debate on it after this trial is over."

"Thank you, m'lord."

*   *   *

Mirrin moved, leaning forward as Kate leaned back.

349

"It's him," Kate murmured. "Oh, God, Willie. Lamont's come."

"It's all right, now. It's all right." Willie patted her hand. "Drew knows what he's doin'."

Lamont climbed into the witness stand, raised his hand and repeated the solemn oath upon the Bible. He wore a dark coat and morning trousers and, Mirrin thought, might easily have passed for a lawyer. Drew and he were one of a kind, with nothing at all to separate them, to boast of Lamont's lineage of privilege, ownership and responsibility in constrast to Stalker's inheritance of ambition, determination and pride.

She watched her brother come forward.

In the dock, Neill was sitting bolt upright, staring at Lamont as if he was some executioner come to do the deed upon him there and then. It was the first really positive reaction that Neill had given in the two days of the trial. For the rest he had watched and listened with great attention. Only Rob's testimony had so far had any visible effect upon him. He had not protested his innocence in the face of lies; nor did he now give any sign that he sensed himself to be free. He trusted his father, and his father's skill, and was obedient to that trust. She saw, though, how Houston looked at the dock, not hurriedly, not furtively, but with a strange lopsided wistfulness that nobody but she, perhaps, could interpret.

There would be more strife, more bitterness yet between masters and servants; yet Mirrin was aware that she was watching the last act of a long drama, that this was its high point. After men like Lamont were gone, who would succeed them? The Stalkers of this world, perhaps? Men like her brother, men with few scruples? And after them, the colliers themselves might come into their own, under men like Rob? Would that, she wondered, pave the path to the golden age?

As he began to give evidence, in Houston she saw the predator, whose doom is part of nature, caught in the spiral of time. In fifty years, there would be none of his kind left. She did not want to see him humiliated. She prayed that Drew would understand the magnitude, and the ramifications, of the coalmaster's debt.

"You are Houston Lamont, principal partner in the Blacklaw

350

Colliery Company, owners and operators of the pits of Blacklaw, Northrigg and Eastlagg, and other pits and mineral properties in Lanarkshire."

"I am."

"Do you know the accused?"

"I do."

"How well do you know him?"

"Not well; he is an employee."

"You know his family?"

"I do."

"At one time, Mr. Lamont, you knew his family well?"

"At one time, I knew all my colliers' families."

"At one time?"

"My holdings are too large for that now."

"I see."

"Do you consider the accused to be honest, hard-working and reliable?"

"I have heard no report to the contrary."

"Who would be most liable to bring such a report?"

"My partner and General Manager, Sydney Thrush."

"He did not bring it?"

"No."

"When you discovered that Neill Stalker had committed a violent act, were you surprised?"

"I was surprised, perhaps, that it was Stalker."

"But not that violence had erupted at the pit?"

"No."

"You anticipated that violence might occur."

"I did."

"At any time, or on the morning of July eighteenth in particular?"

"On that morning."

"Why, on that morning?"

"In accordance with the law that permits me to hew coal on my own properties and leases without impediment, I had taken steps to resume production."

"What steps, sir?"

"I had employed eighty casual labourers, recruited through a Glasgow agent known to me as reliable in such matters."

"How much does a casual labourer earn?"

"I cannot speak in general. I was asked to pay a guinea per man for a half day's work—that is, for taking the pit. After that, the wage, for most jobs, is twice that of the standard rate."

"Twice that of the wage of an employed collier?"

"Yes."

"So, Mr. Lamont, you purchased a labour force of eighty men to re-enter and possess your Blacklaw pit?"

"I required coal. I could not afford not to hew coal."

"But you knew that the colliers, the strikers, would try to prevent the casual labourers taking over the pit?"

"I knew it," said Lamont. "I accept responsibility for the decision."

"Now, sir, who gave you the news that a special constable had been killed?"

"Mr. Dunlop; later Mr. Thrush."

"There was, presumably, some discussion of the incident."

"It may save the court's time," Lamont said, "if I tell the court that it was my decision to aid the police in finding sufficient evidence to sustain a charge of murder against the accused."

"Did you feel justified in this course, Mr. Lamont?"

"I knew that it would bring my colliers to their senses. It was expedient to return to full normal working as soon as possible, and without further violence."

Drew said, "And what of Neill Campbell Stalker? Did you not spare at least a passing thought for his plight?"

"At that time, I cherished the belief that he had killed the policeman out of malice."

"At that time?"

"I am . . . less sure now."

"Yet you did everything in your power, through the services of Thrush and Dunlop, your managers, to assist the police in gathering enough evidence to hang the boy?"

"I did not wish the boy to hang. I merely wanted an example made of him."

"To serve your own purposes?"

"I admit it."

"Through Dunlop, you applied pressure upon several of your

miners, including Henderson, to revise and consolidate their accounts of what they saw that morning?"

"Yes."

"Thus ensuring that Neill Stalker would remain under threat of sentence of a capital crime, while your pits went back into full production?"

"Yes."

"Mr. Lamont, let me ask you now, do you believe that Neill Stalker, with deliberate malice and knowledge of consequence, killed the special constable in the manner charged?"

"No, I do not."

"May I ask the reason for your change of opinion?"

Houston Lamont did not answer. Mirrin scanned his face for some sign that he had reached the limit, that his pride had restored itself again. So far his honesty had been scathing.

Drew said, "What changed your mind, Mr. Lamont?"

"You did."

"I?"

"You chose to defend the accused. You, Mr. Stalker, would not have done so had you not been utterly convinced of his innocence."

"That is hardly a reason, Mr. Lamont," McSherry said quietly.

"It is my opinion," Lamont said, "that guilt or innocence matter less in law than a belief in guilt or innocence. You, Mr. Stalker, would not have risked defending your son, or in suing your peers for permission to do so, if you had not been moved by a belief in truth. It was your action that made me regret mine."

"I . . . I am not . . ." Drew said.

"At one time," said Lamont, "I would have known the boy, and I would not have acted as I did, not to save fifty pits or a dozen mining companies."

"A last question, Mr. Lamont," said Drew, dropping the words into the silence that had formed in the well of the court, the breathless attention of the throng flooding down upon him. "Without the tampered evidence of the eye-witnesses would, in your opinion, there have been a case to answer?"

"From what I know of law," Lamont said, raising his voice

as Lauder and Mellish bellowed their objections, "there would have been no case of murder, whatever else."

"Thank you, Mr. Lamont."

Amid the uproar, with Lauder rushing to the bench and Mellish hurling imprecations at Drew, Mirrin noticed how Lamont looked not at judge, jury, lawyers or the public in the gallery but only at the prisoner, at Neill, and how the young man, sitting upright, stared back—unafraid.

*　　*　　*

In the midst of the chaos, the Lord Justice-Clerk prudently adjourned the court for lunch. It was two-thirty in the afternoon when Patrick Lauder got to his feet to make his final address to the jury. If he knew that he was beaten, he gave no sign of it, though his demand for justice under law was pitched in a lower key than usual. As a preliminary, he gave a few pointers of law, opening to the jury the possibility of returning a verdict of guilty of manslaughter in preference to that of homicide. He said that his lordship would impart closer direction in the course of his summing-up.

"At the close of this important trial, it is my duty to address you on behalf of the Crown and ask you to look at the indictment that is placed before you. I know I need not point out to you the tremendous responsibility that rests with you at this juncture; a life is at stake—a life, you might think, no less precious than that of the young constable of police that was brutally and summarily taken from him while in the performance of his duty. Make no mistake, gentlemen of the jury, the complexities that have been introduced into this case are not of the Crown's making. There is but one person on trial, and that person is the accused, Neill Campbell Stalker."

Bit by bit Lauder guided the jury through the evidence, interpreting it as required, adjuring more than once that only the accused was on trial.

After forty minutes, he concluded, "And so I say to you that, despite the diversions that the defending counsel has seen fit to raise in the hope of confusing the issue in your minds, one fact and one fact alone stands clear before you—that the prisoner did throw the hammer that killed poor Constable

Ronald. Whether he did so, as we have heard from several of his colleagues, with intent to do harm is for you to decide. I do not doubt that my learned friend for the defence will raise the issue of master versus man, but it is not that issue that is at stake. It is, I say, your duty to confine yourselves to a consideration of the facts, bleak as they are. The facts laid before you are sufficient—amply sufficient—to convict the prisoner at the bar. I made no appeal to your emotions, gentlemen of the jury. We have been drowned in emotion as it is, treated to sentiment in excess. Sentiment must have no part in your verdict. Weigh everything upon the evidence given, leave nothing to be determined without proof. For myself, I see no way out for this unhappy youth. If you reach the same conclusion as I have done, there is but one course open to you and that is to return a verdict of guilty of the charge."

There was, at that moment, a freakish blink of sunlight over Edinburgh, rays of pale gold slanting into the cavernous courtroom. The atmosphere throughout the trial had been taut but, as Andrew Stalker rose to make his closing address to the jury, it became electric.

"Gentlemen of the jury, the charge against the prisoner is murder, and the punishment of murder is death," Drew began. "That simple statement is sufficient to recall to you the awful solemnity of the occasion that brings you here to discharge your duties as citizens.

"It is customary at this point for the defence counsel to steer the course of the trial with a view to drawing your attention to the aspects of its evidence most favourable to his client's case. The Advocate-Depute, in his address, has endeavoured to persuade you that all that you should consider in respect of the commission of the crime is the act of the crime itself—if crime, indeed, it be. That there was a death, a tragic death, there is no doubt whatsoever. That the death of Constable Ronald was caused by a blow from a hammer, there is also no doubt. But that, gentlemen, is not enough, by way of plain fact and admission, to condemn my client, Neill Stalker, on *any* charge, whether of murder or of manslaughter.

"Now, you may already suppose, in the light of testimony

355

retracted by certain prosecution witnesses, that all evidence given by the witnesses for the Crown is suspect and false. This is manifestly not so. The fundamental element in the testimony of the eye-witnesses—and that which must be weighed by you with greatest care—concerns the manner in which the hammer was thrown. Did the accused know where he was throwing it, or was he, as we have heard, dazed from a blow?

"Manslaughter, though a lesser charge than murder and not a charge that demands a man's life, may carry the penalty of fifteen years in prison. Fifteen years, gentlemen of the jury; the whole term of youth. If you contemplate returning a verdict of guilty of manslaughter, I wish you to bear in mind that you would be robbing this young man of something almost as important as his life; you would be robbing him of his youth and the fulfilment of the opportunities of his youth.

"What of manslaughter? The Lord Justice-Clerk will direct you as to its precise definition and explain how it relates to this case. However, to enable you to understand the evidence that has been brought before you and to which I will refer in the course of this address, let me make it plain, as my learned colleague for the Crown has not, that it is the duty of the prosecution to *prove* the prisoner's guilt. If any reasonable doubt, created by the evidence, remains in your minds that the prisoner killed the deceased with a malicious intention, the prosecution has not made a case and the prisoner is entitled to acquittal. When dealing with a charge of murder the Crown must consequently prove death as the result of a voluntary act of the accused and—either expressly or by implication— the malice of the accused. If evidence of death and malice has been given—and this is for you to decide—the accused is entitled to show by evidence or *examination of the circumstances of the crime*—mark that well, gentlemen—that the act on his part which caused death was either unintentional or provoked. If you are satisfied with his explanation or, upon reviewing the evidence, are left in reasonable doubt as to whether or not the act was unintentional or provoked, the prisoner is entitled to be acquitted.

"Unintentional? Can you doubt that the accused's action

was unintentional. He *discarded* the weapon; he did not turn it upon the man who had struck him with it. If he, the accused, had really been livid with fury, would it not have seemed more rational to strike at the nearest living object in vengeance, to *retalliate*. It is true, as the prosecution has pointed out, that the accused had not been provoked by the deceased—the deceased had only just appeared upon the scene—but in the light of all that you have heard, can you doubt that Neill Campbell Stalker *was* provoked? I submit to you, however, that he is a rational young man and, though dazed, was sensible enough to *throw away* that potentially dangerous weapon, the sledge hammer. That it struck Constable Ronald was an act of pure misfortune, an accident.

"Now, you may say, if the accused had not been upon the scene, had not run to the pit-gate that morning, had behaved more circumspectly and in a law-abiding manner, then he would not have put himself in a position to commit any hurtful action at all. To that I say, that you must apply the same criterion to the victim, to the deceased. Constable Ronald was there as a *volunteer*. Remember that fact: it is important. As a special constable he was not ordered to Blacklaw Colliery; he was paid extra for the duty, and went of his own volition. It is not for me to condemn the motives of the dead, but, in deference to my client's case, I must point out that Constable Ronald's motives were for gain. Neill Campbell's motives were loyalty and anger in a situation that he—not without justification—construed as unjust. The collusion of these two forces is unfortunate in its results; one man is dead and another stands on trial for his life.

"Provocation? You have heard what the pit means to a young man like the accused. It may not be within your experience, gentlemen of the jury, to identify with such a strange passion, such an attachment. But can you doubt that it is genuine, or that it is valid, not only in the light of what you have heard from the witness Ewing but from the lips of witness Henderson, and in the demeanour of the other colliers who have appeared before you? What *is* provocation? In this instance, provocation was a quality of injustice, a breakdown in the system, in the balance between master and servant. In the making of a scapegoat, is there not provocation?

"The prosecution have pointed out that you must consider the action of the accused in a kind of vacuum, in isolation. If you do that, then you may find that evidence proves him guilty. *In isolation?* No man, collier, grocer, carpenter, brewer, labourer or lawyer, exists in isolation, commits one action, whatever that action, in isolation, in a vacuum. We are all—you and I as well as the accused—bound into a circle of consequence, of cause and effect. Therefore you must give due regard to the circumstances that lead the accused to that pit-gate and created in him that mood. You must also give regard to the character of the accused, and his youth. Is it not remarkable that he was ever charged with murder at all? You may think so. Indeed, in view of the testimony given by Minister Laird, by the negligence shown on the part of the authorities, in particular by the Police Surgeon who did not even know that the prisoner had been injured, and by others, you are right to ask, *Why* was the prisoner ever charged with murder? I think, gentlemen of the jury, that you have heard the answer to that question from the lips of the coalmaster, Houston Lamont. It was *expedient*. It was *necessary*. Are these, I ask you, reasons for occupying the court? Are these pointers for the guidance of our society? Are these sound reasons for threatening the life of a young man, for bringing grief and suffering to him and to his family?"

Drew had been pacing slowly along the line of the jury enclosure. Now he came to a halt close to the dock and, with his hand raised, looked back over his shoulder at the jurors.

"The charge of the Crown is not based upon evidence but upon betrayal," Drew said. "The motive is not justice, but pique."

Muttering ran through the crowded court, though the jury gave no sign at all of how his speech impressed them. They might have been waxworks seated there. Drew paused until silence settled once more. He did not move: that spot on the floor below the dock seemed to have become his private territory.

"No, gentlemen of the jury," he said, at length, "do not

suppose that because the accused is hardly more than a boy
that the issues in this case are trivial. Do not suppose, I beg
of you, that all the evidence is the evidence of your eyes and
ears, that the words spoken in this court are logical. Some
things defy logical explanation, and the charge against Neill
Campbell Stalker is one of them.

"Betrayal, I said: the unforgivable sin. Betrayal by
workmates, by class. What does the Bible say—"An eye for
an eye." Yes, a life for a life is the demand of the moral law
as well as the civil. But what damage does that law do to those
who seek to enforce it? Surely, you would not set such a low
premium on this young man's life as that." Drew paused
again. "Freedom stands there in the dock; the freedom of a
man to operate within the same system of values as his
employers, to remain an individual in the establishment of
society. Now, I will tell you the truth that lies behind the
Crown's accusation; that part of it that has puzzled you. I will
tell you why, in all conscience, I may ask that you acknowledge
this young man's innocence by acquittal."

Drew's head flicked. For a split-second, he was staring at
the gallery, directly, unerringly at Kate. He looked back at the
jury.

"If he has been betrayed by the law, gentlemen of the jury,
will you support that law and carry and compound the injustice
of it further? How dare I, servant of the law, say that to you
without fear of reprimand, without making the law seem an
ass? The law of this land of ours is dispassionate. It is both
master and servant. The law is for all of us. It must not be
flouted by self-seeking in the quest for power. I have
lived by the law, gentlemen, as this young man has lived by
the law. You have heard from witness Lamont that Neill
Campbell Stalker is my son. That is correct. He is my son
elsewhere, but not here. Here, in this court of justice, I am
advocate first and father second. Yet I feel myself less father
to him than betrayer, because I have been brought to this bar
in this court to defend him of a crime that was no crime,
to shield him from a stigma that is no stigma, to be sure that
truth and justice might flourish from lies, treachery and
deceit; in the belief that you will serve us all with impartiality

and return a verdict that acquits him unblemished from the bar."

Reporters bolted for the swing doors, charging past the ushers. The listeners in the gallery broke out in a babble of chatter in which Kate Kellock's tears went unnoticed.

In the well of the court, Advocate Stalker slid onto the chair beside his colleague.

"Good God, Stalker," said Kinnemouth. "What on earth have you done?"

"Got him off," Drew said. "They won't dare convict him now."

"No, it's you they'll hang instead."

"Let them."

"Andrew, don't you care about your career?"

Straightening his wig, Drew said, "Not in the least. My son isn't the only prisoner who will soon be set free."

*　　*　　*

The judge's charge to the jurors dispelled all doubt from their minds. Lord McSherry left only two courses open—to find the prisoner guilty of manslaughter, which he did not advise, or to acquit him completely.

The jury were gone from court for eighteen minutes.

They returned at ten minutes to five o'clock.

"Gentlemen," the Clerk of the Court intoned, "what is your verdict?"

"My lord," the Foreman answered, "the jury are unanimously of the opinion that the prisoner is not guilty."

Advocate Stalker spoke his last words in a Scottish court of Law. "M'lord, I move for the prisoner's immediate release."

McSherry answered, "The prisoner is so released."

As Neill Campbell Stalker stepped down from the dock, his father, grim and unsmiling, thrust from the courtroom, boarded the cab that Horn had waiting, and, to all intents and purposes, vanished from the capital.

December

In Perthshire, the Christmas season was invariably white.
Pine forests and high hills stood sharp in the clean cold air.
In the first weeks of her exile, Betsy had felt penned by
the mountains, threatened by the huge rolling expanses of
moorland; now however she found their beauty exhilarating.
Wrapped in furs, like a Russian princess, her daughters in the
open seat behind her, she drove the two-wheeled gig sedately
down the winding road from Pearsehill to the tiny railroad
station in ample time to meet the noon train from Edinburgh.
Her cheeks glowed with the effect of the weather. She had a
sense of well-being that she had not experienced for many
years; though, as her dresses proved, she was putting on rather
too much weight, thanks, no doubt, to the quantities of wholesome food that Lady Isobel, her mother-in-law, forced upon
her, as if she was an invalid recovering from an illness.

Christmas had been very quiet indeed, with only a few close
friends spending the weekend. With no grand ball and no
shooting parties to organise Lady Isobel had turned her
attention to the children and they, at least, had thoroughly
enjoyed themselves. Looking back on it now, Betsy realised
that she too had taken greater pleasure in that Christmas than
in any spent in the whirlygig of Edinburgh where the frenetic
pace of pleasure-seeking hardly left one any time to enjoy
oneself.

At first, during the early weeks of 'the holiday', Betsy
repeatedly told herself that being sent packing to Pearsehill was
a punishment and that, like a jail sentence, it would not last
forever. Now, though, she contemplated an eventual return to

the city with apprehension and had already laid plans to spend more time at Pearsehill in spring and summer. Fraser said that they might look out for a place of their own, a lodge or small country house; that he, with the Sprotts' consent, might even open a branch office in nearby Perth. A governess had been employed, a cheerful young woman, to attend to the girls' education. Removed from the stuffy confinements of Edinburgh, the children too had blossomed. In fact, Betsy grudgingly confessed, they really were rather good company— in small doses.

"There's Papa; there's Papa," Lisbeth cried, standing up in the carriage and waving. "He has so much luggage."

Her sister pulled her down, as the carriage rocked over the hard rutted road.

Lisbeth's voice had contained so much excitement at seeing her father—who had only been gone three days—that some of it conveyed itself to Betsy and, taking one hand from the reins, she waved too.

Fraser raised both arms and, like a signaller, shaped out a greeting.

"What's he saying? What's he saying?" demanded Lisbeth, who was going through a repetitious phase.

"He is saying," her sister told her, having been recently introduced to the mysteries of semaphore, "that he is glad to be back with us."

"Tell him that we are glad he is back; go on, go on," said Lisbeth.

Roberta did as bidden, and the erractic waving went on all down the last slope to the station.

The station roof was brilliant red, like a jewel in the rays of the waning sun, the moorland stretching away in fretted white towards a line of mountains etched white against the deep blue winter sky.

"New Year: New Year: happy New Year, Papa," Lisbeth called happily when her father swung her from the seat and hugged her.

As the railway porter, who, in spite of regulations about uniform, wore a cock-feather in his hat, loaded up the baggage, Fraser put his daughter back beside her sister and climbed up by Betsy on the deep front seat. A tartan travelling rug was wrapped round her knees. She unloosed it and brought him in by her to share the warmth.

"New Year: New Year: New Year," Lisbeth chanted.

"Not until the day after tomorrow, silly," her sister told her, then, when the porter passed, said in a ladylike voice, "May I wish you a prosperous New Year—when it comes—Mr. McTavish."

"Aye, thank ye, lass," McTavish said, and, as Fraser passed down two florins, said, with a good deal more enthusiasm, "An' *thank* ye, sir. May eighteen-ninety-seven gang weel wi' ye all at Pearsehill."

Fraser leaned over and shook the porter's hand, then touched Betsy's knee with his. She lifted the whip and slapped the horses' cruppers inexpertly; driving traps and gigs was a newly-learned skill.

"Shall I take the reins?" said Fraser.

"No, you sit back and relax after your busy week in Edinburgh."

"Relax," said Fraser, stetching out his hands. "Who on earth can relax in this beautiful scene; who would want to? How has the weather been?"

"Like this," said Betsy. "Very cold at night."

"How is mother?"

"Well; very well."

"God, but I'm glad to be back. Really, there are times when I would give the world not to have to return to Edinburgh at all. It smells so. And that fog . . . Bbbbbrrrrrrr."

"Papa: Papa?" said Lisbeth. "Grandmama says that we may stay up tomorrow night and hear the kirk ring its bells."

"And drink a toast in wine," put in Roberta.

"May we: may we, Papa?"

"If you both have a nap in the afternoon—perhaps." Fraser turned in his seat and tucked a rug around their knees. Within their fur-lined hoods their faces were prettier than ever, eyes sparkling and cheeks, like Betsy's, glowing. "Now, sit a little more peacefully, please; the horses have quite enough work to do pulling us up this slippery hill without you distracting them."

"Yes, Papa," said Roberta, placing her arm about her little sister's shoulders to hold her motionless.

The gig slowed as the slope steepened. Ahead a gap in the treeline framed a section of the sky to the west, the sun tinting the blue with a winey red. From the top of the hill, they would look down into the pleasant valley, to the policies of Pearsehill, with the small baronial house that Fraser's father had bought planted in the centre.

Fraser said, "Elizabeth, Andrew is back."

Betsy caught her breath and, for a second, lost control of the gig. It swayed towards the verge, then the horses brought it into line as Fraser tightened the reins, his hand on his wife's hands.

"I asked him to come here, to celebrate with us, but, apparently, he is going off again directly."

"Going off where? And where has he been?"

Fraser said, "He's been in London."

"All this while?"

"It was wise of him to clear out of Scotland. After all, he left far too many awkward questions unanswered. I can't say that I blame him for doing a bunk."

"But his law practice . . .?"

"He is retiring from the law."

"I thought that was only talk."

Moving closer, and lowering his voice, Fraser said, "He has not been idle these last six weeks, Elizabeth. He asked me to make his apologies to you, and to deliver his fondest regards."

"That," said Elizabeth, "sounds as if he doesn't intend to return."

"Who knows!" said Fraser. "Will you miss him?"

"Yes," said Betsy. "I suppose I will, rather."

"So shall I—rather," said Fraser. "He is in Edinburgh only on a flying visit, to settle his affairs. He left reams of instructions with us. We are to sell the house and the library, to find good posts for Corby and his other servants."

"Then he really doesn't intend to return?"

"He's setting off for America, Pennsylvania, I believe, though he was not exactly gushing with information about his plans."

364

"Knowing my brother, he will have something positive in view."

"He's bought into a company; that much he did impart. Some fellow in London sold him shares."

"What sort of company?"

"I really couldn't say. All I do know, Elizabeth, is that he's liquidating *all* his assets and having his wealth transferred abroad."

"Drew never does things by halfs," said Elizabeth. "And all because of that boy."

"I wonder," said Fraser.

"About what, dear?" said Elizabeth.

"Drew's true reason for doing what he did. Do you know what he said to us, to Innes, Balfour and I, when he left us this morning? He said, 'Don't think that I'm being noble. You know me better than that'."

"How odd," said Betsy, who did not think it odd at all.

"He also said, 'The working class will always battle to escape what they are, but when they succeed, they will seize on the first opportunity to cast themselves down again'. Then, would you believe, he quoted Shakespeare: 'The fault is not in our stars but in ourselves, that we are the underlings'."

"Did you believe him?"

"Well, the sentiments are honest, but coming from Andrew . . ." Fraser smiled uncertainly at his wife, "they do sound rather false."

"He means not a word of it," Betsy declared. "He never, ever considered himself an underling."

"And never will?" Fraser asked.

"Unless some woman changes him."

"Ah, yes," said Fraser, as the gig rolled to the breast of the hill and the view of his family's estate opened out before him, "that reminds me. In parting, he gave me one last piece of fraternal advice: he warned me to keep a close eye on you."

Beneath the rug, Fraser's knee pressed against her thigh.

To her surprise, Betsy experienced a need for her husband that she had supposed had gone for good.

"Trust him!" she said. "He always had gall."

365

"But," said Fraser, kissing her on the lips, "he was always so much cleverer than me that, perhaps, I'll take the hint."

"Oh? And how closely will you watch me, Fraser?"

"Very closely, indeed."

Betsy leaned her head on his shoulder. "Not," she said, "before time."

Behind her, her daughters giggled, Roberta rather knowingly, and Lisbeth simply because she was happy.

* * *

The Moray Place chambers already seemed remote and empty. Drew no longer felt comfortable there. Perhaps the very tidiness of the tables and desk gave that effect. Corby had been thorough in his maintenance of the house, and firm with the servants. Besides, Daniel Horn had been in almost daily, as he, and he alone, had served as Drew's link with the city and the more formal aspects of his business.

In Glasgow, George Arnold Craddick had also been alerted to his employer's intentions and had begun the process of hiving off stock held in Drew's name, selling it where possible by private bargain. Letters were exchanged between agent and advocate through an address in a dull temperance hotel in Salmon Grove, Islington, London. Craddick's enquiry as to what was to be done with the Blacklaw stock received a curt postscript in the next communication from London, stating that the Blacklaw stock had already been sold.

Though Stalker did not invite the information Craddick put in such snippets of gossip as came to him through the commercial grapevine concerning Houston Lamont and Sydney Thrush.

It seemed that Mr. Thrush was no longer managing the Blacklaw Colliery Company, and had been, as Craddick put it, 'deposed'. Thrush was hardly begging for crusts, of course. Rumour indicated that Lamont had paid sweetly for his partner's share of the stock and, of necessity, had sold off *en bloc* many of his anciliary holdings, including three of the seven pits. Innocently, Craddick enquired if Drew was interested in making a bid. The reply to that question was a blunt *No*.

Thrush and his sister had left Blacklaw shortly before Christmas; the exact date of departure was not recorded. Lamont himself took over as General Manager, and appointed a team of four deputy-managers, all of them young and with college training, to deal with the day-to-day running of the pits. Like Drew, Lamont had moved quickly and positively, inward into boardrooms, into the ground-floor study of Strathmore, rudely rebuffing every attack made on his privacy, by rich and poor, press, public and peers. His wife made one frantic assault on Glasgow society, was snubbed everywhere, retired to lick her wounds and, last that Craddick had heard, was vainly trying to find a role for herself in local Church society.

In time, of course, the scandal would be forgotten. But time was relative, and both Edith and Houston Lamont, in their declining years, would not again attain the position that they had held in established society.

From Horn, Drew learned of matters closer to his heart. Neill and Edward had been sacked from Blacklaw pit. Dunlop had been pensioned off and had gone to live with a married daughter, and her nine children, in Clydebank. Rob Ewing had been offered a remunerated post as district convener with the U.F.M. and had until January to make up his mind. Rob had not been paid off. He went out on his shift, as he had always done, and returned to sleep in his empty house. Henderson had left Blacklaw to be trained as a checker in an engineering firm in Springburn. Somebody had taken pity on him, seeing him, perhaps, as a victim of tyranny: perhaps it was Lamont himself. He wasn't much missed in the mining village. Willie Kellock had found jobs for Neill and Edward about the bakehouse, though business was slack in the wake of the trial, colliers being a damned wary bunch about things like that. The young men were considering making application for a three-year course of mining study in Hamilton College of Industrial Crafts, encouraged in this direction by Kate, Lily and Rob.

How Horn had acquired all this information, Drew did not feel entitled to enquire. Even now, the less he knew of Horn's methods, the better for both of them.

Of Mirrin, Tom and Hazelrig, Horn wrote nothing. If it interested him, Drew must find that out for himself.

Rum and chocolate for Horn, port wine for Drew, provided an unsentimental toast; the hour was appropriately late, the fire low. The men might have been discussing a tricky brief, or the problem of extricating a wealthy client from the results of his own folly, as they had done a thousand times over the years. But the atmosphere was altered, Drew's restlessness palpable. He could not be at ease. He rose to poke the fire, to refill his glass, to scan the rows of books for any title that he might wish to keep. In that hour of conversation, his big winged chair mostly remained unoccupied.

"You were wise t'get out as fast as you did," said Horn. "There was a horde o'newspaper reporters clamouring for titbits o' gossip. The big question was about the mother."

"I trust that you told them nothing."

"Not a blessed word, Drew."

"I suppose they descended like locusts upon my relatives in Blacklaw?"

"I hear they got short shrift there too."

"Good," said Drew. "Now it's all past: a nine days' wonder."

"Best keep your head low, though."

"I intend to," said Drew. "What briefs have we been offered since the trial?"

"As you predicted, you could become the workin' man's champion. You could be pleadin' cases in every court from here t'the Orkney Isles, defending every kind o' crime that the lower orders commit, from wife beatin' to poachin', from drunken assault to petty theft."

"All at the most miserable of fees, or no fee at all."

"Naturally," said Horn. "Defenders o' justice are supposed t'live on air, it seems."

"Were there no briefs from 'old friends'?"

"Not one."

"It's just as well. What did you reply to the others?"

"I did as you instructed, told them you were not acceptin' briefs for the next session, an' let it go at that."

Drew nodded. "I will, it appears, leave Scotland without any responsibilities and damned few regrets."

"None?"

"Well, only in leaving good friends like you behind, Daniel."
Drew studied the bookshelves, his voice matter-of-fact.

"I'm . . . I'm not that keen t'stay here, either,"·Horn said.

Drew did not look round. "You'll find another position
without much bother, Daniel. I can make an arrangement with
Kinnemouth if you wish."

Horn finished the rum and chocolate and put the cup down
on the side table. He did not look at the Advocate as he
said, "I think I might have a shot at America too."

"Hoh!" said Drew. "What a coincidence."

"Association with you has been good for me," said Horn.
"I'm not exactly hard up. I've a shilling or two put away,
an' I'm still active enough t'adjust to a change of scene."

"Are you hinting, Horn?"

"Me? Hintin'?"

"What do you know of America?"

"It's the land o' opportunity."

Drew laughed. "They tell me the girls are very pretty."

"I'm comin' out o' my adolescent period, I think," said
Horn. "Could you see your way t' givin me a position in any
new venture you might be startin', sir?"

"Sir? You're a 'smarmy' devil, Daniel, as my sister would
put it. You have only been as faithful and honest to me as
suited you. I'm not inclined to spend the next twenty years
keeping one eye on what you're up to behind my back."

"I'm not sure I know what y'mean."

"God, Horn, you're made of poor parchment. I see through
you so easily."

For once, Horn was non-plussed. Drew came over from
the shelves and stood by the hearth, arm on the back of
the chair. "How much did you screw out of friend Lauder,
Daniel?"

"Och, no, I wouldn't have any secret dealin's with the likes
o' him, Drew."

"He wrote to me, you know. He told me about you, what
you'd done, told me about Elizabeth, too."

Horn's gaunt, hawk-like face lengthened. He peered at Drew
from the tops of his eyes. "When?"

"Soon after I accepted the Stalker brief. I think it was Mellish's idea, to undermine my confidence, to rob me of my dependence on you as general factotum."

"Seems the plot failed," Horn muttered.

"Certainly," said Drew. "Elizabeth only got what she asked for. As for you, when it came down to the last bite, I gather that you just couldn't swallow it."

Horn nodded. "Couldn't do it. I don't know why."

"Perhaps you finally sorted out your priorities, Daniel."

"Like you did?"

"Yes," said Drew. "Perhaps."

"Will you . . . will you not take me t' America with you?"

"My ship sails from Southampton on the fourteenth of January," said Drew. "If you happen to be on it, with your passage paid, I'll consider it."

"Where are we headed?"

"To Pittsburg," said Drew, "in South West Pennsylvania."

"And what'll we do there, might I ask?"

"I have bought a company," said Drew. "In a small town some fifty miles from Pittsburg itself. In Blue River Falls to be exact."

"A company?"

"I think I'll register it simply as the Stalker Mining Company."

Horn's features split in a grin. "Mining? And what do they happen t'mine in Blue River Falls?"

"Coal," Drew Stalker told him.

⋆   ⋆   ⋆

It was Hogmanay, and Willie's products were much in demand, business having picked up again over the festive season. The shop was stocked with bread and buns, biscuits and fancy cakes. Trade was brisk all day long. Kate served behind the counter, Flora too. Lily drove the bread van to the pit-gates in Blacklaw, Northrigg Claypark, and Eastlagg, making one round in the morning, and another in the afternoon. At home, in Kellock's Square, wine and spirits, black bun and shortbreads were already set out in the parlour to welcome first-foots, though the Kellocks would not be at home when midnight came. They would be at Hazelrig, all together at the farm.

The weather was cold but bright, the hills lying passive in the far distance, speckled with light snow, the elevations of the mine workings, all across the plain, sharp against the winter colourings. Sounds too were vivid, each identifiable to the two young men, exiles from the seams, who sat together on the board of the flatbed cart and rode, rocking, along the back road from the corn-mills at Sheen.in Ford. Sacks of flour lay solid upon the cart. The vigorous young horse hauled them along effortlessly. The young men were talking, as young men will, of the future, of that night's festivities and the crate of bottled beer that Malcolm had hidden in the barn, of the girls they would meet, and of the town of Hamilton and the difficulties they might experience in those first weeks of the new term—all subjects of importance but shaken, jumbled and leisurely, like the rhythm of the cart.

It was a fine curtain, Edward and Neill agreed later, that sudden appearance by the side of the road, out of nowhere and, too quickly to suit them, back into nowhere. The heavy Ulster tweed travelling coat, Homburg hat and polished shoes were never designed for the rough outskirts of Blacklaw. Though the mystery of how he found them was later explained by Lily—who had encountered him outside Claypark Halt and told him where the boys were—the impression of it remained, the effect of pleasure and surprise. He could not be as sour as all that, Neill decided and, oddly, when he spoke of his father in the years to come he would present him as something of a wag.

"Hey, look at that man!" said Neill.

"It looks like your . . . like Mr. Stalker."

"Good God, it is him! What's he doin' here?"

"Whoa, there, Tar.. Whoa, lad." Edward steered the cart slowly, wheels running in the old gutter along the side of the curb. He brought the horse to a halt abreast of Andrew Stalker.

Drew was standing at the corner, one hand in his pocket, the other holding a black cheroot to his mouth, like some plump dandy spying out girls on a Haymarket beat. But there were no awnings or bright lights, no gay passersby, only a stray dog limping along the earth bank, and a bent old woman in a shawl crabbing home from her daughter's house in Claypark, a dribble of coal-damp dross in a sack under her arm. On the drying greens behind the thorns a half mile of washing was draped like bunting on the ropes and the women, though almost indistinguishable from the backs of the houses, gave a human dimension that was both decently remote and comforting.

"Mr. Stalker," said Neill, awkward now in this familiar setting and conscious of his shabby clothing. "What're y'doin' here?"

"I came to speak with you."

"Climb aboard, then," said Edward. "We'll give y'a ride back t'the house."

"No. I haven't time for that. I came to see you, that's all."

"But Mam and Willie will want t'thank . . ." Neill began.

"Is the station out of your way?" Drew asked. "Claypark."

"It's only ten minutes away," Edward said.

"Then, if you will, I'd be glad of a ride."

"Give's your hand, Mr. Stalker," Edward said.

Drew glanced right and left along the empty backstreets then, clumsily, put his shoe on the wheel, grasped Edward's hand and let the young man pull him onto the board seat. He wrapped his coat around his knees and stared at the horse's rump.

"Claypark Halt?" said Edward.

"Please."

The cart rocked off again, Drew gripping the iron flange of the seat as if it was a chariot that might tip and throw him off.

Neill cleared his throat. "I . . . I came t'see you in Edinburgh, Mr. Stalker, but you were gone, an' your man, Mr. Horn, he told me he didn't think you'd be back,"

"I'm leaving again tomorrow morning."

"Leavin' Scotland?" Edward asked.

"Yes—for some considerable time."

"I . . . I wanted t'thank you," Neill said. "I know that m'Mam an' Willie wanted that too. Mam wrote y'a letter."

"I got it," said Drew. "Be good enough to tell your mother,

372

Neill, that there is no charge whatsoever for my services."

The Claypark road ran parallel with Blacklaw's main street, and Drew, head turned, stared at the familiar freize of houses, at the kirk steeple and, just as the cart veered right, at the tower of the schoolhouse across the field by the Poulter's burn. He said nothing, gave no indication of any sentiment that might have lurked in him. Respecting his silence, for a while the boys did not speak.

At length, when the horse pulled along between the flat fields and Blacklaw lay behind him, Drew put his hand into his breast pocket and took out an envelope. He gave it to Neill.

The boy did not open it.

Drew said, "That is a gift, young man. It is not for your mother—for Kate. It's for you, both of you. One hundred pounds each."

"But Mr. Stalker, we can't possibly take any more," Neill began.

Edward dug his cousin in the ribs. "College fees, Mr. Stalker?"

"Yes," said Drew. "One hundred pounds will cover your fees for the next three years. It might buy you the odd tipple of wine in the Hamilton pubs."

"Beer," said Neill. "We're beer men."

Drew did not smile. He remained taut, and restless.

"Mr. Stalker, I'm . . . sorry."

"Sorry—for what?"

Edward said, "I think y'know what Neill means."

"Aye," Neill said. "If it hadn't been for me . . ."

"If it hadn't been for you," said Drew, "all of you, I would not have changed. I don't consider that change is bad. On the contrary, all that is bad stems from fear of change, from the failure to square up to one's options. I learned that early in my life. I learned it from your grandfather, from your father, Edward, from your mother, Neill—I mean, from my sister. Most of all, perhaps, I learned it from your Aunt Mirrin. You are, you can be, what you choose to be."

"It's a struggle, though," said Neill.

"Certainly," Drew agreed. "A struggle against prejudice, laziness and wilful ignorance."

"Mr. Stalker, d'you . . . despise us, like Kate always says?" Edward asked.

"I scorn much of what you are, but only with my head, Edward. At least," Drew said, "that is my excuse. I was given too much."

"What?" said Neill.

"Perhaps I should say that I took too much," said Drew. "But I may have paid it back—no, I don't mean to you, Neill, or to my sisters, but to . . . oh, people that are dead, and mostly forgotten."

Claypark Halt came suddenly upon them, appearing from behind the ragged hedge. Whitewash weathered into the brick, the faded letters of a slogan declared, FIGHT THE BOSSES.

Seeing it, Drew smiled and shook his head.

"The bosses," he said. "It seems that the legendary monster has a new name now."

Neill laughed. "Well, call them b'any name, Mr. Stalker, it'll no' be me that does the fightin' from now on."

"No?" said Drew.

Steadying himself, as the cart halted, he got down, glancing left towards Glasgow, the direction from which the train would appear.

Edward put his hand on his cousin's shoulder. "I'll wait here for you, Neill."

The boy was momentarily confused and, turning to his father, looked to him for advice.

"Come, then," said Drew.

They walked together out of Edward's sight onto the short platform behind the small brick building. Even as they vanished, the hoot and whistle of the train sounded down line at the Inchpit junction, dragging up from the city, smoke coiling thickly against the clear afternoon sky.

On the platform, Neill suddenly blurted out, "I want t'thank you, no' just for the money, an' for what y'did—I mean, gettin' me off an' out o' the jail—but for . . . well, I don't know how t'say it."

"You thanked me before," said Drew. "Look after your mother, Neill, that's all I ask. Look after Kate."

"I'll always do that."

374

The train squealed and rolled up to the platform, hissing steam from its cylinders bringing a smell of coal-smoke and hot metal like the breath of the past, and an augury of the future.

Neill stuck out his hand.

Drew took it then, on impulse, pulled the boy to him and embraced him briefly. Turning away, he jerked open the carriage door and got up into the grubby third-class compartment.

Neill stepped forward. "Mr. Stalker, Mr. Stalker, where are y'goin' to. Please, tell me that?"

The door slammed. The Ulster coat filled the space in the window.

"Da?"

Drew's face appeared, Homburg canted at a raffish angle by the frame.

"America, son," he said, as the train heaved into motion. "I think it's improbable that we'll ever meet again."

Neill's face was wide open, his eyes round. He lifted his hand in a hesitant gesture of farewell then, as coupling-links tightened and the carriages rumbled forward to trail the engine out of the station, he ran along the platform and, hands cupped to his mouth, shouted.

"You never know, Da. You just never know."

*　　*　　*

Tom opened his eyes. Each morning for the past couple of weeks he had performed the action with calculation, filled with a mixture of exultation and dread. Shifting his head on the pillow so that it would be turned towards the window ready to absorb the growing light, he waited for the regular shape upon the retina that told him that Parfitt had been right and he had been wrong. Suspicious of optimism, he said nothing to anyone, holding off until there could be no doubt at all that sight was returning, slowly but with certainty, to both eyes.

Now, on the morning of the last day of the year, he had been roused from deep sleep and, without thinking, opened his eyes. He saw only darkness. Pinned by fear, he held his breath and blinked. Still there was nothing, nothing but darkness pressed against his pupils.

375

"Da, are y'awake?" a muffled voice said. He heard a tentative rapping on the bedroom door and realised that that had awakened him.

"Malcolm?"

"Aye."

"What's wrong?"

Suddenly the shape of the bedroom door was carved out of that awful stunning blackness. To Tom's relief, he saw his son's anxious face, and the red and yellow of his plaid shirt—the new one that Mirrin had bought him as a Christmas gift. Startled by the clarity, Tom sat bolt upright.

"What time is it?"

"No' four yet."

"What the hell are y'doin' up then?"

Mirrin stirred beside her husband, her arm coming over his thigh. He glanced down at her, seeing her hair spilled out on the pale pillow, the shadows, soft and shapely, along her arm.

"Wha . . . what's that, Tom?"

"Nothin' love. Go back t'sleep."

Quickly, Tom slid from the bed and, reaching his clothes from the chair, bundled them in his arms and crept out of the bedroom into the kitchen. It was a radiant world, much more defined and colourful than it had been yesterday. He looked at his son, at the worried expression, but said nothing.

"Can you . . . can you *see* me?" asked Malcolm.

"Faintly."

"That's great; how long?"

"Couple o' weeks."

"That's really great, Da. Does Mam know?"

"Not yet."

"Look, I'm sorry. I should've told y'before."

"Told me what?"

"There's a ewe in lamb."

"On the thirty-first o' December? *Bloody hell!* None o'them are supposed t'be due 'til the end o' February," Tom growled. "Can't leave anythin' t'you pair it seems. Why did y'not tell me before?"

"We weren't sure she was in lamb. It's one o'the Suffolks.

It happened last July, when things were so upset. She got out the pasture an' in wi' the ram."

"I'll be the bloody laughin'-stock o' Crosstrees." Tom pulled on his clothes as he spoke. He did not feel dismayed. The return of vision was too exciting. Besides, it had happened before on Hazelrig, this early unexpected lambing. However, he did not choose to remind Malcolm of those other 'accidents'.

"It's no' your fault; it's mine," said Malcolm.

"Where's Sandy?"

"I left him asleep."

"That was thoughtful, wasn't it? The sheep're his responsibility too. Where's the bloody ewe, then?"

"In the wee pen at the side o'the barn. I fetched her in last night. She full o'lambs by the look o'her. I've got the straw bales out."

"Lamps?"

"Two."

"Soap?"

"In the jar."

"Did y'have a go yoursel'?"

"Aye."

"So she's stuck bad, is she?"

"Wee hoofs an' legs an' heads everywhere inside her. I didn't want t'damage her. You've got the smallest hands, Da. I'm too muckle-fisted for difficult deliveries."

Shaking his head and complaining, in spite of his eagerness, Tom wound a scarf round his throat and started across the kitchen.

Sleepily, Mirrin appeared at that moment in the bedroom doorway.

"What's wrong?"

"There's a damned ewe in lamb' an' this ham-fisted idiot can't get in far enough. Lambin', at *this* time o'the year! I don't know how he ever expects t'be a farmer."

Mirrin said, "I'll come."

Tom said, "I suppose y'knew about this?"

"I thought the beast was just gettin' fat," said Mirrin. "Wi' all the good feed we give her."

"Aye, that'll be right," Tom said, and, without waiting for

377

his wife or son, pushed through the corridor and out into the yard.

A patch of golden light from the hanging oil-lamp guided him easily to the pen.

The ewe was a big sooty-woolled Suffolk with a velvet black face and a duchess expression. She cast a disapproving look at Tom as he entered the tiny slope-roofed pen that Malcolm had thoughtfully quilted with bales of straw. There was a pan of bruised barley and a pail of fresh water in the stone trough by the wall, four lengths of twine laid across the straw and a clasp-knife stuck in the wood of the pen post. A jar of Brander's Best Lambing Soap, half scooped out, was on the floor.

The ewe kicked skittishly and butted her head on the bales. Tom stepped over the straw and, with his knees, drove the animal round. He lifted her tail, and saw a protruding hoof, like a tusk, set in the scalded pink of the ewe's vulva. The fact that he could make it out without stooping to within an inch of the tail delighted him but he gave no indication of his pleasure, merely grunting and, as the ewe let out a bellow of indignation and discomfort, peeled off his jacket, tossed it over the barrier and rolled his shirt sleeves up to his shoulders.

Malcolm said, "She's awful tight, Da."

"I can see that. It's as well y'didn't damage her, son. Right, we'll get her over the bale an' see what's inside."

"A pair, at least."

"A pair's enough, this season o'the year."

"They feel big."

Expertly, Tom caught the ewe by the forelegs and turned her over. Amid loud and pathetic protests, with Malcolm's help, he lifted the swollen animal bodily onto the straw bale. The young man moved round his father and pinned the rear legs, pushing them wide, smothering the boxing forelegs with his hip.

"Can y'*really see* well enough for this?" Malcolm asked as Tom laved soap on his hands and arms.

"Aye. Now, hold her still, son."

Tom bent and gently inserted his right hand into the ewe, exploring the tangle of wet slippery limbs. Membranes compressed his wrist painfully as his fingers slid deeper. He could feel the thrusting of the ewe against his flesh. His fingers were cramped. He could not find enough space in that spongy cavity to turn his hand. He could quite understand why the boy had been defeated. "Aye," he conceded. "It's a right mess the wee buggers have got themselves into."

"How many?"

"Feels like twenty bloody legs," Tom said. "But it's two lambs, son, both twisted."

"Can y'manage them, Da?"

Tom did not reply.

Pressure on his arm and hand was becoming painful, but he had found the position of the limbs, the curled woollen wrinkles of the shoulder, the smoother line of a jaw. With great skill, he began to sort out the living creatures within the womb and to present them for birth. Instinctively he knew that they were both alive, and good big lambs at that.

Extracting arm and hand he brought out a lamb's head and another forefoot, covered in the tobacco-coloured jelly of the birth-sac. The head hung limp. Gripping the legs with fingers and thumbs, Tom drew the lamb out. The Suffolk pressed. The creature came away with a slithering plop and landed on the straw. Tom turned it on its side. The ewe was bleating now on a different note, rearing to lift its head from Malcolm's side to get at the lamb, to lick and mother it.

"No' yet, lass. In a wee minute," Malcolm said.

Tom stripped jelly from the lamb's mouth and nostrils, saw its sides sag with the first sigh of breath and heard the burble as its tubes cleared. "Aye, a bonnie big lamb," he said. "Even if it is early."

Slipping his hand into the ewe once more, Tom brought out the second lamb, more easily than the first. He released it so that the sheep could do the work, thrusting the long-bodied little creature out onto the straw. Soon, the second lamb was breathing, and the pair, almost in unison, gave a surprisingly strong blethering bleat that drove the ewe into a struggling frenzy.

Tom eased the strings of cleanings from the womb mouth

and, stepping back over the bale, said, "She's fine, son. Let her up an' see if she takes them."

Malcolm turned the ewe and hopped over the bale too and together the farmers watched the sheep sniff and then, delightedly, begin to clean her offspring.

Just as Mirrin arrived, the first-born lamb struggled to its feet and, blunt black tongue vibrating, bleated for a suck at the teat.

Smiling, Mirrin leaned over and inspected the new arrivals.

"Those," she said, "are about the best things t'come out o' eighteen ninety-six."

"Accidents," said Tom.

"Accidents or not, they're welcome," Mirrin said. "Maybe they'll bring us luck in the year ahead."

"An' a shillin' or two at the market," said Malcolm.

Walking to the far corner Tom stooped to the pail that Malcolm had put there for the purpose and sluiced his hands and arms thoroughly in the freezing cold water. He towelled them vigorously on a piece of clean sacking, squinting across the pen at his wife.

"Hey, flower," he said. "That's a bonnie cardigan you're wearin'."

Mirrin looked up from the lambs. There was no sound in the shed save for the soft rustling of the ewe as she moved on the straw.

"What did y'say?"

"A bonnie garment," Tom said. "Red was always a good colour for a woman like you."

"Red?"

"All right," said Tom. "Mauve, if y'must have it accurate."

Mirrin's hand flew to her mouth. "Oh, God, Tom; what is it?"

"It's comin' back, Mirrin," her husband told her. "Very slow, but very sure; my sight's comin' back."

"Oh, Tom: Tom." She wept.

"I'll . . . I'll . . ." Malcolm said, inching towards the door.

"You go an' rumble Hurley out o'his bed, son," Tom told him and, as Malcolm left, took Mirrin in his arms.

380

She touched his eyelids with her fingertips, staring up at him.

He could see her face clearly even by lantern light.

It seemed as beautiful to him as it had ever been.

"How much sight will b'given me, an' how long it'll last, I don't know," he said.

"Each day now as it comes, Tom."

"Aye, flower, each day as it comes." '

"What a way t'end a year, this year o'them all."

"Next year'll be better, you'll see."

"Next year," said Mirrin, "always is."

★   ★   ★

It wanted now but a minute to midnight. All the crowd, young and old, gathered in the Armstrongs' big kitchen had fallen silent, each with a nestle of special thoughts in the last tick of the old year; remembrances, regrets, plans and expectations for the brave days of the future. In the chair by the hearth, Flora thought, as she always did at this time, of her husband and the sons she had lost to the pit. Mirrin too, and Kate, remembered them, and recalled the pain of doubt and sadness, the trials of those years, and the changes that had come about because of them.

Willie Kellock studied his watch, as if the New Year was a cake that must be taken from the oven bang on time. Lily stood by Rob who, spruced up and less grim than anyone could remember him in the lonely years since his wife's death, had even dared to put his arm about her waist. Lily did not look at the clock or at the door as the others did, she looked up at Rob, very steadily, waiting for the kiss that would tell her, and all the folk that mattered in her life, if her year would bring a wedding.

Though aware of his mother's intention, Edward felt no resentment. He treated it with rueful amusement as if it was a bit of a joke that people as old as that could share the future with the young. That night, Edward had other things on his mind. So too had Malcolm, Neill and even Sandy. Much to Mirrin's surprise, the Lauries had turned up from the farm across the hill—Will Laurie, a widower, and his four daughters, come to

381

escape from the loneliness of their steading, expressly at Malcolm's invitation.

"Four daughters, Tom! Look at them! If ever I saw lassies with matrimony on their minds, it's that lot," Mirrin had whispered.

"All lassies have matrimony on their minds," Tom had told her.

"But look at that dark-haired one, Maisie. Look't the eyes she's makin' at our Malcolm."

"Lucky lad."

"Don't brush it aside," Mirrin had said. "She's far too old for him."

"Aye," Tom had agreed, face straight. "She's all o'twenty."

They had claimed the corner by the window, the Laurie girls and Stalker boys, and had filled the kitchen with their laughter throughout the evening. In that minute to the hour of twelve, however, even they were quiet and thoughtful, as if the weight of their lives, for sixty seconds only, bore upon them and they saw clearly in that room what they in their time would become.

The kitchen was clean and warm, the table spread with food. The flames of the fire reflected in the dishes and the fat, copper jelly-pans that lorded it on the shelf. Glasses stood ready. Bottles of wine and whisky and the squat barrel of beer that Willie had brought were laid out for toasts to come. Mirrin glanced round, to make sure everything was in its proper place, when she saw that Davie and Kitten had crept down from their beds and sat now on Flora's chair, their arms about their Gran'ma as if she was a rock that even Mirrin did not dare defy.

The clock in the corner ticked.

"Hurley," said Tom. "Open the door."

"Aye, gaffer." Hurley leapt from the chair by the laden table, ran to the outside door and threw it wide.

The air was cold and sweet.

Fleck barked. The big horses whinnied. The ewe and her new lambs, wakened from sleep, bleated a little in the pen by the barn.

The clock struck twelve.

In the still cold air, over the dark pastures, into the farmhouse came the sounds of kirk bells in distant towns, bells and colliery hooters, sounding out of shift.

On the last stroke, there was uproar, a wishing of good health, a kissing all round, and a shaking of hands.

Willie tapped the beer barrel. Tom uncorked the whisky and the wine. Filled glasses were handed round. Malcolm, who was on the verge of losing his head, kissed Maisie Laurie for the fourth time that new year, while Neill confided to Jean Laurie that he was really too young to get serious but if she wouldn't mind holdin' off for three years, there was no sayin' what would happen. Edward kept his arm round Eileen Laurie's waist and wondered about the girls he might meet in Hamilton. Sandy, who was entering a gentlemanly phase, gave fifteen-year-old Bea a glass of ginger wine, and, bowing, blushed.

The lords of the dance, indeed; Mirrin thought. Her apprehension vanished. Willie handed her a glass.

"Now, friends," Tom shouted. "Now—a toast. First t'the New Year. May it bring health, wealth an' happiness t' each an' every one o' us."

"Ne'erday," said Willie. The company drank.

"Tonight," Tom went on, thumb in the pocket of his cardigan, head lifted, "I ask that we all give a special thought t' the toast t' absent friends. In fact, it would not be too much, I think, if we drink t' Andrew Stalker."

"Andrew Stalker," Willie said.

Mirrin saw Kate's face dissolve, saw her turn and, darting between chairs and table, take refuge in the back bedroom.

"Oh, dear me," said Tom. "It seems that my sister-in-law is a wee bit overcome."

"She's just upset," said Mirrin. "Lily, serve supper now, an' I'll go in t'see Kate."

The bedroom was lit only by a wedge of light from the open door. Kate sat on the bed with her back to Mirrin, hands to her face, weeping.

Outside Fleck still barked. From the kitchen, gathering volume, came the cheerful sounds of the young folk singing to the unmusical notes of Hurley Pritchard's mouth organ.

Kneeling on the bed, Mirrin touched Kate's shoulder.

"You can't hold a grudge against Drew now, love," she

said. "Tom's right. Nobody deserves a toast more than Drew. We owe him this night, aye, an' a good lot else besides—for whatever reason."

"I know, I know," Kate sobbed. "It's not that I grudge him anythin', Mirrin. I just wish he was here, an' our Betsy too, so that we could all be together again."

"We've got our own families now."

"An' he has nobody."

Kate leaned her head against Mirrin's breast, and sighed.

"I wonder," said Mirrin, "if we Stalkers were lead t'expect too much of each other, aye, an' too much of life."

Kate sniffed and rubbed her nose on her sleeve. "How we've changed, Mirrin. We're all gettin' old, an' I'm afraid of tomorrow."

"Come on, Kate. None o'that." Mirrin took her sister's hand and lifted her from the bed. "Look, we live in a house where the roof doesn't leak. We have food on the table, an' warm clothes on our backs. Children who love us. What more could you an' I want?"

"Aye," said Kate. "But Neill—what does he think o'me now?"

"He still loves you. He always has."

"He was meant t'be my son, Mirrin."

Mirrin put her fingers to Kate's cheek and turned her face to the lighted doorway. "Drew knew that. What he did was his way of saying it, his way of saying that he trusted us, and will always trust us."

"Aye, Mirrin, you're right, as usual," Kate said. "I'm just bein' foolish. It's odd, y'know, but I really pity our Drew."

"God help us," Mirrin said. "I pity America."

For a moment there was no sound, then Kate laughed and, arm in arm, laughing, the Stalker girls returned to the party.